More praise for
HONOR AND DUTY

"DEEPLY MOVING ... The novel rises to an astonishing power ... and confronts issues that trouble many Americans today, including how they feel about their country. ... It stands up to the best of Amy Tan for insights into the Chinese community in this country and its emotional tug-of-war among generations."
—*The San Diego Union-Tribune*

"OVERPOWERING ... PHILOSOPHICALLY RICH ... A PLEASURE ... It has been a long time since anyone has wrestled as profoundly with what we owe family, friends and institutions. ... Kai Ting earns his peace dearly; he is a classic hero."
—*New York Daily News*

"WONDERFUL ... ALLURING ... Gus Lee churns a great story. ... Pages melt away like ice in springtime. An environment few readers have experienced quickly feels familiar as a favorite old pair of jeans."
—*Denver Post*

"ENTHRALLING ... Confirming the promise of his first novel, *China Boy*, Lee has produced another insightful, moving tale ... [and] fashions a convincing first-person narrative in Kai's voice, skillfully drawing the reader into each of his young narrator's painful dilemmas."
—*Publishers Weekly*

HONOR
AND DUTY

Gus Lee

IVY BOOKS • NEW YORK

Ivy Books
Published by Ballantine Books
Copyright © 1994 by Gus Lee

Grateful acknowledgment is made to the following for permission to reprint previously published material:
Paul Simon Music: Excerpt from
"The Fifty-ninth Street Bridge Song (Feelin' Groovy)"
by Paul Simon, copyright © 1966 by Paul Simon.

Library of Congress Catalog Card Number: 92-42711

ISBN 0-8041-1004-2

This edition published by arrangement with Alfred A. Knopf, Inc.

Manufactured in the United States of America

First Ballantine Books Edition: February 1995

10 9 8 7 6 5 4 3

To Amazing Grace and
To the USMA Class of 1968, who will always honor

DONALD ROBERT COLGLAZIER
JOHN THOMAS MARTIN III
JAMES DEAN KELLY
RICHARD MELVIN MASON
DAVID LEE ALEXANDER
HENRY MERSHON SPENGLER III
KENNETH PAUL KNITT
PETER MICHAEL CONNOR
JAMES JOHN STETTLER
LOUIS JOHN SPEIDEL
WILLIAM FRANCIS REICHERT
DENNY LAYTON JOHNSON
DOUGLAS TERRELL WHELESS
DONALD FRANCIS VANCOOK, JR.
DAVID THORNTON MADDUX
WILLIAM FORSSELL ERICSON II
WILLIAM FRANCIS LITTLE III
ROY WILLIAM MASE
JOHN EDWARD DARLING, JR.
ROBERT GEORGE MACDONALD
JEFFREY RANDAL RIEK
ERNEST WILLIAM FLOWERS II
DON RENAY WORKMAN
HARRY ELLIS HAYES
DONALD JOHN DARMODY
JAMES ALFRED GAISER
MICHAEL ANTHONY DIBENEDETTO, JR.
KENNETH THADDEST CUMMINGS
DAVID LEE SACKETT
RICHARD ASPINALL HAWLEY, JR.

To Companies H, 1st Regiment, and A, 3rd Regiment, U.S. Corps of Cadets: Jim Adams, Jim Altemose, Jon Anderson, Tim Balliet, Jim Beahm, Tony Cerne, Steve Childers, Bruce Erion, Jim Forquerean, Jon Gardner, Jim Higgins, Bob Hunt, Barry Hittner, Fred Klein, Jim Llewellyn, Bob Lorbeer, Marvin Markley, Mike Murphy, Steve Murphy, Tom Pence, Mike Peters, Lew Robertson, Lou Speer, Jon Stolp, Art Torres, and George Williams, who stayed the course and served. And to all the Immortals, with a Present Arms to Danny Guigan, David Bue, Paul Coulter, and Bobby J.

The sad things that happened long ago will always remain part of who we are ... but instead of being a burden of guilt, recrimination, and regret that make us constantly stumble ... even the saddest things can become, once we have made peace with them, a source of wisdom and strength for the journey that still lies ahead. It is through memory that we are able to reclaim much of our lives that we have long since written off by finding that in everything that has happened to us over the years God was offering us possibilities of new life and healing which, though we may have missed them at the time, we can still ... be brought to life by and healed by all these years later.

—Frederick Buechner, *Telling Secrets*

CONTENTS

Acknowledgments

To Diane, Jena, and Eric, for everything.

To my father, Tsung-chi Lee; to my sisters, Lee Hause, Ying Lee Kelley, and Dr. Ming Zhu, M.D., and John, Lars, Max, Sara, Anna, and Eva; Lon-Lon, Jane, and Lulu; to the memory of my mothers, Da-tsien and Edith.

To Toussaint Maceo Streat; Charles Alex Murray; Lawrence Anthony Rapisarda; Robert Carl Lorbeer; Michael Warren Bain; Professor George Kagiwada, Asian American Studies, University of California, Davis; Professor Kwang-Ching Liu, Department of History, University of California, Davis, with deep appreciation for his teaching and for *Orthodoxy in Late Imperial China* (University of California Press, 1990); to my Christian covenant brothers Frank Ramirez, Barry Shiller, Paul Benchener, and Paul Gustaf Watermulder; and to the wonderful family of the First Presbyterian Church of Burlingame.

With thanks to Gary G. Hamilton and Wang Zheng for their translation of Fei Xiaotong's *Xiangtu Zhongguo: From the Soil*; to sister Amy Tan; to the Molly Giles Flying Circus and Tahoe Cabin Crew; to Pinoy Punsalong; to Daisy Tan; to Herbert M. Rosenthal, Mark T. Harris, and Diane C. Yu; to the faculty and staff of the U.S. Military Academy, with particular thanks to H. Norman Schwarzkopf, Robert Yerks, Pennell Joseph Hickey, Wallace William Noll, John "Buzz" Calabro, and Ray Aalbue; to my editor Ash Green and my publishers Sonny Mehta and Leona Nevler; to my peerless agent Jane Dystel of Acton, Dystel, Leone & Jaffe, New York; to Miriam Goderich; to Steven Douglas Childers and Arthur Frank Torres; to Monina Ramos; to the Boys and Girls Club of North San Mateo; to Valerie Rice of North Utilities; to Kevin Bourke; and to the Corps, which will weather all changes, and always be there for the protection of the Republic.

1

BEAST

United States Military Academy, West Point,
July 1, 1964

It was the most beautiful morning in my life. A warm and gentle breeze caressed my face and rustled my shirt as I walked up the winding river road toward West Point. It was late dawn of Reception Day for a thousand men and boys. No one wanted to be here more than I. Sunlight glittered on the Hudson and birds trilled in deep green oaks and maples as I followed the stone wall of Thayer Road to the beat of my pounding heart. I swung the suitcase to the lilt of imaginary bagpipes and the murmur of distant drums. The bag, filled with my worldly goods, was light. I was going to trade it and my past for a new life. I wanted to be the first to report.

An imposing array of tall, granite towers and stark, gray battlements came into view. Their majestic austerity consumed my vision with each nearing step. I inhaled history. After all the years of hope, I was here. This was America's Hanlin Academy, its Forest of Pens, designed by Washington, built by Jefferson. It was the object of my father's desire; here I would fulfill his dreams. The outline of spires seemed to be etchings from his spiritual blueprint, in which I was the human ink.

The grand oaks whispered sibilantly, carrying away my father's expectations. For a precious, golden moment, West Point was my dream. I heard the paratrooper captain from the Academy entrance exams say, "West Point is a school in the mountains and the clouds. There, at the River and the Rock, young men are bound to each other not by hopes of fame but by pledges to honor. A West Pointer is an honest man, all his life. He always strives to do the right thing."

I was seventeen and thirsted for redemption from more wrongs than I could admit. The air was different, and I paused. American flags waved softly, and I imagined the yellow pen-

1

nons of the Ch'ing emperors snapping across the years of history in the face of gritty Manchurian winds. I saw the great Chinese military hero Guan Yu and his red face and barrel chest. I stood straighter, flexing the arms that had worked in a YMCA weight room for ten years, preparing for this day. I was strong and ready. I exercised one of my talents, learned only this year: I smiled from an inner pleasure. Sparrows whistled in high, five-note calls and a deep and distant buzzer rang. Heat came down and the earth began to warm.

A mile later, I obeyed the sign "Candidates Report Here." I stood alone at the great doors to a gray-stoned building. A tall, silver-haired janitor with a badly scarred face stood with his mop and stared at me, a Negro elder studying a Chinese youth at the gateway to West Point. "Good luck to you, young man," he said as I entered. "Thank you, sir," I replied, warmed by his kindness.

The building was a vast gymnasium. I was processed through tables manned by straight-postured Army sergeants. I filled out an ID tags form (Ting, Kai/O-positive/religion: none), surrendered cash ($18.61), received inoculations, and did pull-ups. I could normally do fifty. Unnerved by the observing sergeants, I did forty-two, but I basked in their admiration. I was photographed in a jockstrap, which could not cloak my scoliosis, the curvature of the spine.

The candidate buses unloaded, and my status of being the first was lost. The reminder, in echoing tones, of a five-year service obligation after graduation, induced a few to leave, beginning a process of attrition that would last for over three years. The grim words invited me to belong to something honorable; there was no going back. We were briefed on the oath of service and directed to Central Area. I was the only Chinese I saw.

As we left with our bags to meet our fates, the sergeants gazed at us as if we were boys instead of projections of parental ambition. The Negro janitor and I exchanged a glance. He was solemn, as if he were saying farewell to someone he knew. I nodded, appreciating his presence, wishing he knew that I had been raised as a Negro youth, knowing that, for an American, I always dipped my head too low in deference to China.

We stepped into the bright and angry flare of a day that was now alarmingly hot. The heat broiled my skin. I was entering a huge quadrangle filled with a deep, primitive roar of voices.

A breathtakingly immaculate cadet awaited me. He thrust his

intensely focused features directly into my face and I jerked. Man—too close! "Hi," I gulped, "my name's Kai and—"

"DROP THAT BAG!" he roared, and I recoiled as my unguarded mind took his angry words like punches to the head. I gaped as my smarts fled before this *yu chao,* bad omen. I placed my luggage at my feet. Others began to drop their bags in small "whaps" across the Area.

"PICK IT UP!" the cadet screamed, then bellowed, "DROP THAT BAG!" I winced as the bag smashed onto the concrete: it contained my father's carefully preserved Colt super .38 automatic pistol. "PICK IT UP!" I picked it up, faster. "DROP THAT BAG!" I dropped it. "PICK IT UP!" I recovered it before the "UP!" I had become a human marionette, bobbing at my master, disarmed by the emotion.

"MISTER!" the cadet shouted. "YOU WILL IMMEDIATELY EXECUTE THE COMMAND GIVEN. DO YOU UNDERSTAND?!"

"Yes," I said, voice quavering, eardrums ringing.

"MISTER! You have THREE ANSWERS: 'YES, SIR,' 'NO, SIR,' AND 'NO EXCUSE, SIR.' DO YOU UNDERSTAND?!"

"Uh, yes, sir," I said, politely.

He was impeccable in a starched white shirt with blue, gold-striped shoulder epaulets; a bright, black-visored, snow-white cap; razor-sharp, black-striped gray pants; brilliant shoes; and advertising-quality white gloves. His name tag said "Rice," a name I liked. I had never seen anyone so marvelously perfect.

"I CANNOT HEAR YOU, SMACKHEAD!" he bellowed, as if I were back at the hotel rather than an inch from his clanging tonsils.

"Yes, sir," I said, pupils and testicles contracting.

"POP OFF, MISTER! KNOCK YOUR EQUIPMENT TOGETHER! YOU SOUND LIKE A WEEPING GIRL! DO YOU HEAR ME?! DROP THAT BAG!" he screamed.

"YES, SIR!" I cried, wincing at my own voice, the bag slapping the concrete. His face filled my vision. Uncle Shim believed that shouting was for thoughtless men. To my mother, shouting was a mortal sin. A street ditty inanely ran through my addled brain:

> *Step on a crack, break yo' momma's back.*
> *Yell at her face, lose all yo' grace.*

"BRACE, MISTER! You are CROOKED! PUSH that neck IN! KEEP YOUR EYES *UP—SQUASH* THAT NECK BACK! MAKE WRINKLES IN YOUR CHIN! CRAM IT IN! *ROLL* YOUR SHOULDERS BACK! *PUFF* OUT THAT PUNY, BIRDLIKE CHEST! HEELS TOGETHER, FEET AT FORTY-FIVE DEGREES! ELBOWS IN! THUMBS BEHIND THE SEAMS OF YOUR TROUSERS! KEEP YOUR HEAD STRAIGHT! ROLL YOUR HIPS UNDER! How old are you, SMACKHEAD!?"

I balked. He had almost spit in my face. "Se-seventeen," I said. Ten years in the ring spoke to me: take your stance, gloves high, and box this bully with the Godzilla voice. It was an old tune: China boy trips in and bingo from the jump, it's Fist City.

"*IRP!*—IMMEDIATE RESPONSE, PLEASE! 'SEVEN-TEEN, *SIR,*' *RIGHT?!* NOT 'Se-seventeen.' " The *"IRP!"* was the dark, sonorous belch of a thunder lizard; *"RIGHT?!"* was the sound of silk being slit by a sharp butcher knife. The cadence and emphasis of his speech were almost Negro, but there was no comfort in it.

"Yessir, seventeen, SIR, YESSIR!!"

"CROTHEAD," he hissed, "I WANT *SEVENTEEN* WRIN-KLES! PICK UP THAT BAG! *BRACE! ROLL* YOUR SHOULDERS DOWN AND BACK! *LIFT* YOUR HEAD UP! *CRAM* YOUR NECK IN! BRACING IS THE MILITARY POSTURE FOR A MEMBER OF THE FOURTH CLASS! IF YOU SURVIVE BEAST, YOU WILL BRACE FOR ONE YEAR! DO YOU UNDERSTAND ME, DUMBJOHNWILLIE CROT!? SOUND-OFF!"

"YES, SIR!" I cried.

"*KEEP* YOUR BEADY LITTLE EYES STRAIGHT AHEAD! NEW CADETS ARE NOT AUTHORIZED TO GAZE AROUND! REPORT TO THE MAN IN THE RED SASH AND SAY, 'Sir, New Cadet X reports to the Man in the Red Sash as ordered.' PRESENT ARMS—SALUTE HIM. DO YOU UNDERSTAND, CROTWASTE!"

"YES, SIR!" I screamed, catching only the inner threat of his incomprehensible speech. I struggled with the seventeen parts of bracing while recovering my luggage and trying to breathe the bad air and survive the truly awful lack of *ho*, har-mony, in this place.

"NEW CADETS DOUBLE-TIME WHEN THEY ARE ABOUT THEIR DUTIES. 'DOUBLE-TIME' MEANS YOU

WILL RUN IN A MILITARY MANNER, FOREARMS PAR-
ALLEL TO THE GROUND, HEAD IN. *POST,* MISTER!" he
bellowed, and I trembled isometrically in exaggerated rigidity,
trying to simulate an American picket fence post, stiff,
unbreathing, and white.

"*POST,* MISTER! DO NOT SPAZ ON ME! TAKE YOUR
POST AND GET YOUR SORRY UNMILITARY WAYS
OUT OF MY AREA! *MOVE IT!*"

I bolted and crashed into someone. "Oof," he said. I
bounced off, staggered sideways in the staccato minuet of a
bracing wino confused by the rotation of the earth. I cleverly
dropped my bag and tripped over it backward and crashed
awkwardly. My victim smashed hard into the Area, nose down,
hurling his bag into another candidate, who went down like a
lone pin plucked by a speeding bowling ball. "OW!" said this
one. The admission of pain drew cadre like shoppers to bar-
gains and they descended on him with rabid enthusiasm. The
man I had hit was Sonny Rappa, whom I had met yesterday at
the Hotel Thayer. I helped him up while making seventeen
wrinkles. I wanted to apologize but it wasn't one of my three
answers. I mouthed "Sorry," my pantomime making his cheeks
redden, his cheeks swelling. He guffawed. He covered his
mouth.

A horde of upperclassmen shouted at us so intimately they
seemed to be in our clothes. Sonny's bellows and my shouts
echoed within the gray rock fortress. We screamed with these
dapper nightmare men until the world became a single, blinding roar. I was blamed for knocking down a classmate. Sonny
was blamed for laughing without authorization and for looking
like Sal Mineo. I began to feel personally responsible for the
national debt, the tensions of the cold war, and the oppressive-
ness of a New York summer.

They shouted accusations; we shrieked "YES, SIR!" like
stuck records. Any prohibitions about yelling at elders died in
that hot, sweaty square. Here, a failure to yell at superiors
could lead to whatever followed torture—the kind of punishment one deserves for doing something really wrong, like will-
fully burning down Paris.

One cadet, motivated by our stirring interpretation of Laurel
and Hardy at West Point, began to psychically sandblast us
with howling halitosis and flying spit. He yelled with an intent
that would outlast the words, as if he wanted to reach my past
and allow me to wear the marks of his voice forever, with an

imprinting I thought only parents possessed. "YOU ARE IN IT NOW, *CREEP!* YOU ARE IN THE *PAIN PALACE,* THE *HURT HOOCH,* THE *OUCH POUCH,* THE *BRUISE BAG*— THE LAST PLACE YOU EVER WANTED! YOU *NEVER* WIPE OUT A CLASSMATE, CROTHEAD SMACKCREEP! I WILL NOT FORGET *YOU,* SHITFACE! I AM MR. O'WARE! POST, MARS-MAN!" I trembled with my foul luck.

We braced in line with others who once had been promising young Americans, awaiting the pleasure of the Man in the Red Sash. I kept my beady little eyes straight ahead and puffed out my puny, birdlike chest. The din of five hundred boys scream- ing at the cadre resounded from the tall, dun battlements. The maelstrom of screams grew as the morning passed, disturbing the calm of the cloudless blue sky. Luggage fell in random har- monies across the concrete of the Area. This was more than freshman registration for classes; I knew we were being pre- pared for war. I missed the West Point of *The Long Gray Line,* with boxing and camaraderie. It had reminded me of a China and a Chinese academy I had never known, a place of honor and of belonging, a school in the mountains and the clouds.

It was my turn, contorting as I threw a stupendously athlet- ic and unmilitary salute based on a lifetime's study of war movies.

"SIR! NEW CADET TING REPORTS TO THE SASH WITH THE RED MAN AS ORDERED!" Oh, *crap!* English! I grimaced and frowned, as if fierceness in expression could erase my words.

The Sash man was a stone-cold dude with a black shield on his sky-blue epaulet. Dark, visor-shaded eyes of murderous flint bore into me, augers into young wood. I trembled. The Man in the Red Sash fixed me with his frigid, cobralike gaze. I wasn't a candidate or a new cadet. I wasn't blood Chinese or inner Colored boy. I was a little, terrified bunny rabbit who had fallen through a crack and landed in Crocodile City, no longer competent in English, twitching with fear, wondering if they'd snap my neck before they ate me.

"SCREW IN THAT DUMBCROT NECK! TRY THAT AGAIN, *SMACKHEAD!*"

He delivered the last word with a ringing, baritone reso- nance that loosened the grip of my glasses on my head. I mas- tered the salute after he corrected my arms, shoulders, elbows, wrist, hand, fingers, thumb, eyeballs, chin, neck, and head.

"MISTER! GLASSES IMPLY WEAKNESS AND INVITE WEAK MARKSMANSHIP! THAT INVITES DEFEAT IN BATTLE! WHY ARE YOU WEARING *GLASSES?!*" he roared, the tassel on his red sash swaying.

"NO EXCUSE, SIR!" Wearing glasses—or being Chinese or Negro or in any way different—was always dangerous. But he treated me just as he had the others: with a crushing lack of human regard, with an authority that exceeded the inculcation of simple shock.

"ARE YOU SCARED, MISTER?!" he roared.

I was ready to die of fear. This was a question about heart. "NO, SIR!" I screamed.

"WHAT IS YOUR NAME, CROTHEAD?"

I only had three answers, so I thought it was a trick question. "SIR, MY NAME IS TING!" He looked at his clipboard.

"CROT! You are in Fourth New Cadet Company, tenth division of barracks. REPORT TO YOUR COMPANY FIRST SERGEANT. POST!"

I ran; skidded to a stop with both shoes; avoided another near crash with Sonny while he saluted; recovered my bag; and ran with the refined, continental suaveness of a myopic, spavined, bespectacled, perspiring, jet-lagged, bracing jackass with a suitcase, a military manner, and an enemy named Mr. O'Ware.

More new cadets entered the ancient gray stone tunnel, passing from the banal, gentrified urbanity of Thayer Road into the consuming, bone-crushing buzzsaw of the cadre.

Inside the stone quadrangle of Central Area, hundreds of us double-timed while bracing and searching for signs in a world laced tight with torment and abusive accusation. We were like casualties from a giant train wreck, in which all coincidentally had emerged with identical orthopedic injuries. We looked like science fiction zombies. I felt as if we were being used as stuffing for sausages, and the factory management had decided to allow us to scream in unison as we were being compressed into the skin.

I found a sign that said "4th New Cadet Company" hammered to a long stone barracks stoop atop a single flight of steps. I kept my chin in, my chest out, trying to breathe and hold my eyes and head locked to the front while doubletiming. It was like juggling pachyderms while dogs chewed at your ankles, your mother screamed at you, and a gasoline fire began to spread in your pants.

"YOU MOVE LIKE A CHICKEN! CLUCK YOUR WAY UP THOSE STAIRS!"

I stopped, goggle-eyed. I did not know what "cluck" meant.

"CLUCK! MAKE LIKE A CHICKEN!" cried an upperclassman.

"Cluck, sir?" I said. I was not a *t'u*, a rabbit. I was not a sausage, not a *lopchong*. I was a chicken, *hsiaochi*.

"POP OFF, MISTER! I CAN'T HEAR YOU! GIVE ME TWO CLUCKS! NOW CLUCK YOUR MISERABLE DUMBJOHN BODY UP THOSE STAIRS!"

"YES, SIR! CLUCK-CLUCK, SIR! CLUCK-CLUCK, SIR!"

The sky fell and I fluttered into a building resounding with the cries of final distress. I wanted to flee, but I surrendered to my *yeh*, my fate as a Chinese Chicken Little, marching to the sounds of carnivorous consumption, entering the room as would an undevout soul with foul karma. I was *da ru saba chun di yuh*, beaten into the eighteenth level of Buddhist hell for eighteen previous bad lives. Here, the cacophonous, volcanic bellowing in the sweltering room defeated any message that may have lain within it. A lava of fury and terror crawled over us like a live, serpentine evil. Everyone screamed in an accelerating tempo punctuated by the crash of bodies against walls and fists against metal. When was someone going to offer a hand and say, "Just kidding. Welcome to West Point. Sure is hot, isn't it? Have a lemonade"? Please, God. Then I remembered that I made wishes only to Chinese deities. They had the power.

Outside, upperclassmen wore white hats and yelled precisely. As one ventured deeper into the cauldron, conditions worsened. Hats came off, bodies fell, apostrophes appeared, dangling modifiers would follow, and soon all hope would be lost. Flames would lick higher, flesh and bone would congeal; sausages, rabbits, and chickens would be flambéed as smoking sacrifices to military gods.

"WHAT'RE YOU DOING, CROTHEAD?! *FUNCTION*, MISTER, DON'T *SPAZ* ON ME!" screamed a dark, unhatted cadet seated behind a desk, the veins in his exceptionally thick neck competing with flexing tendons and muscles for space. He was very agitated. Agitated at me.

I saluted and screamed, "SIR, NEW CADET TING REPORTS TO THE FIRST SERGEANT OF FOURTH NEW

CADET COMPANY!" I had no idea what words would pop from my mouth.

"MISTER, YOU LEFT OUT 'AS ORDERED'! TRY AGAIN, *CROT!*" The first sergeant stood and leaned into me, his face so close that my eyeballs bulged from the gravitational pull of his corneas. He was like the others: angry, clean-cut, and white, his features the products of sharp chiseling. Compared to his cropped hair, my crew cut looked like malicious error. Now he was so close he had to know I was Chinese. So now it begins. Remember, you're American, *ch'uan hsin ch'uan i*—with whole heart and mind. No going back.

"SIR, NEW CADET TING REPORTS TO THE FIRST SERGEANT OF FOURTH NEW CADET COMPANY, AS ORDERED, SIR!"

"ONLY *ONE* 'SIR' IN A STATEMENT!" he screamed. "CRAM THAT NECK *IN!* GIMME MORE WRINKLES, YOU SORRY STINKING GROSSED-OUT KNOB!"

I pressed my chin through my jaw, my throat, my neck, trying to merge it with my spine. Maybe, if I braced hard enough, I might pass into another room; perhaps, into another dimension. My eyes began to roll around in my head like lost and unrelated marbles.

The first sergeant looked at a roster. "You're in Third Squad, First Platoon," he snarled. "Room ten-forty-one. Squad leader's Mr. Alsop." He suddenly lunged at me and screamed, "WHAT SQUAD, BEANHEAD?!" I recoiled and instinctively formed fists.

"YOU *FLINCHED*, YOU SORRY GROSS CROT! WHAT SQUAD'RE YOU IN?!"

"SIR, I AM IN FIRST SQUAD!" I shouted, trying to control my compressed throat, which was pulsating without my wishing it to.

"*THAT'S* WRONG, *CRAPHEAD!*" he screamed in that unique, Negro-like, military meter, rocketing the first word, banging his fist onto the hollow metal desk and making the roster—and half the world and most of the chambers of my heart—jump. "YOU'RE IN *THIRD* SQUAD, *FIRST* PLATOON!" He lifted his chin, making an announcement to the world: "THE BEASTS IN THIS, THE FINEST FRIGGING COMPANY IN FIRST DETAIL, AREN'T GONNA EAT, SLEEP, OR BE VERY *DAMNED MERRY* THIS FINE SUMMER, YOU GOT THAT, *CROTHEAD?!*"

"YES, SIR!" I cried, as someone new began to roar at me.

He had Henry Fonda's flat midwestern twang, with the volume turned up.

"THAT'S THE GROSSEST PIECE OF DOGCRAP SPECK *EVER* DISPLAYED IN BEAST! YOU PROBABLY CAN'T REMEMBER YOUR OWN *NAME!* YOU'RE GOING TO BE LUCKY TO *SEE* FOOD THIS SUMMER, YOU GOT THAT, *CROT*BEAN!!?"

"YES, SIR!" I screamed.

"*I CAN'T HEAR YOU! POP OFF,* MISTER!" cried the first sergeant.

I screamed again in an escalating fury, using all my lung air to speak. It was as if everyone were yelling to each other from distant mountaintops, trying to explain that their hair was aflame. All these white guys screaming at me. And had he really said no food this summer?

I lived for food and cared little for perspiration. Tony Barraza, my boxing coach, had marveled at my ability to work hard and to sweat little. Now I was bracing at West Point, sweat pouring from me like rats from a holed freighter. The human body was 80 percent water, and my brain was shrinking. At this rate I could be in very big trouble, very quickly.

Kai Ting, you funny-lookin' China-boy crapforbrains, you *are* in major-league, *very big* trouble. No food for the summer. Mr. Alsop. Room ten-something. Third Squad, First Platoon. Glasses are not welcome here. My name is Ting. My name used to be Ting.

The first sergeant was pasting angry shouts all over the next victim in the Fourth New Cadet Company lineup, teaching him how to throw his rigid body against a wall to allow an upperclassman to pass. "*HIT* THAT WALL, MISTER! *KISS* IT WITH YOUR BACKSIDE, YOU SORRY CROT! WHEN I WALK, I WANNA HEAR YOUR BODY *SLAM* THAT WALL! I DON'T WANT YOUR SORRY DISREPUTABLE UNMILITARY BEANHEAD CORPSE NEAR ME!"

Henry Fonda's voice said to me, "Report to your room. Deposit your luggage. FALL OUT INTO THE COMPANY STREET IN CENTRAL AREA AND REPORT TO THE MAN IN THE RED SASH! *DO YOU UNDERSTAND ME?!*"

"YES, SIR!" I cried, responding with the automatic compliance of the abused. The Sash man directed me to barbers who buzzed my hair to the skull. I donned T-shirt, gym shorts, black shoes, and knee-high socks—the first outfit which ex-

ceeded the imposed poor taste of my mother's school clothes.
I accented the ensemble with a quivering West Point brace that
began in Central Area and reached my ancestral home in
Shanghai. A paper laundry tag marked "TING" dangled from
a safety pin on my shorts. Tiny spikes of cut hair pricked my
sweating skin. I looked like a fugitive from a hotel fire and felt
like a sofa that had been thrown, burning, from the top floor,
over which an engine company of booted, axe-toting firefight-
ers had trod on their way to something important. My stomach
grumbled angrily and emptily.

A multitude of Men in Red Sashes met our needs with the
bonhomie of surly Parisian waiters encountering Bermuda-
shorted, tobacco-spitting, gum-chewing American tourists. We
learned facing movements and close-order drill. The Sash men
marked off each Herculean task on our laundry tags. We were
the wash, caught in a perpetual spin cycle, high wet heat, no
rinse, all original colors merging into plebeian new cadet
sludge, the true American melting crucible fueled by a broiling
sun and a consuming white male anger. "POST INTO THAT
SALLY PORT, MISTER!" shouted a Sash man.

Who was Sally Port? What was a girl doing here?

"IT IS A FORTIFIED PASSAGE FOR TROOPS, LIKE A
TUNNEL. *POST!*"

I basked in the coolness. Screams were thinned by the tunnel's depth, and I took a cool breath of air for the first time in
hours.

Three men waited for me, backlit by the bright sun. I
thought of rumbles in the dune tunnels on the Great Highway
by the Pacific Ocean, where punks fought hoods without the
honor of single combat. White boys had yelled "Skinny yellow
ching-chong Chinaman chink" at me and "Wooly-headed
skinny nigger boy" at Toussaint LaRue, my best friend. I had
raised my fists, trying to parry their words from hurting us
deep, the way punches never could. I learned to fight ugly,
bloody words with skinny, hard-knuckled, weeping fists.

Now, three men: one tall, one big, and one huge. I had never
fought with my neck stuck in. My poor eyes adjusted to the
dark.

"SIR, MR. TING REPORTS TO THE SALLY PORT AS
ORDERED!" The tunnel magnified my voice—like the showers at the Y, without the shampoo, the water, the laughter, or
the goodwill.

Tall returned the salute. "Singing experience!" he said.

"SIR, I TOOK SEVENTH-GRADE VOCAL CLASS!"

"This is choir tryout!" said Huge. "State religion!"

I hesitated, fearful of saying "None."

"Protestant, Catholic, or Jewish?" asked Tall in a deep voice that filled the tunnel. He had delicate features and translucent skin that seemed immune from the hot, beating New York summer sun. His name tag said "Fideli." He hadn't mentioned Taoism, and Confucianism wasn't a faith. Tony Barraza's rosary was in my pocket, for luck. I thought of the only church I had liked.

"SIR, I AM PROTESTANT!"

"Sing," he said, "the following lines:

> *Amazing grace, how sweet the sound*
> *That saved a wretch like me.*
> *I once was lost, but now am found,*
> *Was blind, but now I see."*

His voice was rich and textured and seemed to fill gaps in an imperfect universe. Even today, his singing echoes in my mind. "Fall out. Let your neck out. Sing, Mr. Ting," he said.

I let my neck relax and immediately felt something bad was going to happen. I sang. When I got to "lost" in the third line, Large said, "STOP! Mister, you *normally* sing like this?"

"YES, SIR! 'Yes, sir; Yes, sir,'" echoed my voice.

The three looked at each other.

"Amusing voice," said Huge.

"'Amusing Grace,'" said Mr. Fideli. He smiled and I felt a wave of instant affection for him, followed by guilt. My mother knew that I was emotionally frail. Screw that crap. I frowned. Mr. Fideli studied my face. I heard the roar outside the sally port.

"Dismissed. Report to the Man in the Red Sash," said Large.

Again, Mr. Fideli smiled. "And please take your voice with you."

My next task was a mad shopping tour for bedding, uniforms, equipment, and books that, when lifted, inevitably reflected the atomic weight of lead. Now I was lost, betrayed by my terrible sense of direction, a lunatic in an open-doored asylum, running with my neck in, bearing heavy barracks bags. I joined a mob of other new cadets who moved purposefully. I was back in Central Area, breathing a sigh of amazed relief when I saw the "4th New Cadet Company" sign. I dumped the gear in my room and reported back to the orderly room, wherein lurked the awful first sergeant.

I ached with hunger. Food was first in my hierarchy of needs. Eating was second and having thirds was next. Because I feared hunger, I presumed that the ultimate test of American manhood would be starvation. Of course, I was wrong; the tests that awaited me in this school possessed roots even deeper than my appetite.

"Git outa mah road, damn Yankee *scum*." His deep, growling intensity and sinister regionalism undercut the vortex of thumping bodies and mortal screams. It was familiar and strange, as if a white man were speaking the colored dialect of Negro streets. I saw him in my fearful mind—a pissed white bogeyman, running through the night with all the authority of a bad cop. We jumped like jammed holiday shoppers from a rabid dog, crashing our sorry knob bodies into inadequate wall spaces to flee teeth. Fear seized my guts. I knew, of all these boys in the room, he would pick me.

A lean, hard face filled my vision. The remnants of the hairs on my neck bristled. I regretted my childhood campaign to become a successful Negro youth. This man would hate my effort at blackness, my eclecticism, my pure Asiatic blood, my Chinese- and Spanish-speaking tongue, my love of Asian foods. This was no time to look like the United Nations rolled into a small, clucking rabbit.

The closeness of his face blurred my vision. Everyone seemed as myopic as I, pushing their eyeballs into my eye sockets to get a better look. He wore Aqua Velva. I shaved once a week whether I needed to or not. I knew details about razors and shaving colognes. Schick. Gillette. Old Spice, Mennen. Burley. Canoe. Blood.

He frowned, waves of forehead ridges bunching angrily, his eyeballs crawling over the features of my face. Time stopped.

"Whaat," he drawled slowly at me, pulling the words like taffy on a cold day, "inna name a good *GOD hail* are *yeew?*"

I knew what he was asking. Verify your alien nature so we can hang your Chinaman body from a tall tree, fair and square. I wanted to say, "I AM AN *AMERICAN*—JUST LIKE EVERYONE ELSE!"—but my purpose had wilted in this white, crystalline blast furnace. "SIR, I AM CHINESE-AMERICAN!" I shouted, ready, with teeth-gnashing determination, to endure the test, to take the words, face the rope, and show the skill. Where I came from, children yelled as a prelude to fists and men grew silent before taking blood. The roar dropped. I saw his name tag: Alsop. *Yu chao.* He was my squad leader.

"Jehezus. No beans? Pure Chi-nese?"

"YES, SIR!"

"Waall ... whup mah ever-lovin', long-livin', stand-up-straight *unit!* Ah ain't *never* seen no *Chi-nese* built lahk *yeew* afore. *Damn!* Y'all's a *big* sonofabitch! What's it lahk bein' *Chi-nese?*"

"IT IS NOT VERY MERRY, SIR!" I shouted.

His face softened, the features sliding, changing, his face so old. "Good fer you," he said with a smile. "CRACK YO' HEAD IN, CROT!" he screamed. "DON'T YOU *DARE* BE BJ ON R-DAY! YOU AIN'T GONNA BE VERY MERRY— I'LL SHEW YOU *NOT VERY MERRY!* GONNA FILL YOU UP WITH FOURTH-CLASS KNOWLEDGE, YOU *CHI-NESE YANKEE SCUMBAG CROTHEAD DOOWILLIE DUMBJOHN!!*" His shouts filled my ears, my brain pan, the room, the Western Hemisphere, the Gulf of Po Hai. He stopped fuming. "WHY'D Y'ALL DECIDE TA BE A *CHI-NESE?*" he roared.

"NO EXCUSE, SIR!" I cried.

He smiled. "BJ means '*Be*-fore June,' 1965—year frum now, if y'all fortunate—when y'all be *reckanized* by the upper classes. Y'all be Yearlin's an' we'll shake your damn Yankee hands." He made his imitation grin, and then it disappeared without memory. "*THAT'S* WHEN Y'ALL CAN FIX TA SPOUT BJ WO-ORDS LAHK 'MERRY'!" he roared, his head jacking up and down as if he were going to take a bite out of my head. "TILL THEN, Y'ALL BRACE LIKE A DANG FOOT-DRAGGIN', TAIL-BUSTED, LONG-TONGUED YELLER *DAWG*—YA'LL *GOT* THAT!?"

"YES, SIR!"

"Listen up, crothead. *NEXT* TIME, Y'ALL CHOOSE TA BE FRUM *MISSISSIPPI, YOU HEAR ME?*"

"YES, SIR!" I screamed, with total sincerity.

2

EXODUS

Sunset District, San Francisco, May 1964

I understood Buddhist *yeh*, karma. I had wondered who I was and who, in the prior rotation, I had been. I feared I was descending the slope of respent lives, following the progression from man to woman, of woman to lower animal, lower animal to insect. I expected an assistant Buddha to tell me someday that this was my last trip.

Two months before wandering into Central Area like Typhoid Mary—colliding with classmates, horrifying the public with my singing, and making enemies on sight—my stout English teacher, Mrs. Marshall, touched me. I recoiled; I didn't like to be touched.

"Your mother called, Kai. You've been accepted at West Point."

Shouts rang as friends beat on my back and shook my hand. "Way to go, Kai!" "Cool rules!" "Bitchin', man!" "All right!" I was going to West Point! Me, in a place like that! I was round and full with American status. I tried to control my face, but had to smile as I shook hands with Randy Reed, John Estrella, Pat Hogan, and the others, expanding my chest as Cindy McCreedy, Katie Martin, Berta Lowry, Jane Accampo, and Molly Bokelund cried "Congratulations!" I felt pleasure. I felt fear, disbelief, joy, and unworthiness, the distress of an unlucky person becoming noticed, a failure being subjected to the risks of recognition. But I had been given a golden ladder to scale success. I had wanted so badly to win the appointment, and I had been convinced that my very desire was a fatal impediment to its realization. What one wanted invited its opposite to appear. Gods frustrated human wishes, turning dreams into vapor. My mother had been proof of that. Whatever I openly liked, she uncannily took.

15

"Do not," said Uncle Shim, "ever speak unpromisingly about family. This is *ji hui*, inauspicious words to be avoided, where speaking sourness invites it, and uttering desires chases them away. One receives rewards by not wanting. To ask for something directly is bad manners and exceptionally bad luck."

In the Negro neighborhood where I had grown up, Reverend Stamina Jones had led prayers in the storefront church for Kingdom Come. But Chinese spirits were superior to the gods of Western faith; they had *yuing chi*, life fortune, *sze*, death, *jing ji*, taboo, *ji hui*, inauspicious thoughts, and *k'ung hsu*, living abandonment, while Baptists awaited Grace in a world that disliked black skin.

I had told four people—Coach Barraza, Toussaint LaRue, Jack Peeve, and Christine Carlson—my secret of wanting to go to West Point. With each admission, each more hazardous than the one preceding it, I had known that I accordingly could not go.

Jack Peeve had also wanted to go to West Point, but had been eliminated because of a history of scarlet fever. I had trouble telling him the good news, but he had no trouble hearing it.

My father, the former Colonel Ting Kuo-fan of the Chinese Nationalist Army, wanted me to go to the Academy. To him, West Point was escape from diaspora and attainment of America itself.

"Go to West Point. *Must.*" It was his refrain.

"Sit up straight, like a West Point cadet, like the cadet you'll never be," hissed my mother, providing the coda.

I had always wanted to leave. Years before, Toussaint and I sat on the tin-roofed sheds of the Empire Metal Works in the South Mission yards, studying the freights, watching 4–6–2s pulling long strings and little 0–8–0s humping cars in the yard, light gray smoke merging with the dun mist. We were from the Panhandle, a Negro neighborhood similar to South Mission on the other side of San Francisco, but the draw of locomotives on youth knew no boundaries. I was the only Chinese at the yards, but Mission boys customarily put up with me if I didn't pretend to own the view.

"What's a China boy doin' here?" asked a kid one day. He was built like a big, rectangular caboose with rhino-sized limbs.

Toussaint had taught me to leave my new glasses be when

trouble called. I made my hands quiet, fingers itching as the glasses slid down the modest bridge of my nose.

"Aw, he's cool. Boy thinks he's colored," said another.

"He don' *look* colored," said Caboose. "He look *white*."

"Ain't white," I said in my high voice. "See, I'm colored."

"Bool-shit!" spat Caboose, frowning.

"He's colored," said Toos quietly. He had heart and knuckles. It looked like a lot of work to take on those fists, having that strong, high-cheekboned face bent on putting the hurt on you.

Caboose poked the insides of his mouth with his tongue, inventorying teeth and thinking, while Toos ran his cool icebox gaze around the challenger's profile, getting ready for fate.

I hated those pulsing eternities before a fight, when breathing stopped and sparks and silence filled the air as the heart pounded in the anticipation of losing blood. I hated this more than I hated the tussles. Fear would put cotton in my brain and pump all my circulation into my ventricles and atria.

I remembered Toos's advice. "Don't jump to fist or to scat. Give words a chance. And don't scream China stuff at 'em." That was easy for him to say. When he spoke, talking came out and people nodded. "China, look 'em inna eyes and talk it real slow."

Later, Coach Barraza trained me. The first round, when anxiety ruled, was my worst; in the third, when I was working too hard on saving my life to worry, I fought in accord with *ho,* sweet harmony, which drew left hooks and countering rights from me like long noodles from a good-fortune dish.

Please, I said to all the listening gods, let's not fight Caboose and his brothers. He's as big as a house, and it'll be five to two on this here tin roof, and heights make me like to faint and I'm gonna fall for sure, way down there, where some train'll flatten me and my glasses. I looked down, the bottom of my stomach dropping from me in anticipation, my gorge rising.

"Yeah, right," sighed Caboose, peering through thin fog toward the downtown skyscrapers. "What I said—he's jus' light."

I took a deep breath.

"But he surely do look like a damn China boy to *me,*" he added, to no one in particular.

The yards were Jump City for flight out. But Toos only joked about running, and I was never serious about my chances on distant tracks without him. In my running fever, I did not know that leaving Egypt would be hard. Exodus meant making farewells, and this was not one of my skills. I wanted to belong, never to be separated, to be made to stand alone, isolated, hopelessly different, and required to act or to suffer— ever again.

I was fourteen when we moved out of the Negro Panhandle, where I had been born and the family had lived since fleeing China. I felt like I was already ten feet under quicksand, and said nothing to Toos, Alvin Sharpes, Titus McGovern, or Earline Ribbons, or to anyone. I denied the split. I'll be back— soon, I said to myself.

"What's happenin'?" asked Toos. He frowned at the truck while my father and friend Hector Pueblo moved our furniture out.

I shook my head, no words in my mouth. We spit in our hands and shook. I was weak, unable to take the comfort of his strength. I was losing my best friend. There would never be another like him. This was where *yeh* played its bitter hand. If I had been more deserving, I wouldn't have had to leave him and my young heart.

Now, three long years later, at seventeen, I wanted to leave with the fervor of a Hebrew held in Egypt. I wanted to flee San Francisco, a city I loved, so I could escape my mother, whom I secretly disliked. My mother was Edna McGurk Ting, and to me she was Pharaoh, skilled in abuse and quick with the whip. I was seven when she had come into our family with a reign of cultural terror that ended the Chinese nature of our family. She was from Philadelphia society, and I was her hopeless social project.

"I hope you do well at the Point," Edna said to me when I came home the day I was accepted. Her cool eyes were sharply observant. "Your chances are poor. Jim Latre, a very bright, handsome, ex-beau of mine, got shingles and failed that first summer, drawing our sympathy." She smiled, remembering. Then the frown.

"Lift your drooping shoulder. West Point is the most diffi- cult school in the world. What possessed us to send you? They will throw you out on your ear. You are so woeful in math, so lacking in ambition, your mind so pitifully *mediocre,* you can- not miss a *single* thing. There, you cannot succeed by laughing or going crazy.

"But it is that pitiful Negroid neighborhood background that will always hold you back. You may not be sufficiently American. I have given you your best chance. But your affection for failure, your penchant for associating with those with no future, will haunt you all your days." She was talking about Toos and Tony Barraza.

She ran a green dust rag from a pocket in her peach-toned sweater across the bindings of my beloved books. *Ben Hur, Beau Geste, Captains Courageous, The Adventures of Huckleberry Finn, Romance of the Three Kingdoms, Pride and Prejudice.* She had taught me English, and I had quickly grasped paradox and irony.

She sighed. "I had to cleanse you of singing 'Jesus Loves Me' in *Chinese*. Then you employed that horrid Negro speech. Now your English is quite correct, thank you, but you still hesitate, your mouth filled with marbles and confusion. He who hesitates is lost. You hesitate." She sighed, burdened by my shortcomings. "Your father and I have savings, enough for one of us to attend your graduation from West Point."

In Philadelphia, silent table manners justified continued life. My family was from Shanghai, where the roar of omnivorous consumption shook seaports around the world. I was from San Francisco, rocked by sharp earthquakes, soothed by mournful foghorns, surrounded by Dungeness crabs, blessed with modest weather, and populated by citizens of the world. I was packing to leave the City, which to me had become the Pyramids.

I did not know what to say to her, and was experiencing the normal reactions of a boy whose brain was being flogged. It was a cool and foggy day, but I perspired, back aching. I wondered if I had polio from the polio god who had taken my friend Connie Dureaux. I must have done something very bad in my earlier life to have deserved these talks with my mother.

I was a teenager, tormented by profound doubt. I wore an unwanted Chinese face in Negro streets and white avenues. I was cursed by a tongue that misspoke to elders and was handicapped by an endless host of cultural stupidities. I secretly answered to every god known. To my credit, I had friends, got good grades, could box, and play basketball, but because I was not a genius, and I was not handsome, I knew I was on a karmic roller coaster that was headed, with all deliberate speed, down, and south.

"Pack your school clothes," she said.

In the Sunset, boys wore Keds, tight, peg-legged jeans, and plaid shirts. I wore black baggy wool slacks, black shoes, and

a white shirt. School clothes, Edna said. To me, they were for
funerals—Chinese wore white, and Negroes wore black.

Jack Peeve, my friend in this new neighborhood, gave me
his cast-offs. At his house, on the way to school, I'd change
into an outfit that wouldn't suggest suicide.

Jack, like Toos, had all the freedoms and skills I envied. He
could talk without making his mother scream, use the telephone, be cool in front of a girl he liked, swat curveballs out
of the park, recover instantly from gruesome, mind-weakening
injuries, and lick nearly any comer in arm wrestling. Jack
could beat most men, except for Uncle Yorchich Votan and his
dad.

Jack's dad was short, thin haired, and broad shouldered. He
smiled a lot, and he and Jack used to clap each other on the
back every few minutes, making the same kind of sound that
a house must make when it falls on a car. I did that once to
Mr. Peeve, and it was like hitting the lumber in the basement.

Uncle Yorch lived in the Peeves' dark garage. He displayed
shark jaws, deer antlers, ram horns, assorted truck parts, and
bullet-punctured German Wehrmacht helmets on the walls. He
liked to play catch with a car tire with the wheel still in it. His
head was as big as a medicine ball, and he used to punch Jack
with a massive fist to keep him alert. "Hurtcha?" he'd ask.

"No way!" Jack would shout, rising at the opposite end of
the garage, the debris from his collision with the memorabilia
from his uncle's campaigns against all animals and Nazis still
jangling onto the oil-stained concrete of his living room floor.
Being with them was like watching an unchoreographed John
Ford western bar brawl. I knew how to box, but hated to fight.

"Ouch," I would say in sympathy.

"Arm-wrestle?" Uncle Yorch asked me, eyes bright with
hope.

I shook my head. Not with *my* hand.

I think Jack awakened one morning at the age of twelve
with whiskers and the musculature of an adult. I thought this
was because Mr. Peeve was a chef, with lots of food at home.
Jack said it was because he was Bulgarian. With the Germans
so close, they couldn't mess around with growing up, so they
did it overnight.

I had been walking to Lincoln when he had said, "Nice
clothes."

I sized him up and knew, with a sinking heart, that even

with all my years in the ring, this guy could pound me. He had a toughness that did not come from effort, but from the gods.

"I'm Jack. Want some a my old clothes?"

"Yeah," I said. Then I smiled, although Toos was the only one who could tell when I did. He said something happened in my eyes.

"Burt Lancaster would wear clothes like this," I said. He was my number-one cinema hero. I liked his smile. Jack looked like him.

I hoped the clothes would make me look white. They didn't—any more than I had turned Negro from hanging with Toos. But the clothes helped; I didn't look like the sad, lame, emasculated Chinese in American movies, bound for Chinese and Negro funerals, dressed by a mother who saw life as more than a challenge.

After school I took the L car downtown to my YMCA job in the Tenderloin, then returned the clothes to the Peeves' on the way home, racing through the clothing change. "Fast, huh?" I said.

"Yeah," said Jack. "Get moolah for changing clothes fast."

"You *do?*" I asked, excited about my skills.

Jack shook his head, grinning. "Nope. Just kidding," he said, clapping me thunderously on the back.

"Wish Jack would dress up like that," said Mrs. Peeve, appraising me in the formality of Edna's school clothes.

"No thanks, Ma," said Jack. "I'd rather go to school naked."

"I'm done with school clothes," I said now as I packed, my heart in my throat, feeling like Oliver asking for more porridge. I finally had gotten up the nerve to bring Jack's cast-offs home. I did it the way our cat, Silly Dilly, used to bring in birds, worried about the reaction of the home folk.

"What do *you* know about *anything?*" Edna asked through closed teeth. "Where did you get these?"

"Jack Peeve's give-aways." I felt anticipatory fear. Now would come woe and the return of the garments to Jack under scrutiny of press, cops, and neighbors. I awaited the conventional destruction of my spirit or of my model planes that hung from the ceiling. She would claw them out of the sky with her antiaircraft broom and then jump on them with a vehemence that arrested breath. Four planes had survived her blitz. Silence. I prepared for sadness.

"Predictably, Christine has not thanked you," she said. "She should send flowers to *us,* for our appointment to West Point."

I slammed the suitcase lid on my fingers. *Our* appointment. My heart slugged, vision blurred, stomach soured, back ached, polio bloomed. I could not argue or raise my voice to her.

I had asked Dear Abby if it was correct for me to send flowers to a girl I loved who did not love me. Edna was aware of the flowers and knew that I had received no answer from Christine. An old and familiar anger surged through me. "You can't read my mail! It's against the law!" I had yelled when I discovered she had been reading my letters for years. I had made the claim hysterically, without thought, as if I were worthy of having an opinion.

"I AM YOUR *MOTHER!*" she screamed. "There are bad influences in this world—much of it in the mail! DON'T YOU *DARE* RAISE YOUR VOICE TO ME! How dare you toss the law at me as if you were a *lawyer? DO YOU WANT YOUR FATHER TO FIND ME WITH A STROKE?!*"

I couldn't believe how stupid I had been. Of course, she had read my Dear Abby correspondence. She was my mother.

I had not always kowtowed to her. I was almost nine when I had held my fists up to her, left foot and left profile leading in accord with the Marquis of Queensberry and the teachings of Tony the Tiger Barraza. I didn't want her to hit me anymore. She took to her bed in a dignified retreat that probably made the funeral procession for Queen Victoria look like the drunken 49er riots at Kezar after another bitter loss to Detroit.

One morning, after breakfast, she called me to their room. "You gave me a stroke," she said calmly, her voice brimming with ancient pains. Her careful articulation was a weapon against my imprecise speech. Weak sunlight fell on the bed, leaving her face in shadow. I stood at near attention, facing the rope, the consequences of my prior bad lives, of standing up for myself.

"I am your mother. *Not* your stepmother. Give the picture of the Other Woman to your sister. *Never, ever* make a fist or *raise your voice to me!*" she cried. "Refer to me as 'my mother,' or 'my real mother.' Obey and I will not hit you. Stand straighter, you *pitiful*, wretched, ugly, fat-lipped thing. Wipe that expression from your face *this moment*." Megan, middle of my three *tsiatsia*, older sisters, had given me Mahmee's photo only weeks earlier. Edna was offering a trade. If I gave it to Janie, the youngest of my sisters, she wouldn't hit me anymore. I didn't know that raising my guard to her had already accomplished what she now offered. All I knew was that she hated me, and it was my *yeh* to live with it.

"Deal," I said, edging closer, offering my hand, without spit.

We shook, her pale eyes and pallid features eloquently accusing me; I was a hood who had tried to knuckle his own mom. I was the cause of her ills, her poor animation, her industry in correcting and guiding me through a ceaseless process of examination and criticism. I felt bad, and tried, and old. The strength of her handshake made me wonder. In time, overcome by the small events of life, I forgot the photo.

Edna's postal concern was not related to Howdy Doody flexi-straws or Davy Crockett coonskin hats; it was worse than my frowning face, my trouble with the gymnastics of English, or my Chinese habit of eating noisily. I had looked at Sears bra ads.

"Girls distract boys and diminish your woeful native capacity for schoolwork. Girls are cruel, you are far from handsome, and they will hurt you terribly. Rely on us for affection. Animals are kinder than people. You are so frail and emotionally stunted . . . the slightest comment drives you into a frenzy. You can't even speak without my help. Change that expression *this instant!* I can't *stand* that ugly, despicable scowl. Don't you *dare* defy me with your horrid face. You are *sick* and vile for looking at these—these *pictures*. Your interest is unnatural! Other boys do not look at women in their underwear! If only you could see yourself as others see you. You're despicable! Just because you're now larger in frame does *not* mean that you do not have to mind me."

She was in rhythm now, chanting ills in synchronicity with *ho,* the greater harmony, flurrying verbal Sunday punches with no jabs and all right crosses, hooks, and uppercuts. All I felt was hurt, pinned to the ropes, without a ref, a bell, or a god to intervene. I leaked blood from my brain and regretted my life. Her voice knifed into my brain, where it vibrated and keened painfully, and I prayed for the emptiness that comes to those with patience.

"I should've called Juvenile Hall and had you arrested! You're *terrible,* ungodly, disgusting, with fat lips and small, frowning, squinty eyes. No girl could like you! You're going to West Point and don't even see it is *I* who made this possible and now you're going as if *you* earned it! You are so ungrateful and full of venomous, stupid, *teenaged* nonsense! Oh, yes, show me that bland, ugly, stupid, expressionless face. It will hurt you more than me."

3

ROCK

Chinatown, May 20, 1964

"*Dababa,* Uncle, you ever have a bad relationship with anyone?" Uncle Shim was not my true blood uncle, but he was my Old World elder in all of life.

"Ding hao!"—highest best! He liked my question. We were in the On-On Cafe on Grant Avenue after my Saturday shift at the Y. He sipped long-steeped, thick, oily black tea while I ate the house specialty of *hoy yaw ngauyuhk fan,* succulent, aromatic oyster beef over steamed, fluffy white rice, along with *do see dofu hom nyeuw,* the sharply salted, tender fish with soft bean curd in thick black bean sauce that Chinese had used for centuries to build muscles, and *gai chowfun,* chicken with wide, flat, richly seasoned rice noodles. It was a meal for four or five and barely enough for me.

The waiter said, "Hey, *fan toong.*" Rice garbage can.

Chinese food was a tonic to my ills. When Edna called Christine names, I wanted to scream to the heavens and jump up and down; but I couldn't, so I ran to the basement and punched wood in crossing combinations with bare knuckles until the pain went away.

"Able Student," Uncle Shim said, smiling, "you have asked a *very* excellent question. Maintaining positive *gahng* and *lun,* bonds and relationships, is the essence of the moral and superior man. You have no existence outside the network of your *gahng,* the constellation of your duties. I am very happy with your question." He showed me his teeth. I smiled back, chewing industriously.

He cleared his thin throat, adjusting a perfectly knotted jade bow tie. He looked about through his thick-lensed apothecary spectacles that brightly reflected light like Archimedes' mirror. The cafe was awash in the bubbling talk of the high-tea lunch crowd as patrons argued, yelled, chewed, sucked soup and tea, and filled the air with lush, fourteen-toned Cantonese dialects. No one cared what we said, or could hear us if they tried.

Uncle Shim hid his teeth, frowned, pain in his eyes, distaste in his mouth. He looked down and said, in his soft, spare voice, "You know, *I* am in bad relationships."

This was like Mrs. Marshall saying she loathed Shakespeare's effete writing, or President Johnson saying he disliked Texas.

"Yes!" he cried against my disbelief. "I tell you the truth!" He sucked in breath. "Young Ting, I failed in my relationship to my parents, to my son, to my wife, and to my daughters, to the *entire clan*. I could not stop their deaths. Is this not the most awful thing that an elder can tell a youth? Someday I will tell you the story of my failure." He brought his face up. "All my learning, and my parents' efforts, to no avail. *Wo ts'o liao!* I am to blame!"

"Uncle—"

"So," he sighed. "Please believe me. Our learning in this mystery of *gahng* and *lun* is never done. This is why we must be students of the Master, for all our days. And as regrettable a man as I am, I have not ceased in my effort to be a good student."

He adjusted the alignment of his unused *kwaidz,* chopsticks. His thick, graying eyebrows were skewed, his thin cheeks hollowing, his eyes large and liquid, burning brightly with oils of pain and remorse. Now he spoke to himself, again the uncle of my early childhood, the reciter of Ming poetry, the cantor of sad rhymes from another age, speaking to graves.

"My heart is a cold stove, my life the cup filled with dust."

"I don't remember that one, *Dababa,*" I said. My uncle avoided saying new things. He liked to review the fundamentals.

"Words just came; I made them up. Now they are gone." He sipped his tea and looked at me. "Why do you ask this essential question about *gahng* and *lun?*" he asked softly.

"*Dababa*—the war wasn't your fault. If China had an army—"

"Why do you ask this essential question about *gahng* and *lun?*"

I wanted to say: if China had had a West Point, it could've

resisted the foreign powers, saved the slain from death, and kept my uncle from savoring his failures. The foreign destruction of China's spirit could have been avoided. One must fight evil.

"It's my mother," I said, closing my eyes in primitive fear. "I have a bad relationship with her." I sucked in breath. I was violating *ji hui,* speaking inauspiciously and disturbing the geomancy, causing bad words to come to life. It was unfair that negatives waited in muscular ambush to pounce on our stupid words, while the good was hidden in the secret, hidden folds of life.

"I'm supposed to love her. I don't even know how. I want to yell at her." I omitted the part about beating up the house.

He sucked his breath. "Shouting is for men without brains. This is indeed a failing, to raise your voice against your mother." He shook his gray head and I could no longer enjoy the wafting cafe aromas. "Think of Cheng Han-cheng's disrespectful wife."

I looked at him blankly.

"Do you not remember her? She struck her mother-in-law and was stripped of her skin, sliced and burned? Truly, to have a mind with no gripping at all—a brain made of hard rocks."

I grimaced for Mrs. Cheng and smiled at his description of me.

"And now you smile! Ayyy—yes, thank you," he said to our red-jacketed waiter, who delivered hot tea, nodding blandly at the ritual of elders chastising the young, trying to pour their life lessons into the empty and nonabsorbent vessels of youth.

"See here, young Ting. The love of parents is not a Sung canticle of romance, for the lute or mandolin, for poets who yearn for the moon and shed tears for the mystery of the tides. It has nothing to do with *gan ch'ing*—human emotion.

"*Hausheng,* Able Student, it is *duty.* Do not worry about feelings. Think of your *obligations.* It is such a mistake to call this relationship a matter of love. This is Western silliness and foreign nonsense, which do not cover the truth of duty.

"There is no dreamy softness inside the heavy burden of *shiao,* of piety to parents. It is a huge rock. You can try all your life and never encircle this rock with your arms or with your life.

"It is the mountain of obligation you can never carry and never drop, for you are bound by duty to your father and all fathers before. *This* is what it means to honor your birthright.

"You must create in your father a sense of harmony, of *ho,* in his heart! This is the unending duty of sons! To place his thoughts before yours, his needs before all others." He sighed deeply, attempting to calm the exclamations my statement about Edna had excited from him. The vein in his temple darkened to a deep blue. He sipped tea loudly, trying to drown the bitter air at the table. I did not give my parents a sense of harmony. I had raised my fists to Edna. I wanted to yell at her. It did not matter what she did to me; I had to honor her. Yet, deep down, I knew truly that I hated her, breaching *shiao* and failing in duty. I was without honor or value. I lowered my face in hot, red shame and put down my *kwaidz,* unworthy of human respect, undeserving of good or plentiful food.

"Bonds and relationships," he said softly, "*gahng* and *lun,* tie you to others and give you the purpose of life. Duty, *dzeren,* filial piety, *shiao,* bind you to those you must honor. In serving *gahng* and *lun,* you honor the life your parents gave you. Without this, you are dishonored. It cannot be simpler. Do you see?"

"Yes, *Dababa,*" I said, looking at my old shoes.

"So whose fault is this lack of *ho,* this absence of harmony with your living mother?" he asked. I looked up.

"Mine, *Dababa,*" I said. The dark blue vein in his head pulsed.

"And how can you rectify this failing?" he asked.

"I will leave," I said firmly.

He smiled wanly. "The worst, perhaps, of all thoughtful choices." It was a mild day, but Uncle Shim held the teacup in both hands, taking its warmth. He looked at me as if seeing me from afar.

"Are there not others whom you *will* miss," he said slowly, "when you leave for the moon, for the outer stars?" He could not bear to say the name of my actual destination, that "military school"—two words that produced an immediate contradiction. This place in distant New York that could not be an academy of thought and scholarship if it also had guns and taught killing. "Good emperors with armies are more evil," he had said, "than bad scholars with poor brushes."

"I'll miss Christine Carlson," I said.

"Who is this?" he said, for perhaps the tenth time.

"Christine." I flourished her photo, as always.

"She does not remind one of Hsi Shih, the famous beauty who sat watching the quiet river in ancient times, does she," he said, not even expending a *shihma,* a question mark. "She is not Chinese," he said, and I stiffened. He sucked the tea loudly, offering the most powerful punctuation available. "You have romantic fondness for her? Affection which she does not return to you?" he asked.

"Yes, Uncle. No, Uncle," I said.

"Ah ha," he said. "You are quite smart in these matters. You have given all your affection to a white-haired girl without family, who detests you." He looked at his impeccable nails and found dust on a cuticle. He looked up. "She does not know the *San-gahng,* the Three Bonds, the *Wu-ch'ang,* Five Constant Virtues, the Three Followings, and the Four Female Virtues?"

"Americans don't know that," I said. Edna was independent with my father. She was not a Chinese wife with small feet and small voice and five steps back. My father was American.

"All the more important, then, young Ting, to select a woman who *does* know them. Is she willing to learn?"

Christine submitting herself to her dad, then to her husband, and then, in widowhood, to her son. Cultivating obedience, appropriateness, seemliness, and the home? I didn't think so.

"Ha!" cried my uncle, startling me. "Is she of a free spirit—an unconventional thinker? Different than most girls you know?"

"Yes," I said. "That's her."

He nodded. "Your Mah-mee was the same." He beamed until he realized he was smiling. He furrowed his brows.

I poured him tea. I placed the empty pot with its lid canted near the edge of the table and waved to the waiter.

"*Hausheng.* Honoring your duties, it will take years to build. You cannot recover your relational skills in that . . . *place.*"

He cleared his face of the bitterness of these truths. "You know. There are no Chinese there. No Chinese food. No customs or rituals. No *dababa,* Chinese uncles. No one to speak to about matters of the mind, of duty, of honor." He looked sadly into my face, studying me through his frameless spectacles. It meant I had provided another incorrect answer.

"I just want to go," I said.

Silence. My fault. Say something. "Uncle," I said, "I think West Point is like the Hanlin Kuan, the Hanlin Academy, of the *Wen-lin,* the forest of culture." What he called the Forest of Pens.

The fabled green-and-orange-tiled Hanlin Academy had

stood for centuries before T'ien An Men Gate in the Forbidden City. Six years before my father's birth, British troops burned and looted its storied courtyards and gazebos, its antiquities, and its irreplaceable national library archives, turning the northern sky black with the ruin of China's ancient scholastic heritage.

He looked at me as if I had thrown reeking ox dung onto his white hotel-living-room rug. He shuddered, then gathered himself, much as I would after taking a wicked right cross in the chops.

"So," he said, imposing sentence with one syllable. "This is the result of Chinese youth in a foreign land trying to think." He hissed. "Ssss! *Hausheng*—foreign *ping* burned the Hanlin Academy! Foreign soldiers fabricated stories of Chinese Boxers killing foreigners—and used those lies to pillage and burn the Summer Palace and the Hanlin Kuan. The stink of it still shames all Chinese men." He lowered his head, grieving for losses never to be salved. "That *you* would join their army!" He closed his eyes.

"What was Master K'ung Fu-tzu's central message?" I welcomed his change of subject: what he called *wong ku tso yu ehr yen t'a*—talking to the left and right.

" 'Moderation in all things,' " I recited.

"*Hausheng*. Can a soldier"—he curled his lip, bristling his mustache—"be moderate? Can a soldier *moderately* attack his enemy and use *moderation* in cutting off the head of the enemy general, then *moderately* stake the bleeding skull onto a tall spear?"

"No, *Dababa*," I said, recoiling from his words. "But you want me to exert with the Chinese stuff—without moderation."

"Yes, use all muscles in your brain. This is duty—resulting in excellent thinking, which benefits society. But soldiers kill innocents and burn books. They stole China's eleven-thousand-volume national encyclopedia after burning all the copies."

"West Point would not teach its officers to do such a thing."

"*Hausheng,* the American *ping* who attacked the Forbidden City were led by General Chaffee. He killed Indians and Filipinos before he killed Chinese. Your father knows."

"Then he was wrong," I said. "Not the school."

He cleared his throat and repeated what had become a favorite aphorism of his—"Good iron is not used for nails"—followed quickly by *"Hau nan bu dang bin."* That he had said

"Good boys do not become soldiers" in Chinese seemed to emphasize its truth.

"Tsong yong shi dao," he said evenly, drowning me in Chinese, punishing me with Confucian heavy artillery. Walk the middle path. In it there are no *ping,* no soldiers.

I was unhappy with this lecture and brought my shoulders up.

"Who was China's greatest thinker and scholar? Clearly, the Master K'ung. Who was the greatest soldier in Chinese history?"

"Guan Yu," I said, naming my barrel-chested, red-faced hero.

He shook his head, no.

"Tso Tsung-tang—who had fought the Taipings and the Muslims?" I tried. "Li Hung-chang? . . . Tseng Kuo-fan?"

"It was Chingis Khan," he said, "who conquered Asia and Europe, from Turkey to Poland and Hungary, filled Russia with almond-eyed people, drank tea on the Mediterranean, in Moscow and Baghdad. All feared him. He was never defeated. He died in 1227 and his able grandson Kublai conquered China, where he settled. Do you know how the Mongol soldier defined pleasure?"

I shook my head.

"Listen to these erudite words: 'Pleasure is crushing your enemies, taking their property, making their families weep bitter tears, riding their horses, and ravishing their women.' You wish to train to be a *ping?* Be a Mongol—tied to a horse at three, given bow, lance, and sword at five! Join the army at fourteen and look forward to death in a short life of battle!"

He sensed that this did not sound as bad as he wished it to. *"Hausheng,* for a young person as yourself, with muscles coming out of your body as if you wanted to be a horse instead of a man, what I say about myself also applies to you. You are a Chinese youth, Able Student. You sound so foreign, and think so foreign, but you are Chinese. The *only* way of remaining intact and not going crazy without the clan to sustain us in this foreign land is to honor the teachings of your past with even greater fervor. Do you see?"

"Yes, Uncle," I said. But I did not believe him. I was American, like my father. I was going to West Point, a place that took only true Americans, a status to which my birth certificate attested. I spoke English almost like my Caucasian true mother, had read hundreds of books in the English language, and was in love with an American girl named Christine whose very brightness was an unmistakable message to my myopic eyes. Even if she rejected me, that pain was confirmation of my existence and made me similar to so many other American boys who also sought her heart. West Point represented American culture and artful escape. West Point—between a wide, sparkling azure river and hard-rocked, deep-green-forested mountains, with regiments of armed marching men in gray—appeared to be a sanctuary. It had food, sports, an all-male faculty, and uniforms that made everyone look alike. It was surrounded by fortified walls with cannons. It was three thousand miles from my mother, but it felt to me, somehow, that both she and my father had stowed away in the airplane and followed me there.

4

SPROUTS

Beast Barracks, July 1, 1964

"TA-AAKE *SEATS!*" cried a voice from above. The vast, high-ceilinged, stone-castled dining hall seemed to have held its breath during grace. In an instant it roared with two hundred cadre and a thousand agitated former civilians screaming at each other.

We were at rectangular tables of ten. First Sergeant Stoner sat at the head, flanked by two squad leaders. Fourth New Cadet Company's tables were under the high balcony whence the command to be seated had issued. Seven sweating, bracing, disoriented, thirsty and hungry new cadets occupied the other seats. We were in a sea of anxious, high-pitched, fear-fueled human static.

"I'm Mr. Armentrot," said the man to the left of Mr. Stoner. "Mr. Arvin, King of Beasts, gave grace and the order to sit. You are Beasts; he is Commander, First Detail, New Cadet Barracks.

"Sit on the first six inches of the chair, one fist from the table, hands grounded on laps. Ground hands after each task. Pick up knife and fork, cut one small bite, ground silverware in parallel diagonals at rear of plate, ground hands. Pick up fork, select small morsel, place in mouth by a right angle to the spine, elbow up. Retrack fork to table, then to back of plate. Ground hands. Chew, swallow, silently, mouth shut, ears open, eyes down.

"Take small bites. Chew six times for adequate digestion by your dumbwillie GI tracts. Six times, six inches, one fist. Keep eyeballs on the Academy crest at twelve o'clock on your plate.

"Three at the bottom are gunner, cold beverage, and hot beverage corporals." He explained how to pass platters. "GOT IT?"

"YES, SIR!" we screamed back. I longed for the cold beverage, but I would have guzzled mud and fought over milk of magnesia.

"Knob in the middle is gunner." Guns at the table? "Gunner announces food. Look up." We left the crest on our plates to look, stiff-necked and bracing, like a clutch of overfed turkeys invited to dine with Pilgrims bearing knives. Mr. Armentrot was bald, with shoulders that could be used for cots, cool in his crisp white uniform shirt. Mr. Stoner was the thick-necked first sergeant, tall and dark, with jet-black hair and deep creases where humans kept dimples. He looked as cruel as a heartless buccaneer. He was the one I had vexed in the orderly room by forgetting the words "as ordered." My fearful heart dropped into my empty stomach; the other squad leader was the halitoxic Mr. O'Ware who had called me "shitface-Marsman" and had promised that he would remember me. He had the face of a ferret with four tight shoes on its paws.

Mr. Armentrot held his plate above his right epaulet with both hands. Next to him, the plate looked like a coffee cup saucer. "Say this is potatoes au gratin, delivered by the mess hall waiter. Gunner holds it away from mouth, head up, eyes on his plate crest, and announces in a manly voice: 'SIR, THE VEGETABLE DISH FOR LUNCH TODAY IS POTATOES AU GRATIN. POTATOES AU GRATIN TO THE HEAD OF THE TABLE FOR INSPECTION, PLEASE, SIR!' Gunner passes with his left hand to the hot beverage corporal, who receives it in his right. The rest of you sorry knobs will pass it up to Mr. Stoner, the table commandant, for his inspection. That's the easy part."

We strained to hear him above the roar in the hall, and he had a huge voice. My neck ached from the contortion of bracing. I spied a huge, colorful mural of war covering an entire wall, state flags, ancient, cathedral-like windows, and many old portraits of exceptionally stern-looking white men.

"Gunner prepares dessert." Mr. Armentrot smiled. Inside, we smiled. He had reason to; we did not. "Gunner announces dessert and inquires who wishes dessert. You want, present right fist, forearm at a right angle to the vertical upper arm. Gunner counts and divides it into *exactly* equal, Strac portions. Should he fail to cut equal portions, all manner of misfortune will befall him unto the third generation of little dumbjohn crothead gunners. You share in the success and failures of your classmates, so you all get it in the neck if he ties up. You *will* work together, and cooperate. DO YOU UNDERSTAND?!" he bellowed, and we cried "YES, SIR!" as our twisted bodies lurched with effort and fear, wondering what a "Strac" portion was. Was that bigger or smaller than equal?

Lunch was my best meal since it was the one I consistently ate away from my mother's criticism. I was relieved to be in the middle of the table, without a job. I was not boss of beverages or desserts. It was a good omen. Waiters brought platters.

"SIR!" cried the gunner, in an Hispanic accent. "THE VEGIE-TABLE DISH FOR LUNCH TOday . . . is . . ." We all died a little as his voice trailed off, swallowed by uncertainty. Name the veggie! I urged silently. You were so close!

"IRP, MISTER!" "POP-OFF!" "FUNCTION, CROT-SPAZ!!" cried our upperclassmen as they pounded their big fists on the table, so eager to assist the gunner that they screamed advice at the same time, causing my internal organs to shuffle positions as the flatware and condiments jumped.

"SIR," cried the new cadet, "THE VEGIE-TABLE DISH FOR LUNCH TODAY IS . . . IS . . . *LEETLE CABBAGES!* LEETLE CABBAGES TO THE HEAD OF THE TABLE, FOR INSPECTION, PLEASE, SIR!"

"THAT'S WRONG!" screamed Mr. O'Ware. "WHERE THE FUCK DID *YOU* COME FROM—NEW GUINEA? HOW THE HELL DID YOU—"

"Frenchy," advised Mr. Stoner quietly. "MISTER, THAT WAS *GROSS!* TRY IT AGAIN!"

"SIR," the new cadet cried confidently. "THE VEGIE-TABLE FOR LUNCH TODAY IS *LEETLE GROSSES!*

LEETLE GROSSES TO THE HEAD OF THE TABLE FOR INSPECTION, PLEASE, SIR!"

Ice water sprayed over the table as Messrs. Armentrot and Stoner roared, screamed, coughed, and guffawed.

"What's your name and where you from, Mister?" asked Mr. Armentrot, wiping his eyes and wetly clearing his throat.

"SIR, MY NAME IS MR. VARGA. SIR, I AM A FOREIGN CADET FROM THE NATION OF ARGENTINA!"

"Varga," said Mr. Stoner. "These shitty little things are not 'leetle cabbages.' They're 'brussels sprouts.' This is the big, badassed sprout patch of the Western world. You're the sprouts. Welcome to America and cram in your stupid little crot neck."

The cold beverage corporal distributed milk and water; the upperclassmen fisted for the hot beverage corporal's announcement of coffee. The food went up to the top of the table and came around for us. We passed and received correctly. It was a team drill, and we operated under a collective will of seven crots sweating to make it, to help each other, to do it right. One screwup would endanger us all. It was Chinese *pao-chia*, collective responsibility—all of us profit, or all of us lose.

I received cold cuts, brussels sprouts, and melon. Task by task, I built a modest sandwich, my plate crest free of food for my faithful gaze. Small bites, chew six times. I could do that.

Neck muscles ached. A glass of milk stood tall above the point of my knife, the empty carton by its side. We had said grace; we had passed correctly; we had not broken crockery or taken the Lord's name in vain; we had survived the attack of the killer brussels sprouts. Edna would have approved. Well, maybe not Edna.

"When the worker crots are done," said Mr. Armentrot, "gunner says, 'Sir, may I ask a question?' With permission, he says, 'Sir, the new cadets at this table have completed their tasks. Sir, may the new cadets at this table have permission to eat?'

Now I had four answers: I could also say, 'Sir, may I ask a question?' At this rate, I could orate by Christmas.

"SIR, MAY I ASK A QUESTION?" yelled Mr. Varga.

"Absolutely," said Mr. Stoner.

"SIR, THE NEW CADETS AT THEES TABLE HAVE COMPLETED THEIR TASKS. SIR, MAY THE NEW CADETS AT THEES TABLE HAVE PERMISSION TO EAT?" We cheered silently. Way to go—word for word!

"Well done, gunner. EAT!" cried Mr. Stoner, and seven hun-

gry hands dove with lightning speed for forks, glasses, or sandwiches.

"TOO SLOW!! SIT UP!!" screamed Mr. Armentrot.

Shocked, we returned our hands to our laps.

"YOU BEANHEADS BLEW IT! I figured you smacks to
be hungry enough to sniff buffalo chips! Your Care Factor's
down! You're indifferent to the fine meal the Quartermaster
Corps prepared!"

I care! my stomach screamed.

"CUT UP YOUR MEAL! PLACE IT IN SMALL BITE-
SIZED MORSELS IN YOUR EMPTY MILK CARTONS! IF
IT WON'T FIT, WE'LL KNOW YOU DICKED THE FOOD
FOR YOURSELF! THAT YOU SCREWED YOUR CLASS-
MATES! YOU WILL *NEVER* SCREW A CLASSMATE OR
LET HIM DOWN! DO YOU UNDERSTAND ME?"

"YES, SIR!" we cried.

I recalled the best meal of my life—three servings of beef stro-
ganoff, green beans amandine, dinner salad, tapioca, brownies,
and no brussels sprouts, twenty thousand feet up. The stewardesses had fed me all the way across America. That had been
yesterday.

The aging Trans World Airways Super Constellation had
taken me east, toward the school that my father and his friend
Na-men so revered, toward what I hoped would be the Promised Land.

I was feeling physical distance from my past and mistook it
for the psychic freedom that it resembled. The plane was faster
than the Santa Fe freights in the Mission yards, but I bounced
in my seat to help the airliner take me out of California. The
Super Constellation was an old but sleek, silver, four-engined
aircraft with a triple-ruddered tail and an elegant swoop to its
fuselage.

I wore a sport coat from the Ting Family Association in Chinatown, tailored to my scoliosis-induced low right shoulder and
bodybuilding torso. I carried my Academy appointment letter.

"You are to be congratulated on this opportunity for admission to the Military Academy, for it comes only to a select few
of America's youth. It represents a challenge that will demand
your best effort. Therefore, it is suggested that you give serious
thought to your desire for a military career as, without proper
motivation, you may find it difficult to conform to what may
be a new way of life." Signed, J. C. Lambert, The Adjutant

General of the United States Army. I kept touching the letter
and the photo while I reread my 1908 Harper & Brothers half-
leather copy of *Ben-Hur*.

The TWA stewardesses were pretty, and I expanded my
chest and flexed my biceps whenever they passed. They provided food on request, and I liked to think this was in reaction
to the influence of my muscles. As I finished my fourth bag of
salted cashews and third Coke, and anticipated lunch, I
thought: This is too good to be true. *Ji hui.* Maybe it wasn't
true. Nick Kleiner would change his mind. I would have to return my appointment to him.

After months of arduous testing, Nick had won one of our
two congressional West Point slots. Applicants had to be U.S.
citizens, between the ages of seventeen and twenty-two at the
time of admission, and possessing leadership skills, competitive grades, and top Scholastic Aptitude Test scores. Leadership skills meant student body or class president, varsity
captain, or Eagle Scout. Competitive grades meant an "A" average. SAT scores had to be in the top 95th percentile. The
process began when our congressmen reviewed the field of applicants, eliminated the unqualified, and sent the list of survivors to the Army.

The Army invited the hundreds of qualifying applicants from
all the neighboring congressional districts to the Presidio of San
Francisco to test our medical and physical qualifications.

It would take three days, and began with a briefing about
West Point. A handsome, athletic captain named Bue, wearing
silver Airborne wings on his chest with a bright yellow Ranger
shoulder tab, spoke to us in Harmon Hall, near Crissy Army
Air Field.

"The Academy is famous for its graduates—Thayer, Lee,
Grant, Scott, Sheridan, Sherman, Longstreet, Stuart, Jefferson
Davis, Jackson, Pershing, Goethals, MacArthur, Darby,
Stilwell, Bradley, Patton, Arnold, Groves, Eisenhower, Van
Fleet, Ridgway, Taylor, Gavin, Dawkins, Carpenter. No school
has more renowned graduates. Imagine that West Point is a
school in the mountains and the clouds. There, at the River and
the Rock, young men are bound to each other not by hopes of
fame but by pledges to honor. A West Pointer is a brave and
honest man. He always strives to do the right thing."

I sat on the edge of the bleachers, barely breathing. Here
was where K'ung Fu-tzu and Guan Yu came together. Be hon-

orable. Do your duty. Be correct. Have courage. Do not be selfish. Subdue the self.

The physical was akin to performing every event in the Olympics, followed by being asked to defeat Napoleon at Borodino and to reconstruct the Grand Canal of China. I had practiced at the Y. At the Presidio, I did fifty-one pull-ups, a hundred push-ups, ninety sit-ups in one minute, fifty parallel-bar dips, a four-second legless rope climb, a ten-second hundred, and a two-minute-ten half-mile. I was convinced with all the assurance of uninformed youth that competence with my arms, legs, and abdominals would compensate for a lack of other aptitudes.

My asthma raised eyebrows, as two doctors listened to my chest and heard wheezing. Going to the Y had lessened the symptoms.

"Asthma is psychosomatic," Edna had said to me when I began wheezing after her arrival in our home. "You have chosen to have this to defy me. I am taking you from that loud, rowdy Negro church. Henceforth, you are a Christian Scientist. Doctors are too expensive. Read Mary Baker Eddy. You *will* end your asthma."

Then, the eye exam. "Son," said the doctor, "you're twenty over eight hundred, legally blind. You're 4-F, can't be drafted, or enlisted. You show asthma symptoms. You're big for an Oriental, but forget the Point. It's not a school for the handicapped."

They studied the drooping right shoulder which made my right hand hang four inches lower than my left. "Scoliosis, another 4-F disqualifer. . . . And, son, you have flat feet."

The Army was to be my ticket out of my family. While I knew that getting into West Point was practically impossible, I never thought I couldn't be a common soldier. I had trouble sleeping.

The congressman wrote, "The Army has informed me of your medical tests and I have requested waivers from the surgeon general of the Army. I have never seen three granted before. Best wishes."

I wrote back, thanking Congressman Mailliard for his assistance and restating my intent to attend the Academy.

The waivers were granted, and I was able to join fewer than a hundred who had passed the Presidio tests, to take an eight-hour Civil Service achievement exam at the Federal Building on Market. This was the final test. From this, the eight top cumulative scorers would be selected, from which the top two would go. Eight, *ba,* was a lucky number, round and full in sound and shape.

Some congressmen ignored scores and selected sons of patrons. Ours did not. This was lucky, since the Ting family influenced Congress the way I influenced the gravity of the sun. William S. Mailliard, Sixth U.S. Congressional District, posted his list of eight candidates in the early spring of 1964, which was printed in all local papers. The top two would be appointed to the U.S. Military Academy at West Point. The other six were alternates, who could use that status as a basis for joining the Army and applying to the U.S. Military Academy Preparatory School in Virginia. USMAPS grads could then compete for direct Army appointments to the Academy. I assumed that this would be my path; my congressman had already recommended that I not go to West Point at age seventeen.

I had placed third. Nick Kleiner and Hank Spence won the spots. Nick was Washington's student body president and football captain and the all-city quarterback. He looked like William Holden. He and Hank, who attended academically elite Lowell High, were National Science Foundation scholars. I figured that last summer one had found the true source of the Nile and the other had helped Dr. Salk invent a new vaccine. But Nick declined his appointment in order to go to Princeton, moving me up. That's when Edna received the telegram from West Point and, in a burst of goodwill, called Lincoln High with the news.

I called Nick that afternoon from the Y pay phone. "This is Kai Ting—from the West Point exams. . . . Yeah, the Chinese guy. Way to go on Princeton. And thanks—it moved me up."

"Hey," he said, "you got the waivers. You earned it—you made 'em drop dead during the tests. Ever think of football?"

I laughed. "Sure, if I were bigger, stronger, smarter, braver. With eyes. Gonna play for Princeton?"

"It's not playing for Dietzel at Army, but I'll start. Good luck." Nick hesitated. "You oughta know . . . my older brother's at the Academy—he's a senior, a Firstie. He says it is *no* fun."

Fun was flying to West Point through the clouds at three hundred miles an hour with an open kitchen. I was answering the Academy's invitation to undertake the "irksome and difficult" task of becoming a member of the U.S. Corps of Cadets. There I would be a continent away from all that I disliked, and separated from all that I knew. I would not see any other Chinese people.

I had brought my icons: my photo of Christine, plastic cup, wooden *liang-jiang,* Chinese linked fighting sticks, and my father's Colt super .38 automatic in its shoulder holster with his letter to his American Army patron, Na-men. Other things— ancient times, *goo dai,* and Chinese duty—accompanied me as well, and I felt their weight. In my pocket was Tony's old rosary.

I had often wondered what my father thought of Tony. Whenever I spoke of him, or Pinoy, or Barney Lewis, my father was silent.

5

FATHER

San Francisco, 1964

Chinese fathers—for me, such a mystical, frightening term, full of ancient fogs, aeons of deeply ingrained custom and ritual. None of that American let's-play-catch interaction which was always advertised in film and so absent in life. None of that teen-aged talking-back, gimme-the-car-keys, rock-and-roll rebellion. Chinese fathers inspired deep obedience—*deep* obedience.

"What did the emperor Ch'in Shih Huang Ti tell his subjects?" asked Uncle Shim.

"Build me a great big wall," I quipped.

Uncle Shim's brows knitted and he pursed his lips in profound disapproval. I grimaced and rolled my shoulders.

" *'Lin tsun'*—tremblingly obey," he said. "This directive closed imperial edicts, requiring subjects to obey the emperor, as sons must revere fathers. This is reflected in your actions, your thoughts, and your speech. In all you do. In all you do *not* do. You regard him with awe; you speak to him with clarity."

I was more likely to put hippos on roller skates than to speak with ease with my father. The thought of it invited panic. I tried to form questions and fell into chaos when I spoke. It was as if the gods had seized the cards in which I had organized my thoughts and shuffled them in a loud advertisement of my weaknesses.

My father was formal, detached, and remote. My speech, actions, and failures to act were all variations on a dirge. I was a Chinese candidate stuck at the first level of examinations, the page who could never be a knight, the boy who would always be made of wood. Our *gahng* arose not from sociology but paleontology, an archeological dig of unknown boundaries and unplumbed meanings, whose hold on the both of us was strengthened by silence.

I could play sports and no longer feared the sight of my own blood; Toos and Jack were my friends; I communed with animals in the zoo; I could earn money; I crazily loved food and Christine Carlson. I was *jook sing* and a *fan toong,* an American-born Chinese and a garbage can for rice. I was different, and always would be. That's what I could read in the open pages of my small life story.

My father's life was a secret, so I harbored my own ciphers. I disliked my mother. I disliked being Chinese, preferring either Negro or white. I liked the lingerie models in the Sears catalog. I had been crazy once, when the insanity god had lived inside me when I was ten. The god made me laugh when nothing was funny.

Once, the god appeared at a banquet at Johnny Kan's restaurant in Chinatown. Beautiful Chinese ladies in soft, padded peach, azure, and saffron silk cheongsams encircled me and said "*Bougwai!* Precious!" and touched my cheeks, bathing me in glittering smiles. I loved their touch, and the god arrived, making me giggle, falling into the mad grip of insane laughter. Each laugh forced a beautiful lady to back away, the insanity god separating me from her affection, her smile turning from shock to hurt and fear, until there were none left, and I was alone, laughing with tears.

By this time in my life, I had achieved threshold acceptance as a struggling Negro youth, and no longer wore the tattoos of lost fights on my body. This incident, of hurting Chinese ladies, became my most painful memory, which I could not expunge because I was reminded of them and their pain in my dreams. A woman with soft, kind brown eyes, a small red rosebud mouth, and jet-black hair, dressed in a peach cheongsam, smiled at me, and wept when I began to laugh. When I awoke, she was gone. Later, I would dream of a mur-

dered man who blamed me for his death, and he would chase
the Chinese woman from my sleep for all time.

The secrecy of my father's life convinced me that he harbored within himself a wealth of deep confidences and myster-
ies. I imagined his life to be the best book in the world, and
one I would never be sufficiently smart or qualified to read.

I had within me murky half-memories, superstitious shadows
of belief and event, fractured impressions of connection, cratered
concepts of separation and pain, abandonment and death.

I could not distinguish memory from dream, boundary from
custom, fact from fear, East from West. It was a long and dark
tunnel, with no landmarks in the offing or light at its end.

I watched my father in the parlor, reading about West Point
and the Panama Canal, Cheops and the Pyramids, Queen
Anne's War, the discovery of the helix, and the banking secrets
of Geneva, his pipe clamped tightly, the pages turning with a
steady rhythm. He was more disciplined every day than I was
in my wildest dreams.

I knew that my father, the proud warrior who loved to jump
from American airplanes and tramp Chinese river roads in pursuit of the enemy, was finding refuge in books, as surely as my
friend Sippy Suds, our most famous drunk, found solace in the
bottle.

As a pledge to America, Father read only in English and
never in Chinese. He was immobile while he read, as if he, the
inanimate book, the table lamp, and his cushioned living room
chair were an ensemble as secure as Napoleon, his great maps,
his courageous marshals, and his old green coat. I read books
about war, but they weighed little against Father's encyclope-
dic grasp of the world.

I used to ask him about China, his childhood, his war years,
his family. I asked him about his father.

Puffing on his pipe, he never answered. If pressed, he would
lift his eyes and look off into the great beyond, giving the Gaze.
It took him from the present world to places unknown. If I had
the discourtesy to persist, he would maintain the Gaze, or say,
"This is America," and my briefing on the history of our family,
the character of its members, the moral lessons they learned
from life, and the nature of Chinese civilization was concluded.

His strong grasp of the things that pressed inside me, things
that beat bright brass Chinese gongs in the pocket of the brain
where questions are formed, was closed to me, as inaccessible
as Red China, as mysterious as romance or the dark side of the

moon. China was his secret. He guarded it with care, using it
to court Edna with selected stories of family history, of the es-
tates and servants of his *gung-gung,* grandfather. He told her of
the dawn conferences in the Forbidden City under imperial
roofs lined with the figures of bad Prince Min and the parade
of marching animals, of the predawn work regimens of scholars in the Hanlin Academy, of the cycles of agriculture in the
valleys of the Yellow River. Edna shared morsels of these stories with me, sufficient to inspire taste, never enough to digest,
proof of his distrust of my mind. When my father spoke to
Edna about China, he was wistful. The two of them had a
close but private relationship, full of passion, conversation, and
privacy. When Father looked at me, he was sad and silent, as
if I reminded him of ancient pains and lost hopes.

I wanted to know his history, certain in the belief that this
knowledge was part of my preparation for later events. I believed, primordially, that his telling me his past would lend me
some of his great power, and that somehow the telling could
even lighten the rock that he himself bore through the length
of his weighty American days. I was the child at the fire, looking up at my father with curiosity and faith, waiting for the
stories that represented the chain of life.

At the wooded campfires at Camp Tolowa in the Santa Cruz
Mountains, my boxing coaches, Barney Lewis and Tony
Barraza, spoke under a canopy of stars to boys who were not
their sons. Tony had last seen his child when the boy was four.
Tony Jr. and I had been born in the same year. I imagined my
father and me sharing singed marshmallows, throwing moss
kindling into a crackling fire, watching sparks fly into the
nighttime sky. Here, under the cloak of dark, under Wen-
ch'ang, the celestial god of scholarship, whose presence was
known in the West as the Big Dipper.

When I was nine, I got glasses, and Uncle Shim pointed out
what he called the Literacy Arc. "See, *Hausheng,* Wen-ch'ang,
god of the literati, in the form of the Bear. Below him, the four
stars of his chariot with Wen-ch'ang's principal assistant,
K'uei-hsing, the ugly fellow who gives the grades. Inside the
chariot, unseen, is Chu-i, who gives good luck to lackluster, ill-
prepared students.

"*Hausheng,* never trust Chu-i, god of the inept. Honor Wen-
ch'ang as I honored you with your name, Able Student. As an
advocate of the *Wen-lin,* I urge upon you scholarship and literacy."

In my daydreams, Father would tell me the stories of his life—his childhood, his victories, his enjoyments—tutoring me under the kind and ancient Arc of Literacy and its three gods. Here, his urge for mathematical genius and Uncle Shim's Old World beliefs, Tony's training about rules, my Negro heart and Chinese blood, and the wishes and hopes of fathers and sons could commune and be safe with one another, fortified against any harm or any change.

On the night before I left, we stood in the dank and poorly lit garage. Here he found quiet refuge. When the pressures of his life became too weighty for reading, he would clang his pipe against an old, large glass ashtray and walk down the narrow hallway to the door that led to the garage.

Using hand tools, he made inlaid stools, ornate end tables, and cabinets of a quality that was beyond his training. He had a gift, which appeared in many things that he did. It was in this respect—demonstration of competence—that I was not his son. He was a capable man; I was always slow, myopic, hard of hearing, stupid, awkward, poorly tongued, hesitant in speech and uttering inarticulate Chinese when I should have been silent, putting up fists when I should have been doing kowtow, raging with horrible anger against my own parents, blurring my Chinese, Negro, and American boundaries, unable to laugh except when mad.

I came down twice every morning to do pull-ups, six sets of twenty, thirty seconds apart, on an old metal pipe, driven by the need to escape. My arms were my wings. I practiced with the *liang-jiang*, the two octagonally beveled rods of pine that resembled dynamite sticks connected by a thong. Chinese fighting sticks. I practiced the double-hand whipping, attacking, blocking, and hand switches taught me by Pinoy Punsalong at the Y. When I could not cope with life, I came here to punch the beams.

"Come," he said, standing, and I followed him downstairs.

On a high shelf, surrounded by small cardboard boxes of wood screws and hinges, was his Colt super .38 automatic, two shelves above my *liang-jiang*. His old Army sweater strained as he reached. It was moth-eaten, stretched thin around his shoulders, the fragile fabric requiring him to don it as if it were made from the webs of spiders. His baldness had quickened, but he was trimly athletic, his posture exemplary; his handsome face had softened as the war years grew distant. I thought of asking him about West Point.

"Clean," he said, handing the gun to me, watching as I disassembled and cleaned it with an old undershirt and an oiled gun cloth. I held the barrel to the light, checking for lint in the bore. I glanced at him quickly. He was lost in his thoughts. I knew that my *gahng*, my bond to him, had been a test for both of us. The purpose of the test and how I might pass it were never clear. Now this duty of son to father—the first of the *San-gahng*, the high Three Bonds identified by K'ung Futzu—was changing, seemingly before the test had been administered. I was relieved in a way; I did not want the grade that K'uei-hsing—or Chu-i—would give me.

I cleaned the slide. I was leaving in the morning—to go to the one place on earth that seemed to embody all that he believed, all that he had hoped for in both of our lives. Now that I had obtained what he had always wanted, he seemed more withdrawn and secretive. Something was angering him. It had to be me.

He inspected the pieces. He nodded, and I began reassembly. What does the gun mean to him? Had he killed with it? When I was seven, and learning the basics of street fighting, I wanted to believe that he had killed. Now I was less sure.

My mouth fought itself. "Uh . . . so, uh, when you wore it—uh, you know, the gun—did you put a round . . . in the chamber with, you know, a full clip, or did you just, uh, load it with, you know, the magazine? Alone? So it had, you know, extra—an extra round?"

He came out of his thoughts. He rubbed his square jaw, and made a gesture with his hand: Finish your work.

When I finished, he inspected it, closing the action with a loud metallic snap. He slapped the empty magazine into the handle well. "You know how safety work," he said.

"Yes, Dad."

"Leave chamber empty. Child find, she can die," he said.

"Yes, Dad."

"During war, I keep extra round in chamber, under hammer. Extra clip, all places—in boots. Canteen carrier. Pockets, rucksack. Sergeant Kress, Infantry School, say, 'Never no such thing, too much ammo.' Now, no war. Leave empty."

"Yes, Dad." He carried extra clips for the gun, in the war, the way Teddy Roosevelt carried nineteen pairs of extra glasses up San Juan Hill. TR also had suffered from asthma. My mouth moved, looking for words, wanting to be the portal for a hundred questions while my mind clattered against itself. Maybe he would say more.

"Kai, this yours." He pushed the heavy gun into my hand.

He cleared his throat. "Na-men give to me. I put letter for you, mail to her when you get there. In holster. Na-men will smile when she see West Point postmark on stamp. She will like letter from her old friend from China days, mailed by her only son." Many Chinese confused the feminine third-person pronoun with the masculine; in Chinese there is no distinction. This difference had caused comic mayhem with Dad's instructions when my sisters were part of the family. With Edna in the house, their visits were now infrequent.

"Na-men" was H. Norman Schwarzhedd, who had fought alongside my father during the Second World War. Na-men now wore the two stars of a major general, and commanded the Second U.S. Infantry along the DMZ in Korea. Na-men was a Chinese-speaking West Pointer.

Na-men had judged men by what my father called "Western way"—by action. My father's upbringing had taught him to judge men by their classical education, social status, and birth order. During the war in China, when my father became an expert judge of the character of men in the Western way, he looked carefully at Major Na-men Schwarzhedd and decided that if he, Major Ting Kuo-fan, ever had a son, the son should be a West Pointer as well.

"Dad, this is your gun," I said, feeling its weight, returning it. His hands came up suddenly, pushing the gun into my chest.

"No, no more. Is her army make it. Now, *your* army." He patted it, as if, in a way, he were patting me.

"You know, I *love* U.S. Army! *Yess! All* American soldier *gallant gentlemen!* Eat last, sleep last, up hill first, die first!" His eyes moistened. "Best men! Good you go to Army. No money for college." He laughed in a way that was not sad, but close to a thing of pleasure, surprising me.

"*West Point!*" he said. "This the way! Army college, pay *you!*" His eyes beamed. "American Army West Pointer! Ahhh!

"My dream," he said.

"I'll send money home, Dad."

He frowned. "No! No! You need. Books. Ammunition, uniform. Don't need your money. No worry. Work, pay raise. Buy less food, you gone! You do good. No fail. Edna and I come for graduation. Edna, very proud of you."

So many words for him, to me. Fortified, I blurted, "Dad, what would your father think of my going to West Point?"

It was too dark for the Gaze. He walked to the bench and rummaged for his old pipe, filled it with Edgeworth, and lit it. This was a powerful message: Do not ask. He hated this old pipe but he hated my question more. Long, uneasy moments passed. I had to break the spell I had caused. "I should send a little money."

He looked at me. "Edna very proud," he said. "*Very* proud."

"Okay," I said, frowning. He loved her. I couldn't.

"*I am your father!*" he shouted, enunciating each word as if it were Shanghainese and not English. "Chinese or American—I am *father!* YOU NOT STUDY!" he cried, waving his hand at me in a fury of expression. "Draw airplane picture! Read book about war! Get grades by brains and luck without work! You work at Y not at math! Do boxing, play sport all time! You sit and hold your knees! You talk zoo elephants out loud! Bad at math! How can climb American ladder without math!"

I backed up, blinking.

"No fail," he hissed angrily. He stood in front of me, and I saw him in his tan field uniform with the Sam Browne belt, soaked in sweat, standing in front of his men, the automatic in his holster, somewhere in Asia, where war was the business at hand and talk was not Jane Austen; it had been Edgar Rice Burroughs.

Dad never looked directly at me. Now he did, and it seemed to be a matter of effort, of his will, to fix his eyes directly on mine, and I trembled for so many reasons, all unclear.

"Work hard," he said in a strained voice, the muscles in his face taut, his lean face hard and flinty, death on his breath.

I began shaking.

"I, engineer. Your father's father, *he* tell everyone—be *engineer!* Education, math!"

"Your father's father," my grandfather, *gung-gung,* Ah-Tiah. "You cannot say the name of your father, or of your father's father," Uncle Shim had said. "Do not ask me the name of your father's father. He is his rank; he is *gung-gung.*"

"Work," my father said, "to point of bitter pain, *k'u-li*—what American call 'coolie'—understand? Be *very* good engineer, for family. Fear *nothing* in head or heart. *So much riding on your head!* This our dream! For *America!* You are only son!" He nodded his head. "*Ch'uan hsin ch'uan i!*"

I didn't understand. *Ch'uan,* I thought, might mean "everything." I looked at him, unknowing, unbreathing, unsteady.

"With whole heart and whole mind." He coughed. "Make us proud. Please, please," he said, laying upon me a vast and ancient weight reaching back to my mysterious, unknown grandfather, wanting his issue to be engineers. Math. That's why my father so valued it.

Fear nothing in head or heart, he had said. Yet I feared him in head, heart, stomach, liver, ear canal, and pancreas. And I feared my mother. Even on the airplane, it was this combined weight upon all my organs that seemed to aid gravity, delay forward movement, and invite a numbing detachment.

I knew what to do. I flexed my neck and arms, flared my lats, waved casually at the stewardess, and asked plaintively for a third dinner.

The cold beverage corporal served water. Mr. Stoner provided us two salt tablets, two glasses of water, and a "Bon appétit." I took the water in small, regulated sips, my body singing in ecstasy.

But I feared I had seen my last meal. In my rush to be the first candidate through the gate, I had bypassed breakfast that morning. My last lunch and last supper had been yesterday, June 30, at the Thayer Hotel, at the threshold of the Academy reservation.

6

THAYER

U.S. Hotel Thayer, West Point, June 30, 1964

"I hear they torture you," a voice had said from the back.

Our letters of instruction directed candidates to report to the West Point Gymnasium in the morning. There were two groups at this government hotel at the edge of the post. One was brash about the next day's challenges; the other was anxious about them and scared of the unknown. I was anxious, scared, and hungry.

College should not begin in July. After what we had done to win appointments, it was unnerving to be called "candidates." We were a multitude in the dining room, our hubbub transforming its dignified, dark-wooded colonial formality into the roar of a public school cafeteria. Hundreds of us, lumbars stiff and bottoms sore from bus and airplane travel, were pressed together by tens at round tables. The brash spoke of the past while the anxious ruminated about the future. All I saw were white. I ate.

This was lunch, but I read the dinner menu the way some read the ends of novels first, unable to resist the desserts of the last chapter. "Broiled Rock Lobster Tail with Drawn Butter, Snowflake Potatoes, Asparagus Hollandaise, and California Sunshine Salade," preceded by "chicken liver pâté, V8 cocktail, melon in season, marinated herring, Crème Vichyssoise in Tasse or split green pea soup": at three dollars and fifty cents, it was more than pricey. The lunch highlight was a club with soup and coleslaw for ninety-five cents, not including an automatic 10 percent gratuity. I had landed in the social upper crust.

Newcomers crowded the lobby. They were uniform in height, age, and build. Still no Negro, Hispanic, or Asiatic faces, reinforcing the familiar feeling of unfitness. Through no lack of effort, I had seldom passed for a Negro, however light skinned. I was going to blend in like Pancho Villa at a Texas Ranger convention.

Three years before, I had hated leaving the 'hood for the jangling anxiety of white streets. Lincoln High was not a nation of Ednas, but kids had achieved material paradise in possessions. No ringworm, tuberculosis, vomit, or blood; lots of dental braces, TVs, and new clothes. They ate well and had limited experience with violence. Fist City was not the governance theme. I had not been pitched a new fight card to set status. The school was clean and the teachers were not asked to be cops. Again I mimicked, switching adjectives, gestures, and attitudes, putting one more cultural mile between me and my Chinese youth and the fading borders of my recent past.

This was the Sunset district. People didn't live on top of each other, sharing arguments, passions, and deep bass tones as the music pounded through common walls, everyone merging pleasures, disagreements, bad habits, scents, and garbage.

"Found a friend, Toos," I said. "Name's Jack."

"That's cool," he said. "You in the same 'hood?"

"No 'hood here."

"Say what?" he said. "No 'hood? You livin' in a tent?"

"It's a house with a little lawn and a backyard. Houses have *trees*. Little plants everywhere. No turf, no—no nothin'."

"Damn," he said, thinking on it. "They pickin' on you?"

"No one picks on no one, Toos," I said. "If I picked one, there'd be no action. Grown-ups don't fight. No noise. No winos. Everyone's polite. White kids talk like people at church."

"Sounds good, China," he said.

"Spooky," I said. "Don't know what they're thinkin'."

"Know what *Jack* thinks?" he asked.

I thought I did. I was sort of good at that.

"That's all you need," he said.

Through the jabber of the congregated future generals of America, came a pure, sharp-angled New York, Bowery Boys accent, rich with confidence and as thick as new concrete: "Let's order." I admired his priorities and liked him instantly. He looked like Sal Mineo, short with dark eyebrows, wearing a blue button-down shirt and dark slacks. He talked like a cab-driver and I wondered if he had enough smarts to get through the Academy.

"Why'dja come here," he asked, without using a question mark.

"Free education," I said, chewing. Better than, I'm running away from home 'cause I don't like my mother. "You?"

A waitress served salads with bright orange Kraft French, and I was done before the others had found forks. She was in her forties and moved fast while speaking little, in a voice I found charming just because she served food. She wore a black dress with a white starched collar, a white lace apron, and a little white hat. Her small brown name tag said "Jean." She had near-green eyes and almost-red hair with white roots in a tight bun. She ignored us, as if, in a defiance of reason, she were refusing to recognize our remarkable status as West Point new cadet candidates.

"Slow down, ma'am," said one of the diners in a fascinating drawl reminiscent of Southern gentry in *Gone With the Wind*. "Number a us heah ah fixin' ta be gen'rals. Stay a space an' y'all be able ta recall mah face when they put it on the new dollah bill."

Jean looked at the person next to him. "Look to your left and to your right. One of these boys won't be here four years from now." She looked back at the speaker. "General," she added.

"Love math," my neighbor was saying. The catalog's description of freshman calculus had upset my stomach: "set theory, rigorous treatment of differential and integral calculus of single variable algebraic functions, calculus of transcendental functions, polar coordinates, ninety minutes a day, six days a week."

Across from me was a man in his twenties. He ate vigorously and I was warmed by the hint of a kindred spirit. He was large and tan and wore expensive clothes. A widow's peak, a pronounced triangular wedge of hair, pointed into his forehead. He had a prominent, lean, and noble nose that reminded me of Louis Calhern, the tall, patrician actor who had played Julius Caesar to Marlon Brando's Mark Antony. His imperious beak pointed and flared, his aristocratic head haloed by the bright summer light that glared through red and blue painted glass windows and black wrought-iron borders. He had ice-cold eyes that gave me a start. *Ave, Imperator.*

"Bet you're good at that math shit," he said to me. "NSF finalist, right?" He openly chewed lettuce flecked with carrots.

I shook my head. I liked Western literature and loved movies.

"What, don't speak English?" He laughed. "Math's not gonna be the drill *tomorrow*. Won't be any stinkin' trig problems buffin' their shoes and jackin' rounds for us tonight!" What did that mean? I ate saltines, Ritz crackers next. It was hot, and I drank like Sippy Suds at a free beer tap. Boxers took eight water tumblers a day, and now I drank for the comfort of the familiar. Jean left the water pitcher for me.

"What's 'buffin' shoes' mean?" asked the Southerner. Julius Caesar ignored him and bore down on his salad.

"What's gonna be the problem tomorrow," asked Sal Mineo, no longer eating. I wanted to ask for his salad, crispy, neglected, murmuring to me about its loneliness. I restrained myself.

"Beast detail. Upperclassmen," said Caesar. "Going to hassle us *all* goddamned year. Gonna haze the holy shit outa us and screw us in the ear. Beast sucks. Only way to win is to form our own team." He studied us, one by one, as he pulled a pack of Winstons from his pale blue sport coat, tapped one out, and lit it with a sharp snap from a Zippo. He was an adult. He ate as smoke blew from his nostrils, cloaking his plate in haze as he studied and discarded each of us from his prospective, independent team.

"How you know so much?" asked a distressed kid, his mouth, eyes, and nose in nervous motion, ready to pose more questions before the first was answered. His high-pitched voice was absorbed by the general clamor from other tables, from the lobby, and from my still nearly empty stomach. Deep down, I recognized his fear.

Caesar laughed. "I didn't watch *West Point Story*. I'm a 'poop schooler.' Already *in* the Army. Means I went to Yoos-Maps—West Point Prep, Fort Belvoir. I've been preppin' *all* goddamned year for this, gettin' the straight poop, doin' the math shit and pull-ups and the M-14 drill while you young studs were drinkin' beer and gettin' laid in high school."

Getting laid in high school?

"Sonny Rappa," said Sal Mineo. "I'm a good Catholic boy, and have definitely not been laid. I've confessed to a beer." He offered his hand across the table. Caesar hesitated, put down his fork, dangling his smoke from his lower lip, and shook with the enthusiasm with which New York cabbies greet syphilitic fares.

"Luther Troth," he said. "Duke to you, Squirt."

Sonny's grip was firm; Mike Benjamin's was calloused. I also shook with five other guys—including the one who foresaw himself as the future adornment of the American dollar bill—none of whom were to survive Beast Barracks. "Kai Ting," I said to Duke, gripping his big, nicotine-yellowed mitt, fearing what he would call me.

"*Kai Ting?*" laughed Duke Troth. "Sounds like an accident in a fuckin' Chinese kitchen." A few laughed. Sonny and Mike, on either side of me, did not. An acidic message circuited my gut. Troth added nothing to soften the comment. He smiled through his smoke and food, and the weight of silence fell on me.

This was familiar country; bullies had smelled me, a Chinese kid in a black-and-white city, like frogs found flies. The slur was ugly spit on cold concrete—an invitation to later tests. Toussaint had taught me deterrence. Best to say from the jump that I wouldn't swallow words now so I could eat crap later. The risks were fishes, worsening over time.

I edged back, checking for knives, spans of reach, and Samaritans. Was he all mouth or was he going to pound me? Hot fear and cornered anger surged, and bile pumped in my hands. I cleared my throat; five seconds had passed. Look him inna eye. Talk slow. Give words a chance. Now. "Want to discuss family names with me?"

He put down his fork and cigarette, chewing a big mouthful. "Touchy, aren't you?" he asked thickly through my glare.

Rude to talk with your mouth full, I thought, observant of manners. My mother was a monster for etiquette. I was her son. Our table fell silent within a sea of clattering diners. Duke was big, but he showed no Fist City response. I was glad.

"Hey, cool. Ting's a *good* name," said Sonny Rappa. "Let's sweat these upperclassmen and not pick fights, know what I mean?"

Troth snorted. "Yeah. I want *no* part of that Oriental bullshit fighting, that karate hand-chop crap. *That* shit isn't fair. Bet you're good with that Oriental shit, right? Well, *screw you in the ear.*" He looked around the table, grinning falsely. Plates clacked as Jean brought my club sandwich with coleslaw and barley soup. The food gods did not want a fight, and forced a smile from me. My hands, heavy with purpose, relaxed. I picked up my soup spoon. "Right," I said. Troth thought I was a math whiz and a karate expert. Pinoy Punsalong was as happy with the purity of my Western-polluted *wing chun gong fu,* Chinese boxing, as Uncle Shim was with my Chinese scholarship. I applauded the equivalency between Troth's fighting spirit and his insight. I immediately typecast, classified, and pigeonholed him as a stereotyper; a big guy who bullied but did not enjoy fighting; a guy who enjoyed advantages over others; someone not to forget: Caesar.

I ate as always—as if the building were on fire and I would never see food again. I was done, pointedly ignoring Duke Troth, and nodding at Sonny and Mike as I left. I appreciated them; they had not laughed at me.

The hotel bustled with young men befriending each other. I walked across the vast area of Cavalry Field and thought about Christine, Jack Peeve, and Toussaint LaRue. It struck me that the people I was closest to had come from very different streets, and had never met each other. My father had never met

Tony, Barney, or Pinoy. He had never seen a bout, a game, a swim match.

Later, alone, I ate the huge dinner I had previewed, my last civilian meal. I passed through the heavily flagged lobby now filled with boys who had become friends, and stepped into the late dusk of a warm New York summer night. I looked up at the building—five stories of gray towered stone. From its promontory and high ramp I saw the Hudson and the quiet little winding road that had led to the future of thousands of young men and influenced the course of world history. To the north, up the banks of the Hudson, below the forested mountains that rustled softly like rippling velvet in the hot summer wind, lay the school that Washington had conceived, Jefferson had authorized, Benedict Arnold had betrayed, and Sylvanus Thayer had made in his own image. The catalog said that Thayer—West Point Class of 1808 and "Father of the Military Academy"—was founder of the Thayer Academic System, wherein every cadet is examined in every course, every day, six days a week. To honor this excess, the academic system, the biggest road, the only hotel, the main academic hall, and a major statue were named after him. It simplified navigation.

What am I doing here? Like I was one of these angular-faced white guys who looked like models for heroic statuary. I didn't belong here; anyone could see that. I was going to be arrested for fraud. I had the wrong face. I was ugly, wrong in color and culture. I wasn't smart enough. A school in the mountains and the clouds, to do the right thing. I, a boy who always did wrong, who was without honor, in a school commemorated to it. I felt alone. I wondered if I could do West Point all by myself.

Mike Benjamin joined me. "Dad's a colonel. He brought me here when I was a kid." He was my height, but his shoulders and chest pushed him over two hundred pounds. He reminded me of a famous actor, but in the dark, humid air and under the weight of history, I couldn't remember which one. He spoke rapidly, constantly moving, cracking his knuckles, full of nervous, muscular energy.

"There," he said. "Hundred years ago, when they heard about Fort Sumter, Southern cadets marched down the road, past this knoll, waving to the Northern cadets. A dry, dusty day. Knowing they'd kill each other later. The young, nameless lieutenants."

"Why'd your father want you to come here?" I asked.

"Best school in the world." He looked at the river. "Grampa was an immigrant. Can't believe I'm here." He looked at the road. "Like the Southern cadets couldn't believe they were leaving."

I knew what he meant; my father looked up to West Point as he would at the heavens. No, it was higher. That's why I'm here.

"How hard do you think this is going to be?" I asked.

"Damn hard. One of Dad's best friends came here and flunked Plebe math. And he was real smart." He pulled out a pack of Marlboros. "Always wanted to try this." He lit up, inhaled, and blew it out. "Jesus!" he said, clearing his throat. "Man, that's bad! Want one? Why'd you *really* want to come here? We all had free education, scholarships. Lots of them."

A school in the mountains and the clouds. Honor. I cleared my throat, as if I were choking on smoke. I hadn't applied to any other college. It was here or the Army. "I wanted to leave home."

He looked at me carefully. "Not sure this is going to be better. Going to be a career officer," he said. "Used to a ration of crap a day. Dad got me ready. This'll be more than homework."

I wasn't any good at homework. Edna revered it and I accordingly equated it with immorality. I defied her by reading novels instead of studying. If I couldn't figure a lesson intuitively, I dropped it, before the insanity god showed up. Putting out in sports, for class projects, had to be what would count at West Point. That was the only way I was going to make it.

"Don't you think if a guy learns fast, it'll be enough?"

"Heck no," he said. "Sure you don't want a smoke? You oughta try it. It's absolutely the pits."

The members of the West Point Class of 1968 came from every state of the Union. We averaged six feet in height and 700 on the verbal and math portions of the Scholastic Aptitude Test. Three out of four members of the class had been student body presidents *and* varsity team captains, weighted toward football, the classic corporate American blood sport; half had been Eagle Scouts. I thought all the tall, broad-shouldered, straight-nosed blond guys with good grades in America had come. Most were Protestants from middle-class homes with good skin and smooth consciences who had been the pride of their high schools. We began as a thousand car-crazy, nonvoting, rock-and-rolling, high-achieving, clean-cut children of World War II veterans who still missed John F. Kennedy and Ritchie Valens, had not yet welcomed the Beatles and the British Invasion, wondering if we would make any West Point varsity teams, and ready to protect America against all comers.

I did not fit the profile. I believed in protecting the Republic and had scored 700s in English aptitude, but I had a high 500 in math—an ominously low figure for a rigorous engineering college. I had been a class officer. An inch below six feet, I was a steady playmaking junior varsity basketball guard and a boxer. I was superstitiously Taoist and remotely Christian, ethnically Chinese, culturally quasi-Negro, trained to the table etiquette of Main Line Philadelphia, and blessed with a linguistic bouillabaisse of Shanghainese, Mandarin, and Spanish, African, and European English. I was physically strong, socially inept, intellectually underdeveloped, spiritually muddled, and politically untested. My father had come from wealth, but we were now of the economic underclass. I possessed a troubled conscience, hoped I was growing in height, and was clueless about girls. Actually, I knew a lot about girls; I had read Jane Austen and Jade Snow Wong and seen the Sears ads. I just didn't know what to do about them.

I was behind the American social curve. I had never dated, driven a car, been to a dance, a sock hop, a party, or played a record player. I was a Chinese colored boy with a Pennsylvanian Puritan upbringing who was *fan toong,* an overeater of Kwangtung food, who always wanted to be accepted, and would always have trouble finding people who were similarly situated. I was one of thirty members of the Class of 1968 who were something other than Western European Caucasoid. We were a small subgroup of Negroes, Hispanics, Orientals, and foreign cadets from the governments of the Philippines and Argentina.

"How do you feel about being here?" Mike asked.

His question snapped me out of my thoughts. What a weird question, especially out loud. What do feelings have to do with it. *Ji hui,* inauspicious talk. I didn't know. It was an honor to be accepted at one of the world's most famous schools. My parents wanted me to be a West Pointer more than anything, causing me to doubt my own wishes. I had to honor my parents but had resisted them in my secret heart. I defied my mother by not being studious, and had committed capital crimes. I angered my father and was not a good son. Uncle Shim was in misery because I was here. I loved a girl who would never miss me. I hadn't said goodbye to Toussaint. In view of this, my feelings mattered not at all.

"Duke makes me think I should've taken Yale or Stanford."

"How come?" I asked.

"He's a bigot who knows the score. I thought being an Army brat meant I knew the Army. But a guy who's actually *been* in the Army, getting ready to be a cadet for a year, has a big jump."

"You can take him; he won't pick on you. He's not a fighter."

"Sure I can take him, but the hell he won't. He won't do it alone—he's forming a mob. And I'm a Jew." He smiled. "So's everyone in my family. You're not exactly small, and he went after you without even thinking. So he's crazy, and has a plan. You see him, trying to pick a team in there at lunch? He looked at us—a Jew, a Chinese, and an Italian—and said 'Drop dead.' Bad omen."

Yu chao. "You superstitious?" I fingered Tony's rosary.

"Mom is. Thinks God saved Dad in the war, but will take me if there's another one. Wants me to be a Yale doctor. Says there'll be an omen soon about West Point. I have a very bad feeling about that guy Troth." He studied the cigarette, squinting at the smoke. *Command Decision, It Happened One Night, Gone With the Wind.*

"Anyone ever say you look like Clark Gable?"

"Girls do. You're part Chinese, aren't you?"

"Hundred percent."

"No kidding? You don't look it. Why think of actors?"

Edna's crusade to drive me from the house had led me to the YMCA, many of the churches, and most of the movie houses in San Francisco. Armed with free Y movie passes and glasses, I entered a world where good guys carried guns and won every ninety minutes. I emulated Burt Lancaster, who smiled and walked and shot guns the way I wanted to. I adored Grace Kelly, whom Christine Carlson so closely resembled, and it was simple to love them both. In *David Copperfield, The Bad Seed,* and the Dead End Kids, I recognized life.

"Movies are like truth," I said solemnly.

Mike laughed. "I don't think so," he said. "Anyway, the trick here isn't going to be drama. The key is not standing out."

"Oh," I said, gulping. "Hey, what kind of omen do you expect?"

"Communists are going to make a move," he said.

"Berlin or Prague!" I cried. "This time we'll fight, not like Budapest—Ike's big mistake. Won't be Indochina; we're too smart to get sucked up like the French." I said that in three seconds. What I didn't say was: Please, no more wars with Asians.

"It'll be Laos and Vietnam," he said. "But Eisenhower's screwup was opposing Israel at the Suez." He studied his smoke. "So how come you don't know how you feel about being here? Proud? Bad? Here 'cause of your dad? Scared shitless? Or dream come true?"

"Yes," I said.

I thought that making the right decisions on the battlefield might be my special skill. I made good basketball decisions, finding the open man and filling the lanes, so I was hopeful. My possession of this knowledge was a secret. I hoped someday it would be forced from me, resulting in the salvation of the Free World. I would be successful, famous. But if I said that now, or even thought it with any clarity, *ji hui* would bleed me.

Saving the nation seemed easier than living with my family. I thought of Uncle Shim teaching me that the sole reason for living, the only justification for my mother's pain of birth and the cost of children, was to benefit the clan. I was not a good member of my family, and had tried not to think what others thought of me, fearful of the conclusions they ought to reach.

Now I had a new start. I had been invited to merge directly into the white tapestry of American history. I could pretend to be a person who had never known privation of spirit, stomach, heart, or neighborhood, who had never sinned, made bad decisions, produced bad thoughts of *ji hui,* or caused others to die. I could pretend to be happy, a boy who knew how to smile without outer cause. For once, on this special day, I wondered how others saw me.

The stars began to emerge in a darkening sky. It was eight, a propitious hour. The Eight Immortals, the Eight Ch'ing Banner Armies, the Eight Breezes, the eight Academy candidates. I had been born on the eighth of August, double-eight, double luck.

"Why'd you ask about how I feel?" I asked Mike.

"My gramma says: 'Know your feelings, make wise decisions.' "

I didn't have grandparents. "Feelings have nothing to do with it," I said. "I think feelings can screw things up. Like, how can you *think* if you try to figure out how you *feel?* And if you figure it out, who *cares?* What if you feel *bad* about something? It doesn't matter." I took a deep breath.

"I *had* to come here," I said.

"Yeah," said Mike. "You can give up thinking like that. We're out of high school. The diplomas make us adults. We don't have to do *anything* we don't want to do."

I looked up the road, toward the Academy. I was an adult. In the morning, I would experience what grown-ups get— respect. I would be a West Point new cadet. I would thrust out my chest like Guan Yu, forget that my mother criticized all I did, and start a new life.

"Mike, it'll be great," I said.

"It'll probably be hard," he said, putting his hand out.

We shook. I didn't care. I had made a friend, and felt I was about to enter the script of a very good movie, a Clark Gable film, in which the good guys couldn't help but win. I had arrived in America.

7

PUNG-YOH

Mr. Alsop's Room, July 1, 1964

Third Squad reported to Mr. Alsop's room at 2030 hours —8:30 P.M. I had been at West Point for twelve hours and it felt like ten years. Three hours ago, we had been learning close-order drill with rifles, and a cannon had fired. We were ordered to face the tall American flag at the end of the Plain and to present arms. A bugler played retreat, a haunting, melancholy solo as the flag came down. It sounded like the tune of my life, echoing in my mind.

Mr. Alsop had ordered me to return in my next life as a Mississippian. If they didn't feed me soon, I would be able to comply. He sat in a spotless uniform; we marveled at his relaxed state, his nonchalance riveting. We braced, lousy with sweat.

He stood. "Ah'm Mr. Alsop. First Detail squad leader, the mos' 'portant human bein' in yo' sorry little crot lives. If yew were a rifle squad, Ah'd be charged with yo' success. Here, Ah haze those who wish ta be here." His jaw muscles flexed. "Not fond a screamin'. Don't take this ta mean Ah'm soft. Factually, Ah'm as hard a man as y'all know." He placed his muscular hands on the desk and leaned forward on lean arms that seemed to be all tendon.

"Y'all been told the truth. 'A cadet does not lie, cheat, or steal, or tolerate those who do.' Y'all began livin' that with immediate effect. *Nuthin'* is ever goin' ta be the same. Honor is *personal* ta *yew*. Y'all can be slow with a rifle an' better at football 'n' track, prefer math ta English. But Honor—yew young gen'l'men must be *perfect* at it. Yew cannot lie, cheat, or steal."

He walked slowly by each of us. "It's the way at West Point. *The way*. Honor Code an' System belong to the United States Corps a Cadets. Corps runs the Honor System. Yew can do so much here, long as ya'll don' *cheat*. Cheat or lie, y'all face sword point an' leave with your tail down lahk lowlife, animal shit-scum. Questions?"

I had a question about false bravado, but I was afraid to stand out. A fist appeared to my right. A new cadet asked if it was an Honor violation to say you were not scared when you were.

"Questions 'bout motivation, Care Factor an' morale—y'all can try ta pump yo'self with a spirited answer. If y'all can't tell the difference, state: 'Sir, may I ask a question?' and ask it. 'Member, y'all gonna be hazed ta hell an back, all year, *anyway*, an' trust me most deeply, gen'lmen: there ain't *nuthin'* worse than violatin' the Honor Code and gettin' your young butt handed to ya onna tip of an Academy saber, fornicated for life."

We listened to distant screams. I hated rules about school clothes and posture, table manners, restrictions—Edna's rules. I respected the rules in the ring, in sports, on the street. Honor. I was bracing, but I wanted to smile. I was in a terrible place for food and comfort, but the architecture was correct.

"I present y'all Mr. Spillaney. Your boys, sir."

Spillaney had no neck. A football player, snarling like Old Evil, the terrible, child-eating bulldog in the Panhandle. Bad omen. I shivered. *All* the upperclassmen were *yu chao,* bearers of hunger, anger, fear, and disharmony. But I still had hope. Maybe he'd discuss food.

"Thank you, sir," he said. "YOU PUKING CROTS MAKE ME SICK!!" he screamed, spit flying. My guts jumped, my heart stopped, and my pulse went up. We quivered and braced, stuck rigidly in various corners and open spaces of walls like two-by-fours in a house to be framed, raw wood waiting for iron nails. After a day of Kafkaesque panic, dining à la Torquemada, and de Sadeian social conditioning, Mr. Spillaney's fury inspired gallons of new adrenal fluid to rush through our drained smackhead bodies.

We had marched to Trophy Point dressed in gray trousers, short-sleeved shirts, empty epaulets, and white gloves. A band had played marches full of emotion which had tickled my heart. We had stood at Trophy Point's Battle Monument to take the oath at the river with gloveless right hands, and we had crossed a boundary into another country, trembling with the weight of our pledge to protect the nation. I remembered Guan Yu. I thought: Now things will get better.

"THERE'S ONE REASON YOU'RE ALIVE—WHY I DON'T KILL ALL OF YOU!" he cried. Our eyes popped with attentiveness.

"I HATE NAVY WORSE THAN I HATE YOU! You might make it to do the President's bidding, or you'll be scabby-assed, money-sucking civilians. But either way, that damned Squid U, Crab State, will still be stinkin' up the Severn River AND TRYING TO BEAT US SIX YEARS STRAIGHT!" He took a deep breath, which deprived much of upper New York State of oxygen.

"Say again after me: 'I HATE NAVY AND ROGER STAUBACH!' "

"I HATE NAVY AND ROGER STAUBACH!!"

"Rotate your stupid knob noggins and look at each other. Six a you stupid little knobs aren't going to make it to the Navy game. Four knobs in this room are going to leave during Beast! My lung air's wasted on the half of you who're low on Care Factor!" He glared at us, circling the room. I was swamped in feelings. I felt guilty, hungry, fearful, exhausted, thirsty, confused, beleaguered. And hungrier than before I started the inventory.

Six little knobs out of fourteen? We had heard one in three. Now it was nearly one in two? What had happened since yesterday? Did our futures fluctuate with the Dow Jones? Was it my fault?

"I wanted AOT Carson to be with my OAO. But ole Spike got shafted and I got Beast One and *you* puking tools." His face was Tragedy's, the alphabet soup alarming. Who was AOT Carson?

"Honor, A Squad ball, and beating the living *crap* outa Navy—that's West Point. The rest of it's crap. Well, you can't get it. You will. Don't think I hate you *personally;* I just *hate* you."

He blinked. "You got these." He held up what looked like a small address book. "*Bugle Notes*. Spec it; start on page one-twelve. Be prepared to spout it cold. Get *nothing* wrong. You spaz, more gets laid on you till you bounce out on a carpet of quill."

He inspected us, studying the bodies of the football players. "Dirty little grunged-out knobs are beat, starving, pissed, and scared. *I* wasn't scared, 'cause I was gonna play Navy and pay them back for everything that's ever gone wrong in my life. Listen up.

"One. Crap here causes constipation. You don't eat, so you might not brush your stupid little knob teeth. Humidity's bad, so you might think showering's not doing any good. REPORT TO YOUR SQUAD LEADER BEFORE TAPS THAT YOU HAVE SHOWERED, BRUSHED YOUR TEETH, THAT YOU HAVE, OR HAVE NOT, MOVED YOUR KNOBBY LITTLE BOWELS IN THE LAST TWENTY-FOUR HOURS! DO YOU UNDERSTAND?!"

"YES, SIR!" we shouted.

He smiled vacuously. "Write a letter to your congressman, or to the President, whoever appointed you to this *marvelous* frigging place, thanking His Magnificence, pledging to uphold his unwarranted high expectations of you. That's 'cause they don't know what a hard thing it is they've done to you. Think you came to cotillion dances where girls throw you room keys. Haven't understood since Ike was President. This place is hard."

Shower, teeth, bowels, letter to Congressman Mailliard, I

said to myself. Let's see, S-T-B-C. There was something else . . . someone else I was supposed to write to.

"Who here got an AAA letter?" asked Mr. Spillaney.

The Automobile Association of America? My father had gotten an AAA letter, asking him to join. Fists came out, mine among them.

"What sport, Ting?" asked Mr. Spillaney.

Oh, God. Sport? "SIR, I DO NOT UNDERSTAND!" I cried.

"What *sport,* KNUCKLEHEAD, did Triple A recruit you for?"

"SIR, I MADE A MISTAKE!"

"WHADDAYA MEAN! YOU DIDN'T CONFUSE THE HOLY *ARMY ATHLETIC ASSOCIATION* FOR THE AMERICAN AUTO ASSOCIATION, DID YOU?!"

"YES, SIR!" Some of the other fists withdrew.

"THERE'S ALWAYS TEN PERCENT THAT DON'T GET THE WORD! WHEN YOU TIE UP, SPOUT, 'SIR, MAY I MAKE A CORRECTION?' TING! I'M GONNA REMEMBER *YOU!* YOU JUST CRAPPED ON A HUNDRED YEARS OF ARMY ATHLETICS! PUSH IT IN, CRAPHEAD. YOU GOT THE BRAINS OF A BORE BRUSH! DROP AND GIMME FIFTY PUSH-UPS, CALLING 'EM OUT FOR THE ARMY TEAM!! Last," he said with great equanimity while I shouted "ONE, ARMY TEAM! TWO, ARMY TEAM!" "You will learn this line, and you will repeat it now, after me: 'SIR. ALL THAT I AM, AND ALL THAT I CAN EVER HOPE TO BE, I OWE TO MR. ALSOP, MY FIRST DETAIL BEAST BARRACKS SQUAD LEADER!' NOW *BANG 'EM TOGETHER!!*"

"SIR, ALL THAT I AM, AND ALL THAT I CAN EVER HOPE TO BE, I OWE TO MR. ALSOP, MY FIRST DETAIL BEAST BARRACKS SQUAD LEADER!!"

"Clint Bestier." He was a young, scrubbed Gary Cooper, tall, nauseatingly handsome, and unnaturally self-assured. Guys like him reminded me why I had not a chance with Christine Carlson.

"Kai Ting," I said, shaking hands.

"Mick McCloud. Pee Wee," said a huge, Ernest Borgnine–like guy who had a slow, thick, comically dumb voice that was only two tics above Goofy's. Instantly, I felt smarter, if not handsomer.

"Stew Mersey. This sucks," said the third roommate, tall and angry with a long nose. He had looked like a blond surfer until the shears had met his skull and taken no prisoners. We felt the unfamiliar contours of our own shorn heads. They studied themselves in the sink mirror, awed by the changes. I didn't look; I knew what I looked like, and being reminded gave me no pleasure. I was accustomed to bad do's; my mother had dictated the style.

"I'd like to part my hair," I had said to her. "Please."

Edna had accompanied me to the barbershop. "Cut it very short so it conforms to the shape of his head," she had told the barber. "Cut it as always, regardless of what he says."

"Look a tad better different, ma'am," the barber had said.

She had glared at him, and I had felt sorry for both of us.

I smiled at my roommates. My bad haircut now had company.

"Like petting a skinned, sweating cat," said Bestier, smiling. He even sounded like the young Gary Cooper—innocent and earnest.

Never before had I sweated so much without being in a gym. White salt residue spotted armpits and the centers of chests. We looked like fugitives from a chain gang. I would've preferred a rock quarry. Ball and chain, armed guards, and snarling dogs would have represented an improvement, because at some point, prisoners got hardtack with their water.

We had a sink and took turns sucking from the faucet, sounding like rude drunks struggling for peace at a beer tap. I retrieved Momma LaRue's green plastic cup from my suitcase and we used it like pilgrims at Lourdes. Everyone but Pee Wee French-bathed in the sink, groaning as the cold water hit our lathered skin.

"Don't like water," said Pee Wee in his slow, moronic voice.

"Sure feels good," I said, remembering my talk with Mike about feelings. I wondered what company he and Sonny Rappa were in.

"I don't like water," said Pee Wee, louder.

I collapsed on a cot and studied the room. It had old ceiling lights and windowpanes, a light transom above the door, a partition creating two alcoves with bunk beds in each, four steel lockers against the plain walls, and metal desks in the middle. It was coldly bare on a hot night. Occasional new-cadet screams pierced the night. These were the barracks occupied by Sheridan, Sherman, MacArthur, Stilwell, Patton, and Na-men, my father's friend.

"I'm eighteen and they did this crap to me," said Mersey, lying on the floor. He sat up, leaving a puddle of sweat. "Gonna write to my hometown paper and expose West Point."

I laughed, but he was serious. Our equipment resembled everything in a Sears store after a big quake. I had read libraries of military works, but the gear—some of it modern military equipment and some of it eighteenth century—made little sense. We had banked like indiscriminate chipmunks, storing madly for winter shortages yet to be announced. Their strangeness was threatening. We had everything here except food, freedom, and comprehension.

"Unbelievable crap!" muttered Stew Mersey. "After all the shit to get here—all for 'Drop that bag!' Shoulda told them to screw off, turned around, and walked out." Some had.

Bestier, the quintessential white boy, listened attentively. His clear, bright eyes had witnessed success in life. His physique had been well fed and well trained. I thought that nothing bad had ever happened to him. Bestier was the young man I had always wanted to be, able to fit in; tall and fit for the street, with a cinematic Caucasian face that could be used for aftershave ads or a target for a girl's kisses. Edna would never have picked on me if I had looked like him. She always flirted with Jack Peeve.

"Let's get to work," Bestier said. He began folding clothes and placing them in a locker according to a chart that listed hundreds of items, like "helmet, steel, one each; helmet cover, camouflage, jungle, one each; helmet liner, one each."

"Want to know how to do this, watch me. Gotta hustle." He moved faster with each repeated task. His long and narrow, aquiline face was shaded by a growing beard. He slowed down, showing me how to fold the drollies, the undershirts, the cartridge belts. Heat came from everywhere, including my own confused body.

Toussaint had told me years ago that the South was hot. The East was no slouch. I looked at my new roommates. It was as if the gods had given me three strong friends with whom to share this hard experience. I thought of Toos, whom I hadn't seen in three years.

"You *pung-yoh*. Number-One *Pung-yoh*," I had said to him once.

"Whachu mean, 'pung you'?" asked Toussaint.

"*Pung-yoh*—friend," I said. "In Chinese."

"Aw, China! Thought you were cussin' me! I was gonna say, 'Well, *pung you*, you *punk!*'"

We laughed.

"See, China—you can laugh, real good."

"China," he had hissed at me when I was seven, "don' laugh! That boy done cut you *bad!* He's *laughin'* at you. Don't help him out!" Later, "You hear that, China?" he whispered. "*That's* funny. *Now* laugh. You 'member this sound"—and he laughed his high, wonderful cackle, and I joined him sounding like a jaw-busted jackass, while he coached me on the sounds of human joy.

"Lissen, China. When the ball come in, don't hit it with your face. Use the *hands*. Catch it like this, cradle it in, like it was a friend. See? Don't be jukin' your head back and forth. Hands up and *think* it in. Can't catch *nuthin'* with your mouth.

"Hey! Don't hold the bat like that! Hitchuself that ball! Lookit that pitcher! Give 'im the eye! No, man—he's over *there!*"

"No, no. China. Momma says, don't say 'dat' or 'dem' or 'dese.' Say it like this—see, move your lips: 'that,' 'them.'"

I made a face. "I don' talk like dat," I said.

"Right, China—surely you don't," he said.

I would look at his face to figure out my mood. If men drew blades or dogs coupled, I'd study his face so I could set mine. Toos was always explaining things to me. He told me on the way out of the Strand Theater on Market that the movie we'd just seen, *Pinocchio*, was about me.

I didn't get it. But I was a boy tied up in strings, trying to be real and to think at the same time. Toos saw that Tony Barraza, my Y coach, was Gepetto, an adoptive father trying to form new limbs for me through the human carpentry of iron bodybuilding. Toos was in the role of a blond fairy godmother in a pastel blue dress with a magic wand, giving me second chances from ages seven to fourteen.

When we were ten, I found Toos crying behind a wall on the Anza yard. The sight of tear tracks on his strong dark cheeks shot pains into my heart and guts and made me pant while standing still.

"Toos—what's wrong?" My eyes got wet because his were.

"Nothin'. Double nothin'." He wiped his face with his sleeves. "Nothin'. You hear? I *do not cry*." He looked away.

"What?" I asked.

He was quiet for a spell, just breathing. "Your daddy gets killed in the war. You get another daddy. And then he leaves for good, wouldn't mean *nuthin'*, right?"

Fathers. Big omen. "You don' cry. You're strong," I said.

He nodded at me, hitting my little fist with his big one. "I'm a man and I do not cry," he said, while I said, "You a man and you don' cry," and we repeated it until our eyes dried.

But something had happened. You can look at our classroom pictures, at Toussaint's smile after fourth grade, and see it, that although the smile was real, it had been robbed of a parent—a loss that children cannot restore without great outside help. The whole question about Toos's survival, and mine, was whether that help would come.

But he was always there for me. Toos even explained life to me. "Somethin's wrong," I whined, ripe with panic and rich with embarrassment. "My . . . thing. It—it gets . . ."

Toos looked confused until he saw where I was pointing. I was gesturing the way fishermen advertise the catch of a lifetime. Exaggeration began early for us.

"Aw, you're gettin' a big boner. Normal, man! Ain't gonna kill ya." He laughed. Then he frowned. "Leastways, don' think so."

"Hurts," I said.

"Don' give it no mind. It'll check out after an hour or two. That's how babies get made."

I gave him my funniest look, which made him hit me so I'd change it. "How?" I asked.

"Haven't figgered that. Somethin' to do with the moon."

"Oh, I know dat." I used to sit next to Sippy Suds on the LaRues' steps, next to Brooks Mortuary. Once he had babbled about women. "They's like heaven," he had breathed. "Oh, God, sweet *heaven!*" I knew that the goddess Gwan Yin lived in the night sky, in the celestial firmament, sitting on the moon and deciding who got boy babies. She had sent me into the Ting family. I wondered how Sippy knew this without Uncle Shim explaining it to him.

Toos and I had hidden inside a closet in the apartment, with Edna unaware that we had managed to enter through the unlocked back door. My heart slugged with fear. If she caught us . . .

We had entered the closet to tell each other a *mimi*, a secret. "You first," I said under my breath. "What's yo' secret?"

"Nawww!" he whispered. "I figured the door. *You* go first."

I hitched closer to him. We were wet with sweat from a day of running from the McAllister Car Barn to Sears, Roebuck on Geary, and back to Anza to shoot buckets. I had dribbled the ball a couple miles and played three-on-three, shooting fair and passing good.

"Go ahead!" Toos urged.

"I wanna go ta West Point," I whispered, below the ears of *wupo,* ghosts. They were in the closet, in the dark, with us.

"Huh?" he said.

"Shh! Wanna go ta West Point. Be a paratroopa. Don't tell *no one*." *Ji hui.* The gods had to have heard that. Years from now, they might kill me as I came out of the airplane. I looked into the dark, seeing nothing. Edna's long coat was in my face. Mothballs. Pitch-black.

"Dang, China," he whispered. "That Army place?"

I nodded my head vigorously up and down in the dark. Toos and I had talked about being jump-booted paratroopers when we grew up, swaggering like big men down McAllister past Cutty's Garage.

"That Army place?" he said, louder.

"Yeah! Shhh!" I whispered.

Toos turned the idea around. "Be a soldier," he said.

I thought of Guan Yu. I nodded. Toussaint's daddy had been a soldier, too.

"Huh," he said.

"Good idea?" I whispered. Silence. "Good idea, Toos?" I said.

"Oh, yeah, China, sure," he whispered lightly. He believed in ghosts, too.

"Don' tell, cross heart."

I heard his finger trace loudly, twice, across his old, tattered flannel shirt. "Your turn," I said.

"China . . ."

"Yeah."

"China . . ."

"Say it!" I hissed.

"Sshhhh!" he answered.

I giggled nervously.

"China. Don' laugh, man. This is a *dream*."

He cleared his throat, making a sound like a roaring Chinese dragon, and I flinched in the dark.

"I want to be a . . . docta."

We laughed in a pure way that preceded the days when I associated laughter with madness. That was crazy—Toos being a doctor! We almost died, stuffing our fists into our mouths, biting them, writhing on the floor, kicking each other, drumming our feet, trying to be silent. We laughed so hard, so physically, in that tiny closet, that we wept. When tears came out of my eyes I got scared, fearing that laughing had busted something inside me, that I had used some muscles or feelings I wasn't supposed to be messing with and the gods had punished me for the happiness. Later, when we crept out of the house and onto the street, our eyes still wet, we started laughing all over again, unable to stop until we hit each other. Never, ever, had I ever failed to laugh with him.

Toussaint and I had taken many steps in our youth. He had taught me the big ones. But he had not given me the little plastic cup. It was from his mother, on the day I gave her flowers. That had been last Saturday, a day before I had left for West Point.

Dear Abby had answered my letter with a form letter on flowers. Red roses meant love. I had walked to Podesta Baldocchi's near Maiden Lane. I couldn't afford their prices, but I couldn't afford to not get the best, and wired red roses to Christine in Berkeley. I spent two hours writing, correcting, and restructuring the sentiment, the counter littered with my errors. So much rested on the choice of words. Cyrano and Li Po never worked harder. Forget Roxane, Juliet, Dulcinea, Scarlett, Hsi Shih of the Warring States, or Brigitte Bardot and France Nuyen. Christine would read this letter. With the right words, someday she might marry me.

The final product was replete with the fundamental truths of affection, brimming with honest good cheer to last a season, robust with hidden meanings, forthright in its identification of parties and purpose, and not overly verbose:

Dear Christine,
   Have a great summer.
Love,
Kai

"Anything else?" the clerk asked.
"Flowers for a mother," I had said.

* * *

Mrs. LaRue looked at me for a moment. It had been three years.

"It's me, Kai Ting," I said.

"Oh, Lord, it's *you!* All grown!" she cried, putting hands to her cheeks, then stepping onto the porch and opening her arms.

"Hi, Mrs. LaRue." She was the only woman who hugged me, and now she did it with great purpose. I made myself relax and accepted her strong warmth, letting it take me, holding her, not breathing, weakened by the irrepressible surging of *gan ch'ing,* human emotion.

"What's this 'Mrs. LaRue'?" She separated herself from me. "Now, Kai Ting—*what* have I done to . . . to fall from your grace?"

"Momma," I said. "How are you?"

"Fine! Just a touch of bursitis! I'm *so* happy you visited! Reminds me of the old times, when you and Toos were just little children." She smoothed her hair, then her dress, a faded purple down-to-the-floor, probably a discard from one of the households she cleaned. It had an open collar with a missing button. Against her skin lay an old gold necklace with a cross centered on her throat. Her hair had gray, but her youthfully smooth and pretty face and her symmetrical frame had remained largely unchanged in the last decade. She had a tiny mole on her left eyelid, and I smiled when I saw it. "I'm a lot older, and my hair's a mess."

"You're the prettiest lady in the 'hood, Momma." I handed her the bouquet, called "Spring Glory."

"Oh, Lord," she breathed. "You are a *case.* Thank you, Kai," she said, holding the flowers at different angles, smelling the yellow roses and the gardenias, the sprigs of green, smiling at them. "Sit, where everybody can see us." Here, folks visited in the open air. It promoted neighborliness, allowed women to chat while watching their children, and supported accurate gossip.

Forties big-band music came winding out of her open door from the Emerson radio which Toos had bought her with his first paycheck from the now aged Petrini Plaza Market.

"Momma. Where's Toussaint?"

"He's at summer school in L.A. You've been gone—how long? Four years?"

"Three years, Momma," I said.

"Three years, chile! Be sure you come back next week."

My heart sank. Los Angeles! "Can't, Momma. I'm leaving—I got into West Point. I'm leaving tomorrow."

"Oh, Kai—that's *fantastic* news! That was your *dream*, wasn't it? Your daddy has to be so proud of you! You be sure to write Toos! After all these years . . . you best write letters."

"Toos tell you that?" I asked laughing. "It was a secret."

She smiled. "You told me, chile, all the time. You wait here."

She left. Kids ran in the street, tossing balls and thumping bodies, occasionally pausing to check out the Chinese guy on the LaRue steps. One kid came up the steps, squinting at me.

"I 'member you. You Toos's fren'."

"Hi," I said. "Denise's brother, Alfred. You're gettin' big."

"Yeah," he smiled. "I am." He rejoined his buddies, confirming his identification of me. Here, no bikes, trikes, or Flexis; lots of juice and spit while the winos worked their bags. School had been out for a week. Many others had gotten out much sooner.

"Bread from a cold toaster" was the way Reverend Jones said it. Some had moved out; some already had kids, some were pregnant; others were at Youth Authority or in jail. Many were sick with a host of addictions and health ailments abetted by local liquor stores. Willie Mack, the tough, tormenting bully of my early youth, had just up and disappeared, years before. A few, like Lucky and Maurice, who had always flirted with the wild side, had been buried in cold earth before I left. Years before, we had filled the street like a Lion's Dance parade down Grant Avenue on Chinese New Year.

Two neighbors passed, and I called out, "Hi, Mrs. Green—hello, Mrs. Gibson!" They waved back hesitantly. I could see them saying, Is that the Chinese boy who used to live here?

This had been home—ninety proof whiskey, a hundred proof cement, and 10 percent the Lord Jesus, with the rest in the hands, or the paws, of the rats and the trash-can dogs.

The music stepped up. Momma sat next to me and handed me a newspaper-wrapped package, a gardenia in her hair. It smelled sweet. I kept looking at her. She had a large, rounded forehead that led smoothly into her strong, angular, smart, knowing nose.

It was a worn, green plastic cup—a cousin to the one that had become my personal cup when Toos and I were second-graders. That had been the beginning of my life, when Toussaint had brought me within the embrace of his mother and the sanctuary of their poor apartment with the sureness of a lifeguard throwing a rope.

"Toussaint's daddy, John LaRue, was a man who shared his

water. You remember that, 'cause it's the spirit of the good Lord Jesus, Kai," she said, with bright eyes. "You take that with you to the Army. Give me comfort, thinkin' on you drinkin' from it."

"Thank you, Momma," I said, holding it in both hands. "I will never lose it." I used to sit here at night, while Sippy slept next to me. I hadn't seen him, and I didn't see his signs on the steps.

"Where's Sippy? And Mrs. Hall?" We never knew her true name. Toos called her that because she lived in the hallway.

Momma looked down. "Mrs. Hall, she died last winter. Sippy, he's *fine*. Sweeps up at the church. Name's now Deloitte. He from 'Sippi, but he pretends now to be Louisiana folk. Like you passin' for a colored, his tryin' to be uptown N'Orlins. Sippy says that Mr. Suds died and went to Kingdom Come. Deloitte is here to work for the Lord. He's done with fightin' the bottle. Sleeps in the church with the good Lord, who always forgave him his bad smell."

She rubbed her hands together, making a rasping noise between her palms, getting ready to say something. "Toos helped me take care of Mrs. Hall. Right painful for him." She put her head down, and then started to stand. I helped her. "You as strong as Toos! Dang, chile—you got rocks in your arm! Look how tall you are! Time's surely passin'."

She squinted off toward the park. Petrini Plaza was doing business putting the hurt on Mrs. Timm's failing Reliance Market a block away. UC Hospital sat off on Parnassus Hill.

The nurse who had defined for me the two nations of America had come from UC Hospital. In the thicket of the park, a thug had beaten and raped her, taking one eye and her peace.

Toos and I had stood on Fell and watched a magical army of never-before-seen City workers clearing trees and bushes from the Panhandle at Baker Street. "How come?" I asked Toos.

"Nurse lady from the hospital got hurt in there."

"Folk get cut in there evera night," I said.

"They ain't white," he said.

When we came back from school, the crews had reached Shrader Street. The tall eucalyptuses and pines of our forbidden forest, the divider between the kid gangs of the 'Handle and the Haight, were gone. The axes fell into living wood, and saws toppled trees; and suddenly now, this place where so many had been killed and hurt at night was open and almost indecently naked. It was then I noticed the hate in the white workers' eyes as they surveyed us, looking at us, muttering and swinging angry axes.

"Mrs. Hall," said Momma LaRue, "would've loved to see your face before she passed on to the Maker. Mrs. Hall missed you.

"Listen, sweetnin', this is Momma talkin'. Ain't right, driftin' in an' out of people's lives. Some men are that way but you got to be *different*. I know you lost your momma and your daddy works hard, but you are not trash." She looked at me, and I felt hollow, and bad. She poked me with an iron finger to drive the point deeper.

"I'm sorry. I can't believe she's dead. She was so *tough*. She used to wear those old, men's shoes without the laces, walking with those sticks." I was not comfortable thinking about her, a dead woman who had cared for me. "Glad for Sippy."

"Deloitte," she said. "You say hello to him. He's one of the folk who asks after you. Wouldn't be right, you visitin' me and not him." She smiled. "You know, there was some who never took a cotton to you. But not him. He *always* said you were special."

I nodded. Sippy Suds. I liked him when I was little, charmed by his unrated pro-welterweight past, warmed by his acceptance of me. But as I grew older I saw him more clearly: he was a smelly old drunk who messed his own pants and couldn't walk a straight line for a free drink. But Toos had always liked him.

Toos was in L.A. I had to see him. I couldn't *not* see him.

"I know you tryin' ta speak. No need. I know your feelin's, and it warms my heart. Just hold on to *all* those good feelin's. Now don' drift away. You hear me? Now, 'nuff scoldin' you. You've grown so! Put your young man's arms around me, and give Momma a *big* hug."

We embraced, and I moaned as she rubbed my back.

"You'd best write, Kai. Don' drift out on us. Promise me now."

"I do," I said, not wanting to leave, not even for West Point.

I watched him on the bench. I had been his least promising pupil. But he had never told me to take a hike, to jump in a lake, to take a flying leap. Now I was leaving him, and I didn't know how to do it. I tried to say hello, but couldn't. I tried again.

"Hi, Tony."

"Pass yur duties ta Johnny Moore?"

"Yeah, sure," I said.

Johnny was the next president of the Junior Leaders. He would assign Leaders to the Y classes. The hard part was training my replacement in the men's locker room. The new guy fumbled with the register, forgot members' names and habits. I felt bad leaving Leroy and the counter. It was my job, and now I was leaving.

"Kid, gimme a spot. Gettin' old and it's pissin' me off."

He had six 45-pound Yorks and two quarter plates on a standard bar—365 pounds. Tony believed that any normal person should bench a pound for every day of the year.

The bald spot was growing in the middle of a jet-black scalp. The thick muscles forced between his big frame corded while he steadily pressed the bar. Fourteen years out of the ring, he was still 225 pounds of gristle and bone graced by a relentless beard and enough body hair for twenty of me. I grimaced as he exhaled bitter *bagnacauda* fumes from his lunch. He did ten reps without help, banged down the bar, and sat up. "Yur leavin'. Well, shit, kid." He looked down.

"Gee, Tony, thanks for the good word."

" 'Member what I told you, 'bout war?"

"I know it's hard," I said.

"*Hard?* Hey, it's fuckin' *impossible,* 'scuse my French. It don' mean spit ta study it. And it don' mean spit there ain't no war *now,* cuz there's always a friggin' war *later.* Know what I mean?"

I frowned. This is not what I wanted from him.

"Look, kid. Ya never wanted to hear this." He drew his forearm across his nose while flexing his nasal passages. He was squinting.

"Excuse me, are you using that bench?" asked a new member.

"Yeah, I'm usin' it ta sit," said Tony without looking up. "Ya got skills but ya ain't a fighter. Toe ta toe with a fighter, yur screwed twelve outa ten. And *shit*—it's all my goddamm fault."

"Whaddya mean?" I asked. "I help teach it!"

"Aw, shit, kid. Yur a good coach, patient as a dead man. Not sayin' this ta bust yur bones. Tryin' ta tell ya who ya are. Ya got no taste fer blood. I know why ya get inna ring," he said, his face twisted. "Ya get in there fer me. The Science saved yur skinny butt ten years ago, when that bully come inta yur life. Now the ring's yur church. Me, I'm the fuckin' priest, 'scuse my French. 'Cept I ain't a goddamm peacemaker. Shit, kid. You are."

"I'm as good as anyone in the program." My voice was high.

"Tito put the big hurt on ya. Ya missed the finals. Wills made ya look bad. They ain't blind like youse an' they ain't got no *relations* and no funny-lookin' pencil-neck Chinese *uncles* draggin' on their gloves, givin' 'em the tsk-tsk shit fer the Duke's rules! Tito, he'd knock out his gramma ta get another fight! Shit! You fight, ya gotta go bow ta yur uncle an' mumble Chinese rosaries." He snorted. "Ya got try. But yur family crap's bigger 'n yur try."

"But you taught me that *trying's* bigger than winning!" I shouted. Others stared.

"Yeah, an' 'at's the flat truth. Lookit ya! Ya got a body! Ya got good arms and a man's chest! Ya look like a fuckin' piece a work! Ya got *great* try, great heart! But shit, ya started with *nothin'*. . . . Aw, shit, fergit it. I'm only makin' it worse." He looked down at his black gym shoes, moving his mouth silently. He was practicing a speech. He looked up, the smaller, left eye glinting, the larger one flat and lizardlike, the scar tissue livid in the dull light from the grated windows. Tony smelled of effort and garlic. A cabbie leaned on his horn, six floors down, making other cars honk back while pigeons took flight in a clatter of wings.

"Don' know nothin' 'bout West Point. Don' even know where the hell it is. But it makes officers, which, ya ask me, are all turds.

"West Point's prob'ly like the Corps. Marines, they like *killers*. Kid, you could do it. Lotsa kids can do it. But it'd be ugly fer ya. Lookit me. I came from bad youth, Hell's Kitchen, fuckin' bottom drawer, fulla sin, foul mouth, killed the Nips and screwed lots—aw, shit." He shook his big, rocklike head. "None a that helped me with Clara or my boy." He snorted, blew his nose on the old floor behind the bench. He had said too much. "Kid. Yur like yur Uncle Shingus." He paused. "I'm hurtin' yur feelin's."

"No," I said, my voice barely audible.

"Kid, ya don' wanna be an old, achin', busted-down, soft-eared, bad-mouthed *bum,* livin' in a hotel eatin' goop from a can. Couldn't even keep my goddamn dog alive. Ya wanna be a smart college man with a tie and a hat, a car and money in the bank, like yur Uncle Shingus, or yur dad. Meals. A roof. A future."

That was not true. "I want to be like you," I said.

"Oh, hell, like *crap* you do!" he bellowed. Men began to move away. "Ya gimme *porca miseria*, pig pain in my heart, talkin' like that! Ya don' like garlic sausage, ya spit out the best *bagnacauda* in North Beach, ya can't play bocce ball ta save the Virgin Mary, an' ya ain't true Catholic even when ya show off my rosary an' recite yur damn venal sins. Ya don' cross yurself 'fore a bout or thank the goddammed Lord fer a stinkin' meal, ya don' give crap to yur patron saint, an' ya don' speak paisan excep' fer the *'Che fai.'* An' ya got too many brains in yur headgear ta be a good fighter. So *fergit it.* Ya gonna stand there lookin' pretty, or ya gonna work out?!"

"I—I just wanted to say goodbye. And hear your good word."

He put out his huge, calloused mitt. His hand felt like an old piece of cold concrete with a leather cover. "Okay, great."

I shook his hand with great emotion, making his big shoulder bounce. His fingers had lost feeling two decades ago. I did the gripping for both of us. I didn't want to let go of him.

"Okay, kid. Here's my goddamm good word. Put two more quarters on. Goin' fer fifteen reps with four-fifteen—and fer Christ's sake, don' make no faces when I blow out my air.

"Goddammed peacemaker. Shit—can't even *tell* you how pissed I'm gonna be if you get killed in some shitface war. Now, help me with this stinkin' bar an' don' forget ta take my rosary with ya."

8

RITUALS

Central Area, West Point, July 1, 1964

I rummaged for grub and there was none. Tony used to eat food out of the can in his hotel room, and I continued to envy him.

"Got more uniforms," said big Pee Wee slowly. "Think

they're multiplying." I expected him to chuckle "Uh-huuh," like Goofy.

"At least someone's having fun," said Clint Bestier.

I didn't get it. Then I did, and giggled. " 'Multiplying.' "

"Need a shower," said Stew Mersey. "I'm, like, ripe."

He was. "Anyone see any food?" I drank more water.

"Wouldn't do that," said Bestier. "You're going to have to use the latrine. Latrine's in the sinks."

I looked at our sink, puzzled. I wouldn't go in there.

"Sinks. Five floors down. Latrines are in the basement, where we stowed gym gear about four hours ago." It seemed like last year.

There was a mass of insanely deranged, screaming upperclassmen between my bladder and the sinks. I could wait, maybe a year.

"Not going to be any food until Christmas," said Bestier.

I made a deep, squealing noise. "Hey—someone said we wouldn't eat for the *summer*." I was whining.

"Beast's the worst," he said. "We'll get a little food in the fall." I closed my mouth; no nutrition was going to enter it. Dinner had been an encore of lunch: moving food into milk cartons while testing the bouquet of water and savoring salt tablets.

"I could eat the tail off a hobbyhorse," said Pee Wee. I saw Mersey look at Bestier, secretly laughing at Pee Wee's funny voice. I didn't like him doing that.

"Won't we get rickets or scurvy?" I asked, hoping that a medical justification might spontaneously create grits. I thought of Angie's burgers and cold vanilla shakes with ice in the bottom.

"Where you guys from?" Bestier asked.

"Escanaba, Upper Peninsula, Michigan," said Mersey.

"San Francisco," I said.

"Washington, D.C.," said McCloud methodically. "You?"

"Fort Huachuca, Arizona," said Bestier. "I'm an Army brat. Dad's been prepping me for Beast and Plebe year since I was five." He smiled, dimples deepening. "I knew what would happen today."

The door exploded in a colossal crash as someone struck, opened, and bashed it into the wall. We hopped like the Four Stooges being goosed by cattle prods. The heavy door vibrated from its battering as Bestier shouted, "ROOM, ATTEN-HUT!"

and braced, quivering at attention, eyes straight ahead. We followed suit.

"WHAT ARE YOU DOOWILLIES TALKING ABOUT?!" screamed Mr. Spillaney. My mind fumbled as I tried to form an answer. I couldn't remember. He looked angry. I wondered if he had been born that way.

He turned his back to us, facing our open door. "LOOK AT THIS LOCKER! EQUIPMENT'S IMPROPERLY DISPLAYED!" he bellowed. He turned into the room, took three giant steps like a fearsome hulk in a torture chamber, his eyes glaring like headlights in a big truck, and seized Bestier's locker. He jerked it, shotgunning its carefully folded contents and throwing the locker down face first. It crashed horribly, like a living thing, in a great metallic boom. He turned to the door. Mersey closed his eyes, the horror too great. My eyes bulged with fear. That locker could have been us.

"TAPS IN THIRTY MINUTES, 2200 HOURS! SQUARE AWAY EQUIPMENT, READY FOR MORNING INSPECTION! REVEILLE IS 0500, UNIFORM IS BRAVO WITH DRESS SHOES, *SMACKHEADS!* DO YOU HEAR ME?!"

"YES, SIR!" we screamed as he left. We respected lockers at the Y. "Lockercide," I said, looking at it, starting to breathe again. Stew Mersey was shaking. We ran our hands over our bald heads, creating a soft rasping. "He has a big voice," I added.

We picked up Bestier's locker and gear. The locker still had its rivets. Bestier began refolding the T-shirts, the boxer underwear, the socks, in the prescribed pattern, with the same speed and dexterity he had demonstrated before.

"Why us?" I asked as I began folding mine.

"Might be me," Bestier said. "My dad's a general. Or you, being Chinese. Or the room, cuz it's the best place to speak to the floor. Here, he says it once instead of four times."

"Man," I said. "They'd do that? Because of me being Chinese?"

"Not good to stand out," he said.

Mr. O'Ware had said he would remember me. So had Mr. Spillaney. I felt white ghosts moving across my heart.

"My dad's General Ira Costain McCloud," said Pee Wee, taking about five minutes to say it. "Your dad's Pierce Bestier? We probably went to grade school together, in Fort Lewis, when they were majors." Clint nodded.

"My shit luck!" cried Mersey. "Stuck with two guys they

hate cuz they know the score, and with a guy they hate cuz he's Chinese. Goddammit, this is no way to start college."

"Look," said Bestier to me. "Center and fold to this width, so it reaches to here on the shelf. The drollies—boxer shorts—go next. Just like the chart. Dad showed me all of this."

"Man," I said, "don't you feel . . . discouraged?"

"A little," he sighed. "Remember, we're in the Army."

"Oh, God," moaned Mersey. "I'm in the Army."

He had reshelved everything. "Pick up the pace, but don't tie up the alignment of the folds, or the display. It's all geometric."

We heard haunting, random cries, echoing distantly throughout Central Area while we struggled with the rules, the tasks, and the waiting, watching anger. It all seemed new but somehow familiar.

A bugle sounded taps. Bestier switched off the lights as we heard "LIGHTS OUT!" Thirty minutes had gone in an instant. Everything was stowed, none of it better than Bestier's. Mersey's was second best. Mine and Pee Wee's looked like the work of inebriated chimps using spoons in an effort to make televisions.

"What do we do now?" I asked.

"Go to bed," whispered Bestier. "That's what taps means."

"I know what it means," I said. "I went to YMCA summer camp."

"Oh, *wow*," whispered Stew Mersey.

I lay down in a sea of aches. It was still hot. My neck was stiff from fourteen hours of compression, my back was sore from hitting walls, and my throat was raw from yelling, but my empty gut was most articulate in its complaints at the day's events, or lack of events. It *had* been a day. Eruptions of overinformation, hunger, demands, criticism, and anger. The Honor lecture in air-conditioned Thayer Hall. Never again could I lie, about *anything*. I couldn't even *accept* lying in another. I didn't think that was fair. How could you turn in a buddy? *Pao-chia*, each responsible for all. I remembered each mistake in the day. West Point was the Hanlin, with model standards. It also seemed like Edna. West Point made California seem like a new invention. The Academy was bigger, older, and harder than I had imagined, like being belowdecks in a Roman galley. Bracing was like oaring under verbal whips. I remembered clippers running across my scalp like a psycho lawn mower, the cascade of hair down my back, the barber asking "More off the top?" My favorite tune "Garry Owens," so gay while we marched in tight ranks out of the sally ports, our left heels hitting the pavement with each strike of the deep drums, across the Plain to Battle Monument for the oath before a huge throng—proud of us, of America, and of the bright flag that whipped in the river wind in front of that grand vista of the Hudson. I was taking big steps into the heart of America, out of the slum of my prior life with poverty and Edna. Troops of kids had run alongside us past iron-backed MP sergeants in white hats and white gloves as we took the curve toward the Hudson. The drums beat, and I trembled in a crescendo of unknown emotions. Life was changing. We swore to support the Constitution of the United States, to bear true allegiance to the national government. Guan Yu had made a pledge like that in Peach Orchard by the Yangtze River. Later, he had died, protecting honor.

I had been singled out, asked what I was. I wasn't an American, but a Chinese-American, a citizen with a hyphen. The hard cot creaked as I tried to find a comfortable position. The pillow smelled old. I tried to imagine my father doing this at Fort Benning. How had he dealt with being the only Chinese? Here, I felt alone. I squelched the feeling. Doesn't mean anything, I said, flexing arms, crossing them against my chest, curling my body on its side, flaring my lats and shoulders in my conventional position of sleep, ready to take unseen blows. Reading *Ben-Hur* on the airliner was an age ago. His mother and sister in a secret, sealed cell for eight years.

" 'A woman of Israel, entombed here with her daughter. Help us quickly, or we die.'

" 'Thou shalt have relief, woman,' said the new guard. 'I will send thee food and drink.' " Someone was shouting. I smiled for the food and drink. The lights were on. I was on my feet with my glasses on. Our door was open, bright light on the old floor.

Mr. Fideli, the tall, aesthetic, aristocratic singing cadet from the tunnel of summer songs, was in our room. "MOVE YOUR KNOBBY BUTTS!" he roared with a voice that boomed like the new speakers in the Fox Theater, louder than Spillaney, filling the room, as loud as God. "UNIFORM BRAVO! TWO MINUTES AND YOU'RE LATE!"

I stared at him, uncomprehending. What did he say? The door slammed, the force slapping air in my face. Dress! We moved like boys with hot coals under our feet, Mersey whimpering when he fell on the floor from performing the complex task of putting on pants.

"Remember dress-offs," cried Bestier, as we folded the excess shirt fabric across our backs to create formfitting contours. I had trained for this, changing into Jack's cast-offs. I was the first dressed. "Oh, crap," Pee Wee grunted deeply. Outside, the sounds of purgatory or a pork slaughterhouse filled Central Area.

The entire barracks thumped with a thousand half-dressed boys fighting unfamiliar clothing while the cadre screamed advice and threw wastebaskets down hallways to encourage cooperation and a positive attitude.

For all his slow speech, Pee Wee was also ready. Bestier was next. "Garrison cap!" he shouted, holding the one that looked like a taco. "Wait for Mersey," he said. We put on our hats.

"It's one-thirty—I thought it was morning!" said Mersey.

"It *is* morning," hissed Clint. "Now *move it!*" We pounded down the staircase, forearms parallel to the ground, necks in. Central Area was alive with verbal violence. Mr. Alsop and Mr. Spillaney, white-gloved in khakis and combat boots, waited for us, screaming us into a squad line by height.

"LOOK DOWN! REMEMBER YOUR SPOT ON THE AREA!" screamed Mr. Spillaney. Between my shoes was an intersection between a concrete line and a small pockmark, my nose aligned with the fourth window from the door. I imagined Grant and Stilwell using these marks to find their places. A good omen. One fellow was last into the formation, and five cadremen converged, screaming at him, calling him a "shit magnet" until he seemed to disappear, his screams seeming more real than his physical presence. The entire class was bracing at attention in company formations. A huge cadet who resembled a Greek god stood on the stoops in the center of the barracks. There were thirteen hundred people assembled. West Point was unearthily silent in the moonlight and in the cool river breeze.

"GENTLEMEN, I AM MR. ARVIN, KING OF BEASTS," shouted the big man. "YOU ARE DISREPUTABLE. YOU LACK ALIGNMENT, DRESS-OFFS, AND KNOWLEDGE. CHANGE YOUR WAYS AND YOUR UNIFORMS."

A cadet with a rack of black bars on his collar stood in front of our company. Seven other cadets spoke in front of their companies, arrayed across the width of the Area.

"I AM CADET CAPTAIN COSWELL, COMMANDER, FOURTH NEW CADET COMPANY. I HAVE NEVER LOST AT *ANYTHING* IN MY LIFE! I WILL NOT *TOLERATE* LESS THAN FIRST PLACE IN THIS CLOTHING FORMATION!

"THE NEXT UNIFORM IS SWEATSHIRTS OVER FATIGUES WITH SHOWER CLOGS WITH GARRISON CAPS, UNDER ARMS. YOU WILL HAVE THREE MINUTES. YOU WILL BE DISMISSED BY FLOORS. WHAT'S YOUR COMPANY MOTTO, MEN?"

" 'STUDS GO FOURTH,' SIR!" A sign with those curious words sat on the first sergeant's desk in the orderly room. I could hear "First in the Corps!" and "Second to none!" in the echo of our shout. I tried to decode the uniform prescription. Shower clogs under arms?

Mr. Coswell hesitated, looking to Mr. Arvin, who raised his right arm and dropped it with the precision of a Chinese executioner swinging a headsman's axe. "FIFTH FLOOR, POST!!"

The penthouse dwellers jerked, then ran, as did their mates from other companies. This was my sport. Triple A recruited me for clothing competition! I'm fast! I smiled, and no one caught me.

"FOURTH FLOOR, POST!" I sprinted in that spastic, upright form while bracing. Up the stoop stairs, past Mr. Fideli in his stiffly starched khakis, through the door. I was about to leap up the stairs when all the new cadets from the fifth floor came flying down them, to the sinks. Our sweatshirts were with the gym gear, in the sinks. Down the stairs, to the gym lockers; then up the stairs four flights, the pounding of military shoes taking the authorized single steps, no skipping, creating an imbecilic single-beat drumming; into the room.

Our lockers were on the floor, gear intermixed in heaps, as if King Kong had souffléed the room with an eggbeater the size of the Eiffel Tower. The alcove wall hangers were contorted in angles of mayhem, resembling the stripped and pitiful bones of animals that had been caught by an omnivorous predator. Godzilla had dropped by for a visit, with a technique I knew from living with my mother.

"Crap!" cried Bestier. He stripped and sorted through the debris. The rest of us were immobile, overwhelmed, defeated.

"Goddammit! Why the *hell* are they *doing* this?!" cried Mersey.

"Pee Wee, Kai—here are larges. Put 'em on! Clock's running!"

"ROOM, ATTEN-HUT!" cried McCloud, as fast as he could.

Mr. Fideli stepped into the room. He was in fatigues over a sweatshirt, garrison cap, with his saber, Sam Browne belt, and not our simple clogs—but with fully laced combat boots.

"You are slow," he said in a low tone, making our hearts pound faster. Speaking softly? Big sticks were next. "Why has your militarily disreputable room become Grand Central Station?"

I'm Chinese, I thought. It's cuz he's Chinese, Mersey thought. McCloud thought: Oh, crap, it's because Ting's Chinese!

"You were to report before taps the condition of your knob bodies. As a result, you will memorize not only *Bugle Notes* but also individual Fourth Class knowledge, assigned by me.

"Let us say, crotheads, I am your acting squad leader."

What to do? Time was running out. We had to be changing.

"SIR!" cried Stew Mersey. "Uh, NEW CADET MERSEY REPORTS HE HAS NOT BRUSHED HIS TEETH, HAS NOT—UH—MOVED HIS BOWELS, AND THAT HE HAS NOT SHOWERED, IN THE LAST—oh, maybe I did—"

"BANG THAT HEAD IN, MERSEY! THAT WAS GROSS! I DON'T WANT *PUNY* REPORTS FROM *THIS* DISREPUTABLE ROOM! REPORT YOUR SHOWER, TEETH, AND BOWELS IN THAT ORDER, WITHOUT THE BABBLE! *GOT THAT, SMACKBEAN?!*"

"YESSIR!" cried Stew.

"Your Care Factor as a room is low. Buck it up. Otherwise, Beast could become *unpleasant*. Do not let me catch you behind me on the next uniform. WORK!" he shouted. The door banged shut.

"God, he changed fast," murmured Bestier.

Stew Mersey wandered, fingering his shirt, studying the carnage.

"Hurry, guys," said Bestier. "We're dead if we don't try."

After much stumbling and excavating, we fell in ranks in the curious attire. We grimaced as we heard a few new cadets fall down the stairs with their rifles in a terrible clashing of bodies, wood, and steel. One of us was carried out by a cadre member.

"GENTLEMEN. THE NEXT UNIFORM IS UNIFORM INDIA WITH PONCHO, COMBAT BOOTS, PROPERLY LACED AND UNBLOUSED, AND HELMET LINERS. YOU HAVE FOUR MINUTES. FIFTH FLOOR, POST!"

We had just entered the room when Mr. Fideli appeared in the new uniform, looking like a million bucks in coattails.

"ROOM, ATTEN-HUT!" I screamed.

"Too slow, knobs," he said. "How can you succeed without clothes?" He exited, making us jump when he slammed the door.

This went on all night. Each time we ran like crazed men up the stairs and began to strip the former uniforms, Mr. Fideli would enter, impeccably in the next uniform, without a hint of effort.

"Asshole must be made outa zippers," muttered Mersey.

After three hours we had become beaten galley slaves, gasping, sweating, wheezing, and coughing in ranks. Dizzy with effort, dazed from hazing, starving, we were near the end of our ability to function. I was done in from our attempt to imitate *Vogue* models on West Point's fashion runway. We were like them: thin, underfed, exploited, overscrutinized, and clothed in outrageous taste.

"THIS WAS A SORRY EXPERIENCE," called Mr. Arvin. "IF I AM TO BE RESPONSIBLE FOR YOU AS MEMBERS OF THE UNITED STATES ARMY, YOU MUST GET THIS EXERCISE RIGHT. WE WILL HAVE TO DO THIS AGAIN."

A soft moan ran through ranks. Mr. Fideli, like the other upperclassmen, looked calm, as if Mr. Arvin had said tomorrow would bring sunlight, milk and cookies, iced tea with mint for the adults, and plenty for everyone.

"I WILL INFORM YOU WHEN. COMPANY COMMANDERS, TAKE COMMAND OF YOUR COMPANIES!"

"FIFTH FLOOR, POST! CLEAN UP YOUR ROOMS! FOURTH FLOOR, POST! DRINK WATER! THIRD FLOOR, POST! SECOND AND FIRST FLOORS, POST!"

We were in our room. I looked at my Timex. It was 3:34 A.M.; 12:34 in California. I kept drinking water from my green cup.

Bestier pointed at his cot. "Our pal here: the rack." Flat, like our spirits; sallow, like our hopes; institutionally Spartan, like West Point, the International Center for Quick Dieting, Clothing Abuse, and Sleep Deprivation. I had slept in the rack for three hours, but felt none of its benefits.

"It's a goddamned nightmare," said Mersey.

I hadn't experienced my normal, recurring nightmare about murder in the 'hood. I had dreamed about Ben-Hur's mother and sister. The hazing was unbelievable, but I was enduring it with a thousand other guys. This wasn't the result of an angry woman's hate; Thayer and George Washington were testing me, seeing if I was fit, if I could change clothes, and other things, with sufficient skill to be allowed to stay. It was the test of my life.

"This nightmare only lasts a year," said Bestier.

I could do that. I used to imagine running away on an S.P. freight, asking Toos where trains came from while he wondered where they were headed. I had made good my escape, believing that anywhere would be an improvement. Today had been a test of that proposition. "Man, I'm glad you're here," I said to Bestier.

"Aw, *crap*," said Mersey. "*I'm* not. This *sucks!*"

Bestier laughed, and so did McCloud, too loudly. Then Mersey.

"Still sucks," he said. "These fuckin' rituals eat it big."

"The *li,* the rituals, *Hausheng,*" said Uncle Shim, "are to honor your *gahng* and *lun,* bonds and relationships. You must adhere to the teachings of the Master K'ung, who said, *'k'e ji fu li.'* Subdue the self, and honor the rituals. Do the correct thing."

Mr. Alsop had said, "the Honor Code. It is the way."

To him, I had repeated, I owed all that I was, and all that I would ever be.

9

HOME

Second Detail, Beast Barracks, August 20, 1964

"Six goddamned weeks. Gotta get *outa* here!" cried Mersey.

I wanted to help. "What would your dad say?"

"Who gives a shit? What'd *your* dad say if *you* quit?"

I shook my head. It'd be easier to report my death.

"I don't give a crap!" he cried. "It's *my* life. *He's* not here! 'My son, West Point cadet'—bragging at the country club while we got guys trying to kill themselves by drinking Brasso. You thought that guy was nuts for attacking Sowerby. *Shit!* I know how he coulda done it! *I* could've killed him! *Easy,* see?"

Last week, the first class had taught us the Spirit of the Bayonet. We used the M-14 like a medieval multipurpose halberd, stabbing and slashing with the blade, clubbing and bashing with the rifle butt, lunging with the grace permitted by a twelve-pound pointed club in the horizontal butt-stroke series, the high parry, and the straight-armed thrust, none of which was useful without a throat-stripping roar as we dismembered the imaginary enemy. I did not feel like d'Artagnan. Then one of our classmates had gone nuts and attacked Mr. Sowerby with his bayonet. He had been butt-stroked, clubbed, hospitalized, arrested, and separated from Beast.

"WHAT'S THE SPIRIT OF THE BAYONET?" Sowerby had screamed.

"TO KILL, SIR!" we had cried back.

"And the jodies, singing while we march," spat Mersey. "What crap. 'Everywhere we go, people want to know, who we are, so we tell them, we are Fourth, Mighty Mighty Fourth,'" he mimicked in a high voice. "Bullshit!" Mersey paced, a POW in his own army. "That goddamned *asshole*

85

O'Ware—he's a goddamn *sadist!* If he orders another shower formation, I'll kill him!"

Ferret-faced Mr. O'Ware had become Norman Bates in cadet gray, the psycho motel clerk authorized to carry knives and make raiding parties on the guests. He relished pain, found our hurting parts and spiked them with lye and malice. He was the only cadre who hazed from the side, screaming sour spittle into our cheeks. He was still not a candidate for dental hygiene poster boy. He was the sort who would chop off your foot and then write you up for limping at parade. He called Stew "Spazzed-Little-Girl-Emotional-Crap-Your-Pants-Douchebag Puke Mersey." He required recitations of the Definitions of Leather and Concrete, the Days, MacArthur's Message from the Far East, and Battalion Orders. Perhaps Einstein could have spouted errorless poop; we couldn't. Mersey was being ground down. We tried helping, but he fought us instead.

O'Ware liked shower formations. They began on the top floor, in a bathrobe with a towel folded on the extended left forearm and a soap dish in the left hand. We looked like failed English butlers with bad haircuts, working for tyrannical lords. We sweated pennies to the wall with our backs. The more you sweated, the more floors you descended, until, drenched with your own sweat, you reached the sinks for a ten-second cold shower. Refreshed, you could retire for three hours' sleep before reveille. I was beginning to have dreams about sleeping.

O'Ware called Clint Bestier "Gary Cooper" and called me "Mars-man." He called Pee Wee McCloud "Goofy Gomer Pyle." He ordered me to report to his room two hours after taps on evenings not blessed with clothing or shower formations. Without an alarm clock, I fought narcotic sleepfulness, trying to stay awake.

His door was open and I stood in it while he wrote in a log at his desk. His roommate was Mr. Spillaney, whose snoring sounded like the bellows of hell. The desk lamp placed deep, haunting shadows on Mr. O'Ware's face. It was like looking at Lucifer.

"Fishfaced douchebag hunchback," he whispered, "your mother have any children who lived? Don't like your looks." I wondered if he had paid copyright fees to my mother for the last remark. I wondered what a "douchebag" was.

"Rack your ugly, flat-face neck in, cretin," he hissed. "Your type doesn't have emotion. Gimme the Definition of Duty. I'll kick your yellow ass out of the Academy if you wake up Mr. Spike."

"Sir, the Definition of Duty," I whispered. " 'Duty may be defined as the sense of obligation which motivates one to do, to the best of his ability, what is expected of him in a certain position or station. This, sir, is the Definition of Duty."

"Your duty is to suffer, shithead." He asked other questions, as the mood affected him, without looking at me. "Think you can muck it through West Point?" He laughed at me. "I don't think so."

"Gonna get him," Mersey said. He was playing with his bayonet.

"Put it down," said Bestier. "In the fall, you can call him out. Plebes can challenge upperclassmen to box. The problem is, when you beat him, you have to box his classmates."

Mersey smiled, for the first time in Beast. "No shit? He's *mine*. And I was starting to think there was nothing good here."

Once, I had held my fists up to my mother. Uncle Shim would say that boxing an elder would be very *jing ji*, taboo, and violate the *Wu-lun*, the Five Personal Relationships. I fought when I had to; here, I only had to know the poop. As hungry as I was, this was better than home, for suffering had a purpose and hunger made me feel noble. I was with Washington's ragtag army at Valley Forge, in the middle of summer, proving my patriotism as a measure of self. There was no honor in fighting your mother.

"Stew," I said, "it's like we're trying to do what Kennedy asked—doing something for our country, something bigger than just . . . college. It's home, now." Bestier nodded.

"You stupid shit," said Mersey. "You think *this* is *home*? Mother screw! You musta come from a fuckin' *prison* to think *that!*"

I felt like arguing, but Beast was better than living with Edna. A cadet does not lie, cheat, or steal. "Yeah," I said.

"You guys know what my best friend is doing this summer?" Mersey said, trying to make up.

"Yup," Bestier said. "Getting laid. You already said that."

"But think of it!" he exhorted. "He's *getting laid*."

"Don't wanna think about it," said Pee Wee McCloud, his nearly invisible eyebrows rising, then falling into a frown.

"Hey, guys," I said. "In ten days the Corps returns, we join our regular companies, and we might get some *food*."

"You're havin' a cow over *food*," said Mersey, "while our pals are gettin' nookie and havin' a blast at Beach Boys concerts, seein' Ann-Margret in *Viva Las Vegas*. We're shinin' shoes and yakkin' about *food!* This crap started in *July*—while everyone we know is havin' the *best* goddamned summer in their lives! Does this *suck* or not?"

"It sucks," said Pee Wee slowly, nodding his big head.

Bestier smiled. "I eat this up," he said. "I wanted to come here so bad, I don't sweat this stuff."

"Yeah, fine, eat it up," said Stew. "You're *nuts*. You look at each other? We're *disappearing*. I couldn't *compete* right now. You were big," he said to me. "Now you're a skinny Chinaman!"

I put down my shoeshine rag. "That's not a good word."

"So what the hell do I call you?" he asked.

" 'Kai' is good. So's 'Ting,' or 'American.' 'Chinese' is good. 'Chinese-American,' that's okay. That other word, that's *not* good."

Silence. I had emphasized my difference to them.

"Hey," said Pee Wee, grinning at me. "What about 'crot'? Or 'doo-willie'? Or 'bean-head.' Or 'dumb john crot willie smackhead'?"

I had written Christine four exotically long letters, describing the flight across America, the skyscrapers and taxis in New York, and the trip up the Hudson. "I have a roommate who looks like Gary Cooper, another who resembles Ernest Borgnine but sounds like Goofy, and one who cackles while sharpening his bayonet as he considers murdering the upperclassmen." In my last letter, I had said that I needed to hear from her, about anything.

I look out the window at Central Area at the stars. The only illumination comes from soft yellow streetlamps on Thayer Road, on the other side of tall granite fortress walls formed into a hollow square. A tall clock tower stands in the middle of the Area. I see the stars three hours earlier than you, knowing they are looking down at you, and I think of your face, and your laugh, and your thoughts, hoping that you are safe, and happy, and doing the things that you wanted to do.

I had pledged undying love, forever, to Christine Anne Carlson, the most beautiful girl in the world. I used to pine for

her while we ate lunch together. Her blondness reminded me
of every idealized actress in Hollywood. I knew her birthday,
the name of her cat and her older brother, that her father
worked for *The San Francisco Chronicle,* and that Mrs.
Carlson was glamorous and was active in church and community.

Christine was a National Merit Scholar who was accepted at
Stanford but picked Cal. Indifferent to cliques, she preferred
girlfriends to boyfriends. She turned hallways dark with smoke
when she burned cookies in home economics, worked on the
school paper, loved literature and drama, starred in school
plays, and sang.

I breathed her name, a sound that scraped at the roof of
heaven and conjured mystic powers of creation and storm. If I
said her name for two minutes, I would hyperventilate, and the
constellations would come out at high noon.

" 'At's a lotta crap," said Tony Barraza. "Yur mind quits *before* that. Ya get giddy thinkin' 'bout her. It's stoopid."

"But Tony, I told you—she's like *Grace Kelly.* Beautiful!
She's *beyond beautiful.* You oughta see her with the sun on her
hair and her eyes. And she's smart. You're always saying *I'm*
smart. She's a hundred times smarter'n I am."

"Kid, that's obvious. Friggin' spit bucket knows ya got no
brains. Take it back, sayin' yur smart. Yur punch-drunk. Rattle
on like yur shacked up an' she's already been givin' ya—"

"Antonio Barraza, don't you *dare* complete that sentence,"
said Barney Lewis, chief of instruction.

"Right—sorry, Barney. Look, kid. Do me a big friggin' favor. Lemme give youse the good word: let off on this *dame*
crap. Trust me. Ya ain't built fer it. Ya got a face like mine."
He winced, his craggy, boulderlike head, reshaped with blows
and laced with ring scars, cracked open as he laughed. His
false teeth, yellowed over the years, slipped a bit.

Tony was the perennial favorite of the Y secretaries. Built
like a tall Rocky Marciano and armed with a Burt Lancaster
smile, he was dark and brooding, square jawed, broad shouldered, and uncured, a challenge for any single woman interested in the impossible. Tony gave me hope; he had neither
wife nor family, riches nor gold, and somehow he was loved
and well fed.

"Ladies like your looks. Your wife was beautiful," I said.

Barney was writing ring grades. He stopped without looking
up, his breath condensed. Talk about Clara was strictly off-

limits. Eleven years ago, Clara had tired of Tony's dalliances: she had scooped up Tony Jr. and his teddy bear, her rosary, extensive wardrobe, and cosmetics, and walked out, forever.

Tony was at his desk, aimlessly sorting glove laces, Ace hand wraps, old keys, chits, busted mouthpieces, carpenters' pencils, fossilized pieces of chewed gum and old food, back and forth, his huge, hamlike hands moving with an ageless speed, an inborn dexterity. Tony could thread a needle with those hands, throw a wad of bills into the collection plate at St. Boniface's from two pews back, and punch two-by-fours into toothpicks; but he had trouble writing and shaking hands. Big piles of desk junk became small piles, then changed back into big ones. Whenever he thought he ought to clean out his desk—which usually followed a hundredth attempt to find the liniment closet key—he made piles. It was the same scarred metal desk he had when I met him, ten years before.

He stopped and looked up at me. "Jeezus, kid. Sometimes yur legs shake. But yur mouth has no friggin' fear, *none*."

Barney resumed writing. Sweat was on my brow. I smiled thinly.

"Clara," continued Tony, "an' dames, chased me cuz I had a name, I could cook. Had a footlocker fulla cash. I had press. I had front seats at Bimbo's 365 an' Ernie's an' Tarantino's. Arthur Constance and Herb Caen, they wrote about me in the paper. The afternoon dailies used ta interview me when I belched.

"Ya got a name? No, ya ain't got a name. Any money? No, Master Kai Ting, ya ain't got one thin dime. So ferget the fancy dames. *Grace Kelly?* Who ya tryin' to kid?" He opened the desk drawer and with his trunklike arm swept the piles on the desktop into it, and with a ferocious flick of his wrist, he closed it with a metallic screech and a resounding boom that sounded like a bad car crash.

"Nah, nah. Don' show me her freakin' pitture again!"

"Tony! At least *admit* she's beautiful," I urged.

"It's a freakin' pitture. How can youse tell anythin'? Ya pull 'at dam' thing out like it was the one good clippin' fer yur only good fight. I saw it. *You* oughta *read* it. It says 'Yur good fren'.' I ain't educated, but I get it. Means youse ain't gonna be *Mr.* Grace Kelly. Means the atomic bomb goes off an' kayos the world ta full count an' it's a two a ya left under a desk, ya still ain't gonna be Mr. Whoosis. Ya still gonna be 'good fren'.'"

"Tony," said Barney, "I believe Kai got your main thought. You're ahead on points and swinging after the bell."

I knew, with the prescience of the *I Ching,* the Book of Changes, that Christine exceeded reality. Sitting next to her in history caused my heart to pound as if I were going to sprint or box. I wanted to be American, and she was Miss America. I looked at her school photo for hours the way other kids watched TV, making the experience more personal by speaking to her in imaginary conversations in which I violated *ji hui* by speaking of my strengths. The beauty of her perfectly proportioned face on the front of the photo overcame the paucity of affection on its back. There was the promise of a future in her words "*good* friend."

For three years I had asked her every question about herself I could imagine. I could not know too much about her. She asked me about China and my family. "Doesn't your mom talk about it?"

"She doesn't know much about it," I said. "I mean, my first mother died when I was real little. I hardly knew her."

"So you have a stepmother," she said.

"She's my mother, my true mother," I recited. "She taught me English. My first mother was not a very good person."

"Why do you say that?" she asked.

"She was superstitious, and primitive. And a complete religious fanatic—a crazy, illiterate Christian."

"Do you remember her that way?"

I sighed. "I don't remember her at all. I mean, I don't even know what she looked like." I had said too much.

"But she must have loved you very much."

"I don't think so. She was corrupt. She didn't love me. My real mother raised me, made a lot of sacrifices for me. She taught me English, and—discipline." I had almost said, "and table manners so I don't eat like a Chinese."

"That sounds so harsh, so biased," she said, frowning.

I shook my head. Edna told the truth. She was my mother. "I'm biased about you," I said reverently.

Christine had glanced at the noon, lunch yard basketball game. I had left it in an instant to sit by her.

"Boys like me for my looks." Her eyes were shaped in large and perfect almonds, almost like Chinese eyes. Her mouth was wondrous mystery. She was breathtaking. Her smile could break a heart from fifty yards, the range of my visual acuity. I nodded vigorously.

She shook her head. "Going on about my looks, about going steady . . . boys want all your time, to consume you. That's what I like about you. You don't care about looks and appearances."

I gulped. "But your boyfriends are the best-looking guys."

She waved away the observation that I could not ignore.

On one of those rare sunny days in the fog belt, sitting next to her on the lunch yard steps, I saw our reflection in the cafeteria windows. She was a blond goddess, Grace Kelly in *The Swan*. My appearance was heartbreaking. Even in my cool Jack Peeve cast-offs, I looked like the kitchen help, an unattractive, broad-shouldered Chinese kid in glasses with a death-row-inmate haircut. I hated what I saw, feeling unworthy to be seated so close to her.

When I passed the locker room mirror on the way to Y boxing class, I faced myself. "You're an ugly piece a dark, squinty-eyed, fat-lip shit, and you're stupid thinkin' you could be with her." I appreciated my muscles and disliked my face. All that work on my body, and it meant nothing. "You're revolting," I added.

"Kid," said Tony, looking at me, "stow it. Don't let no one talk to ya like that, even you."

Christine and I had been good friends until I could no longer contain myself and had to commit social suicide in her presence. I confessed that I loved her, more than humanity had planned or the cosmos or the gods of the East or the West had contemplated. Any normal boy would love her, but even I was surprised by the force of my declaration of affection.

She looked sad. "No, Kai. *Please* say you're not serious."

I looked at her, absorbing her intensity. I was special, and I was like everyone else. I held to this moment of joy and pain.

"I've always loved you. I always will. You're the most beautiful girl in the world. I'm in love with you." I could never take it back. I was exhilarated and brokenhearted.

Christine was from a world filled with soft borders, elastic materials, and pastels. I had fallen in love with her when I heard her sing the theme from *A Summer Place* in accompaniment to the cafeteria jukebox. Her voice was clear and bright, the voice of angels. The sweetness and grace in her voice caused me to close my eyes so I could savor the sound. Christine's voice and face were more dreamlike than my imagination. It was clear that whoever this girl picked would have a happy life, forever after; I wanted something of her to rub off on me, as if whatever she possessed could be communicated to others, like measles. She was the *yin*, female, side of America, as much as West Point was the *yang*. Together, they represented happiness and belonging. Her lack of interest in me only confirmed the wisdom of my taste; it was never easy becoming American. I had not understood in those days the distinction between image and reality, love and affliction.

"Kai—oh, please—don't change our friendship." Her face was radiant, her fingers gripping my forearm, studying my muscles, neither of us particularly experienced with touching.

I looked at her hand touching me. It made the pain go away. But the confession was a blow I had landed on the simple nature of our unromantic friendship. I had been special by being Chinese and unique in apparently evading her global spell on boys. Now I was like all the others, in the worst way, emphasizing the dissonance of my Negro 'hood sliding around her Swedish-Irish roots and Upper West Portal rose gardens. She was the love of my life; as a mature teenager, she resisted commitments, dedicating loyalty to deceased Germans. "I can't stand school; it has no adults," she said. She read Immanuel Kant, studied Kierkegaard, and admired Heidegger. "I can't wait to start college." Her voice was the call of sirens, delivering laments. She had criticized boxing and my teaching younger kids the Sweet Science. She did not understand that boxing had saved my life, that by learning a code of fighting I had found physical courage and, ironically, a way to avoid bloodshed. She disliked West Point on general principle.

Christine graduated six months early, in the middle of our senior year. Early graduation was in the gym, and I watched her go the way Abelard must have watched Heloise after the knife fell. Her absence from my own graduation, with a thousand of us at the Masonic Auditorium, seemed a greater reality than the moment when my name was called with other scholarship students, and I received the applause of my classmates, so pleased, so uncomfortable, and so lonely for her.

An old sensation with formless edges and no bottom, a thing that seemed foreboding and enclosing, a thing that sucked air and denied thought and caused pain, welled up in me, expanding through my chest and into the small corners where I tried to hide.

I had selected for the love of my life someone who was more dream than girl, someone utterly beyond my reach. She was drawn to me for every cause except romance. I hoped to have improved myself in her eyes by being accepted at the toughest of American schools, and it had only pushed me farther away.

I was proud of my self-control, for I had told her only once how luminously beautiful she was.

The only mail I received was a letter from Major General Schwarzhedd and a note from someone whose name I did not at first recognize. The letter from Na-men congratulated me on my appointment. "Beast Barracks," he wrote,

was one of the hardest times of my life. This may seem unlikely to those enduring it, but my classmates and I still genuinely laugh about the horrors of Beast. I am very proud of you, and I know that my pride is only a fraction of what your father feels. During the dark days of the war we used to talk about his someday having a son. I prayed for that. I believe he prayed, in his own way, that his son would be who you are. I know how happy he is, because I too, through the Grace of the God and my own good blessings, have a son, who is also a West Pointer. Godspeed, and do not give up.
H. "Na-men" Schwarzhedd.

The other letter seemed to be from a child, corrected by an adult; with the cross-outs, it was hard to read. It was signed "Deloitte." I realized that it was from Sippy Suds.

How you Kai? you boxing what weight? Keep lef hand hi abt yo head + chin down! Jesus love me + sav me frm drnk. He wok wit me + tok wit me and love you to. you her me boy! R. Jones sa hello. mis you boy. Deloitte.

"ROOM ATTEN-HUT!!" screamed Mersey and Pee Wee McCloud.

It was Mr. Fideli. On August 1, First Detail Beast had departed for summer leave. Messrs. Alsop, Arvin, Spillaney, Armentrot, Stoner, and the other modern Inquisitors had done a final inspection in ranks, openly wondering who would survive Second Beast. Then they left, leaving only Mr. Fideli to serve a second tour. Why him? we wondered. Bad *yeh*, very bad karma.

He gave me special Plebe poop to spec. It wasn't military, but nonsense from Broadway plays, like *A Funny Thing Hap-*

pened on the Way to the Forum. He usually arrived to give me more.

"Sir, a little song, a little dance, a little seltzer down our pants. Sir, you have heard minor tones and middling chords, but mine are wretched, odious, and creaking. It is auditory Armageddon, screechy, off-key, and forlornly Ting-y."

He smiled. "Are you writing in your journal? Quietly, please."

"Yes, sir."

"Good." He pointed his fine chin at me. "Two decades after Beethoven sketched an idea it became an opus. I think of him when I hear you sing, because Beethoven was as deaf as an old shoe. I commend to you the painting of him, listening to a storm that bends trees, but he cannot hear. Mr. Ting, you actively fraternize with your classmates, all over Beast. Were you always a social maven?"

"No, sir."

"Why not?"

I hesitated. "Sir, I worked. Sir, my mother did not allow me to—socialize."

"Allow me to understand you. Are you saying that you now possess more social freedoms than you did as a high school senior?"

"Yes, sir," I said. Bestier and McCloud blinked.

"Well. Was I the first to critique your singing?"

"No, sir. Sir, when I was twelve, singing in a Baptist church, a little girl said to me, 'Y'all don' havta sing *evera* song.' "

Mr. Fideli laughed. "Thespis does not hold your future." He faced my roomies. "Heed—I dub New Cadet Ting—'Caruso.' Nicknames are almost obligatory here, Caruso. Down Thespis, up Mars. Who knows what happened in Southeast Asia this month?"

No fists emerged. He paced, his expression thoughtful, his brilliantly shined shoes hitting our floor. "Two weeks ago, North Vietnamese patrol boats attacked the U.S. destroyers *Maddox* and the *C. Turner Joy* in Tonkin Gulf. We retaliated with air strikes on North Vietnamese naval ports. Gentlemen, we are about to enter a ground war in Asia, against all good military advice."

The American army fighting Asians. I would look like the enemy. I had prayed to the gods that this would not happen.

Three companies were drilling under cadre commands to fifes and drums, making the sharp music of five hundred rifles slapping from hands to shoulders with the sound of a huge mechanical beast throwing steel. We had six minutes to gym formation under arms.

"Mr. Bestier, your father is Major General Pierce Bestier. Is it true that he has prepared you since infancy for the Point?"

"Yes, sir," Clint said.

"What's the most important lesson he imparted to you?"

"To take care of my classmates, sir."

Fideli turned to Pee Wee. "We all know and admire your father, General Ira Costain McCloud. What lesson did he give you?"

"Sir," he said in that cartoonish voice, "the same thing."

The buzzer rang, rattling my teeth. The minute caller called five minutes to formation.

"Are you gentlemen going to make it through Beast?"

Clint, Pee Wee, and I said yes. Mersey remained silent.

"You are now fretting about permanent regimental assignments after Beast. Do not. These are mere details. Worry instead about Honor and the Corps. 'Let Duty be well performed, Honor be e'er untarned,' " he quoted from the school song. "Sound off," he said.

" 'LET DUTY BE WELL PERFORMED, HONOR BE E'ER UNTARNED!' "

Mr. Fidel's omnipresent smile was absent, which sent an electric chill down my spine. He looked into our eyes. I did not see a jocular, baritoned cadet, but the bright eyes of a true believer, a man who sang and joked, but took life most seriously.

We always worked in the dark, after taps, to complete duties. After an hour of preparing our gear, we were able to crawl into our bunks. We were worried about our regimental assignments.

"We don't want First Regiment," Clint said quietly after taps, referring to his notebook by the light from his Zippo. "It's awful, hard-core, full of Grayhog butt-kickers like Spillaney and Stoner. Second Regiment's Greenwich Village, beatniks, like Fideli." Clint flipped pages. "Companies H, B, G, and A are Hell-One, Bitch-One, Guts-One, and Aches-One. In the Second Regiment, they're Happy-Two, Beach-Two, Gomer-Two, and Aloha-Two. We'll get our assignments tomorrow."

"Hope we get Second Regiment," I said fervently, closing my eyes and praying to Wen-ch'ang, the scholarship god.

Some minutes passed. Mersey was snoring and I couldn't sleep, even though I didn't have to report to Mr. O'Ware. "Clint," I said softly, "you ever have the same nightmare, over and over again?"

"No," he whispered. "You?"

"Used to. A guy I knew and his dad died when I was a kid. Used to dream about him every night. Clint—you afraid of anything?"

He thought. "No, but I worry about academics." He fell silent as an upperclassman walked down the hall. "I'm not real good," he whispered. "But I've never failed at anything. And my dad expects me to succeed. So I will, whatever it takes."

Ji hui. He shouldn't have said that. I curled up, providing a smaller profile for both of us from watching gods. I kept seeing Leo Washington's face. Here, where I had roommates, a rifle, a bayonet, and walls, the nightmare had evaporated. I wondered if I would dream of Leo if I were alone again. I realized how much Clint's presence had meant to me during Beast. I put on my glasses.

"Clint," I whispered.

"Hmm," he said sleepily.

"Think we'll always be friends?"

Clint turned in his cot. "Uh-huh," he murmured.

I nodded. I thought of Toos. "I'll always be yours," I said.

"I'll be your bud," said Pee Wee slowly, "if you go to sleep."

In the morning, before physical training, we braced in the south sally port and reviewed the lists of regimental assignments into regular West Point companies. Pee Wee was the only one to get Second Regiment. I was in First Regiment, Company H. These were my mates for the next four years.

David Neil Alduss	Jackson Flynn Latimer II
James Ryan Barisone	Robert Myres Lorbus
Jeffrey True Bartels	Leigh Sachs McSon
Clinton David Bestier	Peck Levine Mankoff
James Drew Butte	Earl Tecumseh Mims
Jeremy Odette Conoyer III	Saul Hoeck Patterson
Sponson Charles DeVries	Joseph NMN Rensler II
Terrence Phillip Dirkette	Matthew McBall Rodgers

Chad King Enders	Deke Ross Schibsted
David Benjamin Glick	William Christian Shine
Robert Thought Hamblin	Kai NMN Ting
Luke Ansara Hansen	Acheson Rey Torres
Richard Mause Hoggatt	Anthony Mercury Ziegler

It was great to see Clint on the list, but I worried what the subsequent cost of such good *foo chi,* fortune, would be.

I, Caruso, was about to live with guys named Tree, Zoo Keeper, Spoon, Moon, The Man, Curve Wrecker, Pensive, Moose, Big Bus, Meatball, and Rocket Scientist.

I learned that Mike Benjamin and Sonny Rappa were also in First Regiment. I had taken great risks to remain in contact with them throughout Beast; I would do the same during Plebe year, whatever it took.

10

DAYS

Mess Hall, September 11, 1964

"Rensler, how's the cow?" asked Mr. Grabzchek.

"Sir, she walks, she talks, she's full of chalk; the lacteal fluid extracted from the female of the bovine species is highly prolific to the fourth degree!" That is, we had four milks left.

We were no longer Beasts and new cadets; we were Plebes, which was like a Sing Sing inmate bragging about having graduated to Devil's Island. We had despaired on the first day of the fall term, when two thousand boomingly well-fed upperclassmen returned to West Point and descended on us like Goths on Rome. They outnumbered us, three to one. We now had academics, athletics, parades, reviews, tactical officers, quill and demerits, and games of risk.

"Who wants to go Big Dick?" asked Mr. Kunselman. As a Yearling who had been a Plebe two months ago, he was predictably reckless. In Big Dick, all ten cadets spun knives; those landing with their cutting edges toward the plates were "in" and would divide the entire dessert between them. The "outs" received none. It was a game of risk designed to advance greed.

"Nah," said Mr. Grabzchek, a Cow squad leader, "it's just stinkin' sheet cake."

A bigger risk was requesting a Fall-out with Big Bites. If one of the Plebes had won a bout or could tell a winning joke, the table com might grant a Fall-out and Big Bites—releasing us from bracing so we could eat like pigs. But if the offering was deemed "puny" or inadequately amusing, wrath, catcalls, punishment, and endless recitations would replace nutrition.

Yesterday, Joey Rensler had told the "Thayer" joke. "Sir, permission ta tell a joke for a Fall-out with Big Bites!" he had cried in his wildly rampant Bronx accent.

"Better be good, Rensler," warned Mr. Kirchhoff.

"Sir! Two officers in de Amazon get captured by dese seriously giant tribesmen, who tie 'em up an' take 'em to de chief. Chief's surrounded by hundreds a giant warriahs. De chief points a big spear in de first guy's face an' screams: *Thayer or death?*

"Now dis officer, he's OCS an' he ain't educated an' he says, 'Crap, given dis choice, I'll take Thayer, whoever de hell it is.'

"Tribesmen, dey pull de guy's pants down, spreadeagle 'im on de ground, an' the whole tribe takes turns, sodomizin' 'im."

Groans rose from the upperclassmen. All of us Plebes for tables around crammed our chins deeper into our necks, fearing something more than losing our lunches from this joke.

"So de chief," continued Joey, "he turns to de second guy. Second guy, he's a West Pointer. *'Thayer or death?'* demands de chief. West Pointer, he puffs out his manly chest, an' pops off inna military manner, 'SCREW ALL A YA. GIMME DEATH!'

"De warriahs, dey beat dere spears ona ground goin' 'Ooohh!' in deep respec', admirin' the West Pointer's big guts.

" 'All right!' de chief says, pattin' de guy on de shoulder. 'Death! Good! Hey—yur brave! But first, *Thayer!*' "

Silence.

"Rensler," said Mr. Kirchhoff. "You may have a Fall-out with Big Bites. If you never tell that joke again."

Now, I was gunner, as correctly in my place as Judas at the Last Supper. I had no joke that could alter the course of the meal. One of our upperclassmen was in the hospital, and I had cut the Martha Washington sheet cake into nine stunningly equal, proudly Euclidean, rectilinear pieces. I opened my mouth to announce it.

"Gentlemen, remain seated. Mr. K., may I join you for lunch?" It was Major Robert "Yoiks" Yerks, our company tactical officer. He was spare, unassuming, caring, and hungry, and he sat in the empty chair. In three years, he would win twenty-two combat decorations in Vietnam. He would retire as a four-star general who still remembered the first names of his cadets from the 1960s.

I heard Mr. Kirchhoff say, "Mr. Ting, cut ten pieces."

Sweat appeared on my forehead. Without a twitch, my brain went through a floor exercise that was the internal equivalent of rubbing my scalp, contemplating the skull of Yorick, screaming for a cab in a Manhattan downpour, and dropping my trousers in Times Square while doing a hat dance around my freshly dug grave. I quickly smoothed over the cuts, pushing the icing around in hard sworls to cover the marks, hoping against all of Newton's laws that stitching the surface would reunify the divided cake beneath.

Joey Rensler uttered semiaudible squeaks of sympathy in a miniaturized version of a Three Stooges whine. It was all I had going for me. I announced the cake and passed it up.

"Let me serve you some cake, sir," said Mr. K. "What the . . . TING! THIS IS AN *ATROCITY!* WHAT'D YOU DO—CUT IT WITH A *HAMMER?*"

"NO, SIR!" I cried. Joey Rensler said, "Meep, meep."

"LOOK UP HERE!" Mr. Kirchhoff was looking at me with the heaviest, blackest eyebrows in the Corps and one of those classic expressions cherished by Bela Lugosi fans everywhere. He filled me with the deep willies. That darkly underworld gaze, his large, menacing, suspended eyeballs floating in the bright white sclera under a dark roof of hairy brow, induced wienie-shortening fear.

"REPORT HERE AND BRING YOUR HAT! Take this to Washington's statue and ask the Father of Your Country for forgiveness for having *butchered* his wife's cake! NOW POST!"

In those days, Washington was northeast of the Plain, where he had a panoramic view of the wide, sparkling Hudson as it took a hard left around the dark green forests on Constitution Island. Today, he's in front of the Mess Hall, making it far easier for Plebes impaired in the cutlery arts to report their failures.

Chinese want burial where the geomantic forces of wind and water, *fengshui,* are kind, permitting a view of the neighboring real estate. General Washington had good *fengshui.* This was the general who had willed that America would have a military academy to defend against foreign invasion, who had headquartered here to keep the British from dividing the Colonies. He had led frozen, chilblained farmers and boys in rags to face Europe's best army. He was the father of the entire nation. It was an overpowering mixture of icons, and I trembled superstitiously.

"Sir, Mr. Ting reports to the President as ordered." I offered the cake. "Sir, I apologize for butchering Mrs. Washington's sheet cake." It had taken seventeen cuts, the last nine the unkindest.

He looked the same as the face on the dollar bill—quiet, reliable, steady, and green. I didn't compare him to any actor because he looked like George Washington. Silence. Wind brushing through the trees at the edge of the Plain, the water deep and still in its blueness, the air fresh from the river. In his face I saw my father's Gaze, as he would look into the distance at China. This was similar to my conversations with him, experiencing a monolithic silence while anticipating a burst of anger.

How often had the Father of Our Country seen Plebes offering ruptured cakes? If I hadn't taken the Confucian position to his side, it would look as if he were reaching for the cake. I wondered if Washington had ever seen an Oriental in the span of his rich life. I wondered how he felt about a Chinese West Point cadet. Would true acceptance here mean that I would look at Washington and think only American thoughts, and not think of old Chinese ways?

The late-summer day embraced me. The emerging oranges and yellows of the valley soothed the memory of the abusive din of the mess hall. The wind whipped the flags and flag cords. The pleasure of being alone and so near the river overcame the awkwardness of conversing with a cold and unresponsive mass of melted metals forged into the shape of an unreachable father.

Through tremendous good fortune, Clint Bestier and I had not only been assigned to Company H-1, but also had ended up in the same room. Our two new roomies were Joey Rensler, a sharp-featured, sun-sensitive, Danny Kaye look-alike from the Bronx, and Bob Lorbus, a big, cheerful, country music–loving, broad-shouldered Kansan who began every sentence with the words, "Hiya, buddy!" I missed Pee Wee, Sonny, and Mike, but they were great friends to have while facing Plebe year.

Something buzzed in my ear and I started punching my pillow. I found an alarm clock and switched it off. It was quarter to five, I had laundry duty, and I hadn't awakened my roommates.

H-1 occupied three divisions, or vertical floors, in Old South Barracks. Davey "Curve Wrecker" Glick, Matt McBall "Meatball" Rodgers, and I began collecting the dirty laundry bags with their inventories and running them down to the stoops. One bag was torn. When we were done, I exchanged it in the sinks for a new one. A BP—a barracks policeman, a civilian janitor—was rummaging through the spilled contents of a consolidated garbage can. "Oh, sorry, young man," he said, scooping up the garbage from the floor to put it back in the can. "Looking for a Texas football program."

He was scarred and I recognized him as the silver-haired janitor at the gym on R-Day who had wished me good luck. I saw his name tag: Scoggin. "Mr. Scoggin, I'm Kai Ting. I was the first guy to report in. You were standing by the door of the Post Gym on one July." We used military date timing: the number before the month.

He smiled, and we shook hands. "Elmer," he said.

Like other BPs, Elmer emptied our waste cans, which we placed outside our doors in the morning before class. He mopped rooms and hallways once a week; we cleaned our floors the other six. Upperclassmen handled classified military assignments. Thus, BPs could not scrounge our garbage.

"I'll give you mine," I said.

"Oh, son, that'd be beautiful." Texas was number one in the country. Rollie Stichweh, our quarterback, had almost beaten them.

"Can I pay you?" he asked after I gave him my program.

I shook my head. "Want me to get you programs for the games?"

"No, sir. Only if they play Texas again. . . . Hey, Mr. Ting. Thank you *most* kindly, and bless you. You're a real gentleman."

I returned to my room feeling quite pleased with myself.

Our door was open. Clint Bestier, Joey Rensler, and Bob Lorbus were bracing stiffly in our darkened room, facing me and the open door. Oh, God, I thought: it's Mr. O'Ware with a message from hell and now I'm going to pay for having felt good about something. I stood in the door, bracing hard.

It was Mr. Fideli. He smiled. I moved the corners of my mouth.

He said, "Please meet my brother, Mario."

Another Mr. Fideli stepped from behind the door. I blinked. My eyes popped. I braced harder. There were *two* identical Mr. Fidelis. In the dim light in our room, they appeared more duplicate than duplicates. That's how they had changed clothes so quickly during Beast; there had been two of them. My roommates and the Fideli twins looked at my comically compressed, eyeball-swelling, shocked face and burst into laughter, joined by the Fidelis, and I nearly ruptured myself hee-hawing while bracing, shoulders rising and falling like pistons.

"Caruso, don't just stand there," the Fidelis said simultaneously.

"Sir," I said, "a little song, a little dance, a little seltzer down our pants."

11

SHIM

His Journal, San Francisco, October 3, 1964

I, Shim, am a man alone, the last leaf on a dying tree, bending in a foreign wind. I cannot honor the graves of the beforeborns. There is no sweet music of grandchildren. The household women do not fuss over me when I appear for meals; nor am I the center of attention with all screaming to Heaven when a grandson piddles on my knee. I customarily eat alone.

Of all the things and sounds of China, I miss most the laughter of my son. This is a surprise; I thought that the loss of my scholastic discernment, or my library, would have hurt most. All Chinese should know the future by knowing the past. But I, a man of learning and moral habit, did not know all I should have known.

I miss the expressions and the faces of my family, so full of life, ringing of laughter, finding all the signs of strong *foo chi*, good fortune, at the dinner table, where food pleased so many mouths, and all ate to celebrate the continuation of the line!

"My son, the fish cheek," I used to say. "Take it, and its luck." He would laugh as only ten-year-olds can. The symphony of twenty people of your blood and *lun*, eating and celebrating the fruits of the earth. *That* is China. That is what I miss.

I miss the delicate hand of my wife on my arm as we walked along the Whangpu River, listening to the water warble to us, as she told me her thoughts. I am the picture of loneliness! All men of Han have memories. We are reminded of the failure to be with the others, or to have saved them, or to have died with them. If I shed a thousand tears, *ch'eng ch'ien ch'eng wan*, it would not be enough.

The consequences of never using my mouth and eyes for laughter are now etched in my face. I am a learned man, I am far from China, and I must pay the price. I do not know how much longer I can live in this foreign country, this America.

The Chess Club has disbanded, its writing tradition ended. Today, I write for myself, and I am an unappreciative reader. Or perhaps I am writing for an unknown reader, whom I do not know and therefore cannot trust. This last idea is particularly displeasing.

We played *shiang-chi*, chess, trying to create *ch'a lu t'ung k'u*, the Fork of Pain, where however your opponent moves, he moves into defeat. I was good at this tactic—the stratagems of five layers at three depths, the moves behind moves, one move now to make six later. Now we cough and are slowly dying without family.

I never believed in Buddhist *yeh*, karma, but I feel it closing in on me now. My life has been played on a chessboard, and I have faced the Fork of Pain. I was in China, with so many of us dying from war and murder. I was not with my family in Shanghai in their moment of danger. I was at the boundary of the game, in Nanjing.

I had two choices. I could attempt escape and earn money to bring them to safety. Or I could stay in Nanjing, wait for the Japanese, and die. There was defeat in either move. *Ch'a lu t'ung ku.* I ran, and earned money. But they were all dead before I could help. Better, I think, to have stayed in China, for I would be with them now. I would know the experience of death and the underground life of the dead. I would not be alone. I have cash, but am poorer than a landless peasant in drought with one relative.

I have striven to be a man of moral rectitude. My life has been like my learning, toward the single path of correct conduct. But this was to occur within my society, not here. My learning means nothing in this culture. I must ask: Is the lesson of my life a deterrence to others? Am I being punished with solitary life to warn a hundred others to never leave the Middle Kingdom? Is there a Buddha who will compel me to return in regenerated life as a woman or a lower animal for my failures as a man? Or is there a Christian god who will forgive me for having run when I should have remained, for having lived emptily when I should have died with those to whom I owed loyalty and duty?

K'e ji fu li. As a Confucian, all I need remember is to subdue self and honor rituals. Yet I feel fear for whatever follows life, as if, despite all my schooling, all my effort, I have failed.

I am sitting at my desk in my room, on the third floor of the Beverly Plaza Hotel in Chinatown at the base of Dupont *gai,* which the foreigners have renamed Grant Avenue. Outside I hear the jangle of streets which remind me so powerfully of Avenue Joffre in the French Concession of Shanghai.

The Ming poets said: "Measure a man by his memories." Mine is filled with lovely things, full of smiles, and good food shared with family fellowship, the sounds of the young joining in harmony with the creaking of the old, lubricating our ancient voices with the cries of childhood and the music of a good kitchen.

Family records should be for sons. My son is dead, as are my daughters, and their children. What can be sadder—all their deaths, the end of our clan, with its last member here, on a far shore, unable to practice the rites.

Did not the Master say: "Honor the past, honor your parents, honor your teachers." To see the future, look over your shoulder and examine the path of your ancestors. He who breaks with the past is himself a brittle thing, easily washed away by wind and water.

Writing now, I am a boy waving a toy hammer at Lu Ban, the great architect. May my forebears respect my effort to preserve memory, and not criticize me for my lack of skill. Do they watch me now? My years in the Western world make me question this. But I feel their presence, and it is not my imagination or my loneliness doing this. Other Chinese men have felt it, too.

I have gone to the *ta'i ping yang,* Pacific Ocean, standing on the San Francisco beach, peering at China. My best friend used to go there to yell at her clan in Shanghai, thirty thousand *li* away. I used to deride her for yelling across the sea with the gulls.

How wrong I was. I should have stood shoulder to shoulder with her and howled into the western winds, my voice joining with hers to reach across the water to our beloved Shanghai, its western lights, and a million fish in the two rivers.

Her husband, K. F. Ting, Ting Kuo-fan, is now my only true remaining friend. But he has abandoned the old ways and is utterly foreign and even has a foreign wife. He and I went to St. John's, a Western Christian college in Shanghai, after our tutors taught us the ways of Master K'ung. I came from scholars; he has soldiers in his heritage. I was a child magistrate when the Empire fell.

Ting used his classical education and his Western schooling to become a soldier, which is like using an emerald to buy a cup of old millet. *Hau nan bu dang bin.* Good youth do not become soldiers.

Ting walks faster than the foreigners, knows their history better than they. He watches their cinema, studies their habits, and embraces them with the vigor of a drowning man seizing floating wood. Yet he is alone in this world, with none like him in all of the Western world or in China. He is as lonely as a mythic dragon, a person of endurance and strange and almost magical uniqueness, wrestling with his mind and his past.

Ting comes from a line of old soldiers and magistrates who valued privacy above all. Ting's own father came from a family of terrible loneliness. Solitude has been their mark.

Ting's wife, Ting *taitai,* Mar Dai-li, was a sparkling connoisseur of literature, an amusing storyteller, an enchanting person filled with great inner energy and utterly peasant in her superstitions. She was also Christian, so fond of her lord, the Jewish teacher Jesu. Ting *taitai* was possessed of powerful *ren yuan,* charisma, something that she passed to her daughters.

Ting *taitai* and I used to argue about poetry, innuendo, and Taoism and Christianity with fluidity. She argued for Mo-Tzu's undifferentiated love of all people; I reminded her of the pre-eminence of *li*, ritual, in all human relationships. I saw only precision and earnestness in our debates. She knew the mind could bring pleasure as well as understanding. I did not.

"C.K., this is so much *fun!*" she used to say in the middle of hot debate. Now I hope this was all very true. I hear her words and remember her energy, and I smile, all by myself.

She came here during the war, to America, bringing her three daughters, with all the enemies of China on her heels. Unlike my dear wife, she had detested walking, yet she strode across China. She had loathed the idea of war, and she became a lady warrior in the protection of her daughters and their path to Free China and beyond. She loved China and Shanghai, and crossed the Pacific to live in San Francisco. She was raised to be a fabled princess of Chinese society, and left it forever.

The separation from parents and clan was too great. She could not survive on Gold Mountain, what my Kwangtung brothers call *gum san*. Her faith in the Christian god could not sustain her—proving, I think, its weakness. She took comfort in her producing at least one son, not knowing he would receive an American *chimu*, abandon Chinese ways, and not accept me as his tutor.

I used to think that the Christian missionaries who captivated her imagination in Shanghai had changed her. Now I do not think so. The Christians made her more romantic. A believer in poetry and good deeds, a believer in life's mystery. A forgiver, which is a most foreign habit. Who with power forgives enemies? Nonsense!

I miss her. If she were here today, I would ask how someone who has acted as poorly as I could be forgiven by any god. It is only in her absence that I realize what she meant to me and my days. She was a woman. She was my closest friend.

How unlucky of me to have one friend left in the world, a rebel to all which I have ever held dear, married to a foreign woman, who appreciates China no more than a Mongol soldier.

This great rebel, however, has a son. I hope that the son can be my courier, taking this writing to my family graves. But he is like his father, chasing after soldiers. Where is the honor in this? I am losing the effort to save his Chinese essence. He is seventeen and already a *ping*, in a palace of soldiers. His becoming a soldier worries me; I fear he cannot recover, for with every sunrise he grows farther from the reach of the Master's ways. Looking at him, I see a youth of neither the foreign land nor our old ways in China. He is neither of this world nor of the next, part Chinese, part foreign. Half of him here, half of him waiting to arrive later. He has the body of a common worker, the scholastic diligence of an infant, and the mind of a rock.

The boy remembers nothing of his mother. My *dzeren*, duty, and *lun*, connection, to his father prohibit me from telling her story to him. He has forgotten his sister, Janie Ming-li. As a child, she served as his mother after their Mah-mee died. Tragically, Janie ran away. I have purchased detective agencies to find her, but she is lost. It is in this respect that Ding Kai, what he would be called in China, shows so little promise: he has no memory. I cannot pour China back into his hard, foreign bones.

I have told him many of the important stories of China, of Lu Ban the builder, scholars Chang Tsai, Chu Hsi, and Wang Fu-chih, novelists Li Ju-chen and Lo Kuan-chung, fortune seeker Su Ch'in, selfish Yang Tsu, Golden Age rulers Yao and Shun, the all-loving Mo-Tzu, stark painter Ni Tsan, who never painted petty humans against great mountains, and the stories of piety and the sacrifice of sons. He should remember the forty-three thousand poems of the Emperor Ch'ien-lung, wandering to southeast China, pretending to be a humble poet. But I do not know if any of these moral points have touched the boy's already hardened foreign heart.

It is hard to teach him. Boys in this foreign country are wild, without deep culture. They lack the large extended family to pool the adult labor necessary to raise them. Foreign elders and parents abandon their children, and children think they own their own lives, which are of course, the property of parents.

Teaching young Ting, whom I named Able Student at birth, and who has been consumed by foreign ways, has been the challenge of my late years.

Yet, I have hope for him. He is lazy with Chinese, but reads aggressively in English. He is forgetful, but he looks at me with genuine affection, and respects his friends, if not his family. He is striving to please his father.

Yet, this does not matter. His mother has commanded me to remain loyal to him, to not regard scholarship as the basis for relationship. This is hard for me, but I loved my friend dearly.

12

VALLS

Old South Barracks, West Point, October 18, 1964

I looked at my watch: three minutes to go.

"Kai," said Clint Bestier, "he'll ask about your health and about Plebe sports. He'll try to get you to box for the company. He'll talk about your grades. Then he'll ask you 'spirit' questions—whether you like the Infantry, jumping out of airplanes, slitting people's throats, drinking blood, you know, things like that."

"Drinking blood?" I asked.

"Like 'Would you drink enemy blood?' or 'Are you a killer?' "

"Sir, Mr. Ting reports to his squad leader as ordered!"

"ENTER!" he bellowed. Mr. McWalters, an Arkansan, was probing *Macbeth*'s deeper meaning by poking his tongue from the corner of his mouth. His roommates cranked formula for electrical engineering while cursing the heritage, progeny, and anatomy of Juice in a blue fog of creative, scatalogical profanity. How could I whip a course that hard? Why struggle now, merely to face that course later? McWalters scribbled a margin note on Harrison's *Shakespeare* and removed his Squad Book.

"Weight?" McWalters was one of a large continent of beefy cadets who could pass as bouncers in any bar south of Market. He was a goat, nonacademically inclined. But he was a thorough squad leader. He resembled George C. Scott, the actor from *The Hustler*. He had a very big nose through which he sniffed frequently.

"Sir, I weigh one hundred and fifty pounds."

"Up five pounds—still fifteen down. How's your body?"

"Sir, I am good." I had taken the dull ache of hunger the way moose heads accept wall mounts. Eating had been my skill, and it was my *yeh* to know hunger in a society with ample food.

He sniffed. "Constipated? Shoulders?" The conventional questions. Flushed with maturity, we no longer reported bowel movements and teeth brushing. But matters had not improved. When everything went to hell in a biblical chain of disciplinary, academic, and athletic disasters, Joey Rensler would say in Bronx, "It's been a Thayer sort a day."

"A fifty-thousand-dollar education," added Pee Wee slowly.

"Crammed up our asses, a nickel at a time," recited Bestier.

The pressure of being "fourth estate" subserfs in a feudal society, overburdened with torment and too much work, and deprived of food, sleep, and comfort, would incite revolution in other societies. At West Point, it caused constipation.

Away from our bottoms and closer to our compressed, dumbjohn doo-willie skulls, bracing sometimes induced "brace palsy," where the shoulder muscles, stressed from months of isometric tension, collapsed. A palsied Plebe looked like Pinocchio after the strings had been cut, and was "profiled"— excused medically—from bracing. This seemed, initially, to be a Good Deal. But the brace profiles were pursued by gangs of upperclassmen who sought to compensate for the Plebe's loss of a full Academy experience. I had somehow evaded these plagues of our modern age.

"You validated boxing," McWalters said happily. Plebe athletics had a full menu of masculine pastimes: boxing, wrestling, survival swimming, and gymnastics, which we called bleeding, groping, drowning, and spasmatics. If you could pass an early skills test in any one of these courses, you were "validated"—granted early course completion—and rewarded with a class in the more refined pursuits of scuba, golf, squash, or tennis.

"Gonna box for us in the winter?" he asked, blood almost dripping from his mouth in hearty anticipation.

"Sir, I do not know." I had boxed for ten years, but technique wasn't the stuff of victory at West Point. Once, I had no choice in fighting. Now I did. I knew McWalters wanted me to box. I wasn't sure what to do. Tony had wanted me to quit. He had been telling me to leave boxing for something else.

I had entered the South Boxing Room as if I were visiting a shrine. The lights, smells, ring, and apparatus inspired a strange reverence, connecting me to Tony. It was something I knew. When I was seven, I feared the very sight of the Y ring.

Now, its counterpart at the Academy was a comfort, brimming with the habitual and the prosaic. I had paid the mortgage on boxing floors and knew them the way helmsmen know tides.

We had spent the first weeks on the basics: stance, hand positions, movements, punches, jabs, and parries, taught en masse in long lines, like ballroom dancing in Cullum Hall, but infinitely easier. West Point had more heavy body bags than any gym I'd seen.

Coach F. N. Fabrizi was a former middleweight with a flat nose. I felt like saying that I had been trained by Antonio Cemore "Tony the Tiger" Barraza, also known as "Dr. Hook," but I knew this would be very un-Chinese, very unplebeian, and very stupid. ("Oh, Willie Mays taught you to bat? No kidding? Okay, *Ace,* let's see your stuff. . . .")

Coach Fabrizi used me as an example. "Lookit body position. The chin. See him smooth left toe up? Liftin' and glidin' heel back, no herky-jerky. Lift, glide, lift, glide trailin' foot, circle left, circle right. Lookit the high left hand, springin' jabs. See it return, same place, after? Lookit the hook. *Whap!* Head up, opposite hand up, chin down—use the hip! Do it like that!"

This was the first thing, besides being hungry and Chinese, in which I had excelled here. My classmates were great athletic specimens, and some had dabbled with the Sweet Science, but no others in my group had boxed in a Y program. They clodhopped, dropped guards, and telegraphed punches, unsure where to place heads, arms, gloves, and feet, sapped by malnutrition and a lack of sleep. Helping classmates with the techniques was a job I knew.

Coach spoke to me in my corner after my first round.

"Ting. Ya bin inna ring. This ain't the ring, it's *West Point.* You're backin' up from your man. In my book, you're losin'."

I pulled out my mouthpiece. "Coach—he's dead meat. Split his lip and I'm wearing his blood. You can throw in the towel, Coach. He's not standing for the third."

"You're backin' up. Ya back up at the Point, ya lose."

I had gone into the second and third rounds advancing, and gotten chewed up. I had won, but my guts ached from a steady rain of blows from a rookie boxer who stood his ground and waited for me to come to him, poking through my no longer perfect guard. I beat him because I knew combination punching, and he didn't.

Coach Fabrizi was right; this wasn't the ring. It was pure aggression. No skill, just advancing. No Sweet Science; this was Bash City. That's what I knew before I learned boxing.

Tony Barraza's last good word still rang in my ears. He had said to me, "Ya ain't a killer." I was better at defense than offense. I was a counterpuncher. I didn't like hitting friends.

"Coach," I said, "what if I box for two rounds, beatin' the crap outa him and losing points, and then advance in the third. Work for you?"

Coach pulled me aside after two weeks of fights. "Stand here. Gonna validate ya. Your trainer taught ya ta exploit your gifts."

I smiled. "Yeah, Coach—bad eyes and no vision."

"Don't shortchange him. West Point ain't a palooka gym with fifty-buck purses onna way ta Madison Square Garden. This is jus' ta teach young gen'l'men ta be *aggressive*. That's *it*. Your trainer was a pro, right? Colored, Latin, or paisan?"

"Paisan, Coach."

"Good! He built ya a system. Speed, counterpunchin' hooks an' your left to getchur way inta the body. Rich stuff for this gym." He laid a hand on my shoulder. "I'll miss ya as a demonstrator."

I basked in his good words.

"I ever hear a your trainer?" he asked.

"Tony Barraza," I said.

"The Tiger? No kiddin'! Saw him fight. When—'47? Just after Hank Casey. At Winterland. Piece a work. He still out on the Coast? What's he doin' trainin' *Chinese?*"

"He's at a black-and-white Y. I was the only Chinese."

"Well, you had one a the best." He pulled on his nose. "And he got ya a ticket outa here. Now they'll teach ya some pansy crap like squash or tennis or scuba. Hell, that ain't even English." He looked at the class.

"Skills ain't the ticket here. The Point just wants a guy who'll wade in for blood." He made a face. "Who's ta say they're wrong? They grew up some good fighters. The system, it ain't gonna change. Be curious ta see if ya box here." He pulled on an old, broken ear. "Havta live off your right 'steada your left. You can do it. Gimme your hand. Took my direction good. You run inta Barraza, tell 'im Fabrizi remembers from Winterland."

I filled out a preference card, with scuba followed by tennis and squash. I didn't even know what squash was. I got squash.

After squash, I would enter the ring and practice a straight, attacking style. For ten years I had circled left and right, feinted, advanced, backed up, each of these moves setting up counterpunching combinations as my opponent looked for the alleys. I could follow a glove I had parried because I could feel it. Going straight in with my eyesight was awkward. It was like running blindfolded. I couldn't see the glove if I walked into it.

"Hey, Ting!" growled McWalters. "Don't drift while I'm talkin' to you! Crack your skull in! Ya gonna box or not? Be decisive, beanhead!"

"Sir, I will box if I do not make the gymnastics team."

"Fair enough," said McWalters. "You validated swimming. Where the hell'd you learn to swim so good?"

"Sir, I learned at the YMCA." I had learned everything there.

We heard that Plebes drowned at West Point like lemmings in season. Our enemy was not the water, or climbing from the water on swaying steel chain ladders to jump from little postage-stamp platforms to retrieve rifles on the pool bottom, struggling down the swim lanes with our rifles while outfitted in full field gear—spongy fatigues, boots, and brick-filled field packs. Our enemy was the Teutonic presence of Mr. Flauck. Flauck made Frederick the Great look like Bob Hope and Chingis Khan look like a comedian.

He was lean, bald, clear-eyed, high-cheekboned, and Prussian. He taught survival swimming, Erich von Stroheim at West Point, parading the length of the pool in his black uniform, swagger stick, and silent black sneakers while we performed like steel girders in a high sea. I learned to swallow pool water and like it.

I was a good swimmer, but keeping the rifle dry while wearing a pack and boots gave me the flotation profile of a red brick. Whenever we faltered, and reached desperately for the edge of the pool to avoid drowning, Mr. Flauck struck our hands and wrists and arms with his hard, sharp, welting swagger stick. Whack! Whack! "ZERE ARE NO *VALLS* IN DER OCEAN!" he boomed. "VAT ARE YOU GOING TO DO VEN YOUR ASSAULT CRAFT SINKS? CLIMB OUT OF DER POOL?"

I had almost gone under at one point, but Mercury "Rocket Scientist" Ziegler, in the lane next to mine, hissed, "Do it!"

It was all I needed. "Thanks, Rocket," I gasped to him after I finished the laps, spitting out the water I couldn't swallow.

"Do the same for me," he said.

I shook my head. "Not enough air to help you," I said weakly.

"YOU VANT *HELP*, MISTER?! *CHATTING* IN MY POOL! GIVE ME ANOZER LAP MIT DER RIFLE! BOSE OF YOU!"

No one could help Pee Wee McCloud. A phobic fear of water meant that his aquatic background never graduated past shallow baths with a highly trusted rubber ducky. He joined the drowners, the Rock Squad, learned the rudiments of the Australian crawl through sheer willpower, and was prepared for testing. In the platform event, Pee Wee had frozen. Halfway up the ladder, the fear of drowning had met the fear of heights. He locked on to the ladder with limbs and teeth with such commitment that it was difficult to see where he ended and the ladder began.

"Whew!" hissed Peck "Ravine" Mankoff. "If he could wrap his dick around a rung, I think he'd do it."

Pee Wee panted as the ladder swung high above the pool, the ladder jerking with every flex of his large, grunting form. The idea of climbing up so he could drown in twenty feet of cold, chlorinated water failed to inspire him to greater heights.

"YOU COME DOWN FROM ZERE RIGHT NOW, YOU KNUCKLEHEAD PLEBE!" cried Mr. Flauck, threatening with his stick. "CLIMB OR JUMP! YOU ARE BLOCKING MY LADDER!"

Pee Wee released the steel rung from his small mouth to scream, with great candor, "NO, SIR!"

A young lieutenant, four years out of the Academy, pulled off sweats, dove in, and climbed up. He spoke quietly to Pee Wee, who moaned, his eyes tightly shut, his teeth ready to pop from his gums under the pressure of his mandible on the rung. The lieutenant spoke more emphatically. The lieutenant yelled. He screamed. "May I touch you?" he roared. Plebes could be starved, sweated to walls, push-upped to death, tormented, and kept awake for months, but they could not be touched without consent. Pee Wee sort of nodded.

The officer would free one finger, then two, and the original finger would lock around the ladder. Nothing West Point could do—finger torts, psychic torture, starvation, recitation, mass abuse, punishment slugs, sleep deprivation, loss of football

privileges, court-martial, or firing squad—could compare to releasing the ladder. The survival-swimming program had en-
countered primordial fear and played it to a tie in double over-
time.

"Who knows this man?" asked the lieutenant. My fist came
out.

I was sent to retrieve Pee Wee. I didn't mention to anyone
my hysterical fear of heights, first discovered on the roof of the
Empire Metal Works in the Mission rail yards, and barely conquered when I had done the platform event. Oh, man, I get to
do it again. I dove in and climbed, trembling, heart frail, loins
weak.

"Hey, Pee Wee." I faced him from the other side of the ladder. Both of us were cold. It was difficult for me to hold on,
because his body had merged into the ladder, leaving little to
grasp.

He released the rung from his teeth, his eyes scrunched
closed. "Kai?" he said, teeth clamping on to the rung again.

"Yo. Climb down with me. We'll go one rung at a time."
I adjusted my grip, and the ladder swung. Pee Wee groaned
"no."

"Okay, I'll jump first. I'll be in the water with the lieutenant
and a swim ring. Then you. We put the ring on you and pull
you to the edge. Mr. Flauck'll even let you climb out on his
'valls.' C'mon, man." I looked down, my gorge rising. I closed
my eyes. "Whatever you do, don't look down."

He looked down. "Oh, shit," he said slowly. "Go 'way," he
whispered.

I couldn't leave him. Time passed. "Pee Wee. This duck
comes into the O Club and says, 'A round for the whole
house. Put it on my bill.' "

Pee Wee opened one eye. I made like Groucho Marx, holding on with one hand while fluttering eyebrows and dusting an
imaginary cigar. I smiled brilliantly while teetering. He shut
his eye.

"Duck goes to the commissary," I said. "Duck says, 'Give
me a box of rubbers.' The clerk says, 'Shall I put that on your
bill?' The duck says, 'I'm sorry, I'm not that kind of duck.' "

Pee Wee's face closed up like a wet fist. He shook, and we
swayed, the ladder's metal pins clacking hollowly. He forced
his eyes open, blinking, his pupils huge. His saliva was everywhere. "Get down," he hissed. "Too heavy. We'll fall!"

I closed my eyes. "Pee Wee," I said, my voice unsteady. "I'm scared too. C'mon. We'll go together."

He violently shook his head. "No. Go 'way," he hissed.

I had failed. I wanted to climb down, but this was West Point. I'd be expected to climb the ladder. "Take care, Pee Wee." I climbed to the top and dropped, for a long time, until I hit the pool, hoping the sound would invite him. It didn't.

Mr. Flauck and the lieutenant sat in vigil at poolside, taking lunch, dinner, and a vat of coffee. They took turns sleeping. At four sharp the following morning, Pee Wee McCloud fell asleep and dropped into the pool as if Kansas had landed in a bathtub. With a classic, world-record-setting cannonball impact, Pee Wee emptied the hated pool of half its wretched contents. A drenched Mr. Flauck and lieutenant pulled him out before any water got in his lungs. Flauck filled him with hot chocolate and sandwiches. Pee Wee kept pulling on his teeth with trembling, rigid fingers, his body shaking. His teeth and gums hurt from chewing steel.

Mr. Flauck patted him kindly. "Izz okay, young Plebe. Dreenk chocolate."

The lieutenant stared at Mr. Flauck. This was the man who would detain him from diving into the water to rescue a drowning Plebe until the last possible moment. "*Nein, nein—vait, vait!* Bubbles, *ja?* I zink he still moves."

Pee Wee was placed in the hospital for an overnight psychiatric evaluation. I had introduced him to Mike Benjamin and Sonny Rappa during the Plebe Encampment at Lake Fredericks, and I gathered them for a visit to the one-bed psych ward.

As our heels echoed hollowly down the hall, Mike said, "You know, after graduation, I want to be a doctor." Sonny and I stopped, open-mouthed. We were being trained to be warriors, not healers.

"Ya picked a doozy of a pre-med program," said Sonny.

Pee Wee was eating strawberry Jell-O. I wanted some. Mike and Sonny said a few words and left.

"You guys were my first visitors," said Pee Wee methodically. "If I get stuck up there again, just shoot me. Or, tell me another joke, which'll have the same effect." When the shrinks let him out, Pee Wee would have to face Mr. Flauck and the ladder.

"Hope I didn't make it worse for you."

He turned his head away. "I just fucked up," he said.

"You know, Pee Wee, when I was a kid, I went crazy."

He looked at me. "I thought you went nuts after you got here."

I laughed. I remembered the insanity god and the kind Chinese woman I used to dream of before Leo Washington took over my nightmares. "I used to laugh when nothing was funny. I couldn't stop. It happened at the worst times. In public. With my dad." I was becoming very confessional. Tony would be proud of me. I had never told anyone this. "After a while it went away. This thing—it's nothing. You'll beat the ladder. I got better—you will, too."

"Look at yourself. You call that better?" We laughed. I rubbed my face. He belched and I smelled chlorine. We shook hands, nodding at each other. On my way out, my heart went cold as I passed Duke Troth, the bigot from the Thayer Hotel. Against my own admonition, I had forgotten about him. What did he want with Pee Wee? Troth looked at me the way dogs look at cats as he entered the ward. Remember him, I said to myself.

I doubted my own skills in swimming, but Mr. Flauck validated me, giving me another shot at scuba training. I wanted to learn what frogmen knew. By now it was November and colder than anything I had experienced in San Francisco. I got golf. Golf was not a sport for a Chinese kid. Chinese people couldn't get into half the golf courses in San Francisco unless it was to empty the trash.

Mr. McWalters raised his eyebrows at my grades. "You're good in everything 'cept math. How come?"

"Sir, I am not good at mathematics."

"Whaddyou mean, you're not good at math? Aren't you Chinese?"

"Mr. Ting!" called Captain Dozier.

"Yes, sir!" I stood at attention before his desk, some of the chalk from my badly butchered math problem dusting my gray trou. We recited math problems at large, numbered chalkboards which covered the section walls. We were assigned calculus problems based on staggered boards, odd and even, to avoid inadvertent glances at other solutions. Many of the boards, I was sure, were replete with equations marching in rigid horizontal lines of progressive derivation leading to the notation "Q.E.D." on the bottom, for *quod erat demonstrandum*, "which was to be demonstrated."

I had placed a "Q.E.D." on my board, but there were no

equations of value between my name on top and the Latin initials on the bottom.

"Mr. Ting, this is a routine differential equation. You okay?"

"Yes, sir."

He lowered his voice. "Having trouble at home? Someone sick?"

"No, sir."

"Well, did you get a 'Dear John' letter? Something like that? Or some upperclassman really on your tail—signature calls?"

"No, sir," I said.

"Ting, are you *really* Chinese?" he asked.

"You a virgin?" asked Mr. McWalters. "You're turnin' red!"

"Sir, I believe I am," I said. Clint hadn't warned me about this question.

"You *believe* you are—what? Turning red, or a virgin?"

"Sir, I do not know if I am a virgin."

"Whaddyou mean, you don't know? You mean *you don't know?*" His roommates looked up.

"No, sir," I said.

He laughed. "Well, Ting, have you been laid?"

"No, sir," I said.

"Wow, you really are no rocket scientist, are you?"

"No, sir," I said.

"Well, I never figured *you* for a goat. You're in top sections in everything but math. All right. Papa McWalters is gonna give you the straight poop: Wet dreams, Mr. Smack, do *not* count. That's a big negative. They're not so bad—hell, they're not scheduled. Prevent white-out, internal drowning. But good as they are, when it's over, you're still a bona fide government-issue Virgin, one each, capital V. If you haven't been laid, you're a virgin. Now, that's as good as Webster. You're eighteen, right?"

"Yes, sir," I said.

"You a *killer,* smackhead?"

"Yes, sir!" I shouted.

"Ever kill anyone, Mr. Ting?" he asked, smiling broadly. "IRP!" he shouted.

"SIR, I DO NOT KNOW!" I cried.

He stared at me. "You wanna explain *that* one? No. As you were: I don't wanna know. Need a damn encyclopedia for every friggin' question I ask you. What are you—a damn Eastern mystic or something?"

13

LUCKY

Golden Gate Park, November 22, 1960

Kennedy had been elected President. Edna, my father, and I heard Kennedy speak at the Cow Palace during the primary. That's where, after the war, Tony Barraza used to fight in front of adoring fans. Siciliano cries for blood and Piedmontese oaths were so loud that he threw torso-crushing combinations into his opponent in time to their rhythmic chants of "Ti-ger, Ti-ger, Ti-ger!"

"My coach used to fight here," I said without thinking.

"Hush and keep your mouth closed," said Edna.

Kennedy had mesmerized the audience. The Irish, Italians, Negroes, Hispanics, Slavs, and Japanese, the Filipinos and the Basques, the Russians and the Jews, and the powerful Cantonese political organization of Chinatown had arrived skeptical of a man so young and so Catholic. By the middle of his speech about a new generation of Americans pledged to a world of idealism and freedom, who would use athletic spirit, vigor, and youth to keep America first in the world, San Francisco was his. He spoke of racial equality, and I had developed a political view.

I was happy as I pitched rocks high over Stow Lake—happy about Kennedy, because he had made it clear that he was a friend of the Negro, and I was sort of a Negro, and I was hopeful that he would like me. I was also happy with my arm. It had been lifting iron for seven years; I could beat everyone except for Toos and Markie in rock throwing for distance.

"Kennedy's a good man," Markie T. had said. "Rich white

dude on the side a colored people." He blew a big bubble of Bazooka gum. "Don't know why he that way, but he is."

"Kai," said Toos as I pitched rocks. "C'mere."

Jerome "Lucky" Washington was waiting for me. His left eye was puffed, trying to clot from a lot of bleeding. Something very hard had hit him, splitting his lip and canting him to the left. So Leo Washington was back. Leo, the sour-bellied, weather-bitching pool cheat, nocturnal groin kicker, daylight sucker puncher, wife beater, and child stomper, cursed the whole 'hood and could kill you with his breath. He was a mean drinker with hard boots, the ambulatory nightmare of the Pandhandle. Leo was Lucky's father.

Toos was solemn and I cooled my face. Lucky looked like he had been spit out of an old meat grinder. Early on, if there had been two kids and one of them looked like Lucky did now, it would have been me. But Lucky had foul *yeh*, karma, and I had whipped him in a nighttime fistfight; he wore the tar of being the China boy's first dunce like a permanent shiner. Now, six years later, as my fortunes rose and his fell, he still had no use for me.

"Hey, Lucky," I said.

"Hey," he managed, thickly.

Lucky's tongue ran over his ripped lip. "Yo' daddy has a gun. I want it, bad. Jus' one time, man." His shoulders quaked and he looked away, quickly swabbing his eyes with a forearm.

I looked away. I felt sorry for him. It wasn't the first time.

"He gonna kill my momma," Lucky said. "Gotta stop that sonofabitch. He gonna git her when she come home tonight. Gimme yo' daddy's gun, China. I gotta shoot 'im ta stop 'im."

Titus B., Markie T., and Alvin Sharpes had joined in. I didn't know what to say. I shook my head, violently. I wasn't allowed to have my elbows on the table—how the heck was he going to get away with shooting his daddy? My face showed my doubts.

"Oh, man!" moaned Lucky.

"Yo' daddy's gun *work?*" asked Titus. "It's not all rusted up?"

I nodded, then shook my head.

"Then let Lucky use it, chump!"

"Fergit it!" said Markie T. "We ain't killin' *nobody*." Markie was like Toussaint—a peacemaker.

"What do I do, Toos?" I asked, panic in my voice. They didn't ask me for much—to play skins on a cold day or to re-

trieve long-hit balls over a fence—I didn't mind. Saying no
could be *ji hui*, bad luck, and take from me the acceptance I
had earned. I didn't want to be *k'ung hsu*, abandoned, again.

"Gonna tell you again, Lucky," said Toos. "Pack yo' bags
and *git*. Tell yo' momma to meet at my place. Momma'll know
what to do. May have to crash with us. Maybe at the church.
But don't go back there with no *gun*."

"Toos," said Lucky, his low voice gravelly, "he gonna kill
us. He like a dog who can track. He find us! He find us at yo'
place, he kill you *and* yo' momma. At the church, he kill the
Rev'rend."

He looked at Toos, his left eye a bolus of red meat. "Help
me, man." He pointed at me with an arm that was shadowed
in darkening bruises. "Git 'im ta gimme his daddy's gun!
Can't kill 'im wif my hands. I pull a knife, he'll cut me till I'm
dead."

"Gun's no better than a knife, Lucky," said Toos. "Besides,
I know Mr. Ting. He ain't *never* gonna let us do this. Lucky,
you ain't gonna make this boy *steal* from his own daddy.
Mr. Ting ain't gonna help you kill Leo."

I nodded. Yes, that was the right thing to say.

"An' I ain't either," said Mark T. softly. "Ain't the answer."

"Then I gonna die!" Lucky cried, his face in anguish.

"My momma," said Toos, "told me that Leo Washington's
gonna die by his own hand. An' that's what's gonna be. No
guns."

"Poison the mothafucka," said Titus B. in his hard, high
voice. "Put roach and rat poison in his drink. Leo, he like
Sippy—he drink *anything*. Lucky, don't he drink after he beat
you?"

Lucky nodded. "Red plum wine," he said.

"You gotta let him hit you, Jerome," said Titus. "It gonna
hurt like a bitch, your eye all fucked up. Hell, you could lose
it. But then you know he take his slug, and you know what be
in it." He looked at Toos. I worked my mouth, which was dry.

"Let's get Hector Pueblo an' them to help," I squeaked.

"No way!" spat Lucky. "No growed man gonna cotton ta
helpin' kids kill. Hector, he's cool, but he go pop his muscles
in fronta my daddy an' that'll be the end a *me!* That's *suicide!*"

"You know, Hector, he'd say this is wrong," said Alvin
Sharpes. "I gotta tell you straight. My daddy, he'd think this is
bad shit, and *not* to be done." Everyone looked up to Mr.

Sharpes. He drove a Muni rail car and didn't drink. There was silence.

"Dead on, Alvin Sharpes," said Toos. "Lucky, don' try killin' yo' daddy, even if he be Leo Washington. Get yo' momma outa town. He won't follow. He'll find someone else to beat on close by. He's too lazy to chase."

"Toussaint," said Lucky, "he track down his firs' wife and baby girl and *killed* them *dead!* They was in Atlanta, and she run from him and he caught 'em in *De-troit.* Sometime he hit my momma he call her the same name, an that firs' woman, she's *dead.*"

"Okay, Lucky," said Toos, "I help you run. But God tol' Moses to say 'Thou shalt not kill,' an' I lissen to that. *You* lissen to that."

Alvin Sharpes said, "Amen to that."

"Don' be using the Book on him!" shouted Titus, his rasping voice cracking with emphasis. "Tha's fo' *grown-up* people, an' *prob'ly* for grown-up *white* people. God don' give a *shit* 'bout us. We's goin' up against *Leo.* It's be David an' that big shit-kickin' black nigga mothafucka *Go-liath!* Toos, you's *all* wrong 'bout this. Lookit here—Lucky's got *no* room to move—*no* room, man! Man, all he askin' for is a *slingshot* to go up against *Leo!*" He paced, raising clouds of fine red dust from the trail as Toos, Markie, and Alvin Sharpes argued with Titus.

I didn't want to hear it—not about beatings, or killings, or guns, or the Good Book. Where were the men? Where was Uncle Shim's *changgiao t'ungchih*—rule by elders? Where was a place where this didn't happen? This was the biggest trouble since Leo knifed Mathey Roache, back when Mathey had just returned from the Korean War and I had cried when I saw Leo throw Lucky's momma down the hard stairs into the street. I didn't want to be here. I wanted to jump a freight with Toos. This didn't happen in the Hanlin Kuan, in the Pen Forest. We shouldn't have to hope for God to avoid murder. I had to do something, to stop this bitter, bad luck talk.

"I can call the po-lice," I said.

"Oh, shit—screw them!" hissed Lucky. "They won't do *nuthin'.* Figger it's a man's right, beat his wife."

We were quiet for a moment. I didn't know the answer to that. Dave Neumark at the Y was a cop. He wouldn't let this happen.

"*I* know a cop," I said, "who don't think like that."

They looked at me. Kai Ting from China knows a cop. I was always full of surprises.

"Well, *I* don't," said Lucky. " 'Nuff flappin' lip. Gonna take Leo down tonight or die tryin'. Gonna keep my momma out of it. You serious, my momma can stay wif you?" he asked Toos. "Or wif you?"

Markie T. nodded. "You got it." Toos nodded.

"My place, too, if my daddy says okay," said Alvin Sharpes.

"Don't mean nothin'," whispered Toos, hitting Lucky on his arm. Lucky's uninjured eye blazed with weeping hurt. That's how it had been for me when I had to fight Lucky, six years back: no way out. I wanted to ask Toos what I should do, but Titus was yelling at Toos and Markie about everyone ganging up on Leo with baseball bats, renewing the argument, and they left, leaving me at the lakeshore.

I stood on the red gravel path, fingering a round rock, wanting to throw it over the moon, wanting to call Dave Neumark and tell him that murder was going to happen. I wanted him to fix things. I remembered that cops had come into the Haight, gone into the wrong apartment and shot the wrong person, seeing no difference between Negro killer and Negro victim.

But Dave Neumark would get it right; he was smart, and worked as a cop volunteer for Barney Lewis, chief of instruction at the Y. Barney was a Negro. Dave Neumark would approach Leo, telling him to be cool. Leo was a bully; he'd smile and make jokes, shake hands and talk about the weather. Later, he'd kill me.

I imagined calling Tony, Barney, or Pinoy. I knew what they'd say: tell your father. Chinese fathers were out of reach. All evening long, I looked at the phone at the Y, and later, I stared at the one in the living room. I touched it, but couldn't call, stopped by the terror of facing Leo, of imagining Edna while I tried to explain this problem to my father. I knew it wouldn't save Lucky and would somehow make everything far worse.

I lay in my bed and spoke to Dave Neumark a hundred times, silently, each time telling him more and more about Leo and what he did to his son and wife. I tried to imagine why Leo was this way. I figured his daddy beat him. I imagined a place where kids didn't have to think so hard.

Leo Washington came home, drank a good portion of a bottle of plum wine, and became ill. He dumped the bottle into a bowl in the kitchen and found a residue in it. He went looking for Lucky.

In the morning, Momma LaRue and Mrs. Timm found fourteen-year-old Jerome "Lucky" Washington in the hallway outside his door. He had been dead for a while, cut and stabbed beyond the reach of earthly pain, further bad fortune, and the pains of foul *yuing chi*. Leo was in his living room, without wife or son to hamper his wandering ways, his swollen purple tongue filling his gaping mouth, stained by cheap wine vomitus that had choked him to death. Leo had been done in by his own hand.

Was I a killer? Mr. McWalter's question would not go away.

And so I dreamed of Leo drinking his wine and dying. He would pop his suspenders and belch as the first waves of pain hit, and he would get sick. Or he would be bent over with gut pain, slapping the wood floor with his large hands, retching onto his Big Ben overalls, his big, ugly head down. He would hunt down Lucky with a knife. Lucky, his eye swollen, put his unschooled fists up to his father as he had put them up to me, six years before.

At the end, Leo would always cry, "China boy, you lame little streak a yella chink crap, why didn't you call the *po-lice?!* I'm dyin' in my gut an it's your doin'! You had a phone!"

14

DUKE

West Point, November 1964

The winter gods smiled on me, shedding *foo chi,* good fortune. I moved to Corps Squad gymnastics training tables in the deep alcove in the center of Washington Hall. I was the worst high-bar man in college athletics, but I ate a nightly supper that would have filled the Trojan horse and the hulls of the Greek fleet. I squirreled food and distributed it to classmates.

"Damn, son," said Fitz McBay, the Southern traditionalist table com. "You eat like a starvin' potbellied pig!"

The presidential election consumed the front pages of *The New York Times*. Johnson ran on a platform of rationality and peace, and painted Senator Goldwater of Arizona as a militaristic warmonger. The President announced that he would not send "American boys to fight a war that ought to be fought by Asian boys."

There were four other Asians in the Class of 1968.

"I guess," I said to Mike Benjamin during the bonfire rally before the Navy game, "he's just going to send me and the other four Asians to Vietnam, so you don't have to go."

"Mighty white of you," said Arch Torres, a classmate from New Mexico who was a better boxer than I.

"Thanks, buddy!" said Bob Lorbus as he thumped me on my chest hard enough to evacuate my air, while Joey Rensler whacked my back, exclaiming, "Yeah, outstandin'!"

"Anytime," I squeaked.

On November 3, Lyndon Johnson would defeat Barry Goldwater and remain in the White House. Robert Francis Kennedy would be elected senator from New York. Both would draw 90 percent of the black vote. I couldn't vote, and I wasn't black, but I felt I was part of it, even if I ended up being one of a tiny minority of Asian-American soldiers who were going to be sent to Vietnam so white boys wouldn't have to go.

But the larger event, by far, in the historic month of November 1964 was the 74th Army-Navy Game in Veterans Memorial Stadium, Philadelphia. The Army team, three-touchdown underdogs, had defeated the highly touted Navy squad with stout defense and blitzes. Army's Rollie Stichweh, the unsung star quarterback, had outplayed Heisman Trophy winner Roger Staubach. The Corps, the Army team's "twelfth man," had willed victory through our demented screams led by Marco Matteo Fideli. It had helped that the team was rich in defensive talent and coached by Paul Dietzel, one of the country's best coaches. Army had the tradition. Red Blaik had defined Army football of the twentieth century, and college football of the forties and fifties. Vince Lombardi had been an assistant coach, and now everyone was excited about a big, bluff line coach named Bill Parcells, whose brother was on the team.

The buses returned from Philadelphia on November 28, 1964, and the band played, chapel bells pealed, faculty and staff families honked car horns, and everyone, throats stripped raw from hours of screaming, once again sang "On Brave Old Army Team" as if it were the new national anthem. It felt as if we had won World War II, singing for all that was good, all our suffering as cadets redeemed by a game that represented so much more than a pigskin in fall.

I, a basketball player who had never mastered football, had become an uncompromising football fanatic. The season had absorbed our personas, suspended our cares. I answered Marco Fideli's spirited cheers as if they were calls from Odin, the Norse high god, to whom Plebes prayed in long, haunting chants, for parade-canceling thunderstorms. I donated my *yuing chi*, my fortune, and my *yeh*, karma, to all the Scandinavian and Chinese gods. I offered my few good credits in return for first downs or enemy punts. Just let us get one touchdown here, on *this* drive, and I'll expect nothing else of my life, I whispered amidst the roar of the Corps. The Army victory over Navy had been an answer to prayers, more significant than our march across the Plain to join our companies at the end of Beast. The victory in 1964 had ended Navy's stunning ability, in six consecutive years, to hand talented Army teams bitter defeats in Philadelphia. The curse had ended, and we were to share in riches beyond measure.

Mr. Arvin had been named First Captain of the Corps, following in the long-striding footsteps of Robert E. Lee, John Pershing, Douglas MacArthur, and Pete Dawkins. "IN RECOGNITION OF ARMY'S DEFEAT OF NAVY," he boomed from the Poop Deck, "MEMBERS OF THE FOURTH CLASS ARE GRANTED A FALL-OUT AT ALL MEALS, WITH IMMEDIATE EFFECT, UNTIL RETURN OF THE CORPS FOLLOWING CHRISTMAS LEAVE!"

"CHEER, BOYS, CHEER!" shouted Fitz McBay. "There's been nuthin' like this since a days a Dawkins, Ca'penter, Hol'afield, Red Blaik, Blanchard an' Davis, an' the National Championships. Talk about yo' West Point Good Deal! Y'all got it made!"

Pandemonium erupted as we screamed, reliving Champi's TD catch from Stichweh, Nickerson's kick, Staubach's safety and his negative twenty-eight yards rushing. Plebes ate without bracing, and I would no longer have to spirit grub from the mess hall for starving classmates. Arvin was a god, a modern Hector or Diomedes.

And so we entered December, round with victory over ancient enemies and cheered by a dramatic drop in temperature that prefaced the arrival of Christmas. We were going home for Yuletide, the first Plebe Class ever to do so. This was my first eastern winter, the snowfall was light—and I had found a pool table, a modern version of a boy's rock-throwing lake.

"I hear you're famous," said Duke Troth.

"You have me confused with someone else," I said, chalking the cue and bending over the table. "Six ball, side pocket."

I stroked it softly, the six falling into the hole, creating a sweet little drumroll as it followed the chute across the underside of the table into the tray. The cue ball rolled to the far rail slowly. Instead of caroming to give me shape and space on the three, it hugged the rail, producing a tough shot. "Hmm," I said to myself. I was not happy to see Duke.

At Wedemeyer's Billiards in the Tenderloin, Bennie Davis would say, "Play loose, don't lose your cool." He could make his play, double-banking a cushion-running ball, while a San Francisco quake shook the slate and his four ex-wives screamed at him for the rent.

We were in Nininger Hall, the generously described Fourth Class Club. Lieutenant Alexander R. Nininger, Class of 1941, was the first West Pointer to receive the Medal of Honor in World War II. He had died while fighting with the 57th Infantry, Philippine Scouts. Nininger Hall was a long room on the third floor above the north sally port in Central Area. It had one small TV, an old pool table, bad lights, and an assembly of furniture that had been rejected by that other army—the Salvation. Nininger was more than sufficient entertainment for eight hundred men who spelled "recreation" with the letters S-L-E-E-P. Ten of us were in Nininger on a Sunday following chapel and before supper formation because of the halcyon days created by Army's epic game. The rest were blissfully asleep in brown boys, the pedestrian-issue comforters which, along with being able to go to the bathroom without someone screaming at us, provided us our simple pleasures.

I had waited two hours for the table, memorizing the Days until my turn arrived. I was playing eight ball with Bill Reichert, the winner for the last five games. Bill had also been in Fourth New Cadet Company. I was playing well and was three balls behind.

"Three ball, corner pocket," I said.

"Never make it," said Troth.

I blew out air. "Your opinion don't matter." I stroked the cue ball, too hard—it took too much off the three, which caromed off the left margin of the pocket and left the cue ball in fair shape for Bill's fifteen. Sorry, Bennie Davis; I lost my cool. I dusted chalk dust from the apron.

"Tough shot," said Bill, offering comfort.

"Someone said I wouldn't make it, and I listened to him. Good luck on yours," I said.

"Shit!" laughed Troth. "You society bitches playing bridge? 'Good luck on yours,'" he mimicked. "You guys married?"

"Yes," I said. "It was in all the papers."

Duke Troth glared at me. He pulled down a pool cue as if it were a rifle from a gun rack. My heartbeat picked up. He reversed the cue stick, blunt end forward. But he didn't move, staying out of my reach. I turned my cue around as well, holding it a shoulder width apart, and faced him, my heart pounding. "No wonder you're no good in pool," I said. "You're holding it wrong."

He barked a laugh. "I could fuckin' kill your ass," he hissed.

"All you could do," I said, "is *talk* someone to death."

"Screw you. Finish your game, geek. Then let's talk." He hurled the stick in the corner. My heart fluttered as the stick clattered against old wood and hollowly bounced on the floor.

Some classmates were playing chess and watching the tube, and they jumped. "Don't be a jerk," said one.

"Fuck *you*, asshole, in the ear," replied Troth.

Bill lifted his eyebrows at me.

"Beats me," I said quietly.

"You know he's crazy," said Bill.

"I figured." My left quadricep had a small muscular quiver. Troth had to be crazy. Plebe year and the dominion of the upper classes left no room for intramural animosity. Everyone did his best for himself and for his classmates. Troth seemed outside the system, as if he were not a Plebe but a young lord in a nation of hoboes. My heart slugged with the possibility of fighting him. I shook my head. Plebes don't fight each other. We could call out an upperclassman into the ring, but not each other. He had called me a "geek." It sounded like "gook."

I wondered how he got away with it. In Hell-One, my company, a BJ Plebe like Troth would be a shit magnet, drawing the ire of the upper classes like blasphemy in the Vatican.

"Fifteen in the corner," said Bill, "eight in the side." The music of sinking balls began, and I racked my pool cue.

Troth was reclined on the sofa, smoking. He had popped

open the dress-gray winter jacket's high black collar, which had a white, snap-on, starched cotton insert. Troth's was worn black, obviously unchanged for days. His uniform and body were saturated in the stale, sour imprint of a chain-smoker. I thought: What do you want with me, you unwashed, dirtbag, bigoted, anti-Semitic pig?

"I hear you're a celebrity yourself," I said.

"Whaddya hear?" he asked, taking his gaze from the snow-shrouded window and the view of the steam grates to look up at me.

"I hear you sponge off small classmates."

"Rumors! They're a bitch. But it's true, growing boys gotta eat. Why pick on flankers when you can snip runts?" He smiled with big teeth, his prominent nose aiming at me, his hard, muscular face shadowed by the hall's old lights. Plebe year had placed accents into his features, making it look maliciously mature. Caesar.

"So talk." I sat on one of those sofas not designed for sitting, and it resisted me.

Troth wasn't going to fight. It would be insane to do it here, even with the delirium of the Navy game still thick in the air, like a rich, redolent cologne that clouded and powdered West Point's severe Calvinism. Troth had a bad reputation; I didn't. If we were to scrap, it'd be his neck, not mine.

He lit another cigarette and blew smoke rings at the window. He took pleasure from their little implosions against the cold, iron-runged glass, as if the smoke rings were little furry creatures that he enjoyed killing.

I tried to estimate the size of his arms beneath his tunic. I estimated effort in the ring by measuring the size of an opponent's arms. Tony Barraza's were huge, and all my life I'd tried to make mine look like his. Winter dress gray was made of a heavy and rough wool; it had taken all the hair off our legs. It was too thick for me to read Troth's arms, but he clearly had not been hungry for a while, and he was not a Corps Squader.

"Contacts," Troth said, smiling. He ran the thumb of his right hand across its fingertips, starting with the little finger and ending with the index, then running them back. It was a simple movement, but his leering smile made it seem sordid and uncleanly obscene.

"Contacts. The whole friggin' world's made of *contacts*. It ain't what you know, it's *who* you know. And *who* you know is based on what you can *trade*. Know what I mean? Learned in the Army: 'Take command.' " He smiled, showing teeth. "I'm takin' command."

"Okay," I said.

"You're just an Oriental, but you got contacts. Bo Kleiner was a hero in the Navy game and is all-East, and he talks about you like you were an asshole buddy. You know the Fideli twins—the ones who confused the shit out of us during Beast—and they sing opera in New York during the summer, with their names in *The New York Times*. And Marco Fideli's head Rabble Rouser and has *adopted* your ass. You run all over the goddamn Academy talkin' to guys who were in your Beast company, listenin' to their gripes and B-aches. I'm building a team, and everywhere I go I hear about some Oriental in glasses who got there first. Can you believe that crap?"

"I don't know about that," I said.

"Aw, the hell you don't! You eat it up, slidin' around on your special ticket. Guys think you're *interesting*. Okay, hotshot. I want to meet Kleiner and the Fidelis. I won't forget it. I'll help you when you need something. That's what *classmates* are all about."

"You're nuts," I said. "Plebes don't introduce Plebes to upperclassmen like—like this was some sort of *club*. I can't say, 'Hi, sir, I want you to meet a buddy of mine.' Look, Kleiner's younger brother turned down the appointment I got. We talked *once*. The Fidelis—well, they got their reasons for picking me out. But it's up to them, not us. You know that. You know all this stuff better than I do. You're a poop schooler."

I looked over at the table. Bill was playing Mike DiBenedetto, who was patiently waiting for Bill's first miss. Both looked up at me, concerned. I was awed. That's what classmates are for. I was instantly proud to know them, to be here. Here, my dreams of Leo Washington had evaporated. I was inside a castle, a fort, the Hanlin Academy. Here, people were encouraged to do the right thing. We had promised at the river to be good men.

"Okay," Troth said in a low voice, bending toward me, his smoke curling around my face. "I'll trade. How'd you like to have all your papers *Times*? Or get outa laundry duty? That's beautiful—a fuckin' *Chinese* guy not havin' laundry detail! Is that chichi or not? I can't do a thing about minute calling, or latrine warming. You're on your own for those shit details."

I looked at him, brows at work. "What are you talking

about?" I was hearing his words, but they weren't making sense. "We're not even in the same regiment—we couldn't swap duties."

Cadet upperclassmen received two dailies—*The New York Times* and a good, obscure, and unpopular upstate paper. Plebe details gathered them from stoops before reveille and delivered them to the doors of the sleeping upperclassman. There were never enough copies of the *Times,* and there was hell to pay when a Firstie or a Cow, a junior, got the *Gazette* instead. Plebes divided the *Times* so the criticism could be distributed, producing optimum shared success under deficient circumstances. (I vowed, if I got through Plebe year, to be an upperclassman who would always ask for the *Gazette*.) In reality, of course, it wasn't a big deal, but in a world when you can't decide how or when to get up seven mornings a week, picking your newspaper became a Good Deal. How could Troth get only the *Times?* How could he trade duties like they were stocks?

"I'm not talkin' about swapping, douchebag! Damn, you're dense! I'll get knobs to do it for you! You don't do a damn thing."

"You'll get knobs to do it? What the hell are you—a freakin' *upperclassman* all of a sudden?" I asked.

"Keep your goddamn voice down!" he hissed.

"How the hell would you get your classmates to—? Oh, wow," I said, getting it. He would get them to do his jobs like he got them to share their food: he used his fists—or pool cues. I twisted on the sofa, making it complain. "You're unbelievable."

"Pretty fuckin' neat hat-trick, *right?*" he asked, punching me on my arm. He was only half through his smoke, but he discarded it and lit another, glinting at me through the haze. "Figured this out in the Army. At Sandhurst, the Brit academy, upperclassman got *valets* to take care of their shit, to pack their ditty bags and spit-shine their shoes. Now, *that's* chichi. Haven't gotten the goddamn system to work yet, but I will. Just a matter of contacts, building the team. You can help. The Fidelis, they can help."

He ran his ice-cold gaze around the room. I studied him in amazement. He lowered his voice so much he almost croaked. "Whoever sticks with me now, I'll remember later. Whoever pisses me off, I'm gonna butcher—tomorrow, maybe the day after, but the asshole'll get it in the ear when he's not looking.

Let's not shit around. The only reason I'm in this sucking, chickenshit place is to *win*."

He was waiting. All I could do was stare. I kept looking at his uniform. I often wondered how I had managed to get into this exclusive White Men's Club. How did *he?*

"I don't want anything to do with you," I said. I stood.

He leaned across the sofa. "Listen, Red Ryder," he said, rasping. "You don't get it. You don't know what you're missing. Don't be dense. Don't you know who I am? I could get you *laid*. This is your only chance, meathead! You're not exactly model material. And they're *beautiful*. How about *that?*"

I coughed. For a moment, the idea of actually having physical congress with a girl stopped the creaky little wheels in my brain. I remembered the Tenderloin pimps and the hard, unhappy, painted ladies of Turk Street, their dislike of boys who stared and had no cash or interest. They had terrible lives orchestrated by their managers. It was better to be rejected by Christine or to be a lifetime monk.

"Tell me," I said. "You enjoy pimping?" I left.

"You fuckin' *jerk!* You're walking away from a Good Deal! Fuck you in the ear! You're gonna get it in the ass! I'm not gonna forget you. Keep your fuckin' slant eyes open, asshole!"

I walked back to him, my adrenal system pumping fear and rage. After all of the pent-up repressions of Plebe year, to have this guy slap me in the face . . . "Stand up," I said.

"Fuck off," he growled.

"Park it and get up! Piss me off. Pickin' on little guys. You'd better stand—it's gonna hurt more sitting there than *doing* it." I wasn't a fighter, nor someone who even started fights. But I couldn't turn my back on a guy who said I'd get it when I wasn't looking. I'd rather fight than wait for it.

"He's not worth it," said Bill. "C'mon! They'll kick a Plebe out for something like this." He grabbed my arm and I threw him off, recovering my stance, left leg leading, left profile up.

What system—boxing from Tony Barraza or Chinese *wing chun gong fu* from Pinoy Punsalong? My muscles were taut, accumulating energy for release. I'd use both: right leg-front kick to groin, to chin as it came down; right cross to the head; lefts, rights, left hooks to the temples; full hip. If he was still standing after that, I'd improvise. I liked it. I wanted it. Yes, I said, showing teeth, deepening my stance.

"Kai—knock it off, man!" urged Mike D. "You're gonna get in a shitload of trouble."

"I got trouble if I don't dunce him, *right* now."

Troth was looking around, looking for space, getting ready to get up, the rodent in him scurrying for the guts to take a bite out of the cat before the lights went out.

The Plebes in Nininger were up, a few of them clearing the hall so they would not be part of the investigation that would follow a fight between Plebes. Rapid, fading footfalls echoed down the narrow staircase. I edged closer.

"Cool it right now!" shouted someone.

"Okay, okay! *Asshole,*" hissed Troth, baring his teeth and leaning back. "Take a freakin' joke. You're fuckin' *crazy.* I'm not gonna screw with you."

"Then stay away from me. And don't play pool," I added, flushed with victory. "And stay away from my friends." And leave town before sunset, I wanted to say.

"How the fuck am I supposed to know who your friends are?!"

"They don't like you," I said.

I returned to barracks, my neck in, sloshing through the snow.

Why had I done that? Was I too thin-skinned, too sensitive about being what I felt deep down—a misfit, a yellow-colored man who ate too much while awaiting final rejection? I was surprised by how much anger I had in me. This was the second time I had offered to fight him over words. I wondered what my friends would have done. Toos wouldn't have suffered Troth's insults. Jack Peeve wouldn't have, either.

"Tony," I said, "this toad said I'd get it in the butt. So I called him out, in a place where we're not supposed to fight. Did I do the right thing?" I saw Tony Barraza's big head. He'd say, "Kid, what choice ya got?" I remembered Bill's and Mike's faces, afraid I had gone crazy. It was the look of my father.

As I entered barracks, Mr. Kunselman, the Yearling CQ, in charge of quarters, stopped me. "Ting, you have a visitor at Grant Hall. You're authorized to go before supper formation."

"Thank you, sir," I said.

I walked into Grant, mystified. Who would visit me? I knew no one who might drop in unannounced. I scanned the hall, the severe generals gazing back. There, under Marshall's portrait, was a familiar face.

"Jack!" I cried. "Good God, Jack Peeve! God, I was just thinking about you!"

We shook hands vigorously, grinning and then laughing as he clapped me on the back and I beat on his big arms. He was dressed in a navy pea jacket, hadn't shaved for several days, and smelled like an old truck. He looked like a man, and not a college student.

"How'd you get here?" I asked. "Why didn't you tell me you were coming? I could've arranged something."

"Hitchhiked," he said. "Why call? Wasn't sure I was gonna make it." He laughed. "Damned big country!"

I marveled at him. He had just thumbed his way across the United States. Jack and I used to hitchhike around San Francisco. The City was seven by seven miles square.

I couldn't stop smiling. "How long did it take?"

"Nine days. One guy got lost, took me too far south. Hey, you got any food? I'm outa dough. Haven't eaten in a couple days."

"Wait right here!" I yelled. "Don't move."

I sprinted back to barracks and asked for Bestier's advice and Mr. Kunselman's help. I filled my overcoat and ran back to Grant.

"First," I said, "shave. God, you have so much hair . . . here's the latrine. Gotta cut your hair. I can take you to the gymnastics table. You can eat like a horse. Pretend to be a cadet. I brought a uniform of a Yearling who's going to help you out. My Honor rep says it's a prank. If we get caught, they'll skin me, but probably won't kick me out." He lathered and started shaving.

"Jack, being a cadet is like being in a different country. I'm just figuring it out. Shave faster! I gotta make formation. Enter the mess hall with the hockey team and find table sixteen in the Corps Squad alcove. Walk tall, military. Here's a map of your route, the door, the alcove, and the tables. The hockey team will come singly, here . . . merge with them, here," I said pointing.

"God, I have so much to teach you. Lotta people here are pissed and silent. It's a hard place. Don't say *anything!* Grunt and nod like you're in *The Guns of Navarone,* in German-occupied Greece, and you don't speak any of the languages."

"You mean like you?" he asked.

I laughed with him. "Yeah. You open your trap, they'll know you don't fit in, and we're dead."

* * *

"Dang," said Fitz McBay. "Who cut yo' hair?"

Jack and I ate like we had been raised at the same trough. He shrugged his shoulders in a tight-fitting dress-gray tunic.

"Mranghl," he said, chewing fast.

"Mah feelin's exactly," said Mr. McBay. "You a floater?" A floater's team table had filled, and he "floated" for a seat.

Jack wasn't under the Honor Code. He nodded.

"Big talker, huh?" asked Fitz.

Jack shook his head, grunted, and downed his milk. I poured him another.

"You're going to eat more than Ting," said Jake Kimure, team captain, fascinated with a cadet he had never laid eyes upon before.

"Hmm-mm," said Jack.

"You know, there may be nothin' *ruder* than a Yearlin' Corps Squad floater," said Fitz.

"Got that right," said Jack in his thick, heavy speech, ending the conversation with a confident and baleful stare.

"How you getting back to the City?" We were in the lobby of the USMA Library. I had showed him as much of the Academy as I could. He had really liked the museum in Thayer. Hall had studied Goering's baton, Yamashita's sword, Mussolini's little black cap, Robert E. Lee's sash, and Stilwell's campaign hat and diary.

"Same way," he said. He stretched his thick neck and belched.

"Jack, you're staying in the Thayer Hotel. I could try to sneak you into barracks, but it's too risky."

He shook his head. "I don't take charity," he said. "I'll sleep in the truck park, or in the library."

"Can't, Jack." I crammed some money into his pocket. "Think of how many clothes you handed down to me."

"Yeah," he said. "Worth, altogether, at least five bucks."

"Man, it was worth a million to me. Don't fight. Just take it. You sleep anywhere else at West Point, you'll get me in trouble."

He nodded. "Okay. Just wanted to see the place. You like it?"

"Better than being at home." I felt a spark of guilt. Jack had also wanted to come to West Point. Somehow, this generous, powerful athlete had not made it, and I, the Chinese kid, had.

"I wish you were here with me, Jack."

He shrugged his shoulders. There was an uncomfortable silence.

I broke it by explaining the incident with Duke Troth. "Was I wrong?" I asked.

"Oh, crap, the asshole's a *jerk*. You went easy on 'im!"

"What would you have done?"

He grinned. How I envied that expression, brimming with deep emotional self-assurance. Duke wouldn't consider crossing a guy with a smile like that. When I was a kid, I used to imitate Burt Lancaster's gleaming smile, but I convinced no one while worrying others. As a boy, I had wanted to be a tough, unshaven, silently dangerous man, as tough as Hector Pueblo and Tony Barraza.

"I woulda said," said Jack, " 'If I light this cue stick on fire, will you make it disappear up your ass? Now duck-walk outa here, buttface!' "

I laughed. "That's Keats, isn't it?"

He laughed. "Kai."

"Yeah, Jack?"

"I woulda hated it here."

15

Mockingbird

English 101B, February 1965

The Mighty Nine stone warriors in the Academic Board Room did not blink when the synchronized second hand of the boardroom chronometer struck twelve. Along the broad and brightly lit wainscoted corridors on three floors of Thayer, in Washington, and the old wooden halls of Bartlett, uniformed faculty in neatly pressed greens entered their section rooms.

"Section, Atten-HUT!" shouted section leaders throughout the Academy's classrooms. The ten of us in English Section 2 sprang to attention, eyes ahead, shoulders back, heels together, feet at forty-five degrees. We did not have to brace, which made us feel practically nonchalant.

"Sir, the section is present and accounted for," announced Deke Schibsted. We looked like hell. Ravine Mankoff was green and nauseous from drowning under Mr. Flauck's watchful gaze; Curve Wrecker Glick and Spoon DeVries had boxing nosebleeds. My head was abraded from wrestling-mat burns and Robert Thought "Pensive" Hamblin wobbled, recovering from gymnastic apparatus falls. Only Jackson Flynn "Hawk" Latimer, the basketball player, seemed sound.

Section 2 was near the top of the class, and Deke was the number-one cadet in the section. We were periodically resectioned based on cumulative, daily grading. Mike Benjamin was number one in Section I—first in the class in English. Joey Rensler was at the bottom of the class, and Clint Bestier was right next to him.

"Take seats," said Captain MacPellsin. Most of the faculty were youthful and tall, but Captain Mac was middle-aged and had successfully copied Mickey Rooney's height. Many were handsome; our professor displayed the face of Uriah Heep, the ears of Jughead, and the hair of Harpo Marx. Mesmerizingly, he also spoke with Laurence Olivier's British-accented voice. On his upper right sleeve he wore the World War II unit patch that my father had worn: the China-Burma-India theater. I felt a familial connection between us, silent but tangible, always wanting my teachers to like me.

His intensely pale face was highlighted by dark, age-lined eyes which were earnest in speech and ironic while listening. The disorganized light gray hair that rose from the top of his head was evidence of the riot of rich thought I imagined lay below. While seated, he seemed ghostlike and unearthly, a sepia-toned still life that could have been painted by James Abbot McNeill Whistler, USMA Class of 1855. I thought, *Whistler's Lit Professor*.

Captain Mac taught Fourth Class English, focusing upon logic, ethics, aesthetics, and expression. He was respectful of poetry and committed to argument. Between defeating the Axis powers and holding the Reds at bay, Captain Mac had earned a master's in English lit from Columbia. Like all good teachers, he brought all that he was into his lessons.

I enjoyed the lessons more than I did his authors. The Academy was enamored of Faulkner, who, late in life, had visited West Point to read from *The Reivers*. He offered the English department a touch of panache in a traditional school of well-oiled slide rules and room-filling, worship-seeking, card-reading analog computers.

Captain Mac never inspected our shoes, our belt buckles, the knots in our black ties, or the press in our charcoal class shirts while we stood to attention in his section, as was the habit of many math professors. Captain Mac petitioned us to push what he called the "outer edge of the envelopes of our beings. *Thinking,* gentlemen, may not be enough in this section." That filled us with nagging fear. What the hell else was there?

Captain Mac's essay topics went to the heart, and sometimes the buttocks, of the Academy experience. "Pros and Cons of Hazing: Evaluating the Fourth Class System," required us to translate our social woes into essay. I wondered: could a heretic critique the Inquisition—and still get a good grade?

I couldn't believe my own answer. The system that starved, shocked, and shackled me was "a worthy exercise for young men in which the desire to belong is implacably tested. The pride and belief produced by commonly enduring the stresses and toils of such a system may be unique in modern American education. As a consequence of this experience, cadets are prepared to aid each other to an unusual degree, a condition common to few schools. Hardship creates bonds. This truth can only be of benefit to the National Security."

"I just wrote an essay in support of *hazing.*"

My roommates looked at me. Joey smiled. "Bang yur stupid crot neck in an' gimme fifty push-ups an' de Days, smackhead."

"The Arguments Pro and Con: Submission of Cadet Grades to Parents" drew strong negative responses from the section. "We are either adults, prepared to defend the Nation, or not," I wrote.

The essay "Should Toleration of Cheating Be the Equal of Cheating Itself?" was the most difficult for me. The Honor Code invoked strict liability; a slight infraction brought the most horrific penalty: expulsion from the Corps under the most painful conditions. A cadet Honor Board took evidence. You would be called into the boardroom in a midnight hearing to face a sword. If the hilt was offered, you were innocent—a grade far above "not guilty." If you faced the sword point, you were dishonorably separated from the Corps, and cadets could not, ever after, speak of you. If found on honor by the Honor Board but reinstated by a successful officers' appeal, no cadets could speak to you during cadetship and for all time, unto death. You would be "silenced," sentenced to live without relationships—a lifetime curse imposed by the school in the mountains and the clouds.

Uncle Shim had told me that this system existed in China. "The worst punishment on earth, *Hausheng*, is *k'ung hsu*, to be ignored and socially abandoned. A person without *gahng* and *lun*, bonds and relationships to others, is a living ghost, unworthy of life."

I had been raised under the rules of Draco and was opposed to his culture, but I wrote, "A failure to attack cheating is as reprehensible as the original crime by the first offender."

Captain Mac wrote: "What if the original offender is your best friend?" Smugly, I wrote above his comment in large capitals, "MY FRIENDS WOULDN'T CHEAT."

It was the topic "Should Chapel Be Mandatory at West Point?" that taught me that emotions were part of life. I hated chapel but was afraid to give an honest answer; this was about the white Christian God, and his house, and could involve any number of consequences. Superstitious fear tugged at my heart. I wrote a cowardly essay in support of mandatory chapel. I realized that if I turned it in, it could be a breach of the Honor Code. I tried again, savaging the system with a fervor that reminded me of Edna's antichurch beliefs. It was hysterical. Again I rewrote it, arguing for abolishment with a logical, clinical objectivity appropriate, I thought, to my dignified maturity.

"Mr. Ting?" called Captain Mac in his refined English accent. I stood at attention before his table, where he sat at the head of a U-shaped array of cadet desks and flanked by the chalkboard walls. There we performed individual recitations, for grades, every day, acting out Sylvanus Thayer's vision of rampant scholasticism.

"Are you in favor of abolishing mandatory chapel?"

"Yes, sir."

"I disagree. You dedicate six pages in support, three against. I am influenced by the fact that you conclude with the argument against, but I found your reasoning for to be more compelling. Please explain the ambiguity."

"Sir, I—I felt a—conflict in writing this essay."

"Mr. Ting, it is my statement to that effect that brought you before my desk. I am not asking you to restate my inquiry. Please answer my questions." Captain Mac's wide face was wrinkled from brow to chin. His crow's-footed eyes had squinted for years, having seen the China that I had not. He slowly rolled his spare, square shoulders—a sign, I thought, of impatience.

"Sir—I—hate mandatory chapel. In my first try, I came out for it, thinking it was the approved solution. Then I realized it could have been an Honor violation. In my second try, I *attacked* mandatory chapel, and got sort of emotional. In my third try, I corrected that, trying to be more—reasonable, sir."

"Yes, Mr. Ting. By all means let us not be *emotional*. Emotion might spring from passion, and passion from conviction. And we cannot have that, can we?" He looked at me.

I thought of the Academy motto: "Duty, Honor, Country."

"Sir, we operate from conviction."

"Good. Take your seat, Mr. Ting." He stood.

"Gentlemen. I expect you to push the outer edge of the envelopes of your *beings*. I have stated that thinking may not be enough in this section room. The question is clear: What else is there, besides thinking, for future officers of the United States Army?" He looked around the U.

"Ah, yes, Mr. Ting. I believe you did not have your hand up. Give us your thoughts about what else there might be."

"Sir," I said. "There's conviction, and passion, and—uh—emotion. I think, sir, under all that is belief."

"Good, Mr. Ting. Thank you. Let me pose another question. Why, in weapons train-fire, are you not provided competition ear covers to block out sound to permit better aiming? Mr. Ziegler."

"Sir," said Rocket Scientist, "we have to aim during combat. You want us to feel our emotions, and operate on our beliefs—our values—not just our intellects."

"Splendid and three-oh, Mr. Ziegler. Thank you. Who here knows something of his classmates in this section?"

All hands went up.

"And who knows something of my background?"

I was surprised to be the only one with my hand up. I liked to research my teachers. I thought everyone did.

"Gentlemen, herein begins the lecture.

"You may find me in the *Register of Graduates and Former Cadets of the U.S. Military Academy* and *Howitzer*. You can study my ribbons, wonder about the sources of all those wrinkles in my old, beat-up face, and surmise at the forces of nature that forced my ears from my head in flaps-up, air-brakes-out fashion." We laughed.

"But that is a small part of the story. Let me tell you about who I am." He sat on his desk.

"I am the son of a crowned regent, taught the ways of war by Sir James, a man of iron. I am a millionaire's son who fell into the sea, where I was rescued by a Portuguese fisherman with a great heart. I know of the time that men must spend with boys," he said, nodding, "if boys are to be men. I rode the Mississippi with Big Jim and sailed the Mediterranean as a Jewish prince condemned to the galleys. I ventured into the heart of darkness to define courage, wielded a musketeer's rapier in countless duels of shallow honor for my vain queen, fled in blind fear from a screaming Rebel charge, and watched Achilles the Achaean indecently drag the slain body of Hector around the walls of Priam's Troy.

"As Cordelia, I yearned for my father's lost love. I was a fifth Chinese daughter; I was Portia, honorable in restraint and sympathetic to the suffering; I was Desdemona, slain by my husband's blindness. I tramped the sewers of Paris with the police hot on my trail. I was Boo Radley's faithful neighbor, but left Maycomb County to travel to Colonus to see the god-blessed monster. In 1984, I resided in room 101, and I was the Savage in a brave new world. I cry for the innocents, shout for the merciful. I experience the pleasures and aches of love, and separation, and loyalty refused, of life given, and patriotism expressed.

"That's who Captain MacPellsin is. I am a reader of books, a fool for libraries, and a sorry, sniveling patsy for Book-of-the-Month Club salesmen. I absorb the instruction in books and retain them for my own use. Someday, on some battlefield, in some crisis, in the stewardship of my children or in my marriage, I will need the lessons of some of their lives to solve the problems in mine."

He stood and circled the U, peering at us. "Gentlemen! This is not merely English 101B. This is *life*. Do not view this as the weak and vague side of your West Point education. All of you in the top sections are excellent students, superior cadet engineers, enamored of numbers and approved solutions." I squirmed in my seat.

"*Feel,* gentlemen! Let passion beat within you! Do you *truly* think the great captains of West Point were just *engineers?* Negative, gentlemen. Any fool with a sword can risk his life for his regent, for his commander-in-chief. No, these were men who sweated, stank, dug maggots out of hardtack, cursed, and struggled—*to protect their men.* Well, perhaps Robert E. Lee did not curse.

"They were great leaders," he said crisply, "because *they loved their men* by acting in their interests. They were morally committed not only to Country but to the honor of dutiful service and to the survival of their people. Cicero said: 'In the observance of duty lies all that is honorable, and in the neglect of it is all that is dishonorable.'

"A leader who does not know the passions of history, or the morality of literature, or the emotions of his soldiers, marches away from the observance of duty and compromises his nation.

"Gentlemen, without Homer, the Trojan War was a domestic spat with boats and some discordant dialogue in Asia Minor. But an old, blind poet, a storyteller of moral tales, has given us a fable for the ages. As soldiers, we can identify with the wise Nestor, the vain and gifted prima donna Achilles, the steady Ajax, the intrepid Diomedes, the loyal Hector, the handsome, frivolous Paris.

"Gentlemen, heed this: passion in the defense of a moral position is consistent with the moral man. It is also linked to your grade in this course. It is no accident that passion contributed to the formation of this country, and of this school, and of well-thought solutions for all human endeavor.

"Lads, you will not learn the ethics of leadership from psychology. Nor can you grasp the wisdom of military leaders who preceded you by studying their movements on bloodless maps and tactics sand tables. You cannot learn about the leading of men without grasping the tapestry of the entire human experience.

"You get that here, in the study of English. English embodies the human condition. You will need this, because outside these walls, you will lead *people,* not *equations.*" He stood, straightened his tunic, and grinned at us.

"End of lecture. Questions? . . . Very good. Stagger desks. For a three-point writ, explain 'The Pros and Cons of Emotion in the Military Leader.' Begin work."

"Captain Mac teaches us to think," I said to Clint Bestier.

"This is West Point," he said. "If they wanted you to think, they wouldn't have given you a slide rule."

"He's that old guy, right?" asked Joey Rensler.

"Watch who you call old," said Bob Lorbus, age twenty-two.

"He must be forty. Why's he only a captain?" asked Clint.

"Flew P-5Is in World War Two," I said. "Three DFCs, Air Medals, Purple Heart, and now is Infantry. Must've been hurt bad to lose flight status. He was in the same unit my father was."

That ended it. It was funny how my roommates gibed each other about everything—girlfriends, buddies, brothers, sisters, sex, politics, private organs, religion, and even mothers. But there was no ribaldry, sarcasm, or ribbing about dads. It was as if everyone were a Chinese son. It had been exactly the opposite in the 'hood, where it was open season on badmouthing fathers, and cursing someone's mother was an invitation to a fight to the finish.

The next essay addressed West Point's academic policy of expelling a cadet for failure in a single course. Joey, Clint, and I were holding on to the Academy with our teeth. They were at risk in English, and I in math, for legend had it that math, the great cadet slayer, would flush all of the lower math sections, where I resided. Major Yerks, our Tac, informed us that another two hundred classmates would be "found"—separated—this year. Plebe athletics, first semester math, and English already had flunked scores of us. We felt the cold breath of failure, seeking victims.

"I miss Stew," I said as I began typing. Stew Mersey and his cursing, his bad moods, his quick mind, his abiding sense of unfair treatment. He showed the feelings I tried to control.

"Anyone could tell Stew was going to quit," said Clint.

"He was always so quick on his feet. He would've done well."

"Nope," said Clint. He licked his lips and coughed. "Stew was only here for his dad. Can't make it here on that alone."

"Who won the Pulitzer Prize for fiction in 1961?" asked Captain Mac. "Mr. Rodgers."

"Sir, it was Miss Harper Lee," said Matthew McBall "Meatball" Rodgers in his distinguished Southern accent.

"Who is Boo Radley?" asked Captain Mac.

"Sir," said Curve Wrecker Davey Glick, "Mr. Radley's your next-door neighbor in Maycomb County, before you left for Colonus."

"Good memory, Mr. Glick. It is my pleasure to inform you that the next assignment is *To Kill a Mockingbird*. You will answer the question, 'Who Is Boo Radley?'"

"We will have the rare pleasure of the author's presence next week. She will address us, and may answer the question herself. This is an honor for West Point. Miss Lee is an exceptional author who has categorically declined all college speaking invitations.

"Gentlemen, this is a coup. A female Pulitzer Prize winner in fiction is coming to West Point. Enjoy this experience to the hilt." He beamed at us, his dark eyes afire. I twitched in my chair under his bright gaze. I had no interest in white Southern authors.

"Mr. Mankoff."

"Sir," said Ravine Mankoff, "what if my answer differs from hers? She has to be the undisputed master of the correct solution. Can I max the writ if I write something different?"

"Mr. Mankoff. You can cold max the writ, so long as—" and Captain Mac raised both arms to the section—

"WE PUSH THE OUTER EDGE OF THE ENVELOPE OF OUR BEINGS!" we chorused, somewhat raggedly.

I read *To Kill a Mockingbird* in one night. I waited until the last possible evening to pick it up. It did not transform my life with the power of religious vision or atomic war, but it was close. I was exhausted when the cannon went off, the buzzer rang, the building shook, and the band's Hellcats broke into the fury of that marvelously stirring hit and perennial favorite, reveille.

I hated the tune. It was cheery and energetic, befitting lambs prancing down a wooded country lane in late spring, eating ivy, looking forward to a day of gentle grazing.

"Piss me off . . . hate dat damn gun . . . too early . . . get up ta dis crap . . . buzzer an' dat bullcrap-eatin' tune . . . miserable, lousy, assbite Army musicians . . . play too loud . . . where the *hell* are my frickin' socks?" Joey's Bronx cheer never appeared at dawn.

"Hiya, buddy!" said Bob Lorbus, grinning as he thumped Joey on his chest. I had slept less than an hour, but churning thickly through my tired blood and math-beaten brain were the spirits of Scout, Jem, Atticus, Tom Robinson, Calpurnia, and Boo. I had been touched by an author who saw evil in familiarity, and hope within an old culture predicated in so many ways on despair. I realized that I had known nothing about the South, despite having read *Gone with the Wind*.

An old tune ran through my sluggish mind, and I smiled. It

was an old 'hood song, chanted by kids and mommas alike. Its structure was like storytelling, allowing anyone to throw in his own stanza, so long as it rhymed. I used to call it the "Papa Ditty," but it was more commonly known as the mockingbird song.

> *Well, I'll tell you what I learned*
> *Papa gonna buy me a mockinbird.*
> *If that mockinbird don' sing,*
> *Papa's gonna buy me a diamond ring.*
> *If that diamond ring don' shine,*
> *Papa's gonna buy me a bottle a wine.*
> *If that bottle a wine don't pour . . .*

To Kill a Mockingbird indicted a way of life in San Francisco. My old neighborhood had been an urban version of the shantytown where the Robinsons lived, shunted off and away from white people. And folks in the 'hood had been hard on Sippy Suds just like the folks in Maycomb had been bad to Boo Radley.

I felt as if I had a read a book with fire in its pages, scourging prejudice in any form.

Atticus, the lawyer, had liked his children. Lawyers defended the poor, the weak, the victims of prejudice and unfairness and abuses of power. There were lawyers in the Army.

Mockingbird became my standard for judging books. I wrote more energetically in my journal, and was no longer inclined to judge a book before I read it.

I asked "Pensive" Hamblin what he thought of it. Pensive was from Meridian, Mississippi. "Segregation was sin, but integration's killin' us. Story like that, it coulda happened. Prob'ly did." He shook his head sadly. "If so, things gotta change. But I surely hate a damn Yankee captain ta tell me about it."

"Stagger desks, gentlemen," said Captain Mac. "Answer the question: 'Who Is Boo Radley?' " Desks were shifted to disarm inadvertent glances.

I was too tired to remember the ecstasy of the story. Soporifically, I remembered "critical analysis." I was transformed. I could write English and change lives. I was going to be analytical. Boo Radley, I wrote, was a symbol for the wretched of the earth, whose goodness could only be perceived by a child still in a state of innocence. Frightened by an abusive world,

Boo Radley was reduced to being able to relate, at a distance, only to children. "The Harper Leeaic Voice," I opined, "utilizes Boo Radley as the perigee of social hierarchy. The apogee is Atticus Finch, Father, Attorney, Arbiter of Justice and Advocate for the Weak. Scout is the mechanism of realization."

Thirty minutes passed. "Cease work!" ordered Captain Mac. A cascade of pens fell onto desktops, since continuing to write after the cease-work order constituted an Honor violation.

I received a 2.4—a miserable grade, similar to a C-plus. Captain Mac had not been impressed:

Why try for academic criticism or mastery of the obtuse? You write as if you are firing Roget's machine gun, belt-fed from a NASA thesaurus. Boo Radley is many things to many people, based on their unique feelings and individual experiences. He is a loner. We are a band of individuals being formed into a community. He is the outsider, within. Have you ever felt the outsider? Who is Boo Radley to Kai Ting the person? I care little about Kai Ting, Critical Essayist. The author wrote about social injustice. Where's the passion? Where's the outer edge of your envelope? Push the throttle, Mr. Ting.
CPT Mac

I was deflated. I thought I had found some truths and had used some exceptionally fancy English to express them. Harper Lee, I thought, was not as fantastic as I'd originally imagined.

I returned to Shakespeare with relief. Following Harper Lee's upcoming lecture, we were going to be examined on three of the Bard's tragedies. Joey and Clint were trying to avoid becoming two more of them. Captain Mac informed us that one of the exam points would be the use of irony.

"How'd Shakespeare use irony?" I asked. Blank faces. "What's ironic about *Romeo and Juliet?*"

"Girl an' boy," said Joey in his rich Bronx tones, which were beginning to affect my highly absorbent speech patterns. "Here, dat's irony."

"Girl, boy, and no sex," said Clint. "Here, that's *not* irony."

"Try again," I said.

"All dem fancy clothes, an' no ironin' at all," said Joey.

"How about love instigating hate?" I asked, looking at him. He clapped his hand to his forehead. "Got it," he said.

I smiled. "Okay, *Othello?*"

"Black and white," said Joey.

"Good," I said. "Now, one level deeper."

Two blank faces, four shrugging shoulders.

"Othello's a Muslim general," I said, "defending Venetian Christians against fellow Muslims. Weird, right? Okay, think about *Julius Caesar*. Think about Mark Antony."

Nothing. "Clint?" I said. He shook his head.

"Antony," I said, "in front of his Romans and countrymen, compliments Brutus for killing Caesar. But what really happens?"

"He tells the Thayer joke and dey get a Fall-out with Big Bites," said Joey.

"Doesn't the mob get pissed at Brutus?" asked Clint.

"Right! Antony uses irony to nail Brutus!" I said.

"I need an equation for dis crap," said Joey. "Who gives a shit 'bout irony, copper, brass, or any of that stuff?"

"Kai—enough," said Clint. "Shakespeare, Byron, Keats— what a bunch of rot. Hey—we're gonna be late. I woulda thought you'd be first there. You *like* this junk."

"Aw," I said, "she's just an author."

The irony of their having a Chinese-American roommate who enjoyed the class that could flunk them out of West Point was something over which Joey, Clint, and I often kidded.

"Too bad we don't have to take *Chinese*," Clint said. "I'd probably do better'n you."

South Aud—or Odd—South Auditorium in Thayer Hall— was a new, twelve-hundred-seat theater wired for sound and light. Here, during Beast, had come instruction on the Honor Code, on the Code of Conduct for POWs, and on the objectives of tactics instruction. Here, next month, the Firsties, the seniors, would learn which branch—Infantry, Armor, Artillery, Signal Corps, or Engineers—was to be theirs to serve as second lieutenants. Beyond the walls waited MACV, Military Assistance Command, Vietnam—which needed Infantry platoon leaders.

When the aud seated upperclassmen, it boomed with the deep, bright bass of high-hormoned males. With us, it hummed with the whispers and low tones of muted voices. Tonight, under subdued lighting fit for a state funeral, we were even quieter. I sat with Clint, Joey, Bob, Arch Torres, tall Hawk Latimer, and Pee Wee McCloud. There were ample seats due to class attrition. We used to fill the aud. I remembered the absent ones, how they had looked in soaked fatigues during the scorching days of Beast, trying to hold on, trying to meet expectations, trying not to be the boys who left West Point in a summer that was too hot. The lights dimmed.

Colonel Sutherland, the mustached head of the Department of English, approached the podium on the high stage below us. He was a lean patrician with high, angular shoulders, walking with a stateliness born to royalty or induced by bad knees. He had been an Infantry officer in Europe and had become a Doctor of Philosophy from the University of Pennsylvania. He looked like Don Quijote.

Colonel Sutherland welcomed us to "a signal event." Limited, he said, by the modesty of our guest, he was merely going to introduce her. He then described the unprecedented honors that had been paid Harper Lee for her work. He did not complain that the Superintendent had failed to direct the entire Corps to appear for the lecture. Appropriate applause was delivered, and Clint, Joey, and other English goats settled deeper into the comfortable padding of their seats, preparing to catch some badly needed rest. Plebe year operated on the axiom that an hour in the rack was an hour away from West Point. There was a gentle snort as classmates awoke someone who had already collapsed into the arms of Morpheus, even before the arrival of the Harper Leeaic voice.

Miss Harper Lee sat at a small table on stage.

"Good evening, General Jannarone, Colonel Sutherland, faculty of the Department of English, ladies and gentlemen, and gentlemen of the Fourth Class of the Corps of Cadets."

She was a small person, conservatively garbed in a simple dark dress, her hair wrapped into a conservative bun atop her head. Her voice was softly Southern, with high musical notes, and crystal clear in a hall that was utterly silent. It reminded me of someone, and I sat up, breathing rapidly.

"This is very exciting," she said slowly, "because I do not speak at colleges. The prospect of it is too intimidating. Surely, it's obvious—rows of bright, intense, focused students, some even of the sciences, all of them analyzing my every word and staring fixedly at me—this would terrify a person such as myself.

"So, I wisely agreed to come here, where the atmosphere would be far more relaxing and welcoming than on a rigid, strict, rule-bound, and severely disciplined college campus."

The auditorium erupted in laughter, something we had not yet done together, and it released tensions that had begun on

Reception Day, had increased through the rigors of Beast and Plebe year and the loss of friends, and until now had not been freed. I laughed until Clint hit me to shut up. We applauded thunderously, which probably confused her.

"She's great," I breathed.

"If we were blessed with parents who love, and who love others," she said a while later, "we have souls who will live within us for all our lives. They fortify us in times of need, strengthening our hearts when we need strengthening most. Most of you young men are in this category, of having been loved by family, aided and cared for by people who know you best."

I thought of Toos and his mother, Tony, Uncle Shim. I thought of Jack Peeve and his parents, and all the people at the Y.

"Today we are urged to live beyond our homes, in industry, education, the professions. Here we are in the midst of some who do not love, do not cherish our quaint habits, and are uncaring about our needs. This experience need not be sad, but it is clearly different than being with family."

She took a small sip of water from the tumbler on the table.

"When we seek to replace family in new environs, we seek to reestablish trust, and love, and comfort.

"But all too often, we end up establishing difference instead of love. We like to have all our comforts and familiars about us, and tend to push away that which is different, and worrisome.

"That is what happened to Boo Radley, and to Tom Robinson.

"They were not set apart by evil men, or evil women, or evil thoughts. They were set apart by an evil past, which good people in the present were ill equipped to change.

"The irony is, if we divide ourselves for our own comfort, *no one* will have comfort. It means we must bury our pasts by seeing them, and destroy our differences through learning another way.

"Of course, many people, not including a *soul* present tonight, come from families that include members who do not like change, do not love their neighbors, detest their own children, despise people of other colors, and loathe those from other states.

"As a writer, I am fascinated with these people, cursed with hate, overladen with dislikes. For they contain within their souls the foibles and weaknesses of us all."

I sighed.

"Our response to these people represents our earthly test. And I think," she said, speaking to the small microphone before her, her hands crossed on her lap, her head at a small angle, as if she were studying it, "that these people enrich the wonder of our lives. It is they who most need our kindness, *because* they seem less deserving. After all, *anyone* can love people who are lovely."

I thought of Christine, who was lovely, and not easy to love.

"Are these principles for life? Perhaps. Some of this affected me when I wrote *To Kill a Mockingbird*. To me, it is a simple love story about family and honoring that which is good."

Love. A lecture on love and tolerance at the United States Military Academy, from a woman novelist speaking to a society of men. I could hear the air ducts dusting the air in the auditorium. An unoiled chair distantly squeaked near the back of the aud.

"People in the press have asked me if this book is descriptive of my own childhood, or of my own family.

"Is this very important? I am simply one who had time and chance to write. I was that person before, and no one in the press much cared about the details of my life. I am yet that same person now, who only misses her former anonymity.

"So I tell people, because curiosity is both natural and wonderful, that in every character who appears in any story, the author draws from life some who are known to her, and some whom she has met through her reading of other, more capable authors."

Soon it was time for the questions. Five of the top cadets, who had written superior essays on Boo Radley, took seats behind a table on the right of the stage: Mike Benjamin, Sonny "Rap" Rappa, Davey Curve Wrecker Glick, Rocket Scientist Mercury Ziegler, and "Gentleman" Jules Green.

"Good evening, Miss Lee. I am Cadet Fourth Classman Michael Warren Benjamin. The members of the Fourth Class *uniformly*"—he paused, smiling his bright Clark Gable grin— "enjoyed your book. We were asked by our professors to answer the question 'Who Is Boo Radley?' I have taken a composite of the answers to form a question: Does Boo Radley represent a tension of transference, and the failure of social mobility between the lower classes and the nobility, or does he represent the ultimate demise of the vanishing classical hero, or is he an icon of the continuing tension between Locke and Hobbes?"

Crap! I thought. What a question!

"Goodness, Mr. Benjamin," she said, laughing. "I recall Boo Radley as the poor, lonely fellow who lived in that house next door to the Finches."

Again the class roared in laughter. I felt like crying. Her voice and softly spoken, musical words caressed my brain, encouraging tears. I felt as if I were losing control as nameless emotions surged wildly and feared I was going crazy and would begin laughing uncontrollably. Focus—look for Captain Mac. He was in the first row on the right. I studied the woman with short brown hair with him, and the boy on his lap. A girl, maybe eight, leaned on his shoulder. He seemed happy to have his children so physically close to him. He was smiling openly at Harper Lee. His smile was infectiously warm. I took a deep, shuddering breath.

I thought of the multitude of answers we could produce that Captain Mac would deem correct, as long as we were honest and tried to reach beyond our conventional limits. Math did not seek honesty; it sought precision in accordance with proven principle. Calculus produced a single approved solution. Engineering reminded me of many things I did not like.

Miss Lee spoke of writing family stories, and thought those with pain and disorder were more engaging than those without. I figured that was going too far, but my warm admiration for her, confirmed by Captain Mac's smile, was boundless.

As we marched back, bracing, eyes straight ahead, we whispered, hissing speech escaping from the corners of our mouths.

"Arch," I asked, "how can I love a woman who's so old?"

"Heck," he whispered, "since R-Day, I love *all* women. Jean at the Thayer. Mrs. Holland, the cadet hostess. The statue of Fame on Battle Monument. I like Blondie in the comics. Models in *The New York Times*. I love all the secretaries."

"This is different."

"That's cuz *being here* is different," he hissed.

"Her voice remind you of someone?" I asked. Arch had dated more girls than I had met.

"Southern ladies," he said.

"She reminds me of someone I knew, a long time ago," I said. "Can't remember who. It's her voice, how musical it is. I mean, that voice really got to me. But I didn't know anyone white from the South. It wasn't the accent, it was the tone. Damn, that's so strange. Arch—think she'd write back if I wrote her?"

We passed under the dual streetlights at Thayer Road and shut up until we entered the dark alley to New South Barracks.

"Right!" he hissed. " 'Dear Miss Lee, I'm one of eight hundred faceless cadets in dress gray you spoke to at West Point. Please write. And send food. Your big fan, Kai.' Fat chance. I got a better chance of getting a date with Queen Elizabeth."

"Didn't know ya were tryin'," said Joey.

"Hey. Aim low, hit low," he whispered.

16

LOSS

Old South Barracks, West Point, May 1965

It was in May, when the upper classes radiate benevolence, when Plebes are BJ and robins serenade in five-note calls, that the debonaire Marco Matteo Fideli came calling. I was writing a letter to Christine when he bashed in our door and Clint, Joey, and I responded like the Three Little Pigs.

"SLAM BODIES ON THE WALL!" Pens, books, Kiwi polish cans, and shoe-shine rags flew in the air as we thundered against the wall.

"I just heard that you are D in math," he hissed like a hungry, malevolent wolf. "And that Rensler and Bestier are D in English. DID I HEAR INCORRECTLY?"

"NO, SIR!" we squealed.

"YOU WILL HIVE 'TIL THE RHODES COMMITTEE SINGS YOUR PRAISE! Mr. Ting, drive your goat brains to Trophy Point after Chapel."

Under the broad shade of Battle Monument, he asked if I knew how stupid it would be for me to be found. The day was hot. I remembered the morning sun on the river road, a year ago, when my life seemed full of unlimited promise.

"The fates are flirting with you, preparing to write your name on the list of the Immortals." Immortals were former cadets, expelled or separated from the Academy for deficiencies in brains, brawn, or will. Many simply had quit and walked away. They were frozen in the memories of their classmates as last seen—boys in the stasis of nascent manhood, forever young, forever separated from the collective.

"To be an Immortal is no grand objective," he said. "It is the one way to achieve notoriety without talent." He was so handsome, and I imagined the breathless beauty of his girlfriend.

"Caruso, Boethius was a fellow paisan who gave us *De consolatione philosophiae*. If he were with us, he'd recognize Fame." Mr. Fideli pointed up, to the figure of the winged, scantily clad, golden girl. "Below her, the dead." He motioned to the monument to the 2,230 men and officers of the Regular Army killed in the Civil War, consecrated by their surviving comrades. He turned to face Thayer and Bartlett Halls, the playing fields. "There, Endeavor and Strength. In the admin building management meets, but really they pray to Athena for Wisdom." He smiled thinly. "She comes when she will." He looked at the flag. "Duty, Patria. Up there, on the rock, with the chapels, Boethius gives way to St. Augustine's Faith, Hope, and Love. In the barracks is our collective heart—Brotherhood and Honor."

He faced east. "The river is Providence and Grace, too grand to be understood by us." He exhaled. "It'd be the failing of your young life to get found. Caruso, you're fighting a demon. I don't know its name. Nor may you. No doubt it's from your past." He nodded at the river and the rock. "This is now. Make it bigger and stronger than your old demon. Engineer a solution. And hurry."

Clint, Joey, and I began to muck. "No more wisecrack answers," I said. They agreed. We reviewed the basic structure of essay writing. Clint got it and Joey didn't. Miss Harper Lee's appearance meant that *Mockingbird* would appear prominently in the heart of the WFR, written final review, or whufer, so we retraced the plot, broke down the characters, and established the probable thematic messages, intended or not. Clint got it and Joey didn't.

"Pop's prouda me," Joey said. "I'm gonna get the college degree and commission he didn't get."

"Don't say that," I said. "Indulge my Chinese superstitions."

Joey smiled, just like Danny Kaye. "Okay," he said dubiously.

Clint passed. Joey and ten other members of our company Plebes didn't, and faced a final "turn out" exam. If they passed, they were in. If they failed, they were out. Curve Wrecker Glick, Mercury Ziegler, and I worked on prepping Joey.

I passed math. Mr. McWalters congratulated me by allowing me, Curve Wrecker, and Rocket Scientist to eat leftovers from other tables with Big Bites. I was at work when Mr. Fideli sat beside me.

"Pray continue. I dare not interfere with art. I'm delighted that Athena smiled on you. No, I don't want any more beef ragout." He smiled brightly. "Report to my room after Grad Parade. I'm giving you my shako. Use it to carry a tune. I will miss our talks and your Broadway ditties." He gazed at the cavernous mess hall, where only the chowhounds were at labor. His time here was short. I would miss him. I almost put down my fork. I felt his nostalgia. He was going to give me his plumed full-dress cadet helmet.

"Do you know why I adopted you?"

I chewed and swallowed. "Sir, my sense of humor. My dash, my cultured suaveness, my table manners and dainty eating habits?"

"It was your frown during the first clothing formation. Never before had I seen one of such intensity, such *gravity*—a frown of pure Grecian pathos. I decided, despite the fact that your singing bore the promise of long-dead fish, I would try to make you smile."

"You did that, sir." The words "Tragedy tomorrow, Comedy tonight!" rang through my mind. A little song, a little dance, a little seltzer down our pants. I grinned with a mouthful of food.

"Well, we're off to win a war. I wish you well, Kai Ting. Good luck. Don't forget to drop by after P-rade."

"Best of luck to you, shir," I said, my mouth full.

Clint ran into the mess hall, bracing. "Hurry!" he hissed.

On the H-1 company bulletin board was a list of academically disqualified cadets passed down by the Academic Board:

David Neil Alduss/found: mathematics
Jeremy Odette Conoyer III/found: mathematics
Terrence Phillip Dirkette/found: English and German
Peck Levine Mankoff/found: physical education (swimming)
Earl Tecumseh Mims/found: English

Joseph NMN Rensler II/found: English

When Clint and I returned to the room, Joey was packing, his cot rolled, and Bob had his head down, praying. I shook my head. Man, what good would that do?

Joey shook my hand. "Thanks, Kai, for helpin' me."

I shook my head. "Not good enough," I said.

"Hey, I tried, honest."

"*I'm* not good enough," I said.

"Hey, book outa here!" said Joey. "You're great. De greatest! Watch—dey'll require Chinese. I'll come back an' do ya proud!"

I couldn't say anything.

"I'll jus be down de block in de Bronx." He was going into the Infantry as a private first class, eligible for Vietnam.

The thirty of us had become twenty. Jean at the Thayer Hotel had been right; we had lost one out of three. Then I remembered the losses from Beast, before academics had even begun, and physics, chemistry, Juice, nuclear physics, and more math awaited us.

The companies stood in massed formation of gray and white, gold and steel, for Graduation Parade. The Firsties, sabers drawn, broke ranks and marched out as a class toward the north end of the plain and the river, leaving the Corps behind to the heart-pounding tune of the West Point March. It was a song that brought a tear to the hardest heart, the most cynical Plebe, the oldest soldier, its irresistible melody impressing upon us the timelessness of an Academy graduation, and the significance of losing classmates and the seniors, the Class of 1965. They would always be giants to me.

"Bye, Pete!" "See ya, Bill!" "So long, Johnny!" called out the Cows and Yearlings, in a traditional valediction that, through the crash of drums and bugles, the deafening cheers and applause, the forty thousand in attendance never heard. Goodbye, I whispered. Bye Marco and Mario Fideli, Bo Kleiner, "Bela Lugosi" Kirchhoff, Big Jim Stoner the heartless pirate, Jake Kimure, captain of the gym team, Roger Stichweh, our quarterback, and Fitz McBay, Southern Traditionalist. Guan Yu, keep your big spear above their heads.

The Class of '68 had done its last bracing. In Recognition, the final exercise of Plebe year, we stood at attention and extended our arms above our heads, holding our rifles high while the upper classes bashed in our shiny brass breastplates with their rifle butts and etched their names into the metal with their sabers. I felt like the cherry tree under George Washington's axe. Then they shook our hands, telling us their first names. It was a surprise that some of those people even *had* first names.

Most of us managed to avoid Mr. O'Ware's offered hand. Arch and I had not been so lucky. "Frenchy O'Ware," he said, offering to shake, his white glove off: the glove that had found dust where there was none; the glove with the pointing digit, illuminating failures, or differences that were our weaknesses; the glove of a bigot who had taken pleasure from our fears.

"Kai Ting." I thought of the names he had called Stew Mersey, the nights he had taken from me because he didn't like my face.

"Arch Torres," he said, shaking O'Ware's hand firmly. "That's for public consumption." He smiled. "Frenchy, you ever screw with any Plebes like you did us, I'll kick your sorry ass from here to the river."

All of the Hell-One's former Plebes gathered in the middle of the hallway in the central division of company barracks.

"We made it, guys," said Bob "Big Bus" Lorbus. He put his hand out in the middle, palm down, and twenty hands piled on top.

"Absent friends and comrades," said Bob, and we repeated it, loudly and with great force, shaking the walls, my voice the loudest.

Arch Torres and Deke Schibsted joined Lorbus and me in our room. We all collapsed on the floor, happy to let the earth support us, feeling like survivors from a year-long airplane crash. We had become upperclassmen. By working nineteen hours a day and by carrying twenty semester hours while dancing with the TD, dodging OPE, taking military training and a pre-Olympics sports schedule, we had squeezed two and a half years of life and two years of college into twelve months. That was why I missed Joey Rensler, Ravine Mankoff, Tecumseh Mims, and the others, so much.

There were shouts in the hallway. With a big roar, most of our classmates squeezed into the room, led by Clint. "Man, we just dropped a Mountain BA on Frenchy O'Ware—it grossed him so bad he fell down the stairs!"

"It was *atomic!*" shouted Chad "The Man" Enders.

"Nuclear," cried Jimmy Buns Butte. "Five man base, three on the second row, one on top, and four on the side for dressing!"

"It was perfect!" crooned Rocket Man Ziegler. "O'Ware chugs those stairs, head down. He crests the steps and eyeballs thirteen bare derrieres pointed at him, dead-on, in the cross hairs—then Chad takes his picture with a Polaroid flash."

"Frenchy just upped and died," drawled Meatball Rodgers. "Threw his rifle in the air and commenced to bounce down the whole damn staircase."

"It was outa sight," said Moon Shine reverently.

Clint spoke quietly in my ear while the crowd passed around the Polaroid. "He'll never call you names again," said Clint.

Most of the Corps had left. I was a pinger, a fast mover through cadet tasks, but now I dawdled. I didn't want to go home. Clint said he'd go with me over to Second Regiment to visit Pee Wee McCloud.

"Stay in shape for Buckner," said Bob. "It's gonna be real physical." Buckner would teach us advanced infantry skills and patrolling. It sounded serious. It was the stuff my father knew.

I would run on the beach every day. I would go home for that. I was going to ask Christine for a date. I was going to see Tony and tell him about Coach Fabrizi. Winterland, '47. I looked out our window; never again would the clock tower seem so foreboding, such an enemy of overspent Plebe time. Although tens of thousands of exulting celebrants were here, West Point seemed quiet and subdued.

The Firsties were gone. They and the Great American Public were at Michie Stadium, listening to the address by the Chairman of the Joint Chiefs, General Earle Wheeler. In thirty minutes, First Captain Robert Arvin would call the Class of '65 to attention and dismiss them. They would scream and throw their white cadet hats in the air, members of the Long Gray Line.

After packing, Clint and I strode through the unique quiet of the Academy, through the ghostly hush of Central Area, to Second Regiment's East Barracks.

"Guys," said Pee Wee slowly in his deep voice, "stay for retreat. Promised Dad I'd remember our classmates who didn't make it, at retreat, last day of Plebe year." Pee Wee's size and goofy voice had drawn hazing, but when the upperclassmen realized that Pee Wee was a hive and tutor to others in all subjects, they had felt affection for the buffoonish-sounding genius who played excellent football and beat everyone in chess.

We stood at attention on the Plain, no longer bracing. The cannon boomed and we saluted as the lone bugler played retreat against the falling summer sun. The melancholy, almost tragic, echoing bugle call wafted through the low hills of the Academy, and I thought of those now gone who, for many long months, had heard this same bugle at the end of the longest days of their lives. The last note sounded. We ordered arms. "Rituals are important," said Pee Wee thickly. "Hardly have them in America, anymore."

Pee Wee had us do this at Lake Fredericks, the Plebe encampment at the end of Beast. We had stood together, eleven months ago as four Beast roomies, our rifles slung, saluting retreat and wondering if we could last a year of Plebedom. Now we were three—two sons of generals and a son of a Chinese colonel.

On the way to Marco Fideli's room, Clint said, "Makes me wonder if Joey woulda passed, if you weren't also coaching me."

Marco Fideli's room was full of spanking-new second lieutenants and I saluted. One of them, Lars McCreary, smiled and gave me a dollar bill as a certificate of having been the first to salute him. All of them had elected Infantry. Mr. Fideli's tar bucket hat was on his desk. In it was a large, rolled envelope.

"Open it later, Caruso." He shook hands, recognizing us.

"Good luck in Vietnam, Marco, and thank you." I crushed his hand in mine, and had the same feeling I had experienced when I left Tony the year before. Clint and Pee Wee watched us.

I later put the envelope in my B-4 bag. Sonny, Mike, and I caught a C-141 from McGuire to Kelly Air Force Base in San Antonio to spend a week together in the home of Colonel and Mrs. Benjamin. On the 141, while eating a second box lunch, I opened it.

When you feel like frowning, sing. Hold my tarbucket, remember my voice, and don't worry—just sing in round, full tones, fearing nothing. Sing "Amazing Grace" or "Sons of Slum and Gravy." When you sing, God's with you, and there can be no despair. When you feel contemplative, write. You have the hearing that Beethoven lacked. Read Augustine's *Enchiridion*, grasp Seneca's sordid appreciation of Honor, and strive to write *satura*—prose with poetry—as Boethius. I am so glad that you will be a West Pointer. We need you. God bless you.
Marco

Behind the letter was a black-and-white etching: *Beethoven Listening to the Storm*. He sat, uncaring, with his sketchbook against a tree bending perilously in a gusting wind, composing.

I imagined telling Tony: "I met a paisan who adopted me last year. He sings Italian opera and he nicknamed me 'Caruso.' "

"Good name fer ya," he'd say. "Ya sing like a ruptured duck."

The flight landed at Travis before dawn, and I entered the Y as it was opening its doors at seven for the Saturday crowd. I watched Leroy and his new assistant. They took valuables, rang up sales, passed towels and basketballs, and answered the phone. The new guy was not as good as I had been. He made people wait too long, didn't smile at anyone, and wasn't enjoying himself. After a year that had seemed so much longer, Leroy was moving with greater method. He was slowing down. I felt that this was my fault. I shouldn't have left. I waited in line, smiled broadly as Leroy said, "Hey!" and shook my hand in his soft mitt. He and I never said much; our companionship was formed by work and not by words. He winked, I shook hands with the new guy and went to the elevator.

The ring was empty. Tony would be at his desk struggling with fight evaluation cards. He wrote the way I would if I used my feet.

"Paisan, che a!" I shouted as I entered the office. It was empty. Tony's desk was so clean it looked dead. I opened the old drawers. They were empty. I was blinking a lot, looking around the tiny office for an explanation. I rubbed my short scalp. Oh, God. I walked around and sat slowly in his chair, as if he were in it. I rubbed the top of the desk and my hands were deep in dust.

"Junggworen," I said. "How's the Junior Leaders?"

"Hey! Kai Ting!" said Pinoy Punsalong, the intermediate boxing instructor. Pinoy was part *junggworen*—Chinese. He was also part Japanese, part French, part Filipino, and all heart. He rose from the lobby office desk. We shook hands. He was unchanged, his wide face youthfully round and tautly smooth, his eyes limpidly bright. Omar Sharif in *Lawrence of Arabia* had Punsalong eyes.

"You look great, Pinoy. And yeah, I look skinny again."

"Is okay. I *like* skinny. Only you, and Tony, like *muscle-*

bound. Skinny mean *speed*. *Move*. Junior Leaders do fine. Hey! Everybody!" he shouted. "This Kai Ting—last year, president, Junior Leaders. Now, West Point cadet!" The light music of Ping-Pong ended as paddles clattered on the thin wood tables, and the kids playing checkers rose from the tables to stand around me. My picture was still on the wall. I thought I looked goofy, as if my face and my arms didn't belong to the same body.

"Kai Ting!"

"Hi, Bobby . . . Michael! How you, bloods?" I shook hands with them all, and with the Junior Leaders, the old and the new, glad to be back. It smelled like boys. I remembered the first time I had entered the lobby. I was seven, barely able to open the door. The trophies had looked like cups for giants, and the Ping-Pong tables like aircraft carriers.

"How hard is it, man?" asked Joe Davis, the third of four brothers. A bodybuilder, he had doubled his size.

"Hey, are you lookin' good?" I said as he smiled with all his teeth, proud of his work. "It was hard," I said. "No food."

Everyone's eyes opened wide. "That what happen in the Army?"

"Just West Point," I said. "Only West Point does that. When you get drafted in the Army, they'll feed you."

"You know how ta kill people?" asked a rookie seven-year-old member.

"Not really," I said, jarred by the question. "I'm good with a rifle. But Mr. P. teaches more unarmed fighting than I learned at the Academy so far. But I've only been there a year."

"You like it?" asked Mike Fox.

I thought for a moment. "Yes, I do like it." I smiled. "I like it a great deal now that Plebe year's over." I was aware that I was speaking formally, the way Captain Mac spoke. "Now I can eat."

They studied me. I sensed the weight of a passing year, of the coin that Plebe year at West Point carried for them, for many boys in America. I was no longer one of them. The year had traversed twelve months, and it felt like a lifetime, as if I had returned from a distant land and romantic wars.

"Okay, everybody buzz away—we're talking," said Pinoy, waving his arm. The group disbanded. Pinoy put his hands on his hips. "You study your *wu-shu*, Chinese martial art?" he asked.

"Just the *liang-jiang*." I looked at him. He read my face.

He nodded. "Tony take vacation. *First* time, ever." He stepped into me on silent feet, inside the reach of my arms in a flashing moment, as if he were in the ring and I were dead meat for the picking of his fists. I was taller, but he lowered his head. "Tony gone look for the boy, Tony Jr.," he whispered. "His boy your age. Man now. He go Italy, look, *real* hard. May stay." He backed up.

Tony gone . . . may stay. I had trouble breathing.

Pinoy studied me. "Proud of you," he said.

Tony had lost his boy, and now I had lost him.

"You light candle at St. Boniface, for Connie?" he asked.

"No," I said quietly.

"You come with me, light candle with me," he urged.

"Okay."

"You worse Catholic I ever know, whole world."

"I'm not Catholic," I said.

"Ayyy! *See?* You confess that in front of God?"

He grabbed my arm, shaking it, making my head wobble. "Come, do *wing chun gong fu*—arm-blocking drill. Like old days. And, buy me donuts for breakfast at Angie's an' say hi to Sally Craft. They happy to see you! Then, go church, pray to patron saint." St. Jude, patron saint of lost causes, once the most unpopular of all saints because people had confused him with Judas.

"You not so orphan no more. You owe him, *plenty*. Right?"

I nodded my head. "Tony, too. And you, and Barney," I said.

Pinoy looked at me. "Okay," he said, "we pray St. Jude for Tony and his boy. Sure, you miss him. Hey. Don't be sad! Tony okay. You know, Barney not here, either. He big boss now at Oakland Y."

Barney and Tony, gone. "They say anything about me before leaving?" I asked.

Pinoy hit my arm hard. "You forget what YMCA is. This place for street kids. Otherwise, they drink, fight knives, go to hell. You grown man now. Little boys, they need Tony and Barney. Not you. Besides, you know—Tony not real sentimental."

In the garage below lay shark jaws, deer antlers, rams' horns, old Chevy engines, and punctured German helmets. I knocked.

"Hi, Mrs. Peeve." I hardly recoiled as she hugged me.

"Oh, don't cry!" I urged.

She shook her head as she pulled a hanky from her apron and blew her nose. "Papa and Uncle Yorch are at work. Jack's gone. He's at Fort Lewis, Washington State. He didn't write you, did he?"

I shook my head.

"It's so lonely without him. And the war. God, if anything happens to him . . ." She began to cry. "Come in," she said wetly.

"I really can't. Haven't been home yet. Just wanted to say hi. Can I have Jack's address? I'm sorry I didn't write." Oh, man, I thought, looking at her. I hadn't written to Momma LaRue or Toussaint.

"Where have you been? How did you get here so early?"

"Hello." My ears began to ring deep inside my head.

"You probably came back to see Christine. What have you been doing? How long will you stay? Have you told your father that you've arrived? Didn't school let out over a week ago?"

"Yes. I've been with Mike Benjamin's family in San Antonio. He's a classmate. I haven't called Dad yet. I'm staying for a week, then I'm heading back. I want to see Christine. And eat. I didn't want to come home at first. But I left St. Boniface and just jumped on the L car, without thinking. Is Dad at work?"

"I dislike your tone. This is so *rude*, showing up without the *slightest* notice. You were probably with those Italian and Negro people at the Y. What were you doing at St. Boniface? Your last church was Christian Science."

I looked at her face, handsome but angry, familiar, pain inflicting, smoldering from our history of discord.

"You're frowning," she said.

"I am being rude. I should've called, but I didn't. I'm sorry. I won't blame you if you want me to leave. I can stay at the Bachelor Officers Quarters at the Presidio." I hadn't been sincere in my apologies to her. "I'm sorry," I would hiss, between clenched teeth—sorry I screwed up one of your stupid, illogical, unfair, tyrannical, and petty little stinking rules. Hollow offerings, worth nothing. She was angry.

"Going to bust an airplane?" I asked, charitably.

Edna drew in breath, her mouth open. I had learned in the last year how to face anger. I put on my inscrutable Plebe face, through which no emotion leaked and no pain was visible. I could endure Beast, march with a rifle, steel pot, and fifty pounds on my back up heartbreaking hills, recite MacArthur, sweat pennies, go without food, sleep, or rest, or raise a table-limits pot on the fourth round for a pair of threes. I could stay up late and could somehow pass the first year of a college engineering curriculum while undergoing more discipline than the boys on Alcatraz.

She had gained weight, but her lean and cool aspect was unperturbed. She wore a simple navy dress, against which her brightly blond hair produced a two-tone rainbow of blue and gold.

"You look nice," I said.

She closed her mouth. "Well, thank you. That is a handsome uniform. I am astonished; you look good in it."

"Can I come in?"

She backed up. I entered and took off my garrison cap. The living room, the flowered couch, the ashtray, Dad's large reading chair, where he absorbed the books of the world, the television—all looked the same, but smaller.

"I got the flowers you sent through your friend Duke."

She stepped away and returned with a letter. It was from Luther "Duke" Troth, in New York City, to me. She had tried to reseal the envelope, but it opened easily the moment I touched it.

This is for your mother. Sorry for any misunderstandings. I'll give you a call during leave. I hope we can be friends. Best wishes, Duke

"They were lovely," said Edna. "They're dead now; had you returned earlier, you could have seen them."

"I didn't send them and he's no friend."

"Oh, do make up with him. He sent his picture, in uniform, which I kept. He's quite—presentable—a lovely friend." She smiled. "I think you should forgive him for his imagined wrongs."

"Christine, this is Kai. How are you?" I was in the living room of my parents' home, sitting back in a chair, with one leg crossed over the other, as if sitting in my own house and using the telephone to call a girl were normal events. This, I thought, was how John Glenn felt circling the earth.

Edna sat next to me, malignantly. I knew Christine's number like the number stamped on the receiver of my rifle.

Christine's voice. "Kai! Oh, Kai—hello, hello! Are you home? How *are* you?" Her voice was so sweet, so rich with passion and my heart pounded as it flowed out of the phone into my ear. Edna's glare became imposingly brilliant, for this was her very own weird problem child, that strange Chinese boy Kai Ting, talking with a girl on a telephone *in her house*. This should have hit my alarm bells and induced a stutter or a sudden recitation of preadolescent nonsense, or laughter, or polio. Only the buzz in my ear persisted. Somehow, Mr. Spillaney, the Man in the Red Sash, Mr. Arvin, Mr. Armentrot, Mr. O'Ware, Plebe math, Mr. Flauck, and the Spirit of the Bayonet had been more intimidating. I wanted to marvel at this accomplishment, and perhaps call the press, but all I could do was hear Christine's voice, and rejoice.

"I'm great, Christine. It's wonderful to hear your voice, to have your voice come out of this telephone. Can I see you?"

"Are you home for the summer?" she asked.

"I have a week," I said. "What are you doing tonight?"

"Oh, I'm busy," she said. "Remember Kyle Bush?"

"How about tomorrow?"

"Kai, let's get together Tuesday; I don't have a thing."

That was four days from now. I could do a lot of running and weightlifting. "Okay. I'll see you at breakfast at eight, for lunch, twelve noon, and for dinner, at five, on Tuesday."

She laughed. "You want to see me three times?"

I laughed. "For starters."

I stepped into my room. The four model airplanes hung from the ceiling, heavy with dust. I stepped to the window. The view of the backyard was the same, although the flowers, whose names I had never learned, seemed brighter and healthier. I put Marco Fideli's etching of Beethoven and the storm on the shelf, then shook my head and put it back in my bag. It didn't belong here.

Edna entered after I showered and was changing into civvies. "You are all sinew and muscle," she said. "They truly didn't feed you much, did they." She put down a plate of Underwood devilled ham sandwiches and a glass of milk. "You're a man now, and can have food in your room," she said simply. "Can I get you anything else?"

"No. Thanks very much," I said. "So we're starting over."

"We both missed you, more than you can believe," she said.

I started to argue. I was confused, my resistance to her in jeopardy. I didn't know what to do with her kindness. I looked again at the bed, where Silly Dilly had slept, and was comforted by my old loathing of her, for what had happened to the cat. "Thanks for the sandwiches."

I brushed my teeth and donned my dark blue Rogers Peet blazer with blue button-down shirt, narrow red-striped tie, and gray trousers. The phone rang and Edna said it was for me.

"Kai, Duke Troth." Hollow echoes of long-distance calling. I paused. "My mother liked the flowers."

"Congrats on math. Hey, I was a *shit*." He laughed. "Probably shouldn't swear on leave. Plebe year, you know. Sorry."

"No problem," I said. A silence. He wanted something.

"Want some help with *contacts?*" I asked.

"Aw, hey, I don't do that anymore. I'm apologizing to *everyone*. We're upperclassmen now. No reason to shit on anyone. I owe you a cherry Coke at Doris Barth Hall at Camp Buckner. Hey, you're all right. Let's not crap on each other. What do you say?"

"Cool," I said. "I don't like having enemies."

"Well, look, that's great. See you at Buckner."

I looked at my watch. I could make it. "Going to call Dad for lunch," I said to Edna. It would've been better if I could've seen Tony first. Pinoy had said, "Little boys need Tony and Barney." I was eighteen, a grown-up. I had to give up my things of childhood.

"That'd be wonderful, Kai," she said.

17

TALK

San Francisco, June 12, 1965

He was working on a Saturday. I waited in the lobby.

He appeared, smiling, nodding, unchanged. He wore English regimental ties with neatly pressed suits and brilliantly shined shoes. He had shined them ever since Edna announced that a gentleman could be gauged by his shoes. My hand compressed in his powerful grip, and he glowed as he introduced me to his co-workers. "My West Point cadet!" he exclaimed. I endured it manfully, but my discomfort from being his possession was a palpable, living thing that consumed my inconstant, shaky identity.

Dad's job with Soboleski was new. I had never seen his office before. I realized that the disaster area composed of successive layers of sedimentary buildup, of squirreling, and a relentless refusal to discard anything, was his. I expected it to be neater. It looked like my desk after poker, or Tony Barraza's desk before he swept it clean, or New York on a good day. It looked like my brain before a math writ.

Talk it slow. "How's the job?" I asked. The words came out smoothly, as if I were a familiar friend. His office had a clear view of the City. I watched tiny cars twinkling in the late-morning sun as they crossed the San Francisco–Oakland Bay Bridge.

"Good," he said, lighting his pipe.

I had asked something, and he had responded to me.

"I like your desk," I said. "Looks like mine."

"You going to graduate?"

"I hope so," I said.

"Must," he said.

I nodded.

"Cannot *tell* you how much, *must*." He twisted his blue, aquamarine Infantry School ring. The gold eagle and crossed rifles had been worn smooth in the twenty-three years since it was attached to his finger in Fort Benning. It had been the best weeks of his military career, going through the Infantry Officer Basic Course with American lieutenants. He had been a major in the Chinese infantry, and was the beau ideal of the class: he had been in combat and they hadn't. The American officers had bought him drinks and meals and toasted the success of his army against Japan.

I stared at the old ring that made him more American than his citizenship papers. He had been a brother, honored by the Army he had loved so much. Nothing could compare to it. I broke my gaze.

"Many fail, right?" he asked.

"Yes, too many." I thought of Stew Mersey, Joey Rensler, and Ravine Mankoff, of Alduss, Conoyer, Dirkette, and the others.

"They not so smart, not work so hard."

"They worked hard. Some were a lot smarter, better, than me."

There were clouds in the East Bay, where Christine went to college. I frowned with the view. With a start, I realized my middle sister, Megan, was over there. She was a schoolteacher in Berkeley. I wondered how she was. Suddenly, I wanted to see her. My heart began pounding; Edna forbade contact with her. How could I do that? But I'm an adult now. I can talk to my father. I could call her. Like I called Christine—in the open. I looked through the mass of debris on my father's desk and saw his telephone.

"Come," he said. "I take you to lunch, Blue Fox."

I took a breath. "Dad—could we go to Kuo Wah? And I'll pay."

He frowned. "Kuo Wah. Pay—ridiculous! Don't take pleasure!"

Andy Young, Kuo Wah's proprietor, was a tall and dashing man who could have run for governor on the strength of his smile and the beauty of his wife and daughters.

"Hey," he said, "how's our general? Richard! Your best patron is here! How are you, Mr. Ting?" he said, bowing to my father.

Richard Loo, the refined waiter, had always served our family. Seeing him was like Noah seeing the dove and dry land.

"Mr. Ting, how are you, sir? Ah, young master," he said to me. "You look wiser and very hungry! Come. Favorite table and dishes!"

"Doggone it, Richard," I said, "I sure missed you."

He smiled with all his teeth, laughing a little, looking down. "Yes, yes, young master. We miss you too." He seated us in our usual booth near the kitchen, closest to the hottest dishes.

The luncheon was constantly interrupted as a variety of people I could not remember, or perhaps had never met, came to the table to greet the West Point cadet.

"Where your uniform?" asked a stockbroker from Hooker and Fay.

"I don't have to wear it on leave, sir," I said.

"Should wear it," he grunted. "Show off uniform, for all of us. You only Chinese cadet from City!"

"Thank you, sir," I said flatly, trying not to think of the duty he described. I had enough expectations.

As usual, I had foolishly presumed that when people are

near food, the only business at hand is eating. My father, like all table commandants, had a different agenda.

"What they say about Southern Lands, Viet-Nam, at West Point?"

I was enjoying the use of *kwaidz,* chopsticks, and the savoring of food. I liked eating at my own pace, without any semblance of Western manners and without the Fourth Class mess hall light being illuminated for my departure from an unmeal. Then it hit me: my father had asked me a real question. I swallowed.

"We get briefings, but we don't know that much yet. I know basic infantry skills. This summer, we'll learn advanced skills for Vietnam. Lots of patrolling, night patrols."

"You know, China fight Viet-Nam. Never win. *Nam* is Cantonese for *nan,* 'south.' " I nodded. " *'An-nan'* mean 'pacify south.' Whole people, name for warlike natures. They *always* trouble! Han, T'ang, Sung, Yuan, and even Ming—all Chinese armies try rule An-nan, Champa, Viet-Nam. Viet kill all. Chinese, Mongol, Manchu, shock army, Golden Horde, Bannermen—Viet kill Chinese soldiers for thousand year! More hero than China. Dinh Bo Linh! Le Loi! Vo Nguyen Giap."

I remembered hearing about the Chinese army's thousand-year war in Champa, which they renamed An-nan. I didn't want to think about it. Deep down, I was unhappy we had gone in. We were clearly going to win, but my father's talk worried me. "There's not going to be trouble over there, is there?" I asked.

"Already have trouble. To beat them, we must fight a thousand years. You stop eat. Don't. Eat more."

He was talking to me but wasn't eating, watching me devour platefuls of food. Chinese food was the best. Besides tasting better than the best steak and having more complex tastes and sensory memories than the most sophisticated French sauce, it was spiritual sustenance, and wonderfully communal. What I ate was superior in taste, but it did not come from the extraordinary sacrifice of a French chef who had dedicated his life to perfecting a special dish. What I loved about Chinese food was its wondrous merging of the extraordinary with the common, the hard and the soft, the sour and the sweet, the pleasures of one with the pleasures of all. As I ate this food, I was joined in spirit with the great Black Haired people, who recognized in meals the celebration of life, and family, and community, a father talking to his son, hearing his questions. I served him, selecting the cheek and eye of the fish, the most succulent black mushrooms, the darkest, most compact pieces of meat. Some of the delicacies, like sea slugs, were easy for me to surrender.

"How many Chinese in your class?" he asked.

"One other. Three Japanese-Americans. Fifteen are black and Hispanic, a couple from foreign countries."

"You box, play basketball?" he asked.

Surprised, I put down my chopsticks. We had no history of discussing my sports. "I was a good athlete in high school and the Y. At the Academy, I'm average. Except for boxing." I looked at my hands. "I'll never be a great fighter. I can only go so far with my eyes. My vision really stinks."

He frowned. "But you so big, strong, tall. Hard for Chinese, Japanese?"

"It's hard on everyone." I didn't say that it felt harder because I was different. He knew that, better than I: he still had to fight his accent whenever he spoke; we attracted negative attention. Our accomplishments, and our failings, were magnified by our difference. Some people simply didn't like our looks, and never would. Some upperclassmen had stared at me as if I were an animal during open season. We would always be aliens, constantly in a state of unspecified jeopardy from bigots.

"The school is very white, but it's not racist," I said.

"See, I'm right, about U.S. Army," he said. "Best!"

"Yes, Dad, absolutely," I said. I remembered how difficult it was for him and Edna, members of a unique mixed marriage. My father would get up from the table in restaurants and I knew that the management had decided not to serve us. Kids threw rocks and chanted the snake charmer's tune, "Na na na na na, na na nana nana na." Even with Frenchy O'Ware, West Point was better.

"Dad, shouldn't you eat?"

"I watch you," he said.

I felt the God-given courage of Achilles. "Are you happy?"

"Pretty happy," he said, smiling, watching me.

"Dad, thanks for talking to me," I said.

"Ah ha," he said, "eat."

"Megan? This is Kai. Your brother."

"Kai! How wonderful to hear your voice. Is something wrong?"

"No," I said. "I just wanted to call you and see how you are."

"Oh, I'm fine!" she said in her English accent, the indelible mark of having learned from British and Indian teachers. "Tell me, please," she said, "that you've quit West Point." She checked herself. "I'm sorry. I shouldn't have said that. Dad's so proud."

"What do you have against West Point?"

"Kai, we don't know each other. We're sixteen years apart. As the second daughter, I've never been important, and I'd rather have Dad's indifference than his demands. I don't count to him.

"Ever since the war in China, I've been a pacifist, and I'm brokenhearted that you've chosen to be a soldier—a killer." She took a breath. "I'm *very* disturbed by the Tonkin Gulf Resolution, and I *despise* the American army's war on Vietnamese peasants."

"Megan, the Reds are assassinating village leaders. We're only protecting them. And Dad cares about you." I didn't understand her words about not being important, about his indifference.

"Kai, Kai—I'm sorry. No arguments. This is the first time we've ever spoken, just the two of us. Let me ask you a favor. Please respect my view of my relationship to my father. Our father.

"Now. How are you? Are you back for summer vacation?"

"Just for a few days."

"Can you visit, or can we get together?"

"Probably not this time," I said, afraid to argue with her, to hear about her *gahng* with Dad. "Nice talking to you," I said.

"Oh, sure! All I did was criticize and depress you. I hear it in your voice. Please, come over and I'll cook some great *baodze* and long bean *dofu* for you. I'd *really* love to see my *didi*, my baby brother."

I shuffled through the narrow aisles of the San Bo Company. It smelled of rosewood, teak, and stale shipping confetti. I picked two Guan Yus, one to pack and one for an elder. Each of them was a dollar sixty-five. "Can I have them in two boxes?" I asked.

"You speak Chinese?" the man asked.

I shook my head. Three years of Chinese school and no retention of *sam yep*. A childhood of speaking Shanghai and

Mandarin, and nothing remembered except food. Now I spoke English, like Edna, and was estranged from the people whose faces I shared, whose culture had produced me and my clan.

"So sad, you lose Chinese. You look like Guan Yu!" He slapped my arm, startling me with the contact, and boxed each figurine. "Hey, young master, you pray Guan Ti, Lord Guan, then you speak Chinese again."

I looked at the figurines going into the boxes. Guan Yu's great, expansive chest seemed less imposing, his ferocity compromised by being laid horizontal.

He looked like Tony Barraza. When the clerk closed the box, I closed my eyes.

18

PURPOSE

San Francisco, June 15, 1965

Uncle Shim was working half-time in the China Lights Bank on Jackson Street. He had told me that he would be at Sigmund Stern Grove, a small park not far from the Pacific Ocean, where free concerts were held on summer Sundays amidst an impressive stand of stately eucalyptus trees. Here, for years, he had studiously tutored me in the ways of China, while the sun glinted through the trees, the birds chirped, and the eyeballs rolled in my head.

I knew that by going to West Point I had been unfaithful to his creed. "The purpose of learning is to help others," he had said. "The purpose of soldiering is to kill. Yes, yes, I know you say it is to 'protect.' But the way soldiers protect is to kill."

Stern Grove usually had more fog than sun. Today the sun was bright, and more brittle than warm. Shim *baba* now had a small, delicate, ebony cane, upon which he rested both hands as he watched bushy-tailed squirrels take peanuts from his feet.

He smiled and his head moved stiffly with each of their lightning moves. Uncle had shrunk, his frame gaunt inside the soft gray flannel suit of which he was so fond. The collar and cuffs of his white shirt encircled his thin neck and wrists like carelessly loose shackles on an old, forgotten prisoner. For the first time in memory, I noticed that his collar and cuffs were worn. He had always been flawless in his dress. The gay brightness of his familiar jade bow tie emphasized the pallor of his skin.

It was painful seeing him. Had he aged so much in only one year? Or had the year in the company of oversized, physically vigorous, athletic Western men altered my perception?

His brightly cleaned, metal-rimmed spectacles caught the sunlight in blinding beacons as he looked toward me. He put out a hand and waved it, palm down, in the conventional Eastern way of invitation, of beckoning. Friends in the 'hood were always confused by the gesture, which looked like waving goodbye instead of "Come here." The squirrels saw me and fled.

"I bow to you, *Dababa*," I said, bowing, smiling as the pleasure of his company overcame the pain of studying his frailty.

"*Hausheng*. What a pleasant surprise. I find you looking very round, very full, very lucky, and a strong credit to your family. Actually, have you lost weight? Ah! Is that food?" he asked, sniffing the *kuotieh,* pork-filled pot-sticker dumplings, and the flat rice-noodle shrimp *chowfun* that I had brought in a take-out bag from Kuo Wah. I reached into the bag and pulled out my gifts for him. " 'The weight of this is light, but the feeling in my heart is like a mountain,' " I said. In it was a Guan Yu figurine.

Uncle Shim smiled, blinking rapidly. "Ah ha, thank you, *Hausheng*. Very nice gift. Very clever of you, to give me a household god, but not Wench'ang, for scholarship. Instead, Guan Yu, the warrior." He nodded. "Put him on the ground."

I did. The squirrels rushed over to the great red-faced spearman, sniffing, grasping him. Guan Yu stood tall, his widely spread feet resisting, his spear held firm. I was proud of him.

"Guan Yu was the great Asian soldier, *Dababa,* not Chingis Khan." I removed the containers and began to divide the servings onto plates. "Millions of Chinese people honor him and his sense of duty, and honor. That is what West Point is helping me become."

"Yes, no doubt," he said gruffly. "You may do what he accomplished. Which is, to kill and to die by the sword."

"*Dweila*—right," I said automatically. I passed him a plate of steaming noodles and pot-stickers.

"Yes, *syesye.* First. Please remember, through all your foreign thinking and your foreign ways, that you are not in this world alone, one young man on the flatland dirt of the world beneath the Heavens. Oh, no! You are connected by blood and tissue"—he said "tiss-you"—"to every person in your family by the *San-gahng* and *Wu-lun,* the Three Bonds of trust and Five Personal Relationships. You all represent one collective creature. To be without them—well, it is to be like me. Cut out from the world."

He deftly scraped the wooden chopsticks against each other, smoothing them, then nimbly secured one of the steaming, slippery pot-stickers and took a bite, chewing, full of gusto and enthusiasm.

I felt his hurt, but was happy that he was still a man of China. Even when depressed, he ate like a horse. Food, after all, was a celebration in itself. I smiled as if I had cooked it.

"I'm sorry, Uncle," I said. The squirrels returned, sniffing, standing up on hind legs, hopeful. As a child and as a crotheaded Plebe, I had known how they felt: hungry. I broke a fortune cookie and offered the fragments. The squirrels boldly snatched them and stepped away, eating with those little hypersonic movements.

If this fortune says "Love is in your future," then Christine will kiss me before I go back to the Academy, I thought. It said "You are cordial and perceptive." I wondered if she would ever kiss me. Uncle was talking and I was daydreaming again.

"*Hausheng,* do not be sorry. It is not your fault! You did not cause the Ch'ing to lose the *T'ien Ming,* the Mandate of Heaven, to lose the power to govern people. You did not choose to be born here. But you often choose to forget who you are.

"So. Second, I owe *you* an apology." He looked down while I wondered what was happening. Chinese men do not apologize.

"When you called the bank and tried to say goodbye to me last spring, I was very hurt that you were choosing to follow in your father's footsteps, eager to be a soldier. All this teaching of you, to come to that. I felt very sad, and most alone."

"I'm sorry, Uncle," I said, pained.

"Yes. This, to apologize to me for this, is acceptable, although I am confessing my wrongs, not yours, and you of course did the correct thing. You honored your father."

It was summer in San Francisco and the bench was cold. I was warmed by the food, hoping that he did not notice how ferociously the light ginger sauce in the *kuotieh* squirted when I bit into it.

"Against the wishes of your father, nothing can compete but the judgment of Heaven. So the wishes of an old, outside uncle, are nothing against the authority of the *fu-ch'in*.

"But," he said slowly, "your father has abandoned the way of the Master. It truly is a terrible problem. It is what the English call Hobson's choice. What I have always called the *ch'a lu t'ung k'u*. Do you remember this expression?"

I shook my head, chewing. "Notrly," I said with my mouth full, which was acceptable when eating Chinese food.

He put down his chopsticks. "It is the Fork of Pain, the Choice with No Choices. You see, for me to support and aid your father's wishes to make you a soldier offends all that I have learned. But to *not* support your father's wishes also offends all that I have taught you, and either outcome produced dishonor. I could not solve the puzzle. Where does the duty lie? This is, of course, a terrible reflection on me, and on my scholarship."

His face was torn with intellectual pains. I shut my eyes, not wanting to see my uncle humbled.

"So I closed my door. I did not give you my elderly words. I did not give you a gift to remember the honor you paid me as a sometime, lackluster student. I asked Secretary Hannah to tell you I was out, when I was in. I did not act with skill, or wisdom. It was as if I were the youth, and you the elder." He chewed, his mustache flaring, put down his *kwaidz*, and adjusted his cane.

"So, *Haushusheng*, I am very sorry. Please be more courteous to me than I was to you, and accept this."

He reached into a pocket. He opened my palm and placed his gold Piaget Swiss watch in it, his cool, thin fingers bending around mine to enclose it. He had never touched me before.

"Here. Do not argue, for I will not bend. No polite refusals, three times, until I forbear upon you. I forbear now. I employ the same aphorism: 'The weight of the gift is as a feather, but its meaning in my heart is like a huge rock.' There. All said.

"I only wore a watch because Madame Cheng expected her staff to wear them, to be so American, even me. This was frankly silly of her; there were clocks on all the walls, and ancient Chinese timepieces in the hallways—then she gave us little gold clocks for our desks. Ai-yaa!—so many reminders of death! It is such a modern thing, and I am now almost retired. It ticks too loudly; I hear it at night, calling to me, like the small voices of all the dead in my family. It now ticks with a rhythm of a bad heart. Very, very—uh—*eccentric*. If I silence it by not winding it, I feel a deep guilt to Madame Cheng. I do not wear a watch at all now. I am late for any number of things, and I enjoy the privileges of being old. No one at the bank can criticize me, for they all call me 'Father.' "

It was true. I could not imagine anyone in the bank, or anyone in the world, criticizing a Chinese elder like Uncle Shim.

"You always gazed at it," he said. "I taught you how to read time with it. Do you remember? I used to say to you: '*Hausheng,* the numbers on the face of this watch are only for the small hand. The big hand *does not care* about numbers. The big hand is literary, and sees no numbers, but imagines the numbers one through sixty in its literary mind. The little hand, it is a small accountant or banker, fond of counting, of abacus, and it reads the numbers on the dial.'

"No? Oh, *Hausheng,* talking with you is like speaking to half of you. Your memory is such a weak, unhealthy thing, so filled with huge holes. But ah, I really did not come here to criticize you.

"It would warm the heart to think that young Ting enjoys its noises. And it now falls from my wrist, as if I were already a ghost in my underground residence, not of this earth. I truly do not want it anymore."

"Uncle—"

"No! No! Do not kill me with politeness! Please. No American stupidities. Indulge me and accept it gently."

I put on the watch. It was too small at its widest, pinching my wrist. It was a fine watch, made magnificent by its former owner, and the honorable tasks he had completed in total disregard for Western time. The watch was a symbol of change, and he had never wanted it.

"Now, third," he said softly, "for my wise words of advice." He smiled to himself. "I do not believe in advice. I believe in a life of learning, of steady scholarship. Of constant inquiry in the presence of elders. Advice is what is given when the daily routines of life call for the thoughts of elders.

"I have given you my thoughts about your going to a school

for soldiers. Now, it is too late. You already have the look, the short hair of a monk with the jaw of a warlord, full of iron will. This is a particularly nasty combination of appearances. You look like your father when he finished at Paoting Military Academy, like Chiang Kai-shek when he returned from the Japanese military school. It changes young men. It hardens their hearts."

"I look hard 'cause I didn't have Chinese food for a year."

He sighed, looking at the lake. The ducks were also having lunch, the older ones no doubt frustrated with the limited insight of the young. "What is the *purpose* of life? Young Man Ting, I will tell you, now.

"It is that you subdue yourself and honor the rituals. The rituals and proprieties require you to respect the relationships which are older than time.

"First, to your father. Second, to the emperor. The emperor is alive, but not on the throne. Do not worry about him. 'Heaven is high, and the emperor is truly far away.' Third, in the time of your marriage, your wife to you. *Hausheng,* marry a good Chinese girl. Your father did so, as did I, to our infinite happiness," he said, his face stricken with grief.

He looked away from me. "I do not say this to your face. I say this to the Eight Breezes. 'Look at the trouble when your father married a foreign woman!' Of course, I could not say this to any human being." He cleared his throat, and did not look at me.

I gulped, feeling *ji hui* everywhere.

"Fourth, does not matter, for you do not have an older brother to respect and answer to, which is grand luck, please believe me.

"Of course, in life, you will find such a person. The older brother. It is what your own father did, finding two of them: one, a brother of the Cheng clan, who gave your father his name; second, that American son of Christian missionaries with the German name. The soldier," he said, sadly.

"Na-men Schwarzhedd," I said.

"Fifth," he said quickly, "is the respecting of friends, which is the least of the *Wu-lun,* the Five Personal Relationships. You have always had these friends, these *pung-yoh,* but none of them have been Chinese scholars."

Santino Rappa and Michael Benjamin, I thought.

"In times of life change—birth, marriage, death—and in times of trouble—floods, disease, war, famine, drought, locusts, earthquake, typhoon, or crime—the rituals, the *San-gahng* and the *Wu-lun*, are your truths. This will be true after I am dead.

"You have gone to a school that this foreign society regards as the Hanlin." He shook his head so violently on his thin neck that all the squirrels ran away again, their little claws shooting acorns and eucalyptus leaves in their wakes. Ducks honked.

"I did not realize what an honor it was, in this country, for you to be in that school. Your father swells with pride because of it. He is very active with Chinatown society, bragging about you. It has given him great life, and great *t'i-mien*, force, as is fitting for a father regarding the accomplishments of his only son.

"He owns you, *Hausheng*. He *is* you. You are the arrow shot from his bow. He has given you life; therefore, your successes are his and your failures are yours alone. You are his son—only to obey and please and serve him!" he said shrilly, causing the ducks to flap away from shore.

"Ai-yaa! You do not pay attention. You stare at the trees."

"I'm sorry, Uncle. I heard you."

"No," he said. "You do not hear me. You do not look at me. *Mian dui mian*. Face to face."

I stood, my face red and hot. The squirrels were caught between cookie hopes and fear of Uncle Shim's powerful emotions.

"You might think your father has not served his role as well as he should. Bah!" he cried. "How would *you* do in China, raising children in a land that is not yours, without a wife to tend to home and the little ones. And in China, you would have a face that would make you welcome everywhere. Here, he looks like *he* is the foreigner. What if you lost your family and your wealth and your status, and had to get by using your skills as a Chinese man? You would be quickly dead in a fantastic and most miserable hurry!

"He has done *miracles* by finding work in this land. And by marrying a foreign woman to make you equally foreign.

"This, of course, I would not have done. But he is your father, and it is his duty to do what he knows is best.

"Do not ever be so carefree with the mention of your father again. If I speak of your father, you should be supremely attentive. In China, you would kneel, your head below the feet of grasshoppers. Sit."

"Yes, *Dababa*," I said, pained.

"*Chung,* loyalty, *gahng,* bonds, *lun,* links, *dzeren,* duty, *Hausheng,*" he gasped, his breathing labored, his forehead bright.

"Look at what you have done. You consort with brutish professional fistfighters, the big black and Italian men who urge you to punch your fellow classmates! You have forgotten Chinese. You do not perform *ch'ingming* rituals for ancestors. You do not know the third day, third month. You forget *shiao,* filial piety! You do not know any of the rites or understand memory tablets!

"You do not speak to the grave of your mother! You have no hair on your head, and you are a young man! I am too excited," he said, breathlessly.

"Please rest," I said, watching his chest, remembering my resuscitation training.

His mustache flared at me. "Try to remember what I say."

"Yes, Uncle."

"Can you do that, young Ting? Do that for me, and for all the before-borns I represent? I feel so lonely, the only human who remembers the Master K'ung in this foreign world. . . . Can you be dutiful to his memory, and mine? Can part of your foreign brain remember to use reason in the face of force, to honor *gahng* and *lun* above self-gain, to always seek the righteous path?"

I nodded. *K'e ji fu li,* subdue the self and honor the rituals and proprieties. *Gahng* and *lun,* bonds and human relationships above gain. Rule by elders, the before-borns, walking the righteous path.

"Please, say yes."

"Yes, *Dababa,*" I said.

"Make your promise to the Heavens," he said fiercely, his eyes burning past this moment in the grove. It was a Chinese sky, composed of the celestial blues of the Far East, accented by long, thin, diaphanous clouds that came from a measureless past—a Chinese sky that had overseen the Tings before me. The sky seemed weighted, bearing down upon me. I was young and small, and a host of Chinese male elders pointed their gossamer fingers at me through the body of my uncle, urging me to my duty. I thought of the cathedral of the Cadet Chapel and its mournful organ prelude before worship, when I felt the undefined deficiencies of my life. I thought of Mr. Alsop's words: "But Honor, you must be *perfect* at it."

I hardened my face, knowing how serious this was for him

and for me. "Yes, Uncle," I said, looking at him. *Mian dui mian.* "On my honor."

19

CHRISTINE

San Francisco, June 15, 1965

We were at Zim's on Taraval and I looked at her with all my hope compressed into the forward curve of my myopic corneas. We had ambled through conversational foreplay: my trying to seduce her with West Point, to little effect, and her avid descriptions of the Cal student-power and antiwar movements, which had left me cold. Christine had become a full participant in "the movement."

Her blue eyes looked carefully at me. "I would rather die than kill someone else. Your life is in front of you, and you're so bright—you could do so much. It's not fair." She shook her head.

I tightened my jaw. I knew I was frowning. "There are lots of places where that kind of thinking works. There are more where it doesn't. You walk into the Panhandle or Bed-Sty and offer your life up and someone'll take it. If you know how to fight, no one fights. If you signal weakness, the taking starts.

"What are you going to do when all that's between your daughter and a guy with a knife is the fact that you can tell him that she has her life in front of her, and that she's bright?"

"That's not fair," she said.

"Life's not," I said with blinding wisdom. "It happens. When it does, protesting won't help. You need skills, right then."

"That's not the same," she said. "Kierkegaard says—"

"It's the same. Can I have some of your fries?"

She frowned, nodded, and almost smiled.

My feelings were like a huge, festering boil pressing against an unkind combat boot on a twenty-five-mile march, a thing developed not by volition but by circumstance, magnified by isolation, made true by its own force. I didn't think she'd enjoy the analogy. "Christine, I like being with you. I love you."

"Kai, don't love me. That's not smart. I want you to be different. Boys are wonderful and fun and exciting, but I need a friend—someone who's not pawing at me and trying—all of that."

"Great."

"Don't be disappointed. We have something *far* better. Kai, why do you think we're here, and given life?"

"For me to gaze at you, endlessly," I said.

She laughed. The dark cloud in my heart began to dissipate, and I returned to cleaning her plate.

"Not very existential. No, please, why are we here?"

"To serve our country. To do what Jack Kennedy talked about."

"That's so—chivalrous," she said. "And antiquated."

"Service isn't obsolete. Why do you think we're here?"

"For love and learning," she said. "And *feeling. Being. Experiencing.*"

I snorted over a fry. "That's for rich folk."

"That's not fair! The world should be a kind and soft place for *everyone,* not just struggle and stupid competition and heartache and war and conflict. There has to be a better way—and it's up to us to find it! I would *die* for a better world!"

I nodded at her. "That's what I'm committed to." I wondered what Tony would think if he heard this conversation. He'd probably say, "Never heard so much drizzly crap since a medic with a needle told me ta drop my drawers an' bend over, an' that I'd like it."

She took my hand in hers, caressing it, exploring it, her affection so direct, so simple. Self-consciously, I looked around the restaurant. A few people studied us, the bright blond in the beige sweater and white pants massaging the hand of the Chinese guy without hair who was eating all her food.

She leaned forward. "No more of this. You and I are special. I loved your letters. Cal is full of life, and exploration, and learning, and *being*—it's the most *alive* thing in the whole world! The rest of the planet is *insane*—only Berkeley makes sense."

She looked at me. "Everything you've described at West Point is inhuman. You're learning how to lead men to kill other human beings. At Cal I met a boy who had left West

Point, and he talked to me, a lot. He told me about such torture and pain. He said that Beast Barracks was absolute hell. Such *sadism*. These horrible male rituals of—of extorting effort to test loyalty to stupid values. Everything I fear and dislike." She licked her lips. "I love your letters. I read them and pretend you're in Paris."

"Paris?" I asked.

"I pretend you're on the Rive Gauche, an eccentric poet. It makes me hope that I can change how you think—I want you to agree with me. I want you to quit West Point and be with me."

Christine ran her tongue around her spectacular upper lip, making me forget everything. "What do you mean, 'be with me'?"

Her hands stopped massaging mine. "Oh, Kai, I don't know. I'd probably do *anything* to get you out of there. I really care for you! I *love* you—not romantically, but—like a special human being loves another special human being. Part of me's very attracted to you, physically. You have a sweet face." She gazed into my eyes. Then she looked down.

"But love of that sort is a—there's an instant knowledge of physical attraction. Anything else, any disturbing of the internal psyche for something that *isn't* instant knowledge—that would be disastrous, a huge, incredible, painful, mistake."

"Loving me would be a mistake," I said.

"No, Kai. Loving you *that* way would be."

"But you might do it to save me from West Point?"

She ran her tongue along her teeth. "I might," she said, her voice laden not with desire or love, but with sacrifice.

Like an ostrich, I closed my eyes, hoping that when I opened them she would say something different. The lights in Zim's seemed darker. I was so stupid, so lame, to try to win her love. Such an idiot. But no one loved her more. I saw that if I could endure her regally unrealistic view of the world, I could do anything, like remain committed to her until the end of time. I understood life while she lived in the bubble of the white middle class. I had known unhappiness and could embrace the joy of her company with soulful conviction. I was now at the Academy, in the center of the traditional white, American male experience, and would have all the tools to protect her when the time of the wolves arrived. Then I remembered that she had said I had a sweet face.

"I'm good, Christine," I said, trying to find my voice be-

tween seizures of unspeakable human worthlessness and surges
of princely, martial splendor. Aim low, hit low, Arch had said.

I looked at her intently. "Christine, I'd be so good for you."

She looked back at me with large, luminous eyes. She
looked at me as if I had told her I had terminal cancer instead
of an affliction of the heart.

On my last night in the City, Christine and I walked north
along the beach, the long string of coastal lights winking into
the distant night fog behind us. Ahead was the tall, brooding,
brightly lit Gothic restaurant, the Cliff House. It was high tide,
and we had a band of only ten or fifteen feet on the edge of
the seawall on which to walk. I inhaled the strong, pungent
scent of the beach, the seaweed which now looked black, the
smell of a living ocean, caressing the earth. I thought of the
Hudson, stroking the banks of West Point. I loved this place,
this border where sea met land, and I did not know why.

"Look, Kai. Look at the crescent moon—how the clouds
move across it. The sky's filled with clouds we can't see. The
stars are so bright above us, and they fade as they approach the
horizon. You can't really see where the sky ends and the ocean
begins."

The sky that had seemed so heavy and Chinese in the grove
was now dark but without weight. " 'When the heavens separated from the earth,' " I said.

"What was that?" she asked.

"How Chinese storytellers begin their stories, their version
of 'once upon a time.' " I looked at the seamless edge of the
world. The Chinese side of my family would be looking east
at our horizon, while we looked west at theirs.

"That's beautiful," she said, shivering in the cold sea-wind,
holding my hand in both of hers, leaning into me. I freed my
hand and wrapped her to me, pressing my biceps into her soft
shoulder.

"I love you so much," I said into her billowing hair as it
wrapped around my face, the blond tips catching the moonlight. I placed my cheek against hers, my heart pounding.

"I love being with you so much. I truly do," she said, rubbing her smooth cheek against mine. She did not say, "And I
feel the instant knowledge of consuming love for you, for
which, in this instant, I surrender myself to you."

She leaned against me, careful to keep the point of her hip
against mine, and I knew she knew more about boys than I

knew about girls. I saw fragments of constellations. The moon appeared from the clouds, dimming the stars, creating small holes and relics of light.

"Look," she said into the roar of the surf, pointing at the track of the moon's reflection on the Pacific. "That path, it's like a bridge, that runs between you and me, from the East to the West, from us to the *infinite,* a path across the water. That's how it feels to me to be your friend."

The moon was my old friend in a black sky. When I was a kid, I used to think that it followed me, wherever I went. Now it cast a fragile bridge of fleeting, shimmering light on the black water.

"Look at me," she said. I did. I put my hands on her waist, and she placed her hands on mine.

"To walk on moonlit waters," she said, smiling up at me, looking into my eyes, "To a horizon, ever near/Come to me on waves/Walk to me on its path/Hold moonbeams and kiss the moon." She smiled. "Like it?" she asked. "I just made it up."

"It's beautiful." I remembered Uncle Shim's poetry about an empty stove. "I inspire people around me to poetry, but they don't want to tear their clothes off and kiss until the moon sets."

She giggled. "I've always wanted to be able to compose poetry while looking into the eyes of passion," she said, smiling. "And your eyes are passionate . . . I do love how you adore me . . . but we have purity and innocence . . . there's nothing I have to apologize to my mother and father for."

She turned away from me, blinking into the wind. "And although it's not real poetry, I just did something like it. Isn't this *wonderful*—like being in love, without sex, or jealousy, or worry, or guilt? When I can take risks with poetry, and you can write me long and glorious letters. And all the petty things mean nothing, and we're still free to be absorbed by the universe, to be consumed by muses." She smiled gaily, her Grace Kelly–like visage dazzling in the moonlight. She was impossibly beautiful.

I didn't want to be consumed by the muses. I wanted to kiss her. "Christine, I've always wanted to be your boyfriend."

She nodded at me solemnly, watching me, breathing fast.

"Now I learn we're better off as big-time, handshaking buddies, with you as a virgin poetess and I a platonic audience, throwing roses at your moonlight poetry." I made a face.

"Oh, Kai, oh Kai, thank you!" she cried, her eyes burning

and liquid, her face, her lips offered to me, wet with the salt
of the sea, and I kissed her. Her lips were soft and merged
seamlessly with mine, and angels sang both near and far. I felt
her fingertips on my cheek and felt myself breathing in a way
I had never breathed before. She half-opened her eyes and
looked so softly, so dreamily into mine that I kissed her again,
gently folding her into me, and I was in love. Her hands
touched my face and my arms, as she opened her mouth to me,
teaching me an internal dance possessed of rhythms and rhap-
sodies borne only of instant knowledge. She made small, need-
ful, urgent hums in her throat that carried me to the moon,
where the goddess Gwan Yin brushed my heart and my life
with sparkling light, filling me with a sweet music that was
joy. I was consumed by her mouth, by her taste and smell. I
kissed her deeply with unmeasured passions, making her
whimper and grasp me. Panting, she pulled away, her chest
heaving.

"Christine," I said, "oh, Christine," reaching for her.

"No," she breathed, stepping back awkwardly, her long hair
blowing across her face, her beautiful face full of heat. "I will
not be *consumed* by this!" she exclaimed, tears in her eyes.
"It's too strong. It's too—too—oh, damn it!"

She walked away from me, toward the surf. She was stunning.

I closed my eyes, remembering the kiss, remembering to
breathe, the image of her beauty by the sea overwhelming. The
kiss had been too incredible to be undone by her retreat, and
I returned to its memory, astonished at the height of my good
fortune and at the depth of the bad. I joined her near the water.

"Tell me," I said, "that wasn't 'instant knowledge.' "

"It wasn't," she breathed.

I memorized her mouth, her eyes, her face. I was leaving in
the morning, and only my ability to remember her face would
sustain me for another six months or a year. She was achingly
gorgeous. No one could be more desirable. "Christine." She
turned away from me.

I hated this. What the hell am I doing, messing around with
someone beyond my reach who was also nuts? I'm a blooming
idiot. I've done torture. I lived with Edna for a decade and endured Plebe year.

"Can't do this," I said. "I can't be your platonic buddy. I
want to love you, always, forever. To be the man who honors
you and cherishes you ... made better by you ... singing

about you from mountaintops." I cleared my throat. "And I can't sing."

She looked at me with such sadness, shaking her lovely face in the wind. "Once I give myself to you, I'd be without power, without inspiration, without hope, burdened by you and your needs. You're—you're an anachronism. Like Don Quijote! A throwback to a day that doesn't even exist anymore." She crossed her arms across her chest in the cold, biting wind of the sea. "You'd stop my life before it's even begun. I *can't* allow that to happen."

"By being with you I feel I can do anything," I said. "How come it has the opposite effect on you?"

She looked at the horizon. "I believe in instant knowledge. Please don't let me hurt your feelings—but when it occurs, there's no talking, no debate." The small, fine muscle along her jaw flexed. "I'm trying to be in control, and to be moral." She brushed her long hair from her face. "Instant knowledge is correct because it naturally defeats reason, and control, and can't be helped." She wouldn't look at me. She waited for my answer.

"Okay, we don't have it. Let's call it 'slow knowledge.' Okay? Can we call it something so I have a chance with you?" She looked at me and I smiled broadly. "Smile, Christine, please. We've been friends so long, and I've been so patient trying to be worthy of you, and you kissed me as if you loved me. Please, smile."

She shook her head. "No, Kai. We're not right for each other this way. It would be a disaster."

I breathed deeply from the sea. This kiss from heaven signaled for me life and joy. For her it was tragedy. I couldn't help thinking it was because I was Chinese, that I was too different to generate in her the countdown sequence for her hated instant knowledge. I tried to look at the sea but couldn't keep my eyes from her. I again felt the strange sensation of missing her while I was in her company.

She stepped closer, still breathing rapidly, her lips parted, staring at my mouth, and I knew we could kiss again, magically, and then she would pull away, and tell me that we had just avoided catastrophe. How could she kiss me like that and still have reservations about anything? I wanted to pick her up and carry her to the dunes and kiss her, hold her, touch her.

"Why did you kiss me like that if you don't love me?" I asked.

"I'm sorry, Kai. I lost control," she said. "I didn't mean to."
I moved toward her and she backed away.

Irresistibly, I heard Edna telling me that I was ugly, revolting, and unlovable. Christine had said I had a sweet face. I didn't know who was right, but Edna was never wrong.

The thought "It doesn't mean anything" came to me from my past. I tried to say, "You mean everything to me" but I knew if I opened my mouth, I would weep. I ground my molars.

I am a man and I do not cry, I repeated to myself, trying to soothe an unreachable hurt through repetition of fictional strengths. I couldn't look at her and survive the night.

I hardened my face and looked at the moon, seeing nothing, trying not to love her, trying to escape this place I loved, with this impossible, perplexing girl I adored. I tried to find a moment of comfort, an icon of sanctuary, and pictured the gray eminence of the chapel overlooking West Point, waiting for the numbness that always came.

20

SOCIETY

West Point Bachelor Officers Quarters, April 16, 1966

"See you—raise five." I was a bold Yearling night patrol-leader, a nineteen-year-old apprentice infantryman, pulsing with the raw drive of a fearless, take-no-prisoners poker player. Yearlings rebelled against the system by dressing ineptly and playing at the outer bounds of military decorum. My shoes were nearly gross, my trousers lacked their spoony creases, and my sleeves were rolled up to advertise my biceps. To make it easier on Plebes, I ordered the *Gazette* and not *The New York Times*.

Colonel Smits had two rules: no cap on bumps, and bets to table limits, which was no limit, and booze was gratis if you paid, which was hardly free. His table was covered with a

coarse Army olive drab blanket. We were in casual dress—
T-shirts and trou.

I had jacks and nines with four of us still in.

"Out," said Colonel Smits, banging down his hand and taking a big slug of Bushmills from a dirty tumbler. The pot was
right. I lay down my two pairs, beating Clint's kings. Duke had
three sixes and a big smile as he scooped the chips with large
arms.

The room was thick with smoke and rank with the thick
aroma of pepperoni pizza, whiskey, beer belches, and warming
bodies. Colonel Smits had a weak oscillating fan from his recent Vietnam tour, and from a small bookcase it pushed the
bad air around like a tired traffic cop. The window was open,
but little help came from it on a warm April night.

Lieutenant Colonel Franz Alonzo Smits was attached to Post
Command, West Point. He was our Wild Hairy Renegade. He
had a rancid mouth, foul armpits, excess body hair, bachelor
quarters he shared with cadets, and all the bad habits that
young men admire. He had a large, semiflat, closed face that
could have been shaped on an irregular cookie sheet in high
heat. His nose had been broken at least twice by different
forces bearing from different directions. Something sharp had
tried to chop off his chin, leaving a pale incision where the
hair grew with less abundance. The dark eyes were hooded, injured, reptilian. He was Bluto in the "Popeye" cartoons, with
the predatory grin but without the good cheer.

He had been a member of the 1952 Army grid team, but his
tour in Vietnam had been compared to the play of snakes in
Ireland. He had gone to MACV to win the Medal of Honor
and had returned to West Point with a Combat Infantryman's
Badge and a Purple Heart, and no other decorations of distinction to match an enduring anger. The CIB and Purple Heart
were revered awards, but they were not enough for him. He
was six feet three and overly broad, with a chest designed for
a lifetime of medals—all preferably centered on the constellation of stars on a dark blue field that denoted the nation's highest award.

Rumor Control said that he loved one person—Coach Red
Blaik—and that this distant connection had been sufficient for
him to overcome a bad combat tour and get posted to the
Academy staff. Legend had it that in the fifties, assistant coach
Vince Lombardi had applauded Smits's talent but had prayed

for his soul. Coach Blaik had seen the gold in Franz Smits and had never lost faith.

After the Navy game last year, Smits invited Duke and Clint and other cadets to use his BOQ for poker, pizza, and drinking. Having access to this type of facility—bursting with food and stamped with the tattoos of adulthood—was an undeniable take-Big-Bites Good Deal for cadets.

Officers were encouraged to develop relationships with cadets to facilitate the transfer of values and to provide a sense of kin. Officers served in a range of roles, from offering housing for cadet dates to direct, long-term mentorship. The Academy might have reconsidered the practice had it observed the Poker Society.

Duke had introduced me to the Saturday Night Poker Society after we finished our advanced infantry and patrol training at Camp Buckner. We returned to West Point and its new four-regiment organization to accommodate the further-expanded Class of 1969. Company H-1 had been reorganized as Company A-3. Hell-One had become Aches-in-Three-Places. Hellraisers had become Avengers.

Colonel Smits's rotgut could be used as the poison you'd give a horse before you shot it with an unreliable gun. I was smug in rejecting it. Then Smits introduced me to Irish whiskey blended with brandy and chocolate ice cream—the Velvet Hammer. I drank Hammers like Popeye took spinach. It was candy with a kiss inside; I discovered the joys of inebriation: existential angst, incoherent speech, Falstaffian pronouncements, pounding headaches, and Olympian retching. My first binge was nothing to remember.

"Big buddy, you threw up all night," said Bob Lorbus.

"Talked Chinese," said Clint. "Had us worried, but we had to leave you in the showers or you'd tank the room."

"Was I—was I embarrassing?" I asked.

"If I'm ever that blotto," said Bob, "slit my throat."

"Don't be a Snuffy's Special," said Deke Schibsted. We couldn't drink within ten miles of the Academy, and Snuffy's was uncannily located just beyond the ten-mile perimeter line. Drinking with an officer in his quarters was not prohibited; the presumption was that a glass of port might enhance a lace-tablecloth dinner.

I liked being drunk, pleased by the sensation of my brains sliding out of my ears. I liked the absence of tension, the giggling. Laughing had kept other demons from me. I felt quite adult, sophisticated, philosophical, and liberated.

"Why, *Hausheng*," Uncle Shim had asked, "were poets drunks? They put *goliang* in their bellies to forget *gahng, lun,* and duty. They paid homage to the gods of poetry and writing. In their wine cups, they could enter the Other World, where they could feel pity and emotion and forget themselves. Think of the poet Li Po, who habitually drank to excess. He drowned when he leaned over his boat to kiss his own image in the water, and fell in."

I had many Confucian relationships to maintain, but I was like Li Po; when the Irish whiskey went in, the *gahng* and *lun* went out.

"Why do you mess with Smits and alcohol?" asked Mike Benjamin.

"I kin handle it," I said, embracing the commode like a baby koala holds its mother, trying to focus my bloodshot eyeballs. I used my best adult voice. "I'm, upperclassman."

"You're trying to drink like an Irishman. Knock it off. You're blowing away brain cells like Hitler killed Jews."

Mike set a rumbling tumbler of Alka-Seltzer next to me. I tried to think through the violent popping and fizzing. "Not nice comp'rison," I said.

"Wasn't meant to be," he said.

"Wanna come ta Society, play cars—*cards?*" I asked.

"I wouldn't go there if I were dead," he said.

"Number-one drink of the gods," Smits mumbled, pouring the sludge of the Hammer into my beer mug. "Cures all ills. Cleanses the soul, stitches up sucking chest wounds. Keeps your dick hard."

Smits was a music fan. He played the Animals, Tom Jones, and Johnny Rivers at decibel levels that invited concussions and hearing loss. Sometimes, over my cards, I studied his hard, darkly bloated, crooked face as he mulled his whiskey, blinking from his blaring music, wondering why he favored us with his freedoms.

I had brought Arch Torres and Bob Lorbus along tonight to bring the Society to a perfect seven for poker, joining the colonel, Clint Zoo Keeper Bestier, Duke Troth, and Miles Brodie. Bob and Arch had observed the aftereffects of the Society's temperance habits. They wanted to "see the elephant" and his dark, bohemian den. In the stairwell of the Q, we felt the vibrations of a stereo system and heard the words to "Secret Agent Man." We were all tall, fit, trained as killers, and dark to varying degrees. We identified with Agent 007, James Bond, the Man of our time. His enjoying the favors of many women I recognized as fantasy; that only happened to Arch and Bob. I liked James Bond because he ate like a starving restaurant critic wherever he went.

When we came through the door, Smits seemed to be seeing me for the first time. His eyes narrowed in suspicion. He was looking at the spic and the Chinaman.

Arch looked at him steadily. "Too many of us, sir?"

"Hell no," he growled in a voice abused by yelling over artillery, imbibing over the limit, and living past reason. "Siddown. Whaddya drinkin'?"

Arch's skill at seven-card stud lifted the level of play. We had finished the Velvet Hammers and had been at the Schlitz for a couple hours. I was drinking Bushmills and feeling no pain.

"Three, no help," Arch said. He flipped up the fourth card for Clint with the sharp dealer's snap that cracked like a dry branch on night patrol. *Snap.* "Club, flush," he said to Duke. *Snap.* "Nine, straightening," to the colonel. *Snap.* "Pair of eights up, four to the flush," to Bob. *Snap.* "Ace, no help," to me. I had stayed in to show guts and help the pot, but now I had two aces. *Snap.* "Pair of fours," to Miles. "Ten, no help," to himself. Arch led and Clint followed. I lagged with my average hand.

"Down and dirty," Arch said, dealing the seventh card.

I intermixed the cards and fanned them: three aces, two down. Maybe two full houses, Arch showing three jacks and Lorbus with three eights and no flush. Duke had no flush. My bet. I threw in a modest I-am-still-here bet. Lorbus bumped again. I sweated his flush, feeling full houses.

"The problem is, no one's getting laid," Colonel Smits said. I couldn't tell if he was complaining or cheering.

"The problem is," said Arch, "I see the five, the five, the five, and ten more," tossing in red chips the way Tony used to throw garlic, onion, sugar, and oregano into the vat of gurgling spaghetti sauce during the YMCA sleep-overs on the gym floor. The bets went around again, leaving Arch, Bob, Smits, and me.

"Oughta bet on women," said Duke. Duke had set drags, or dates, for many in the Poker Society. Arch and Bob needed help with women the way Tony Barraza needed boxing lessons.

"Three aces," I said, laying them out and waiting for the full houses. Smits's two pairs were the only threat, and he looked at me balefully as I gathered the chips. We had two decks, and Clint began dealing five-card stud while Arch shuffled.

"Arch," said Miles Brodie, a wiry man from West Virginia, "that was a fine dish y'all dragged to the hop."

"I'd low-crawl a mile to sniff her bicycle seat," said Troth, who always handled his cards before the deal was completed.

"Uck," I said.

"Makin' Ting airsick again," said Colonel Smits. There was laughter. My expertise with women was limited.

"Don't like bicycles," I said. Miles had king high showing and led the betting, everyone in.

"Her name's Jill, and I think I'm in love," said Arch.

"She ask about me?" asked Clint.

"Well," said Arch. "When she was helping me unhook the bra, she broke a nail. She said 'son of a Bestier!' "

"Don't mind being associated with her bra," said Clint.

"She was thinking of female dogs, Zoo Keeper."

Clint was our zoologist. At Buckner, I had spent precious time coating all the movable metal in our gear with masking tape. In our final problem, I led the night patrol into an aggressor camp slowly and silently, creeping a few feet a minute in the final assault past their listening post. The paratroopers had been startled by our silent rising from the grass, our weapons on them. Clint had been on the right flank, but now he was missing. Billy Bader had been assistant patrol leader, and we both ran a one-eighty on our attack line. Several hundred meters back I saw the faint glow of a red-lens flashlight. Clint was on the ground, the earth about him uprooted. He had a baby starling in his hand and was feeding it parts of an earthworm, then dripping water from his canteen into its beak. "Little guy fell from the nest, and I crawled over him," he said. "Made this peep. Damn near killed him."

"You missed the attack, Clint. The lane grader's busted you."

"Damn worm's no good—help find me another, Kai, quick."

Duke was low man, with a deuce and a seven, close to folding. He turned to Miles, now with a pair of kings. "Lay your girl yet?"

Miles frowned. "What kinda bool-shit question is that?"

"Didn't ask if she was good," he said. "Asked if she put out."

"Screw you, dirtbag," said Miles, looking hard at Duke.

"Hey, pretty fuckin' touchy, Brodie," said Duke.

"It's none a yore business. Ever hear a privacy?"

"Privacy!" snorted Colonel Smits, who also had a bad hand. "What the screw you know about *privacy!* You're in the god-damned Army! Get a fartsack dream 'bout your squeeze, every swingin' dick in the Corps knows her name. Shit—whadyya think this is, the British Army?" He blew smoke. "So, Miles. She any good?"

Miles jerked. "Hey, it's nothing, Miles," said Bob Lorbus.

"Bullshit it's nothin'," Miles said. He glared at Smits, who looked back with dead, hooded eyes. I thought he was restraining a smirk. I looked at Bob and Arch for guidance. They looked at Smits. Clint dealt the last card, down. I had nothing and folded as Miles led the betting and angrily took the pot with two pairs. Duke began dealing five-card draw as Clint shuffled.

"Listen, women are standard issue," said Smits, betting heavily. "Same layout. Don't need a doctorate to know *that* shit. Greeks, they got it right. Women're slaves. No brains, no guts, just handy. Don't go nuclear, Brodie—you wouldn't care if people talked about your car, would ya? Ting—don't Orientals treat women like chattel?"

"I don't," I said, my cheeks blushing with anger. Confucian teachings focused on the moral man, and said little about women. Women appeared in the *Wu-lun* only as wives owing duty to their husbands. What would Uncle Shim say to someone like Smits?

"You ever been married, sir?" asked Arch, matching the bet.

"Do I look like an *idiot?*" asked Smits. "Pot's right. I'll take three," he said, throwing his discards hard into the table, blaming Duke with a glance for his bad hand as he stood. He cranked the stereo volume up as it played "Seventh Son." The pictures on the wall rattled, humming harmonically in accompaniment to the alcoholic buzz in my brain. The pictures were of the temples of Angkor Wat, of Cholon, the Chinese district of Saigon, and of a firebase somewhere in Vietnam, which showed a hairy, smoking, barechested Smits. He had a flat butt and a large gut.

"And them Oriental women in their *ao-dais*, . . ." he said, sitting and smiling falsely at me with all his teeth. "They're *sooo* fine! What kinda stuff ya want most, Scrounger?" Smits asked Duke. Duke disliked the nickname; I disliked the question. I took three cards, needing all kinds of help. I felt Arch had the cards.

"I'd like a stuck-up Hebe with lots of money," said Troth.

I looked at Duke. "Jesus, you sorry—," I said.

"Like to lay a darkie," said Smits.

"Oh, man," said Duke. "I wouldn't even wanna *touch* one a them. They're all like—"

"Like WHAT?" I exploded.

"Fuckin' A, Ting, cool it!" said Duke. "Don't go ape on me again. God, you are so fucked up! You're not a kike or a ninny!"

I stood, the chair scraping sourly. "Go to hell, Troth."

"Get a handle, man," said Duke, frowning and leaning back.

I wanted him to take it back, and I wanted him to say it again so I could hurt him. I was hot with booze. Nameless angers raged.

"Shit, Ting," said Smits, "you got a black momma, or what?"

The room went out of focus. There stood Momma LaRue, in the faded purple down-to-the-floor, with her smooth, handsome face, touching my cheek.

"Yes," I said, in a gravelly voice I didn't recognize as I moved. Lorbus grabbed my arm and I tore it free, liking the action, the room turning red. I didn't know math worth crap, but I knew this. "Cool it," hissed Bob. "You're in a Q and if you brawl you'll get booted. I heard you almost did this as a Plebe! Now can it!"

I blinked, heart still pounding, blind, raging, homicidal adrenaline surging through my arms and fists. I couldn't think, my mind full of unworkable ooze. I wanted to hit Troth's and Smits's dirty, ugly, white mouths. There had been no physical contact and I tasted blood in my mouth and Toos and I were backed up against five white boys and no joke or smart remark could end this. I moved for Troth.

A fist pounded on the door and I hesitated. "Screw 'em," said Smits.

The door opened. A bearlike man in an Army athletic shirt and sweats filled the doorway. He made Smits look small. The red dissipated and my vision returned, details announcing themselves. The rotating fan had a bullet hole in its base. My cards were on the floor and I had a large number of red chips, neatly stacked. Through the upbeat and mourning voice of Johnny Rivers, I heard the bearlike man say, "Sir, please turn down the music." His voice was thinner than his frame, but it was crystal clear.

Colonel Smits looked up. Smirking, he walked slowly. BOQ rooms were small. He took his time. He turned the volume down slightly.

"More would be great, sir," said the bear at the door.

Smits turned the volume back up, grinning at us as eardrums popped and the pictures shimmied. Smits grinned.

"Less," said the bear, and then he smiled hugely, his teeth glinting in the light of the cheap crimson Japanese table lamps. It was the smile of a man who would never be troubled by the minutiae of life. He was younger than Smits, a lot bigger, with more blood in the brain, more vinegar in his fists, judgment in his stance. He had a barrel chest, broad, well-defined shoulders, thick arms, and a reddening face—Guan Yu in the flesh. A new tension, older and sharper than the one sparking between me and Troth and Smits, filled the room. There was a link between Smits and this big man. Like the one between the Capulets and the Montagues.

Smits turned the volume down. I blinked, and took a deep breath against my hammering heart. I had been ready to screw things up. I was in my stance, as stupid as stupid could be. I quietly sat down.

"Just playin' cards, *Major*," Smits said. "Saturday-night R&R in the *privacy* of our shitty Q too rich for your blue blood?"

"Not at all, sir," he said. "Good to play cards. Good to be a good neighbor. Need sodas or hot dogs, sir? I got extra."

"Negative. Don't need a goddamned thing, *Major*," said Smits. "Hope we didn't fuck up your beauty sleep."

The bear smiled. "Good night, sir." He closed the door.

"Who was that?" asked Clint.

"That," said Duke, "was Major H. Norman Schwarzhedd."

"Jesus Christ," I said.

"Ohhh," said some.

H. Norman Schwarzhedd, the same name as the renowned Na-men—he was the son of the general, the son of my father's wartime friend. I looked at the door, wanting it to reopen. But I had seen him, and heard him, felt his presence. I looked at Troth, emptily.

Duke looked away from me as he spoke rapidly. "He got

put in for the Medal of Honor but got a second Silver Star. Gotta be one of the Point's most decorated graduates, just reeking of *contacts*. Damn, is he *big?*" Trying to be cheerful.

"I heard he was coming," said Bob, who patted my shoulder. "Calm down, buddy," he said.

"He's a fuckin' blowhard," growled Smits. "Jerk thinks livin' in a mousetrap is all right. He's a suckin' mouse chaser. I got boh-coo bad-mouth for this Q. This Q is *number ten!* This Q *sucks*. Had better in Nam—can you believe that shit? You boys see where married officers live? Up the hill? Squeezeville! They live like the damn Queen a Sheba. Treat us like number-ten dogshit. Goddamn Army scrags your ribbons and gives you a goddamn *house* cuz you were sucking stupid enough to marry two legs joined in the middle. And he fucked up our game. Shit! I woulda taken this hand, too."

A silence came over the table. An officer bad-mouthing another officer? Duncing *all* women? And calling a war hero a blowhard?

"Yeah, married idiots got it licked, boh-coo," affirmed Duke.

"Let me tell you boys something," said Smits. "The world's an anus. It's all that it's cracked up to be, and it's out there, ready to come *di di mau* and get you in the cheeks. Can't trust one butthole in the setup," he said. "Asshole careerists in charge are only out to do you. Don't *even* waste your time tryin' to figure it. No suckin' answer. You're gonna be Airborne Ranger engineers, the best and the brightest, and they're gonna fart you boys out and zip you up in body bags before you can say 'Slope City.'"

I stared at Smits. The more he drank, the more he had a black meter to his speech, the placement of emphasis not the pattern of a white man's speech.

"Win this shit, gotta take the *offensive,* not pass gas in the fuckin' hurricane. We're just fartin' in the wind, so the whole thing eats it *big*." He pulled down more Bushmills.

"Like that song," he said softly. It was "The House of the Rising Sun." "Many a poor boy . . ." He leaned forward and belched wetly, his red eyes searching our faces, looking for friends.

"Build defilades, brothers. Do your own rules. Run up the Jolly Roger." He held up two fingers. "Two standards. *Two* suckin' worlds. You gotta be cool on this West Point shit, and be cool in a big suckin' boh-coo hurry or it'll eat your livin' guts."

Only Duke nodded his head. I shook mine. Lorbus and Torres were tight-lipped. I thought of the smiling, bearlike major who also had returned from Vietnam, but could not be more different from Smits. In the silence, Miles collected the cards, returned bets, and dealt seven-card, no-look sweat.

I bet blindly, wondering what Major Schwarzhedd was doing. I wondered if he looked like his father. The major was probably about the same age as the first Major Schwarzhedd was when he was running around in the bush with Major Ting of the Chinese Army. I was ready to leave.

Arch bet harder and won with three kings. "That's it for me, hombres," he said, "Gotta book. You want to get some air, Kai?" he asked.

I cashed out. Smits was staring into the bottom of his glass.

"Thanks again, sir, for inviting us," Arch said.

"Then don't leave early, soldier, takin' our winnings," he said thickly, looking at me quizzically, the booze changing him.

"Gotta go. I'm a goat," I said.

"What's your excuse, Torres," mumbled Smits.

"Aim low, hit low," said Arch.

"So leave already," said Duke.

"Turn up the volume on the way out," said Smits.

I went to the stereo, Arch and I putting on our dress-gray tunics. The dial was set at three. I moved the dial to three and a half and left a ten in the cup.

21

BEAR

West Point Library, September 7, 1966

Major H. Norman Schwarzhedd became my P in the mechanics of solids, yet another break-my-heart Cow engineering course. He taught the second-from-the-cellar section, where I was the second-from-the-bottom man. He gave no hint of knowing about my father.

Legends followed Schwarzhedd like iron filings after magnets. He had been the first cadet since MacArthur to break down the reveille cannon and reassemble it atop Central Barracks, and had succeeded in turning back the clock tower in East Barracks thirteen minutes in distant salute to George Orwell. In Vietnam, he had fought like Napoleon in fatigues. Reportedly, he possessed a fulminating anger.

"You're NOT AUTHORIZED to be indifferent to this course!" he shouted, crashing the classroom pointer on my desk, fragmenting it and raining splinters on the blackboard and his carefully drafted bridging diagrams while my heart seized in imitated infarction.

In a faculty composed of war heroes, canal architects, all-American athletes, nuclear engineers, nation builders, espionage masters, Heisman Trophy winners, Rhodes scholars, and rocket scientists, Schwarzhedd drew an affectionately romanticized reputation among the Corps. Wild rumors abounded to explain the sources of his many nicknames—"the Bear," "the Blitz," "Hannibal." In a school where Honor was all and honesty was presumed, we relished tall tales about the man with the pretzled name. He had graduated high, played football, lettered in track and field, and been a member of the Dialectic Society, founded in 1816. I joined the society, as those without charisma seek its growth through association. I helped write the system-razzing skit for the Hundredth Night Play, held a hundred days before graduation.

The major was of a size that suggested the bigger-than-life statues that populated West Point like penguins at the South Pole. He had a large torso, big feet, and a booming voice. His head was the result of geometry at work. The square jaw, sheer-sided cheeks, and wide temples suggested he had been formed by a large-bladed hatchet wielded by a sculptor who had focused on the big parts. His fierce, penetrating eyes under strong, animated brows seemed at odds with his neatly linear mouth, which teased at the edge of an outlaw smirk, a nighttime-raiding smile that could crawl up your drainpipes and leave laughter in the middle of a bad storm. I liked that part. I didn't like the burning eyes, the brows beetling with muscular intent.

En route to the library, I passed George Patton in bronze, his

pearl-handled revolvers on his hips. In an air pocket within the
hands were four of his stars—small secrets held inside, like a
Taoist spirit. River winds keened through his profile. I always
thought it was because he had spent five years at the Academy; he had flunked a course and been given the ""turnback"
option—repeating an entire year.

I was reading a pristine copy of Fairbank's *East Asia: The
Modern Transformation* in the third-floor reading room when a
deep voice said, "None of that is on tomorrow's writ."

I looked up. Major Schwarzhedd was sitting serenely, as if
he were a part of the library, waiting for pigeons to alight. I
was surprised by his presence and by his silence; in my experience, there was little he did without ample dynamism. I, who
prided myself on my silence in the woods, had been surprised
by a man as large as South Aud and as quiet as a tactical
atomic weapon.

The banked lights in the tall ceiling illuminated the brightly
burning eyes of Ulysses S. Grant and H. Norman Schwarzhedd. The four orbs fixed me in dark, steely gazes. I wasn't
happy to see the major. I knew this because I had stopped
breathing, sweat was on my upper lip, and my shoes and
Jockey shorts had shrunk. He had come by to check on the
halt, the lame, and the dumb, and had found all three in one
body, studying Chinese history.

"Hi, sir," I said, blushing a little.

"And a very cheery good evening to you," he said, his
mouth smiling for an instant. "Is this how you pass your
time?"

"No, sir. Usually, I'm in the military section. This is a new
book from Harvard's Yenching Institute. My uncle recommended it."

He looked at me, expressionless, and I was reminded of my
dababa. Actually, it was like looking at three Uncle Shims
while sitting in a pool of water as live power lines sparked,
which aptly described my progress in engineering as well as
my success in adhering to the ancient ways of my heritage. I
heard the high wind whistling over Patton's statue outside the
granite walls.

"What does the book tell you?" he asked politely.

"Sir, China is all families, in ritualized relationships, based
on obligation and duty. Duty is done by honoring others."

I looked at him. He was still listening.

"Here, we try to make money, be successful, and look good."

He smiled.

"K'ung Fu-tzu, Confucius, said, 'Subdue the self, honor the rituals, and benefit society. Do not work for individual gain.' "

"Interesting," he said. "Perhaps the sages knew something we rediscovered a couple hundred years ago. Or perhaps there are life principles which transcend times and nations."

I surveyed the colorful collage on his chest: the sky blue Combat Infantryman's Badge; the bright silver U.S. Master Parachutist wings; the red, white, and blues of the Silver Star and Bronze Star, each with bright gold, oak-leaf clusters; the green and white Army Commendation Medal with gold "V" devices for valor; the deep burgundy and bright white of the Purple Heart; the blue and gold Air Medals; and the greens, yellows, and reds of the Vietnam service medals. On the right were golden Vietnamese Jumpmaster wings. On his shoulders were the black, gray, and gold USMA patch with the Helmet of Athena, the bright yellow and black Ranger Tab, and the bright red, double-A patch of the all-American, 82nd Airborne Division. The colors of brass, and courage. I looked at them and imagined their cost in fear, pressure, and anguish.

As Plebes we had memorized the ribbons. They sold for a nickel in the post exchange, but to wear them, we had learned in tactics, one had to have protected his men, served his mission, confronted fear, and conquered the tendency for disorganization while the Grim Reaper called the tune, enemy steel filled the air, and men screamed from the hideous carnage done to their bodies and souls.

I thought I knew him from the eloquence of his awards and the force of his lectures. Now, alone with him, it struck me that I didn't know him at all. His large, rectangular face was still, his sunburned complexion darkening through a very short scalp.

"You have done what Sun Tzu recommends," he said. "You have confused your enemy with misinformation."

"Who's my enemy, sir?"

"Engineering," he said. "Half the academic departments think you're gifted. The other half want to send you back to elementary school. Your classmate Mr. Benjamin says you spend sixteen hours a day not studying, and the other eight avoiding books."

"Scurrilous innuendo, sir. I read books," I said.

"Yes, but nothing you read is examinable. Mr. Ting, prepare to receive a reprimand. Ready?"

I nodded, gulping loudly. "Yes, sir."

His large, squarish hands were quietly crossed in front of him. There were little blond hairs on them. "We're giving you an excellent work protocol to sustain you all your life. But you're not receiving; you spend study time on rec reading. You're slacking off. THAT," he said loudly, his body seeming to rise from the table, "gives *me* a pain in my Southern *neck*. It oughta give YOU cause to use Preparation H. Now, absorb *that*." He sighed, his large chest relaxing into its normal barrel expansion, his tunic no longer straining against his shoulders.

"This was an excellent reprimand. It was short, concise, and sincerely delivered. I expect our discussion to change your ways, for all time. Do you agree?" he asked flatly.

"Yes, sir," I said.

"Feel better, now that your life has been restructured into a model that future leaders of America will be inspired to emulate?"

"Absolutely, sir," I said.

"Let me ask you a riddle," he said. "Why don't you study?"

"Sir, I don't really know," I said.

His eyes narrowed. "You surprise me. I'd expect a person who gets such fine grades in the other subjects, someone as well read as you, to provide something creative."

"Sir, maybe my slide rule was damaged in a fall. So the cursor doesn't read on a true axis, and this skew creates a disparity in, and a uniqueness to, my answers. So, meanwhile, I should avail myself of one of the best military libraries in the world."

The corners of his mouth rose slightly. "WHERE THE HELL DO YOU THINK YOU ARE—ON A CRUISE SHIP, PLAYING SHUFFLEBOARD 'CAUSE YOU THINK BINGO HAS TOO MUCH MATH? Does it make sense for you to be in the top sections in nonengineering and then get *found* in solids?"

Jeff "Tree" Bartels, Buns Butte, and Moose Hoggatt were next to us. When they saw who was yelling, Moose said "Oh, boy" and scooped his papers and books. Buns and Tree cleared their throats, slammed books shut, and they all moved smartly out of the room, as if they had just set short det cord into a brick of C-4 plastique and amatol at the base of an enemy bridge.

"No, sir," I said.

"You're not sure why you don't study," he said.

"No, sir." I licked my lips, my face warm, trying to swallow.

"Think that might be an issue of some interest, given that this institution's underlying motto is 'Work, Labor, Sweat'?"

"Yes, sir."

"You're a noise-sensitive artilleryman, a palsied demolitionist, a misanthropic minister. Want a classic internal contradiction? *Lazy cadet.* That's because there are only *former* lazy cadets. Think you can pass solids without hiving it?"

"No, sir."

"*Want* to flunk out?" he asked.

"No, sir."

"I'm confused," he said quietly. "Help me out. Do something extraordinary: make your incomprehensible condition understandable to an amateur in the listening arts." His eyes opened wide in an effort to understand whatever I might say and I wanted him to stop this so I could laugh with him and he could tell me about his life.

I sighed. "Sir, I'm blocked. I sit down with the texts—and I open them, and I don't see anything. Nothing sticks. My mind goes blank." It was like writing with a hard piece of chalk that makes noise but leaves no mark. "Then the whufers come. I stay up all night, sitting with my books." I licked my lips. "I probably pray to Chinese gods more than study. I memorize parts. I take the writs, I pass. I'm still here.

"Early in Yearling year I found the Mil Sci Reading Room. That's why I came to West Point. To learn that. Gettysburg, Midway, Chosin Reservoir, Dien Bien Phu, Blenheim. That's the part that I'll need when I get out of here. I don't think that villagers trying to decide between us and the VC are going to care if I can figure out a Thevenin circuit." I stopped, knowing I had gone too far. The young turtle's neck was offered to the hunting eagle.

Silence. He wanted more neck.

"I've read most of the series works there, sir," I said.

"Like *History of the United States Army?*" he asked.

"Yes, sir. Karig's *Battle Report,* Morison's *History of U.S. Naval Operations. The Study of U.S. Strategic Bombing in World War II.* Stilwell's *Letters.* Eisenhower's *Crusade in Europe.* Foreman's *A History of the U.S. Military Academy.* I'm doing *The West Point Atlas of the Napoleonic Wars* now."

"Unfortunately, they have nothing to do with Cow curriculum. What will your family say when you get found in academics?"

It was the question of my life, enhanced because it was posed by the professor who could be the supervisor of the outcome.

"My father will disown me, sir. I mean, there's no money—it's a relationship thing. But, well, he won't be able to handle it. The disappointment. The dishonor, the shame."

"Can *you?*"

"I'll have to, sir," I said.

"You may, at that. Character building." He looked at me. "You accept defeat too quickly, Mr. Ting. I don't like that one bit. It's an unattractive condition in a soldier. You enjoy losing?"

"No, sir," I said.

He studied me. "How do you think Lee felt after Gettysburg?"

"Bad, sir. Like Pompey at Pharsalus, Kimmel after Pearl Harbor, Yamamoto at Midway, Navarre after Dien Bien Phu, von Rundstedt at Normandy. They all knew they had blown it."

"Damn me for a monkey in tights. You keep a list of all the damn losers, excuse my French . . . why are you *smiling?*"

"Sir, a coach said 'Excuse my French' to me for ten years."

"I don't wonder. You irk him by refusing *his* training, too?"

"No, sir, I did it. That was boxing. It wasn't math."

"Ah, of course. Math's only sixty percent of the curriculum. What will you do in Vietnam, DECIDE IF YOU DON'T LIKE THE NATIVE TONGUE YOU'LL TALK TO EVERYONE IN PIG LATIN?"

I stood up, the chair dragging screechingly along the smooth floor. High *mu,* coefficient of friction.

"Sir, I have no excuse for my lack of diligence in your course, or in any of the engineering subjects."

"That's a start. I'll make you a deal. Study solids tonight. Don't just sit there, chanting you can't do it. Use your mind and cut through the resistance in your spirit and *do your duty* with the assignment." He peered at me.

"Yes, sir," I said.

"Later, after you show progress, report to my quarters. I'll teach you tactics, to never underestimate your foe. That's Sun Tzu. So, if you get found, causing the Academy deep remorse for losing a Second Classman, and a corporal at that, you'll at least have some specific tactical poop when we make you a sergeant of infantry and send you to Vietnam to see the elephant."

I brightened. "Roger that, sir. And thank you, sir!"

"You seem very chipper about what I would term a bad outcome."

"Sir, I really hate engineering. I don't mind the field."

"You're not worried about that? Going to Vietnam as an NCO?"

"No, sir!" I said emphatically. A question about heart.

"Well, you *OUGHTA BE!*" he shouted, hitting me with his wind. "My section room may be hard, but it won't *kill* you. Of all the miserable, knock-brained people in the world—I get a guy who can't tell a nuclear family from a hydrogen bomb! YOU THINK COMBAT'S JUST ANOTHER ACADEMY COURSE?" With great athletic grace, he snapped out of his chair, seized his briefcase, and was in the main aisle leading to the doors, striding away.

Then he stopped and turned, his mouth compressed into a small, tight crease of stored energy. "KEEP YOUR VOICE DOWN!" he roared, causing the lights to buzz while I jumped in place.

"THIS IS A DAMN *LIBRARY!*" His voice echoed through the room.

A librarian came running, worry creasing her face. I looked at her as she glanced at me and then stared at the major as he marched with long strides down the hall.

She smiled broadly at him, showing all of her pretty teeth. It was obvious that, with his back turned to me, he was smiling hugely.

22

LAIR

West Point, October 8, 1966

It was Saturday after parade. I was dressing after the shower, studying my squad book before the Plebes reported.

"They're afraid of you," said Clint.

"Hey, I'm their big, manly chested squad leader."

"They're afraid 'cause you're Chinese. What's the name of the tall, skinny crot with pimples?"

"Owen Spanner," I said.

"Spanner's never seen an Asian in his life. First one he meets is his hard-core, Third Regiment squad leader. He's freaked."

"You were the first animal nut I ever met. I wasn't scared."

"I wasn't your squad leader," he said.

They reported and filed in. It was true; they *were* scared.

"Know how lucky you are that I'm your squad leader?" I asked.

Half heard it as a spirit question and shouted, "YES, SIR!" The other half thought it was Socratic and shouted, "NO, SIR."

I laughed. "You're lucky. To me, you all look alike." I smiled, which authorized them to smirk. Most of them grinned.

They were so young—just kids. Mr. Spanner was taking to West Point like the *Titanic* adjusted to icebergs. Mr. Parthes made John Calvin look like a beachboy. Both continued to frown.

"Small joke," I said to them, quietly.

"Very small," offered Clint.

"Fall out. Tell me in which area," I said, "you are doing best, and worst—academics, athletics, and Tactical Department. Conclude by stating what worries you most about your Plebe experience. Mr. Schmidt."

"Sir, I am doing best in earth, space and graphic sciences. Sir, I am doing poorly in boxing. Sir, I worry I am going to get bone disease or rickets from not eating. I think about food, sir."

Schmidt had come in overweight by ten pounds, but I nodded in sympathy. I hated hunger. They each reported, not wanting to confess performance weaknesses or to admit to anxiety; but everything they had already accomplished, and all that lay before them, had been, and would be, no less difficult.

Mr. Zerl, a presidential scholar and high school all-American, was headed for starman, a status reserved for the top academic 5 percent. He would probably start next year at halfback, was validating all his courses, had mastered spit-shining, and now struggled to admit a concern. He may have been fretting about his tan. At the other end of the spectrum was Mr. Spanner, who was trying to flunk mathematics and English and drown in Mr. Flauck's pool. He was the company's shit magnet, and was getting porcupined with quill even from hard-core First Regiment upperclassmen as he braced his way to ES&GS in distant Washington Hall. With ample cause, he was worrying about everything.

Mr. Parthes was average in all aspects, which, when I thought about it, was hardly average. "Sir," he said, "I worry about Mr. Spanner. Sir, he does not brush his teeth. Sir, he picks his toes instead of studying. Sir, I believe he is urinating in our sink at night to avoid contact with upperclassmen. Sir, I worry that I am going to attack Mr. Spanner and hurt him."

"Who's responsible if Mr. Spanner doesn't make it?" I asked.

They all twitched.

"That is right," I said. "We all are. I, as his squad leader. You, because he's your classmate. His habits are different than yours, and he's not doing great, but he's your classmate. He may in fact be revolting and disgusting, but he's your classmate.

"There is a basic principle here. The Army is not a pickup game where you choose up sides and some do not play. You play everyone. You bring as many through as possible. Not because they are like you, or because you like them. Do it because this is the Army and you are not alone. You are a team or you are nothing.

"Mr. Zerl, I want you to tutor Mr. Spanner in math or English. What's your pleasure?"

He took math. "Sir," he said, "I can also teach Mr. Spanner how to spit-shine."

"Thank you, Mr. Zerl." My spit-shine AI had failed. I asked Mr. Caleb to tutor Mr. Spanner in English, and told him to stay behind with Mr. Spanner. I would impart what I'd learned with Joey Rensler, Clint, and Captain Mac. I would tutor the boxing goats. Mr. McFee, who was doggedly combative in all he did, would help me tutor the Rock Squaders in survival swimming.

"Mr. Spanner, if Mr. Parthes suspects you of abusing the sink, I will require you to memorize a MacArthur speech. Understand?"

"Yes, sir," said Mr. Spanner.

"If, however, you respect the sink, I will escort you to ES&GS to keep the First Regiment from quilling you to death. Okay?"

"Yes, sir," he said, his voice cracking.

Clint and I looked away from him. "Long after you've forgotten your grade in some course," I said, "you'll remember that you helped someone else, or that someone helped you."

"Mr. Ting helped me pass Plebe English," said Clint.

"And Mr. Bestier helped me pass Beast," I said. "And taught me Zoology 101. For which I have never forgiven him."

Murphy, author of the famous law, was alive and well, routinely fed, steadily pampered, and in command of human affairs. I wanted to avoid Colonel Smits, and had now received an invitation to enter his country once again.

Cadet Ting:
    I would appreciate the honor of your presence in my Q, Bldg. 149 #39 (extension 2591), after Parade. I have popcorn, hot dogs and sodas. Call only regrets.
    MAJ Schwarzhedd, Inf.

Major Schwarzhedd had developed a new reputation. It was added, like rings in a sequoia, to his many existing ones: he invited goats to his quarters for academic counseling. He was said to be a great reader of books. I went with trepidation and excitement, still wondering if he knew that my father had been friends with his. I did not sense that he was being secretive, for the major was as covert as a Fourth of July parade.

I looked up from rereading the note in time to render a salute to the chief recreation officer and grab-ass commander of the West Point Saturday Night Poker Society.

"Here to see me?" Colonel Smits asked, his tunic smelling of cigarettes, his breath sour. He did not return my salute.

"No, sir," I said.

He spec'ed me with his cold, reptile eyes. For an instant I had a sense of what it would be like to be a woman in his presence. "Then screw off," he said in his rockslide voice, smiling omnivorously as he stepped away on metal-tapped heels.

The distaste remained. I watched him walk away, not willing to present him with my back. Birds quarreled in the trees. Of all the many people on the sphere, I have to run into him: Murphy's Law.

Major Schwarzhedd's BOQ door was open and I heard music. I thought it was classical because it lacked lyrics and exhibited the pace of something that would last longer than three minutes.

From the door I saw the major in gray sweats, writing at his desk, left handed. He was built to the ideal specifications for cadets, career officers, professional football players, and permanent brick structures. On the desk were neat piles of papers, reports and manuals, and a double-photo-frame set of what I presumed were his parents—Na-men and his wife. I was surprised by the smallness and the simplicity of his poorly lit room. It was not only that his size dwarfed his quarters; the place was small—less than half of what Smits occupied next door. Here, in the relative dark, a neighbor's loud music could approach auditory persecution, where one would consider changing religions and admitting mythical mortal sins for a reduction in volume.

I hadn't made a sound. "Thanks for coming, Mr. Ting. Have a seat," he said over his shoulder, motioning with his head toward a metal folding chair near the old, whitewashed, paint-peeling door with the number 39. "I'll be with you in a moment."

The room was lined with bookcases, filled from floor to ceiling with books of all sizes and titles, ages and colors. Books lay in organized stacks on the hardwood floor. In the far corner, books, notebooks, and papers were in piles arrayed in a mazelike radial pattern. I could trace his reading from the inner circle to the outer, with a gap in the pattern to allow passage. The books were scholarly—Latin American, European, Middle Eastern, Asian, ancient—the kind that collect dust on the shelves of lesser men.

A robust rotating fan hummed busily as it riffled the many papers on his desk, on his bed, and on his bulletin boards, creating a small, cyclic pattern of fluttering. Differently colored sheets with personal notes lay inside them, and they sang like an orchestra of small birds with each sweep of the fan, beating occasionally in harmony with the music. To the right was a small cot and a nightstand with a radio, an old brass lamp, and Hendrik Van Loon's *Tolerance*. To the left was a kitchen area that would have been small in Lilliput.

He closed a binder, placed it on a shelf above the small desk, and reached down to an old icebox about as attractive as a brown, beaten Lister bag on an abandoned battlefield. He pulled out two bottles of Tab and offered me one.

"Thanks, sir," I said, reminded of Tony Barraza's dank YMCA hotel room in San Francisco's Tenderloin, with the neon sign out the window, the streets owned by hookers and winos. The soda was very cold; the major had a million books and played sophisticated music. The room was all his, and it was next to a majestic river, with birds and trees and sunlight. I liked it. If I lived here, I would keep the books and the ice-box, and play Brenda Lee, Skeeter Davis, the Everly Brothers, Lenny Welch, and Marianne Faithfull, and their songs of per-petual tragedy and lonely, romantic woe.

"I hope we can talk about tactics, homework, cabbages and kings. Let's start with your father. Tell me about him," he said.

So he knows. But my father, like engineering, was not one of my areas of expertise. I reviewed my gleanings from sixteen years of Uncle Shim's calculated sayings and Edna's offhanded remarks.

The music stopped. A radio announcer whispered, as if he were afraid that someone would hear him, as if he were doing the KDET reveille radio show in a soft, noninvasive voice, try-ing not to disturb the *ho*, the harmony, of the Corps as it fell out of bunks for the cannon, the buzzer, and the band.

"Sir, my father was the second of two sons, born in Yangzhou, at the confluence of the Grand Canal and the Yangtze River in northern China." I looked at the tracks of my fingers on the bottle's condensation. "His grandfather was a wealthy magistrate who had his own army. My father was born in the same year and same month as Henry P'u-yi, the last em-peror of China. My father grew up, and lived through, revolu-tion, the warlords, invasion, world war, civil war.

"Later, the family moved to Shanghai, where my father completed a classical Chinese education and attended St. John's University, an American school for rich Chinese sons. He got an engineering degree. Later, he joined the Nationalist Army, which was a radical thing for an aristocrat's son. He flew an old Vought biplane against the Communists and the Japanese. He was detailed to the Infantry School and took IOBC and Jump School at Benning. He later joined Stilwell's headquarters, and was in the field with a number of American officers."

One of whom was your father, Na-men. Schwarzhedd looked at me attentively. Maybe he didn't know. What should I do? I saw the face of Uncle Shim, and knew the answer. Re-member the *Wu-lun,* the Five Personal Relationships. Elders raise issues, not subordinates.

His linear, finely engineered mouth was now on the edge of a grin. *"Ni hau ma?"* he asked. His Chinese was strong and confident.

"Hau, syesyenin, nin hau ma?" I said. Fine, and you?

"Hau," he said. *"Yi shwo jung-gwo hwa ma?"* Do you speak Chinese?

"Bu-shr," I said. No.

"A shame," he said.

"Sir, I think that every time I'm in a Chinese restaurant. Where did you learn Chinese?"

"My father taught me," he said. "His Dad was a China missionary in Anhwei province. Your parents speak Shanghainese and Mandarin?"

"Yes, sir."

He nodded. "I'd find that deficiency painful."

"Sir, a correction. My mother doesn't speak it. She and I are the ones who don't speak Chinese, although I used to as a kid."

"She was born here?" he asked.

"Philadelphia, sir."

"How'd your siblings speak it if she didn't?"

"Sir, she's actually my stepmother, a *chimu*. She's Caucasian. I promised her a long time ago that I'd always refer to her as my mother. You know, I've been tying up on this relationship between my biological mother and my *chimu* for years."

"Understandable," he said softly. "A matter of loyalty. She'd want a chance to be accepted by her new children." He sipped his soda. "My family's from Germany. As a visitor there, I was glad I had learned it. Dad was a connoisseur of languages. It's helped me all my life. Wherever you're assigned, it's a good idea to learn the tongue." He emptied his bottle and tossed it deftly into a garbage can. "Want popcorn? Or a hot dog?"

"You bet, sir!" I said enthusiastically.

He laughed. "Study this," he said as he handed me a hand-drawn map with a blue, rectangular, friendly unit marker for an airborne infantry company. Its TAOR, tactical area of responsibility, was thick jungle with three-hundred-meter north-south ridges and a river that ran on a SW-NE axis. It covered two ten-thousand-meter grids, an immense amount of real estate for a company of 155 men. West and parallel of the ridge was the FEBA, forward edge of the battle area. West of the FEBA was an infantry battalion unit marker, in enemy red, four times the strength of the blue infantry company.

"An enemy battalion," he said, "has established a thin defense along the FEBA. Through it, the enemy pushes supplies and night strikes, killing your people. After hitting you, the en-

emy recrosses the FEBA. Under the rules, that's sanctuary for
them. Want the works—relish, mustard, ketchup?"

I nodded. Sanctuary. This looked like the Iadrang. The major pulled out franks and condiments from his icebox. He
looked like a bear drawing nuts from a sapling. The franks
were big, the kind that squirt juice on uniforms like *kuotieh*,
pot-stickers, and represent a meal in themselves for boys with
smaller tummies than mine. He put the franks into a tiny portable electric oven on a small counter next to his desk, and began to dress the buns with the works. He had a small window
which overlooked the river. Through it came the calls of sparrows, warbling as background to the classical music, which
was now powerful and emphatic.

"The river's the Iadrang; the FEBA is the Cambodian border. You can't cross it. To stop the enemy raids, you set a good
series of A- and U-shaped ambushes in depth on your side of
the border. The enemy battalion walks into them. You have
them in cross fire, forcing them to retrograde back into Cambodia, giving up terrific losses as they run. You chase on
planned pursuit lanes." His face was animated. This was no
theoretical problem; he had been there.

"You got 'em in a three-prong pincer and now they're coming into your preregistered artillery. You're about to give the
call for the final fire mission when the first sergeant informs
you that you've crossed the border. You've got the enemy in
your hands, but you're in Cambodia." He crossed his arms.
"What do you do?"

I knew the answer. You have to follow orders. That's what
we had been trained so well to do. That's an international border. I can't cross it. Don't break a rule or bust an order.

"Order disengagement, sir," I said. "Can't cross the line."

He flexed his jaw slowly, looking at me as if he were able
to see my viscera, my ganglia, my veinous system. He shook
his head.

"I don't think so. Your duty's to your men. They're not
safe with the enemy cutting them in the night, hiding later
in a safety zone. I'd risk my career for my men, every time.
Heck, what the hell does one little officer's career matter, anywhere?

"You pick up your handset," he said, imitating the motion,
"give your call signs, and say, 'Fire for effect!' Then you order
your platoons to close on the remains of the enemy, *wherever*
he is, and destroy him. In your after-action report, you tell your

battalion CO that you crossed the border. Then Honor is served twice—by your doing the right thing, and by being honest about busting the rule. Forget your career. You protected your men."

He pulled his rolling chair closer to me. "Your duty's to them and their families. Your country expects you to do that duty. Honor means doing it right. Tactics is destroying the enemy with superior information and judgment." He leaned forward. "Use your brains, earn your pay by *thinking*. Destroy the enemy. But protect your men. A careerist wouldn't—he'd cover his own tail—instead of his men's." He slapped his knee. "Got it?"

"Yes, sir," I said. I stared at the map, so rich with lessons.

"You always been a chowhound?" he asked.

"Sir, can I just sort of sit here for a moment? I want to let what you said sink in."

He nodded. Honor in action, honor in speech. Forget your career; think of your men. Subdue the self, honor the rituals, cross the border, break the rule if necessary and report clearly, but serve your men.

The dogs were cooking. He returned to his tiny kitchen and pulled out a one-ring burner, an old, battered pot, and a jar of popcorn. He was authorized a popcorn popper, and didn't have one. We weren't supposed to have one, and did. "I do not miss the TD and the system," he said. "Hated getting quill." He stood there, looking at his old pot. "Mind if I don't make popcorn?" I didn't mind. Rumor had it that Schwarzhedd had never walked an hour on the Area. I had walked ten. "How many dogs you want?"

"How many you willing to requisition, sir?"

"Eight each," he said. "Then I'm out and we call for pizza."

"Eight's a good number, sir."

"Big appetite," he said.

"Sir, I've been a chowhound since I was seven. Sir, you ever walk the Area?" I was getting very personal.

"No," he said. "I have Century Club classmates who claim, as a result, that I never really attended West Point." The Club was for cadets who had served at least a hundred punishment tours.

He gave me four on a paper plate while cooking the others.

"Pig heaven, Good Deal, woof-woof," I said. "Thank you, sir." I had half of one in my mouth when he said, "Want me to say grace?"

All meals at the Academy were preceded by prayer from the Poop Deck, the high medieval balcony where the Supe and the First Captain had lunch, and could watch over the Corps with the same stately ease as the watching warriors on the massive mural of Great Battles. I never prayed before we ate contraband popcorn or boodle in barracks. Lorbus always did, and Arch always crossed himself.

I forced the food into one cheek, cleared my throat, put my head down, and closed my eyes.

"God, thank you for the fellowship of Christian men. For your gifts, for your love, for your forgiveness of our inadequacies and our forgiveness of others, for giving us here at West Point the opportunity to learn how to serve, for the food you place before us, let us use it to your purposes. In your Son's name, Amen."

"Amn." I began chewing again. I remembered Mr. Armentrot on R-Day, skulls shaven, necks in, stomachs empty, small bites and chew six times, on imaginary food. Armentrot was in Vietnam.

He grinned at my hoggish appreciation. "*C'est magnifique!* Am I a chef, or what?"

"Yr a shf," I garbled. I swallowed. "Have to invite you over to barracks for soup, sir."

"Soup?" he said.

"Sir, we make real good soup, using mess kits and coffee heating coils. Start with a base of chicken broth from kosher stores in the City, stored in our boots. Add vegetables which dates bring in, salami from the laundry bag. Cut them up with Gerber jungle knives on the reverse side of the desk blotter padded with a laundry shirt board. Add one tin of C-rats 'beef and rocks'—beef and potatoes—with the cream, salt, pepper, and sugar from the accessory pack—bring to simmer and serve in java cups."

"Obviously," he said, "I graduated too early."

I smiled so hard it surprised me.

"I feel a little like Fagin," he said, "collecting urchins and giving them leadership." He ate with greater dignity than I, which, on analysis, was saying little. "Define leadership."

I swallowed. "Influencing the behavior of others toward an organizational goal." He wanted to influence me toward good grades.

"I want to influence you toward conscious behavior," he said.

I lifted my eyebrows in surprise, while still chewing, which was like my dismounting the high bar and landing on my feet.

"If you don't study, it's for a reason. And if you do study, it's also for a reason, either of which is understood by you."

This was an astonishing proposition. Why would I need to understand the reasons for anything? At West Point, we did not ask why, since the question was irrelevant. At West Point, one must simply function, perform, execute, and obey. We were performers, not logicians.

"What's the big deal with conscious behavior, sir?"

"Ah, always begin with basics. If you're conscious, you can be accountable. Ethics flows from accountability. I learned that from my father and my sisters. I learned it from my mother.

"Even though the Academy emphasizes a variety of rote behaviors, we're really urging you to think, to understand."

"What did your father teach you, sir?" I asked, blinking when I realized the gravity of the inquiry. I was being impertinent.

He looked at me. "What did your father teach *you?*"

Fathers. *Lin tsun,* tremblingly obey. "To obey. To be respectful. To work hard. To be American. To admire West Point. I'd never really thought about it before, sir. This is the first time I've ever said this."

Major Schwarzhedd passed me another Tab. "My dad taught me to honor the concept of a calling. He was a servant."

"A servant?" I said.

"He didn't live for his advancement. He served my mother, my sisters, me—his men, his president, the Army, the nation."

I took a breath. "Sir, did your father like you?"

Schwarzhedd smiled. "A childhood chum of mine, back in New Jersey, came from a strict religious family. When he was little, his father lined up the kids and told them to remember two things. 'One, fear and obey God, and me. Two, I am not your friend.'

"I don't agree with that," he said. "I don't think parents can be peers with their kids. But the trust, the knowing, the affection that go with friendship—they should be in there." He studied his large hands. "They have to be there."

He looked at me while I mulled over his answer. "Your father trusted you?" I asked. "And really knew you?"

He nodded, his eyes on me but focused on the past. "I was blessed. The trick though, is to focus on what you can do for others—*not* on what others may not have done for you."

What I can do for others. The papers riffled musically.

"Someone must've helped you," he said. "Boys don't end up at West Point under independent steam."

"My mother—my stepmother—gave me English. My father gave me West Point as the objective. My boxing coach—who always said 'Excuse my French'—gave me his time and his skills." I sighed. "For ten years." I realized that it was enough, that I had gotten more than most kids.

"Sir, my first friend gave me hope. When I'm in chapel, I think about the black Baptist church I used to go to—a Chinese kid in a sea of black faces, singing songs I didn't understand." I remembered that I used to cry to the sound of that congregation singing. I cleared my throat. "I really didn't know how to fight back then. Or to talk." I was talking too much. "I was just a kid. It's sort of a mystery."

"No mystery," he said. He looked at me as if I were as normal a fixture in his Q as his books. "My best pal was Jewish. I celebrated Seder with him every Passover and could sing with him in Hebrew. When Dad was assigned to Paris, I learned French. Had friends from all over Europe, on both sides of the Iron Curtain, from Ethiopia, survivors of the Holocaust. Each language, each new friendship, each cuisine—and some pretty amazing delicacies—opened a wider world for me. I saw the world as having all the colors, all the faiths, so many tongues, and all one face.

"When I reported to the Academy on R-Day in 1952, during the Korean War and in the wake of the cheating scandal, I had already seen a world larger than West Point.

"In Vietnam, I got to serve with selfless patriots fighting for their country." He put his head down and his voice caught. "I saw courage to make the songs of Homer pale." His eyes were moist. My heart pounded, caught between discomfort and wonder. Schwarzhedd, man of men, crying?

He raised his right forearm, shaking the watchband, making a noise like the small black ammunition links falling from the ejector in a chattering M-60 machine gun.

"Good men died for a noble cause, their sacrifices slandered by our countrymen who know no better." His eyes narrowed in pain and wisdom. "My father taught me to know what I'm doing, and why I'm doing it. Leaders have to know that. People should know that.

"Cadets should consciously know why they're here. A lot are here because their fathers sent them. This," he said, waving at the world outside his window, "is a whole lot of horse hooey to put up with for your father. Is that why you're here?"

I put my head down, looking at my empty plate. Major Schwarzhedd filled it with the other franks.

"I don't know, sir," I said. "I hate the engineering. But I really love it here, more than any place I've ever known. But somehow, my father always wants it more than I do." I scratched my itching neck. I wanted a drink. "I don't know why I'm here."

"I never met your father. Dad told me that Colonel Ting's son was in the Class of '68. When I saw that you were part of Alonzo Smits's pirate crew, I backed off." He looked down. "I thought if I introduced myself, you'd be caught between conflicting loyalties, between Smits and me. If you needed to walk the dark side of Doctor Death, as he calls it, well, having the son of your father's best friend trying to intercede would not have been instructive."

"You know, sir, I went to his Q for most of Yearling year. Killed brain cells. But I was never really part of it."

"I'm glad to hear that. Smits is a good man, but he's an injured soul. He's trying to heal the wrong way. Well, Dad told me a lot about your father. He's obviously a very special man, using willpower to change from a Confucian to an American at the age of thirty-five." The major stood, stretching his back. He was in obvious pain, and it was also obvious that he did not want to discuss it. I saw his tunic with the Purple Heart in a small armoire. "If I tried to even *understand* what it means to be a Buddhist or a Zoroastrian now, I don't think I could do it."

It struck me that Major Schwarzhedd might know more about my father than I did.

He grunted in pain. "How could you hold to 'submission of self and honoring ritual,' *and* to individual 'life, liberty, and the pursuit of happiness'? It would be war, Sherman's kind of war. I know about war, now. I did it for a year." He contemplated the view. "Imagine your father, fighting a war of values, every day."

I saw him sitting in his chair, reading books in English, forcing them into the lobes of his mind. He had given me to Edna to make me American, make or break. He had pointed me to the Academy to give me true American citizenship. I lacked his willpower, his drive, his skills, his confidence.

I looked at Major H. Norman Schwarzhedd as he tried to

stretch an obviously wretched back. I liked this man. I admired him. I wanted to be like him.

A realization came to me and I scrunched my eyes shut and lowered my face as I measured the truth of it.

For all the *gahng* and *shiao*, the math and Confucius, the hunger and hard times, I just wanted my dad to like me.

23

PEARL

New York, October 1966

I had three life goals: to study solids; to give up on Christine, who was dating others; and to bench-press three hundred pounds.

"What's your max?" asked Duke Troth.

The last time I had spoken to him, at Smits's BOQ six months ago, I had considered killing him. "Two-eighty-five," I said.

"Put up two-ninety. I'll spot," he said.

We loaded the forty-fives, twenty-fives, fives, and two-and-a-half plates. I lay flat, loading up on oxygen. I had already worked out. I wondered if he'd drop the bar on me.

I lifted and lowered it slowly so it would not bounce, and pressed upward. My shoulders complained under the load as I kept my back flat. The plates rattled against the collars as my arms shook. The first four inches above the chest represented the most difficult lift zone, and I cleared it, my face feeling red. Just before I straightened my arms, everything I had in my arms quit, and I could go no further. Duke helped me finish the press.

"Umph," I gasped, "thanks for the spot."

"Didn't lift an ounce."

"Bull," I breathed, "I was stuck."

"Anyone asks me, you benched two-ninety clean."

I stood up. "Hope no one asks you."

"You're not one of them Honor freaks, are you?" he asked.

I breathed deeply. "What brings you to Iron City?"

"Want you to join our study group," he said.

"English? Social sciences? Psych? Tactics?"

"Juice," he said.

I chuckled. "Duke, goats are supposed to study with hives, not other goats. What good could I do you in Juice?"

He shrugged his shoulders. "It's a way to schmooz. You've dropped outa the Society." His ice-cold eyes looked perfectly sincere. I studied his strong, hard, adult face. My own face was hardening with time. I picked up the eighty-pound bell and did tricep presses.

"Can't figure you," I gasped. "Being in a goats' Juice group'd be like eating crepes at a dump." I thought of that April night, when Schwarzhedd appeared and Smits and Troth announced themselves as bigots. "Which, on occasion," I said, "I have done with you."

"Tonight, fourth-floor reading room, after call to quarters," he said. "Good group. Sonny Rappa's our smart man."

I had trouble imagining them together. I didn't like it. He was forming a team. "Thanks, but I don't study Juice that much."

Juice depended on integral and differential calculus, whose intricacies I had barely learned and instantly forgotten in the previous academic years. Calculus employed sentences without English. It was a dark art, described in graphs rampant with round and sharp-edge squiggles, ancient totems of thunder dragons and small symbols of Egyptian hieroglyphs, black lines which took erratic perpendicular turns, boxes within rectangles filled with vicious glyphs, nonsensical gates, and legends with arrows which pointed to incomprehension. So much for studying more.

That left Christine. I had seen her for Christmas and summer leave. Her opposition to the military, and my commitment to it, had hardened like an old and treasured wound equal to the scarring of her physical rejection of me. I still loved her, devastated by the pain of being separated. Last spring, we had met in New York for six glorious days of sightseeing and restauranting. I spent all my money and had to borrow some from Deke and Arch. We stayed in separate rooms in the Manhattan Hotel. She kissed me passionately when she arrived, and when she left I watched her plane lift off from La Guardia and knew that there was to be no romance between us. I had been given my chance, and she had said no, but I did not know how to end it in my heart.

It was after midnight, Deke "Ping" Schibsted and I had split the winners' pot in our barracks Friday-night poker game, where I had won despite the distraction of William "Moon" Shine's endless playing of every album cut by Buck Owens and the Buckaroos.

"Hey," Moon had said to a chorus of hoots. "This is *real* music, not that weak crap that comes from the coasts."

We were sacked in our racks, communing with our brown boys. Clint and Bob were snoring like M-113 diesel engines. Deke was another disgustingly handsome, athletic white guy with a lantern jaw and a fine mind. He had whipped me in every wrestling match we ever had. Prisons have riots; the Academy had wrestling RFs—rat fornication parties—free-for-all, no-sides, everyone's-my-enemy pandemonia of flying elbows and fists that were imitations of "the Pit" at Camp Buckner. Deke and Bob "Big Bus" Lorbus were RF champs, able to toss bodies from the mound of cadet humanity like farmers husk corn. In the midst of a hyperaggressive, super-male environment, Deke remained at heart as kind and mild mannered as a divinity student. He was a great roomie. Deke and I had been squad leaders for First Detail Beast and had taken leave at Fort DeRussey on Waikiki, where I had healed my heart by developing a world-class tan. "Life is good. This is home."

"Ho boy," he said. "Gray hog alert!"

"Naw, it's just cool. We're all going to make it. What can go wrong from here? Haven't you always wanted to be part of a great band of brothers, committed to doing the right thing? It's like the *Romance of the Three Kingdoms,* this old story about three best friends who swore in a peach orchard to be brothers, always."

The harvest moon looked down over Cadet Hilton, casting shadows from battlement rooftops. "I worry about Vietnam," he said.

"Forget Vietnam—this is special. Never be this good again. Think about Captain Mac, kids to feed, bills, debt. We're single, no kids or wives or families to pull us down, hold us back, make us worry. Never had so much food or freedom. So many *friends.* All we have is each other, pulling together. Football games. Walking back from the mess hall, through the snow, after fourths on Wednesday steak." I even enjoyed singing Christmas carols in the chapel.

"Dream about Vietnam," he said. "About dying. Punji stakes, land mines, bouncing bettys, tripwires, AK-47s, snakes, RPGs, lost airbursts. Wake up and think I'm dead. Or a POW." Bouncing bettys were land mines that sprang up to groin level before detonating.

I thought of Asians holding my roommates prisoner. I imagined what the VC would do to me. "You'll make it, Deke. You're smart and quick and run like the devil. Hey, you think you'd have buddies like this if you were in *college?*"

"Yeah," he sighed. "I just wish we had more privileges."

"You should've joined the Spanish Club."

"I hate taking the bus back," murmured Mike Benjamin. Mike and Sonny Rappa were starmen, in the top 5 percent of the class. They hived 3.0 writs while the rest of us fell asleep during punishing nuclear-physics lectures on de Lorentz and the nuclides, which I thought should be the name of a rock group. My notes degraded from elegant calligraphy into ever-diminishing spirals until there was a wild skid mark down the notebook as the Rack Monster conked me in the head and took my depleted consciousness from the lecture hall. Once, I fell instantly asleep, my head crashing backward into the desk behind me, scattering papers with a huge sonic clap, making me lurch upward with the noise, standing while still snoring, wondering why everyone was seated and staring at me.

"Static equilibrium," said Sonny. "The wind blowing outa West Point is equal in force to the wind that sucks inside it. Despite the stasis, returning still sucks."

"Oh, man, that is so negative," Arch said. "We're goin' to New York, we're not even there and you're moonin' about comin' back."

"I like to be prepared," said Mike.

We were going to New York in our finest threads. We had folding money and matches for the society women we might meet. Some of us had condoms as good-luck charms designed to influence outcomes. Others carried them for their intended purpose. I had none. A panoply of watching spirits, and Edna's enduring presence, expected me to be above the testosterone message. I wondered how I could persuade a girl into something I didn't really understand.

"Describe your perfect girl," said Arch to Big Bus.

"Feed me, drive me, tuck me in at night," he said, grinning.

"Zoo Keeper?" said Arch. No one was handsomer than Clint, but he never had a steady girlfriend.

"Three-oh in looks," said Clint, "hornier than a Texas toad and responds to the orders 'Drive me in your car' and 'Don't scream so loud.' "

"Mike?"

"She's at Smith or Vassar. Dark hair, dark eyes. Has read Willa Cather, prefers Thomas Mann. Writes great, long, deep letters. Very funny. Thinks I'm funny. Can stay up late, talking."

There were loud boos from all but Pee Wee McCloud, who said, "Rabble. If you find her, let me know if she has a sister." Pee Wee had been named to the all-East team as a guard. Sports writers found it hard to believe that someone who was built like a human anvil and talked like Goofy could be a top scholar, but he was.

Mike grinned. "Yeah, but you'll want the smarter one."

"Kai?" asked Arch.

"Feed me, burp me, feed me," I said.

In last year's Armed Forces Day Parade, war protesters had thrown garbage at us. The year before, New Yorkers had thrown ticker tape. I couldn't believe that a war protester would think that West Point had started the Vietnam War. We were the servants who fasted for a year, went to school six days a week, did nothing but follow orders, without any sex, and would be the first to die.

"Hay que hablar español, chicos," said Mike. *"Es un requisito del club."* We have to speak Spanish. It's a club rule.

"Yo, forget it, Mike," said Farren McWhiff, our main soup chef. "We're gonna be talkin' spic all night. Owwww!" he cried as Arch, Mike, and I rubbed our knuckles in his scalp while Pee Wee held him still in his uncontestable mass.

"Farren," said Mike, "this method of behavior modification is admittedly primitive. But you are a base character, evidenced by your ignorance of race relations. This is a reminder to never underestimate the leadership potential of a well-placed noogie."

We were on an Army club bus, embarking on a West Point Good Deal—getting out of the Academy. We had all joined for a variety of reasons. For me, the most important was Sonny and Mike were members. Only Big Bus had joined in error; his mother was Irish. In the rush of activity sign-ups, he had mistaken the Iberia for the Hibernia Society, and was taken aback when everyone began speaking Spanish. ("Hey, buddies, this is a joke, right?" he had asked).

"Mike, I was a little wrong about the next war."

"Oh, you might say that," he replied. "You picked Eastern Europe. Berlin, à la Budapest. You said it would *not* be Indochina."

"Okay, so I was a little off," I said.

"Had to be Indochina," said Sonny. "Look at the world's weather systems. It's the only other place outside the Point where the wind doesn't blow, it sucks."

"Static equilibrium?" I said.

"Negative," said Sonny. "Dynamic imbalance. Nothing but suck."

"Why do you say that?" I asked.

"The country's not behind the war. That's like studying Juice without believing it." He looked at me, hard.

"Whoa. That bad?" I asked. He nodded.

"Kai. This is an Asian war. What do you think?" asked Mike.

"We gotta be ready to stay for a long time. My father said that Vietnam fought the imperial Chinese armies for a thousand years. The Vietnamese never gave up. In the end, they won. The French lasted eighty years. If we want to win, we're going to have to pick the winner, instead of trying to get the loser to win. And the winner is whoever most of the people want. You know, like in a democracy." The bus hit a bump on the Palisades and all of us imitated pogo-stick commuters. "My dad's army didn't do that. Tried to win with logistics; didn't work. We help Tito in Yugoslavia." I took a deep breath. "Oughta pick Ho Chi Minh. The guy *hates* the Red Chinese."

"I can't believe you said that," said Farren. "The South Vietnamese are real patriots."

"But they don't have the masses. They crapped on their own democratic movement."

Mike rubbed his chin. "If Ho hates Peking, then you're right. *Realpolitik*."

"Who cares," said Clint. "We're gonna wipe their butts." I nodded. It was true. For a moment, I felt sorry for the VC.

The bus was taking us to New York City today; later, a similar bus would take us to Saigon. There was a silence.

"Yo, I've been a good cadet. I want to get laid tonight," said Farren. "Who's got a tip for me to score the big one tonight?"

"Use someone else's methods," said Bob.

"Use someone else's personality," said Mike.

"Use somebody else's *dick*," said Arch.

"I'm going to take a chance with life," I said.

"Oh, no," said Mike. "You're going to try to dance again."

"Michael! It's okay!" said "Astaire" Arch. "I've been giving him some AI. Giving him some of that original El Paso *el paso*. The man is beginning to look absolutely Latino."

"Man oh man!" said Clint. "I'm so sick of that song they use. If I hear 'My Girl' one more time I'm gonna puke. You know that Kai and Arch play that for about three hours every damn night!"

We hesitated two counts. Then we all belted out, "I've got sunshine, on a cloudy day . . . ," while Clint cursed us energetically.

A clutch of brightly dressed girls watched us as we trooped through the grand lobby. "Look," someone said, "West Point cadets!" I saw her, amidst all the girls, next to the black, nine-foot-tall, two-ton Waldorf-Astoria clock. Her eyes were large and alert in a very pretty face, a pretty figure in a blue chiffon gown. She looked like Lana Turner. The girls were called first; we followed them to the mezzanine for the reception line. They studied us over their bare shoulders. She looked in my direction, and I reversed field down the stairs and ran from the hotel. I sprinted back, joining the reception line breathless. The hall was immense, gaudy, and high ceilinged, filled with men in tuxedos and women in formals, dark-suited waiters with trays full of champagne flutes, and VIPs in red cummerbunds. An ensemble played classical music. I made sure my fly was zipped.

"Where'd you go? What's that in your hand?" Bob asked.

"Señor Lorbus," said the official line greeter, reading Bob's name tag, shaking his hand, inclining his head very close to his, and stating with great courtliness, *"Tengo mucho gusto conocerle. Me llamo Carlos Iturbe, del . . ."* It is my pleasure to meet you. My name is Carlos Iturbe, of . . .

"It's a corsage," I whispered in Bob's ear, still panting.

"Señor Corsage," said Bob, *"el gusto es mio."*

After enduring the common surprise regarding a Chinese West Point cadet speaking Spanish, I sought the girl in light blue.

Clint and "Meatball" Rodgers were talking to her. They had never looked better: Gary Cooper and Jimmy Stewart talking to Lana Turner, and now I disliked Clint's good looks and Meatball's gentle, self-effacing personality. They were laughing, and she was smiling, showing interest and surprise, quickly grasping a flute of champagne from a passing waiter, sipping it and looking at the coffered ceiling, the chandeliers, the crowd. She fit with Clint and Meatball. I edged in. She glanced at me and touched Clint's arm and did not look at me again.

I left the room, scooping two glasses of champagne for myself, and sat on a soft green sofa on the mezzanine. I felt sorry for myself. I felt like the color of the sofa. I felt like smoking. I saw myself in the multifaceted mirrors of a tall column. I looked good in uniform, but still felt ugly. I was supposed to have a sweet face. I drank fast to numb my doubts and self-dislike.

Someone sat down next to me, someone light in weight. I blinked as two very large eyes in a lovely face framed by shoulder-length black hair gazed intently at me. She was so intent that I thought she was looking at someone behind me. I turned and looked to see who it was. We were alone, and she was Chinese.

She laughed, strong and naturally, without the strains of deliberate practice, the pulls of restraint which colored my laugh.

"You must be very thirsty and on your way to a prom," she said, looking at the flutes and the corsage in my hands. Her voice had bells in it, and a full, round articulation that invited attention. The large, bright eyes dominated a smooth face complemented by a strong nose, a well-formed mouth, elegant eyebrows, and a pronounced jawline with prominent corners. She was tall and slender. The paleness of her face, throat, and arms was accented by a sleeveless black dress, a strand of pearls that looked anything but cheap, and disturbingly noticeable legs. Intelligence shimmered from her like summer heat waves. I was blinking at her and her signals, my addled brain struggling with the data, embarrassed by an involuntary reaction that made standing inappropriate. She was here because of me. I put down the glasses.

"How do you do?" I said. "My name is Kai Ting, and I am delighted to meet you. Please pardon me for not standing."

"Cathy Pearl Yee," she said, offering her hand, which I held, jittery with the realization that her fingers were so alive.

"I believe this is for you," I said, offering the corsage.

She studied it carefully, as if it were something more complicated than a flower. "I don't know you," she said. "Am I safe in accepting this?" Her voice was like a radio message. I would have listened to her if she were giving weather reports from Nome.

"Incredibly," I said.

She took it and pinned it to her dress.

"What generation—?" she asked.

"What genera—?" I asked at the same time, and we laughed. Chinese begin by establishing birth order. "You first," I said.

"I'm first generation, New York. Originally, the family's from Singapore. Shipping business. I'm the firstborn," she said in a way that was so familiar and so new.

"I'm also first. San Francisco. My family's from Shanghai, no family business. Poor as church mice. I'm the only son, and lastborn." I tried not to look at her too hard.

She faced me. "Do you know Townsend Fan Yee?"

"No," I said.

She smiled.

"Who is he?" I asked.

"How did you get into West Point?" she asked.

Nice answer, I thought. "My father was Kuomintang Army. He raised me to go to the Academy. Where do you go to school?"

She leaned forward, close to me, studying my face carefully. I almost squirmed. "What if I was a working girl?"

"Then it would have been a stupid question," I said.

"I take classes," she said, choosing her words carefully. "But I'll be very disappointed if you ask me my major."

College students selected majors. Mine had been selected by Sylvanus Thayer and my father, before my birth. I wanted to know what she studied, but I didn't want to disappoint her.

"Why are you worried about being safe? Safe from what?"

"People," she said. "I like them to stay away. But I also like coming to parties in New York, to look at the people, to study how they act. New York is theater."

"Why do you want people to stay away?" I asked.

"Caucasian boys ask all the same questions," she said.

I shook my head. "That black dress isn't going to ward off anyone. It might make the cops come. Do white guys ask you what generation you are?"

"No. They ask, 'When did your parents come to America?' "

"It's the same question," I said.

"Not from them it's not," she said.

I offered her one of the champagnes and emptied mine. "I've been around white people. I probably ask white-guy questions."

"Yes. I saw you chasing the buxom blond. But you didn't ask her anything."

"She wasn't buxom."

"All blonds are buxom. If she were here now, I don't think I'd be wearing the corsage."

"That's not true," I said.

"Why should I believe you?" she asked.

"Because I don't lie."

She studied my eyes. "Will you dance with me?" she asked.

"I'm not very good," I said.

"Oh, then forget it." She looked down and sipped champagne.

It was safe to stand. I offered my hand. "Cathy Pearl Yee, may I have this dance so I can gently stomp all over your toes?"

I discreetly adjusted my trou. We entered the ballroom, found space, and I took her in my arms, fiercely concentrated to find the beat, and began. She was about five feet six; her waist was very small, her fingertips soft and warm; and she danced very well, adjusting fluidly to me while her large eyes studied me. Somehow, I knew I would not step on her feet and cause her to say "Eek!"

"You're not that bad," she said. "But you're frowning."

I quickly lifted my eyebrows, and she laughed.

"You're very funny," she said.

"What every guy wants to hear while he's waltzing."

"Ding Kai," she said, using the correct and traditional Chinese pronunciation, "we are *not* waltzing."

"No wonder I was frowning."

"Why am I incredibly safe with you?" she asked.

"I'm a gentleman," I said.

"That means you're not married or engaged, right?" she asked.

"Cadets can't be married." Something changed in her face.

"Do you have a girlfriend?" she asked.

"No," I sighed. "I've loved a girl for six years, but she's not interested. How about you?"

"I have too many girlfriends to count," she said, smiling and surveying the crowd. "Your friends are admiring us."

"They're admiring you," I said.

"No, it's us, together. You're tall and muscular. Not a great dancer but you're coordinated, accustomed to using your body."

"How do you know?" I asked.

"I study ballet." I felt the muscles in her back.

"Do you have a boyfriend?" I asked. "And is he here?"

She nestled into me, and I took deep, rapid breaths as I held her, feeling her warmth, her closeness a third party with whom I had to cope, the corsage pressing into me, my heart beating loud enough to interfere with the band. At the end of the number I thanked her. "May I have the pleasure of the next dance?"

She turned and walked away, and I forced myself not to study her undeniably elegant back. I followed her to the sofa and we sat. She leaned toward me, the strand of pearls as white as her skin sliding with a mystic sensuality, resting against the corsage. She looked into my eyes. I imagined feeling her breath on my face. For a moment, I thought she was going to kiss me.

"You're not used to girls, are you?" she asked.

"Yes. No," I said. Her mouth was lovely.

"Are you nice, Ding Kai?"

"I'm a gentleman."

"What does that mean?" she asked.

"I'm trustworthy, loyal, helpful, friendly, courteous, kind, obedient, cheerful, thrifty, brave, clean, reverent."

"Where did you learn to be a gentleman?" she asked.

"My father, I think. And from a woman in my neighborhood."

She laughed. "You may call me Pearl."

"Because I'm nice?" I asked.

"Yes," she said, almost inaudibly. "Do you speak Chinese?"

"I hate that question," I said.

"Me, too," she said. "Although I speak some. Even Mandarin."

I nodded. "Questions which are not answered," I said, "worry me. Who is Townsend Fan Yee? And tell me about your boyfriend."

"I don't think so," she said.

I made a wry face at her and she laughed. "You're very

funny! Not like the men I've known." Not a good sign, my face making her laugh so hard. I wondered how many men she had known.

She read my face. "I'm complimenting you. All my fiancés have been pigs. Oh—if you could see your face! You're so funny!" She laughed, her elegant chin raised, giggling, covering her mouth in a Chinese laugh, and I couldn't help laughing with her. It was all Toussaint's fault; he had made me vulnerable to the contagion of giggling, even if I was its cause.

She had a boyfriend and a history of fiancés. She was a woman.

"How old are you?" she asked. I had felt the question coming.

"I'm twenty." I wanted to say twenty and a half.

"I'm twenty-four," she said. "You're a child. I don't like many men; I'm not sure I like boys."

"Why don't you like men?"

"Men's brains are completely deranged for sex, and men like to give orders. I don't enjoy following them. Pearl's first rule: Only follow orders you must." She sighed. "Men don't understand."

I had jumped internally with her assessment of my brain. "That sounds like me," I said.

"Men don't admit it. You're different—you do." She smiled. "You even said you don't know a lot about girls. I like a little uncertainty in men."

"I'm not that uncertain," I said.

"Don't ruin a good thing," she said. "Please, could I have another champagne." She said it New York—no question mark.

I returned with a tray of twelve flutes. "I'm no good in math."

She raised her eyebrows at me. "You *are* trying to be different, aren't you?" She watched me drink. "Do you have a drinking problem?" she asked softly.

I looked at her, at her still-full second glass. I looked at the tray, beckoning to me. I stood and left with it. When I returned empty-handed, I said, "Not anymore, I don't."

"Do they teach decisiveness at West Point?"

"Any decision is better than none. But I learned about drinking from you. And some of my buddies."

She smiled effortlessly. "I wish I were more decisive."

"About what?" I asked.

She leaned away from me. "Being a good Chinese daughter," she said softly. She sighed. "Or being American."

"Ah-ha," I said automatically. A Chinese acknowledgment. "Why not be both?"

She looked at her pretty hands, caressing her bare left ring finger. Cole Porter's "I've Got You Under My Skin" wafted through the open doors above the smooth roar of the genteel crowd.

"Not possible," she said. "I think you know that. Either I obey my father and give up my own life to him, or I can do what I want to do and lose him."

"Ah-ha," I said again. *Ch'a lu t'ung ku*, the Fork of Pain. In an instant I knew that she should captain her own life. I wondered if that applied to me. I wanted to tell her that I was not a very good Chinese son, but I wanted more for her to think highly of me, to think that I was good and worthy.

"What is it that you want to do?" I asked.

"I want to be free," she said. "It's being free to do whatever I want to do."

To do whatever she wanted to do. So much American thought. I raised an eyebrow. Obviously, I couldn't arch it the way she did, because she laughed, and I couldn't help smiling.

"You have a most amusing face." She giggled at me. "Dance with me, Ding Kai, right here, in the hallway. Pretend that we're old friends, happy to be together again. That we're gay and happy and there's no tomorrow."

"We just met. You've called me funny and laughed at my face." I took her in my arms. We danced to Gershwin and I had Arch's feet.

"I used to daydream about a Chinese warrior prince with a kind heart who would teach me about China," she said, tossing her long hair. I was holding her, without other couples near, and it made our touching more personal, more intimate, riskier. "In the picture books, he looked a little like you. Big, robust, thick black eyebrows. All you're missing is the red face and the beard."

"Guan Yu," I said. "I remind you of him?"

"A little, but you're not really Chinese," she said. "You're not like white men. You're strange."

I was a Chinese colored kid with a white *chimu* who was supposed to be a quiet Confucian scholar and an Airborne Ranger. I liked to read English novels and Chinese history texts in a white school for engineers. "Yes," I said. "I am."

She nodded. I tried to imagine her without makeup. I suspected she was flirting with a lack of health, for reasons unclear.

"Are you healthy?" I asked.

Her eyebrows arched. "What a question! You should ask, instead, what year I am."

"Okay. I'm Year of the Dog. You?"

She smiled. "Horse. Both of us should marry tiger people." Her hand on my back caressed me.

"Guess we don't need to waste any more time with each other."

She laughed. "But dog is also recommended. My doctor says I'd be stronger if I ate more. I don't like Western food. Is it the same for you?"

"I miss Chinese food, but I eat anything that doesn't fight me." She looked at me to see if I had been serious.

"Do you miss your family?" she asked.

I laughed involuntarily, too loudly, took a deep breath and shook my head, too emphatically. "You?"

"You are a mystery, Ding Kai. I miss my mother, and my youngest brother, very much. I'm not a good Chinese daughter."

I took a breath. "I'm not a good Chinese son."

She gazed at me. I think her eyes twinkled.

"Do you like Chinese girls, Ding Kai?" she asked.

I didn't like the question. Her eyes consumed me. Her hand on my back stopped moving. I loved her face.

"You're very beautiful," I said. "Really, breathtaking."

"You don't," she said.

"I don't know," I said. "Grew up with blacks and whites. Never had a real girlfriend. I've tried, for almost six years now, with one girl, who won't have me. Never known a Chinese girl, except for my sisters. And I haven't seen them in a long time." I didn't want her to think I didn't like her, but telling her I cared was too much *ji hui*. I took a deep breath.

"I like you," I said, my voice strained. She was warm and strong. Her eyes danced over my face and I felt the length of her against me.

"I could teach you a lot," she said. "Would you like me to teach you?"

I licked my lips. "I don't know," I said. I looked at her very sternly, curling an eyebrow. I was becoming very expressive.

"Am I safe with you?" I asked in a low voice. "Are you nice?"

She lifted her small chin and laughed, leaning backward. She enjoyed leaning on my arm, angling away from me, and I was captivated by the provocative posture, her delicate throat, the angle of her smile in repose. Her tongue played with her teeth. "You're strong," she said.

"Like ox," I said in my comically deep Mike Mazurki voice, flexing my arms, shoulders, and chest. "After eat onion and garlic, strong all over!"

She pulled away from me, and I felt relieved and despondent. She held on to the rail and leaned so far forward that I quickly joined her, ready to grab her if she fell. She had gorgeous legs. Facing me, her eyes searching, she parted her lips, closed them, licked them, thinking, building a very big question for me.

"Pretend you're a father. You have a daughter who wanted to marry a Caucasian. Would you permit it?"

I never wanted children. "If she loved him," I said.

"What if you disliked him?" she asked.

"For what reasons?"

"Doesn't matter. You're the father and you just don't like him," she said.

"If my daughter loved him, then I would like him," I said flatly, figuring it out, my spirits deflating. I felt chilled.

Her questions revealed everything; she wasn't interested in me. She wanted to marry a Caucasian. She was angry at her bigoted Chinese father. I didn't remind her of the great Guan Yu; I reminded her of the stonehearted father who disapproved of her white boyfriend. She had been toying with me. I, a stupid boy who knew nothing about girls. I felt old pains, regretting these moments. Forget her, fast; retrograde your military butt out of here, now. I tried to bring my heart back from her face and voice, her touching me, her laugh, her closeness, her connection to hidden parts of me.

A thought that seemed to come from below knifed through me and turned the grand lobby of the Waldorf into a dim and underlit place, and I wondered what I could say so I could leave.

Her lower lip trembled. She was on the verge of crying. "Who made you the way you are?" she asked.

I cleared my throat. "What do you mean? I don't know. . . . Are you okay? Was it something I said?"

"Yes. It's all your doing," she whispered, turning to me, leaning her head against my shoulder. I jumped. "Does this bother you?" she asked.

"A little," I said, and she lifted her head from me, looking both surprised and sad. No one like me had ever rejected her. Perhaps, no one had rejected her ever.

"You have a fiancé. You shouldn't be with me."

She looked puzzled. "Oh, Ding Kai, you took me literally." She nodded, narrowing her eyes.

"My father has engaged me to a man I've never met. Family arrangement. A man in Macao. So I told my father about an imaginary white man I was in love with, hoping the shock, the outrageousness of it would end the arrangement. It didn't work; now my father detests this imaginary, nonexistent person because he is not Han Chinese."

"But you're still engaged," I said.

"You are so sad! I won't marry him. Tonight, I met you—and we may be friends for all our days. I like you more than this man from Macao and all the fiancés in my life. Why are you sad?"

I shook my head.

Pearl grabbed my arm. "Admit it!" she urged. "Don't hold back! Not tonight. Not you. You came to me tonight from my childhood storybooks. Please, Ding Kai, tell me what's in your heart. I want to know. I want to know everything about you. How you came to be so different. I want to know why you are sad."

I shook my head. I could never tell anyone this thought, even though she had nearly shaken it from me like an acorn from a tree.

"Guan Yu would tell me," she whispered, and I looked at her. She came closer. "Tell me softly, in my ear. I will tell no one, ever," she said in a voice that soothed me and disturbed me with equal persuasion. She leaned against me on tiptoe, her smooth, cool cheek against my neck, her face in my shoulder, her ear against my lips. I smelled her. Not her perfume, but her—gentle, evanescent, distantly sweet, scented in old mystery, spiced with *tristeza* and *melancolía,* calling to me. Gently, I held her and she fitted her lean body against me.

I tried to speak and couldn't, all my blood rushing everywhere but to my brain. I cleared my throat, making her recoil with the volume of the sound, and I almost laughed with spastic nervousness.

I would tell this girl, this woman, anything. I moved my lips. At first nothing came. I took a deep breath, my chest moving her away as I inhaled, coming closer as I exhaled.

I spoke and no sound came out.

"Say it," she breathed. "Please, try again, Ding Kai."

"No one loves me," I whispered. I closed my eyes and ground my molars. "Shouldn't matter. Means nothing. So hard to say."

"Yes, I know," she whispered back, and she breathed heavily against me, standing taller on ballerina toes to press her cheek against mine so I could feel her tears. I kept my eyes closed as I began to cry, holding her close to me. She felt me tremble.

"Thank you, Ding Kai. You give me *t'ung-hsin t'ung te*. You make me happy. You are a Chinese man, owned by your parents, ruled by your father, who has let me touch your heart. If you cry for me, I will be happy, and I will try to bring happiness to you."

"What's *t'ung-hsin t'ung te?*" I asked thickly, breathing hard.

" 'One heart, one virtue,' perfect Chinese love," she whispered. "No sourness, no untruths. No bitter love, like what you have with the girl who has turned you away for six years. One heart, one virtue."

Her perfume, her touch, her closeness, her mind, almost too much for me to negotiate. I was in a panic of happiness.

I had done many wrongs. "I'm not virtuous," I said.

"Oh, yes, you are," she whispered. "I speak truth." She looked into my eyes and I felt a vulnerability that weakened my legs. "I know the secrets that allow men and women to be happy. They have nothing to do with what men want, and everything to do with what women want. Do you understand?"

I shook my head.

"I have to go. I loathe goodbyes." She pressed a Waldorf-Astoria matchbook into my hand; her fingertips were warm. On the book she had written "Manhattan" and "Southampton," with phone numbers for each.

She kissed me lightly on my cheek, moist with her tears. I closed my eyes, again, to stem the feelings.

"Thank you, Ding Kai," she said in that clear, musical, memorable, radio voice.

When I opened them, she was gone.

24

LUN

West Point, November 5, 1966

In the week before the huge spirit bonfire and the deranged, apocalyptic, table-stacking, drumbeating, bare-chested mess hall rallies for the Navy game, Zoo Keeper Clint decided to branch into botany and aeronautical engineering.

It was between classes, and Arch Torres, Big Bus Lorbus, Moon Shine, and I were playing hearts while musing about writs. We were sophisticated time managers—studying while card playing, reading while weightlifting, bleeding during sports, fretting during sleep, and sleeping while in class.

"Say hello to Para-rat-trooper and Venus," said Clint. He unveiled a small brown rat and a vicious-looking, insect-eating plant that instantly reminded me of Major Szeden, the meanest Tac in the Academy. "Going to train the little guy to jump from the top bunk with a parachute."

"Gonna train the plant to eat him?" asked Moon.

I hated rats. In the 'hood they had a good chance at being the dominant species. Further, I hated heights so much that there was no pleasure in having even the rat jump.

"Can't have a rat in here," I said. "Put him in the sinks."

"You mean that?" asked Clint, his handsome features pained.

The comparative sizes of Clint and the rat made me think of Tony; I probably looked like a rodent the day he adopted me into the Y program. I sighed with the burden of transferred generosity. "Just kidding, Clint," I said. "Put him on the sill. Let him have a good riverview."

"Mr. Ting, sir, long distance. I think it's family, sir," whispered Mr. Haas, the Plebe runner. The light from the hall flooded the room in a bright, luminous parallelogram.

233

"Thanks, Mr. Haas." I grabbed my B-robe, silently closed the door to protect my roommates' sleep, and ran down the stairs, preparing myself for bad news. I entered the orderly room and waved hello to Denny Haydon, Yearling CQ, in charge of quarters, the Mickey Mantle of the Army Nine. It was his job to take phone calls and evacuate the company if fires began. He looked sympathetic.

I picked up the phone. "Cadet Ting speaking, sir."

"*Haushusheng,* is that you?" The voice was tinny, distant. It was Uncle Shim, probably speaking from the phone kiosk in the lobby of the Beverly Plaza Hotel at the foot of Chinatown, blowing nonexistent lint from his impeccably clean spectacles.

"Why must you take such time to come to the telephone?" he asked. "I only have so many coins." He sounded cranky.

"No excuse, Uncle Shim," I said. "*Dababa,* there's one phone for the company and I'm four floors away. What's wrong? Is it—is something wrong with my father? Or mother?"

"No, no. It is tremendous news. *Tremendous.* I must tell you."

"Tell me what, *Dababa?*" I asked.

"*Hausheng.* What do you remember of your family."

This was the tremendous news—a family exam? I struggled with his meaning, enjoying a sensation altogether too familiar: the swamping anxiety of not knowing the correct answer.

"Did you hear me?" he asked, concerned.

"I'm sorry, Uncle," I said. "Why ask me? I'm the one person in the whole family who knows the least."

I could feel Uncle Shim smiling, pleased that he was about to improve my shallow grasp of my Chinese family. "I will fortify you with the old riddle. What is more important than your family name?"

"My relationship to principal family members," I said.

"And what is the importance of your *lun* to your sisters?"

"It's secondary," I said. The Master K'ung Fu-tzu did not name mothers or sisters in the *gahng,* the primary bonds.

"And what is the health of your *lun* to them?" he asked.

"Uh . . . okay. I don't see them, but I—uh—know where they are, and we get along and everything."

"Where are they?" he asked.

He knew where they were; there was little mystery in this. They were eighteen and sixteen years older than I. "Megan Wai-la's in Berkeley, with her husband and two kids. Jennifer

Sung-ah's in Minneapolis, with her husband and son. Their kids are real neat."

"Oh," he said flatly. "Is there not another sister?"

The air in the orderly room seemed unnaturally still. I had another sister. Janie Ming-li. Little Tail. I frowned as a headache pulsed deep in the base of my brain, and my chest tightened.

"Janie Ming-li," I said. I closed my eyes. She was my sister, my own sister, and I had forgotten her. Like forgetting my head.

"Good, *Hausheng,*" said Uncle Shim. "I recall her in Shanghai. The Little Tail of the Tings. So precious. But born sickly and small. Ting *taitai* smothered her in every kind of medicine, closing off her room from all family, all well-wishers. She called to every Taoist spirit, to the gods of health from every religion, to the Episcopalians and the Catholics and the Presbyterians and to the American cereals, even to the Buddhist gods. She lit joss for *foo chi,* called for *yuing chi,* good fortune, committed *yeh,* good karma, and all her willpower. She made peace with the people in her life. Particularly the women.

"I remember your mother's laughter when she knew Ming-li would live." He laughed gaily, a wonderful sound that for a moment cleared the tension from my innards and allowed my heart to beat again. I saw, through hazy memory, my sister's face. A ponytail.

"I was *dababa* to her before I was uncle to you. Your mother asked me to be her tutor. You know, Master Tang Su-lin had been tutor to your mother's brother, but first was your mother's secret teacher, giving her the gift of male scholarship."

I shook my head into the phone. I hadn't known that he had tutored Janie.

"Oh, *Hausheng,* it was indeed one of the good things of my life, seeing Ming-li at the Embarcadero. It was cold and drizzly. I had been exceptionally sick for an entire week, bouncing on the tall, angry ship, wanting to die from stomach pains. I thought of this little girl, who was to be my student. These women had run through the enemy and lived. My own family had died. I hoped she would remember me.

"There was your mother, tall, with her serious features guarding her face. I was to learn that this had become her permanent face. I was to learn that this was to be my face as well—the face of Chinese who have left their homes.

"Next to her was your sister. She waved at me with a small handkerchief, waving at the uncle who had cared for her so much. It meant, for me, that I could be an uncle, a relative. After all those days and nights of sickness, to see China again in the faces of the women of your family—ah, it was *ding hao,* a fantastically wonderful thing! As good as a later day, when your mother delivered her only son.

"But the flight through war and from China, which Dai-li called the *boh-la,* the Run, had affected them all. Of course, it would. It was a journey for an immortal who can take wings, not for men, much less a woman and her daughters.

"But I became little Ming-li's *chia t'ing chiaoshur,* her tutor. She was more diligent, much more talented, than you. She has an inner brightness which you have most successfully hidden, no offense intended." His voice shrank. I imagined him adjusting his white handkerchief or his jade bow tie, inside the phone booth.

"Your mother, wanting sons and having four girls, losing one girl to death in China, said the best thing in her life was the birth of her only son. Surely, she was correct; this is the duty of women. I will tell you your youngest sister loved you, even though you displaced her as the favored child. She later became your mother, when your mother died.

"So. I ask you. What do you owe Little Tail? I will tell you. You owe her the duty, *dzeren,* the relationship, the *lun,* of her only brother. A younger brother, and almost, of a son."

It was so confusing—the cascading confluence of these powerful words. Sister. Brother. Son. Mother, as in *true* mother. All presented by the great aesthete, Uncle Shim, on a platter steaming with Chinese *gan-ch'ing,* emotion.

He was not arguing about Ming poets or Eight-Legged Essays, the transcendent confusions of Lao-tzu, or the preeminence of ritual. He was talking about the fundamentals of Chinese life: human relationships, as prescribed by the Master K'ung. My uncle had loved my sister. It seemed that he had loved my mother—my first mother. I coughed, and needles of pain shot through my head, the pressure growing in my aching, straining chest. I felt panic in my inability to draw a deep breath. I remembered my childhood asthma; now it had come back, from so far away.

"Uncle, can I call you back? I'm on the official company phone. I'll call you from a pay phone in ten minutes." I had to get a lot of change. I had to think about the past.

"You know," I said to him, ten minutes later, "Janie and my mother didn't get along. I mean, they *hated* each other. Janie left, left the house. Christmas Eve—a long time ago. . . ."

"Ming-li ran away in 1954," said Uncle Shim.

"She was sent away, Uncle Shim," I said. "She did not run away. Did my mother tell you that?"

"Your honorable second mother has said little to me since we were introduced, but she did express her lament that—ah—," and he hesitated, calling upon his magnificent memory—" 'Jane, sick from grief over the death of her mother, has run away, without a note. It is so much like her, to make people worry about her needlessly.' That is, of course, only approximate."

I looked at my right hand, as Lady Macbeth had looked at hers. I was going to break *jing ji,* taboo, leaving an old country to cross a river from which return might never be possible. Break the rule, cross the border, serve your people.

"Uncle. To cross the Rubicon? What's the Chinese equivalent?"

"Ah," he said. "*Jacta alea est,* the die is cast. I learned this in classical languages at Princeton. There is no Rubicon in China, although Hideyoshi crossed the Yalu, with an effect similar to Julius Caesar's. The expression you seek is *p'o fu ch'en chou.* Break the pot and sink the boat. No going back."

I took a deep breath. "Here goes the pot, and the boat.

"I must honor my father and my mother. You said my *chimu* was my mother. You were right. But I have to tell you the truth. This means criticizing my *chimu.*" I licked my lips. He was silent. "My mother ordered Janie to never argue with her."

"An exceptionally wise rule," said Uncle Shim.

"Janie knew better, but she refused to kowtow to Edna. She wanted to fight her, as if she could win. That was so stupid. I was the dumbest kid in the world, but *I* could see Edna would beat her, and the harder that Janie fought, the worse the losing would be."

I hadn't thought of this for a decade. It was a child's story, unfit for children.

Father had set the stage by leaving the table to take a phone call from General Bledsoe, a war buddy. Bledsoe had been Joseph Stilwell's artillery commander in China. Here I was at West Point, where Stilwell and Bledsoe had been cadets. Bledsoe always called on Christmas Eve, on the anniversary of the fall of Hong Kong.

I began to tell Uncle Shim a story told many times, but only to myself in early youth. It was my story, once told with the constancy of a spinning Tibetan prayer wheel, sustained by its own momentum and made acceptable through familiarity. Now, recalling it, I felt as if the ceiling of the Cadet Hilton might collapse, allowing familial wrath and *chimu* fury to crush me for my infidelity. Deep, unspoken fears raged unseen before my eyes. *Ji hui, jing ji.* Forget the past, and its losses.

I began to describe to Uncle Shim the images as they unraveled from the creaky spool of suppressed memory. Edna had been criticizing our mother. Janie had cried in protest, the quality of her voice still undefined in my recollection.

Then Edna screamed, "ENOUGH!" She reached into a pocket and withdrew an expensive-looking necklace. I was nine when this happened. I later described the jewelry to Toos as a "pretty."

"I found this," Edna said, holding it up. "You stole it." I thought she was talking to me, but Janie answered.

"I did not! I wouldn't steal anything! I'm a good girl!" I think she also said, "I'm a Christian girl."

"This cost over a hundred dollars," said Edna, her eyes bright. "You stole this from Gumps. It still has the tags. It doesn't matter that you're a cute little Chinese girl, or whatever. You're not an American citizen, and the police will believe me."

Edna passed Janie an envelope. "Inside, you'll find money and bus fare. I found you a new home, at *great* expense to myself. I had to borrow the money to find a woman insane enough to take you. I can't wait until you drive *her* blood pressure up!

"You have one week to get there. If you start tomorrow, on Christmas Eve, you can make it. If you do not make it, the deal is off, and I'll turn you over to the police and the Immigration people."

Edna still held up the necklace, as if it were a noose. "There are two conditions, young lady. One, you must stay with this woman for two years. After that, I don't care what you do, so long as you obey the second: never call or write to your father or your brother ever again. There is to be *no contact* whatsoever, do you understand? Henceforth, you are no longer a member of this family."

I couldn't see Janie's expression, because she was seated too far away from me. But she argued. Then she said, "Father knows. He knows I wouldn't steal. I've been the best girl! I did all the work here! My father will stop you!"

But for months after my sister's departure, I knew what Janie didn't know. Our father could not help. He would later say, in a household devoid of daughters, that the American woman knew all the answers and that a Chinese man could not know the rules of this new nation. Yes, it was so sad, so hard. But *mai yo ban fa?* What can a person do?

I told Uncle Shim that I used to stand on a wooden crate in the bathroom, telling this story of my sister's banishment, this horror story of *wupo,* witches, to the mirror. That I told the story to myself and to the spirit of the mirror to keep Janie alive, until Edna caught me and the storytelling had ended and I had to lose my sister again.

I breathed into the phone, my chest banded with weights. My father had not laughed for a decade. He had given up a daughter to the fates, and the laughter god had taken his mirth.

"Ah, ah. This is so strange, *Hausheng.* I wish we were in Shanghai, swimming in its busy streets in a double-benched pedicab, eating salted fish and arguing about books. We could pretend our families are still strong and united. Your mother still alive, the Little Tail still a tiny girl with a strong musical voice . . . my wife, waiting for me on the docks of the Whangpu. So, I called to give you news. Instead, you give me news.

"You know, your mother believed in *yeh,* in Buddhist karma. I do not, at least, very little. We used to argue about this. Do you remember? We used to argue about everything."

"No," I said.

"You remember the calligraphy lessons," he said.

"Vaguely," I said.

"You of course remember the *Sheng yu,* the Sacred Edicts of Master K'ung. . . ."

"I learned them from you, right?"

"Ai-yaa! Of course you learned them from me. Do you think your father taught you the Edicts? How is this possible? You were not in the *boh-la,* the Run. You did not see war and invasion and revolution. You were not a young witness to death and bombing. Why is your memory as bad as little Janie's?"

"I don't know. I actually have a pretty good memory. I don't think anyone can remember anything before the age of seven, anyway. I mean, maybe the geniuses . . ."

"See here, this is not true. Everyone remembers those years. Unless they have been in war. Ah!" he exclaimed. "Your mother died. Your memory died with her, as tribute, to honor her life. You and your mother lived in the Chinese language, and now you have lost the language of her memory. It is so clear. Sometimes I think I have the brains of an ox, not thinking at all. I am so sorry. It is time to tell you the tremendous news."

I had wanted to hear, but was now afraid to listen.

The American *jing ji* taboos: No talking about the first Mrs. Ting, who had been known to the Chinatown community as Ting *taitai*, and to my father as Honey, and to me as Mah-mee. No talking about the evil and defiantly double-bad girl who had been my sister. Each of these people had disappeared from my life in the space of a single day, a year apart, without any bidding farewell, any grieving, any rituals of remembrance.

I remembered trying to do this as a child, trying to call up the memory of our family's females. When I was very young, I could remember my mother and my sister. Later, the little stitchings in the mind that connected me to them broke, and I had trouble recalling their faces, voices, and habits. Because Edna's voice had been so angry when she attacked the spirits of these two people, I began to develop a throbbing cerebral pain whenever I thought of them on my own. In time, it was as if my fading recollections of the two people who had been closest to my small life were the products of fairy tales and of fable, not of fact; of wishful thinking, and not of life; of pain, and not of love.

"*Hausheng,* your sister, the Little Tail, Janie Ming-li. I have found her. She has been living in Canada. She is ready to be greeted by you, and to renew your relationship.

"But," he said slowly, "she is different. She has changed her name. Both names. She is not Janie anymore." He cleared his throat. "Her new name is Lisa. She also wears the family name Mar, after your mother. She seeks to change her *yuing chi*, her fortune.

"I asked her if she missed you, her *syau didi*, her baby brother. She said, 'I have no brother.' That is the bad news."

I felt a great pressure behind my eyes. Janie. With surprising clarity I saw her in the old kitchen, pots and pans arrayed on the countertops while she made dinner for Father and me, preparing breakfast, packing lunches. I saw the tip of her tongue, hinting of her effort to run the house. She was putting her hair

into a ponytail, proud of her prettiness. She sat on the lawn of
Brooks Mortuary while I picked daisies for her. She held my
hand so tight as we crossed the street against busy motor traffic, and gave crayons for coloring books about the Lord Jesus.
She was on a picnic blanket in Golden Gate Park, apple
juice streaming down her face and in her hair, thrown there by Edna
for some transgression.

I saw her sitting at the dinner table, holding the envelope
with her fate within it. Janie blinked and was looking at our father's chair, which was empty.

My sister, who had become, after our mother's death, my
mother. Who had been transformed by our new stepmother
into a nonperson, relinquished and forgotten, returned to a
bland and nameless inventory of Chinese ghosts and abandoned spirits, to whom I could neither pray nor honor, or later,
remember. I remembered Pearl's choice: Chinese daughter or
American woman. To honor a Chinese father or to be *k'ung
'hsu,* abandoned.

Now she had returned, without *lun,* ties. But she was my
sister. When she had been an adolescent, caring for me, standing up for me, she had been pushed out, and I had forgotten
her.

"I'm glad that was the bad news," I said. "I don't think I
could've handled it if that was the good part."

"Yes," he said. "You are quite American, trying to laugh at
the destruction of your family. Please, as a favor to an old
man, an old man who is fond of you, do not inflict lighthearted-
edness on me when we are speaking like honorable men to
each other, about our purpose of life. About family.

"It is one thing to endure pain. It is another to laugh at yourself because your head has been chopped off."

25

JANIE

New South Barracks Sinks, November 10, 1966

"May I speak to Lisa Mar? This is Kai Ting, her brother."

A short intake of breath, somehow familiar. "Hello," she said. A precise voice. Neither cheerful nor sad—neutral. Cold, evanescent gray fog in a San Francisco summer morning.

"Janie—is it you?" I asked.

"I don't use that name," she said. "My name is Lisa Mar."

"Can I call you Janie?" I asked.

"No," she said.

"Ah-huh," I said, making the automatic Chinese sound. "Can't believe I'm talking to you. How are you?"

"Fine," she said.

"I mean, *really,* how are you?" I pressed.

"Good."

"Man, it seems—seems like, like it's been forever," I said.

"Eleven years," she said.

"You're twenty-seven, right? What do you do for work?"

"I work in a lab. I'm engaged. You're at West Point?"

"Janie—Lisa—can you visit me at the Academy?"

"I am not related to you."

"Of course you are. Can you visit me?" I asked.

"No," she said. "It's nice to hear your voice. You must be—very healthy, to be at West Point. Do you still have asthma?"

"No. Well, actually, yes, I just got it again. Not as bad."

"Is Silly Dilly still alive?" she asked, in a very small voice. Silence. "Janie. Can you visit me?"

"Did she have a good life?"

"Yes," I said.

"I have to go," she said, slowly, mechanically. It seemed her voice, in my ear, was a ghost's, slipping away from me.

"When's the best time for me to call you, when you can talk?" I rushed the words, frantic to keep her with me.

"Goodbye," she said. She hung up.

Quebec City is not only in a different country; it is in a different nation than the one in which it is located. Quebec seemed to be a pinch of France swimming in a hybrid English potpie. The traffic signs said *"Arrêt."* I imagined I was in Paris: pretty women, artistic fountains, clustered streets and broad boulevards, warm air, bright lights, and Citroëns. I headed for the student hostel, detouring to check the Citadelle, where Wolfe and Montcalm had fought on the Plains of Abraham. Everyone spoke French. I could not miss my hotel: it was once the Petite Bastille, which was as petite as the Pentagon and as Bastille as San Quentin. It looked like a fort that had been under siege for a century and was ready to capitulate. It overlooked the massively elegant Château Frontenac and the deep blue Fleuve Saint-Laurent.

I entered, grimaced with the gouge of two dollars American, and saw I was out of uniform: everyone looked like Jean Valjean on the run, with hair that must have taken years to grow. I was in my Rogers Peet navy Academy blazer and gray trousers, with an Academy tie. "Dig the threads," came a mutter. I entered the dim prison, caught in a relentless cross fire of hostile stares mitigated by mean-hearted chuckles. Loud rock from competing stations seeped from under closed doors and through walls and floors, filled the spiral staircase, and boomed in latrines that housed people and dorm areas that had been used for waste. The station playing the Rolling Stones was beating the competition.

I smelled Indian incense, exotic oils, old wine, warm beer, stale vomit, a nation of armpits, scented candles, and cigarettes, and something I hadn't whiffed since early youth: marijuana. Then it hit me. This wasn't filth; it was the new age—Aquarius.

I found my floor and my bay. A cluster milled about as the Who sang "I hope I die before I get old. . . ." Eerie shadows from old, forgotten, half-gutted chandeliers and wall sconces played on walls rich with French slogans and black-light posters, creating a fixating effect with a poster depicting forms of intercourse.

A guy looked up and pointed at a bunk. "That's free. Has crabs or somethin'. Keep your shit off my crib."

"Right," I said. The bunk had an active growth: greenish with a tinge of blue, and floating oil bubbles.

"Detroit," he added.

"New York," I said.

"You Army?" he asked.

"Got any money, man?" asked another.

"Sleep on yo' wallet an yo' shoes," said Detroit.

"I said, you got any money?"

I turned to the interrogator. "Got any for me?"

The guy cackled. He wore an Army field jacket with a PFC stripe and the unit patch and name tag removed. "Fuck you, asshole," he said to me. "Don't give me that DI look."

I looked at him, and he cursed and bounded up, grabbed a backpack, and sprinted out, his hair flying. Reflexively, I started after him, and stopped as the crowd surrounded me. He was a deserter in Canada. This was his country, not mine.

"Who the hell are you?" asked an Asian guy in my face.

"Kai Ting," I said.

"Shit," he said, "look like a narc."

"He's a *narc?*" screamed several guys, some hiding things as others began to move. Two more fled.

"Hey, tune in, dude. You in the Army, right?" asked Detroit.

Another group gathered gear, and a person walked out briskly. Adult musical chairs. Hate beamed at me from cold and angry eyes. I was getting tired of standing out, of being picked on. The group's malevolence was multiplying.

"Fuck you, you asshole!" shouted a guy displaying a rusted jackknife as if it were a cavalry saber. "What you doin'— screwin' with us? Who the fuck are you?"

"I'm the baddest sonovabitch you'll see this year," I said, "and you got me confused with someone who gives a rat's ass about *anyone.* I have no business with you." I held up the two fingers that used to mean victory. "Peace," I said. "Or, not. Your choice."

Janie agreed to meet me at Le Cordon Berthelot on rue de Jardin. It was filled with hip-huggers, beads, headbands, bell-bottom trousers, bright, half-open paisley shirts, and white hats. I ordered an Oly.

"*Quoi?*" said the bartender.

"Have any Western American beer?" I asked.

He gave me a Schlitz. "This is from Milwaukee," I said.

"Milwaukee is west, m'sieu," he said.

Janie and I had lived together and now I couldn't remember what she looked like. I was nervous, skittish, like the big, simple horses that we rode on the J. P. Morgan ranch on the edge of the Academy.

I thought of Toussaint and Jack, Mike, Arch, Bob Lorbus, and Clint. Cool, confident guys. Hang in. Be calm like Pearl Yee. Lucky to be here on leave. You're happy to see her. You're lucky Major Noll and SGM Klazewski gave you emergency leave from the Academy.

She was in a yellow suit and matching yellow headband. I jumped up. "Hi," I said. Impulsively, I kissed her on the cheek. I realized that this was the first time I had ever kissed one of my sisters.

She leaned away from me stiffly. "Oh," she said.

"You look really good. Beautiful." I beamed at her. "It's great, just great, to see you."

Her mouth was open. Then she smiled for an instant, dimples deepening. I remembered them. We studied each other, searching for clues of the children we had been, the siblings we had lost. She didn't look the least bit like me: a small, delicate nose, common to the three sisters; high, pronounced cheekbones; large eyes; dark, elegant eyebrows; thick, dark black hair, more than halfway down her back. She was about five feet tall.

She patted me on my arm—the old signal to move on. ("*Kwala, kwala.* Time to go. Put down the toy—come, come." Pat, pat.)

"I picked this place," I said, "for the moo shu pork." I grinned; she smiled wanly as we sat. We ordered. With flair, I ordered a French rosé. "Goes with anything," I bragged.

"You're just huge," she said, studying me.

"I'm a lot bigger than when you last saw me."

"No, really. You're *huge*. How did you get so big? Do you take vitamins, or are you on a special diet? You're built like the black men in our old neighborhood in San Francisco."

"I eat anything that isn't alive. A girl I know calls me the adorable glutton. One out of two's not bad."

"What do you mean?" she asked.

" 'Adorable' and 'glutton.' I like the 'adorable' part."

"You're trying to be funny," she said.

I showed my teeth.

"So Edna let you stay at the YMCA and lift weights."

"You know, when I was little, I wanted to be with her and

she had nothing to do with me. When I became a teenager and wanted freedom, she nailed my foot to the floor."

"She did?" she asked in horror.

"Figuratively," I said.

"Oh," she said.

"Janie. Where have you been? Where'd she send you?"

"Edmonton, Alberta. A Christian foster home. I was the oldest of seven, a mother again to smaller kids. Two of us were Chinese, one was Filipino, one was English, one was black, and two were Canadian Indian. It was the Stonehocker family."

"Were they good to you?" I asked.

"They were very nice." She looked around the dining room. "Actually," she said, "they were wonderful." She sighed. "Two years later, Jennifer found me, and I joined her in Minneapolis."

"That's super! Jennifer! I would've *loved* that."

"But I didn't have Dad," she said. "Or you. None of my friends. It wasn't easy for Jennifer to raise me. No money."

"Yeah, but getting away from Edna . . ."

"I didn't *want* to get away from Edna. I wanted to get her out of our home, away from Daddy—from K.F. And you. Kai, we could do that now. You're big enough to do it."

I shook my head. "Bad idea. Why do you call him K.F.?"

"It's his name. He's not my father."

"Whatever happened, he's still our father," I said.

"I am not his daughter. He's not my father. He gave me up. He's *your* father."

Silence. "How long were you with Jennifer?" I asked.

"Until 1957," she said. "You don't know any of this?"

I shook my head.

"I went to Cal. I called Dad. He and Edna visited me for tea, at International House. They said you were fine. I wanted to see you. Megan said they didn't even let you visit *her*, but she saw you when she visited. She said that you didn't talk too much."

I looked at her: so grown, adult, and remote. She was a stranger. My sisters, strangers—as I was to them.

"We're not much of a family, are we?" I said.

She laughed bitterly. "You just figured that out?" It was our father's laugh, the sound of joy offered to the gods of woe, a laugh without a smile—the laugh of Chinese tragedy.

"Yes," I said.

"That's because you followed Edna's orders."

"That's not true," I said.

"You're twenty years old and just realized 'we're not much of a family'? Wake up. You're thinking like her now."

"DON'T COMPARE ME TO HER!" I cried, blinking with the volume of my voice. This wasn't shouting commands; I was yelling. "Sorry," I said, breathing fast. Everyone was staring and someone was wiping up a spilled drink.

I asked about her fiancé.

"His name is Alejandro. First-generation Spanish. He's going to be a doctor." She was wringing her hands together. "It's great," she said. "He and I are so alike. Both of us have only had ourselves. I think his parents hate me."

"Because you argue with them?" I asked.

"Because I'm Chinese," she said.

She worked in a biology lab. She had a master's in biology from Cal Tech. "You got my letters and birthday cards?"

I shook my head. Edna read my mail. She had said, "There are evil influences, and much of it comes through the mail." "Janie. Edna read my mail. She even read my *outgoing* mail."

"But you could've mailed a letter on your own. You could've written to me at school and mailed it on the way home."

"How could I mail you a letter? I didn't know where you were."

She tasted the wine. I had meant to toast but had forgotten. I was going to say, "To lost comrades."

She sat up straighter. "How's K.F.?" she asked.

"Fine," I said. Do not say the name of your father.

She took a deep breath. She swirled the wine in the goblet. "Does he know that you're seeing me?" she asked.

I shook my head. I hadn't even thought of him.

She looked to the side. Large tears filled her eyes and ran down her cheeks. I patted her arm, but she jerked away from me, spilling her glass. I tried to be composed, and began drinking my wine as if it were soda pop. "I'm sorry," I said. "Really sorry."

The soup arrived, but neither of us was hungry.

She let out a big breath of air. "Did he ever ask about me, or talk about me?"

I wanted to say yes, to manufacture conversations or create comments; but there had been none, not to me. I remembered my oath and the Honor Code. It influenced all I did, in my private life and in my military duties. Minimalist social lies were okay: "Mrs. Westmoreland, that is an *exceptional* hat." I embraced the comfort of knowing what to do but shuddered at its cost. For a moment, I hated the Honor Code and its iron-backed inflexibility. It shackled me, weighed me down, caused me to hurt others. "The Harder Right," said the Cadet Prayer.

"No," I said, and I looked away as she began to weep again. I played with my lobster bisque. I watched crackers drown in the soup. She was still shaking. I looked down, awkward, out of place, utterly unsure of what to do. "Please don't cry," I said.

"Oh, thank you," she said, crying. "Don't cry! Why, does this make you uncomfortable?"

"Yes," I said.

"I don't care!" she sobbed, weeping freely. "I'm not very good at accommodating people! I wish I never cried! Wish I hadn't been thrown out like garbage! I wish Daddy remembered me!"

Daddy. When she was a girl, had she called him "Daddy"? Him? "Crying doesn't solve anything," I said.

"Right," she said. "You're a man. Men don't cry. Well, I'm not a man. I'm a worthless Chinese *daughter*." She wept. I cried inside. I worried about anyone seeing her as she wept.

She stopped. "You cry for Mah-mee," she said.

"No," I said.

"Men are terrible," she said. "You're so—*cold*."

"It's important to be in control," I said. "A platoon leader can't weep in front of his troops if his feelings got hurt. Cry in the ring and you lose."

I waited until she finished.

"Feeling better?" I asked.

"I'm the pits," she said. "This is a trip, seeing my little baby brother. You're a giant—a bald giant in a suit." She shook her head, which still produced a veil of tears.

She looked up. "So where were you?" she asked bitterly, her small, delicate mouth turned horribly upside down, her face without color. "Where were you when I left? Why didn't you stop her?" she shrilled, making my eardrums hum as if Edna were talking to me.

"Are you nuts? I couldn't stop her. Stop *Edna*? I was nine!"

"You were the only son! You had *power* and *status*!" she cried. Patrons were split between open gawking and savoir faire.

"You're demented," I said. "I had no power or status. That

woman told me when to go potty, how to go potty, how to fold the toilet paper, and how many minutes I had. She told me when to sleep and in what position, gave me no medicine, ordered me to stop having asthma, and sent me to the Christian Scientists. I only got glasses because Mr. Lew, my teacher, wouldn't let me back in the classroom without them and confronted Edna with my eyesight. She made me Baptist until I liked it, then made me Catholic. Up until my last night at home I couldn't watch TV, have a radio, use the phone, see a girl, or stay up past eight-thirty. She set out my underwear for my flight to West Point. Listen, Janie—I had no power. The only person I could influence was you. I used to beg you not to fight her. But you'd run straight at her. Edna wasn't going to compromise with you. You were a kid, and she was a grown-up. You were going to lose. You *lost* and left me alone with her."

She began to cry again. Great; I've won an argument with my sister, convincing her she was immature when she was fifteen.

"I'm sorry. I wish I could've stopped it. I couldn't."

"That's Chinese man bullshit," she said harshly. "You sound like Edna when you yell at me!"

"Oh, God—DON'T SAY THAT!" I cried.

"Don't say what—'Chinese man bullshit,' or that you sound like Edna?" she asked. "And do not yell at me," she hissed.

"Edna," I said. "I am *not* like her. *No way.* . . . What do you mean, about Chinese men?"

"Not taking responsibility. Kowtowing to status and money, spitting on daughters. You don't know. You weren't born in China. I was little, but I *knew* girls weren't important. Only sons! It's living for surface manners and face! Telling women they can't cry—it might make a male lose face! I had one protector—Mah-mee. No man in China ever helped us. It was always the women who gave up food and shed space for us during the Run." She sighed. "How many girls were left behind! How they cried! God, then Mah-mee died.

"You could've gone to him. After she died, you were the only one. He would've listened to you, the son! We didn't count."

"I don't think so," I said.

"Did you even try?" she cried.

I shook my head. "I couldn't have even imagined doing that."

"*I* would've if they had done this to *you*," she said.

"But I was a kid! You were a teenager."

"You're making Chinese man excuses! It doesn't matter. You were the *son*. If you really cared, you would've done it. You would've just tried. Why did you tell me the truth? Why didn't you lie and tell me you tried even if you didn't? I used to pray to God that you had done this for me—that you had gotten Dad to help. But you didn't even try.

"Don't ever say you were too young. . . . Mah-mee prepared you to do everything before she died. She tutored and taught you to read, told you stories of smart boys. About K'an Tse, who borrowed books and never forgot what he read, the boy who turned the pages without stopping. Mah-mee took Uncle Shim from me to teach you calligraphy and the *tsung cheh,* the old ways. He lived for you. She loved you more than she loved me. . . . She loved you more than anyone."

"What do you mean?" I asked. "That's crazy talk."

She blew her nose, drying her eyes. "I hate this," she said. "God, I hate this. I knew it would be like this, seeing you."

A great physical weight pressed on my chest. A sudden headache lanced from temple to temple. Breathing was labored. I wanted to run away. I felt like dying. I imagined suicide: pulling a grenade pin and bending my head over it in a prayer for relief. I couldn't stand this, drowning, suffocating in my sister's misery. I pulled out my wallet and began extracting bills.

"What are you doing?" she asked.

"I'm leaving," I asked.

"Just like men," she said.

"Jesus!" I hissed. *"Ch'a lu t'ung ku!"*

"Fork pain? What's that?" she asked.

"Chinese chess. Being caught in a dilemma. Stuck if I stay, wrong if I leave."

"Shwa jungwo hwa?" she asked.

I hated that question. I shook my head. *"Bu shr,"* I said. Don't speak. "I've forgotten everything."

We were quiet for a while.

"I must look awful," she said.

"You look great," I said.

She looked at me, thinking of something. "Remember *tseuh?*"

I frowned into my memory. "Yes," I said. "The porridge.

Tseuh. With the shredded pork and pickled somethings—vegetables."

"Remember," she said, "the three of us at the old yellow table in the middle of that old kitchen, eating *tseuh*, next to the large black stove where Mah-mee used to burn toast?"

I nodded. I remembered the table where I had gone mad. "She used to burn toast?" I asked.

"She thought charcoal was healthy. Alejandro thinks it might have induced her cancer."

Mah-mee. Cancer. "The cancer god has taken your mother," Father had said. I was breathing fast and no air was in my lungs, and I was wheezing audibly, coughing unsuccesfully to clear it.

"I told myself that's when you could talk to Daddy. It would just be the two of you, eating *tseuh*, while he read the business section and Herb Caen, and you sat there, silently, next to him.

"You would say to him, in that clear, high, musical boy's voice that Mah-mee taught you: '*Ba-ba*, can't live without Janie Ming-li. You must bring her home.' Eleven words." She repeated them very slowly, with clear pronunciation.

I felt in Janie's voice the music of someone else: an older woman with a high, slow, musical, intense voice, so many things inside it that my small brain could not hold all the nuances, all the emotion of a woman who had loved me and died. I felt a deep, abiding pain inside my chest, my eyes straining to cry for the hole that was inside me, ever growing.

It was the kind voice of Momma LaRue; the soft, gentle voice of Harper Lee; the song of mothers speaking to sons. Janie's voice was hers, and also someone else's: Mah-mee's. I knew that. My whole body was coming apart, against my muscles. Doesn't matter, I said. Means nothing, I said. Through all my childhood inadequacies, I had never been dunced as a momma's boy. I hadn't had a momma to run to. I was vulnerable to a new set of feelings, and I hated it.

"You know," Janie said, more to herself than to me, "I picked the words you'd use, like helping you learn to write. These words are the best. Words you could've used. Should've used." She put her head down again, her shoulders gently shaking. She wiped her face with the napkin. Her cosmetics were smeared around her eyes. She looked at herself in a small mirror, dried her eyes, and reapplied the makeup. I was trembling in a fit of isometric tension, trying to stop the impulse to cry. I focused on her makeup procedure. I watched her. When she applied the makeup to her eyes, she opened her mouth. She glanced at me. For a split second, she smiled.

Through the decade that had separated us and made us strangers to each other, I saw the face of a sister who consistently had set aside her youth to mother her baby brother, quashing her own needs to smile at the questioning little lost boy at her hip.

"So, Kai. You never said that, to him, to Daddy. Did you ever think about saying it to him?"

"Janie, does your voice sound like your mother's? Mahmee's?"

"Do this for me," she said, very intently. "If you had said it, how would you put it?"

"I don't talk to him very well."

"You don't?" she asked. "But you're his son."

"That makes it tougher on both of us," I said. "We mostly have long silences with each other. Lately, he talks to me about politics. Communism." I ground my teeth and the pain subsided.

"Really!" she said, blinking. "He used to talk to you all the time. Ah . . . until Mah-mee died. Then," she said, "then, all he did was read and smoke a pipe."

"You have our mother's voice, don't you?" I wanted her to say yes so I could remember Mah-mee, and to say no, so I couldn't.

"I don't know," she said reflectively. "Maybe."

"I know I missed you. I didn't miss her. I missed you."

"That's impossible," she said. "How could you not remember—and miss—Mah-mee?"

"I don't know," I said. "I just didn't."

"You have a very bad memory," said Janie. "Incredibly bad."

"I remember your Bible lessons. On a felt board, with felt Bible figures. Jesus, and the man who wasn't Jesus . . . the disciple who turned in Christians to the Romans . . . Jesus washing the feet of a bad lady." I laughed. "Wonder who they were. I remember singing. *'Yasu tiahng nu, wah see ching. . . .'* Was I always a lousy singer?"

She shook her head, her hair swaying. She showed her fine teeth for a moment. I thought she was going to smile, so I smiled, imitating her face as if it were Toussaint's.

"God abandoned me," she said. "God made us run from China, and our home, away from our whole family and my amah and my wet nurse and our kitchen, to run on the road like dogs. God killed the Chinese people, using the Japanese Army as His instrument. God littered little Chinese girls in old wells and in bushes and made them cry to me in my sleep. God destroyed our family, ruined China, made us lose everybody. God brought us to this land poor, and He killed Mahmee and brought Edna into our home. God made my father give me up and made my brother forget my name. Daddy stopped laughing and your voice became hoarse and ugly, and you could never sing again."

"Jesus," I breathed.

"Yes, Jesus. Where was he, with all his talk about helping the broken people? *I* was broken! Why didn't he come back? I loved him so *much!* I believed in him! Why didn't he save us? I prayed to him for you to save me with Daddy. That's when I realized Jesus was just another Chinese man. He should've come back, but didn't, and apologizes for nothing! You missed the bombing of Shanghai. The enemy soldiers. The Run out of China. I was only five but I already knew what soldiers did to women and girls. The little dead girls on the road, flies on their eyes . . . America and Canada, they have no problems compared to what we had. We had awful trouble. And we didn't leave it behind. We escaped, but it followed us here. Satan sent Edna for the sins of our great-grandfather."

Sins of our great-grandfather? The magistrate with his own army? What had he done? It didn't matter; I was a soldier so the horror of Nanjing could never happen again. I would protect Asian women. But Janie had followed Edna; neither trusted God, and both saw Satan. I feared *wupo*, witches, and Ts'ao Ts'ao, the evil one.

She pulled on a diamond ring on her hand.

"I don't remember much," I said. "I remember when I started making Dad's lunch, and mine, that I missed you."

"Oh, you just missed my woman *k'u-li*, labor. That's awful!"

"I missed you at dinner. After school, getting my gym bag, looking up the stairs to the attic, knowing you were gone. When I came home from the Y or Chinese school at night, and the place was so empty without you. At bedtime, when we used to brush our teeth together and you always checked mine to make sure I did it right. Remember? Edna's liver and onions would stick between my teeth. . . . I missed your prayers. Couldn't say them without you. Missed you when I got up in the morning and I didn't hear you singing songs to God, it was just me.

"Janie," I breathed. "You used to sing 'Amazing Grace.'" I remembered Marco Fideli asking me to sing it in hard times.

She nodded. "Mah-mee's favorite hymn," she said.

I lurched up and stumbled to the bathroom on feet that were not mine. The pressure behind my eyes, in my head, swelled against the walls. I entered a stall that was too small and pressed my forehead against the cold metal door, gritting my teeth, trying to stop from crying, panting like a lost patrol member racing on a thrashing, branch-snapping run through thick woods with a pack of aggressors in pursuit. Muscles convulsing, I groaned, crushed my mouth with my right hand, knocking my glasses off onto the hard floor of the lavatory as the tears rushed out and noises that were foreign to me escaped from my throat and my ears. I began hitting the door walls until I was weak and wet, quivering on the wall.

When I finished and opened the stall door, three waiters and a cook with a knife were facing me. *"C'est bien?"* asked the cook.

"Fine, great," I said. "Sorry."

"Are you okay?" Janie asked.

I took a deep breath and sat down. "I would have talked to Dad at breakfast." I flexed my face, opening my eyes very wide to not allow any more tears out. I felt bad, and weak, and drained, and immoral, having cried. "I would've said: 'Where Janie? When she come back? You miss her, too, right?'" My voice cracked. I put my head down and began to cry, trying to swallow the sobs and failing, using all my strength to stop the tears, unable to stop, the crystal tinkling against itself as I wept. I hated this, hating myself, my weakness, my incredible bullshit weakness. What was wrong with me? I felt broken. Why was this happening? I no longer felt like a man. I had become a child.

"I *did* say that," I whispered. "I really did. They didn't answer. They never answered. I forgot. I forgot I said it."

After a bit, I looked at her. Janie looked stricken.

"You really don't cry, do you?" she asked. "It sounded like you were dying. I mean, you don't even know how to cry."

"No," I said, "I don't cry," my face wet as I swabbed at it with both coat sleeves. "I try not to cry."

"When did you stop asking about me?" she asked. She awkwardly reached across the table and touched my arm. Pat, pat.

"I was easily defeated then," I said. "Maybe I still am."

"By whom?" she asked.

"Dad," I said. "Edna," I said. "Math."

"Why should you be afraid? You're the son! He loves you—more than you can ever know. And you're *huge*."

"You keep saying that. It doesn't matter. It's only good for boxing and fighting. Sports. It didn't help with Dad."

She looked at me, once again the older sister, the acting mother, the one possessed of greater knowledge.

"Father loved you. You should have seen him, and Mah-mee, when you were born. They went *crazy*. I had no idea that the craziness about sons had anything to do with *us*. But with you, we discovered the truth. Mah-mee, for all her celebrations about us, just wanted a son. After all that stuff about Jesus Christ and Christian equality of women, she was still old-way Chinese. And when I saw what all the fuss was about—it was this little *thing*—this big!" She pressed an angry thumb against the tip of her little finger.

"Gee," I said, "it's grown a bit since then."

"Don't change the subject. They expected great things from Jennifer and you, nothing from Megan, and less from me. Mah-mee used to rub my cheek and say, 'Oh, Little Tail, you are so lovely. So beautiful. Don't worry about school, or grades. Just marry a man with a warm heart, and have many sons!'"

I closed my eyes tightly. Janie's voice was musical, and light, each sound controlling the beating of my heart, threatening to kill me.

"But *you*. You were the genius. She ordered me to take care of you, to keep your genius intact. To make you into K'an Tse."

"Ah," I said, "that's why I'm stupid. You didn't keep my genius intact."

"You're at West Point," she said. "How did you get so big?"

"I lift weights and eat like a potbellied pig."

"You're exactly what Dad wanted," she said.

"I was bad in math and it drove him nuts. He tried to teach me math." I stopped. "Janie, he doesn't like me. I'm just a thing for him to get the things he wants."

"What do you think is the difference between us?" she asked.

"One foot and seventy pounds. You're a lot prettier."

"Did they kick *you* out?" she asked quietly.

The waiter cleared our plates. Only later did I realize I hadn't asked for doggie bags. We drank coffee; mine was mostly cream and sugar, to kill the taste, which Army coffee required.

"Are you going to tell me about my cat?" she asked.

"I don't want to talk about it," I said. "It's really painful. How about if I wrote about it, and mailed it to you?"

"You must be joking," she said.

"No, I'm not," I said.

"Tell me. I already know she's dead. Did Edna kill her?"

"No, I did," I said.

26

DUTY

Bartlett Hall, West Point, December 15, 1966

"Byron" Maher was my Juice P. Like Schwarzhedd, he was one of the few faculty already decorated from service in Vietnam, receiving a Silver Star and Bronze Star with "V" device with oak-leaf cluster. The lore about the Bear dealt with tactical genius; the tales of Byron described a madman pit fighter who lived on fury.

I was barely passing Byron Maher's course, and was only two minutes early—a narrow margin in a society that deemed tardiness close to pederasty. I should have been wondering why he had called, but I ruminated about HMA 273, Revolutionary Warfare, about the French failure to mass at the point of decision and to take the offensive in Indochina. They had gathered in defensive enclaves and were beaten by popular anticolonial, antiwhite nationalism and a lack of French will to protect their empire. I experienced a continuous buzz of low-level anxiety in the bottom of my guts. America was inadvertently following the French plan.

"The major will see you now," said Mrs. Holm, the department secretary. How could such a nice person work for Juice?

His door was open. Only Plebes saluted faculty indoors, but when I saw his expression, I presented arms. Maher normally had a broad smile on a jovial face, but today was not normal.

He returned my salute. Through his window, winter colors made a dim view as barges inched up the ice-encrusted waterway. Christmas was coming, his children's Yuletide art was on his bulletin board, and I felt no joy. I never liked Christmas. He pointed me to the chair.

"Know what's funny, sir?" I asked.

He leaned back in his chair. "Your grades?"

"Sir, a cruel cut. It's that I've hived the answer to a victory in Vietnam, but no one from the Pentagon has called me."

"That *is* funny. Now I know why it was so difficult for me to stem the tide of communism in Asia." He sat up. "Major Noll has excused you from intramurals so we can talk." He opened his briefcase. I smelled applesauce and old milk. He passed me a standard dark green file folder. "Key natural responses of second-order systems and RL circuits are hurting you at boards. ASPs—look at them. No, as you were. *Study* them. Sonny Rappa's our number-one man. We will both help you. He's a good guy, and is going to put out for you. You be sure to put out for him.

"It's my fixed opinion that if you master these, you'll pass the WFRs at end of semester." He was out of his blouse with all the ribbons and steel on it. He rested his harshly crew-cut head on a large hand, the elbow propped on his knee, and studied me. Like most who did so, he frowned. He looked like an older Steve McQueen.

"Thank you very much, sir," I said.

"Know what I liked about Plebe year?" he asked dreamily.

I opened my mouth.

"Not a damn thing," he snapped in his perfect diction. "Plebe year, you're a blind, simple tool, the fates on your back. The American nightmare: no control. Know what I like about life?"

"Food, sir?"

"Everything," he said. "Life after Plebe year is seventh heaven. Even on a battlefield, in a fight not of my choosing, at the worst time for my men, I got more maneuver options than I did as a Plebe. I thank the Academy for that lesson. I remind myself of that whenever I don't appreciate being alive, or fail to be grateful for the big things."

He stood, stopping by the window. I admired his naturally

straight posture. "Now you have choices, the ability to influence events. To do it honorably. People don't know this, 'cause they didn't do Plebe year. You did. Feel lucky."

He looked outside as if checking for eavesdroppers, and then locked the door. He was a muscular, athletically compact, broad-shouldered man, five feet nine, with a ramrod back. His eyes were darkly deep and lined around the corners, where a habit of laughter had carved kindly. His face was squarish. He seemed unhealthily pale, like Pearl Yee, but with a pallor of mood rather than of bacteria. When I watched Schwarzhedd move, I felt his determination. Maher strode with a supremely cocky confidence, the attitude of an indomitable rip-your-face-off street fighter. Tactics taught us the management of war. Schwarzhedd was the manager; Maher was the war.

War sat down. "Going to ask for something very hard," he said. "What's the toughest physical test you've faced here?"

"Stepladder, sir," I said. I hated heights. The Stepladder was a log lattice that went thirty-five feet up. I had climbed it with my eyes screwed shut, imagining my death below.

He laughed, high and funny. "This is tougher than a low night, high-wind jump into the enemy rear. Almost as hard as seeing some of your people hurt by the enemy, because this one's going to come from your own hand. The salient point is," he said deeply, "that you'll do it because I'm a good leader, and no one can resist me." He placed his hands over his eyes, massaging his face, trying, I presumed, to reduce his pallor. His large, gold class ring shined, like Father's Infantry School ring.

"Do you like cheating?" he asked.

I blinked. "No, sir," I said.

"Hate it?" he asked.

"Yes, sir."

"Hate it a lot?"

"Sir, the Honor Code doesn't have gradations. It's binary. So yes, sir, I hate it a lot."

"How strong is the spirit of the Honor Code in your company?"

"Very strong, sir. Rock hard, sir," I said.

"Don't bullshit me. How strong is it in your class?"

"Rock solid, sir." I was barely breathing, not liking this.

"You have classmates who don't share your feelings. I got cheating going on. *In my section*, GODDAMMIT!" His eyes turned glacial, homicidal, and they glared at me as my eyes widened, as if it were my fault. I wondered if it was. Our own section. I looked at him the way mice look at cobras. He was almost cross-eyed with anger, his face reddening. I was sitting entirely too close to him, because it was obvious he wanted to hit something. I did not want this man with so much inner *chi* to hit me. I didn't want to hear any of this. Bad feelings, *jing ji*, taboo. He was talking about my classmates and Honor, and dishonor. Cheating? Not possible.

"Cheating," he said, marveling. "Why tell you? One, I trust you. Usually you're dumber than three lieutenants in a jeep and stupider than shark shit on the ocean floor. But you're not getting any help from anyone. *God's* not helping you. Your answers are preposterous, make-believe, from the 'Twilight Zone.'

"Two, I need you to get them, the planners. Need a cadet who's good in the night. You surprised the paratroopers on your patrol's final assault. I like that. Need a guy who gets along with everyone, who socializes all over the Corps, who communicates. Noll says that's you. You communicate with everyone instead of studying.

"Want you to use those skills to find the cheats. Scope the Corps; find 'em, fix 'em, so the code can dust 'em.

"Three, work with me on this, and some Juice might rub off, and you can graduate. What do you think?"

"I can't imagine any of my classmates cheating, sir," I said.

"Your imagination's not the test. That's why I have to know how your class reads the Code. What's the baseline? Ting, you guys are the leading edge of the war babies. Going to outnumber everyone else in this country, which frankly scares the hell out of me. You're our first expansion class. You guys were born 1945 to '47, when fifteen million GIs and WACs came home and celebrated with the double-backed grapple, giving the world, you."

I cleared my guilty throat.

"West Point's going to be rebuilt as the Corps grows to forty-four hundred. They're even going to move Washington's statue." He looked out at the river. "You grew up pampered—no war, depression, Hitler, Dachau, Bulge, Okinawa. Korea happened when you were sucking formula. Cars and rock and roll, Elvis Presley, hula hoops, transistor radios, TV, Howdy Doody, Hostess Twinkies, and the Beatles. Great prep for shit-kicking Reds."

He looked at me. "If you guys don't buy Honor, I gotta know before I start rolling my jewels around on the tarmac."

The phone rang. "Excuse me. Major Maher speaking, sir."

I rubbed my face the way Maher did. I cleaned my glasses. My hands shook. Cheating in the class. A cabal. An Underground Nation, a tribe in moral exile with a mutinous agenda. How could anyone do that—turn Honor on its ear, and rip off classmates? It was a horrendous thought, like learning how to poison people in cooking school. No, I decided: there was no parallel.

Why me? I made Plebes laugh in a bitter year. I wore the wool, toted the rifle, halfway grubbed the tenths, and did the dance of the Cow squad leader. I almost fit in, and this would blow it. It wouldn't be a cadet duncing others; it'd be that Chinese cadet turning in classmates. Maher was asking me to stand out, to surrender my fitting in. I could say: "Sir, I feel my deficiencies too keenly; I must refuse." But I honored the Code. That, as Major Maher would say, was the salient point. Maybe, the salient point was that I was stupid. Had I mucked more tenths, I'd be in a different section. I had been chosen to serve my country in a special mission, and had been selected from the ranks of the brilliant for my stupidity.

"No more calls, please, Mrs. Holm," and he hung up.

He faced me, making me feel like standing. "What's the salient point?" He glared at me. "Honor. Eighty clicks downriver are twelve million people on a little island who get up every morning so they can beat someone or take something they don't have. That's America out there doing business: buy, kick, scratch, gouge, bribe, screw your way up the ladder. For what? Money! We have a nation with the manners of an organ-grinder and the morals of his monkey.

"We're not going to have an Army like that. Our pay makes us volunteers. We do our management on blue sky and the flag. Best perk's a free funeral, unless they lose your goddamned body on an untidy battlefield. Can't give atomic artillery and tanks to a million testosterone-crazy men and give them managers who operate from self-interest. We need guys who are into sacrifice.

"How do you make guys like that? Ting, I'm glad you asked—I'm going to tell you. Get the best you can find. Test them with cold fire. Beast, Plebe year. Bloodless terror, combat without death, starvation with food on their plates, sacrifices where no one dies. Stress the holy crap out of them, mold them into a team that'll die for the next guy. Teach 'em that values are bigger than education, that Honor's the key to it all, king of the world. Bigger than American success, which is a crock if you look at it close enough.

"This is *not* college. Candidates don't walk in here by filling out a form and cadets don't graduate unless they've trooped down Honor road for four years. Grads are going to be handed feces for pay and fifty-five living human beings to lead in combat. Imagine what kind of Army we'd have if the leadership were thieves. GOOD GOD IN THE SKY!"

He cleared his throat. "Sorry. Didn't mean to make you jump." He reached down and retrieved my hat, which had flown across the room. He went to his file cabinet. "I am now passing you a file." It was labeled "Written Final Reviews 1966/EE 304A" and was marked with a red diagonal slash across its front. Various chop marks, from department head to head of exam committee to Faculty Examinations Work Group, ran down its front in a vertical column of bright red ink. I looked up at him. He put my hat on his desk.

"Open it," he said, and I did. There were the exam questions. Involuntarily, I closed the file, and he laughed.

"Mock-ups. Not the real McCoy. Leaving them in my file cabinet, bait for the bad guys. If there is a cheating ring, and they're using theft, this file of questions will be lifted. And answers prepared. I'm looking for a joker and a hive."

He returned the file to the cabinet and sat down, facing me, leaning on his knees. "Help me find them. I'm calling the first guy Big Dick," he said. "Big Dick" was the dessert risk game.

"I close my eyes, Ting, seeing through the tactical fog. Big Dick's my enemy." His eyes burned. Maher's hands came out, fingers extended stiffly, his teeth showing, and I knew I was inches away from a man who had killed actual people while displaying this exact expression. I cleared my throat.

"I see a joker, a user, a manipulator. A tweaker. Someone who'd go out of his way to tell a woman she was homely, a guy who'd tell Cookie in the chow line that his creamed slop on a shingle tasted bad. A guy who'd take someone else's Swiss watch apart just to screw with it. Likes disorder. Likes to make chaos inside unity. Likes to whack off on the system. See him? I've started to see this dirty sonofabitch every night.

"But Big Dick needs a hive, someone very good in Juice who can answer any problem, who could read that file"—he pointed at me, his chin up, his eyes now closed—"gin the solutions, and pass 'em out. The hive's a damned Good Samaritan who can't draw the line. Doesn't cheat to screw others; he does it to help them. This guy is Big Dick's exact opposite. I don't see this guy so clearly. But he's incidental. His West Point days, his military career, are dead, but he's not the problem. Big Dick, he's the problem." He looked at me. "Help me nab the Dick Brothers, Ting. You're Alfred E. Neuman in Juice, and you're okay in tactics. We can do it."

"Yes, sir," I said, my voice weak, my will uncertain.

"Like fence-sitting? Like that fence up your butt more than you hate cheaters? Don't tell me that! You're going to help me find, fix, and frappé Big Dick before he spits in our soup."

"What do you want me to do, sir?" I asked.

"Good man! First—"

"Sir, I'm sorry. But I'm not sure if I want to help you on this. I just wanted to know what it involved." Honor required me to come clean. "I want to know how much profile there is in this."

He took a deep breath, then blew it out. I shivered a little inside from his building anger.

"How old are you?" he asked.

"Twenty, sir."

"Time to be older. Time to be a company commander, responsible for the lives and deaths of others, not a Cow squad leader with eight little kids who sweat poop, meals, tenths, sports, brace palsy, constipation, and sleep. Major Noll says you're his best squad leader. Fine. That's mouseshit. Time to be a man. To figure out the meaning of *duty*. Who gives a crap about 'profile'? What are you, a careerist in the making?

"Ting, someone's screwing with West Point. That's not as bad as screwing with God or trying to kill the President, but it's still major-league cheap."

He stood up. "Maybe you haven't heard. We have the Code, which I promise you does not exist anywhere else in the world. BY GOD, I'LL NOT HAVE ANY JOKER COME INTO MY SECTION AND DICK IT UP!" He kicked his chair, which bounced off the desk, making the goosenecked lamp collapse and books fall like dominoes on my hat while the chair tipped and crashed to the floor. Maher paced in a tight circle, a panther confined, tortured, by the anonymity of Big Dick. The casters on the upended chair continued to spin. Did all my profs become angry in my presence? What was it about me that inspired them to shout at me? Was it my face? Was I frowning?

He stopped in front of me. I was almost crouched in my chair, my body torn between congratulating him and shaking his hand and jumping through his window into the icy river. He sighed.

"You guys give up so much—women and wine and song at the height of your youth—giving up everything so you can serve in a war where your own country's a bigger pain in the ass than the enemy. You get four years of college in your first three years. You put out too much to allow this thing—this piracy—this *bullshit*—to go on in your face. I'm going to stop it. I just want to do it smart. You *want* this kind of crap happening here?" he demanded.

"No, sir."

"I've got three guys who gave identical answers on every writ I gave last week. My writ file's been moved inside my own cabinet. After I changed a question on the last writ, I still got the approved solution for the original problem.

"I'd can their butts right now, but they're not the problem. They wouldn't break in here. Someone else did. Someone smart enough to hive the answers once they knew the questions. The jokers in the section'd still flunk if they knew the questions. I know you guys are scared shitless of being kicked out, scared of facing your dads and telling them you couldn't finish after making it this far. But humans don't get to be West Pointers. Ony *honorable* humans.

"You want the ring, to graduate and throw the hat, right?"

"Roger that, sir," I said with a thin voice. I saw my father, not as I had seen him last but in his Chinese Army uniform with a high collar like mine, Sam Browne belt strapped across his chest, rigidly upright, shoulders squared, his hard face resolute, showing no pain. What would he do? Could he turn in a comrade?

I saw Uncle Shim. I heard him say, subdue the self, and honor the rituals and proprieties. I breathed deeply; he'd turn them in. And I had made a promise to him in a eucalyptus grove.

"We got a joker in our ranks who's working for all the ass-wrongs in the world. He won't throw himself on a grenade to save his men. This guy'd throw a rifleman on the grenade and then write *himself* up for the Medal of Honor and let people buy him drinks.

"You know how that feels or you don't. It's the difference between being alive and just going through the motions. Feel bad, thinking about a classmate screwing the system?"

"Yes, sir."

"Good. That's duty! Working against your classmates—hell, I know it's hard. Listen up: Big Dick is *not* your classmate. He has no classmates. He gave you guys up. He's the wolf in the coop, taking victims in the night. And he's eatin' it up.

"Want to stop him?" His eyes burned into mine.

"You have options. You can help me. You can fight me. You can tell your classmates in the section that the P has figured their game and they'd better stack arms and fold their tents."

He walked around his chair to look out the window. "Doesn't matter. I'm going to get them. The ones who shot themselves in the foot, they're going to face themselves. The Code's going to get another test, and it's going to sort this one out. That's what *I'm* talking about, and you can write that in your book."

"Sir, why not ask them who's supplying their answers?"

"They're organized, Ting. They won't tell me. See, they've suspended West Point. They're doing something else, something very bad, something from a bad dream. So I blow the whistle, have three guys found on Honor—with Big Dick laughing in the middle of my bedtime prayer. By *God* I want him! This place is for men who feel allegiance to something— not just college jocks and surfers! This guy's shitting in our water supply!"

"How much time do I have to think this over?"

"Take your time." He shrugged his shoulders and made a Maurice Chevalier face of resignation, with an extravagantly cinematic French accent. "West Point, she iss burning down; weedow and orphans, zey are on ze fire. Voilà—you have a fire hose. No problem, m'sieu; I can afford to give you ...." He looked at his watch. "Five minutes."

"How about one day, sir?"

He exhaled loudly. "Okay, it's hard. Think it over during Christmas leave."

Maher extracted my crushed cap from the litter on his desk and passed it to me. He righted his chair and sat in it, heavily. He rubbed his face again. I figured if I remained in his company for long, he wouldn't have any features left.

He removed a notepad from his shirt. He wrote on it, then held it up for me to read. I squinted: OPERATION BENE-

DICT ARNOLD, followed by the names of three sectionmates. The cheaters. My heart sank. He ripped off the sheet, tore it up, then popped a Zippo and burned the shreds in an old metal ashtray.

"No op order for you; no privacy in barracks. I don't want a paper trail that could alert the ene—the cheats. So it's you and me, babes, plus any no-goat buddies you trust, to call in for paragraph 1-b, Friendly Forces.

Clint and Bob were goats, leaving me Mike, Sonny, Arch, Deke, Pee Wee, and Curve Wrecker, with Rocket Scientist, Hawk Latimer, and Spoon in reserve. I felt better.

"Go slow," he said grimly. "Been studying collegiate cheating rings. They begin fraternally. They end in extortion and violence. Here, brilliantly, we've trained the cheaters to kill. You a killer, Kai Ting?"

I took a breath. "I've caused others to die," I said.

27

GUAN YU

Southampton, Long Island, December 19, 1966

"Follow me, sir," said Seff, the driver. I stepped through the lightly falling snow to the colonnaded portico.

"Good afternoon and Merry Christmas, sir," said a large butler at the great entrance. "I am Watkins. May I take your bag?"

"No, thank you," I said. Seff and Watkins wore Academy colors—black suits, gold buttons, gray faces. They were Caucasian, middle-aged, and, but for a vague disapproval, inscrutable. I probably earned a fourth of Seff's income, but I wore my uniform better; his alignment was off, his shoes were scuffed, his salt-and-pepper hair touched his ears. Five demerits, I thought, worried about what I was seeing. The plush Lincoln Continental limo, the gloved chauffeur, the bruising butler, the size of the mansion, the diameter of the columns, suggested architecture by Frank Lloyd Wright and funding by Fort Knox.

From the door came the English hymn adapted from Beethoven's Ninth, "Ode to Joy," which offset the crash of the chilling surf beyond the house.

The entryway led to a cinematically grand, white staircase with a broad, black bannister. Above was a large skylight that might have been a trapdoor to heaven. It was bordered with small, brilliant lights which cheered the wintery morning. The compacted clutter of oversized red vases, turquoise pottery, tall, blooming greenery, and a series of broad teak display tables covered with illuminated objets d'art defeated the openness of the stairs and the skylight. I smelled tea. Beethoven came from all directions. To the left was a large sitting room occupied by more expensive collectibles; to the right was a long, black wainscoted hallway leading to a great library; to my front was the butler Watkins, patient with my circumnavigating, pop-eyed gawk.

"Just like home," I said.

He left me in a sitting room. A snarling, green-splashed, white glazed lion confronted me with its fangs and I bared my teeth at it, saying "Arr!" I was surrounded by a profusion of large, museum-quality Asian art. A fire burned quietly in a magnificent stone fireplace. I heard footfalls and put down my bag.

"Hello, Ding Kai, and welcome to Long Island. You look devilishly handsome out of uniform. 'Civvies,' right?" She approached with a warm smile and dazzling teeth, offering both hands. I took both. I loved her voice, full of energy, ripe with sharp intelligence, laced with hidden meanings I hoped someday to understand.

"Hi. What do I do with your hands?"

"Exactly what you're doing, but now you have to give them back. I'm so glad you came. Was the drive tolerable? Seff is so taciturn." She wore a white linen shirt under a blue cashmere sweater, with old but snug jeans and open-toed sandals. She looked so sensational I felt completely stupid.

"You look great," I said, proud of my understatement.

"Did you bring them?" she whispered.

I nodded. She took my hand and led me quickly through the entryway past a dining room fit for half the Corps Squads, past the gaze of a Chinese maid with raised eyebrows, and an older Chinese woman whose eyebrows were flat with the unrelenting judgment of a stern parent. I wanted to adjust my glasses. Pearl said nothing and we passed a dark, object-filled study that was as European as the sitting room was Asian. We entered a large, white sunroom with red upholstered lacquer chairs. It was simple and uncluttered.

"My favorite place," she said, looking out the great windows. "It's the sea, motioning to me." The ocean was angry, whitecapped, and silent. This sea touched Europe, not Asia. Beyond the windows was a great snow-covered lawn, and maples that in summer would shade mountains.

"Who were they?" I asked, motioning toward the hallway.

"The older woman is Zee *taitai*, my maid." She looked at me. "She was my wet nurse, and has been with me all my life." Pearl smiled hollowly. "She is very protective. It takes all my skill to go to the Waldorf, or visit you at West Point, without her."

She sat down, licking her lips. I opened my Academy overnight bag and gave her the slightly aromatic, tinfoiled package.

She opened it and sighed. "May I?" she pleaded, almost squealing when she bit into the hot dog, drawing my admiration as she deftly combined Chinese enthusiasm with Emily Post delicacy. I had gotten six Coney Island red hots at the Port Authority.

"Ding Kai, come stay with us for Christmas," she had said to me on the phone. "My father wants to meet you. You'll have the best Chinese food in the world. Please do not bring gifts—Father is not Christian. But there is something I want you to get for me. I'm *dying* for red hots. My maid bought them for me at Coney Island when I was a girl, sad that I would make such big noises while eating *gwailo* food. Ding Kai, I eat the best Chinese and French cuisine available, but I can't get hot dogs."

Mrs. Zee entered with a tray of hot tea with crumpets and creamer, English style. She frowned elegantly at the hot dog wrappers, gathering them with surprising violence. She looked at me through the corners of her eyes, reminding me of the pretended indifference of a giant monitor lizard at the zoo as it closed in on dinner.

"*Syesyeni, taitai,*" thank you, I said, showing off.

"*Bu k'e-chi,*" she replied, looking at Pearl. She left with stately speed. We drank without the cream, watching the cold waves.

"Best if you call her 'Ah Wang,' her first name," said Pearl.

"Her husband, who left her when she was a child bride, was Lao Zee." Old Zee. "If I addressed her with the honorific, *taitai*, I could never have accepted her services. *Taitai* is for equals. You must address her correctly."

I listened without blinking.

"This is the summer home. The Lims, our cooks, are not fashionable in our Manhattan place, and easier to hide here. Someday, I hope, the Lims can be accepted in the brownstone."

"Accepted by who? By whom?" I asked.

"The wives of my father's American business associates."

I nodded. I looked at the sunroom ceiling windows. "This is just like the Weapons Room and the bad flicks in the gym."

She smiled. "I enjoy West Point. It's high theater. I enjoy it because I see it through your eyes."

"What's your father like?"

"You mentioned honor."

I was never good in a chair. I stood and leaned against the windows. She stood close to me, and I looked at her face. She looked as good from the side as from the front. She turned and watched me study her. My heart surging, I leaned forward and kissed her gently. Her lips were soft. I liked the well-defined ridge on her lower lip. My heart boomed like one of Odin's summer thunderstorms.

"I missed your smell," I said, our faces very close.

"Chanel Number Five?" she said softly.

"Relish," I said.

She smiled. Her pale skin seemed healthier. She kissed me, testing my restraint, tasting my interest in her, a chef at her stove, making her recipe boil. Her lips were soft peaches and sweet apricots, and I made a sound that merged purring, mewing, and moaning. She stopped, licking her lips, breathing deeply. She delicately cleared her throat. "I like your smell. It's Chinese."

I kissed her, gently folding her into me. She held me with surprising strength, pushing my cheek onto the cold pane. Her kiss was so sweet, her embrace so passionate, that I thought we were still kissing when I realized she had said, "Ding Kai . . . what about honor . . ." I was going to utter something declarative like "uh" when her lips returned urgently. ". . . and duty?" she said into my mouth, her lips warm, breathing fast, lilacs in spring while the snow fell and the ocean roared silently beyond the cold pane that framed my warm cheek. I tasted her and her mouth was honey and my blood was a thick confection as she moaned while subjecting me to her alchemy.

"Oh, sweet God," she murmured, opening her mouth to me and we fit perfectly and I felt I knew all about her and about sublimity as she wrapped herself tightly against me. I was being transformed. I was sliding away from all I knew. My heart pounded and left me, for her.

"I thought," she breathed, "you knew nothing about girls."

"Something," I said. "Not . . . nothing." Again we kissed. She breathed on me like butterflies in spring and we kissed slowly in a void of time. Her hands caressed my back, running over my neck and shoulders to my arms. She squeezed them, kissing me more desperately, moaning, and she pulled away, breathing deeply through her nose, licking her lips, looking deeply into my eyes. "Arms are so hard . . . want to talk. About honor." I kissed her again, wanting to go fast, knowing that we should go slowly.

"Why . . . ask me?" she murmured against my mouth.

"Smarter . . . older," I said, not thinking, amazed I could speak and kiss at the same time.

She pulled back. "Fine thing to say," she said clearly.

I had tied up. "You *are* smarter. You wouldn't have said that."

She smiled. "You kiss very well." She licked her lips. "For a dummy." She stepped away, picked up the teacups and gave me mine. They rattled in high clinking notes. She sat down. I breathed.

"So talk, Dummy *Syensheng*," Mister Dummy, she said.

It was very tough. Closing my eyes made it easier. Honor and duty. I took a deep breath.

"Pearl, we have an Honor Code. 'A cadet does not lie, cheat, or steal, or tolerate those who do.' "

"Vassar has an honor code," she said.

"You go to Vassar?"

She nodded.

"I thought you went to something like night school."

"I didn't want you to think that I'm rich," she said.

"Pearl, I don't think you're rich. You're *past* rich. So how come you wanted to hide this?" I asked.

"My father's wealth has been a liability to me," she said. "We'll talk of this later. Tell me why you're worried about honor."

I gathered my thoughts and explained the basics of Major Maher's request for help.

"Ding Kai, why's this Honor Code so important? There's little cheating at Vassar, but it happens. Copying term papers by a few marginal students. But you talk about it as if it were so serious. Your Honor Code sounds like the old days. You know, Chinese legalism." She made the motion of slitting the throat; Chinese justice meted out death for most offenses. "I think expulsion for knowing about cheating is very unfair, and even unrealistic."

"It's West Point. The Code's the hardest. Pearl, it's like Guan Yu honoring his promise to free Ts'ao Ts'ao, the great evil one, even though it'd later kill him." Ts'ao Ts'ao was the powerful, charismatic minister who illegitimately sought to be emperor during the Three Kingdoms, after the fall of the great Han dynasty. In Chinese lore, he was the equivalent of the Western devil, whose very name inspired superstitious fear.

"Guan Yu was honorable. But Ding Kai, he's from an old fable."

"Pearl, you know the Hanlin Academy, the *Wen-lin*, right?"

"The Culture Forest, the Forest of Pens?"

"Yes! West Point's the Hanlin. We took the pledge of the brothers of different blood in the Peach Orchard by the Yangtze *kang*, except it was at Battle Monument by the Hudson *kang*. Our honor allows us to lead men in battle, to protect others, even unknown and unrelated by blood."

"It sounds quite romantic," she said. I couldn't be sure she was being totally sincere.

"Here's an analogy: Guan Yu made the pledge to his brothers. What if he made a pledge to turn in any cheaters, and the cheater turned out to be one of his brothers—like Liu Bei or Chang Fei? My Honor Code, Pearl, says I have to turn him in."

Pearl Yee's great, penetrating eyes expanded and her mouth opened. "Ding Kai—that *is* Chinese honor."

"Yes. It requires Confucian perfection, larger than any one of us. We're all mutually responsible for protecting Honor."

"So—violating the Honor Code is like forfeiting family honor. You'd breach clan duty."

"Yes," I said. "Dead on."

"Oh." She bit her thumbnail.

"Could I do that for you?" I asked.

"Yes," she said, almost to herself, drinking her cold tea and pouring fresh, then holding the hot cup in both hands. "Guan Yu would protect your school, even if it cost him a brother. He served *chih shan*, moral perfection. Honor is best. I'm surprised that West Point's focused on honor. When I visited you three weeks ago, I thought your school was the most American place I had seen. It also reminded me of a prison, or a monastery. How can you learn about China there?" She sighed. "Who could guess that under all those white faces, is the heart of K'ung Fu-tzu? Well, you should help your professor. Get the cheaters, whoever they are. Ding Kai, please be careful. You know what happened to Guan Yu on the moral path. He had his head handed to him."

"Thank you, Pearl," I said, looking into her confident gaze. "You synthesized the Code."

In the background, "Ode to Joy" ended its fifth or sixth rendition. Now a chorus of heavenly women's voices sang, "Glo——ria, in excelsis Deo, Glo—ria, in excelsis Deo."

"I thought your father wasn't Christian," I said.

"He isn't. I am. Now it's my turn. Let me tell you about my father. Oh, Ding Kai! You've eaten all the crumpets. It was a whole package!"

Townsend Fan Yee was the firstborn son of Brandon Kow Yee of Taishan Shipping Company Ltd., Singapore. Like his father, Townsend had attended Oxford, had more than one wife, and had inherited millions.

"He has more than one wife?" I asked.

"Oh, yes," said Pearl. "My mother is his first wife. My brother is the son of his second wife."

"Does that bother you?" I asked. "How does your mother feel?"

"He is my father," she said. "And she is his wife."

"*Shiao*, filial piety," I said. "The Three Followings and the Four Virtues."

"Of course," she said. For a moment, her beautiful, stilled face looked like one of the cool, expensive objets d'art in the entryway.

"I have trouble seeing you walking with small feet, five steps behind your husband."

She smiled hopefully. "I intend him to take long and powerful strides, to stay with me."

Mr. Yee was a rich man who feared financial risk. As was appropriate to a man with two wives, he had a mistress in New

York and another in Singapore. He changed houses the way I changed the cotton liner in my dress-gray tunic.

She said that she represented his only entrepreneurial impulse. In return for her service as chum for trolling business sharks, Pearl had Zee *taitai*, the lifetime Chinese maid who had followed her to Vassar, an expense account, a Thunderbird convertible, and open charges in most of the stores that counted in New York.

"Is it a good trade?" I asked.

"I don't know," she said. "That's the question."

The father had arranged four engagements for Pearl. When it became clear that she would scuttle them, he helped her break them. Pearl knew that she was becoming a sought-after prize, appealing to the gambling spirit that lives within all men, and increasing the business bounty that would be paid to her father for her hand.

I was going to have dinner with a slave girl and her master.

"He'll ask you the same two questions he posed to my suitors while he was selecting them. A question about politics, to see if you're controlled by it. He likes neutrals but can accept moderates." She looked at me, wondering. "He's a Republican. I'm a Democrat. What are your politics?" she asked.

"I'm an independent. I like Martin Luther King and Bobby Kennedy. I support the war in Vietnam. I like the ACLU and I hate Communists."

"Well," she said, "aren't you easy to categorize! He'll ask you a question about money, to see if you'd risk or conserve. He is most assuredly a conservator. The suitors came from approved families, and he'll ask about that. I hope you tell him more than you've told me."

"Does he think I want to marry you?"

"Yes," she said softly. "But you don't have to."

"I can't imply that if it's not true," I said.

She looked at me, both elegant eyebrows raised. "Guan Yu and the Hanlin, the *Wen-lin*. Chinese honor, right? But you're an American romantic. You want to marry for love."

"I don't want to marry at all," I said.

"Then do what you wish," she said. She stood and leaned against the windows, crossing her trim ankles, the sea frothy and greenish behind her while snow fell on the wintering trees. "I'd be very nice to you," she said, thinking things I could only imagine. "And you'd be rich. But you have to answer his questions. Just, please be nice."

She had a face that could relaunch the Greek fleet and make rational men fight each other with sharp swords for ten years. People would think highly of me for having won a woman so gorgeous. A few weeks ago Pearl had made me reveal that I was weak for being unloved. I blew out my breath. The admission had caused Pearl to pity me the way Clint ached for a busted bird. Crying in front of her. Be nice. I'm rich. What a lot of crap. Doesn't matter.

"I don't like it," I said. "I don't want nice and I don't deserve 'rich.' I don't care about money. You didn't tell me you were setting me up for a marriage exam." I blew out breath. "News about my family would sink all this, anyway."

She closed her eyes in pain and turned her back to me. Slowly her back stiffened, with either anger or resolve, or both. "Just be my friend, Ding Kai," she said in a very controlled voice. "Do not lie—do not pretend to want marriage. But please, be kindhearted."

The rich, captivating aromas of a Chinese banquet and "Joy to the World" filled the entryway. Pearl came down the white staircase in an embroidered, high-collared, pale opaline *chi-pol,* cheongsam, which fit her snugly about the neck and hung straight down from the shoulders to touch a matching pair of satin pumps. Her hair was wrapped atop her head. The long dress set up her radiant face and elegant, deep green jade earrings. I stopped breathing and adjusted my Academy tie.

"These were birthday presents, two years ago, from my father. I'm wearing them for the first time." She seemed vulnerable in her noble outfit, smiling in recognition of my kindhearted look. She touched my hand. She was more nervous than I.

A narrow, white-haired man with a hard, lean face approached us. He wore a precisely tailored charcoal smoking jacket with velvet lapels. He walked carefully, without hurry, on slippered feet that made a Chinese-like, hissing sound on an indigo carpet. He was almost my height. Pearl slightly inclined her head.

"Father, this is Ding Kai, from San Francisco. His family is from Shang-hai. Ding Kai, this is my father, Mr. Townsend Fan Yee."

"I am honored to meet you, sir." His hand was like soft deerskin, making my calloused, weightroom-beaten, pugilist's palm seem like a lizard's. His large, widely spaced eyes were of black ice. He had a face with sharp cheekbones, a large nose, and tight, dark skin beneath a precisely brushed head of medium-length white hair. I saw the source of Pearl's jawline. His mouth was wide, the chin broad. He looked rich and smelled rich, and looked at me the way I inspected Plebes, seeking error.

"Strong," he said in a guttural voice.

"Like ox," I said, and Pearl covered her mouth.

Watkins served the shark-fin soup at a pace akin to Pee Wee McCloud's thick speech. Mr. Yee delivered his questions like a New York cabbie.

"What do you know of business?" he asked.

Leadership was everything. "Management's the prime factor," I said.

"Can you run a business?" he asked.

I raised my eyebrows. "I don't know, sir."

"Brains keep Chinese alive in a foreign world," he said. "Agree?"

"And honor," I said. "K'ung Fu-tzu liked honor."

"Do you approve of racial integration?" he asked.

"Yes, sir," I said. "Even we Han are really a polyglot race."

He leaned forward, although his daughter did it better. "What if this costs us our traditions?"

"Then they are expendable."

"What if this changes who you are?"

Like going to West Point. "Then I'll learn a new life."

In an injured voice he said, "You are Chinese, and say this?"

"But sir, so many of our traditions have changed. Chinese used to listen to the *Sheng yu,* the Edicts, every fifteen days. The daughters of prosperous men had their feet bound. Times change."

He made a dismissive Chinese sound—"Foot binding was *not* tradition. This is Western sensationalism, focusing on a stupid fad! Tradition is the *San-gahng* and the *Wu-lun,* the Three Bonds and the Five Relationships. The Five Virtues of benevolence, duty, ritual, wisdom, and faithfulness. Agree?"

I took a deep breath. The shark-fin soup was probably cold. I figured part of the test was to see if I could recite instead of eat. An old test. "*Gahng* and *lun* omitted mothers and sisters. And daughters."

He sighed. "Should wives honor their husbands?" he asked.

"Yes, sir. And husbands should honor their wives." He had

two mistresses. I felt smug until I realized that I felt a continuing loyalty to Christine. That made no sense.

His next question jarred me: "How would you discipline a disobedient child?" He looked at Pearl. She looked at her soup.

Edna was screaming at me to take Silly Dilly to the vet to be put to sleep. Edna had never known poverty, we were poor, and this was her response—to save fifty cents a day by killing the cat. My income alone would support a nation of pets, and there were scores of people who would take Silly Dilly, but Edna had decided, and she never recanted a decision. I could have our cat put to sleep, or Edna would mismanage Silly's death. *Ch'a lu t'ung k'u.*

I would never have children. "I can't discuss parenting competently, sir," I said, frowning.

He pursed his lips. Pearl smiled at me hopefully.

"Should college students be drafted?"

"Yes, sir," I said. "All citizens should serve the country."

"You are a political extremist," he said. Now he frowned.

"No, sir. I'm an American."

"This is a melodramatic answer," he said.

"Being American is melodrama," I said, tasting the soup. "Great soup," I said, finishing it while he and Pearl watched me.

"Do you know that she has broken three"—he held up the last three fingers of his left hand—"engagements, and each time I lost the dowry?"

"I knew about the engagements. Not the dowries."

He looked at Pearl. "Do you wish to marry her?" he asked.

"I don't know," I said.

He peered at me like a squad leader finding rust in the rifle bore. He looked at Pearl. She smiled at him wanly, lifting an elegant eyebrow. He rubbed his hard, smooth forehead with the first two fingers of his right hand. "Your answer is insulting. She is engaged to a fine man from an excellent family in Macao, the result of months of search and interviews. You have no right in this house unless you provide cause for breaking the engagement."

"I'm sorry. I meant no insult." I adjusted my glasses. "I would like permission to continue to date your daughter. But the best cause for breaking the engagement is your daughter's wish to break it."

He wiped his mouth with a jade-colored napkin, which he crushed like something that had angered him, and left on the table. "Why would you not want to marry my daughter?" He asked it with the same tone as "Why would you not want to breathe?"

"We've known each other for only two months." Honor. I looked at Pearl. "I was in love with another girl for six years." I let out my breath. "Whoever marries Pearl marries, I think, a lot more than Pearl."

"You resist a Chinese family that would welcome you, while you are part of an army that restricts your freedom?" He laughed a joyless Chinese laugh. "I have read of West Point and its famous discipline. What if it orders you to kill Asians? Do you know the American army killed a million Chinese in the Korean War? How many of them do you think were named Ting and Yee?"

"I will go where the Army directs me. They have my promise." I looked at Pearl. "It's an honorable profession. It gives me a purpose in life."

"Can you afford a girl like her?" he asked, his eyes alight. "With 'purpose'?"

I knew it: a math question. The tip of my tongue emerged while I calculated. "Sir, for three dates, I've bought your daughter one corsage, three cherry Cokes, a ticket to an armed forces movie theater for one dollar, two dinners at a government hotel, and six hot dogs. We're within budget."

He tilted his head and moved his crushed napkin. "Six hot dogs?" he said.

I was trying to read book titles, but my view was constantly interrupted by paintings I later learned were Matisses, Vuillards, Maillols, and Picassos. My concentration was broken by Pearl's clear voice. "He's in awe of you. He's proud that a Chinese is at West Point. He understands what it's like to be a Chinese man in a Caucasian school. He admired your courage. You were wonderful. You were honest and strong. You saved me, I think, from the man from Macao."

She crossed her legs beneath the long dress. I wanted to kiss her, but I could feel her father's flat, refrigerated gaze on my desires. It was ten o'clock. I had no idea how I could sleep in this house. I wondered if they had a big weight room. I wondered if I could run back to the Academy from here.

"You did well, if somewhat sarcastically."

"West Point," I said.

"Many men are very interested in marrying me," she said.

I looked at her. "This is news?"

"They think me attractive."

"They never saw you eat a red hot."

"You're not avoiding me, are you?" she called.

I was on the other side of the room. If I went any farther, she'd have to phone me. I returned, which took a while, and sat next to her on the extravagantly soft burgundy sofa. I felt vulnerable, the way Pearl had looked coming down the staircase.

I realized that the company of Chinese women had caused me to cry. My muscles were of no use in these matters. She was more than the sum of chest-thumping intelligence and good looks. She sat there, so dignified, holding keys to a mythological past that I could not know, and a future that was filled with new days. She was, in so many respects, perfect for me. The money didn't matter; she was a Chinese woman and we had walked in each other's shoes. My heart quivered in fear. I'm a loser. I don't want to lose her. No more questions about heart. I've already done too much.

Her eyes were so warm, so close. She filled my vision and my mind. I looked at her mouth. "Are we through talking?" I asked. "Can we kiss now?"

"I hope we're never through talking," she said softly.

"Ach, zere may be no hope for you, young Chinese lady," I said. "Unless, you take ze vater treatment. I have zis teacher, Mr. Flauck, who can help you change your life."

"How, *Herr Doktor?*" she asked.

"You must close your eyes," I said, moving closer.

"You may not kiss me until I know why you won't court me."

I took a deep breath. I could lose her because of honesty. Honor. "I'd be no good as a husband. Worse as a father."

"How can you know that?" she asked.

"I know," I said with great certainty.

"There are books that can help us," she said. She was looking at my mouth. Her eyes were so large and bright, her eyelashes so long. "I'm smart, learn fast, and already know much. Let me help."

"You can't help me with your eyes open," I said.

She closed them. She lifted her chin, her face so strong, so confident, so open, her lips expectant, her pallor gone.

"Don't know if I'm good enough for you," I said.

She opened her eyes. "For this I closed my eyes?" she asked.

"Okay. Close them again," I said.

"Kai. Do you love me?"

Music played. I looked into her penetrating eyes. I looked at her with love and fear. She lifted her elegant chin, offering her mouth as she closed her eyes. Two tears clung to her eyelashes. I kissed her eyes, picking up the teardrops, then caressed her lips.

"Yes," I whispered.

"Oh," she whispered. "I love you. Merry, Merry Christmas, Ding Kai," she said into my mouth, sealing my lips with hers.

28

FORK

West Point, January 4, 1967

"Major Maher speaking, sir."

"Sir, this is Kai Ting. I'm on your team."

"All right, Big Thunder! Good man. Happy New Year!"

"Same to you, sir. You sound cheerful."

"Dammit—I love a good fight! Hell, I can't wait! Congratulations on getting off the goddamn fence. Listen, watch your AO. Only speak to me when you're secure. Remember—we're dealing with a mutiny."

I wasn't sure how I was going to start. I didn't know what was going to happen, but I knew that my comfort quotient was about to be kicked in the teeth. All the Academy buildings looked different. Somewhere, among us, cheaters lived and worked. Ts'ao Ts'ao was alive and living at West Point, cackling as he rubbed his hands.

I checked for messages in the orderly room. There was an envelope from the Catholic chaplin inviting me to a memorial service on Sunday for First Lieutenant Marco Matteo Fideli.

* * *

I had been staring at the Guan Yu figurine and the photo of Pearl on my desk when I realized that Clint had been trying to welcome me back from Christmas leave. Then Clint saw the note. Time stopped.

"Oh, man!" he cried. "Don't do this to me! Not Fideli!"

I couldn't say anything. I appreciated my immobility, and tried to hold on to it.

Pee Wee McCloud came in the door in a civvy sport coat, a new beard on his face. He looked at me with an infinite sadness, then crumpled the chaplain's note he had received, and savagely hurled it into the wastecan. He grabbed me by the open collar to my dress gray and lifted my dead weight bodily from the bunk, carried me to Clint, who was at the window near Para-rat, and embraced both of us, their foreheads touching mine. Pee Wee's shoulders shook and he wept. "He was too good," he said, dragging out each word. "He'd be the guy to pull the others out of the bush. Can't be dead. He and Mario were going to sing at Carnegie next year."

Clint kept shaking his head, and then he began to cry. I did not want to be in this cluster of misery, but Pee Wee's bulk pinned me. "It's a battlefield mistake," I tried.

No one bought it. Pee Wee growled, "We're going to the funeral, Kai. Pay respects. Meet me in my room, thirteen hundred hours."

The three of us trudged silently up Washington Road wearing full overcoats over full dress. Our galoshes made a unified scrunch in the fresh snow. Hundreds of cadets straggled behind. Pee Wee had timed it to allow family and officers to arrive first.

Mr. Fideli was a medium-sized man in a heavy black overcoat. He leaned heavily on Lieutenant Mario Fideli, all of his control swept away in a maelstrom of burst agony. A soft and gentle snow fell. Mrs. Fideli was a tall, patrician woman, struggling to retain control. She kept an arm around the waist of a young woman in black, speaking to her through their veils: Marco had a sister.

The chaplain spoke. A week ago, the Fideli brothers had been in a verdant jungle.... I jolted as the honor guard fired its salute, the sharp cracks of the M-14s echoing across the cold hills and the icy river. After honors, the guard captain passed the folded American flag to Mario. Mario gave it to the young woman in black.

The three of us sighed: the woman was Marco's widow.

Somehow, in the last eighteen months, Marco had married. As the bugler sounded taps, she collapsed in Mario's arms, her slight frame shuddering as she tried to stifle her wails. Her mother-in-law bowed her head and surrendered, weeping with her. I clamped my jaws together and tried to imagine the jungle that the Fidelis had left. Through the snow I saw the face of the enemy. The Vietcong and the NVA, victors over the Japanese and the French. I was a Chinese soldier preparing to fight Reds. I trembled with hate and blood lust. I would kill them all with fire and knife. I crept up on them and cut them down without mercy. The enemy looked like me.

"Mario," I said later, "I'm sorry."

He nodded, his mouth compressed in a massive effort of will to stop his emotions. He was thin and older, pale under sunburned skin. "Thanks, Kai," he said. Tears ran down his face. "Marco's honored that you came." His strong voice tremored. "So am I." He handed me an envelope with my name on it. We shook hands. Later, I would learn, Mario would never sing again.

I started to approach the parents and Marco's widow, and Mario gently, almost imperceptibly, shook his head. My Asian face was unwelcome at this moment, at this American funeral for a son who had been killed by Asians. By gooks. I nodded. "Good luck, Mario," I said, and immediately left the cemetery in long strides, panting, thankful for the heavier pelts of falling snow. I began to run, fleeing the loss, the hatred, the confusion. Clint called and I ran faster. Pee Wee could outsprint me, but he gave up the chase.

I ran all the way to the Thayer. Jean was on duty, and she gave me a table on the lower patio, where no one sat in winter.

God love you, Marco Fideli. Thank you for your warm heart, for your cheering of me in a hard year, for teaching me how to laugh in the face of Beast, for teaching me the geography of my soul. Even if we kill them all, I'll still miss you.

Inside the envelope was a gold lieutenant's bar. It was corroded with the humidity of the Far East, scratched by unknown causes, so unlike the impeccable appearance of its owner. I would be honored to wear it. I leaned forward, holding it to my forehead.

I would never attend another funeral for a Vietnam fatality. I hated funerals with a deep and undefined passion and was not strong enough to do this again. Pain filled me, and I expected blood to run from my ears. Don't mean nothin'. After a while, it was true. By evening, I could no longer remember the theme of the chaplain's eulogy.

I did remember my expected failure of the Juice whufer. I opened the textbook. My mathematical mind, absent since youth, was facing its grandest opportunity to realize what Buddhists seek—nothingness. Beset by an endless siege of invidious calculus problems, battered by three years of bad engineering grades, and finally victimized by my wretched study habits, the architecture of my thinking, such as it was, now approached rubble.

The small, fine edges of linear thought, the clear geometric cutting devices and bright boundary lines that allowed analysis in any subject, were becoming *tseuh*, porridge. My synapses were clogging, the neurons in retreat, and my thinking apparatus assumed a negative personality that sounded like a roll call of the Seven Stupid Dwarfs: Surly, Cranky, Dumb, Dopey, Grouchy, Foolish, and Unprepared. When it came to engineering, I concluded, there was only so much one could do with wishful thinking. Now, it seemed, wishful thinking was no longer in season. If I had a wish, I'd bring Marco back. Thinking about academic failure was more comforting than acknowledging his loss. I slammed the book shut.

I thought of Pearl. "Chinese honor," Pearl had said. "Honor at all costs. It's a sacrifice. The highest value."

Marco's life was the price. He had told us, near the end of Beast, that we were entering a ground war in Asia, against all good military advice. When it was time to go, he had said cheerfully, "We're off to win a war."

I could live to be a hundred and I would not have his great human spark, his strength and mirth, his sense of Honor. He was dead. He had wanted me to forget my fears. Byron Maher wanted me to do my duty by zapping classmates who were cheating. Cathy Pearl Yee wanted me to help Maher, and to be a man not only with emotions, but one who admitted them. She had brought me love. Townsend Fan Yee wanted me to compete for his daughter and to protect his wealth.

My father and Edna wanted me to be an American West Pointer. Schwarzhedd wanted me to be conscious. Tony had wanted me to be a college man with a hat and a briefcase. Uncle Shim wished me to be a Chinese man of letters, opposed to violence and committed to the past. But Tony was gone and Marco was dead, and I didn't know what to do with all these feelings which were rushing to the surface like so many boiling gases.

Sonny was drilling me for the whufer, and my roommates had evacuated to the library to give us workout space. Sonny started with the basics. "It'll hurt more to face your dad if you flunk than to squeeze Juice data into your iron head. Right?"

Sonny presented what he considered to be the standard problems and walked me through them. I understood what he was doing. He then gave me a new problem. With much struggle and a great deal of rote memory work I solved it. He pulled out his red pen and drew a large five-pointed star and circled it. A star from the starman. He grinned, and so did I, with less enthusiasm.

He created a variant problem. But however minor the variation, I had no idea how to proceed. He made hissing noises and ran his hand through his thick black hair, his heavy eyebrows dark with concentration and frustration, tinted with a look of fear.

Clint returned early. I expected him to look as defeated as I felt, but he undressed and racked out quickly. I turned out the ceiling lights and we went to the subdued desk lamps.

"Ready for tomorrow?" I asked.

"Hmm," Clint said.

Sonny Rappa sighed. "Okay. Try it like this," he said, but he lost me. He tried again. By now my mind was in full retreat.

"Back to basics," he said. "Do these differential and integral equations," and he drew out a series of them. I worked them.

"Kai, got two problems. One, your calculus sucks. Two, there's somethin' in your brain that doesn't let the stuff in. You got a series of heavy-duty resistors in line with your reasoning circuits. I can't find connections on your main circuit board. I end around, and I'm in the jungles of Brazil or something. Let's get some of Chad's high-octane java. I need a jolt." Chad "the Man" Enders made the strongest coffee this side of the ordnance lab.

"Works for me," I said. "I need a break."

When we returned, Deke was in the rack. Neither the java nor the break changed matters, as we hacked our way through the uncharted areas of my math-disabled brain. The ten-minute bell before taps sounded.

I shook my head. "Sonny, thanks a lot, really," I said. "I feel like I wasted all your time. You could be working on pulling a cold max."

"Naw" he said. "I know the poop—better I'm here. I *like* buttin' my head up against a brick wall." He hit me on the arm. "Good luck tomorrow. Just grab down some rack. Don't stay up late. This stuff'll come to you—trust me. I know what I'm talkin' about. Just pull seventy-one percent. Your mind'll be clear tomorrow."

"That's my problem," I said. "My mind's always clear; it's 'cause there's nothing *in* it."

"Hiya, buddy!" said Bob Lorbus to Sonny as he came in the door. He smiled and shook his head as he piled his books on his desk. "This stuff is awful."

Sonny grimaced; no one liked his favorite subject. He gathered his books and his slide rule, put on his gray company jacket, and I walked him out. At the stairs, he gave me a thumbs-up, and headed out to return to his barracks on the far side of the Cadet Hilton.

Bob racked out. I stayed up for an hour, shuffling meaninglessly through my notes and Sonny's materials. I stood by the radiator and looked out the window at the Area, avoiding Venus's jaws and letting Para-Rat-Trooper grab my pinkie with his little claws as I shelled a peanut for him. There were only a few other lights on. I knew who they were: goats like me, struggling with tired brains against the challenge of tomorrow's final writ, hoping stupidly that sacrificing sleep and rest would produce results.

At midnight I collapsed on top of my brown boy, wondering what strange twist of fate had led me, a ham-fisted slide-rule klutz, to survive this long in a school that so dearly loved math. Above me, in the upper bunk, snored Deke in his steady, reliable, hypnotic buzz-saw rhythm that meant no Nam nightmares tonight. My eyes followed the sound. Taped to the underside of the bedsprings were some papers. On the top sheet were five electrical engineering problems, surrounded by a great deal of explanatory script.

I stared at them. I thought overconsumption of saltpeter from the mess hall, or too much of Chad's atomic coffee, had induced hallucinatory misperception. I scrunched my eyes closed and rubbed them, but when I opened them, the papers were still there.

I pulled the masking tape from the springs. Ten sheets, each with five problems. They were typed. Homework sets were run off on blue ditto machines, with space to enter your work. In the spaces appeared to be the answers, in neat, approved solution form.

Why were they taped to the bottom of Deke's bunk? Were they for him, or me, or neither? They had been in direct line of sight above my pillow. I went to my desk and examined them.

"Sinusoidal Input to RL and RC Circuits ... Impulse Response ... Sinusoidal Steady-state Solutions of Parallel Circuits ... Automatic Control Systems ... Linear Approximations to Machine Analysis ... Electronic Analog Computers...." This was a roll call of the key topics of second semester—the exam topics of the WFR.

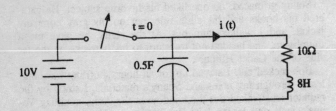

1. For the circuit shown above, find the natural response, i(t), for $t \geq 0$. Hint: Use KVL to write an integro-differential equation in i(t); differentiate to form a 2d order linear homogeneous differential equation.

Solution:

KVL $\qquad V_C(t) = V_R(t) + V_L(t)$

$V_R(t) = Ri(t) = 10i(t)$

$V_L(t) = L\dfrac{di}{dt} = 8\dfrac{di}{dt}$

$V_C(t) = -\dfrac{1}{c}\displaystyle\int_0^t i(\tau)d\tau + V_C(o) = -2\int_0^t i(\tau)d\tau + V_C(o)$

Note: Minus sign because i(t) is UP through the capacitor!

Apply to KVL

$-2\displaystyle\int_0^t i(\tau)d\tau + V_C(o) = 10i(t) + 8\dfrac{di}{dt}$

$o = 8\dfrac{di}{dt} + 10i(t) + 2\displaystyle\int_0^t i(\tau)d\tau - V_C(o)$

Differentiate

$$o = 8\frac{d^2i}{dt^2} + 10\frac{di}{dt} + 2i(t)$$

Characteristic equation

$$o = 8m^2 + 10m + 2$$

$$m = \frac{-10 \pm \sqrt{10^2 - 4 \cdot 8 \cdot 2}}{2 \cdot 8} = \frac{-10 \pm 6}{16}$$

$$m = -0.25, -1$$

Natural response is:

$$\underline{o(t) = Ae^{-0.25+} + Be^{-t} \text{ for } t \geq 0}$$

Each of the problems had an underlined answer, Q.E.D. Looking at the sheet gave me an otherworldly sensation. There were going to be fifty problems on tomorrow's final. Intuitively, I knew I was looking at correct answers to real problems. I was holding department material. It was today's whufer, a pass on tomorrow's final. This wasn't Maher's dummy with the fake problems. It was the real thing.

"Oh, Jesus," I said, suddenly looking around the room, as if I had been under observation. My heart slugged heavily. How'd this thing get here? I had been here all night, leaving only to get Chad's java and to walk Sonny down the hall. Clint had come back early; Deke returned during the coffee break, and Bob walked in as Sonny was leaving. I felt chills. Who could've come in here without one of us seeing him? Ts'ao Ts'ao had stolen the march.

I turned the sheets over. On the backside of the tenth and final page, in red, was a circled star. Sonny was a lefty, and his stars canted to the left, with the two lateral points the largest. I rustled through my notes, finding the one he had given me for my one correct answer. It was his star.

29

Honor

West Point, January 11, 1967

I stood up. I put the papers into a folder.

I looked at the figure of Guan Yu on my desk, casting a small shadow onto the folder with the papers. I thought of Uncle Shim.

> This is a big journey, when you leave the home of your father for the house of the Son of Heaven. Brigands, robbers and misfortune wait in your path, but the Confucian scholar with rectitude knows no fear, and his steps are morally bold and knowing.

This was in Uncle Shim's letter to me during Beast Barracks, in 1964, when he wrote about his departure from home as a youth to take the three days of Confucian tests en route to becoming a "superior man."

"Good evening, *Dababa*," I said into the phone. "This is Kai Ting. I am so sorry to call you so late." It was after ten in California. "How are you?"

"I am happy to hear your young voice. Are you well?"

"*Dababa*, I want you to tell me one of your stories, about someone who faced the Fork of Pain. Where he has two choices—to destroy a friend, a Confucian friend, or to dishonor himself."

"Do you ask for your own moral guidance? Or for someone else?"

"For me," I said.

"How prophetic a woman was your mother."

"Pardon me?" I asked.

"*Hausheng*, your mother said you would ask me someday

for a story of moral guidance. She said you would not ask your father, or your father's second wife. You would ask me."

"She knew my father would remarry?"

"Everyone knew that," he said. "Your father had two small children. Naturally he would find a new mother. It was his duty."

"Did my mother—did she have advice for me?"

"She was your mother," he said.

"Did she ever face the Fork?"

"*Hausheng,* we all do."

"What was her advice?"

"It is already known to you; it caused you to call me."

I hesitated. "Oh, you mean it's one of those general things. So, Uncle, what's the answer?"

"*K'e ji fu li,*" he said.

Silence.

"You think this does not help you? Then you are not thinking. You find no comfort in these words? Then you are not accepting. There is no guidance in the edict? Then I have been a most miserable teacher. Think, *Hausheng.* What does the Master tell you to do?"

I sighed. "To subdue the self and honor the rites, the bonds and relationships. First to the father, then to the emperor, and of the young to elders," I said.

"Your mother, whom you do not know, whose face is no longer known to you, says to you, 'Go forth into the world in peace; be of good courage; hold fast to that which is good; render to no one evil for evil; support the weak; help the afflicted; honor all persons; love and honor God.' "

"Is that Taoism?" I asked.

"It is the teachings of her Jewish Lord Jesu."

I sighed. "That's no help. I'm looking for Chinese guidance. This place is lousy with American, Christian regulations."

"*Hausheng,* I am not trying to help you. I am performing my duty to my friend, who was your mother. She asked me to say those words to you when you requested help. She believed your family would be plagued with inherited problems, reaching down to you, 'unto the third generation.' She saw consequences to entire families over time, instead of Eastern, individual *yeh,* karma. These are not my precepts. They are hers. I have remembered them for fifteen years."

"Is that your advice—*k'e ji fu li* and my mother's Christian stuff?"

He repeated the advice for me. I wrote it down. It had been authored by "the other woman": the bad mother, superstitious, illiterate, crude, confused about God and the gods, a fanatic for Jesus Christ, prone to the passions and death. She had abandoned us by dying.

I felt confused. But his words seemed right, and familiar, and I felt stirrings in the hollow parts of me.

"But *Dababa*," I said. "Master K'ung didn't even mention mothers in the chain of obedience. Only men—the father, the emperor, the elder brother, and the elder friend."

"I am the scholar, not you," he said. "Your mother was learned and I tell you to also honor her by following her advice."

I looked at the advice. Christian liturgy. I smelled Edna.

"You must not lose her face in your mind," he was saying. "Remember her. Goodbye, *Hausheng*."

I hung up. I concentrated, returning in my memory, trying to conjure the face of my first mother. I saw a Chinese woman; it was my sister, Jennifer Sung-ah. She was brushing our mother's hair, smiling. Our mother was laughing next to her, but she had no face.

"Sonny," I whispered. "Wake up."

He jolted up, confused, looking to the right, at me, and then to the left, at the wall. He started to say something, and I clapped my hand over his mouth and held my left index finger across my lips. His eyes were bugged open, uncomprehending. He had been in the best sleep we get, in the hour before reveille.

"Look at this," I said to him in the sinks. I watched him. The color in his face drained. "Where'd you get this?"

"Above my bunk, last night. Look at the back, last page."

"Jesus," he said, twitching, squirming.

"Your star," I said. "Function symbols look like yours."

"Dammit to hell!" he spat. "Sorry. Hail Mary, full of grace. Forgive me, God."

"Sonny," I said, my heart in my throat. If he's cheating, and admits it, I have to turn him in—for helping me. If I don't turn him in, we are animal shit scum, forever. Guys who had spit on the Code, screwed in the inner sanctum of our brains and hearts. In what Uncle Shim called *hsin fa*, the mind-heart system, what Western people called "conscience," but with stronger obligations and duties to doing the correct thing. We would become the servants of Ts'ao Ts'ao.

"What's going on?" I asked.

"I was asked for a star. I gave one, on a blank page." He flipped the paper. "This stuff wasn't on it."

"Who was it?" I asked. "Who asked you?"

He took a breath. "Big Bus. Bob Lorbus."

"Bob wouldn't do anything like this. That's bullshit!"

"My stinkin' star's like a signature." He ran his hand through his thick, dark hair. "Look," he said, "I'm your tutor. This falls in your lap, looks like it's from me. You use it, bust the Code in the chops, and pass. Otherwise, ya gotta turn in a buddy. And that'd be tough, right? Hey, *right?*"

"I'd hate to see you go. Can I have your meal tickets?"

He smiled wanly, rubbing his whiskers. They rasped.

I rubbed mine. I would've sworn I heard something.

"You didn't leave this thing, right?" I asked.

"God, no. We gotta report this."

I sighed in relief. I looked at my watch. "Fifteen minutes before the buzzer." False dawn freshened the sinks.

"Kai. Chad Enders's your company Honor rep. Report it to him, get in sync with the Code. Ask him to meet us ASAP."

"He'll know that Bob couldn't be part of whatever this is."

"That's not the test. Can't go to Chad with *that* load. He's got his duties, we got ours. All of us are in it deep. Including Bob, sweet Mary and the Son of God love him."

"Some expression," I said.

"That's no expression. Want to pray with me?"

I laughed. "No. I'll get Chad. Gotta see my P, Major Maher. Meet me in the A-3 orderly room after breakfast."

We looked at our watches. "Let's meet at oh-six-fifteen," he said. "Scrag breakfast."

I cleared my throat. "I'll eat fast."

"Cheez, forgot who I was talking to." He squirmed, then looked at me. "What would you've done if I cheated for you?"

"I don't know," I said. "Been up all night, mucking it. Turned my brain into tapioca. What would you've done?"

He looked at me, eyes narrowed, as if he were saying goodbye to me. "I'd follow the Code."

Sonny and I retraced the march to the graves, up the high hill of Washington Road, past the Old Cadet Chapel. It was a crisp and clear morning, and we looked upriver at the wall of the long and loamy space of the West Point Cemetery. Here members of the Long Gray Line had been interred since 1817. With so many famous generals buried there, and so many campaigns fought and won, it was strange how we tended to think first of George Armstrong Custer, his brash tactics, unique obelisk grave marker, and his wife, Libby, buried next to him. Now, I would think only of Marco Matteo Fideli's simple white gravestone. How could he be gone? Nothing was worth his loss.

Residents of these quarters could sit on their railed porches on summer evenings and watch the river, thinking about the strange nature of the soldiering profession, where violent death was a player, with the grand cemetery always waiting, stage left.

Sonny looked at the quarters. "Used to be the Old Soldiers Hospital. Inspiring view for old, shot-up vets," he said, looking at the cemetery and the Old Cadet Chapel, where Benedict Arnold was remembered with a cryptic plaque that only said, "Maj Gen b. 1740."

A woman in a red suit opened the door to Quarters 126A. She was athletic, of medium height, with light brown hair and warmly attractive. I thought: Polly Bergen. I heard children and smelled an invitingly robust breakfast. I hadn't eaten for twelve minutes.

"Good morning. I'm Kai Ting; this is Sonny Rappa. I called about seeing Major Maher. Please excuse our intrusion."

"How do you do, Kai and Sonny," she said, shaking our hands. "Please call me Ann. Come in. Would you like some coffee?"

"No, thank you," I said, following her into the entryway. A large living room was to the right.

"Great thundering balls of fire!" announced Major Maher thickly, chewing aggressively. He was in greens, holding a breakfast plate. A large tan dog panted by his leg, licking up an earlier spill and hoping for an accident. "What's up?"

We showed the major the problems that had appeared on the top of my bunk while he scooped his entire breakfast plate into his mouth and closed the dining room doors. It was a technique I knew.

"I didn't study them, but I know the writ, sir," said Sonny. The major looked at me, chewing fast with ballooned cheeks.

"I saw them, too, sir. I looked at them a lot." I shook my

head. "Can't remember anything about them. I of all people hate to say this, but they all looked alike to me."

"This WFR," he said, his normally eloquent voice mushy, "was in my office safe. Disappeared between 1900 hours Tuesday and 0800 yesterday, when I opened it. This is the only copy except for the one in my wallet." He checked it.

"Sir, are you the writ officer?" Sonny asked.

"The Academy has great thinkers. In time of need, however, the forces of good customarily call on me. I don't want to brag." We laughed. "You can't take this writ. I'll write a new one for you."

"Sir," I said, "can we bring Mr. Rappa into the situation?"

"Mr. Rappa, I'm expected to bring the international Communist conspiracy to its knees, mentor the next generation of nuclear Army leaders, and grade some whufers, all, preferably, within seven days. I can use your help. Welcome to a counterconspiracy to save the Honor Code of the United States Military Academy. Doing anything for the next few weeks?"

"Oh, no, sir," said Sonny. "Just tryin' to get Huck Finn here to eat his vegetables and do a little studying." He looked at me.

"Good, Rappa. I have authority to conduct an investigation. I need you gents to have your Honor Rep contact me. We can use help, but remember, we're up against a cheating ring. You're in charge, Ting. Use your discretion and use whom you wish.

"But I promise you this," he said, leaning forward and wiping his mouth with a napkin and showing his teeth. "This mission is going to end up with Honor taking one hellacious, shit-kicking bite out of the southports of the ratscum who are doing this. When we're done, they're gonna walk funny for a long time."

"Chase, *please*," said his wife from around the door.

30

PERFECTION

West Point Museum, January 11, 1967

Chad Enders paced past the glass display of Fort Putnam. His footfalls echoed through the empty, hollow museum in the basement of the Administration Building.

"Maher's the Juice WFR exam officer. He detailed you to find the planners in a cheating ring. Honor belongs to the Corps, not the greensuits. The Committee can win a jurisdiction contest, but that'd waste time. Maher's on to something. I think he's square with the Corps.

"I'll report it to the Committee. Keep me posted. You're working for the Corps, not Maher. I'll talk to him about that."

"He's expecting you," I said.

"Good." Chad rubbed his chin. "Damn, whoever did this has to be nuts. They've crossed a line in the sand. Be careful."

Sonny and I nodded as he left.

"Let's presume a ring," said Sonny. "How'd they do it? Wonder what happened in '51, with the football team. It was a big scandal."

I had heard of that. "Tough to reconstruct something that old," I said. "We can't even talk about guys found on Honor."

"I don't care about who," said Sonny. "Let's sweat the *how*."

"Okay," I said. "How would you get into Maher's safe? Pretend you're a lousy student. And a cheat. How would you get in?"

He closed his eyes, sighing. "Kill myself first," he said.

"For being a bad student? Or a burglar?"

"Hey," he said. "I've been a lousy student. Survival swim and boxin' almost killed me." Boxing was one of the few things I could help him with. He shuddered. "First, let's get into Bartlett. The doors are push locks, with a retracting bar."

He went to the museum door. He pushed on it, opening it. "See—the bottom tongue goes into a hole in the floor. The top into that one, above. Fill 'em with epoxy, and the lock would look good, but wouldn't work. Find a guy with epoxy . . . naw," he said. "Too inconclusive."

"Hide in Bartlett until closing hours," I said.

"Okay, but you're still not into Maher's office. It locks, too."

"I got it," I said. "A UFO lands on the roof of Bartlett. The UFO driver whammies the locks for the cheating ring."

"Can't believe I missed that one," said Sonny.

"Here you go," I said. "A lock pick. San Francisco's lousy with them."

"Know how ta pick a lock?" he asked.

I shook my head.

"And you're smart. How many cadets can pick locks?"

"All you need is one," I said.

"Not a cadet skill. We blow things up, not open 'em. Keys, Kai. Whoever did this had keys to Bartlett and the office."

"Who has them besides profs and department heads?" I asked.

He laughed. "They didn't do it. Who makes the Schlage or Taylor keys? Ah—BPs," he said. The civilian janitors.

"BPs wouldn't give keys to cadets," I said.

"Might if they thought it was innocent," he said.

"That still leaves the safe," I said. "How'd they do that?"

"Oh, easy, Kai, it was a lock pick," he said. "West Point's lousy with lock picks."

"You're a lot of help. Let's ask Mike," I said.

"We have four topics to hive," said Mike Benjamin while I ate. "One, the '51 cheating scandal, for method. Two, keys, for getting into Bartlett and Maher's office. Three, the safe. Four is checking out our classmates who are coming up with canned answers in Kai's section. From these four we derive the planners—Maher's Big Dick and Hive. Maybe, we even get to know *why*. What's your pleasure?"

Mike, Sonny, and I were drinking cherry Cokes and I was eating burgers in the far corner of the Weapons Room, our cadet corporal stripes large and prominent on our lower sleeves. I took reflected pride in the bright bilateral gold stars on their high, black, dress-gray collars. Sonny was sixth in the class and Mike was eighth. By graduation, they'd switch. I was 350th, dead center.

"I'll take keys," said Sonny. "Kai, you oughta take '51— you like history. Mike, why not take the safe."

"Each of us should start watching one of the guys in the section," I said.

"And log contacts," said Mike. "For cross-referencing."

"What are you guys talkin' about?" asked Fritz Palmer, a reserve pitcher from Fourth Regiment.

"How to get the bullion out of the Silver Depository," I said. "We figure that'll keep us in burgers and Cokes till '73." That was when our class would complete its military obligation.

"You're not serious," he said.

"C'mon, Palmer! How'd I afford these drinks if I didn't already dig a tunnel into the silver?"

Sonny and Mike hooted, a simian Greek chorus.

"Don't hurt Doubleday Field during your dig," Fritz said.

"Know what I like about you, Kai?" Mike asked.

"Nothing?" I said.

"You like it here," he said. "You know how many don't like it here? I look at you and think, If he likes it, maybe it's okay."

That made no sense at all, and I frowned at him. He was the starman; I was the court jester. "So what if I like it?" I said.

"You like people," said Mike. "I'm too judgmental of the bigots, the anti-Semites, the nonintellectual athletes."

"Oh, yeah, they're my kind of people," I said.

"No, they're not. But you accept everyone."

"Wish you'd accept Juice," said Sonny.

"It's dumb," I said, "sweating stuff we'll never use. We oughta be learning Vietnamese. Engineering isn't West Point. You guys, the Code, the leadership, the system—*that's* West Point."

"You still got doubts about the war?" asked Sonny.

"Man, anyone who takes HMA 273"—Rev War—"has doubts. All Juice does is make me doubt myself. Air Force zoomies graduate into supercomplicated jets that run on juice and wires, right? They take engineering for two years. We graduate into mud with M-16s, which have no electrical parts, and get stuck with four years of it. Five percent of us go into Engineers and ninety-five percent don't. The 273 course teaches that if we can relate to the Vietnamese, we'll win. If we don't, we lose. So it pisses me off that we keep bustin' our chops on Juice when we oughta be hiving Vietnam."

I looked at them, waiting for the applause.

"So, Soapbox Man," said Sonny, "ready to interview the Class of '51, and learn the meaning of relating?"

I reviewed the *Register of Graduates,* which listed each grad by GOM, general order of merit. Buzz Aldrin, the *Gemini 12* pilot who was scheduled to fly to the moon next year, graduated third in the Class of 1951. Most who had served as faculty had already left the Academy between the years 1962 and 1964. The majority of the current faculty had graduated in the mid-1950s.

The Class of '51 graduated almost two hundred fewer than the class before it and fifty-two fewer than the class after it. In the middle of the Korean War, with an acute need for junior officers, USMA graduated a class that was 30 percent under strength. I read on, into the Class of 1952. Some members were currently on faculty. One in Physics and Chemistry, another in the Tactical Department. One name, near the bottom of the class, jumped out at me.

Franz Alonzo Smits B-CA 8Sep30:FA:7Div 53–54:97 ADA Gp Oki 54–57: 4Msl Cmd Kor 57–59:4Div 59–62 **(CM):**1 Cav Div RVN 62–63**(PH-CI):** USMA Supe 63-

Born in California, commissioned in Field Artillery, served a year with the 7th Infantry in Korea, three years in Air Defense Artillery in Okinawa, two more years in Korea with the 4th Missile Command. He had spent an inordinate amount of time in hard Asian assignments. Either he was hiding from the world, or he had an awesome enemy in assignments branch. After his first tour, he had been transferred to ADA. He had spent three years with the 4th Infantry in Colorado, for which he received a modest award, an Army Commendation Medal, or Arcom. Then the 1st Cavalry in Vietnam, where he won the Purple Heart and the Combat Infantryman's Badge. Then West Point. Those two and a half lines in the *Register* described a military career sparkling in its modesty.

The hallway buzzed with a mélange of unpleasant noises. I passed number 39, Major Schwarzhedd's quarters. I wanted to knock and hear his voice. I imagined the smell of popcorn. It was just after supper. All the noise was coming from the quarters next door.

I knocked on number 40.

"Yeah," said Colonel Smits.

I opened the door, and the Animals' "We Gotta Get Out of This Place" erupted in my eardrums. I entered and closed the door fast, trying to control the sound contamination.

"Screw me to tears. Boy Wonder, sniffin' around Greenwich Village. Ain't this off limits for Boy Scouts?" He was at the table, watching *The Huntley-Brinkley Report* and playing solitaire. I stared; televisions were not part of our world.

"The Black Power Movement," said Chet Huntley, "is opposed to integration, and seeks a separate Black Nation. . . ."

"Buncha crap," he said, rising and turning down the volume and allowing the voice of Moose Hoggatt, Radio KDET's most renowned DJ, to begin competing with the Animals.

"Want a drink?"

"No thank you, sir."

"Get any Chinese food lately?" He laughed and savagely punched open a Burgie with a punch key that he kept in his pocket. He switched off the turntable, making the Animals' tune die while the rotation slowed, as if the band were being strangled. He turned off the radio. Now it felt as if there were only two of us in the room.

"Yes, sir," Pearl brought Chinese food to me.

"Okay, Boy Scout. Shit, talk, or go blind."

"Sir, I want to learn about the cadet cheating ring of 1951."

He looked at me, surprised in the act of sitting down, making him crash into his chair. "The *hell* you say."

"Sir, you're the only member of the Class of '52 I've met."

"I'll be the last. We don't talk about that shit."

"Sir, it's in the best interests of the Military Academy."

He barked a hawking laugh. "Listen, child of West Point. Don't use that *crap* on me! Don't be *completely* stupid."

"Sir, it's your alma mater."

He snorted and banged his can on the table, beer frothing out of the keypunch holes. "Screw you! This goddamned place ratcheted one of Army's best teams. Coulda been as good as the Davis and Blanchard days. Had the horses. How the hell they expect players doin' long practices in Notre Dame week to pass Juice and physics? Hell, we all needed help with that goddamn course."

I blinked. That scandal, sixteen years ago, was also in Juice?

He stopped, catching his breath. He looked at me, gathering himself. "Why the hell do *you* want to know?"

"Cheating's going on. It's organized. I want to know how it works. I want to know how the first one worked."

"So you can nail the cheaters?" he asked flatly.

"Yes, sir."

"Give you a big charge to do that?"

"No, sir."

"Doin' it for 'Duty, Honor, Country'?"

"Something like that."

"What the hell can you give me in return?"

I looked around. "New poker chips. Burgermeister. Lysol." The TV presented a cartoon fish advertising tuna.

"Mouseshit," he said. "Bid higher."

I stood, heart pounding. "Sir, talk is, something bad happened to you in Southeast Asia—something bigger than missing out on the Medal of Honor. I think you got a higher purpose than drinking and swearing and belching in front of cadets and making us go deaf.

"You think cheating's cool, I can't bid what you want. If you don't want cheating here, you'll tell me, 'cause the Academy needs your help."

He looked at me, those cold snake eyes still struggling with the vision of a cadet in dress gray with an Asiatic face.

"You got the brass balls of a bronze ape," he said slowly. "Comin' in here, givin' *me* the bullshit. I ate that burger, you slope-headed monkey. . . . Ahh—didn't like that, did you? You're like Charlie . . . sniffin' on my wire, creepin' in my AO." He smiled crookedly, his head jiggling.

"You think I'm an ignoramus, don't you? Hey, bozo, you're the missin' brick from the full load. You got a chip on your shoulder the size a Bear Mountain—takin' offense for every shitty little minority group in America." He laughed. "I saw you in the open, soldier. Last time, you didn't want Scrounger Duke's butt for his slam on ninnies and Jews—you wanted to *waste him*—and you were thinkin' about takin' *me* down, too." He smiled broadly.

"*Coc dau*, ole' Doctor Death, come to West Point, patrollin' the dark side with an M-79 and a knife, clipped ears danglin' from your LBE." He leaned back and looked up at his grungy ceiling, transported by sweet memory. "Swear to God, ain't no one better at wastin' people than a slant-eye grunt. Run all night in the bush, slit your throat, and drink your blood. Number One!" He looked at me with narrowed eyes, making me look like his image of me. He sat up, his old chair creaking.

"I know who you are, asshole. Your daddy or someone obviously tore the holy shit outa you when you were a squirt. Treated you like dogshit and gave you small-man complex. Now you fuckin' pump weights, kiss ass with Plebes, shoot everyone a shit-eating grin when you're lonely and left out, and try ta jump a room full of white guys for a thought not worth two cents." He cocked an eyebrow. "You think I'm stupid cuz I don't talk pretty." He snorted. "Numbnuts, I'm smarter'n anyone you'll meet this lifetime. I'm a lot smarter'n you. Listen to Papa: you pull the pin on all your touchy feelings while you're in the Nam, you'll kill so many gooks they'll end up givin' *you* the goddamned Medal a Honor."

I said nothing, trying to control my breathing. Did I have a chip on my shoulder? Was I angry? Did I have feelings? Touchy ones?

"Heard you quit the bottle." He laughed. "Well, didja?"

"Yes, sir."

"Didn't like my drink. Don't like Smitty's booze? Well, screw you twice for a goddammed fucking religious ingrate." He opened one liquor cabinet, then another, slamming doors. He banged a bottle of Glenfiddich on the table, almost breaking the container.

"Ever have this?"

I shook my head.

"Single-malt scotch, best in the world. Not as good as Bushmills Irish, but it'll do when resupply crashes on the pad."

He poured long into two dirty tumblers. "Sit. Every shot you down, I'll give you some deep and dark poop on the Scandal a '51."

He smiled and I sat. I had quit for good after drinking wine in Quebec. The booze spoke to me. I lifted the glass and downed it. It burned and was smooth; it kissed and it bit. The warmth of it zipped down my throat, reawakening old needs. I felt like giggling, and it eased aches in my shoulders I had not recognized until the alcohol hit my blood. Cures polio, I thought. I thought of Pearl, admiring my decision to end my attempt to become a silly drunk.

"Cheatin' was a way of life for some a the squad." He sucked his tumbler, licking his lips. "Goddamned Honor freaks! Took out thirty-seven players from the Brave Old Army Team." He poured again, splashing it into the glasses.

"Imagine that shit. Team like Notre Dame, with Seymour and Hanratty, like Syracuse when Jim Brown'd score forty-three points a game. Thirty-seven boys of oak and hearts of gold, doin' what the Academy taught 'em to do—to take care a each other when shit creek rises high. Drink."

I drank. It went straight to my head. I pulled out my notepad and pen and wrote, "37/Army Team, boys of oak, hearts, gold, teamwork, care for ea. other." I felt no pain.

"Corps had only two regiments."

They had expanded to four regiments last year, in 1966. "Drink."

"Sir, there were only two regiments last year. That's not new poop. Tell me about the cheating."

"I *am* telling you, you dirty sonofabitch!" he snapped. He drank, shaking his big head. "I do not like talking about this shit. Pour slow," he said. "Too good to spill."

I poured slowly and held my glass.

"Cross-Corps, cross-regimental," he said. "Drink."

I drank. "Say again, sir?"

"Listen, barfbrains. Hasn't changed. First Regiment has engineering Monday, Wednesday, Friday, humanities and that other shit on Tuesday, Thursday, Saturday, right?"

I nodded.

"Second Regiment had the reverse. Then, in the next semester, they switch schedules. Got it?"

I wrote: "?"

"You *are* a dipshit. Say you're in First and I'm in Second. You take your Juice whufer on Wednesday—I'll take the same, exact goddamm writ on Thursday. Get it? Drink."

I drank. My head buzzed. It seemed complicated.

Smits got up and turned on his Japanese lamps. I looked into the lights. I giggled.

"What's so fuckin' funny?"

"The lights," I said. The insanity god lived in the light.

"You're such a numbnuts. Look, brain surgeon. You take your writ. You bag a copy or write down the problems before you forget. We meet in the library, draggin' butt from drillin' with B Squad and runnin' our plays for Saturday. You give me the writ or the questions you remembered on crib sheets. Then *I* can rest my weary ass in the rack, cuz *I* know what's on tomorrow's whufer.

"*Next* semester, I return the favor, and *you* get to play Sleepin' Beauty during finals. We keep this up until graduation. No one flunks out. Everyone gets the ring and gets to throw the white hat in front a mom and dad. No one's papa puts a hole through his head cuz his boy flunked out. Drink."

I wanted to spill it so it wouldn't go into my head. He had just told me the answer. There was a question mark written on my notepad. I wondered what it was for.

"Drink, you yellow bastard. You made a deal."

I drank carefully. Cross-regiments. First helps Second. Staggered classes. Staggered Cadet Ting. I laughed. Cadets cheating by organization, by plan, by the numbers. A system. Hearts of gold. Helping classmates. Cold hearts, without Honor.

He sighed, long and deep. I wrinkled my nose. "Started with the tutors. Tutors tryin' to save the Team from gettin' found. Ya don't get it. We had the best fuckin' team in the *entire country*. Playin' Notre Dame was bigger'n religion." He blinked. "It *was* religion." He sucked at the scotch, looking sad. "The tutors were tryin' to save God and the Army Team."

I got it. I studied him blearily. "You cheat too, sir?" I asked.

"Drink," he said.

I drank. "Did you?"

"No," he said.

He walked to his window and looked out between the venetian blinds. I didn't know what he saw. I felt four pounds on my wrist, so I knew I was wearing my Rolex. I read it. It meant nothing.

"Ting, this is between you and me. I was B Squad. Not good enough for A Team. Then most of the Team got found, wiping out offense and defense. I made A Squad. Tried to restart the cheating ring. Hell, I was a goat. The whole country was talkin' about it. Cover of *Time*. I had big balls, asking questions after the scandal.

"Coach Blaik pulled me aside." His voice strained. "He said, 'Don't do it, son.' "

I stared at Smits until I figured out that he was waiting at the window until he recovered control. He slowly straightened, smoothing his wildly floral aloha shirt, all the colors running.

"No more Coach Blaiks," he said, his grating voice almost soft. "You go to the Nam and things go south, tits up. Do your homework, spec the problem, recon the map. Supporting units dick it up cuz officers are on a ticket-punch rotation and everyone's new and they leave you high and dry and now it's just you. You kill the gook little people and they keep comin' and now they're bleedin' you bad and you can't kill enough of those little slope bastards, and now no more medevacs and the guns are splashin' all over the grid and half the LTs are too stupid and shot-up to know when to fart." He showed his teeth in a rictus of memory. "No Coach Blaik to tuck you in at night and tell you he loves you."

He poured, then made it a double. "Drink," he said.

"Had enough, sir—too much," I said.

"Drink and I'll tell you the secret to West Point," he said.

I took a breath and drank it. It was wet and smooth, with a small nibble. My head buzzed and I wanted to laugh and say something about little people, about how I wasn't little, and could now bench almost three hundred pounds. I was at two-nine-five.

"Hated greensuits," he said, sour, too close to my face. I saw the pores in his twice-broken nose, the livid scar in his chin where the hair didn't grow, his smell filling my nostrils, infesting my uniform. "Always screwin' with you, dishin' quill, takin' privileges, makin' you walk the Area. Assholes! Now *I'm* a suit. And here to tell you, when you hit the real world, there ain't no Honor Code to help.

"You crocked?"

"Little," I said.

"Yeah, like you're a little stupid. Someone like you came round sniffin' on the Team back in '51, you'd get your curious Chinese rump ripped from top to bottom.

"This tin-soldier shop runs the perfect world. Everything hunky-dory. *Everything's* squared away, marchin' squares, eatin' squares, bandbox reviews with square corners, bells go off on time, the band plays and when the Corps marches it looks like heaven. Never work harder in your life on so many goddammed things. Everyone's a lord, an honest gentleman. Leave your wallet with your pay on the desk, it's there in the morning. Damn BPs are gents.

"Go out in the Regular Army. You're the best. No one stronger, smarter, harder working, more honest, more freakin' earnest, ready to die. But the people *do* you, Ting, 'cause they didn't have the Corps and the Code, and they hate it that you went to West Point for free, the four years a military life comin' off you like BO. Get a combat command and it ain't no band a brothers. You can't keep all your people alive. The shit falls and they die faster'n you can police up dog tags and the op orders carry bullshit from shit-firin' careerists that don't know that maps don't tell the story. That's when I figured that West Point was a big, neat trick.

"Perfection. Ain't *no* such fuckin' thing in the world.

"That's why, Oriental Boy Wonder, we got the Poker Society. Reality. People bein' real in their heads, swearin', takin' no names, no prisoners, none a that fake gentlemen shit! It's no scrimmage after graduation—boh-coo uh-uh! It's your *nuts* they're after. Careerists, women, whores, newspaper men, fellow officers, the slant-eyed gooks and patriots, misinformed Presidents and the goddammed Congress. They love West Point, and like to screw West Pointers. That's what the staffoid dick-with-ears said who nuked my Medal a Honor. Called me a *ringknocker*.

"All this." he said, waving at his bottles, at West Point, "for nothin'. Won't *even* keep your first sergeant alive, or keep the legs on your RTO, or keep a young kid screamin' for his momma. I told Troth that. He understands, poor bastard. But you, you're dumber'n a GI in a whorehouse on payday. Only people off the boat believe in perfection. Americans oughta know better. You wanna be an American, don't believe it. It ain't real.

"Drink, then back outa here. You're like all those slopes. You wear the shit outa me."

"Sir, how would you start on this problem if you were me?"

"I already told you, troop," he snarled. "Go out and kill something, snip its ears an' pin 'em on your LBE." He took a long, angry swig, sighing as it burned into his guts. He blinked at me as if I had just appeared.

"You still here? Unass my AO, yellow soldier." He stood, stumbled over empty beer cans, which banged hollowly across his floor. He switched on his record player, strange sounds emerging as the turntable began rotating and gained speed, bringing the Animals back into quarters 40.

31

Big Dick

West Point Museum, January 15, 1967

"A Frigault 64 Electrical," said Mike, "is a standard Fort Fumble, Pentagon model. It has a five-number set combination and requires two intermediate steps to open the tumblers: a clockwise, dial-down rotation for the second and fourth pins and a ten-second delay on a preset number to allow one tumbler to gravity-fall. It's called a Frigault combination." As usual, Mike was reciting data he'd seen once.

"Three-sixteenths-inch steel plate welded, that'd survive collapse of the building. The slide bolts are uncuttable half-inch steel rods. The silent tumblers defeat a combo search by sound sensing. It's where I should keep my boodle when Kai's around."

"Ha ha," I said.

"I'm serious," he said, rolling his eyes. "Combination's changed annually. But get this: the faculty has two lieutenants." LTs couldn't be faculty. "Ever hear of 'McNamara Monuments'?"

Just what we needed. More statues. We shook our heads.

"Draft calls are up. McNamara's called up advanced-degree people who used up their deferments, getting them into the Pentagon. Some are PhD's. We have six at the Academy—two in Juice, one in social sciences, and three in language. 'McNamara Monuments.' The two Juice Monuments teach Second and Fourth Regiments. Their names are Baker and Nasser."

"They have access to the Frigault?" asked Sonny.

"Roger," said Mike. "All profs have to secure writs in the exam safe before and after grading."

"If I wanted to get into that safe," said Sonny, "I'd trick a

Monument. Use a ruse. Guy wouldn't know the culture or the system. Like, who's gonna suspect cheating at West Point?"

"I'll follow up on the Monuments," said Mike.

"I talked to Colonel Smits," I said.

"Why him?" asked Mike. "You didn't drink with him, did you?"

"He's Class of '52, played football. He knew a lot about the cheating in '51. If I drank, he gave me the poop."

"What an asshole," said Mike.

"I've known meaner drunks. Here's what I remember. The '51 cheating operation wasn't complicated—no thefts of writs from safes or burglaries. It was cross-regimental—copying or spec'ing whufers by First Regiment guys on crib notes, who passed them to the Second Regiment guys, who took the writs one day later. The next semester, when the schedules reversed, they switched roles. It started with the tutors to the football team in Juice. Football became as important as Honor."

Mike and Sonny looked at each other. "If they got enough guys," said Mike, "they could pool their poop by committee. They wouldn't need a hive to figure the answers."

"Still need Big Dick, the planner," said Sonny. "Staggered classes." He shook his head. "Never think a the other regiments till brigade finals. There's a whole world in East Barracks and the Lost Fifties. And the football team—"

"Would cross the regimental barrier," said Mike. "The Team's divided up through all the companies. It's not the Team, is it?"

"These are my sectionmates who had canned writ answers," I said. "None on the Team." I couldn't say their names. I wrote:

> Jeff T. Faubus
> Galen Nocksin
> Farren McWhiff

"Damn!" said Sonny. He had tutored all of them. "Sorry." He exhaled loudly, running fingers through his hair.

"Sonny," said Mike, "you take Jeff T., since he's in your company. Galen's company is next door to mine, so I'll take him. Farren's next to yours," he said to me. "We have to follow them."

"Why'd they do this?" asked Sonny. "It's not logical."

"They want to graduate," I said.

"Let's hope that trailin' 'em leads to Big Dick," said Sonny. He looked at me. "Why'd Kai get the writ copy?"

Mike jittered his right knee. Sonny peered at the ceiling. I adjusted my underwear.

"That'll help you think," said Sonny.

"Free promotion of the ring," said Mike, his knee still. "Pass out free copies of the stolen writ to goats who need help. Do it covertly, in the night—no tracing back to sources. Give hints that the source was the tutor. They take the writ, they're in."

"So why didn't other goats get the writ?" I asked.

"We don't know that they didn't," said Mike.

"Guess we can't worry about that," I said. "We gotta find guys in First and Third who study with guys from Second and Fourth."

"What do you mean 'we,' white man?" asked Sonny. "You're the stud communicator, the Hudson High–Woo Poo schmoozer who raps all over campus. That's why Maher picked you."

"You got the bad detail, Kai," said Mike. "You're point man." He slapped me on the leg. "You know we're in this together. You just get to do it alone."

Nine small orange figurines marched down the roofline of the Hanlin Academy at the gates of the Forbidden City. At the rear, driving the column, is a fierce and rotund dragon. In the lead is Prince Min, the irresponsibly corrupt Han official whose punishment for greed was permanent point man in the walk of life. These nine little figurines served as lightning rods, waiting for storms, to take the blow from heaven for the sake of the noble red roof. Min rode a ridiculous chicken and led the procession for hell, waiting for an ugly fate. I knew how he felt. I was on the chessboard, trying to fork an invisible enemy in the perfection of the Academy, while storm clouds gathered above my head.

"Sonny, what about the keys?" asked Mike.

"Woo Poo's keys are cut by maintenance and held by the PM, the provost marshal. He's got key control and keys for Bartlett and faculty offices are Top A Restricted, no copies authorized. That's been SOP since 1951.

"Faculty offices have individualized keys, not keyed to department. So Maher, the department head, and the PM are the only ones with a key to his office.

"I know Cutler, the department head," said Sonny. "He's a

detail guy. Doesn't lose his keys. Doesn't lend or borrow keys."

"Ben Franklin would like him," I said.

"Everyone got very careful with keys after the scandal," said Mike. "It wrecked a lot more than football."

"What happened in the '51 Navy game?" asked Sonny.

"We crashed and burned, forty-two to seven," I said.

Mike whistled. "Talk about demoralized."

"How many were found in '51?" asked Sonny. I told him.

"Ninety guys." Again, he ran his hand through his hair. "Kai, you mentioned the BPs. Maybe they opened Bartlett for the ring. We got fifty BPs on Post, each with keys to barracks or buildings. The obvious guy is the one who cleans Bartlett. I'll check him out, but I want you guys to take fifteen BPs each; I'll take twenty. We need standard questions, so we don't screw ourselves by pulling random data out of the sample." He scribbled, we corrected, and agreed on a final product.

On the way back to barracks, we stopped in the sally port to check Sonny and my make-up grades on our special Juice WFR. My heart pounded as I tried not to think of the consequences of not getting my needed 43 tenths to pass the course.

A gross Plebe, barely holding a smart Academy brace, was looking at the print-out and writing in a notepad. He heard our shoes scrunching and quickly left the tunnel. I saw the results:

Rappa, Santino A	60.0
Ting, Kai NMN	44.0

Sonny and Mike hit me on my back. Then they dumped me in the snow and hit me with snowballs while we all laughed. I was flattered by their affection for me. Five times I had entered the sally port and learned that I was still a member of the Corps. There was only one tough semester left at West Point: the one that had just begun.

"I *hate* sweating these whufers with you!" shouted Sonny.

"Try it from my shide," I said, snow in my mouth.

I met one by one with each of my lowerclass squad members on the frigid, icy roof of the Cadet Hilton. We had total privacy.

"I am part of an Honor investigation. I need your help. I want the names of Cows who cross the even-odd regiment line to study, i.e., Cows from First or Third who study with Second or Fourth. I want the names of Cows who seem cool on Honor. Talk it over with everyone you trust. But you are not to reveal the purpose of your inquiries with anyone. If you sense physical danger, disengage immediately and retrograde back to me. What are your questions?"

"Good mornin', Kai," said Elmer Scoggin as he hauled trash.

"Top of the morning," I said. "Elmer, can I talk to you?"

"Be with you in a sec. Need some window cleaner?"

"No," I said. "Nothing like that." I turned on the heating coil to offer Elmer some java.

It was a bright and freezing day, with grand piles of thick white snow collecting in the Area, perfect for a snow war between the Cows and the Yearlings that would evolve into an epic wrestling match. Then Deke and Bob could start throwing Yearlings from the pile like garments from a fire sale. The generators were chugging, and great clouds of steam rose from the tunnels and grates of West Point into the dark and overcast sky over the Hudson. There were ghosts in the steam tunnels, lost souls of former cadets, the Immortals who could never leave West Point, imprisoned below the iron grates, trying to complete the years they had never finished at the Academy. The steam defied the cold that had frozen Washington's army at Valley Forge.

"Just sugar," Elmer said. I pulled out a sugar packet from my pocket and poured it in, stirring with a straw which I dried and replaced in the raincoat pocket. Elmer sat in my chair, far more composed and relaxed than I when Major Maher had asked for my help.

Elmer was old, in his late forties. Years ago, something very hot had hit him on the side of his face, cooking the skin around his right temple. He was tall, with a small gut, big ears, big hands, and overlarge, gunboat feet offset by an aristocratic head of silver hair. He wore the BP uniform of greenish gray work clothes and clean, soft old boots. He wore a matching baseball cap, which now rested on his knee. He looked at me kindly, as he had on my first day at West Point. Elmer liked to stand on the steps of the gym on R-Day and watch the entry of the lambs.

"Elmer, if you wanted the key to Bartlett and a key to a prof's office inside Bartlett, could you get them?"

He nodded. "Mm-hmm."

"How?" I asked.

He shrugged his shoulders. "See Sam Marse, Bartlett BP, ask for his keys." His voice had gruff scratches in it.

"Would he ask why?"

"No, sir. Bartlett's got old linoleum that take wax and buff-spinners. Now, Adam Haskitt, he does northeast Central and Grant. Grant has wood floors. Haskitt swaps towels for Marse's brushes.

"In the ole days, used ta trade, but it took two of us ta come on after hours for the swaps. Now we got us an Honor System. Haskitt, or Gene Reddy, who has them old floors in the Lost Fifties, they get Marse's keys and stack solvent or paper towels in Bartlett an' take floor wax and buff brushes. Sometimes they leave a six-pack for consideration." He quietly studied me.

"If I asked for the Bartlett keys, would you give them to me?"

He frowned and put the coffee down, the large, work-stained fingers of his right hand fretting against each other, drumming a tattoo on his leg. He rubbed his scar and leaned in. "Why?"

"What if I left my slide rule in the lab and my notebooks in my P's office, and I needed them?"

Elmer Scoggins squinted, his tongue running around inside his mouth. "I'd give you the keys. You askin' for the keys, Kai?"

"Negative," I said. "Would other BPs give keys to cadets?"

"Don't know," he said. "Not bad," he said. "Used to drink java from a helmet like this working for Gen'ral Patton.

"Years back, after we come up from Bliss ta be the cleaners for West Point, some cadets tried gettin' Bartlett keys by askin' the youngest punk in the cleanin' detail." He shook his head. "He wanted ta give them cadets the keys. It stank. I said no."

"When did this happen?"

He thought for a moment. "Nineteen fifty."

He canted his head to one side and studied me. He coughed drily. "I figure we got a problem. We got a problem?"

"Yes, sir, we do. I'm going to ask a real big favor. Could you ask the other senior BPs if they've lent keys to cadets? Particularly, keys to Bartlett. One of my classmates is going to be talking to Mr. Marse, but I wanted to talk to you, too. I want the names of the cadets who got the keys, Elmer. More than I want to know the names of the BPs."

"That's askin' a lot," he said. "It's a queer question."

"I'm not asking for me. It's for West Point."

He narrowed his eyes. "It's cheatin' again, ain't it?"

I nodded. "Bad cheating, with stealing and organization. They've gotten into Bartlett, a faculty office, and a prof's safe." My brows ached; I had been frowning for a long time. "Whatever you do, please do not talk about this," I said.

He clucked his tongue, scolding me. "Boy, I bin here longer than you bin in pants! I bin takin' care a West Point 'fore you was outa diapers an' pins. You're a squirt, bouncin' to get grown. You say we got some burglars at the Point, stealin' stuff from the professors an' doin' cheatin'—hey, Elmer Scoggin knows what to do!

"Still in the Army, mister. Mustered me in '46—but I'll always be a tanker. So let me ask *you*—you in the chain a command, or you makin' like a comic-book hero with a red cape?"

"I'm in the chain. What rank were you?" I asked.

"I was a firs' loo-tenant. Battlefield commission, Falaise Gap, summer, 1944. And this make me feel like I'm back in ranks."

"Well, sir, for the first time, I feel like we're going to get out of the woods. I surely appreciate it."

"Not at all, Corporal," he said.

"Lieutenant, you remember a football player in the Class of '52 named Franz Smits?"

He shook his head. "Nah. I'm an old man with an old man's memory," he said. "You know how it is. Cadets jus' see an ole black janitor. You're mighty different, but, I'm sorry ta say— when you come back here as an old grad, on your twenty-fifth class reunion, in—," and he counted on his fingers, mumbling—"1993, and I'm still alive—and if you make it through the wars an' all, I won't 'member yo' name."

"I'll remember you, Elmer Scoggin," I said.

He smiled. "If I save West Point, you might at that. *Nice* havin' your coffee. Forgive me if I don't finish it."

I put my hand out and we shook. Paragraph 1.b., Friendly Forces, had just been augmented.

The gym, hoops, and hockey teams were away, and the Saturday-night flick was a West German western. Please, Farren, I hoped: go to the library and consult with Big Dick. Show yourselves.

I followed Farren back to barracks after supper. I watched the Area from my room while Para-Rat chewed gently on my fingers. There was Farren, walking alone in the snow, and I threw on scarf, short overcoat, and gloves and caught up with him in Central Area. He was headed for the gym without gear, so it was the flick. I sat behind him, hidden in a pack of First Regiment Plebes, nervous with my presence.

We were mesmerized by the foulness of the film. Two hundred head-dressed, face-painted Cherokee chiefs shot plastic arrows at a hundred Aryan, gum-chewing, German-drawling, dual-pistoled, white-hatted pilgrims in Roy Rogers shirts. The eventual massacre of the Cherokees to a Wagnerian soundtrack stopped even my appetite.

West Point was peacefully still and preindustrially dark when Farren left the gym and headed for the river. I had to stay well back as the cadet crowds thinned. Few cadets were genuine loners; tonight, Farren and I qualified, and it made us stand out. He looked at his watch; it was 2250 hours.

He turned west off Upton onto Tower Road, going below the rim of the Plain toward the riverbank. Building 665 seemed dark and the Field House was empty. I looked across the black river at the shadow of Constitution Island, where the lights at Warner House twinkled distantly. George Washington had stood here with Thaddeus Kosciuszko, planning Forts Arnold and Putnam. After Benedict's treachery, Arnold would be re-named Clinton. The river whispered like an ancient slumbering giant, breathing in ripples, its old shoulders slowly brushing granite banks.

Nothing was going on down here, except for a rendezvous. Farren entered 665, the old Quartermaster building, a dark, massive, brooding shadow in the night. I waited one minute and silently entered the foyer through twin, rasping, vacuum airlock doors. I smelled sawdust. With poor night vision, I was happy for the faint flickering of a single fluorescent bulb in the tall ceiling. The dim lobby was filled with stacks of building materials. The tile floor was cold as ice and littered with nails and building debris, but I removed my shoes for silence. I avoided the bulk of construction to the left, and moved to the right around sawhorses, workbenches, radial saws, and piled lumber.

I turned into a hallway, entering darkness. I walked blind and stepped onto a stiff plastic floor-covering that crinkled. I froze. Sergeant Smith at Buckner always said, "Stay frozen." This was easy; 665 was like the inside of an ice box. I regulated breathing, becoming a part of the cold floor in a building that was as still as a mausoleum. Where was McWhiff?

In a few minutes, I was shivering and in possession of as much night vision as I could muster; shadows became things. I used my training and looked off-center, seeing unmounted signs that said "Indoor Ranges" and "Rifle & Pistol"—I realized that 665 was going to be the new consolidated range. I saw stacks of crates. One was open, and I put my hand inside: it was a gun box for .45 automatics. Two were missing from the suspension rack.

In the darkness I saw OD ammo boxes but no clips. I knew I would need a weapon. I stripped my gloves, drew a .45 from the open gun box and locked its slide open. I opened an ammo box, its hinges sharply complaining. I removed a single round from a box of fifty, slid it into the breech, and softly released the slide, automatically safetying it. The action was old, but I had one shot. I put a handful of .45 rounds into my overcoat pocket.

I heard sounds in the foyer.

I moved slowly toward the noise, the plastic covering softly crackling under my socks, the gun behind my right leg.

A steady parade of dark, parka-and-overcoated figures with red-lens flashlights quickly passed from the construction area through the rasping airlock doors, the flashlights switching off just before exiting. My heart tripped; there had to be twenty of them. Thirty feet from me, the last two figures stopped in the semilit foyer, sitting on lumber. I heard McWhiff say, "Listen, we don't need guns."

"Yeah, we do. We got mousechasers after us. Guns'll scare 'em off. And it tells everyone we're serious." I recognized the voice. "Galen gives me the sweats. Asshole thinks he's being followed. He's getting hinky."

"What ya gonna do, shoot Galen?" asked McWhiff.

"Nah. Just make 'im pucker." The voice laughed. "This is the Army, Farren. Don't turn soft on me."

"I won't."

They stood and moved for the doors.

"Stop," I said.

A brilliant flashlight exploded in my field of vision. I closed my eyes and jinked, too late, blinded. I unsafetied the gun.

"*Shit*, it's Ting," said Duke Troth. "You *asshole*! What the fuck are you doing here?"

"Chasing rats," I said, my left hand shielding my eyes while pretending that I could see, pointing my face at his voice. "Farren, bad times are coming. Get out, now."

"Goddammit, he followed you! Shit, you sneaky yellow bastard." The flashlight moved off my face. "He's got a gun." The flashlight came back to my head. Troth's .45 glinted in the light, aiming for the beam splash in the middle of my face.

"Yo, Kai," said Farren. "I don't know why you're following Galen an' me, but jes' drop it. Butt out, man."

"Come with me, Farren," I said earnestly.

"Hey," he said, "this involves a helluva lot more'n you know. It's for the good. It's for our classmates. You should be helpin' us. Otherwise, you're gonna screw things up royal. You're gonna hurt people you don't wanta hurt. Just forget whatever the hell it is you think you know. Kai, jes' walk away."

"Can't," I said.

"Why not?" asked Troth. He was on the left, his flashlight quivering. My heart slugged like an old locomotive laboring up a high hill. If he shoots, I thought, I'm shooting back. Aim left, for the chest; don't hit Farren, roll and reload in the hallway. My left hand covered my eyes and I tightened my gun grip, the trigger finger ready, trying to visualize the shot through the psychedelic splotches of illumination trauma left by the flashlight. You'll be blind from his shot. No aiming—raise the gun, point, and shoot.

I licked my dry lips. My mouth was dust. "Walked away before. I let people get hammered. Knew bad times were coming and I didn't tell. Two people died. And, I let a person in my family get hurt." A person to whom I bore *lun*. I blew out a lot of tired air. "Been keeping secrets for free. Took a pledge on the river to do the right thing. So did you. C'mon, Farren. Come back to the Corps. Don't do this to yourself." I watched Troth, hoping he was as good a shot as he was honest.

I blinked as I saw Lucky Washington, his eye a slab of red meat, asking for my father's gun. He was fourteen years old and was going to be stabbed to death that night.

Farren pleaded, "Hey, man, think about what you're doing."

"I am," I said. "Thought about it all my life."

Lucky wouldn't leave 665. I knew why he was with me, and I cursed him because now I couldn't shoot Troth. Troth was rat scum, but I couldn't shoot him. I safetied the automatic. "I'm going to drop the .45, Duke. Watch your trigger finger."

"Shit, don't drop it, Kai!" cried Farren. "It's the only thing savin' ya." He looked at Duke. Duke steadied his aim.

The sound of the gun landing on the old tile floor was like a baseball going through a plate glass window.

We faced each other for a few moments. They whispered intently. Then the flashlight went out and I heard the airlock doors open and close, and I was alone in the building, the gun at my feet.

Captain Martin was a broad-shouldered lawyer from Chicago with a big, deep voice and a sharply analytic mind. Like many of the Judge Advocates, or JAGCs, he was not a West Pointer. He had taught me the basics of issue analysis. He advised the Honor Committee.

After my final tour in his section, I thanked him for the clarity of his instruction, and told him I had appreciated his presence because he wasn't white.

He smiled. "I've been black a long time now," he said.

"I grew up in a black neighborhood. It's been kind of lonely here," I said. "This place is so—white-bread."

"Aw, c'mon, man. There you go, jumping to a conclusion, just because I'm the single black officer on this faculty. Some, like your friend Alonzo Smits, think my being here makes this Harlem."

"My friend?" I asked.

"Hey, I hear you play poker with him in his Q."

"Captain Martin speaking, sir."

"Sir, this is Cadet Kai Ting. Sorry for calling you in quarters. I have a confidential question." I was whispering into the outside pay phone at the Admin Building, where I had a clear view of Thayer Road. My feet were frozen and I was actively shivering.

"Consider the attorney-client relationship formed," he said. I could hear a pen scratching on a pad.

I took an icy breath. "Sir, I'm part of an Honor investigation into a cheating ring. I'm tasked with finding the ringleader. I got a suspect. I want to tape him in his room, talking to other suspects, without their knowledge or consent."

"Okay," he said, as if I had said, "the weather outside is frightful." "State your probable cause and your emergency."

I told him about the canned writ answers, the break-in of Maher's safe, and the entire episode in Building 665.

"Good enough. What's the issue, Kai?"

"Sir, whether I can wiretap and not violate the Code."

"And not violate laws and regulations. Most police failures are products of failed creativity. Think: how else can you get the information you want?"

"Don't know of another way, sir. I guess we could use torture. It's an Academy procedure, but not for getting evidence."

He chuckled. "You oughta see it from the faculty side. Okay. The privacy doctrine in the military is stunted. Wiretaps aren't cool because they're invasive and too broad. A federal wiretap law is coming. I know its direction. If wiretap's your only avenue, minimize its use." He paused. "Trigger a meeting of the suspects. Say something to one of the cheats that would compel them to meet. When they do, listen only to a discussion of the cheating. The moment the topic changes, switch off. I can't advise indiscriminate monitoring or listening. You'd get one shot at it."

"Perhaps, sir, you could use another metaphor."

I called Major Maher and informed him of the evening's events. He suggested I call CID, but we decided that calling them would kill our investigation into Honor. We'd rough it out. No cops.

"Try not to walk anywhere alone," he said.

" 'Don't walk alone?' " said Mike later when we met in Sonny's room. "That's pretty radical. No one's going to shoot anyone."

"We didn't think anyone would cheat," said Sonny. "Kai saw twenty guys in there. Twenty! And there's no other way to explain why they were there. They weren't practicing the obstacle course."

"But only two guns were missing, right?" asked Mike.

"And Troth has one of them," I said. "Let's wire that cheap bigot's room."

"Troth's still one of God's children," said Sonny.

I laughed. "Oh, yeah, sure he is, Sonny. Guy's an asshole."

"Not sure bad-mouthing him's a lot better," said Sonny. "Supposed to love our enemies."

"Sonny," I said. "That makes no sense. What gives? *You* want to be a doctor," I said to Mike. "And now *you're* a pacifist."

"I'm not a pacifist," said Sonny softly. "I believe in protecting the country. I believe in chasin' down cheaters." He studied me. "I'll kill the enemy. But I'm not gonna giggle while I'm doin' it. I don't think you're supposed to hate Troth while we're fighting him."

"Love your enemy and blow him away," I said. Mike grinned.

Sonny took a deep breath. "Look. I know you were in a buncha ca-ca back there. But don't hate Troth. It matters what's in your heart."

"Well, I never found it in my heart to be in a study group with him, like you."

"I was never in a study group with him," said Sonny.

"He said you were."

"That's wrong."

"Rap. Let's wire him before he implicates George Washington."

"Nah. George'd never do it. I'm worried about Dolley Madison."

"Does she read Willa Cather and Thomas Mann?" asked Mike. He was still searching for the perfect, literate girl.

"She bakes a lot," said Sonny.

Events were closing in on us. Troth knew I knew. "How soon can you build the wire?"

"Tonight, by call to quarters."

"Oh, c'mon, Sonny, sooner."

He climbed on a chair with his rifle and hit a ceiling panel with the butt. I didn't know they could be removed. He threw me his rifle. From the hole in the ceiling he pulled down two cardboard boxes. I racked the rifle. He pulled the chair to his desk, and drew rapidly on a piece of paper.

"What's this?" he asked, holding it up.

"That's a piece of paper, with gafarga on it, shaped like elephant condoms. . . . No—as you were—they're circuit diagrams."

"This is our recording machine," he said.

"Uh-uh. I'm no good at electronics, but this little piece of paper will not record anything. Trust me."

He reached into the first cardboard box. "What's this?" he asked, holding up a black metal box with two open sides.

"Black box," I said. Mike laughed.

"And they say ya don't know nothin' about advanced steady-state electronics."

"What's this?" He extracted a metal pole from the same box.

"A whip. That's a damn whip," I said. "Don't like whips."

"Yeah, you're right. Antenna," he said.

"This?" He held up a doowhinghie.

"A doowhinghie, a poor little overworked doowhingie, that you beat with the whip, and then it goes into the black box, whimpering, never to be seen again."

"And this?" he said, holding up a battery.

"Is a battery. C'mon, Sonny. Ask me something hard."

"What are these?" They came from the second box.

"Wires—red, black, white, and green. Which are the national colors of Iraq and Kuwait. Gimme a harder question."

"What's the purpose of Juice?" he asked.

"Good question," said Mike.

"Juice," I said, "was devised by the Antichrist to reduce the numbers of English-lit types who can become West Pointers."

Sonny made the sound of a buzzer. "*URRRHHH!* Wrong. Juice gives us Fender guitars, the Beatles, the Mamas and the Papas. Runs radio stations, lets ya use the phone to call for nighttime pizza drops at the Admin Building, allows ya to talk to Pearl Yee so you can get goofy, gives us ice cream in the Weapons Room on a warm summer night, and lights up Carnegie Hall for your vocal solos."

"You're not being sincere."

"Juice, Kai, exists only to serve mankind."

"Mankind oughta ask for some change back," I said.

"Hey—ya wanna build this black box?" he asked.

"Oh, sure—and kill us all?"

Chad Enders authorized us to miss supper formation for the "business of the Honor Committee." We went to East Barracks and entered Duke Troth's room while Mike observed Troth in the mess hall. Standing on a chair and using masking tape, Sonny installed the mike, transmitter, and power source on the alcove divider beam. He used a long, thin low-resistance copper wire as the antenna, and laid that alongside the long axis of the beam, on its outer, upper edge, aiming it toward our barracks.

"Hope no one hides boodle on the beam," he said. "Hope Mike can get Jefferson Faubus rattled." Mike was going to catch Jeff T. before grace at supper and ask two questions: (1) Jeff T., how come you don't study Juice with me or Sonny anymore? (2) Jeff T., if you had an Honor problem, you'd report it, wouldn't you?

"I hope," said Sonny, "that Jeff T. talks to Big Dick. I hope Massive Richard lives here." He sighed. "Don't look forward to hearing him talk. Never says anything nice."

I wondered what he'd do if he found the wire.

32

SNOW

New South Barracks, January 20, 1967

Sonny and his bunky Alphabet Burkowski monitored the black-box receiver in their room. They had one of the few two-man rooms in the class. If Big Dick began talking to the cabal, Alphabet would get Benjamin. Mike would get me. Mike and I slept in our sweats that Friday night, ready to run through a snowy night.

I was asleep when someone tried to suffocate me. The gloved hand was on my mouth and jaw in an iron grip, and I couldn't pull it off, even after my adrenaline kicked in and I began to struggle with my entire body. I noticed, amidst my death rattle, that I was wearing my glasses. I wondered how I had fallen asleep with them.

Someone was saying "Shh!" It was Mike. He was a wrestler, and it seemed he had ten arms and fifteen elbows, like something out of a Henry Harryhausen special-effects movie. Mike released me and moved out the door, his sweats, black parka, and gloves speckled with liquefying snow. I breathed and enjoyed it. It was one in the morning. Clint, Bob, and Deke were asleep. I grabbed my tennis shoes and parka, unmarked my All Right Card, and closed the door silently.

"OC's on the road here," whispered Mike in the hallway while I tied my shoes. "Looking for me. I left snow tracks." He gave me one of my towels. "Use this when we step into far-side barracks, so we don't track. Going to Sonny's. He's receiving from the mike in East Barracks." He looked up the hall while I looked down the hall. "I put the glasses on you so you wouldn't fight me, knucklehead."

"Sorry. I didn't notice at first. Next time you try to silence me, don't kill me while you're at it. Who's OC tonight?"

"Hope it's not Szeden."

I shivered with the thought. We headed for the stairs and heard muted footsteps in the stair shaft, coming up, fast.

"My room!" I hissed, and we ran silently back down the hall. I marked my card and pointed into the wardrobe, and Mike crept into it. I threw my parka in his face, closed the door after him, pulled off my shoes, placed them hurriedly under the bed, and dove under the covers, my heart pounding against my ribs. I burrowed deeper and faced away from the door, flexed, and forced myself into regular, slow, deep breathing. I took off my glasses.

I couldn't remember hearing the click of the wardrobe door when I closed it, with Mike inside, before diving into the rack.

Only Major Szeden, the dreaded "Super Tac," opened cadet room doors during the night. If the OC checked our room, it was Szeden. If Szeden saw the dresser door ajar, he would know the cadet he had chased had entered the closet, unable to completely close it from the inside. The door ajar would be like the Queen's slip showing during Coronation, or a pair of bright, starched white trousers unzipped during a Full Dress Armed Forces Day Parade down Fifth Avenue. And Szeden, the nocturnal terror, would nuke our little cadet lives into something that would inspire fear for decades.

At 0120, light flooded the room as our door opened.

I imagined the flashlight beam scanning the room, noticing the open wardrobe, the faulty alignment of tennis shoes.

Kip, kip. Two footsteps into our room. I continued to breathe. Through my closed lids I sensed the bright impact of a flashlight on the wall beside my head. *Kip, kip, kip, kip . . . kip, kip.* Major Szeden was in our room, searching, taking the grand tour.

It had been rumored that Szeden, when pursuing night-running cadets, reached into bunks to check the pulses in search of an elevated rate—the telltale sign of a feigning sleeper swamped in anxiety. If the OC grabbed my wrist right now, he'd get a count of an easy 268 beats per minute. Relax, breathe. I remembered Pinoy Punsalong's techniques and lowered my pulse to 200 beats a minute.

A small eternity passed. The door closed. Mike would wait

for me to open the wardrobe. Major Szeden was the father of the sly fox. Sometimes he wore one tennis shoe and one cordovan; when he ran, it sounded as if he were walking. In situations like this, he entered cadet rooms, walked around, huffed, and then closed the door. Everyone would spring out of their beds, ready to try again to go over the wall to Snuffy's for a midnight toff, and find Major Szeden standing in the center of their room, glaring while the cadets prepared for punishment tours until the New Ice Age.

After ten minutes, I stirred and rose as if I had to go to the latrine. He was gone. The door to the wardrobe was securely closed. I opened it and Mike crossed his eyes, put both index fingers into his mouth, stretched it, and stuck his tongue out.

After arguing, we did it Mike's way. It was an old theme: Do you cross your patrol over an enemy road all at once, or one at a time? The answer always depended on tactical circumstances. Mike thought that two of us crossing at the same time represented double the risk in noise and observability. I thought it cut the risk in half, but he was the starman and I was the math goat. Mike ran across the Area cleanly and headed for Sonny's room.

I began to run. "*YOU!!! HAAALT!!!*" cried a big voice.

I sprinted, raising big billows of snow, almost dropping my towel with its "TING A-3" laundry mark. As I entered the far-side barracks, I stamped my feet, leaving large footprints, pushed the swinging doors onto the first floor, removed my shoes, backtracked through the swinging door, giving it a huge push inward, and sprinted madly up the stairs. Sonny was on the third floor.

The doors slammed against their stops as Szeden burst into the building, and I braked. He started up the stairs, making my heart fall. He cursed. His footfalls went down the stairs, following footprints and the swinging door onto the first floor.

I cut off on the second floor and ran to the central staircase, then went up to the third, my thighs pumping while I drove my arms with all my might, compelling my legs to keep pace. I entered Sonny's room in a slide and quietly closed the door.

"What kept you?" asked Mike.

"Szeden saw me crossing and chased me," I gasped.

"God! You didn't lead him here, did you?" asked Mike.

"Guys! Hold it down!" hissed Sonny, scribbling, his ear flush against a small five-inch speaker. "I might get a name. . . ."

I took my towel and tucked it into the bottom jamb of the door, to keep the light from going into the hallway. Upperclassmen had unlimited lights, but I didn't want to draw any attention. Mike Benjamin and I were unauthorized to be here.

"Is it Troth?" I asked quietly.

Sonny's door was opening, pushing the towel along the floor.

"ROOM, TEN-HUT!" cried Alphabet, and we all snapped to attention. Sonny's posture was askew; he was bent over slightly, his eyes agog as he stared at Major Szeden while still listening to the scratchy conversations coming faintly through the speaker.

Major Szeden glared. He had fallen in the snow. It caked his overcoat and had gone up his sleeves, dropping onto the floor. Snow was packed in the space between his cordovans and his socks, on his face, and on the gold oak-leaved visor of his cap. It graced his massively indented brows, his burning, volcanic eyes, his rabid, snarling, salivating mouth. He entered the room. *Kip, kip, kip*.

We were almost the leaders of the Corps and I wondered if I could recite the Days. How is the Cow? Good, sir, and you?

"How many authorized heah?" he asked through his teeth.

"Two, sir," said Alphabet. Their roomie, Jimmy Basphault, had been medically separated after years of sports injuries.

"I don't give a shit who the twerp is, the asshole can be bought off or shoved off. Now who's helping?" said a tinny voice in the speaker.

"Who said that?" asked Major Szeden.

"Sir, I believe Cadet Troth said that," said Sonny.

"Which a yew young gen'l'men is Mistah Troth?" asked the major. His burning eyes fixed on us, he brushed the bright yellow "OC" brassard on his upper arm, sprinkling us with snow.

"Sir, Mr. Troth is not present," said Sonny. "We're hearing his voice, and the voices of others, through this speaker."

"You gen'l'men snowin' me?" he asked.

"No way! We're not takin' this thing one damn step further! It's already wreckin' us! Now you're talking about—what? Beating people up? Killing them? That's bullshit!"

"What in the *hail* is goin' on here?" asked Major Szeden.

"Sir," I said, "we're doing an Honor investigation, acting under an op order issued on 15 December by Major Chase Maher, EE 304A exam officer. Sir, I'm not authorized to be here. I think Honor has precedence over the Blue Book. We have to track the conversation which is coming through this speaker. Sir, I request permission to continue here, and to report to your office tomorrow to be placed on report for unauthorized absence from rooms."

Major Szeden looked at me as if he were watching pigs fly while they sang the Alma Mater in Swahili.

"You watch. There's a chink and a kike doin' this shit. And I bet there's a dago, too. You gonna let *them* push you out of the Academy? They're here 'cause of the Hire the Handicapped program. Screw 'em in the ear!"

"Don't use those names," said a voice.

"Aw, fuck *you* in the ear!"

"Take yo' notes, gen'l'men. *Yew,*" the major said, pointing his gloved finger at my nose, "outside."

I gulped and followed him.

"Mistah, indulge mah curiosity. Yew set any diversions up ta get me ta be in New South tonight?"

"No, sir," I said. "We wouldn't want you anywhere near us. Nothing personal." I couldn't believe we didn't check the OC list. Szeden wrote the biggest slugs in the Academy; he might give me life imprisonment, or the electric chair, or something worse.

"Someone's bin playin' hail with me all night. Customarily, cadets don't fix ta play games when *Ah'm* on duty."

"No, absolutely not, sir," I said.

"Got an anonymous call in the guard room. Said a fire'd be set in east- or westside New South, aftah midnight. Fire marshal's been through both buildings. CQs report nuthin'.

"Signal flares got popped ovah the river by the train station. MPs and Ah ran down theah. On mah way back, Ah saw a cadet runnin' inta the other wing. Ah did a room-ta-room and couldn't find him."

Diversions drew Major Szeden into Third Regiment, while the cabal met in the Fourth.

"How many a yew crossed the Area jus' now?"

"Two, sir."

"Yew were the second fugitive, right?"

"Yes, sir."

"An' how'd y'all proceed ta this room?" He had canted his head sideways, so I was now looking at one of his eyeballs, pronouncedly red, slightly palpitating, bulging in a most ominous manner. I almost expected the eyeball to spit at me. I heard the great Immortal Poe's laugh from the sepulchre of the steam tunnels.

I told him what I had done.

"Ah knew Ah'd bin suckered offa the stairs, but Ah thought there were two a you, split high and low." He shook his head. "Ah knew Ah'd bin had when Ah saw the wet footprints end in the entryway. Still, that was a *fine* chase."

"Sir, how did you track me to the room?"

His smile vanished, and he frowned. I felt like bracing.

"Hate ta surrender tactical secrets, Mistah Ting." He knew my name. He looked at his watch. "It's 0140. Semestah's new an' no whufers in range. Mos' cadets are in dreamland, hunkered undah brown boys. In New South, only one light's on. This room. When Ah lost y'all on the firs' floor, Ah beelined heah. Ah was most confused by no light 'neath the door."

He pulled a stethoscope out of his overcoat pocket. "Ah listened, and heard conversin'."

He appreciated my gaping mouth. Then he leaned forward. "Y'all gonna think this is an ignorant question. All Asians creep in the night like you?"

"But you saw me, sir."

"But Ah couldn't *catch* you. Ah pride mahself on that." He smiled crookedly at me, rubbing his tongue against an eyetooth, his eyes hooded and half shuttered, the gator before his meal.

"Ah'd be honored if ya'll called on me if ya need he'p with yo' situation. No need ta drive two-dash-ones to mah office. Y'all taught me a lesson in city warfare, an' that means the Tactical Department owes you one."

I saluted him. He smiled, snow wet on his face, and returned it. I stood at attention in the hall as he walked away.

"Hey, great news," I said. "We're not getting written up."

I looked at Mike's ashen face.

Sonny's eyes were wet and he was shaking his head. "It's big," he said. "We got fifty classmates in this, easy. All the regiments and most of the companies. But no names." He looked at me. "God help us all."

33

BENEDICT ARNOLD

Post Gym, February 1967

The memory of the siren floated nauseatingly in the empty spaces in my mind where Juice equations could never roost. We had lost to G-1 in water polo by a goal, and the defeat emphasized my fatigue. I worried about Spanner's math grades. I was ready for the end of Gloom and Operation Benedict Arnold, and ready for Pearl to return from Singapore. Every February and March, she went to the Far East, which was why she was still at Vassar after six years.

Mr. Irkson, one of my Plebes, gave me an envelope. Inside were lists of Cows who, according to the Plebes and Yearlings, studied across the regimental line, and who seemed cool on honor. There were sixty-two names, including Faubus, McWhiff, and Nocksin.

"KAI!" I jumped. It was Arch Torres. "Sonny got hit by a car!"

We came out from the Post Gym and Arch pointed. Next to a wide area of badly stomped black slush and dead sidewalk grass were streaks of bright red blood. We sprinted through Central Area, down Thayer past Old and New South, slipping on the salt-encrusted street, grabbing our hats as they sailed off in the wind, sliding on the old, smooth, underlighted hospital corridors to Emergency. Alphabet Burkowski, Nash Matea, Nichols Harrington, and Carroll Blythe were in the hallway. They were some of Sonny's many pals. "Head injury, broken leg," said Alphabet. "He got hit by the damn Newburgh bus. Just took him into surgery."

"Was it an accident?" I asked.

"What?" asked Nash. "Like, did the bus *try* to hit him?"

"Who saw it?" I asked.

"Plebes," said Arch. "Arguing afterward."

323

"See any upperclassmen? Any Cows?"

"No," he said.

"Arch, find out what those Plebes know. Sonny might have been pushed. A Cow may be involved—I gotta warn Benjamin. If he shows up here," I said to the others, "tell him that Sonny was pushed into the bus and to watch his backside. No MPs. We do it."

"What are you talking about?" asked Arch. "What's the deal?"

"Honor," I said. "Arch, I need you. Get those Plebes. Alphabet, Nash, Nichols, Carroll—make sure one of you stays with Sonny all the time. Pretend someone's after him. And keep this right here, deep and dark. There's a cheating ring, and Sonny knows about them. That's all I can say right now. Gotta buzz."

They cranked the data. "Do what you have to," said Alphabet, as the others nodded. "We'll cover the Rap."

I found a house phone and dialed C-3. "This is Second Classman Ting. Get Mike Benjamin to the phone, *right* now!" I smelled ether, the scent of death and failed surgeries. I hated hospitals.

We slogged through the black snow of midwinter toward East Barracks. Mike looked left while I looked right.

"I'm looking for Troth," said Mike.

"Look for buses," I said. "This is the crap the Grande Armée marched through, leaving Moscow and watching for cossacks. This sludge is god-wretched stuff. I hate it. Really hate it."

"Good to be in a positive mood," Mike said, looking behind us.

We were in Second and Fourth Regiment country, the other West Point under the old clock tower. "Up there," I said, pointing to the broad stone walls, laced with dead ivy, echoing with shouts fading in the cold higher air. In the First and Third, the mortal screams of Plebes were as normal as foul weather in the East.

"Mike," I said, "ask the CO's blessing to crawl some of his Plebes. That we know it's not our regiment, that it's Honor."

"Oh, fine," he said. "Give me the easy job."

I followed the shouts. It was a cold day, and Arch had nine crots sweating against the hallway walls on the third floor.

"MISTER! WHAT'S THE BLOND PLEBE'S NAME AND

COMPANY?!" He was nose to nose with a quivering Fourth
Classman I remembered from Beast last summer. Basset.

"SIR, I BELIEVE YOU ARE USING MY HONOR
AGAINST ME!"

"Me allegro mucho," said Arch. "Got me a gringo barracks
lawyer who hasn't seen the fighting end of an electric razor."

"Mr. Basset," I said, "do not fatigue us with your thoughts.
You are a Plebe. You are a tool of the United States Government. You are outranked by small animals that poop in the
woods."

"Using your Honor, mister," said Arch, "is when a superior
asks a body of men for the perpetrator to identify himself."

"No self-incrimination here," I said. "Answer the question."

"Sir," he said, "the other Plebe was Mr. Fors."

"Do not employ vernacular," I said. "And pop off, Mr. Basset."

"SIR! THE OTHER FOURTH CLASSMAN WAS MR.
FORS! SIR, HE IS IN THIS COMPANY!"

"Oh, you smoothie," said Arch to me.

"Any of you beanheads speak or understand Spanish?" No
hands.

*"Arch, ¿Por qué tán pesado? Quizá sería mejor usar una
mano liviana."* Why heavy? Use the light hand.

*"De verás. Cuando empezé, estos jotos eran pero bien 'Be-
Jota.' Me caían como una petada en el culo."* True. When I
started, these ruffians were BJ. This gave me a colossal pain in
the rump. He shrugged his shoulders. *"Adiós, suave,"* he said.

"CRACK YOUR PUNY LITTLE NECKS *IN!"* Arch
roared. "WE'RE GOING—"

Knuckles rapped sharply on the door. It was Mike.

"Basta," I said. Enough.

"Can we talk?" asked Jed Devon, star end of the 150-pound
football team, member of the Class of '67, and company CO.

"May my classmate continue to haze your Plebes?" I asked.

"Oh, please, if you would," he said, with grand largesse.

"Shining your shoes with RAT CRAP? USING THE
TOWER OF PISA FOR ALIGNMENT? THE LINE OF
YOUR CLASS SHIRT HASN'T *MET* THE COINCIDENT
EDGE OF YOUR BUCKLE! THERE ARE DOORSTOPS
MORE MILITARY THAN YOU! *BANG THOSE NECKS IN!*
I'M HERE SO YOU'D HAVE *ONE DAY* AT WEST POINT!"

"If this is Honor," asked Jed, "why are you hazing them?"

"We're representing the real West Point, the one with a

Fourth Class System and esprit, and we don't know better. Jed, you might have a Cow in your company who ordered a Plebe to push Sonny Rappa, one of our classmates, into the New-burgh bus after Intermurder today. Sonny's in the hospital. He and I were doing an Honor investigation." I looked at Mike. "And Mike, too."

Jed made a face. "Sounds ugly. Okay. What about *him?*"

"That's Arch Torres, Brigade welter champ. He's giving your crots memories to share with their grandkids." I smiled. "Jed, it's music—Plebes in Gloom harmonizing with Sylvanus on a perfect Thayer day, bringing a touch of old American military tradition into Easy Country. And, for your troops today, it's free."

"You're a clown. At least use Mr. Basset's room," he said, nodding toward it. "Our lads aren't used to this. Might cause the stock market to crash. Need anything else besides gutting some of my best Plebes?"

"I need Mr. Fors to join the party. I'd like to invite him to our gracious digs for AI."

"No problem. Fors is Basset's roommate. Wipe your slimy Third Regiment dogs before you enter any of my rooms, wash your hands before you touch doorknobs, and let 'em go in time for supper. By the way, clown, we have the best Plebes in the system."

"Okay, Jed," I said. "What can you tell me about Fors?"

"Hard case," he said. "Appointed from the ranks, buck ser-geant, Infantry. He boxes for us, light heavy. From a line of men with no mirth. Bad attitude but very tough. You'll see him in Brigade finals. You're still a middle, right?"

"I'm doing water polo this year," I said. I hated dieting to make weight.

When Jed Devon left, Mike hit me hard on my arm. "You ought to do engineering like you do cadet captains. You let Juice squeeze you by the nuts! What's the difference here?"

"Math," I said.

Mike and Arch hazed Mr. Fors. Mr. Fors had the look of a hungry lizard, acquisitive, bursting with the urge to take in the middle of a year when taking was not authorized. Young Cae-sar with a poor military appearance. Then I recognized him: the Plebe in the sally port who wrote down the names of the re-test cadets—Rappa and Ting.

"*Creo que él es el reo,*" I said. I think he's our boy.

"Seguro," Arch whispered back. *"Lo recuerdo."* I remember him. "Everyone except Mr. Fors, print and sign your name and your company on the pad of paper on the desk, and vamoose," said Arch. "You too, Basset."

Their collective sigh could have lifted a dirigible.

" 'Vamoose.' Damn, Arch, your Spanish is good," said Mike.

As the sun set and the lights of the Academy were illuminated, and as we looked at the grand old clock tower, Mr. Fors continued to face the elephant. Mike and Arch crawled him with a deep-immersion hazing routine, full of sound and fury, signifying doom.

Despite the impassivity required of Plebes, Fors had an active, expressive face. He did not submit to superiors or accept a team. He was here for himself, and the Corps could go throw rocks. He was like me with Edna. But someone had gone far beyond sullen resentment. Someone had closed in on bone-weary Sonny Rappa and, from the safety of a crowd, pushed him into the bus. Fors wouldn't have had to push hard; he was a large, big-boned man.

Fors resisted the hazing. He shouted back, angry but not desperate, in the face of an expert crawling.

"Mr. Fors," I said, "you are being asked simple questions by compassionate men. Do not make me get up and join this fray. Which member of the upper classes is your patron? Your buddy?"

"I don't have a patron. And no buddies. Sir."

"Mr. Torres, Mr. Benjamin, may I?"

"By all means, Mr. Ting," they said, and left, smiling.

"You sir," I said, "are inappropriate, impolite, and given to the habits of snakes. We require cooperation and you spout rank bull. This room stinks of you. You defile the Corps. You lack skill in the military life. Tell me where you learned this."

"I WAS IN THE REAL ARMY, SIR!" he shouted.

"Who is your squad leader, Mr. Fors?"

"Sir, my squad leader is Mr. Bader."

Billy Bader. I was in luck. "Who was Mr. Bader's Buckner and Recondo mate. Whose butt did Mr. Bader save in the Pit?"

"Sir, I do not know."

"You're talking to him. Based on your sterling, helpful performance as a member of the Fourth Class, do you think Mr. Bader will intercede in your behalf, and save you from me?"

Fors hesitated. "No, sir," he said.

"Do you, sir," I said, "believe a cadre of upperclassmen can drive you out by imposing its military will upon you?"

"NO, SIR!" he shouted, trying to spray me with his spit.

"How long, sir," I asked, "can you survive cross-Corps signature calls. How long can your military decorum survive close inspection by the Second Class of the Third Regiment? How long can you endure a deluge of sharp quill upon your poor, stinking, disreputable, selfish, unmilitary, unwashed knob body?"

"Sir, I do not know." His hard features quivered in anger.

"Mister, you're awful lucky, because *I* do. By the grace of every poor Plebe who ever tried his hardest for the Corps, I'm going to share it with you. You'll last till June. You'll endure the whole pleasure of Plebe year residing de jure in the Fabulous Fourth and living de facto in the Thayer Third. In June, you will have received an excess number of demerits and be found for conduct, separated from the Academy after completing the hardest year, at the very gate of upperclass status."

I removed a pad of Forms 2–1 from my shirt pocket, rebuttoned it, and clicked my pen. "First name and cadet number. Sound off."

"SIR, MY FIRST NAME IS GABRIEL. SIR, MY CADET NUMBER IS C-7079!"

"Uniform lacking alignment," I said. "Brass unshined, collar stay showing, shoes unshined—generous understatement—and improperly tied, stain on trou, stain on class shirt, fingerprints on name tag, name tag not aligned with shirt seam, hair unmilitary in appearance and touching the ear. Seven demerits." Seven was the maximum allotment for personal appearance.

I signed the quill for forwarding to the TD. "This didn't take long. I can smell your rifle, your locker, your rack, and your uniforms from here." Each of them could bring another seven. "You are remarkably gross for a man who's been in 'the real Army.' I could ruin your entire year in the next five minutes. How many demerits did you have before I entered this crot cesspool?"

"Sir, I had ten demerits." Resentment.

"Mr. Fors, I was wrong. You do possess skill—skill in quill. You are over the top." I held up the two-dash-one. "You have earned a free pass to the Area for a game of Concrete Fandango. You will be inspected closely prior to serving your punishment tours. Your poor habits will produce more quill, which in turn will generate more hours, and more inspections, which will generate more quill. I might ask for guard duty when you're on the Area, so I can provide AI. I might find lint in your bore, grease in the butt plate, a lack of alignment in your selfish soul. This would have to be reported. It is an ineluctable truth that a Plebe cannot withstand an intention to dismiss him from the Corps on a carpet of poop. How long do you think you can last, Mr. Fors?"

"Sir, I can beat you," he hissed. Fulminating anger, bristling muscular tension. He was very angry. No one had spoken to him like this since Beast. I was picking on him and he wanted to fight.

"You calling me into the ring?" I asked.

"Yes, sir," he said, barely repressing a smile. Triumph.

"I admire that, Mr. Fors. Must I employ further demonstrations to secure your understanding of the jeopardy of your cadet status?"

"No, sir," he said.

"If we fight tonight, no full meal for me. Damn you," I said.

"Sir, Mr. Fors thanks Mr. Ting with all his heart for the warning," he said, smiling through his big teeth.

"Oh, it's great," said Sonny. "Food probably comes from C-rats, mostly ham 'n' eggs. Bedpan's special." He sighed and tried to shift his body, wincing everywhere. "Nurses are good. Competent."

"What happened?" asked Mike.

"After wrestling. Had my ears bound up. Wind was hard. Think I slipped. Don't remember much. Woke up here. Guess no concussion. Leg's busted in two places, had to pin it." He shook his head wearily. "Was havin' a good season."

Mike also liked wrestling. I detested its chance encounters with a sweaty foreign armpit in your nose. Boxing was clean and sanitary. There was a fundamental decency to it. Fors had boxed in the ranks. I was in shape and I had Tony's rosary for good *foo chi*.

Three other cadets were in the ward, all Plebes, uncommonly pleased to be fractured or ill. No bracing, full meals, and nurses.

"What can I bring you?" I asked.

"New head," he said.

"That's your prescription for me," I said.

"Get yourself a new head too."

"Want me to call Barbara?" I asked.

"No. You'd try to lure her west, be a California girl, an' promise her lots of Chinese food. Loves . . . food. . . ."

"Who can blame her?" I asked. "Can you talk?"

"Grog," he said.

"Gotta move, Kai," Mike said. "Or we all end up here."

"You ready, Sonny?" I asked.

"Oh, yeah," he mumbled. "Ready. Readier. Gnorp."

Mike and I looked at each other. He motioned me away.

"Kai," he whispered, "forget the bus. Sonny's too banged up. Let's get them for the cheating. That's what this is about."

I shook my head. "Can't let them get away with this."

"Can you prove it?" he asked.

Recitations at math boards began with the words, "Sir, I am required to prove . . ." So far, I had proven that mathematics and I were not meant for each other, and that I could anger Plebes who were as surly as Mongols after someone had burned their huts.

"Don't know, Mike. Think so."

"Love your confidence. It'd be great to have more time," he whispered, "but let's do it Saturday."

"Saturday . . . Sonny." No reaction. I shook Sonny gently. He opened an eye. "Ow," he said.

"Saturday night 1900 hours. Colonel Smits's Q, the Poker Society. Arch'll help you line up your ducks." I hoped we wouldn't need them, because he didn't have them yet. It wasn't a matter of ducks. We needed artillery or Chinese gods, or both.

He squinted at me, then at Mike. "Saturday night, Smits. Be there . . . be square. . . ." He drifted off. Mike picked up Sonny's uninjured right hand and placed it on top of his. He gestured to me, and I put my hand on top of Sonny's. "Go, Rabble," Mike said. "Rabble" was the nickname for the Corps. Sonny was silent. I thought of our friendly forces: Pearl, the perennial Vassar senior who made my heart pound, Elmer Scoggin, the scarred armor veteran, Captain Mark Martin, the Chicago JAGC, and Major Szeden, the modern version of Chingis Khan. "Go, Rabble," I said.

I was down six bucks. When I swallowed, I felt the swelling in my neck where Fors's long arm had caught me. It had taken three hard, vicious rights for me to figure out that he was aiming for my neck, trying to break it. I had grinned at him through my mouthpiece, feeling only fear, unable to swallow spit in a dry mouth. Now my body hurt north to south, east to west, with red neon signs that resisted the hard and honest work of Army APCs, aspirin.

I reviewed tonight's mnemonic, describing the plan: SSKSMAS—Star, Study, Key, Safe, Mike, Arch, Sonny.

It was Saturday night at the Poker Society, and the gang was here. KDET played "Turn, Turn, Turn," with the volume knob set at four, and Mike and I studiously avoided eye contact. We were the conspirators, and the others were the chickens. The chickens had us outnumbered. It had taken a federal conspiracy to bring Mike to the Society, the center of bohemia and the war against perfection, ripe with inebriation and the criticism of women and minorities.

My floating ribs spoke to me, complaining that I had not protected them adequately. The fight with the long-armed Gabe Fors, a year older and twenty pounds heavier, had been the fastest three rounds in my life. I'd sit in the corner and the bell would ring. "How about a minute between rounds?" I had asked Mike.

"Been a minute," he had said. "This is New York. Go get 'im."

"Where's your dago friend?" asked Duke.

"Pole-vaulting over fish turds," I said.

Duke laughed. "Where's that Vassar gentility, Ting? Or does 'dago' fit with your California anti-American bullshit?"

"Sorry. Forgot you're an asshole," I said.

Mike kicked me under the table. Cool it.

"Want something real to drink?" asked Colonel Smits gruffly.

"No thanks, sir. I'm on the wagon." My mouth had a memory of his Glenfiddich. It had been artfully smooth. Could cure all ills, stitch my chest and torso wounds, cauterize my split lip.

"Hurtin' my feelings, hero," he said, as he dealt stud.

I started to laugh, and saw that he had been serious.

Bets went around, everyone in. Time to put "Q.E.D." on the solution page of Operation Benedict Arnold.

Moose Hoggatt played Sergio Mendes and Brasil '66's moody "Constant Is the Rain" on KDET. For this hairy moment I needed the Army Band and the Official West Point March and everything Beethoven had composed. Mike nodded at Bob Lorbus. Time for star.

"Duke," said Bob, "remember asking me to get a circled star from Sonny Rappa? Remember I gave it to you?"

Duke looked at Bob, then at me. I was the doofus who ended up with that star and the paper—only when I got it, a whole bandit Juice whufer had been written around it. Bob's future had been pitched, slow and straight, to Duke's bat. Duke could implicate Bob as part of a cabal by saying no, or release him with a yes.

Duke leaned back in his chair, huffing, pursing his lips, studying me, then Bob. Oscar Wilde had said that a cynic knew the value of nothing, and the price for everything.

"Yeah," said Duke. "I remember. I asked you for it. So what?"

"So thanks, buddy," said Bob, "for remembering."

That was it. Duke's words had cleared Bob and Sonny. Troth looked at me: I freed Lorbus and Rappa. Now, pay my price: lay off.

Mike left, then returned. Study-key-safe was next. My turn. Toos had said, "Talk slow, and look 'em in the eye." I cleared my aching throat. It was a Thayer kind of day. Tom Jones was singing.

"Worried about Juice?" I asked Duke.

Duke raised his eyes to me slowly. I saw Clint look at Duke, his eyes looking for something. No, Clint: don't look to Duke.

"Hell no," said Troth. "Strange shit coming from you. All you do is hive Vietnam and play Hardy Hardass on Plebes all over campus. Even knobs who aren't yours. Still dee in Juice?"

"Yeah, I am. Duke, what's the *key* to success in Juice?"

He started to answer, then looked hard at me. I wasn't playing along for him. I now had king high, and led the betting, going slow. I felt the winds of chance bending to me.

"Nothin' to it," he said. "Juice is a breeze."

"Feel *safe*," I said, "with Juice whufers coming?"

"What are you getting at, Kai?" asked Clint, sitting tall.

"Pair of kings," I said, "bets ten more." Stay out, Clint.

Clint dropped out, looking tense, his deep dimples sallow. Duke stayed, showing jacks. My kings beat Miles's queens and I gathered the chips. It was time. Duke was ready, and Smits would do what he would do. The Honor Committee would sort it out.

"Duke," I asked, "how do you feel about the Honor Code?"

Duke looked at Colonel Smits, waiting for him to say something. Smits lit a cigarette and looked blandly back at Duke.

"Great—super," Duke said, glancing at the colonel.

"Would you tolerate a violation?" I asked.

"Kai, what are you doing?" asked Clint.

"Would you report yourself for cheating?" I asked.

"You're gonna get reported for fartin' dingleberries in the wind," Duke said.

"Duke," I said. "Have anything to say to the Honor Committee?"

Cards went down and chairs pushed back in tunes of sour scraping. It was like Chinese music, deep, mournful strings of women's lament bound by *gahng* to fathers, husbands, and sons. I felt something strong, old, and traditional, something like China itself, in my veins. A time for moral rectitude. I was on the path of the moral man. Even if I lost, I was in the right place. "I do not worry about dying. I worry about a life not well lived," said Uncle Shim. *Jacta alea est. P'o fu ch'en chou.* Break the pot and sink the boat.

Clint's mouth had become a light crease in the lower half of his face. He had swallowed his lips.

I looked into Troth's eyes. *"Do you?"*

His eyes narrowed. He rubbed his chin with the back of his hand. "You're crazy. Bad crazy. Stop this shit now, Ting."

I pulled out a notepad and pen, which all good officers carry. "Bob. Help me out. Please note time and date."

Bob looked at his Rolex. "2003 hours, 23 February 1967," he said thinly. He and I cleared space on the table.

"Luther Darwin Troth," I said, "I charge you with two Honor Code violations and one of the Uniform Code of Military Justice. I charge you with violating the Code by participating in the theft of an EE 304A WFR from Electrical Engineering, on or about 9 December 1966, at West Point, New York, and of distributing copies of that WFR to other Second Classmen before the review.

"Under the provisions of the UCMJ, I charge you with violating Article 128, Aggravated Battery, in that on 18 February 1967 at West Point, you caused a collision between a bus and Cadet Santino Rappa, on Thayer Road, in order to discourage him from completing an Honor investigation on you. I am obligated to report these accusations and allegations to the Honor Committee, and to the Department of Tactics, for further disposition. Bob?"

"Wait one—got it," said Bob, scribbling madly.

"How say you, Luther Troth, to these charges?" I asked.

"I say you're full a crap. Who you tryin' to be, the first chink Laurence Olivier?"

I thought of Chase Maher. "I don't want to brag," I said.

"I didn't do a goddamn thing," said Duke. "I'm *good* in Juice. You—you asshole—you couldn't figure a Juice writ with Dago Rappa sittin' in your chair. You're the asshole who needs to cheat, not *me*."

"You're a thief in the night, ripping off brothers," I said.

"Actually," said Mike, "you're a thief all the time."

"You're full a shit," said Duke, turning on Mike.

Mike shrugged. "Not really. Your focus is misplaced." He stood, his big chest filling the room, inviting Troth to swing: Clark Gable standing up to Captain Bligh, Fletcher Christian challenging Julius Caesar. Troth blinked. "I need air," Mike said.

He opened the door. A slender civilian with a bad GI haircut entered as if he had too many feet.

"Gentlemen," said Mike. "First Lieutenant Tom Baker, an MIT doctorate and member of the Juice faculty. Sir, this is Lieutenant Colonel Smits, post staff, Messrs. Bestier, Brodie, Ting, Lorbus, and Troth. The lieutenant is a PhD draftee. The Pentagon calls him a McNamara Monument."

"Hello," said First Lieutenant Baker, waving. No sign of recognition of anyone.

"Lieutenant," said Mike. "A cadet asked you to stow a ring in the exams safe. Is that cadet in this room?"

Lieutenant Baker studied us. He looked twice at Troth, thinking. He looked at Bob, and Clint, then back to Troth.

"LT, play some poker," said Smits, hoarsely.

"Uh . . . no," Baker said, trying to place Duke Troth.

Smiths banged down a glass, belched long and wet, smiling with his teeth, scratching himself. Baker seemed to see Smits in the reality of his disrepair for the first time. He sniffed the aromas of old food and anxious men. Baker looked again at Duke, then Bob. Both were tall and large. "He could be here." He shook his head. "I don't remember."

"Take your time, sir," I said, smiling, panic in my guts. C'mon, you got a doctorate. You got a brain. Don't freak 'cause you got Army all around you. The President made you an officer and a gentleman. I bet it was Troth who got you to pop the safe while he scoped the combination. Remember! The LT blinked at me, now trying to figure out why a Chinese guy was in the room. I had distracted him. He looked again, licking his lips nervously, but it was over. He left. He had been our best shot, the strongest of our ducks in a wishful line. No one could've been smarter, and he was the only percipient witness that could put Duke in Maher's office.

"Ting, what the fuck are you doing?" asked Colonel Smits, his voice filtered by the cigarette between his lips.

I tried to swallow the lump of cold defeat in my throat. "You know what I'm doing."

Smits stood. "What do you mean, yellow soldier?"

I stood. "We got people making up their own rules. Rules for cheating and shoving classmates under buses." I couldn't keep my voice flat. "People can't be screwed with like that—no more."

"Listen, idiot, people get screwed every day. All you guys are gonna get it in the Nam." He shook his head, ambled around until he found the Glenfiddich, and banged it on the table. "Ready to quit the bottle again, Ting?" I sat down and he laughed.

There was a thumping in the hallway. Arch Torres stuck his head in the door. "Guys," he said. He helped Sonny hobble in on crutches. Sonny looked bad. I was afraid he was going to barf on Arch before he could reach Duke. I went to help him.

"Hey," Sonny gasped, sweat on his brow. "I was doin' the obstacle course for practice. Good," he said, as he collapsed in Mike's chair. "Came here ta test my faith in a loving and forgiving God." He looked at Duke. "You're it." He put down the crutches.

Duke snorted. "Break my fuckin' heart. Rappa, unass this party and fuck you, in that order. No one invited you."

I moved toward Duke, and Mike stopped me in an iron grip.

"Hey—you can invite him to dance, but I can't?"

"Look at Sonny, Kai," said Mike.

Sonny, who felt like hammered cow feces, was smiling at me. He was doing it sincerely. Sonny had hived the problem. I might never get to dunce Duke Troth, but I smiled, too.

A hard-boned, humorless older man stepped into the room and took off his baseball cap. He looked around sternly, like it was his room and we were all uninvited transients.

"Well, fuck me to tears!" said Smits. "It's really Joe Schmoe the ragman. Who comes after *him*, Ann-Margret, or the Pope?"

"Evening, sir," said the man politely to Colonel Smits, then reached over and gently patted Sonny. "Hey." He had a deep voice.

"Meet Mr. Sam Marse," said Sonny thinly. "Senior BP for Bartlett and keeper of the keys. Mr. Marse is a decorated combat veteran of the European Theater of Operations, where he was a tank commander, credited with three Panther and one Tiger tank kill. Mr. Marse, this is . . . ," and Sonny introduced him to each man.

"Recognize anyone, Mr. Marse?" asked Sonny.

He shook his head. "No, sir," he said.

I looked at Sonny. Sonny was frowning. He looked confused, then said, "Mr. Marse, you lend any cadets keys to Bartlett last month?" The radio played the Hollies' "Bus Stop."

"Yes, sir," he said. "But I wouldn't lend 'em to anyone but a Plebe. No one in this room," he said.

Sonny was thinking. "Why's that, Mr. Marse?"

"Well, with Yearlin's takin' physics an' chemistry, Cows takin' Juice, an Firsties with or'nance, all them tests in there, wouldn't be kosher. Plebes don' have no tests there in January."

"But you lent them to someone," said Sonny.

Sam Marse nodded, looking around the room. "Yes, sir. But I don' see 'im."

"Fuckin' dago bug-pecker bullshit!" muttered Duke. "That's all this is! Get this janitor outa here before someone gets hurt!"

Mr. Marse stiffened. "I'm a barracks policeman, sir, not a janitor."

"Way to go, Scrounger," said Smits. "Now you got BPs on your butt."

"There he is," said Mr. Marse. "Him." He pointed.

Mr. Fors entered the room. I stood. "Come in, Gabe." He entered the Q, as if drawn by Sam Marse's pointing digit.

"That's him," said Marse, studying Fors. "But he looked a lot different." He looked at Sonny, and at the rumpled room. "Seems you young men are havin' a great number of accidents." Marse looked at Sonny again, found an old folding chair, and sat down.

"What happened, Fors?" asked Colonel Smits.

"Sir, I challenged Mr. Ting to meet me in the ring."

"You go three rounds?" asked Smits.

"Yes, sir," he said.

"Good for you. Why's he callin' you by first name?"

"Sir, after the bout, Mr. Ting recognized me."

Smits nodded and lit another cigarette. "Interesting."

Fors looked at me and I tossed him a can of pop. I started

to speak and Sonny waved me off. "Gabe," said Sonny, "you ask Mr. Marse for keys to Bartlett and Major Maher's office?"

"Yes, sir," he said.

"Why?" I asked.

"Back off!" cried Troth at me. "Gabriel, don't let these douchebags screw with you! They're *using* you! They don't give a *crap* about you. C'mon, buddy! You gotta stick with the Duke. I'll see you through this."

Gabe Fors tried to hold his face still.

"Don't screw this up," said Troth. "Screw *them!*" His eyes left Fors and sat on me. "SHUT UP!!" he screamed, fearing I would argue. His jaw muscles articulated, struggling to control his mouth, his breathing. "Look," he said, his voice quiet, reasonable. "It's been a helluva day in a long fucking week. Gabriel, we gotta patch you up. We can take care of that back at the company. I'm sorry if this asshole hurt you. We'll take care of *him* later.

"Why don't we all confess to something?" He ran his hand through his dark hair, disturbing the wedge that pointed into the center of his forehead. "We've all been sweating rumors about something not square in Juice. Guys, I haven't done anything wrong. Gabriel here, he hasn't, either. Now Kai Ting here can run a little parade of horribles, and you can meet civilians in tans, and you can meet old men who are BPs and shot up German tanks, and he'll probably have Ed Sullivan and Topo Gigio and dancing girls in here next who'll sit on your lap for a quarter." He smiled broadly. I thought one of his teeth gleamed.

"Ting's a little confused. He's flunking Juice. Can you beat it? A fuckin' Chinese, flunkin' Juice. For some reason, he wants to take me down with him. Do I deserve this *shit*? Negative! *I* introduced him to the Society. Now I couldn't get him *laid*, but face it—some things you gotta do for yourself." He looked around the room, smiling, teeth brighter. He was warming up.

"We drank too much," he said. "Let's call it a fuckin' day. Kai, go push your Disneyland crap someplace else." He paused. "I want all of you to think real hard about what's coming down here. Let's give it a rest. Then we'll meet and talk it over." He laughed softly. "I'll give you this. You Chinese people sure have a—"

"STOP IT!" cried Fors in a high, piercing voice, the cords in his neck strained and taut. "STOP LYING! I got the keys for a *prank*! You said it didn't involve Honor. That BPs didn't count—you were going to put the reveille cannon on top of Bartlett. That Rappa was setting you up as a cheat and that it was a ritual to knock a lying cadet into the Newburgh bus and to beat a colored person in the ring—that a Chinese would count."

He wiped his eyes. He honked loudly into a tissue as he cleared his pipes, unable to look at me or at Mr. Marse. The corners of Fors's mouth turned violently downward, his lips quivering as he tried to gain control.

"Well," I said, "I did have a black mother."

Mr. Marse raised his eyebrows at me.

"Gabriel, Gabriel," said Duke. "Why do you believe them? Rappa *was* after me. The asshole wired my room, right above my rack. They were the ones who came over to our company and fuckin' crawled your ass—and then beat you up. The keys *were* for a prank."

"Right, Troth," said Fors. "The whole goddamm Second Class showed up at the hospital, watching him around the clock. Kids brought Mr. Rappa cards and wives brought him flowers. Shit! They cried when they saw him. You jerk! He's their Sunday-school teacher. Father Fiala thinks Rappa's God's gift. He's one of those guys in your class who helps others. I keep hearing the bus. This was no prank. You set me up good. Damn near killed one of the best men in the Academy." He squeezed the can in his hand, baring his teeth, grunting, and the tab popped and soda exploded from it to spatter his uniform and his face and he kept squeezing until it was crushed in his grip. I was glad he hadn't done that in the ring.

Duke's left eye developed a tic. He was breathing fast with his mouth open, his expression changing like litmus being subjected to acids. It went from shock and dull hurt to a shining, regal hate. "You fucking asshole knob—you can't shit on me!"

"*Ave Imperator,*" I said. "You flinched."

Fors felt Duke's words, absorbing them. His big fists formed, his neck cording, adrenaline gathering for the kill.

"Don't get into that," I said. "Hey!" He jerked and exhaled.

"Good man," I said. "You don't do this kind of crap anymore."

Duke rubbed his face. He turned to Colonel Smits, hissing to him while the radio played a song none of us could remember later. We breathed like penitents viewing Hades from the hot edge, hearing tridents scraping coals and names being called. Bob took notes with a great continuous scratching, trying to catch up in the silence.

Smits bared his teeth and pushed Troth back to his chair. "I told you," he said in his hoarse, scratchy voice, "the story a '51 so you'd see the system." He ground out his cigarette and lit another. "You dumb shit, you figured you'd do it again. You're such a *tool*. I told you the story so you wouldn't get what the team got. Shit. Instead a walkin' away, you copied the fucker!" He leaned forward, close to Troth's face, his eyes wet and darting, remembering other cadets in other days, peering harder. He sighed and sat back.

"The point to '51 is that Red Blaik saved my young ass. He told me, 'Son, don't do it.' That's the story of '51 and that's what I told you," he growled. "Now you're gettin' kicked out!"

"They can't!" cried Duke. "Not me! I'm smarter than any of 'em! Shit! Some of these guys aren't even *American*."

"You're history," said Smits. The words settled into the room.

"They can't prove that UCMJ shit," Duke pleaded. "They won't believe a fuckin' *Plebe* over a Cow." Please. Please agree.

"Screw the UCMJ. You're dead on Honor," said Smits. "No one gets saved from that, or it ain't West Point. Don't be an asshole."

A small, twisted sound came from Troth's throat. He contorted like a man with a burst appendix. "You *hate* the Honor Code!"

"It's a screamin' bitch, but it's the Point," said Smits. "I hate the Honor freaks." He took a deep inhalation of smoke, looking sideways at me. "But you can't screw with the Code. God, you're stupid. . . . Aw, shit, Troth, it ain't like your dick got cut off. You weren't right for this place, and this place ain't right for you. This place sucks. Stand up like a man and kiss it goodbye."

"You said, make your own rules," said Duke.

"You got *that* right." Smits shook his head. "Don't be totally stupid," he said. "Honor doesn't have any stinkin' rules. It's Honor. Rules is all that other plastic world shit. Jesus Christ, Scrounger—you couldn't tell a barbecued Porky Pig from an incoming eighty-one-mike-mike. Son, you tied this one up by the numbers. You stepped on your dick so many

ways it's gonna take a piccolo player to help you take a leak."
Smits hit Duke hard on the arm.

"Square yourself away," he growled. "West Point doesn't
like your stinkin' dingleberried ass. Don't get sentimental for
somethin' that doesn't like you! For chrissake," he snorted,
"get outa here and go make some money."

Duke sat down and put his head into his hands.

"Aw, shit! Don't cry, Scrounger! Stand up like a man and
kiss it goodbye. If you can't smile, spit at 'em. C'mon, man!
You're embarrassin' me."

I looked at Clint, and his chair was empty. Mike never took
his eyes off Troth. Sonny and Bob were silently praying. I
shook my head. They were as superstitious as Taoist monks.

Sam Marse slowly rose to his feet. He surveyed the room.
It was a BP's nightmare. He loudly cleared his throat.

"You oughta spiff up these here quarters, Colonel," he said.
"This here place is militarily disreputable."

34

SWORD POINT

West Point, Late Winter 1967

The Honor Boards convened. I remembered Mr. Alsop's room,
fourteen of us sweating, hungry, thirsty, tired, and scared, hearing him tell us that we had to be perfect in Honor.

For two months cadets reported to the Committee in Building 720, to stand in front of the long table of twelve Honor
representatives in chilled and austere midnight and mid-
morning hearings. Some were witnesses; too many were suspects. Classmates began disappearing. No one knew how
many, but each of us had our own count. Those charged with
Honor violations could testify, refuse to testify, seek officer and
attorney counsel, or resign. Those who went through with ev-
identiary boards reported to the Twelve at the end to face the
saber. If the sword point of the Committee's saber pointed at

him, the Committee had returned a unanimous finding of guilt, and the cadet was found on Honor and dishonorably separated from the Corps, with immediate effect. If the hilt was offered, the cadet had been acquitted, the result of at least one dissenting vote. Those called before the Committee were ordered not to discuss their testimony. Those dismissed were not to be discussed, ever again.

I had squared away my uniform with particular care.

"Plebes fall out," I said to the squad. "Honor Boards are in session. These are sad days for the Code and the Corps. A lot of emphasis has been placed on things you cannot do. I want you to remember that we busted our rears to get here, to be part of this school, and that this squad protected the Code. We're unified by our pledges to Honor. That will never change. Plebes stand fast, squad dismissed."

"Guys," I said to the Plebes, "thank you again for your help. I want to continue the Fidelis. But if you want a break, put out a fist. Majority rules."

Eight Plebes, no fists. I smiled. "Then give me a Fideli."

"Sir," they said in unison, "Who says, 'My stomach, right or wrong'? *Mr. Schmidt, sir!* Who's got the sweetest disposition? *Mr. Parthes, sir!* Who'd never dream of picking a fight? *Mr. McFee, sir!* Who prays to live in a steeple with a whole buncha Chinese people? *Mr. Spanner, sir!* Who turns left when the squad turns right? *Mr. Quint, sir!* Who makes a big rock look like Esther Williams? *Mr. Caleb, sir!* Who thinks English is a foreign tongue? *Mr. Irkson, sir!* Who in the flock's the dumbest on the block? *Mr. Zerl, sir!*"

"Ya bring a tear to me eye," I said in the worst brogue imaginable. "Ya make me so hoppy I want y'all to give me thirty push-ups. Count 'em out loud now, lads. Call 'em out to Mr. Fideli, sweetly, now."

I knocked. Farren said, "Yo." He had packed the bag he had dropped on the Area on R-Day. He was gathering unused bandit soup ingredients.

"Farren, I'm here to say I'm sorry," I said.

He didn't look at me, waiting for me to leave, his face red. "Do me a favor," he said. "If something really shitty happens to you, so bad you can't laugh, call me. Like havin' your leg ripped off by a frag or gettin' gorked by a booby trap. Somethin' so bad you can't do your standard-issue happy-shit routine. Look me up, hear? Tell me about it. I'll laugh my fuckin' guts out." He hurled the rest of the food into the wastebasket, knocking it over, all the contents spilling onto the floor. He liked the noise as the kosher soup cans rolled against the bunks. "Get the fuck outa my room."

"Why'd you do it?" I asked. "You didn't believe that crap you handed me about doing it for your classmates."

He looked toward the rifle rack. "Didn't you hear me?"

"Yeah, I heard you," I said. "You crap on the Code, screw your classmates, lie to Plebes, break into buildings, steal exams, and set Sonny and Big Bus up as cheaters. You follow a guy who used to beat up our smaller classmates, barters women, almost kills Sonny, and points a gun at someone trying to follow the Code—and you're pissed at me?"

"Hey, I was against the guns. I had nothin' to do with the bus. I was one of the guys against it."

"Yeah, you did a *great* job of being against it. What the *hell* was I thinking about? I'm not apologizing to *you*. Screw you!" I walked out, slammed the door, and drove a fist into it, splintering his nameplate. His paper tag waffled to the floor. I threw open the door.

"Come and get it, McWhiff," I said, trembling with anger.

Farren looked at me with fear and hate. "Damn, you are seriously nuts. Troth was right about you."

Troth. I ran toward Fourth Regiment. Three years of eating his crap was enough. I was going to take him down.

"Hey, Kai," said someone.

I raced up the stairs and Plebes recognized me and almost herniated themselves in an effort to get out of my road. I ran to the room that Sonny had wired for sound and I turned the knob and kicked it in like a Beast squad leader drawing attention, the door banging hollowly as I stepped in with a good stance with no one to stop me. All three beds had been rolled, and rifles placed in armory; the room was ghostly vacant. I looked at the door. There were no name tags where, not long ago, one of them had said in crisp black letters, "TROTH, LD 68." My chest heaved. I had adrenaline and rage and no one to fight but his memory.

Clint, Deke, and I walked to the north sally port, where our grades were posted, and our section assignments changed, to conform to our new class standings in each course.

"You're outa the basement in English," Deke said to Clint. "And you're in ninth section in solids," he said to me. We were trying to pretend that the world had not changed, that the specter of Honor expulsions was not clouding all we did and all we said.

We recorded our other section assignments. I remained in the bottom in Juice and in the upper five sections in econ, Spanish, social sciences, psych, and English. Clint was two sections from the bottom in Juice. Deke was rock steady in the upper ten sections in all courses. Sonny and Mike were in the first section in everything, and I smiled for them, wondering how two guys so close to being number one in the class could so consciously avoid competing for the honor. K'ung Futzu had said that men of genius gather naturally but can never agree. West Point proved him wrong.

"I'm staying a starman so I can get into med school," Mike had said. Sonny was tutoring everyone in the regiment and still got to bed by nine-thirty most nights. "Early to bed, early to bed" was one of his mottoes. Sonny refused to be daunted by the hearings. He continued, through February and March, to operate as if it were normal for the class to be undergoing hardship and attrition.

"Kai, hearts after class?" asked Arch en route to Bartlett the next day.

"You're on. Say, eleven-fifteen."

Plebes saluted as Deke and I approached the Hilton after thermo. Neither Airborne Rat nor Venus was on the windowsill.

Clint's rack was stripped, the mattress rolled on its wire springs. No shoes under the bed, and only two laundry bags hanging from the bedposts instead of three. Clint's desk was empty. Clint's rifle was gone from the gun rack.

Deke unrolled the mattress and sat heavily on Clint's bunk, dropping his books. "Oh, man," he said. "He's gone."

I opened the wardrobe where Mike Benjamin had resided during Major Szeden's search, the night I thought Clint was asleep. On an empty hanger was Airborne Rat's little parachute.

Had Clint cheated directly or tolerated the cheating in others? I had suspected that the voice we heard on Sonny's black-box receiver saying "screw 'em in the ear" was Duke's, and that the voice urging clean speech was Clint's. I might never know.

I didn't play hearts. A lot of us gathered in our room. We

looked like modern art, immobilized by shock. I poured java and reread *To Kill a Mockingbird*, staying in the room, no longer liking the library, where so much of the interregimental cheating had occurred. I felt as if I should stay near Clint's bunk, out of loyalty. I wanted to read something that had given me joy, but I turned the pages and felt nothing. I saw Clint dancing with Pearl at the last hop. I saw him training Para-Rat to jump from the top bunk, his chute billowing, slapping his forehead as he wrestled with the Bard. Exhausted, I turned in early. When I put my head on the pillow, something crinkled. Inside the pillowcase was a letter.

4 April 1967
Kai

You should not have done this to me. What did I do to deserve this? I laughed at your jokes, never made jokes that hurt your feelings or picked on your nationality. You saved my butt in English. Saved me in Shakespeare and turned me in on Honor. I walked into 720 at 0900 hours to face sword point.

I don't know what's right, or ethical. After this, no one'll ask my opinion. I feel like I've been shot, but I'm still alive and walking around. I never would've turned you in. Not you. Both of us have dads who live through us, who brought us up to come here. See, you didn't kick *me* out of West Point. You got Dad. You told me that story about the Chinese soldiers in an orchard who made the pledges to each other. Didn't the leader die for his buddies? I'm not a hot Christian, any more than you. You think West Point will ever forgive me? The hell it will.

You guys can't even talk about me anymore. Suddenly, I never even existed. Why the hell should I forgive you? I never did anything to you. You were like a brother. It's like you weren't different. I didn't even think of you as Chinese. You talked about your uncle. He wouldn't have done what you did. He was all for relationships. So was I. You do all this bold West Point shit with your Plebes about "taking care of your classmates" and look what you did.

During the Honor boards, I didn't say anything. I tried to maintain, even though I knew they were going to dump me. I feel like I don't have a life anymore. I can't face my dad. Know what's funny? When we started the ring, it was to help guys like you—guys who don't study—and me—who study but don't get it. You should know that Duke really tried at first to like you. He teased you about race and minorities because he didn't think it meant anything to you. I mean, you are weird. You take offense when people make Jew jokes and you're not a Jew. I understand about the black thing, cause you told me, but most guys here don't get it. Duke wanted you to be part of it. He didn't need help in Juice; you did.

What we did was like a Widows and Orphans Society, helping those in need. Juice is just a harassment course. You don't need Juice to lead men in combat. You put it best: it lacks "socially redeeming value—no idealism, no belief, just spec and dump." Why'd you do it? You cashed me in for something you hate. You turned me in for bullshit.

You want to know what's really stupid? Duke tried to bring Pee Wee McCloud in as the smart man. Pee Wee was like you; he never liked Duke, and was very big on the Code. He tried to talk Duke out of it. Once we started the ring, Duke told Pee Wee about it. So Pee Wee knew. He turned himself in for tolerating Duke, and now he's gone. He left this morning. I know you and I were buds, but think of what you've done here. Remember when the three of us stood by Lake Fredericks after that march? And did retreat together after Plebe year? You really got *his* dad, too.

See if you can forgive old Clint *the thief*, your lousy, cheating roommate. I took your dad's gun and Mrs. LaRue's plastic cup and your Tony Barraza's rosary. And I took the little Chinese god. Tell me, do you feel cleaned out?

You can have Para-Rat's chute. I hate heights, like you, and they'll have to shoot me before I go to Jump School. But you'll be a good West Pointer and go when they tell you to. Take the Rat chute with you when you jump. Your roomie,
Clint

I called Pee Wee's company. The CQ told me that Mr. McCloud had been separated from the Corps and had left. No, he said, there were neither forwarding address nor notes for anyone. Again, I crossed over to East Barracks. Pee Wee's bunkies were on bunks, silent and stunned, looking, I imagined, like Deke, Bob, and me.

I got the storage-room keys from the CQ and verified that my service footlocker had been forced open. My father's cherished Colt .38 super automatic and shoulder holster were gone. In its place was the blue shield with the golden helmet of Athena with the sword rampant affixed, a name tag with "Bestier," and the collar and epaulet insignia of a West Point Second Classman.

Major Schwarzhedd and I walked from the mess hall across the Plain to his Q. Each of us carried a block of ice from the kitchen.

"Mr. Bestier's tragedy is not your doing," said the major. "He's blaming you for what he alone could dictate."

"Feels bad, sir. Two of them were Beast roommates. Both of them sons of generals. I keep feeling I did it."

"That's understandable. Hard moral stands demand an extreme price. Consider the alternative. A cheating culture." He shook his head, his mouth turned down. "Intolerable."

"Sir, you ever feel you're split? I mean, with half of you feeling things, and the other half thinking, and they don't fit? My mind says I did the right thing. But inside, it feels wrong."

"The dissonance between heart and mind, thought and impulse. It's the struggle between a leader and a careerist. Did you protect your men by doing what you did?"

I thought of my Plebes. "Yes, sir."

"Listen to your own answer. Think of this—did you enjoy taking down Duke Troth?"

I nodded. It felt good to push Troth around that poker table, knowing that Sonny was going to be avenged. I had enjoyed getting inside Gabriel Fors's guard, slipping punches and reshaping his face. Guilt had made me shake his hand after the fight.

Ironically, it was my recognition of him that made him think I was different from Duke. Recognizing him had allowed him to tell the truth, while hazing had only alienated him from Honor. The whole damn thing worked because I opened my hand instead of keeping it closed. I didn't understand; Gabe Fors had shown up at the Poker Society on his own.

"Harder than you can imagine to win, Kai. We're not supposed to really win. We triumph as part of a team, part of a community, bending sail under good winds for high causes. We try to stop ourselves just short of a great personal win, because the high-profile winners are often selfish people. And we know that, and don't want to be that. We taste blood, master the violence of battle, and like it. Then what?

"Good to worry about winning and gloating. Good to be concerned about enjoying victory—knowing your win is ashes in the mouth to the loser, his home burned, crops destroyed, family exposed to death and economic rapine, children left to wander across a burned earth. All this unspeakable misery, to stop war and to delay the next. God's greatest paradox. Here we train you to kill and educate you to love peace. To love your men, and then send them up a hill to die.

"Look at Trophy Point. Beautiful and barbaric. Battle Monument, for the dead. Made up of melted-down enemy cannon. Trophy Point's salted with cannon, grounded in the earth, muzzles down. Imagine if those were your guns, taking from your dead Redlegs. Wellington was right. The only thing worse than defeat is victory. What would Confucian scholars think of what you did?" he asked.

"*K'e ji fu li,*" I said.

"Ah, yes," he said, as we entered the coolness of the BOQ and unloaded the ice. "Subdue self, honor the rites. Well, Mr. Ting, you honored them well. You deserve a reward. Want a soda?"

35

REQUIEM

Thayer Hall, April 1967

Major Sewell asked us to compare Napoleon's "morale to guns" to the Communist "anti-imperialism to foreign weapons" ratios. I argued that the Chinese Civil War and the Philippine Hukbalahaps proved that nationalism could defeat superior arms. Armed with popular support, the People's Liberation Army defeated my father's better-equipped army. Without popular support, the Huks lost to Magsaysay. Most of the class disagreed, believing that nationalism was but one of many ingredients in the counterinsurgency soup. But I had read Lacoutre, Fall, Truong, and Buttinger. I was right.

The major, an Oxford-educated Rhodes scholar, was moving the discussion to the French war in Indochina. I couldn't wait.

Mrs. Malloy, a department secretary, entered, giving him a note. I felt she was trying to look at me in a consoling fashion.

"Mr. Ting, return to your company for a telephone message."

I entered 4-West wing of the University of California Hospital, carrying my overnight bag and a flower bouquet. I had been classified Military Airlift Priority 1B, medical emergency leave/family, and had been booked on a night-flight C-141 from McGuire AFB in New Jersey to Travis AFB. Now, in San Francisco, I was surrounded by a surly hostility. Few said anything, but many looked at me with dislike. I had gone to West Point to become American, and now in the city of my birth, riding public transportation on the way to the med center, I was the enemy.

"You don't get it, do you?" I asked a guy my age with long hair who was trying to drown me in his glower. "If someone attacked us, you'd expect me to die for you."

He turned his head away from me, laughing, making my words sound silly. He made faces to fellow passengers, who agreed with his sentiment. Once again I was the skinny Chinese kid, drawing ugly laughter. Did they think I invented Hitler, Tojo, Chingis Khan, and Stalin? I got off at Parnassus with my face red with anger. I looked like Guan Yu.

I already missed West Point. Mike was coaching Mr. Spanner in English and math. Mr. Zerl had suffered a knee injury and was despondent about his gridiron future, but had managed to teach Mr. Spanner how to shine shoes. Mr. Parthes had seen a picture of Pearl and had joined the Spanish Club. They all might make it.

"Kai," said my father in the corridor, the use of my name evidence of his distress. He looked tired, deep lines of sleepless worry creasing his cheeks and forehead, deepening the sockets of his eyes. My father looked old. We shook hands, but he could not look at me. She had to be very sick. I put down my bag and the flowers. After twelve hours of transportation, I was where I was supposed to be, but I didn't want to go in.

Megan Wai-la, my sister, stepped out from the room, crying softly. "Oh, Little brother!" She threw her arms around me.

It felt great to hold her, and I could've stayed there a long time, enjoying the closeness, but she broke our grip first.

"You're so big!" she whispered. She wanted to smile but was unable to hide her dismay at the sight of my uniform.

"There's nothing wrong with wearing this uniform," I said.

My father was proud of my comment. But I had compounded old wounds in the family, pulling scabs from my sister's psyche, to no one's benefit. It delayed me from seeing Edna. Again, I was seven years old, afraid to enter my stepmother's room.

"I'm sorry," I said to Megan. "You look good."

"Oh, it's okay, you monster," she said, in her fine English accent. "I have no right to judge you; you're my brother. Hurry. She's waiting."

Edna lay in a room with two beds, one empty. She had the window view. A plastic white curtain was partially drawn, and she lay so still I feared she was dead. A television faced her, and muted, meaningless sounds came from a small gray portable speaker by her pillow. He hair was white, her pale skin blanched, her body thin and seemingly without muscle. A tube ran from her nose, and she had an IV in her arm with a bag of clear fluid suspended on a rack above her.

Dad had not been able to tell me what had felled her. All he could do was choke out the words "Edna in the hospital, bad."

I knew it was a stroke—a real one.

"You're not serious," Janie had said.

"This could be a chance to patch things up," I said.

"It's not my job," she said. "It's up to her."

"Look. I don't want to go, but I have to."

"I do not have to," she said. "Nor do you."

"Don't you feel anything? A duty? She's *chimu,* whether we hate her or not. You'd be going to respect her, her status, not her record as a parent."

"*Gahng* and *lun*?" she asked.

"Yes—*gahng* and *lun*."

"I have no *gahng*. I'm the ghost. I feel nothing for her."

"But—you suggested we get rid of her. Now God's doing it for you. I just think it's a good idea to make peace."

She sighed, long and deep. "I'll never have peace because of that woman, dead or alive. What she did was so wrong, so hateful."

She was asleep. I stepped closer. I hadn't washed. I placed the bouquet on the bed, went to the bathroom sink.

"Hello, Kai," she said quietly.

"Hi, Edna. How are you doing?" I said, drying my hands.

Outside, below on the street, a siren wailed, a car honked its horn, and some young man began shouting his anger.

"Fine," she said.

"You look rested," I said.

The Honor Code forbade even social lying. West Point had always striven to be as strict as she, and usually failed. I had been proud of the Honor Code. Lately, it had been making me sad.

"You look wonderful," she said. "Handsome. So presentable."

She had always thought me ugly, but she loved uniforms.

"What happened?" I asked.

"Senile diabetes. It's affected my eating and functions of other parts of my body. Can't eat. Now, my heart."

She tried to wave her hand. She breathed slowly, once, twice. "The truly terrible, terrible thing—things—are the needles. I *hate* them," she said, frowning, her voice weaker with every word, sighing softly from the exertion. It was like watching water shut off from a tap.

"How soon before you get out of here?" I asked.

She raised her eyelids to see me. I moved a chair to her bedside so she could look at me more easily.

"What uniform is that?" she asked.

"Khakis," I said.

"I'm not leaving here." A sigh. "I'm dying."

"Oh, I'm sure that's not true—you're exaggerating."

"I am *not*," she said, with weakened vehemence. "I really do think you gave me a stroke," she said.

I was ready. I sucked in air. "I'm very sorry. Very sorry."

"It's all right," she said, reaching for me, and I held her hand in mine. I looked at it, the way I would look at the paw of an unknown beast. I didn't enjoy the touch, and I felt guilty.

"Strong hand. Just like your father's," she said. "You were always a good boy," she said.

Jesus, don't say that. After all these years of my being the worst thing in your life, you're going to say that? Strength waned in her frail fingers. I had been a bad boy, the worst. I had hated my life. I had hated her. It was my secret identity.

"I should get Dad," I said, taking my hand back.

"No." She moved her lips soundlessly, licking them, resting, getting ready to speak. "Purse," she said.

Her purse lay on the bedside table. It was new and had replaced the old navy blue one she had carried for many years. "It's not a very *handsome* purse," she had said. "But it has exactly the right number of compartments, *exactly* the right amount of space, and the correct *feel* to hang on my arm as I go downtown, and it matches most of my clothes." She used to talk to me like that when she was cheery. I think my father was always enchanted by her free use of emphasis, her explosion of exclamation points. They both spoke with an innate sense of drama, of pressured thought.

I stood and took the purse.

"Open," she said.

Inside was a large envelope that was labeled "Kai Ting." I remembered Janie Ming-li's envelope, as she sat at our dinner table, a lifetime ago, in the twilight of our Chinese family. Did this hold my fate? What would Edna give me?

"Open," she said faintly. "Rest," she murmured, her arm falling off the bed. I put it back on the bedsheets, her fingers flat and unresponsive. I looked at her, so weak and helpless, her chest barely rising and falling as she laboriously drew breath.

She had been the living, sleeping, hounding terror of my life. Her voice kept me in childhood, ever vulnerable, always fearful, always wrong, and stupid, unworthy, hateful, and ugly. She had cuffed me for breathing, cursed me for not ending my asthma, evicted my sister, killed our cat, taken everything from me I valued, made me regret being a male, a Chinese, a person who had a friend. She had never apologized for anything.

In the envelope was a photograph that had been folded in half, with a note.

Dear Kai,

This picture is of your first mother. You could not successfully become an American while this common, uneducated peasant woman held you back with her oodles of superstitions, her gods in the doorbell, trees, and kitchen and the ghosts of ancestors floating down the hall. She wanted to train you to honor dead people in China and to put *actual* food at *altars* to dead people, and to never use your body. To be like a museum piece—just a brain! Honestly! She had a cockeyed view of Christianity. How could a foreign woman be expected to grasp the fine rules and strict laws of an unworkable faith. She thought you could do *anything* and then be forgiven by God! I hardly think so! There in truth is no God, but there is a Hell, and Judgment Day, as certainly as there is evil in the world and cruel people in it.

I truly hated this woman for what she had done to you, keeping you inside the apartment and away from life! Americans cannot live like this! Americans are robust and outdoorsy! I tried to burn this picture, but it would not burn, and for some unknown reason I never threw it away. You are 20 years old now, and mature enough, in my judgement, to have this picture, to do with as you wish.

I don't know why my discipline of you angered you so. Boys have terrible, physical impulses, and it takes a strong will to redirect them. Your sullenness truly broke my heart. I tried to reach you, but your heart is made of stone. Now, I realize, you will probably never marry or be happy. It is not my fault. You are not handsome, and you would have needed all my assistance to compensate for your shortcomings.

I think I will give this to you as a birthday present. When you speak wonderful textbook English, or look at your big shoulders, every time you date a beautiful American girl or read fine literature, whether it's *Ben-Hur* or *Great Expectations,* and whenever you write English, you should think of me, and thank me, and harbor no ill thoughts.

I love you, Kai.
Your mother, Edna

I pulled out the photo and unfolded it. One corner had been charred. It was the picture my sister Megan had given me in Angie's cafe at the Y, on the eve of my fight with Big Willie Mack. After sleeping with the framed photo under my pillow, I had surrendered it when I was eight, on my handshake deal with Edna that had made her my real mother, and had given me a life without her physical punishment, opening the door for psychic abuse. I had given the picture to Janie. Edna had taken it from her.

My Chinese mother looked at me from the old black-and-white photograph. Her large, observing, serene eyes seemed bright. A rosebud mouth was composed so it could, in an instant, smile or laugh. Jet-black hair, parted in the middle, brushed to sweep along the contour of her head. A sculpted face with gentle cheekbones, dark eyebrows, and a round, pretty chin. She wore a light, high-collared Mandarin dress and a large flower in her hair just above her neck. She was beau-

tiful. This was my mother. My Mah-mee. I found in her lovely
face no similarity to me. I used to dream of her.

The photograph had been folded horizontally, and the crease
caused tiny fissures in the photo's dried emulsion.

You do not honor your mother, or speak to her, Uncle Shim
had said. You do not remember her or know her face.

Now I remembered her features. I had a clear, shining image
of my mother, lying in her hospital bed, smiling at me with her
large, luminescent eyes, communicating with me with her face,
without words. She was trying to tell me something, something
important, and I was little, I was six years old and I couldn't
get it. I smelled something horrible. Ether. It smelled like *sze*,
death.

She was my *mu-ch'in*, my mother, Mah-mee, and she would
never tire, never leave me. She was brave and resourceful and
loyal. Everyone said so. Mah-mee kept smiling, nodding,
encouraging, sending, communicating, radiating feelings,
thoughts, assurances.

I love you, my only son, I always will, her eyes had said.

Hands pulled me away from her, down long corridors, and
my eyes couldn't hold her, and through a terrible, horrible
maze of halls and doors and stairs, each step, each turn, each
floor, and every door separating me from her, making me dizzy
as I tried to memorize the patterns on the floor so I could go
back to her, and someone was telling me *"Vyoh puh,"* don't be
afraid, that she would be all right, and I would be all right.
"Kwahla, kwahla!" Hurry, hurry! But we were going the
wrong way and by then I had no idea where Mah-mee was, or
how I could find her again.

I started to cry, and I felt so counterfeit, so bogus, crying for
my Mah-mee when I should be crying for Edna. This true,
honest, clear image of my mother, my only image, shimmered
like a desert mirage and folded into the photo in my hands. I
lowered my forehead and touched it to the picture, bowing to
her, and to the mother behind her, who lay in her deathbed.

I had passed on the picture to Janie through the deal with
Edna, knowing that Janie would guard it as fiercely as I had.
I did not know that Edna was about to erase Janie from our
family tree, void the home of the memory, of the photographs,
of the spoken name, of recollection of the existence of the two
Chinese females who had been, in rapid succession, my mothers.

I sat there for a moment, looking at the photo of Mah-mee,

and then at Edna, and back again, in a form of filial visual rebounding that did not become simpler through repetition. I could not fit them together. I thought of Dad, who had married both of them. Dad, who would tell me nothing, leaving everything to feeble guesswork, to edited, polemic retellings, to vast and dark ignorance.

Edna had hated my Chinese mother and loathed her memory, fearing her more as a ghost than as a woman with a life now ended. My mother from China had died, and now, joining her, was my American mother. Edna had set aside her hatred. Momma LaRue would have said that Edna was trying to make peace with her maker.

"Thank you," I whispered.

"You . . . good . . . boy," Edna murmured. "Don' cry," she said. She sounded like Momma LaRue. She was fading. I stood and found Dad and Megan at the end of the hall. They returned. Dad held Megan's hand. I stood back, adjusting the details of my uniform, doing the familiar, again and again.

I imagined my father putting his arm around Megan when she was fourteen, when they had met for a moment near the end of the Run, the *boh-la*, from Shanghai to Chungking to America. Born in China, raised in China, fled from China. For all their vast differences and their accumulated disappointments, they were connected in ways I could never emulate. They were true Chinese, not *jook sing* like me, and had seen war without end. I was American, and had fought all my battles within my family, both here and at West Point.

Edna was speaking to Dad, and Dad to her, and Megan tried to separate herself, but Dad needed her, needed her arm, and she stayed, weeping. Megan's tears accentuated their absence in me. My father and my American mother said farewell to each other. They had been married fourteen years and should have had many more.

"Sorry . . . for Silly Dilly," Edna said.

"It's okay," I said, surprised by my words. I think she wanted me to say that she had been good for me. I don't think she wanted me to cry for her, although I would never know. I felt a Buddhist nothingness that paradoxically had clear borders, as if part of me had been excoriated not by fire, but by a surgeon's knife. I looked at my father and felt sadness, and loss, and frustration. I admired Megan's spirit, even the part that opposed me. I had so many confused feelings about Janie. I grieved for the Honor crisis, for Tony Barraza searching for his lost boy, for Clint, for Pee Wee, for Pearl's dilemma with her father. I felt sorry for Silly Dilly.

Edna—nothing.

I had hated this woman, and now she was dying. I had caused it. I caused people to die, to bleed, and I felt nothing.

Megan sobbed when she saw the photo of our mother, who had been unaccountably cruel to her. Megan's sadness opened like the gates of heaven, and she wept louder for so many hurts, so long endured. I heard my father crying, a sound utterly new to me.

I clung to my emotional immobility, again noting that even within my own family, I was a minority who could never fit in. When others were stern, I laughed like a madman. When others wept, I felt nothing. My father and Edna would have preferred a different child than me. I realized that I was supposed to have been a nonasthmatic, perfectly visioned, physically beautiful, mathematically endowed Caucasian girl, and not who I was.

My father wept.

"I'll miss you, darling," she said to my father.

36

BELONGING

West Point, May 1967

West Point's Class of 1835 began the American tradition of graduation rings. Ours displayed the high and sharply spread wings of an American eagle, fiercely crouching on the centerpiece "68." Under the numerals appeared a bold "USMA" and the hilts of Academy cavalry sabers. On the opposite side was the Academy crest with a scrolling bilateral streamer reading, "Duty, Honor, Country, West Point, 1802, USMA." Graduates wear the Academy crest inward, emblematic of the school's closeness to the heart.

The L. G. Balfour Company held the Class Ring Expo in

the Post Gym. We made our selections of gold, stone, and in-
scriptions. Most of us picked gold rings. Pearl suggested I
choose white gold. "See," she said, "it goes better with your
skin."

"My father loved his American Infantry ring more than anything else. Look how big it is! A 'crass mass of brass and
glass.' "

The ring symbolized our camaraderie, the bonds and the
brotherhood of West Point, forged by common effort against
uncommon challenges. It was more symbolic of the effort, and
the comradeship, than any building or monument on post, or
any speech, tactics formula, or epithet created or remembered
in its halls. "It's like the whole thing's inside the stone. All the
lifelong friendships are smelted into the gold. A stamp of ap-
proval from the Academy, from your classmates. From all
West Pointers."

"You think this ring will make you American," said Pearl.

I nodded. I filled out the form. I entered the letters "D.L."
for Dai-li, Mah-mee's initials, for the inside. The eagle of my
country, the gold of Honor, the weight of duty, were in its pa-
tent features. But there was more—it emulated my father's
ring. The black onyx saluted the other part of my heritage, and
the gold was chosen by Pearl. The ring would be the unified
icon of my life.

"What do you think?" asked Bill Ericson, who headed up
the Ring and Crest Committee. He was a ramrod-straight Airborne poop schooler with chiseled features. We were looking
at the mock-up.

"It's beautiful," I said.

"Pardon me?" he asked.

"Congratulations, and thanks. You guys did a beautiful job."

Pearl beamed at me. She always liked me when I was emotional.

Deke wanted to play tennis on the river courts, Arch was putting together a touch football game on the practice field, and
Bob was looking to play basketball. I wanted to do it all. It
was a spectacularly sunny spring Saturday afternoon with no
duties; a fine cool breeze blew in through the windows while
the radio played. Sonny was leaning on me to study Juice.

Harper's Bizarre was singing "The 59th Street Bridge Song
(Feelin' Groovy)": "Slow down / You move too fast / You got
to let the morning last. . . ."

"Kai—you gonna play or not?" asked Arch.

"He's not," said Sonny. "Don't ever ask 'im again. He doesn't play *any* games—no hearts, no hoops, no hallway touch, *nothin'*—until he gets past the Juice whufer."

"Good point," said Bob. "You and good times, Kai, just got a divorce." There was a low, indecipherable mumble of common assent.

"Great," I said.

"That sounded insincere," said Mike.

Sonny hung large sections of butcher paper on the walls of my room. They were filled with multicolored Juice problems. "Remember the OMI lesson—that we retain seventy percent more from visuals than through our ears. Here's your visuals."

Mike kept looking at me while I looked at the equations. Black for the problem, red for the derivation, and blue for the solution. I studied the derivations flowing from the problems.

It was nonsense. Satanic scribblings from the ancient Chia dynasty of China. Bone scrawls, cave etchings, blue-dyed tattoos of dead deities left in memory of extinct civilizations, offering explanations to the smiles of sphinxes and the rising of phoenixes.

Sonny looked at me and scratched his healed leg, scrunched his face. "Kai," he said. "Am I a bad tutor?"

"God, no, Sonny. You're the best. I just got sawdust for brains. I'm the scarecrow in *The Wizard of Oz*. There's only so far you can take me before all the stuffing falls out."

He got up, looking at me and Mike, seated at the desks, the room empty now except for the three of us. A gaggle of guys wrestled in the hallway; distant chatter from the Great American Public on Thayer Road crept through the window; and, with the approach of June, some of my Plebes were singing the lyrics to Broadway show tunes at the tops of their lungs for the pleasure of the upper classes. It was mostly quiet.

"Over here," said Sonny, pointing to his right, "is heaven, a month away, as a Firstie with the Good Deal First Class Trip around the U.S., no more hard engineering. Ya get *two* electives an' the best military art, strategy, and tactics courses in the Academy. Stuff ya came here for. You'll get ta write the script for One Hundredth Night an' you'll be a platoon leader, at least. We get rings in two stinkin' months. Turn in our lousy rifles an' pom-poms an' get sabers an' plumes. Unlimited weekends in New York with Pearl—no more stinkin' movies in the gym. The Corvette or T-Bird or whatever ya want. We cheer as the best Army team since Dawkins rolls over the competition. Kai," he said, taking a big breath, "you'll be with your classmates."

"Sounds good," said Mike. "Too bad it's not a real college."

"Over here," said Sonny in a low voice, pointing to his left, "is the nadir in bullshit humiliation and personal defeat."

"Uh, I pick the other side," I said.

"This," he said, "is sayin' hi ta your old man cuz ya got found. *He* doesn't care that ya flunked only one course, or that you're good in other subjects. He just knows ya let him down. Same for your civilian friends—the ones who aren't Communists. In California, that's probably about two people.

"Anyway," he said, cocking his head to the door. "That's Vietnam as an NCO, no control over what kinda platoon leader ya get. That's goin' over without us, which may not be a Good Deal. And if ya get killed over there, you can't even get buried in the cemetery with Custer and Fideli. Bad Deal. Nothingburger. No degree, ring. No class reunions so ya can tell the new Corps they've gone to hell. No chance for ya to come back as faculty and use your lawyer talk to get 'em to make Juice an elective. This," he said, "is giving up the three hardest years in your life, without the *payoff,* the *fun,* the *easy* year. Ya get this? This makin' sense?"

"I get it. I'm a jerk. You've given me a lot of your time."

"Good," he said. "Better'n feelin' *stupid,* and a lot better'n feelin' *kicked out.*"

"Yes, Sonny," said Mike. "If you weren't helping Kai, you could sleep sixteen hours during the day and still get eight hours of rack at night." It was a joke; Sonny tutored everyone.

"You wanta take a break? Come back to this later?"

I nodded. "I need to run," I said.

Running in tennis shoes and shorts was a basic Academy tradition. I was surprised to learn during my summer leaves that this was not true at Cal, or Stanford, or Yale. Pearl thought I was crazy, running voluntarily while no one was chasing me. West Point was a beautiful place to run, and I took the course around the chapels and the cemetery so I could end up at Trophy Point. The view was a reward.

Random thoughts cruised through my consciousness while I ran. I thought of Pearl, how she had established through our dates at the Academy a regular routine of kissing, knowing that much more was at stake; she was still seeking a husband.

Battle Monument was remarkably empty of sightseers. I

stretched, then sat on the pedestal of the huge granite column and huffed.

This was my school. I belonged here. I had friends almost beyond count: hundreds and hundreds—battalions—of talented and idealistic young men who would smile at the sight of my Chinese features. I loved to run all over the Academy, visiting and talking with friends about anything but math. In a hundred conversations I had learned about the fifty states and explored authors and films. In thousands of talks we had fought and designed and won the war in Vietnam, imagined terrible death and hoped for enduring survival.

This was the most remarkable institution in the world, and I was in the heart of it. I was even admired by some, and could count among my acquaintances some of the outstanding members of my class and of West Point's faculty. I had been in the company of some of the best teachers in the world.

This was the Hanlin, with its bright yellow pennons, imposing stone walls, and ancient traditions, all so steady and strong for the good of all. And I was one of its members.

"I might be a surgeon, but I'm thinking about psychiatry." Michael Warren Benjamin, number-six man in the class, was next to me in his running gear. He smiled his Clark Gable grin, ending my rather stunning analysis of the world at hand.

"My best friend wanted to be a doctor," I said. Toos, where are you? "Psychiatry?" I asked.

"Frontier of the mind," he said. "Motivation, pleasure, anger, hope." He laughed, fully, slapping his knee. "It's great! *Nothing* more exciting. Surgery's macho." We had done macho.

"I like psychology," I said. "Say 'conditioned response' and I say 'Pavlov.' Actually, I can't wait for you to have me lie on a couch and tell me about my injured childhood." Pearl had said, "Chinese people in America need a lot of help."

"You gave me that copy of Sun Tzu's *The Art of War*. He says that figuring out yourself and what the other guy is going to do is the essence of the military art. And that," Mike said triumphantly, "is psychology. Right now, I'm trying to figure out why you can't study. Why you're blocked in Juice."

I looked down. "I'm just not that smart," I said.

"You always hate math?" he asked.

I nodded. Then, a jolt. "No, wait," I said, with the unique urgency of the Honor-bound cadet. "I think I liked it until I was, I don't know—ten? Eleven? Young. Long time ago."

"What happened then?" he asked.

I saw the Cadet Chapel, its geometry. "My dad tutored me."

"That didn't help?"

"He got real pissed when I didn't do it right."

Mike smiled, nodding. "Yeah, I know that one."

"It was real important that I get it right. Your dad do that to you?"

"Until I got smart," he said.

"Well, I never got smart."

"But you liked math until he tutored you?"

I gazed at the river. "Never told anyone this before." I looked down at my hands, rubbing against each other. No sparks came out; no answers were writ in the sky. "I sort of went crazy. I was hard to teach. Stupid. It drove my dad sort of nuts. The funny thing is, *I* went crazy."

"What do you mean, 'crazy'?" he asked.

"Crazy. Abnormal, insane, nuts, crazy. Psychotic, or something. Worse than neurotic. I had laughing fits. I couldn't stop laughing." My words floated over the river, toward watching gods.

I had always known the insanity god had more to do with mathematics than was commonly understood.

My father presented bewildering geometry and trig problems. He looked at me the way cynics study palm readers, suspecting the absence of competence. I would look at these carefully drawn figures, knowing that they were one part graphite and two parts blood from his brain. These were very important sheets, very important diagrams. To me, they were gobbling gibberish, what Toos called rank jive.

My father would describe the problems with his unique English, and I would reply in my personal mutation of the language, neither of us understanding the other, neither willing to express truth. The truth was he feared that I was endemically stupid, while my truth was I could do little but fear him.

I was blind with it. I was the classic citizen of China, listening to the emperor, who echoed, "*Lin tsun*, tremblingly obey." I had mastered the trembling part.

My math never met his expectations. The hurt, frustration, and even fear that flowed from my math errors stoked angers in him that could melt coke and iron in the forges of hell. They made me weep at the sight of his face.

The worse I was with his problem sets, the angrier he became.

"Study math now," he said in his deep voice, and my heart would sink into the nether regions of my body, never sure when it was safe to return. We walked down the dark hall to the kitchen. I would not have been surprised to find a guillotine installed atop the old table. Here, my brain and my soul had been examined, again and again, and been found wanting.

"You are born with your character," said Edna. "Boys cannot change. Girls can, and do."

Uncle Shim agreed. "She is most wise for a foreign person. It is true. You are born with your gifts. You cannot order more talents from Heaven." My lack of talents caused madness.

The passing of my mind was witnesssed by the isosceles triangle and cosine function questions that marched across my father's fragile graph papers. Until this night, I had not known of the existence of the insanity god. He arrived at our kitchen table at my moment of greatest need. I did not understand the trig problem and was in the midst of the solution, making sucking noises with my mouth while wildly guessing at a host of unlikely answers. I was ten and had been angering my father for three years, coinciding roughly with my resistance to his second wife. I feared I would not see eleven.

In the midst of abject fear, something made me look up, into the light fixture that hung from the ceiling. It was very bright, and from it came a small and playful spirit that moved inside my stomach and forced from me a silly laugh.

A son, laughing at his father. During a test. Me, dumbest Chinese kid in the world, laughing at my father. The sound of it stopped my father's hand. Again, the spirit forced out a laugh, heartier, fuller, more spirited than the first. It was neither mocking nor triumphant, but ludicrous, jumping with primitive hilarity, possessed of cosmic power and acting without fear. I laughed with the force of guffawing village clowns braying in tearful exuberance. I laughed from stomach, mouth, brain, and heart, from pancreas and thorax. I was a herd of hee-hawing elephants, crying until sheets of tears ran down my face and stained my shirt and my pants, leaving big salty drops on the delicate graph paper with their foreign symbols.

I saw my father staring at me in surprise, horror, and fear.

"Stop!" he cried. "STOP NOW!"

I couldn't. Father no longer owned me; the insanity god had taken possession of my simple mind. Uncle Shim would say I could no more stop the laughter than a man could embrace smoke.

This did not stop the tutoring, but my father sat one chair farther away from me at the table, and no longer lost his temper physically in the face of my continuing mathematical stupidities.

There was no joy in escaping the bad temper I caused in my father. But I was powerless to beckon or dismiss this immature little spirit that knew nothing of my great rock, the heavy duty, the *shiao*, I bore to my father and all that he was. When I laughed without joy, the rock rolled away from me, and I watched my fate darken with a heart that struggled to beat.

I tried once to say it was okay that he had tried to form from me the intellectually heroic structure of a math prodigy, but I lacked the courage, and could not find words—only the riff of stumbling speech. When I turned thirteen and began to grow, the tutoring stopped. I had mixed feelings. Hard as tutoring was, it was what we did together.

Through his furies and losses and sadness, he was not venting his life's disappointments on me. I was, however, one of them.

"Mike, my dad discovered I was really an idiot. When *I* found out, I think I went nuts, by laughing." I blew out air. "I don't want to talk about it anymore."

"Cold Max," said Mike. Leigh "Cold Max" McSon.

"What about him?"

"I could've beaten him. He went on to win Brigade, but I pinned him in Yearling year." Mike's knee was pumping.

"I remember that." I was glad Mike was talking to the left and to the right, and not on that other topic. Cold Max and I had been roommates as Yearlings. "Mike, Cold Max was so angry, he spat. He talked like Donald Duck for weeks. You know—'Holy smokes, how'd that turkey beat me?'" I said, in my best Donald Duck imitation.

Mike laughed. "Kai, I had him in the last match."

I remembered. Mike was up, 10–1. He could only lose by being pinned, which hadn't happened once at the Academy— and Cold Max pinned Mike with fifteen seconds left. Mike was out of the Brigade finals. I had cheered for both of them, wanting both to win and neither to lose.

"Bad luck," I said.

Mike shook his head. "Don't believe in bad luck anymore.

We have inner motivations—hidden op orders—that uncon-
sciously dictate what we do. Omens are road signs that give us
clues about the motivations. Like, when you sit down with
your Juice assignments," said Mike, "do you see your father in
front of you?"

Back to that. "Do you?" he said.

I shook my head and looked down at my tennis shoes.

"I can't believe you're not aware of him. This whole place
is filled with sons of ambitious fathers. We're all platforms for
their hopes, their ambitions. West Point is a father's totem."

"I don't see him in front of me, Mike." I let out a lot of air.
"He's above me. And he's behind me. That's where Chinese
fathers stand. In our pasts, guiding the future."

"Just before Cold Max took me down," Mike said, "I
thought of Dad. How pissed he'd be if I got pinned when I
was up so many points." He licked his lips, sprang up, and
paced.

"Here's the hard part. See, we're supposed to be number
one, beat the hell out of everyone. Smartest, toughest, fastest.
Dads teach that. West Point gives you letters, stars, and patches
for being the best, for beating everyone, for developing the
habits of victory."

I nodded. 'Upon the fields of friendly strife are sown the
seeds that upon other fields, on other days, will bear the fruits
of victory.' It was a MacArthurism.

"But Kai, fathers are—they're like gods. You can't,
shouldn't beat them. Best them. Be the best, but don't beat
Dad."

"That doesn't make any sense," I said.

"It makes sense if you're doing something your dad couldn't
do. My dad was a great runner. Lousy wrestler."

"But my dad's an engineer. Good at math," I said.

"But he was an immigrant, like my grampa. Your dad
couldn't come here. This was the unattainable dream for
them."

I didn't like the argument. "Naw," I said.

"I don't know, Kai. Dad's still as big in my mind as West
Point. I keep getting them mixed up."

I looked at the chapel, the hard hills, the granite buildings.
They stood above us. They were so huge, so inescapable, casting long shadows, so damnably old, reaching back, behind us.
The Hanlin, older than time; Himalayan peaks, embracing
clouds.

"West Point's the biggest freaking father in the world," he said. "I hate to lose. I mean, I *hate* to lose," he growled. "But I lost that match—the most important in my life—when I had it won. Just before Cold Max hit me, I had a feeling I shouldn't win."

"Okay. So you had a random thought that distracted you. That's all that was. Bad luck."

He shook his head. "Look at you. You love West Point more than the rational mind should permit. You *love* it. I don't. You do. You're a permanent corporal and the darling of the tac. You got friends in all the regiments and departments—even in *Juice*. Maher wants to adopt you. You're popular. Friends with Schwarzhedd. Everyone's buddy and good to Plebes, the only squad leader who's prepared his boys for Buckner. You joke all the time, never down, always cheering up the ones who *are* down. People love that. You never complain, except about Juice. You'd be perfect if you didn't eat off of other people's plates."

I smiled, but Mike was intently serious. "You're crazy about West Point. And you might flunk out. And you're in this wrestling match with your dad, over math."

Major Schwarzhedd asked me to meet him in the West Point Room on the fourth floor of the USMA Library on a Saturday afternoon.

He smiled and sat in a gray chair, a gift from an earlier class. "What do you think of these Immortals?" he asked, pointing to the portraits of Edgar Allen Poe and James Abbott McNeill Whistler.

"I guess they weren't meant to be Grads, sir," I said.

"Do you think you are?" he asked.

"I don't know, sir," I said.

Major Schwarzhedd stood, his size casting shadows from the bright portrait spotlights onto the dark-wood table. "You belong here. You love what the Academy stands for. Idealism. Service. Honor. You're not one of them," he said, waving at Poe and Whistler.

"Not entirely bad company, sir," I said.

"No question about their talent, but Poe was troubled."

I nodded. Cadet Poe had trooped out with the Corps for a Saturday parade and had marched off stark naked, without any of his clothes, which he left hanging like a scarecrow's costume, on his rifle, bayoneted into the Plain.

"Both he and Whistler were answering other calls. They weren't soldiers. They didn't leave here to wear the uniform without lieutenant's bars." I thought of Marco Matteo Fideli's gold bar in my valuables box. "You're a soldier, Kai. You care about your people. If they got hurt, you'd wear the scar.

"Use your talent. Remember Napoleon at Austerlitz, and Norm Cota on Omaha Beach, Dowding during the Battle of Britain, Chamberlain at Gettysburg. They almost lost, but when the skies were darkest, they rallied to win the day. They never lost faith."

He leaned on the chair, his shoulders swelling. "Make sure you do the same." He smiled, his face animated, brightening the whole room. "Why do you think I've spent time with you this year?" Marco Fideli had asked me that question. Marco had picked me out because I frowned.

"Sir, you were badly oversupplied in hot dogs and popcorn, and needed someone to help reduce inventory."

"We all face our special lessons. There's a little bit of you in all of us. Wanting to be special, also wanting to be just like everyone else. Being good at some things, bad at others. You are unnaturally poor in math, but have a good grasp of history." He smiled. "I love history. All our lessons are in it.

"Your father really wanted you here, didn't he?" he asked.

"Oh, yes, sir."

"My father never dictated my future," he said. "I had two noble professions to consider—the ministry, which is what my grandfather followed, or the military, my father's calling. Both require leadership. The military art, though, spoke to my soul."

He stood by the window, his hands joined behind his back. "I wanted to be a general of a great army, filled with all the men of the earth, facing an implacable foe of ultimate and un-reasoning evil in a noble war. It would be the dedication and belief of our troops against the hate and acquisitive greed of the enemy, and it would be my military art, that I learned here, at West Point, against the enemy general. We would have to win, and I would have a chance to serve truly.

"I would feint him, confuse him with rages of doubts and bouts of confidence, and envelop him. It would be the second of August, 216 years before Christ, again, at Cannae on the Aufidus River, ten miles inland from the Adriatic, and he would be destroyed, utterly."

I knew Cannae. Hannibal's masterful, unmatched battle of total annihilation in which his polyglot, multiethnic army outmaneuvered the massive, better-trained Roman legions of Paulus and Varro. Cannae changed warfare for two millennia by placing maneuver and tactics above mechanical discipline and redundant drill.

He sighed. "But the age of the great campaigns is past. If we fight one of those huge, sprawling wars, it'll be the end of us all." He shrugged his big shoulders. "Wanting to be a Great Captain, I'm an Infantry officer in an era of brush and guerrilla wars, wars of national liberation where remarkable patriots fight on both sides. It's unfamiliar terrain. Our country's fighting itself, burning its own cities and debating the war while the government commits the troops, one by one. It's the best of times, and the worst of times, to be an American infantryman."

"My father's biggest nightmare," I said. "An army not supported by the people." The fate of his army in China.

"Your father's nightmare," he said, "is you flunking out of West Point." He stood up. "You're ordered to take and to pass it. We do the best we can." He put his hand out. "Do your best. That's all that's ever asked of anyone. You have the brains to make it, to be a damned good West Point graduate, someone everyone will be proud of. You're a good squad leader. You take care of your people. I am also convinced, if you have to see the elephant, the one in Vietnam, before your classmates do, that you will acquit yourself admirably.

"Your Honor is not at stake. It's yours, clean and pristine, polished, in fact, beyond the shine of your average West Pointer. So keep your eyes on the objective, and go get 'em."

37

DREAMS

West Point, May 1967

We entered whufer country as the delirium of June Week approached. Sonny was encouraged as he built small engineering learning blocks and tried to squeeze them into my little brain.

Some stayed, but when analog computers crept in one ear, transistor amplifiers fell out the other. Power-supply circuits replaced tuned circuits on the creaking, short-cycled conveyer belt of my brain.

"Sonny," I said, "too much. Let's gamble on the likeliest exam areas and bulk up on them. Like analogs and digital circuits."

He shook his head. "Rather do principles. Risky to spec Juice. Spec an' you're playin' Russian roulette with three or four rounds in the cylinder."

I remembered the eerie quiet of the pistol range. "I can't hold it all. Solids, fluids, thermo, nuke physics. Too much."

Mike talked to me about honoring our fathers' expectations. Both of us were extensions of our fathers' ambitions, toting unbearable rocks. "Hey, it's as simple as the inclined plane," he said. "Do what you're told until you do what he wants, or until you go insane." Mike was more Chinese than I, and had a better brain.

English, social sciences, military psychology and leadership, tactics, revolutionary warfare, Spanish, and economics were breezes. I squeaked by nuclear physics, did all right in fluids and thermodynamics, and finished strongly in solids.

Chinese legend had it that successful candidates for the imperial civil service examinations made sacrifices to the watching god of scholarship. Guan Yu could bring success in any enterprise, but Wen-ch'ang, K'uei-hsing and Chu-i were the exams gods. I got oranges from the mess hall, but had no incense. On a starry Saturday night, when I felt a double ache from missing Pearl, I walked up to Fort Putnam, where Kosciuszko used to watch for the British fleet, and left the oranges on the hill as I watched the Big Dipper, the Chinese Stars of Literacy Arc.

According to lore, any cadet who appears at exactly midnight before John Sedgwick's statue, north of the Plain, in full dress under arms, and turns the rowels of Sedgwick's spurs, will obtain a passing grade. I did not think I was that superstitious.

I did not plan to rack early that night. I was going to review my sheets of multicolored equations and diagrams like Schliemann searching for the keys to Troy. At 2347 hours, thirteen minutes before midnight, I found myself desperately throwing on my white trousers, FD, crossbelts, breastplate, waistplate, bayonet, and tar bucket, and unracking my rifle. I was moving with the inner panic of a new cadet in a clothing formation.

I unmarked my absence card, left the room, stopped, and ran back. I grabbed matches and Clint's Cow collar brass, the metallic, light blue shield with the helmet of Athena, and ran down the hall, out of the building, behind Central Area to avoid the Guard Room, across the Plain, to John Sedgwick.

Panting, I came to attention, turned his spurs, and looked at my watch. It was 0002 hours. "Damn!" I was two minutes late.

I covered my bets. I dug a hole at the base of his statue, inserted the brass into it, and covered it. I lit the matchbook and held it to the heavens. "Wen-ch'ang," I whispered, awed by the contrast in shadows and light that flickered across Sedgwick's stolid form from the flaming matchbook. "You wouldn't want a Chinese guy to flunk out of West Point in *math*, would you?" I asked. "Where's your pride?"

I looked for a shooting star, a good omen. There was none. I shuddered in the cold night air. I imagined that it was Chu-i, the funny little god who occasionally dispensed good luck to the unworthy, unprepared student, who looked down at me. Wen-ch'ang was occupied with guarding the fortunes of the starmen and the hives.

The heat burned. Sedgwick was a dark shadow again. His statue had been formed from melted cannons captured by his VI Corps in the Battle of the Wilderness. I felt no scholastic warmth emanating from this figure cast from the fires of hell. A sniper had killed him, at the height of his popularity, at the very edge of victory. "They couldn't hit an elephant at this dist—" were "Uncle John" Sedgwick's last words, while studying enemy lines at Spotsylvania, one hundred and three years ago almost to the day.

In the remains of that night, I dreamed of Leo Washington, who called me names as he died of gut pain. I awoke at 0400. I sat at my desk and gazed at Pearl's photograph. She wore a dark turtleneck and looked directly into the camera with large, shining eyes full of confidence. I imagined her taking my Juice whufer. I imagined being alone with her now in the Waldorf.

After breakfast, the room filled with well-wishers. The Plebes reported and lined up in the room.

"Mr. Ting, sir, the Fourth Classmen in your squad request permission to be BJ."

"It would be my honor, Mr. Spanner. Fall out."

Owen Spanner pointed at McFee.

"GO GET 'EM, SIR!" bellowed the combative Mr. McFee. "You can do *anything*, sir!" cried Mr. Spanner. "Can't be up-start Yearlings without you, sir," said Mr. Caleb. "Sir, who else would give us marching orders in Chinese?" asked Mr. Quint, smiling. "Need you to tutor me in English, sir!" said Mr. Irkson. Mr. Schmidt, the chowhound, said reverently, "You're my patron saint, sir. It won't be the same without you." "Please, sir," said Mr. Parthes, economically.

I nodded. I couldn't say anything, and could never forget what they said. As I tightened my tie for the exam, the guys came in.

"Didya see Sedgwick?" asked Meatball Rodgers.

"Yeah," said Deke. "But Kai says he was two minutes late."

"Ah, no sweat," said Meatball, worry creasing his face. "Sedgwick doesn't wear a watch. Kai, good luck, man."

"Knock 'em dead, Caruso!"

"Just do the El Paso, *compañero*. Aim high, hit high."

"Play the platters, ice the grooves, max the wax."

"Hey, good luck, man. Ya got 'em where you want 'em!"

"Save some tenths for your section leader."

"C'mon, Kai, pin that whufer!"

"Thanks Meatball—Curve Wrecker—Arch—Moose—Moon—Buns—Cold Max—Handsome—Spoon—Pensive—Tree. Hey, guys, thanks to all of you," I said. "Hey, good luck to *all* of us in the low sections—and God bless us, every one."

It was a marvelously sunny May morning, the type that causes birds to sing even on empty stomachs. I took this as a positive omen. I figured that Chu-i hadn't received many American military offerings lately. Be with me now, I thought. You helped Uncle Shim sixty years ago. Help me now as I enter the *kaopung*, the testing cubicle, devoid of sun and moon.

I hung my hat on the hook outside the door, carefully centering it, seeking balance, and grace. Major Byron Maher looked up when I entered the classroom, and nodded.

"Top o' the morning, sir," I said.

"And the same, a course, ta you," he said in brogue.

We took seats. The bell rang. The section reported in. The first of five daily writs composing the 60.0 WFR was distributed.

"You have tried very hard this semester, and you all deserve to pass. Good luck and good hunting. Are there any questions? Gentlemen, begin work."

I turned the writ over. None of it dealt with analog computers or digital circuits—it was electromagnetic forces and torque. I was on the tenth problem of fifteen when the cease-work order was issued and we dropped our pencils.

Major Maher looked at me with concern as I left.

I didn't enter the approved solution room.

I was almost insensate while Sonny tried to prepare me for the second day of tests.

Grades were posted in the north sally port three days after the fifth and final whufer. Because I had entered the WFR eight-tenths deficient, I couldn't afford to be negative on the finals. I needed to pass and to pick up eight tenths.

A passing grade on the whufers would be 40.0; a max would be 60.0. I needed to score 48.0 to pass Juice, to become a First Classman, to wear the ring, and to be a West Pointer.

I shined my shoes and brass for my walk to the sally port. I found the section sheet and ran down the list. All but one person in the bottom section had passed—"Ting, Kai NMN . . . 34.0."

I had flunked Juice. I had been turned out.

Sonny prepared me for the turnout. I had a week, and both of us missed much of the frivolity and joy of the end of the year as we created an enclave of Juice and calculus in the Omar N. Bradley Reading Room on the fourth floor of the library.

I held a final meeting with my Plebes.

"I cannot tell you how proud I am of you. Each of you has made it through the most challenging year of your life. You've done it by supporting each other. You've learned things this year that will sustain you all your life.

"This is the final mimeo on how to excel at Buckner. Read it on the way home, and read it again on your return. Have a blast on leave but promise each other that you will recover a good physical conditioning. Fifty push-ups, twenty pull-ups, run four eight-minute miles in boots, lots of fluids, and you're ready.

"Turn to page three. On your final Recondo patrol, be silent. Silence is the key. I want each of you to carry three feet of masking tape in your first-aid pack, and wrap all your movable steel before you cross the line of departure. We've done it before, but I diagrammed how you tape your LBE and your rifle. When you come out of tree line, move like old ghosts. Your mnemonic is 'FORTY-EIGHT STEPS,' for four eight-minute miles, Silence steel, Tape, Exercise Pull-ups, push-ups, Silence again. Gentlemen, I'm going to recognize all of you now."

I shook their hands, enjoying their smiles. I put my hand out and eight slapped on top. "Forty-eight steps. If you say it, do it." They repeated it. I couldn't look at them. I looked down. "I was honored to be your squad leader. I will miss you." I took a breath. "Never forget how you pulled for each other. Never forget a brave lieutenant named Marco Matteo Fideli, a name that should always be a code to you to have good cheer under pressure. Good luck."

Owen Spanner came by my room after Graduation Parade to say goodbye. "First time I saw you, I thought you were a Chinese devil," he said. "I was so scared. Man, I couldn't believe you were gonna be my squad leader. I thought I'd died and gone to hell." He licked his lips. "I think you saved my skinny Arkansas butt. I want to thank you."

"I was honored to serve, Owen."

I took the turnout and flunked it. I said farewell to the Plebes in the company who had failed math and English. None of mine failed. I wondered if I was to be the next to leave with my bags.

I was deemed eligible for a departmental reexamination, and went through the motions of preparing for it. But my brain had left the field. I knew what it meant. I was leaving.

Sonny was called into conference with Major Maher and other senior members of the department.

"Good news," said Sonny. "The reexam will emphasize magnetic fields, circuits, EM forces, torques, and generation of voltages."

I said farewell to my Plebes individually, trying to focus on their futures rather than on mine. On the last night before the First Class Trip, the Avengers of A-3 held a farewell party. Years later, I saw a photo of it—all of us covered with shaving cream, our T-shirts ripped, the hallways a catastrophe of "an everlasting three-oh Fat City rat fornication." I have no memory of it. I was out on my feet, my guard absent, waiting for the knockout punch. With my squad gone, I felt exposed and childlike.

Sonny had surrendered the initial portion of the First Class Trip to stay with me, and we both watched the Class of 1968—the new First Class of West Point—bus out on their tour of the five Combat Arms Centers. The Infantry, Armor, Artillery, Combat Engineers, and Signal Corps would try to lure our classmates to elect their branches next fall. As the buses pulled out from Washington Road, our classmates yelled out from their windows—"See you at Sill!" "Break a leg!" "Knock 'em dead!" "You can do it, Caruso!"—and Sonny and I gave them thumbs-up. I had a great shouting voice, but could say nothing to them as their waving hands disappeared in the distance in a line of silver buses, glinting in the bright June sun until the buses went out of sight around the western curve of Thayer Road. The idea was that we would join up with them later.

Sonny and I were moved to the Boarders' Ward in Central Barracks. By now, everyone who had passed or failed had left the Academy. We were the only two cadets left at West Point.

I failed the reexam.

"Kai," said Sonny, shaking his head and laughing. "Thank God—they're giving you another chance."

I flunked the second reexamination. Upon Major Maher's advocacy, a third reexam was scheduled.

"I guess they want to keep you," said Sonny. "They're gonna keep doing this till you get it right."

It was supposed to be simpler than any I had yet seen.

To this day I cannot recall the final test. I don't know where it occurred, or the time of day, or if I had slept the night before. I don't know what uniform I wore. I know that I ate at a special table at the mess hall, and the cooks went out of their way to prepare a special meal for me and Sonny.

I was given three days' leave while the Academic Board convened to determine my disposition. This meant that I had failed the last reexam. If I had passed, I would not have been given leave but airline tickets to speed me to Fort Sill.

Sonny got his tickets, but he never said goodbye to me. He couldn't do it, and I was glad he spared me the pain.

I had West Point practically to myself. I began to run ten to fifteen miles, and lift weights for three hours a day. I alternated between flats and hills; shoulders, lats and biceps, and chest, triceps, back, and abs. I began to know every corner of the Academy as I never had as an overscheduled cadet, studying the tall medieval architecture, its arcane carvings, gargoyles, and griffins hidden on the facings of the tall granite towers. I ran along the river, by Building 665 where McWhiff had led me to Big Dick. I explored the post exchange and the commissary until I tired of the sad, understanding glances I got from the shoppers. "Oh, Ben, look—a Second Classman—still here in June. He must've been found. And a Chinese, too. It must've been medical—a sports injury."

I was in the weight room when a man in his forties asked if I was Kai Ting.

"Colonel Jerry Galligan," he said as we shook hands. "Academic Board. Have you thought of being turned back?" That would mean joining the Class of 1969, and taking Juice, thermo, nuclear physics, fluids, and solids again, from the bottom.

"Sir, I'm afraid I'd flunk them all, a second time around." I stood up. "My brain is worn out in engineering, sir."

He nodded, wiping the sweat from his brow.

I was called to the office of the Academic Board on 25 June. That was the anniversary of the Battle of Little Bighorn by the greasy grass, which had placed George Armstrong Custer into his permanent residence across the street from Major Maher's quarters.

"Kai," said Lieutenant Colonel Galligan, seated alone at the long table behind which stood the Mighty Nine—Hector, Alexander, Julius Caesar, Joshua, David, King Arthur, Judas Maccabaeus, Charlemagne, Godfrey de Bouillon. I had always thought that Guan Yu, Mohammed II, Crazy Horse, Sun Tzu, and El Cid Campeador; maybe even Chingis Khan should have been there, too.

"Mr. Ting. It is the decision of the Academic Board that you be separated from the Corps of Cadets for academic deficiency. It is with regret that this decision is rendered, for you have traits which would produce a successful graduate of West Point. As you know, each graduate must pass all courses. The Board could not help but note that you are an outstanding student in most of your work, suggesting to us a lack of focused effort."

I tried to smile.

"Formal outprocessing commences now. Do you have anything you wish to say to the Academic Board?"

I had a speech about the superfluousness of Juice in a modern world filled with Vietnams, where it was clear an isolated military solution was inadequate. Cultural understanding of politics, clan structure, Asian *gahng* and *lun,* social network loyalties, rice farming, history, reverence for complicated pantheons of gods, spoken communication, technical assistance in agriculture and medical health, caring and sacrifice for common villagers—these were the ingredients for modern victory in wars of national liberation. West Point had taught me that. Juice wouldn't help in Vietnam. But I had not earned the right to speak of such matters. This was an opportunity to plead extenuating circumstances in my engineering performance. I was down to my last right—the right to leave. "No, sir."

Lieutenant Colonel Galligan handed me a packet. "Outprocessing will take two days. Your military assignment will be made by your regimental sergeant major. Your last station is Warrant Officer West, for the return of your cadet military identification card. The Academic Board, and I, wish you every success. Kai, we'll miss you."

"Thank you, sir," I said, saluting him and leaving the boardroom with meticulous care. In the boardroom waiting area I had to sit down. I felt numb and wounded, intact and ripped from innards to ear. I wanted to cry. I waffled between feeling too much emotion and feeling none. When the latter prevailed, I stood, thanked the secretary, and left the Administration Building.

I sat on my Boarders Ward bunk, staring at the empty room. I forced myself to stand. I had *gahng* and *lun* with my faculty, and had to say farewell to them. It was not one of my skills.

As I walked down the brightly lit hallway of Thayer Hall, the heels of my cordovans clicked in the largely empty building, I found myself saying farewell to familiar classrooms and "lucky" section seats. I realized how many *foo chi*, good fortune, connections I had made in my three years at West Point. I had a lucky coat hook outside Captain MacPellsin's English 101 classroom on the second floor, where I had hung my raincoat during the heavy winter rains of 1964. There was a hall light that used to flicker outside Advanced Economics 321A, which I had interpreted as the well-wishings of Guan Yu's spirit of commerce. I smiled at the bright, polished floor, remembering one afternoon after classes when Arch had used that space to teach me the rumba. I remembered a lengthy Yearling arm-wrestling contest at the lower entrance to Thayer, by the Five Stone Mounted Warriors, where I beat everyone except Mike Benjamin. I remembered exiting those doors as a Plebe, with my neck in, looking straight ahead in the presence of the upper class, saluting everyone, hoping no one would stop me because I stood out in a nation of bracing, faceless knobs.

I remembered Deke Schibsted and I leading a company of new cadets out of South Aud after their first Honor lecture during R-Day in Beast for the Class of 1970, when we saluted a thousand crots a day until I began laughing from the meaningless repetition.

I entered the hushed, awesome silent expanse of South Aud, seeing the seats I had occupied for so many events. I remembered the horrible German westerns. Harper Lee had been on stage, talking about tolerance; Captain Mac had sat in the first row right, holding his children and smiling. I remembered the Vietnam briefings on the Battle of Iadrang Valley in November 1965, and series of operations like Linebacker and Hastings, and the sobering lessons on Red Chinese infantry operations.

Although the corridors in Thayer and Bartlett and Washington halls were empty of cadets, I heard their voices, and felt their energies struggling against an impossible schedule, and knew no school nor any experience in my life could ever match this.

I had arrived with one bag, a letter to General Schwarzhedd, my father's automatic pistol, Momma LaRue's plastic cup, and Tony's old rosary in my pocket. From the first day forward, I had acquired more and more equipment, and now I was shedding it, like a moth returning to chrysalis, and had none of the original assets with which I had arrived.

I had three unbearable pieces of information for my father.

Dad, I flunked out of West Point, in math. I will not have the ring. And I lost your gun. I could write him a letter.

I would have to call him.

I felt nostalgia when I turned in my rifle, serial number 58179; it had accompanied me on hundreds of hikes and marches, and entirely too many parades and reviews on the Plain, and Bandbox Reviews and inspections in Central Area. Never had it closed on my thumb or dropped during a Buckner reveille run or misfired on the range. Its straps and frogs had always held firm against me, inverted under a poncho under heavy summer rains. It had stood loyally by me when I faced Uncle John Sedgwick, two minutes late.

I found Elmer Scoggin in a maintenance shop, cleaning the buff-spinners. "Damn, Kai, I can't believe they'd boot *you* out."

"Can't believe it either," I said. "I did it to myself."

"You gonna be okay?" he asked.

"Oh, yeah," I said, trying to keep my lip from doing a hula. "Take care of yourself, Elmer," I said, shaking his hand.

"Thank you again for protecting West Point when it was in trouble."

"God bless you, Kai Ting. You're a good man."

At the mailroom I received several cards from Pearl, wishing me luck. I couldn't read them. Someone had sent me a corsage. It was black. The card said, "Congratulations on getting found, stupid. Remember me. I'm going to remember you. Duke."

On my last night at the Academy I undertook my conventional soporific of iron works. I benched and did flies. I did tricep extensions three ways and parallel bar dips with a towel holding a ninety-pound bell. I did triple extension curls, military presses, delt raises, and lat pull-downs until my muscles screamed, and then I did more. I hit the body bag for twenty minutes, took two minutes off, and did thirty minutes until I felt pain and moved through it. By this time, I had the weight room and boxing gym all to myself. I studied my pumped body in the mirror. I liked the bulk, the glistening hardness, but I did not admire the man.

I was afraid to enter the shower. In the shower, with all that water, I might cry. I bathed at the sink, making such a mess that I had to laugh, and I felt better.

I still could not sleep, tossing on the cot that I associated with my dual-left-footed Dance of the Seven Veils with Juice. I put on sweats. I still had an absence card, although in the morning I would no longer be a member of the United States Corps of Cadets, subject to the Honor Code.

I stepped into Central Area, my footfalls unnaturally loud in the cavernous silence. Of course, my room was the only one illuminated. I returned and doused the light. In the dark of night, I felt the Academy was mine alone. The four tall, castled towers of the Area seemed to belong to a painting of an imaginary Gothic castle. I could not believe that a place so dynamic could ever be this peaceful. I looked at the naked uniform flag pole, which never again would dictate to me the uniform of the day; the emptiness of the square which the Corps had filled with its smartly precise winter Bandbox Reviews, the sounds of Souza and the coordinated tramp of marching. In a few days, the Area would be occupied by young men dropping their bags to the sound of screams under a humid sun. I turned in a circle. I can't leave. I can't leave you.

What will I do without you?

I stood there, inside a wide-shouldered body I had needed

since childhood. I felt the strength in my shoulders, capable of absorbing heavy blows, the breadth of chest for exchanging oxygen during extremis, the capability in my arms and hands for fending off any bully. I spoke English, and had won many friends.

You should be happy, punk. I felt awful, rejected, unworthy, dunced. A gross failure. How could this be? It wasn't that I had been so full of promise, because I wasn't. I wasn't that good. But my love for West Point should've been enough to get me through. It wasn't right. Some guys who hated it here were going to graduate. I loved it and had been booted out. I remembered Duke's lament—"Some of these guys aren't even American"—and quickly changed my tack. Everyone who graduates deserves it. Everyone who didn't had his own reasons, his own foul *yeh* that made him outcast rather than brother.

But I would have been a good officer for you. I know a lot about Vietnam. You should teach more of that, so we can win, so that losing Marco purchased something.

I poured lighter fluid on Hammond's Juice text and my Juice notebooks, ASPs, and lab books, near the base of the Central clock tower and only a few paces from the small, eccentric concrete pockmark where I had stood in the heat of Beast, when Studs Went Fourth for clothing formations under the orders of Bob Arvin, King of Beasts. I told the Army corporal in the Guard Room that a controlled fire to DX cadet texts was about to occur, and lit it.

I watched the sparks from the flaming books rise above the clock, into the dark night sky, the illumination of the sparks brightened by the darkness of Central Area. The pages crackled. I liked it.

I looked at Uncle Shim's Piaget. "The big hand does not care about numbers. It is literary." I was the big hand, the big fool, who had not cared about math. The guy who made it to West Point, and lost it, the honor of the experience smudged by the final imprint of failure everlasting.

I looked in the skies for an answer, wanting someone up there to receive the smoke and flame of my once and former West Point career. Take the smoke, Chu-i. I was not to be a West Pointer. I never would. I would never wear the ring. All of my closest friends, my brothers, would; and the emptiness on my hand would ache for all my days.

I was going to be a sergeant, an honorable rank—one closer

to my 'hood, where few of the guys had gone to college, and the best of us had up and disappeared like young smoke in an American night sky. Toos, where are you?

Being a sergeant would be closer to my true past—locker room attendant, Vitalis salesboy, assistant lifeguard, assistant gym instructor. I thought of Leroy Johnson running the desk at the Central Y. I thought of Tony Barraza, who had poured his heart and soul into the little fighting hearts of ruffian street urchins. I shouldn't have tried to better them, by doing college, wearing a bright saber and a sash, by having a plume on my tar bucket and a gold ring on my hand. I wasn't that good.

The fire sputtered, then reignited.

Well, God, I have tied up something miserable. I've ruined my relationship to my father and busted the one thing he wanted from me. I helped kill my stepmother. I forgot my real mother and sister, and have screwed up all the Chinese rituals of my life. I'm not so hot with the American ones. I couldn't save my sister, and I should've, and then I just dropped her from my mind for eleven years. My sisters hated war, war killed Uncle Shim's entire family, and I joined the Army. I killed Leo and Lucky. I became an Honor hot dog and ended up pulling the trigger on Clint and Pee Wee and fifty other classmates. I can't study math. I'm not worth wet crap.

God, you didn't do such a hot job watching over me in engineering, so watch over me in war. Damn! Vietnam, just like the French, the Japanese, and the Chinese. They don't give up. Why'd I join the Army when we're in a war against Asian freedom fighters? Why can't the White House see that communism is an accident for them? What they're all about is killing foreigners who mess with their country. What happened to freeing all the people behind the Iron Curtain? Enough. What the hell do I know? I don't know crap. Okay, God, kill me, but don't maim me. Please. I don't want to be maimed. I was a gimp as a kid. Not in the eyes. Not my nuts. I'm still a virgin—wouldn't be fair. Don't do this to me again as an adult. I'm twenty! Let me do one goddamned thing right in my life! Don't let me embarrass West Point again. Make people say, "Yeah, he's good. He went to West Point." Right, I thought. Who the hell do I think I'm talking to? Chu-i or the tooth fairy? The gods do not favor you, you idiot.

Sergeant Ting, Infantry. I'd get the burnished silver Airborne wings of Jump School and the bright yellow Ranger tab. In Vietnam, I'd win the Combat Infantryman's Badge. That was more than enough for a guy who had flirted with failure and then kissed it in broad daylight under the clock tower. I could live with that. I might never be happy, but happiness wasn't everything. I would have three squares a day . . . if I didn't get killed or shot in the mouth.

I took a deep breath, rich with smoke, my shadow flickering on the grounds of Central Area. I presented arms, saluting my absent class and the gods above, remembering Mike Benjamin talking about losing at the edge of winning. I didn't deserve to win, but did I deserve to lose like this? Yes, Monsieur Dickhead, you must have.

"I'm glad you know how to light a fire."

I turned to face Major Schwarzhedd. Next to him was Major Maher. They were both in uniform, in full fig.

"Tomorrow's your last day at West Point," said Major Schwarzhedd. "Let's drink one for Benny Havens, and to the Army, where there's sobriety, and promotion's very slow." Benny was the legendary nineteenth-century tavern master who helped many cadets greet the bottom side of a beer mug, again and again. It was an Irish army and everyone was a friend of the grape and the hops.

Major Schwarzhedd gave me a cold, iceboxed can of Tab. "Can't toast without spirits. Absent comrades," he said, and we drank.

Major Maher gave me a cigar. "Has quinine, cures malaria, which, no doubt, you'll contract over there. God knows I did," he said in his clearly enunciated tones. "I don't want to brag."

"Chase got malaria," said Schwarzhedd, "because he swore so abundantly he bugged the mosquitoes." He also accepted a cigar. "I'll smoke it 'cause we're outdoors, and someone's already turned the night sky black with hydrocarbons."

"Norm, you're right," said Maher. "I should follow your example. You have a clean mouth, hardly swore, and you got amoebic dysentery, double malaria, blown up in a minefield, machine-gunned, cut off and starved in triple-canopy jungle for a week, and shot down in a chopper. Inspiring as hell." Maher crouched and lit the cigar on the flames of my Juice text, and Schwarzhedd and I followed. The flames warmed my cheeks, and I saw pages of curling, browning circuit diagrams smoking and burning. I would never know the difference between a Norton and a Thevenin circuit. I straightened when I smelled my hair burning.

"Great Tab, sir," I said, drinking it to kill the bite of the cigar. Cans were relatively new; soda used to come in bottles.

"Yes, it was a damn good year for Tab," said Maher. "Test the heady bouquet, savor the insouciant body. Don't guzzle like it was sugared water. Take a vintner chevalier's little sip and mull it. Ahhhh! *C'est bien*. We figured," he added, "you'd be feeling lower than shark shit on the bottom of the sea."

"Or beneath the belly button of a lowly Irish reptile," suggested Schwarzhedd. "And lonelier than Lot's wife. So, you might as well be with a bookish bachelor and a man who can curse when things are good. Incidentally, that's him."

"Murphy, the Irish mystic, knows," said Maher, "when things are bad, ta take comfort, knowin' they can only get worse. My sainted father used ta say, 'When things are bad, don't make 'em worse, for they will be quite bad enough without your help.'"

I laughed. "You know, sir, my stepmother was part Irish. The Irish sayings are easier to remember than the Chinese ones."

"That, laddie," said Maher, "is because they've been translated into English."

I took a deep breath, enjoying the cool night air, the conviviality of the campfire built on the ruins of my engineering career. I looked at them, memorizing their strong faces illuminated by fire, their reflecting metal decorations, their interest in me.

"I'm going to miss you," I said thinly, looking at them both. I could not imagine a world without them.

"We're just passing through," said Maher. "That's all life is. Transition between Large Engineering Unknowns. Both of us are returning to Vietnam. We'll request your assignment to our unit. We'll help you go OCS so we can discuss Juice late into the night."

"Oh, good, Chase," said the Bear. "That'll encourage the man to stay in the Army."

The fire sputtered on the hard spine of Hammond's text.

"Go, Army," said Chase Maher in his clear, articulating voice, putting his hand out, palm down. Norman Schwarzhedd placed his hand on top of Maher's, and I put mine on top of his.

"Go, Army," I said.

"Godspeed, Kai," said Schwarzhedd. He was smiling.

I stood next to the dying flames for a full hour after they

left. I felt magical, because in a blink of an eye, I could repro-
duce their images in the Area, remembering their exact gait,
relative position, azimuth and bearing, as they had walked
away. I can still see them, today, the Bear and Byron, casting
long shadows into a night rich with ruin and smoke.

My last true outprocessing station was Regiment, in Building
720. After I spoke to Major Noll about an unspecific future, he
wished me well, gave me his home address, and asked me to
answer his correspondence. He promised to write, and he did.
I didn't. It was the beginning of the numbnuts syndrome.

"Kai, the sergeant major will discuss your duty assignment,"
the major told me.

Sergeant Major Klazewski had not been Zeus at West Point.
That was the Superintendent's job, or the Commandant's. But
Klazewski was like Apollo, the god of sunlight, of music, and
of prophecy. When I had offered my life to the gods the night
before, commending the sparks from Hammond's text to the
heavens, they had wafted through the night air to land on the
sergeant major's desk.

"Ach, come in, come in," he said, polishing his desk with an
old OD towel. "Dis for you, from wife and daughter." He gave
me a tinfoil package of cookies. "Yeah, yeah, it's okay. So stop
thanking me." He rubbed the thin, pale scar on the side of his
cheek with his big, hairy fist.

"Sit. Talk." He adjusted a pen on his meticulous desk, which
he also polished. He had been an outdoors man, a rugged infantryman, and the broad expanse of old wood was a symbol
of accomplishment, of the executive powers of which he was
master.

"Major Noll vill miss you," he said.

"And I him."

"Vant to go to the college?" he asked.

"Someday, Sergeant Major," I said.

"And do vot?" he asked.

"I like history, and political science, and English, and psychology, and I'd probably like sociology. Philosophy. Languages. I want to study China. Why, Sergeant Major?"

"Jost asking. Nosy old man. You remember, ve talk in field
at Buckner, and vhen you vas Beast cadre." The sergeant major was a fiend for the field, taking any excuse to escape garrison and be with the troops, watching us from defilade in the
woods as we performed field exercises. He had said I looked

good. I had been happy to be eating so much in the absence
of math.

He had two envelopes on his desk. "Vere you vant to go?"

"Jump School, Ranger School, 82nd Airborne, Sergeant Major. I want all the training I can get." I preferred the 82nd to
the 101st Airborne; its nickname was "all-American." That
was what I had always wanted to be.

He frowned, shaking his head. "Na, na, Kai Ting. No Jomp,
no Ranger. Eyes," he said, "vorse zan blind *grandmosser*. Hospital test you take yesterday. X ray, urine, bones—goot. Hearing, not so goot. Back, *old man's* back. Eyes, twenty ofer *eight
hundred*! Too blind to see red flag for Buckner Slide for Life.
No parachute for bad-back blind man. Ranger School is night
jomp. Plus, you have *ass-ma!* You locky get *dis* far. You 4-F."

I blinked. Did this mean I couldn't even be in the Army?
Suddenly, I was back at Letterman Hospital at the Presidio,
with the Army doctor telling me that West Point wasn't a
school for the blind. There was no escaping *ji hui;* last night
I had made plans about Vietnam, asking openly for favors, bartering my wounds for concessions from uncaring gods. I
shouldn't have said anything. I would have to deal with being
out of the Academy; I couldn't also lose the Army. What
would I do with my life?

"Sergeant Major, I have waivers. *Get me in!*"

He looked at me hard enough to take my breath away.
"Ohh," he said in a low, gravelly voice, rich with the dark, old
soils of Eastern Europe, "now you tell der Sergeant Major vot
he must do?"

"I'm sorry, Sergeant Major. I'm begging. You can do *anything*. It's the only way I can try to make good. It's just my
bod."

He shook his head. "Now you are wrong. Bod is Uncle
Sam's bod. Too much. Better you ask Gott for new eyes."

"Sergeant Major, I ask Gott, through you, for new eyes."

He roared in laughter. "Gott through *me!*" His chest jumped
with his roaring, and as he slowed down he opened a drawer,
pulled out a tissue, and honked into it. "Come back two hours.
Orders ready." He put the two waiting envelopes inside his
burn bag.

"Maybe you no like zem too much. I vish you all luck in
der vorld, Kai Ting."

He took a deep breath. "You come here like me—foreigner.
In der old country, you and me, ve vould be hanging from

trees. So don' forget, *never*—is great to be young, and alive, in America!"

At the Hotel Thayer, Jean was just coming on duty in the brightly lit dining room, and I told her the news. She hugged me and cried a little. She had dyed her hair blond.

"I had no idea you had school troubles," she said. "I'll miss you and your beautiful girlfriend." She introduced me to a boy, a candidate of the Class of 1971, whose parents had dropped him at the hotel a full week before R-Day. He was worried about his future. I told him all I knew. He looked at me with awe and pity.

I boarded the bus for New York at the Thayer, wearing khakis, carrying my orders and an overnight bag. My books, sealed in gun-box crates, would be shipped with my uniforms to my next station.

I left my cadet uniforms for the guys in the company to divvy up. I thought of saving my tar bucket helmet and my full-dress tunic, and the glorious all-white India uniform, but they were too painful to keep. It would be like saving pictures of the dead. I kept Marco's tar bucket, for reasons I could not explain to myself.

This was all just and right, I thought. *Yeh.* I had hurt others—none of whom could be discussed again. In a way, I felt like them, orphaned by West Point, the parent I would always love, and always miss.

I watched the Academy disappear. The last image I possessed was of Thayer Gate, and the white-gloved, iron-backed MPs saluting officers as they drove onto post. I had the sensation in my guts of a rapidly descending elevator, heading for a basement experience.

Of course, in that moment I did not know that I would reunite with Company A-3 and my classmates—rejoining my brothers, laughing on playing fields and in section rooms, playing hallway touch football, horsing at hearts tables, eating fourths in the mess hall, packing my weekly ration of roast beef sandwiches on Sunday nights, exulting in my reinstatement as a class-ringed Firstie, full of life and promise, running with Mike, Sonny, Big Bus Bob, Arch Astaire, Deke, Tree, Moon, Spoon, Meatball, Curve Wrecker, Moose, Pensive, Hawk, Buns, Handsome, Rocket Scientist, and Clint and a hundred others . . . only to awaken again and again, often with tearing eyes and cries at my weaknesses, my inability to stop the images, realizing that for me, for the rest of my life, reunion would occur only in dreams.

38

SERGEANT

Fort Ord, Monterey County, California, May 1968

Fort Ord is an Army installation on the central California coast that combines Fort Zinderneuf, the lonely, austere Foreign Legion post in the desert of old French Algeria, with flat stretches of the coast of western France. It is endless thick sand and ice plant on a cold and windy sea.

I had come here as penance for my failure. The sergeant major's orders had been a boxer's mojo juke. I had not gone to Vietnam to fight, but to California to train troops to enter the ring. Nor had I been sent to Jump or Ranger school, missing both distinction and risk. I had been assigned to Drill Sergeant School, which was like an Academy refresher, teaching things I already knew without the use of calculus. I got an Army campaign "Smokey the Bear" hat, a whistle on a chain, and a Drill Sergeant badge that was worn on the lower half of the left breast pocket. I was a DI, a tireless, iron-voiced, cadence-calling driver of men with a penchant for sweet parades, jocular troops, a prohibition on hazing, ample push-ups, and allowance for heavy eating.

I had thirty days' leave. Before DI Academy, I had flown to Benning. Near the towers and the cinder-block buildings of TIS, The Infantry School, I met the deputy commandant of the Airborne School. Jump School trainees ran their miles with the Black Hats, chanting jodies full of hopeful pride and tired air.

"You just flunked out of the Point? You got Surgeon General waivers on a bad body, you have no orders to be here, and you want to be Airborne? Forget it, Sergeant!"

I hung around, the cat after the canary, until he relented. He would grant my wish and let the Black Hat cadre kill me.

The first jump was the worst. As stick leader, I stood in the windblown open door of a C-130 to confront my raging acrophobia. The aircraft shook as seven cabin lights turned from red to green, the jump master shouted, "GO!" and, against all my refined judgment and my inflated fears, I leaped from the Hercules into the harsh, gyrating prop wash. I was blown horizontally, jerked by the canopy, floated, fell like a rock, and landed like a sack of wet crap, shaken, rattled, and rolled, but breathing in great bellowing hoots. After six jumps, the Black Hats congratulated us, punching shiny Airborne wings through our fatigue blouses into the skin of our chests. After the fear of falling, it didn't hurt.

"Blood wings," said Sergeant Malo Gomez. "Wear 'em proud."

Jump School was three tough weeks. Ranger School is nine very hard weeks. I debussed with my duffel bag outside Benning at the old barracks of Harmony Church, HQ, Ranger School, my heart slugging as if I were about to jump again.

The deputy commandant told me to go fly a kite. "Heard what you did in Jump School. You and your lousy vision don't belong here. Should be in *Finance*. You lose your glasses in the glade, you'll drown your patrol. You're a blind man lookin' for a place to crash. You're a year of paperwork, waiting for a date. Ever hear of orders? Unass my AO, Sergeant. Dismissed."

I returned to New York for unfinished business, arriving, with impeccable timing, in an August heat wave. The street vendors cursed, stockbrokers elbowed, the taxis played tag with death and fares while the concrete perspired and the heat arrived in wet, angry droves. I entered the cool Waldorf and sat on the green sofa where I had met Cathy Pearl Yee. I was reading C. S. Forester's *The Happy Return*.

Someone lighter than a cadet sat down. She wore a short sheath dress that was the same color as her name and no doubt the equivalent of half a year of sergeant's pay. The long hair wrapped above her head, and the matching heels made her seem even taller. I stood and took both of her hands, her fingers warm and alive.

"What do I do with them?" I asked, and she laughed. I happily studied her large, bright, knowing eyes, and elegant eyebrow raised for me, her strong nose, her perfect mouth, her strong, able jaw. I brought her right hand up and kissed it. Her skin was cool and smooth. The tip of her tongue came out and ran the perimeter of her fine, even teeth. She withdrew her hand and sat, patting the sofa.

"I love you in civilian clothing," she said in her clear voice. "It makes you look free and independent." She sighed. "I missed you. Ding Kai, where did you go?"

"Fort Benning," I said. As I told her, her eyes traveled over my face, as if she were trying to memorize me. "I've never seen your hair so short. What are your plans?"

"I'm going to Ord, as ordered."

"What about us?" she asked.

"Can't beat your father," I said.

"Why not?"

I looked down. "Pearl. I—flunked out."

"So? He knows. He was surprised, but he prefers men without outside allegiances. Kai, it's not a big deal. It means nothing," she said, angling her head. It was a lovely head.

"It means everything," I said.

"It doesn't have to. I know more about you than you think. I know about your eyesight and your bad back. Arch told me. You don't even have to be in the Army—that, really, you *shouldn't* be in the Army. Remember Pearl's First Rule: Follow only orders you must. Get out of the Army, Ding Kai. Do you know how lucky you are? You're alive and you're not going to Vietnam, where you would kill others and see others die and maybe get killed yourself." She squirmed on the sofa.

"Stay here, with me. Enroll in Columbia or audit classes. Find a career. Find two of them. Money's no problem." She raised the eyebrow again, smiling. "We'd have each other, and all the Chinese restaurants in New York and the Lims' cooking. You've worked very hard, Ding Kai. This is your deserved rest."

I looked at her, aching. "Not good enough," I said.

"Okay, what would make it good enough?" she asked.

"*I'm* not good enough." I was rubbing my ring finger. She had done that on this sofa. Janie had rubbed her ring. I stopped.

"You mean you're not good enough for me?" she asked.

I nodded. "Screwed up so bad." I shook my head. "I don't deserve. I have bad *yeh*." I had to redeem myself. I had to serve my exile. I had to do something worthy. I had no idea what that would be. It had been so clear and bright as I had walked up the river road with my bag three years, and a life-time, ago.

"I don't believe in Buddhist karma," she said.

"I do," I said. There was a logic to my life.

"Kai, is there someone else?"

"You mean, like, another girl?"

She nodded, frowning, her lips parted.

"No," I said. "No girl. Just my worthless life."

She sighed. "I have a room here," she said softly. "How long are you staying?"

"I'm manifested on a 2300-hours flight from McGuire."

Silence.

"Can you change the flight?" she asked.

I had four days to kill. For a moment I considered lying by saying no. I wasn't a member of the Corps. I wasn't subject to the Code. I had daydreamed about being with Pearl in the Wal-dorf, before I had been separated from the Academy. I knew there was nothing wrong with her, or with the Code, or with the Waldorf. Only me.

"Yes, but I don't want to."

She closed her eyes. "Are you breaking up with me?" she asked, her voice different.

"I'll always care for you," I said.

She crossed her long legs, and then her arms, leaning for-ward to watch her suspended high-heeled foot jiggling to a rhythm far faster than the pace of my heart. The pain had only begun, and already I was growing numb. She uncrossed her arms, reached into her bag, and gave me a small black velvet box. "This is yours," she said. Her eyes were wet.

Inside was a very close replica of my Academy class ring. My mother's initials were on the inside of the white gold and onyx ring bright with the American eagle and the numerals "68." I looked at it for a long time. I wanted it badly, but I couldn't wear it. A drill sergeant with an Academy ring. There was no way to explain it. I looked at her.

"It's beautiful," I said. "But it's not mine."

"Undeserving, huh," she said in a thick voice.

I nodded and gave it back to her.

"Hold me, Ding Kai," she said, and I did.

"Goodbye, Pearl," I said.

* * *

I wore the three yellow chevrons of a buck sergeant, the crossed rifles of an eleven-bravo infantryman, the silver wings of a paratrooper. I had no Academy ring or bright yellow Ranger tab. I downed a pack of Cēpacol sore-throat tablets a day to lubricate my voice while yelling, encouraging, and singing West Point jodies ("Left my baby in New Orleans / Twenty-four babies and a can of beans / Sound off") to my troops. Some of them were college graduates with more education than I, but most came from ghettos, barrios, and the projects, and were not accustomed to reading map contours, magnetic declinations, rifle battle sights, defense perimeters, or Army English.

At night after a long day of running in the dunes, I asked them about themselves, to tell their stories. At first, there was uneasy silence. I asked questions. Where's home? How many brothers and sisters? Ages, names? Where'd your family come from? What would you be doing now if you weren't in the green? I wanted the troops to become people to each other. I missed Spanner, McFee, Parthes, Zerl, Caleb, Irkson, Quint, and Schmidt.

The demands of an eccentric Chinese DI led white cryptobigots to speak in the company of blacks, angry black separatists to speak in front of sullen whites, and Hispanics and Jews to speak in front of everyone. I paired whites who died on the obstacle course with blacks who needed help with KP, yellow men who cleaned weapons poorly with brown men who made messy bunks, and rotated them, becoming a Matisse of people, creating mosaics of color, blends of cooperation and unity. Everyone was in *my* Army, and everyone was the color of olive drab.

Nights were filled with the same dream of reinstatement at the Academy. At times the dream was so vivid that when I awoke I could not accept the reality of my barracks room, blinking again and again in an effort to change the view. In the first moments I had thought it was Camp Buckner, knowing that Deke, Bob, Arch, Sonny, Mike, and Billy Bader were just outside the door. I missed Mike's rapscallion smile and personality insights, Sonny's New Jersey patter and generosity, Bob's ability to throw people out of wrestling clusters, Arch's wit, Deke's steady presence, the roar of the crowd. I even missed Moon's maniacal obsession with Buck Owens and the Buckaroos, whose tragic songs never sounded sad.

In the squad bays snored my platoon with the snorts and

unsyncopated rhythms of boys of all colors sleeping under a commonly unfamiliar roof. I opened the barracks door. Company A-3 was not in the street. I wasn't at West Point. I never would be.

The fire guard stiffened. "Yes, Drill Sergeant?" he said.

"Nothing," I said, my mouth aching with the word.

Ord was the Sahara, far from my past and removed from the presence and minds of those I had injured or disappointed. The winds blew the sand, the cycles of trainees arrived and left, time slowed, I ran and mongered iron, and I was recovering a confidence that had been absent for what seemed a very long time. My conscious battle with mathematics as a test of my humanity and my worth had ended. I had dropped the rock of *shiao*, filial piety, and watched it roll down the hill, and I could face west, my back to the Hudson and Boethius's principles, and look at the sea when I was lonely.

20 December 1967
Dear Kai,

Merry Christmas! I conjured some historically good eggnog. Earlier this evening, Chase "Byron" Maher, Pennell Hicks, other officers and I toasted the good health and good fortune of absent comrades now in SE Asia, and those with whom we will never again share a nog. We included you in the first group. The SM asked if you had been admitted to college yet.

"I gave zat boy good Christmas present, early," he said.

Our sad news is that Edwin MacPellsin was killed in action in the Iron Triangle. He will be buried in his hometown in Iowa. Daniel Spillaney, who played so heroically against Navy, was killed when his chopper went down near the Cambode border, close to where you worked your border tactics problem. Wasn't he your assistant Beast squad leader? Jack Armentrot lost his legs and one arm. I regret telling you such bad news.

What are your plans? You must be busy, running a BCT schedule: up until midnight writing your troop evals, prepping handouts and lectures; 0500 reveille. If I know you at all, you're drilling your boys as if they were cadets. In your free time, remember not to give up on your college education. Personally, I would hate to have this particular Sergeant Major upset with me. But my life is blessed; I will marry this summer, and have never been happier. In my youth, I must have done something very good.

We three received orders for our second tours in Vietnam. Byron will take his poetry to SE Asia soon; I go with my culinary skills in the fall. Keep the home fires burning (using your unusual fuels). We all send our best. God bless. H. Norman Schwarzhedd

"Mr. Ting," said the admissions clerk, "we have a problem." UC was not inclined to admit me after my academic failure in a major East Coast college. I had an acceptable GPA, but they were confused by my academic disqualification resulting from failing one class and by the number of units earned. After UC had cast out a good number of my Academy courses because no equivalents existed in its catalog—or anywhere else—they gave me 177 quarter-units. I needed only three more to graduate.

"You failed a course," she said, "obviously, because you took too many classes. You could've graduated in junior year. But we can't take you unless someone from engineering recommends you. Your reference sources are humanities and letters. You're not going to study engineering here, but that was your major at that . . . other place." It was 1967. No one in California liked West Point.

I wrote to the Bear, asking for a letter of recommendation. The letter from Major H. Norman Schwarzhedd arrived that week. As his father had helped my father, the son had helped me.

With the new year of 1968, I purchased a slightly dented, mildly blue '55 Chevy for three hundred dollars from a sergeant first class bound for Nam. I was filled with raucous affection for this four-wheeled machine with a radio. I drove up and down the coast with the windows down, visiting San Simeon, William Randolph Hearst's castle, and became a permanent diner at China Moon Cafe in Seaside. I felt an abiding loneliness, which even black-bean chicken *chowfun* and the comfort of the Chevy could not alleviate. I looked at elegant women in Carmel, missing the days when full-dress cadet gray could make me look like I belonged in the upper tier of society. I had possessed a chance to know young women and to be a West Pointer, and realized that I had seen the best days of my life. I thought of Momma LaRue. I imagined hugging her.

I put on a clean uniform and drove up Route 1 to San Francisco, feeling the pull of the old 'hood and the aura of the Pyramids. I was returning to where I had been an ardent would-be black youth, where I had been a slave to a hard queen, where I had failed at family and romance. I was going up the Nile to Egypt.

I thought of Toussaint. I used to practice his walk, imitating the glide in his feet, the angle of his straight back, the strut so quietly hidden in the shoulders and arms, the height of his head. I would try it, and we would laugh so hard. Now, as the Pacific glistened to my left, I turned off the radio and practiced talking to him. "Toussaint. Damn, it's good to see you. Man, I'm such a fool. Sorry I haven't called, or written. . . . Toos— how are you, man? . . . Yeah, I'm a sergeant. See, I flunked out of West Point. . . ." I exhaled, consumed with gnawing fears. I was afraid he was in Vietnam. I feared he was already dead.

I turned off Nineteenth Avenue and drove through Golden Gate Park to the Haight, and started taking my shocks. The Haight was filled with young white people dressed up like East Indian mystics. Hippies. I turned north on Central.

Cutty's Garage had new management. Joe Cutty and Hector Pueblo were not there. Mrs. Timm's Reliance Market was closed and boarded up. The barbershop with its black-and-white linoleum-squared floor was gone and made into an apartment. The Lew Wallace Eatery—with the two angry cooks, Rupert and Dozer, who made the best fries in the City—had been replaced by a dismal hairdresser's shop that seemed headed for the same fate. The whole commerce of the 'Handle had collapsed under the gravitational pull of the "supermarket" of Petrini Plaza. I drove down McAllister, my mind awash in childhood memories, jarred by the sense that I did not belong here, that I would not be remembered or accepted.

I had not attended the church since childhood. All the way up the coast, I wondered if I would go in. I had hated chapel at the Academy, and had vowed after Marco Fideli's memorial to never enter a church unless it was for my own death. I wondered about Reverend Jones and Sippy Suds Deloitte. I wanted them to see me in uniform, but did not want to explain how I came to be here while my class was at West Point. Yet U.S. Army khakis had never been unwelcome in the storefront Third Baptist; its members had offered too many sons and fathers to the same cloth, for patriotism and in the hope of equality, to decry it. Here, being a sergeant was honorable.

I parked on Grove to watch for Toos and Momma, listening
to Motown on KYA. I hadn't been here for four years, and
hadn't been to church for seven. I had trouble remembering
names of the worshipers. I looked for Titus, Alvin, Reginald,
Tyrone, and Aaron. An old expression returned: I was itching
to see Earline Ribbons and Anita Mae Williams. I wondered
what they'd think of me, if they'd accept me all over again. I
felt shivers of guilt. I had left the 'hood and gone to the Academy, where I had lived like them during Plebe year, but for
three years now I had eaten like a king. Who was I to ask for
acceptance from those who had stuck it out with hard times?

I looked at my watch; the Corps would be returning now
from mandatory chapel. Kids entering the church turned to
check out the Chinese soldier in the dented blue car, their mommas saying, "Stop starin' at the man and come along." A lot of
the folk wore buttons that said "Kennedy," and it took me a moment to realize it was Bobby they meant, and not Jack.

Toos and Momma didn't show. Nor did anyone else I knew
by name, as if I had come to the wrong church. The greeter
was a short, straight, fortyish man in a white shirt, shiny black
suit, and white gloves wearing a large blue badge that said
"USHER."

The doors closed. I heard "Jesus Keep Me Near the Cross,"
then silence. Now it would be congregational prayer, members
speaking of those in need, to the loud and comradely affirma-
tion of others. Then the announcements. The choir led in "I
Don't Feel No Way Tired" and "I Want to Be a Christian in
My Heart," the tune remaining with me for longer than I
wished. Now, I figured, Reverend Jones would be sermoning.
I got out of the car, straightened my uniform, and walked to
the church. Quietly, I approached the storefront opening. I took
a mimeographed bulletin from the stack at the door.

Piano Prelude and Invitation to Worship: Deaconess Man-
    chester
Hymns: 383, 487: Congregation
Congregational Prayer: Congregation
Church Announcements: Baptist Union, Sunday School
    Training
Sermon: On Reverend King in Memphis: Reverend Jones
Memorial: Alvin Sharpes Who Died for His Country, Febru-
    ary 14, 1968,
    Ban Me Thuot, South Vietnam: Joseph W. Sharpes

Hymns: "A Great Joy A-Coming," "You've Buried My
Sin": Choir

Alvin Sharpes had been killed in Tet. He had opposed the
idea of killing Leo Washington. He loved his father so much,
he insisted on being called "Alvin Sharpes" instead of "Alvin."

The usher emerged and I introduced myself. He remembered
Charlotte LaRue and her son, but hadn't seen them in years.
Joe Cutty had sold his garage. He didn't know a Hector
Pueblo. Earline Ribbons died of TB five years ago. Anita Mae
Williams was married and a mother, attending S.F. State.
Markie T. had moved to L.A. years ago and Titus B. was in
state prison. He couldn't recall any of the other names.
Deloitte, the usher said, had gone back South.

I quietly entered. The church seemed to have shrunk. A tall
man in a brown suit gripped the lectern. The church had four
new pews in front to supplement the collage of unrelated
wooden folding chairs. The man was crying, unable to stop.
"My son . . . ," he said in a quavering voice, succumbing to
tears as others said, ". . . the Lord love and keep you." I left
and sat on the steps.

After a while, I heard a hymn I'd forgotten since the days
when I carried rock collections in my pockets and daydreamed
with great power about the taste of fresh bubble gum.

> In the depths of the sea
> You carried my guilt far away.
> As far as the East is from the West
> You've removed my transgressions from me,
> Yes You did.
> So I tell of Your mercy and sing of Your grace
> And walk in Your liberty
> And live in the awesome light of Your love
> 'Cause I know I am free.

Service ended, and I returned to the car until the last of the
worshipers had shaken the pastor's hand. As I walked back,
the man in the brown suit embraced his minister, and they
wept in each other's arms. The sight of these two strong men
weeping was hard to view. I looked at my biceps, expecting
them to be gone. I remembered Marco Fideli's parents and
kept my distance. But the man in the suit saw me. He wiped

his face with a crisp white handkerchief from his breast pocket
and walked toward me.

I put my hand out. "Mr. Sharpes, I knew your son. He was
my friend, I'm so sorry." I'm Asian, but I didn't kill your son.

He smiled bravely, eyes wet, cheeks shining, a man wearing
his wounds on the outside. I remembered him as the man who
didn't drink. He appeared to be living without sleep. He shook
my hand in both of his, the moist hanky wrapping around my
fingers. He pulled on his ear the way Alvin Sharpes had when
something puzzled him.

"Knew my son in the Army?" he asked.

"No, sir. Used to live here. We were boyhood pals."

He studied my chest. "Army gave us lots of medals after he
was dead. Haven't been to Vietnam. You going?"

"Don't know, sir. If I get orders."

"Hope not. God keep you. I appreciate your sentiment."

I nodded, my lips compressed. "So sorry," I said.

Reverend Jones smiled as he took my hand in a strong grip.
His face had aged only slightly, his hair was whiter. He was
shorter than I remembered. "Good to have you back," he said
in his rich, deep voice. "I recall you as a tiny boy, swallowed
up by the chair. You're a completely grown man. What a pleasure to see how the Lord has smiled on you. Thank you for
speaking to Mr. Sharpes." He nodded his head, his words like
soft mountain thunder. "Never can take on too much comfort
in grief. You were friends, right?"

I nodded. I found my voice. "Yes. Reverend, have you seen
Toussaint LaRue, or Mrs. LaRue?"

He shook his head. "Gone to I don't know where. Many have
up and gone, some back to the South." He licked his lips. "Hard
times," he said. "This Vietnam is like Korea, all over again."

"Toussaint, and Charlotte, they can't be missing," I said.

He read my name tag. "Sergeant Ting. Kai Ting, isn't it? All
the boys have gone to the Army. Charlotte left town. They
didn't have any relations here in this church."

"Pastor, how can I find them?"

He shook his head. Then he smiled. "Deloitte's a lay minister
in Mississippi. He'd kick himself hard, missing you. . . . I'm
sorry son. Wish I could tell you better. Pray for them, son—pray
that Almighty Jesus is with them. Would you like to sit awhile,
and visit? Well, it was good, seeing you. I always wanted you
to come back. This is your home. The Lord bless you."

I walked downhill to Golden Gate and headed for the old

block. I had hoped someday to be a muscular, athletic paratrooper in bright jump boots with silver Airborne wings. I had
become my childhood dream.

I stood on Indian Head Beach near Range 9, a twenty-five-
meter, 70-point firing range, reading my mail and inventorying
my assets. I had been accepted at the University of California
at Davis, and my military obligation would end before I could
receive orders for Vietnam. Mike Benjamin wrote. He was applying to medical school, although the Army had made it clear
that it had not sent him through West Point to heal people.

A third of us have been removed from each company to
create twelve new ones. New Plebes aren't like us; you have
to be defined "politically" to do something as unpopular as
coming to West Point in the middle of this war.
I can't believe Martin Luther King is dead. I know you
really admired him. I don't understand what's happening.
Everything's in flux. What's it really like out there? Is it as
crazy as it seems in the papers? It sounds like a race war
and Sodom combined.
Sonny and Barbara got engaged. You know how he's always tutoring classmates. Ordnance is a breeze, so all he
can do is tutor Cows in Juice. He does it with a purpose.
You ought to write to him; he thinks it's his fault you got
found.
You know about MacPellsin and Spillaney. We still laugh
about your answer to his AAA question during Beast.
One of our new Tactics Ps was with the 173d Airborne
Bde. He had a big, athletic sergeant with a stupid voice that
sounded like Goofy. The sergeant was wounded twice, was
put in for a DFC and a Silver Star, and was a general's son.
It was Pee Wee. But get this—in a river action, he rescued a
drowning medic. Irony knows no bounds. I told Mr. Flauck.
He looked at me sternly and whapped his leg with his swagger stick. "Hmm. Goot," he said. Sentimental bastard.
Kai, I'm in love with Lynn Lichtenstein, the brilliant girl
who was in Frankfurt and Ft. Sam Houston when my dad
was assigned there. She's read Mann and Cather and likes to
stay up late, talking. To put it in your terms, she looks like
Elizabeth Taylor. She's mature and doesn't eat off my plate.
I got a letter from Pearl Yee, asking for your address. Apparently, she addressed a letter to "Kai Ting, U.S. Army,

Ord, California" and it was returned. Can I give her your address? Or, better yet, why not write her? I know you're in numbnuts land, and that you're stupid in math, but don't be crazy, too. She's very fond of you. Hang in there,
Mike

In the letter was a photo of Pearl and me at a formal hop. I was in uniform India, the all-white snow machine. She wore stunning black with white high-heeled pumps. We looked terrific. Later, I meant to put it with the picture of Mah-mee, but somehow I had lost it in the dunes.

39

THE CORPS

June 5, 1968

I drove the rented Fairlane through Highland Falls while a radio commentator said that if Bobby Kennedy won the California primary tonight, he was expected to become President of the United States. He was against the war in Vietnam, but when he spoke about Martin Luther King and his own slain brother, I felt as if I were listening to Toussaint LaRue.

I drove up to the guard kiosk at Thayer Gate. The MP smiled when he saw we were the same rank, and gave me a visitor's card for the dash. He kept staring at me.

"Used to be a cadet," I said, and he nodded.

"Thought so, Sergeant Ting. Welcome back. It's a beautiful day." He saluted me, and I returned it. "Thank you," I said.

The Thayer Hotel looked tall and proud, its massive chest out and flags flying in the warm breeze. Mike Benjamin and I had stood at the driving turnabout, looking upriver, talking about omens on the night before R-Day.

Cavalry Field was filled with Firstie cars—Corvette Sting Rays, T-Birds, Bonnevilles, Firebirds, and Cougars. The payments would make them poor for years. After having no freedom, Firsties bought highly prestigious sports cars. I thought of my old Chevy, embarrassed. It was a jalopy, a junk heap.

I followed Thayer Road as it bent around the bright, sparkling river. I had walked up this road, swinging my bag, on the most beautiful morning of my life, four years ago.

I felt pain in my eyes, pain everywhere, my ears ringing, my chest constricted. There was no curb and I couldn't pull over, driving blindly, hoping I wouldn't hit anyone. I fought for control against my rebellious body. My heart surged wildly as I approached the Cadet Hilton, scaring me. Is this what a heart attack feels like? Here, before Admin, was a curb, and I stopped. To my left was the Cadet Hilton. A-3 country. I remembered them all.

Hi, guys, I whispered. I hear you. I feel you.

I drove on, surprised to see that Washington Hall's face had been altered, huge additions connected to it, and that Thayer Monument had been moved. The timeless Academy, changing.

I hadn't been able to answer any of my classmates' letters. They told me the news and tried to understate the glory and relief of First Class year and the pain of losing faculty and Grads in Vietnam. I was unable to write. Writing reminded me of my failures. I had thrown away my journal.

I drove around the cannon to Washington Road. The Ford's engine idled in a warm wind as my mind flooded with unchained memories. The three years here seemed like the sum of my life. Endeavor, Wisdom, Patria, Providence, Faith, Love, Hope, the school in the mountains and the clouds, with Clint Bestier's brass buried beneath Sedgwick's spurs, and the little scar in the old concrete of Central Area marking the place where I had stood.

I spent the morning wandering through the cemetery, communing with others who had left the Academy only in the physical sense. Custer, last man in his class. Ed White, the astronaut. Marco Matteo Fideli, who sang to God. I felt strangely comfortable with the dead. I stopped at one plain white stone. It was new, for Robert Arvin, Class of 1965, our First Captain, killed in action in Vietnam, 1 October 1967. He had been a giant, our King of Beasts, ordering us to change clothes while inviting us into the military order of the Academy. The tablet was too small, the air too warm, too kind, too soft, for this view. I remembered the snowy January morning when we watched Marco's widow bid farewell.

I walked along the edge of the cemetery and saw Major

Maher's quarters. I crossed the street. His wife's name was Ann; the boy . . . Shawn. The nameplate said "MAJ F. Carson." Chase Maher had returned for a second tour in Southeast Asia.

After marching in three hundred reviews and inspections, I was about to see my first live West Point parade as an observer. Graduation Parade was the granddad of them all, with its peaking emotion, particularized music, its passage amidst an ecstatic crowd. I stood at the crest of Battle Monument, where Third Regiment would center. I was going to look for the faces of my brothers.

I had been there an hour before the first of some thirty thousand family, faculty, and tourists arrived. As the morning sun rose above the hill and splashed the deep, lush green of the marching plain and the surrounding forests in sparkles of light, the massed gray-and-white battalions appeared to "Stars and Stripes Forever."

The Corps looked magnificent, marching out to the tune "The Girl I Left Behind Me" with aching precision in four full regiments, eight battalions, thirty-six companies, with bright yellow guidons fluttering in the river wind. The sun caught the rifle receivers, the drawn sabers, the rims of tar buckets, the guidon trucks, as if each of the thirty-three hundred cadets were one body. I coached them, seeing one rifle muzzle too high in Third Regiment, one Firstie slowed by a beer too many at Snuffy's. I knew them all from a wounded heart. They were perfect. The crowd watched them openmouthed. Parents helplessly cheered and I stopped breathing, watching them, memorizing them, recognizing the companies by their individual traits, loving this display of what we could do.

The band played "Army Blue" and the Class of 1968 formed front and center, abandoning their old companies to the hoots of their friends, who only now realized how much they would be missed. I saw the new squad leaders—Spanner, McFee, Parthes, Quint, Schmidt, Zerl, Caleb, and Irkson. Schmidt was overweight. I wanted to wave.

Applause from tens of thousands filled the air as the First Classmen stepped out, and cheers rang from the crowd of fathers.

I had trouble seeing. Then, I saw them all, one by one.

The platoon leaders—Big Bus Lorbus, Deke Schibsted, and Arch Torres. Company commander Chad Enders. The flankers—Jackson Hawk Latimer, Mason Meatball Rodgers,

Tree Bartels. Spoon DeVries, Moon Shine, Rocket Scientist Ziegler, Curve Wrecker Glick, Moose Hoggatt, Buns Butte, Cold Max McSon, Pensive Hamblin, Buzz Patterson, and Handsome Hansen, all royal cards in a rich deck, glorious in gray, unchanged by the year, immortal, forever.

The other companies trooped the line. As the class formed for review, I saw Sonny Rappa and Mike Benjamin, Billy Bader, Alphabet Burkowski, and Miles Brodie, and my chest swelled and my heart sang for them, and I no longer minded that I was not out there. They were my classmates, and their honor, and their achievement, their completeness, were enough, on this beautiful day of unfettered joy, for me. I had been one of them. I was here for Clint Bestier, Pee Wee McCloud, Joey Rensler, Ravine Levine Mankoff, and Stew Mersey.

"Pass in Review!" cried Jack Anschutzel, First Captain of the Corps. The band played "the Thumper," the official West Point march that stirred the collective heart of the Academy, and the companies passed the class and rendered eyes right. My classmates presented brilliant steel sabers to what was now the Corps of Cadets.

The Long Gray Line of the class was formed on the Plain. They would never be together like this again, standing before Washington Hall, driving the Academy with its wheels. I could hear Marco Fideli singing to me in his peerless voice.

> *The long gray line of us stretches*
> *Through the years of a century told,*
> *And the last man feels to his marrow*
> *The grip of your far-off hold . . .*
> *While we swear, as you did of yore,*
> *Or living, or dying, to honor*
> *The Corps, and the Corps, and the Corps!*

They were headed for Vietnam, and they would go, and serve, regardless of individual feelings, regardless of doubts, despite any other obligations or responsibilities. They would go because they believed in each other, and honored the bonds that tied them together like ligatures around the stems of their hearts. Many had come here out of duty to their fathers. Now they would go to Vietnam out of a larger and more defined and clearly selfless duty to an indifferent and hostile public, learned inside the old granite walls, on company tables and green-carpeted playing fields. They were not isolated souls, orbiting their memories, on the edge of Graduation Parades, free-floaters without ties, or bonds, or pledges, purposeless, useless. They were the servants of the Republic, its noble Guardians. They had taken the oath, and they wore the ring, and would go where the American government pointed, whether in wisdom or in ignorance. They were absolutely magnificent in gray and white, their plumes fluttering in the breeze, their glittering sabers saluting the Corps, the mountains, and the clouds.

"Mommy," asked a little boy, "why is that man crying? Isn't he a soldier?"

I couldn't stay. I wiped my face, straightened my garrison cap, held my head high, hitched my trou, ground my molars, willed myself to walk like Toussaint, and marched off Thayer Road through the huge throng of chattering well-wishers flooding onto the Plain from the grandstands as the band joyously played "Garry Owens," the tune imprinted upon me as a boy when I had watched *The Long Gray Line.*

I had planned to stay for the graduation exercise at Michie Stadium in the morning, and to hear the Chief of Staff, General Harold Johnson, deliver the address. But it was too artificial to try to hide from the entire Academy community and be a mouse in the corner, high in the stadium seats, to hear Jack announce "Class Dismissed" and watch seven hundred white cadet caps thrown in the air.

The Graduation Hop would take place tonight at the gymnasium, since Cullum was too small, and I smiled, knowing that Sonny and Barbara and Mike and Lynn would be together, dancing with the skill that Arch Torres had tried so desperately to impart to my two left feet. Many classmates were getting married—an act beyond my greatest courage or most reckless imagination.

I had to sidestep violently to avoid a small girl and boy running through the mob, and I smashed into a very hard object that shook me to my timbers.

"Excuse me!" the man said, reaching up to catch his cap.

"Pardon me, sir," I said.

"Well, blast me! Kai Ting!"

"Jesus—Major Schwarzhedd! How are *you,* sir?" I presented arms, and he saluted me handsomely. He was glorious in his summer whites, his rock-hewn face full of light, his broad chest glittering in the colors of courage. He studied me, beaming, looking down while we shook hands, and he gently took his eyes away from mine when he noticed that mine were wet, that I was losing control. I had experienced an urge to hug him.

"Drill Sergeant Ting, Airborne Infantry. You look positively splendid. You're in great shape. Damn, you look good!" His huge chest expanded, his teeth bright. I enjoyed reviewing his five banks of decorations, as if somehow they were mine as well. I had three ribbons. I basked in his brilliant smile.

A small coterie waited for him. Some waved, saying they would see him later.

"Don't let me keep you, sir. I want to thank you for your letter of recommendation. It got me in."

"That's great." He smiled. "One moment." The major stepped over to his company. "Glenda Auden, Colonel Gordon, this is Sergeant Kai Ting, one of my men. Kai, this is Glenda Auden and Colonel Gordon." He had said "one of my men."

Glenda Auden warmly offered her hand, her smile as healing as the sight of the Corps. Colonel Gordon appeared to be from the cover of *Esquire,* muscular and sharply angled. I tried not to stare, but he had the Medal of Honor. He wore the ring and was black.

"I am very happy to meet you both—ma'am . . . sir," I said, sharply saluting the colonel.

"Why don't you head to the reception? I'll meet you there," Major Schwarzhedd said to them. "You're avoiding everyone, aren't you?" he asked me when they had gone.

"Yes, sir," I said.

"Nice touch, coming covertly. Tackling me at Trophy Point."

"Sir, it takes a special NCO to run over his superior and bust the crap out of himself at the same time." I rotated my right arm.

"Let's walk," he said.

We strolled around the Plain and the Super's Quarters and Battle Monument. I remember asking if he had had a pinpoint return assignment in Vietnam, and that he had said no. I thought of Marco Fideli, Captain Mac, Bob Arvin, Dan Spillaney, and his fiancée, Glenda, and fear seized my guts. Not you, please, not you.

"Be sure to make it back, sir. We need you to come back."

He looked at me with private thoughts, smiling enigmatically. He said something in reply, but I cannot remember his words. I'm not sure how long we were together, nor can I recall all that he said. It was too overwhelming for me to be back at the Academy, this strange and powerful school, founded by ancient Honor, Polish engineers, revolutionary Englishmen, Irish songs of strong ale, and the first political Americans, on this brightest and warmest day of all days bright and warm, with this officer who possessed so many connections to my family and to my heart. I basked in the vitality of my *gahng* and *lun* to him. The bonds were beyond my measure. He told me to forgive myself. I inhaled the river air, appreciating every moment. Life was full and I had no wounds, no injuring past, my heart clean and pure.

Somewhere near the end of our time together, the major stopped. "Ever read Churchill's Graduation Address to Sandhurst?"

"No, sir," I said. Sandhurst, Great Britain's West Point, was Churchill's alma mater.

"Churchill was prime minister, and the world press awaited this eloquent man's words, speaking to his old school, where his record had not been the best. Churchill took the podium. He said, crisply, 'Never give up.' Then he lowered his voice. '*Never* give up.' Then he raised it: 'NEVER ... GIVE ... UP!' Then he sat down."

The major put out his hand. We shook. "It's a good world—much to be thankful for. Go into it for all that's good. Don't give up on yourself, and never give up on others," he said. "Serve somewhere. And keep in touch." He smiled and I memorized him.

As I drove down the hill from Washington Road, I passed the BOQ, where I had countered perfection in the company of the Saturday Night Poker Society, where Major Schwarzhedd had fed me, offered me his advice, and lent me his thoughts, trying to pour his immeasurable strength and abundant confidence into me.

I couldn't run from my heart. It had helped to come here, to lend my small applause and heart-bursting admiration to the graduating First Classmen of the USMA Class of 1968. I was proud to know them, proud to have been one of their brothers.

When I drove out Thayer Gate, I wanted to stop and look back, but the heavy press of festive traffic propelled me forward.

I entered La Guardia with a light step, my boots striking the hard floors, pleased with the possibility that I did not have to be sad for all my days. I remembered Schwarzhedd's smiling face, and it lent strength to my stride and lift to my heart. He thought that I had a future. When he spoke of forgiving myself, I had looked at the river and thought about Pearl. He had said "serve somewhere," and I had thought of Bobby Kennedy.

I could extend leave; Sergeant Seeger could cover my platoon for another day. I closed my eyes and remembered Pearl's Manhattan and Southampton phone numbers. My heart surged with an upbeat rhythm and I smiled from inward pleasure. I licked my lips, imagining her voice. I knew somehow that she would forgive me. I was putting a dime into the phone when I heard a woman crying. Clusters of men shook heads while other women sobbed. I wanted to ask what had happened, but the airport had seemed to come to a stop, full of shocked people. Someone said "Kennedy."

I stepped outside. The redcaps and the cabdrivers, most of them black, were weeping with greater force than the passengers in the terminal.

"What happened?" I asked.

"Oh, man," said one. "He won the primary and they shot him dead. They shot Bobby Kennedy in L.A." He looked at my uniform. "He died for you, man."

On the plane to Travis I realized that I had left the phone dangling, the number undialed. Bobby Kennedy had been shot on the day my class had graduated from West Point.

Kennedy was a man beloved by the many-hued colored people of America. But I knew little else about him. So I couldn't understand why I felt like I had been shot, or that his death had been personal to me, my momentarily promising future ended abruptly, once again.

40

HONOR AND DUTY

San Francisco, June 14, 1968

I reread the letter Uncle Shim had written nearly a year ago.

August 30, 1967

Dear *Haushusheng*,

Thank you for your letter.

Indeed, I have sad news for you. You remember what your sister Janie said to me, when I discovered her in Canada. She said your father was not her father, her sisters were not her sisters, her brother not her brother. I am so sorry, young Ting, to tell you that your father has an equal bitterness in his heart.

He and I had dinner last night, at Johnny Kan's. I asked him if he had heard from you. He said nothing. So I said to him, "K.F., is the boy going to the war in Champa, in Vietnam?" I thought this would produce an answer. It did not.

"See here," I said to him. "He is the only son we have in the total of both our families, however miserable and stupid he might be. He has disappointed me so many times, yet he is all we have."

He said to me, "I have no son."

Your failure to become the man he wished himself to be has cut your father to his inner heart, down in its bottom, where his most vivid and personal feelings are kept. His hope bleeds out of him, as it would from any Chinese father whose son has failed. Salt is in his wound because you failed at what he also regards as the American version of the Hanlin.

I confess I am not so sad, for I know, despite your vigorous arguments, that your military school is not the Hanlin. Perhaps, in some ways, it is Chinese, full of *k'e ji fu li*, demanding honor, suppressing individuality, requiring vigorous scholarship and ritual, committed to social good. Yet, it also teaches the violent ways of Chingis Khan. It asks you to be a killer, and to lead other killers.

Your mother birthed you in the year of loyalty, the Dog Year, and all this time I have tried to form from you a moral Confucian gentleman, loyal to Ancient Times. My chances of success, in my waning years, increase when you are not in the uniform of the *ping,* following *Ping-fa, The Art of War,* instead of the *Lun-yu,* the *Analects.*

If you become a student of China and its ways, and rejoin us, all my work with you, however contrary to the wishes of your very honorable father, will not have been wasted.

I suggest patience with him. A true Chinese father would never forget an injury from a son, and would wear the wound well past death. However, he is now American, and may recognize you again as his blood. I do not think he regards you as the emperor regarded Cheng Han-cheng and his wife, the disobedient couple who were skinned and burned as a warning to all others. You are not quite that bad.

As to solving the problem between him and your sister Janie, please wait. You have no influence with him if you do not exist in his mind, and you can only push Janie into a worse situation, interfering with her own path to her father. So, I hope you are in as good spirits as possible, given the injuries you have imparted to him, and to me.

Shim

The lobby of the Beverly Plaza Hotel was quiet. I saw the old wooden enclosed telephone booth from which Uncle Shim had called me when I was a cadet. I was early. I was early for everything, for I had nothing else to do. The euphoria of seeing the Academy, of seeing my class graduate, of visiting with Major Schwarzhedd, had diminished in the wake of Bobby Kennedy's assassination and the violent animosities surrounding the war. As enduring solitude had returned, and I was trying to embrace it as my necessary *yeh* and *yuing chi.* I reminded myself that I had earned them.

I had driven up from Fort Ord to ask Uncle Shim for help with my father. Perhaps, I thought, he could suggest a way to create a peace—not acceptance—but a relief from my continuous guilt, from the sense of being miserably undeserving. When not with my troops, I felt empty inside. I had become nothing. I was *k'ung hsu*, ignored as if unborn, cast out from the living.

The desk clerk approached. "You are nephew to Mr. Shim?" he asked, and I nodded.

"He say meet at Far East Cafe. He there long time now."

"*Uhm goy,*" I said.

The Far East was between Commercial Street, where you can look at the financial district's skyscrapers, the Bay, the Oakland Bay Bridge, and Old St. Mary's Church—a small, dark brown sanctuary for Christians seeking redemption and heathens fleeing cold sea winds as they swirled from the depression below Nob Hill.

Families filled the cafe and I weaved through the tightly packed tables. In the hallway's last private cubicle next to the kitchen, the honored spot, I found the slender Uncle Shim, leaning slightly to his left. Next to him was my father. Both were in their customary suits, Uncle in a polka-dot bow tie. My father looked strong, but pale, and withdrawn; he stiffened as I knocked and entered through the curtain. I was the wound for which there was no poultice.

The gallant Colonel Ting, the pilot and paratrooper, the man with two lives and two wives, one in China and one here, who had lost them both in America. The man who at one time had possessed an only son, who had failed him before the watching world, and now was a man without a wife, with no son, and a ghostlike nondaughter.

"Hello, Dad," I said to my American father.

"*Dababa,*" I said, lowering my head to my Chinese uncle.

The table was filled with dishes, enough for six, but I saw the food as if it were a photograph, without aroma, a cardboard thing without pleasure or reality. My father studied his plate.

"Just us," said Uncle Shim. "Please, *Haushusheng*, be seated."

I sat opposite my father at the round table, six seats away. Father had not acknowledged me or given me permission to approach him. After I became a cadet, he used to stand and shake my hand. My presence reminded him, I thought, of death, of defeat and failure, of a loss of status. My failure had made him more Chinese, more vulnerable, in a land of businesslike Caucasian Americans.

"Father," I said, "I'm sorry for flunking out of West Point. I know that I have deeply disappointed you." I had said those same words to him by telephone, a year ago, enduring his silence. "I've lost your gun," I had added, back then. There will be no ring.

Uncle Shim studied his jade cuff links. Time stopped; breathing was labored. A large rock pressed on my lungs.

My father faced his cold food. He cleared his throat and began to eat slowly, the large Infantry ring bright on his hand.

Uncle Shim nodded and I served. The rich, high sounds of the many Chinese families outside the cubicle created a symphony of continuity. For a moment I was transported to China and was part of her. She was older than West Point, more patrilineal than the Army, where the unworthy son lowers his head to the disapproving father and the community waits to see his skin peeled back and his bones burned. There was a justice to this, a constancy rising from the waters of tradition. I could be a sacrifice, an example to warn a hundred others, as long as I was a part of something.

"I apologize to you, *Dababa*. You trained me to be a better student. I have disgraced the very name you gave me."

"Pour us drinks, Able Student."

I opened the Taipei beer and walked around the table to pour into my father's and uncle's glasses. My father's pain caused him to incline his head slightly. Stiff, unbending, unyielding sternness radiated from him like rigor from the dead.

I poured tea first to myself, then to Uncle, and last to Father, giving him the richest, strongest-steeped tea from the bottom.

"Let us drink to the strength of the clan," said Uncle Shim, his voice vibrating with feeling. "To the continuation of your line and the memory of old ways. Let us subdue ourselves within the great embrace of the men who have preceded us, the Tings and the Shims. We toast the women of the clan who have been our strength, and drink to the two Ting *taitais*, and to Shim *taitai*, all of whom await us in the next world. Think of them, and not our own cares. The future of both lines now rests with the three of us here."

This was a toast to me, technically, the most likely candidate to procreate. *"Gambei,"* said my uncle.

My father did not drink alcohol, and he and I lifted teacups.

The food was delicious and the meal was terrible. There was no *ren yuan*, social pleasure, at the table, giving the dinner the restrained social subjugation of a Western formal diplomatic supper between nations preparing to declare war.

My father was honoring his friendship to Uncle; Uncle Shim

was honoring his *lun* to my father by arranging this uneasy gathering of desultory digestion, with two spoken comments.

"More crab, Father?" I had asked. No answer.

"*Haushusheng*, finish the soup," said Uncle Shim. I nodded.

Our thoughts were unanchored to positive guidance, as disparate as our relationships, and it was these feelings that spiced the meal, more than the rich oyster, black bean, hoisin, or sweetly soured sauces on the ten platters before us. Into this silence that consumed our feelings, I could project every worst fear of my father's judgment of me.

Our cubicle was silent. Later, one of the waiters burst in, expecting an empty table to clear of plates. He jerked, his eyes flying open when he saw the three apparitions silently seated.

"Ohh!" he cried, bowing and backing out.

I felt an old and ancient tug to down the beer as if it were air, but I was tired of defeats.

An hour passed. No one was eating.

"Please allow me to pay for the meal," I said. "I am so much in debt to you. The gesture means nothing, but the weight of obligation is real." I was stilted by being with men I had known all my life, the English words fighting against my mouth. I sounded neither Chinese nor foreign. Speech was now difficult. My brain swirled, confused.

"Unthinkable," said Uncle Shim. "Tonight is my treat."

My father put his hand on Uncle's arm, shaking his head. He would pay, and there would be no argument. With the check came three fortune cookies, left untouched. These American things, words wrapped in pastry, were for pleasure and levity. Not now.

"*Hausheng*, walk me back to my hotel. Your father will drive home. I thank you both for sharing this meal with me, and for your valuable time." He stood stiffly, his thin legs helped by the ebony cane. I noticed that it was scarred, as if it had been dropped.

"Able Student, I find you looking very round, very full, and very lucky. Someday, you will be a strong credit to your family." He smiled broadly, as if we had just finished a ripsnorting collegial roast closed with four choruses of "That's Amore."

I stood away from the door. Dad studied my chest, looking at the Airborne wings, the drill sergeant badge, my three little ribbons, the qualification badges. I wondered if he wanted me to go to Vietnam. I wondered if he wanted me to, if I would go for him.

"Good night, Dad," I said.

He nodded, put on his gray Tyrolean hat, and walked out of the restaurant with his Prussian posture, stiff with the aches of defeat, slowed by the weight of the unworthy.

"*Hausheng*, matters are progressing famously!" We walked slowly through the press of the evening crowds on Grant.

"I must've missed something," I said.

"You missed nothing. Your father will someday forget the wounds you gave him. You must be ready when he is ready."

"Uncle, thank you for your help. I really appreciate it." I took his frail arm as we crossed heavy traffic on Sacramento. "I know it was hard for you to do."

"Ai-yaa!" he cried. "You are so dense. This is my job—helping support the linkages between friend and friend's only son! It did not bother me to do my duty as a Chinese elder."

He breathed heavily until we reached the Beverly Plaza. At the door, he stopped, reached into his coat, and gave me a letter inside an old and stiff plastic envelope. "Read this," he said, "at the Sunset Beach. Indulge me by using strict obedience. Do not read it anywhere else. Go now."

"I will, Uncle," I said. "Thank you."

He nodded, passed the hated elevator as if it were a rude drunk, and methodically climbed the stairs.

I got my car out of Portsmouth Square and drove up Broadway through the new Barbary Coast, past Carol Doda's Condor Club while Richard Harris sang "MacArthur Park." I turned down Van Ness with the Hungry Hippo and its oversized parking lot on my right. At Geary I turned west for the Pacific Ocean as the Band played "The Weight," about a tired man pulling into Nazareth. I switched stations, slowly turning the tuning knob to KABL.

It was a little after nine-thirty, and Sunset Beach was quiet and deserted on a moonlit, fogless night. The lights in the Cliff House were ablaze. Its roof shined in the glare of the round and full moon. The illumination lifted the gloom left in the scarred excavation of Sutro's Baths and Museum, the empty space next to the Cliff House. I drove down Point Lobos past the Cliff House, opposite the space that once held Playland, a beach amusement park. Diagonal parking spaces lined the Great Highway along the tide break, and I parked. When Bill Moen on KABL stopped talking, I turned off the radio.

I heard the suave and cool ocean wind. Here, Laughin' Sal,

a monstrous, calico-dressed mechanical dummy with a garish, broken-toothed mouth, used to laugh like a foreign devil from a glass perch at the entrance to the Fun House. I walked across the sandy sidewalk to lean against the seawall, and looked at the plastic envelope.

It contained two paper envelopes; the smaller bore the characters *hau, shu, sheng*. I opened it. Inside was a small diamond ring with a note.

> Kai,
> This is yours. You can give it to your wife someday.
> Lisa (I used to be Janie)

I remembered Janie pulling on it, in Quebec.

"Right," I said, buttoning it into my right breast pocket.

The second envelope was very old. Written in an elegant, woman's script were the Chinese characters for "Only Son" and *han* and *lin*. I removed a thin parchment letter of several pages, written in a faded blue ink. I turned my body to allow the moon to shine on the top page. It was very old and it crinkled gently in the soft sea breeze.

> April 4. 1952.
> My Darling Only Son.
> You know some humans are bitter? And others are blessed? Some so bitter about bad luck fortune that they wish to spit at their enemies from death, hating with ever so much great power from their graves. I used to dance like American movie actress, my hair floating in the air, but I am not bitter for losses. From my grave, I give you a long and strong and full hugging so to smell your sweet skin and to feel your small heart beat with life all the way reaching back to China and to our home and our house gods.
> I wish you happiness on day of graduating from high school and beginning of American college. You are now 17, bound for *Hanlin Kuan*. Are you going to Harvard or Juilliard? I wish I could stand in your shadow now! You must be most tall and most handsome! Perfect in your looks! This is what drew me to your father! I pinned pictures of Tyrone Power and Robert Taylor on the walls, thinking thoughts of their faces at the correct moments, for you.
> Today is Friday, 4/4, fourth day, fourth month, double-double-bad-bad luck, one meaning death, the other meaning

dying. Double the number, 8/8, double-double good, day you were born. Now I feel other world, the weakness of my life. When I am not of this place, my Lord will help me cross Great Eastern Sea to rejoin our family in China, where once again I be an honoring daughter to my father and mother.

I think from there maybe my thoughts come to you now, ten years later, in 1964. Uncle will give you this letter when you begin college. You compose for piano, yes? You play wind instruments, yes? Teachers compare you to Mozart and weep for joy when they hear your music, yes? Tell me *everything* at the April festivals, and do not visit me only once a year! I have asked your father to bury me in an American cemetery. Not Chinese cemetery, because too many not Christian. Most Americans Christian, there where Jesu can find my immortal soul with Gwan Yin's sisterly help.

If you speak at the grave, I may hear you, maybe not. If you speak at Eastern Sea, I will hear. This is because of Christianity's reach to China, where Jesu found me when I was a girl, and found my father when he was a young man. My Only Son, visit me at beach, where God joins Heaven and Earth.

You are last male in family and only person who can carry the clan; Reds and Japanese kill everyone else. I accept now. I said to your father—stop worry, Reds will lose. So sad, how wrong I was. He always so much better in politics than me.

So education of My Only Son will be American. It does not matter; you have my character, helped by Uncle Shim to honor the Old Ways and Ancient Times. You will always be perfect Chinese inside yourself, living with foreigners.

I have you for almost seven years—first year in my womb—and you will be six years old in August. I did not let you run, or perspire. All of your precious *shigong*, internal energy, has been preserved for music and for learning! You will be a genius! And better in mathematics than your father! How much misery he get because of Western ways.

Janie Ming-li has helped you grow to 12 years old with Christianity teaching, music lessons, good food and warm clothes, and has kept away physical exertion, human sweat, peanuts and ruffians. No rough *k'u-li* work or awful peasant fighting for my son! You are not a fierce man, but a gentle loving boy with so many brains. I pat your head and you lean against me and this is better than all other things. I gave Janie my diamond ring to repay her for her years being your mother. Little Tail will honor her duty to me and to our Lord.

Someday your father will become your teacher. But too late to make you a soldier. How he wants you to be a Western man in Western uniform, Guan Yu again. I cannot express all my joy that this horrible thing is not to be. Praise be to the Christianity God. Character is formed at birth, finished at 12! He can do many magic things, my husband. But not in this regard. You will be K'an Tse, a scholar with good grades and music, not a soldier, jumping out of Western airplanes with a knife in your mouth and chewing American gum!

Uncle has taught you in my place, balancing your father. Your father does not wish you to be Chinese. Uncle joins me in not wishing you to be American. He has kept your tongue smooth and fluid in *gwo-yu* and Shanghainese. Uncle is Hanlin-trained, and is the best. He loves you as his own son. Care for him in old age, and pray he remarries, although I think he will not. Women should pay cash for man like him! He is kind and attentive and enjoys conversation with women.

You now stand at beach I love. I have so very much comfort knowing that C. K. Shim is my friend and will help you when I am dead. Please always remember how we ran on the sand, how I sang to you. How I put my feet in freezing cold water of the sea and spoke to my father in Tsingtao. This closest to China possible.

Now I cry. Cannot tell if cry for my father, or for Jesu, or for leaving you, the tears are the same.

This is last letter. Cannot write again. I send all good blessings and love and Christian forgiveness to your beautiful wife and to your sons and daughters. Honor me with sons like your *Na-gung*, my father. Daughters who remind you of me. Be a man with a kind heart for your daughters and wife. Try to treat them equal of sons. Teach my grandchildren what Jesu teach: Go into world in peace, be of good courage, hold fast to goodness, render no one evil for evil, support weak and help afflicted, honor *all* persons, love and serve the Lord, being so happy in power of His Spirit.

This your duty to me. God is our Heavenly Father. I very tired now. I kiss your sweet face.

Your
Mah-mee

When I finished reading I could remember nothing, staring at the delicately flapping pages as if they were gossamer wings of an exotic bird. I looked at the waves. Over the horizon lay China and my mother's heart.

I reread the letter three times and I understood, nodding, having a sense of everything in the universe. I returned to the car, carefully returned the letter to its envelopes and put it into the least used storage pocket in my B-4 bag.

The deep, profound silence had been replaced by the roar of the surf. I walked along the seawall until I reached the stairs, and descended onto the beach. I began running across the thick sand to the surf, as my mother, her feet unbound from tradition, her soul yearning for her past, had once run, trying to commune with her distant father, across the Pacific, the Great Sea.

She had placed her feet in the freezing water, hoping her father, on the other side of the world, had been doing the same.

I sat in the sand and unlaced my jump boots, put my socks inside them, rolled up my khaki trousers, and walked across the cool, smooth, wet sand into the cold water. I listened for her, turning my ear toward China, trying to remember her voice, her tones. I remembered she sounded like Janie and Harper Lee. I was four years and sixteen seasons late, standing in the Great Eastern Sea. Do the dead wait?

I looked at the horizon, where the heavens separated from the earth. The ocean roared, driven by the moon, whipped by cosmic tides that felt to me like the hand of God.

I closed my eyes to the crash of the waves, the concussion of its encroaching march upon the earth. In its deep, reverberating roar I heard the voice of divinity, the rhythmic chant of celestial harmony. I heard the baying of patriarchs, the clarion bugle calls of the Academy, the heart-stirring crescendo of the West Point march, a distant call to war and to duty beyond family. It was the crashing of the sea, and Providence, and faith.

I heard my father, his strong voice in the thunder of the surf, his artillerylike defiance to the awesome weight of Chinese tradition, rising above the power of our family, rebellious to an unchallengeable past. He was a blindly zealous champion of a different future, a Black Haired man of the Western world.

He too had been given a rock at birth—the rock of filial

duty, of *shiao*. One he could neither lift nor drop. Then had come civil war and an awful invader. To apply his will and hold his fist to the face of evil, he had dropped the rock, had worked with a foreign army, come to a foreign land, and become a foreigner himself. My father had faced his own Fork of Pain, so many times.

The waves crashed all around me. I was alone on the beach.

I looked up at the moon. Uncle Shim had not given me my mother's letter in 1964 because, to him, West Point had not counted. Going to the University of California at Davis—this counted.

When I last spoke to her, it was in Shanghainese, and I had been a small child.

"Mah-mee . . . ," I now said tentatively. "I was at the American Hanlin." I licked my salty lips. "It was all *k'e ji fu li*. It loved honor and cared nothing for money. I dream of this school, every night. We were like the brothers in the Peach Orchard.

"Mah-mee, I'm a *ping*. Going to be an officer. I'm going to UC Davis, seventy miles from here, like from Shanghai to Soochow. Don't be angry." I looked at the moon and I thought a cloud crossed it. "I apologize for not speaking to you, for being a bad son. I'll honor you at *ch'ing ming* and visit the beach and speak to you. I'll try to open my mind to Christian thought." Although, I thought privately, you ask too much. *Ji hui*, I thought.

"I'm sorry," I said. "I should have no secrets from you. I shouldn't lie to you. The Christian stuff is asking a lot, but I will do all I can to honor you." I breathed in the wet sea air. "Mah-mee, I have done so many wrong things. I wasn't good to my *chimu*. Couldn't love her. Couldn't save Janie from her trouble. Kept Janie from keeping her promise to you. I caused a man and his son to die because I didn't call the police. I caused terrible pain to some classmates, by honoring Honor more than them. Mah-mee, I'm a bad student. I flunked out of the American Hanlin, causing my father unbelievable pain. I'm awful at music. I wish I could tell you I'm Chinese and Christian. I wish I could tell my father that I'm American and not Christian. Uncle knows. In your mind, and in the mind of my father, I am all of that, and none of it."

I cleared my throat. I was filled with self-consciousness and awkwardness. It had begun as a rote exercise. Now she was listening to me and I was performing the Shining Bright Duty of *ch'ingming*, reporting to ancestors.

"I'm not married. I don't have any children for you. I don't think I'd be any good at it. . . . I'm sorry that this is what you want. I'd be the worst at it. I mean, besides math," I added.

I felt the next question. It had been in me always. I shut my eyes tight to keep it away, but I was too weak and Honor pressed upon me to confess the inquiry of my life. But instead of saying it, I began to cry. Softly at first, and then with hooping wails that only a child's lament inside a man's lungs could produce.

"Mah-mee. Did I kill you? My *chimu* said I did. Did being pregnant with me cause your cancer? Oh, God, I'm sorry, so sorry, so sorry." I fell on my knees, covering my face. I could not hear the surf, only my own sounds. I wept into a void of sound and time, no longer looking at my weakness. When I was too tired to cry, I stood.

"I want to honor you, my mother. I want to be a good son to my father.

"I've been confused because each of you wants me to be something the other doesn't want. You both brought the old disputes in China here, and it's continued, long after your death. I've been the living argument between your memory and Father's will."

The roar of the surf was louder. My father spoke to me from the ocean, while my mother listened, and tolerated, and accepted me from a bright and silent moon that blacked out the stars and whipped the waves, throwing fine, wet, salty spray into the air.

"I must do the same as you, Mah-mee, and seek my own path, as you did. I've done things to dishonor you. I love the Army and I don't understand anything about music. Thank you for thinking of me, for writing this letter, sixteen years ago."

I had separated from the Academy with silence. But the separation had been a ripping of my soul, a tortured scream at the roof of heaven, as if a mother I had loved had been taken from me.

I had left a place that was all *yang*, male force, and the separation had brought my mother back to life in the bottom of my heart, where the most vivid feelings settle under the weight of living. I began to suspect that many of the deficiencies in my personality had arisen from the death of a mother I had forgotten.

"Thank you," I said, my voice drowned in the surf, "for loving me." I looked at the lights at the Cliff House. My mother had loved me. At one time in my life, I had deserved love.

"Father," I said. "If you had told me about my mother, I would have understood myself a little. My early physical fears, my reluctance to fistfight, my superstitions, my clinging to Chinese ways in a black 'hood. I would not have felt like a *k'ung hsu* ghost, an abandoned, free-floating spirit in this land of white men. I would not have forgotten my own duties, to my sister, to my mother. You can't take a child's past without an explanation, with only the curses and blows of an angry *chimu*, and expect him to be good in mathematics because you demand it. I may not be good, I may not be worthy; but I was a child, and not clay."

I closed my eyes in the surf and faced my father. "You are the father, the *fu-ch'in*," I said. "You have responsibilities. You can't look stern and walk away when times turn hard. When Edna evicted Janie you did not help. All my fights as a kid I carried alone. When Edna hurt me, you were gone. I'm afraid of your roar but that can't be helped."

My Mah-mee was telling me how to face my father. To face his harnessed fury with peace, to be of good courage where all I felt was fear, to hold tight to the good that lay somewhere in our relationship. I would not render to him the banishment he had permitted to befall Janie, or seek to return the pain that Edna had given me. I would support Janie, a low-status Chinese daughter who had been cursed in *k'ung hsu* by an American *chimu*. I would honor my father and my sister with Confucian duty and Western honor. I, a son with paterphobia, would have to apologize to him, and ask him to serve his daughter.

Seven green aircraft lights went on as we arrowed for the DZ. It was time to stand in the door, to take the wind in the face and to jump out, to see if my mother's God felt like inflating a Chinese parachute sewn from ancient, silken *gahng*, stitched upon the bones of broken relationships and sealed with the blood of suspicious hearts, to test the possibility of Christian poetry.

I rang the doorbell and the buzzer sounded. I opened the iron gate, clanged it shut, and walked up the stairs. The light came on, the door opened, and my father appeared in his old Army sweater.

"Kai! What—what is it?"

"Can we talk?" I asked, nervous, trembling from the cold and the proximity to my father. Obey, and tremble. I smelled his pipe.

"You went ocean, feet in water," he said, stepping back.

I nodded as I entered. I was drenched in saltwater, my knees black with sand and grit.

He smiled as if the uptilting of his mouth might cause pain.

"Dad. Let me say two things. First, I'm sorry I wasn't better in math, that I flunked out. I know you were trying to help me with math when I was younger—"

"Kai," he said sadly, "no need."

I was in the apartment where he and Edna had spent their last years together. He industriously had filled the lonely space with high stacks of books and magazines that covered the floor and in some cases reached four feet in height, creating, for me, an even greater impression of solitude. I remembered Major Schwarzhedd's Q, and his icebox, and his great treasury of books with notes fluttering like small birds in the breeze of his rotating fan. I stood straight, trying to match Dad's ramrod posture, standing at parade rest, formal, but subordinated. I took a very deep breath and heard the jump master's call to "Go!"

"Dad, you need to do something about your family, your daughters. You have to fix things with Janie. Dad, you have to take command. You have to do the right thing. No matter how hard."

He narrowed his eyes, moving his jaw back and forth. He turned away from me. There was a long silence.

"WHAT CAN I DO NOW?" he shouted. "TOO LATE! YEARS TOO LATE! Chance gone. Gone, forever."

"I don't believe that," I said. "It's never too late. All you have to do is say you're sorry. Whether they, or she, listens or not. And she'll probably not listen. Not at first."

"She will scorn at me!" he yelled. "So I was wrong! Never can be forgiven! NO! We forget! DROP!"

I gulped. I involuntarily flexed my arms. "Try, Dad."

He paced, full of fury, knocking over stacks of books, like Godzilla flattening Tokyo, shouldering the furniture, a human temblor shaking his world. This was worse than a world of WFRs.

"DO I BEAT HER, MAKE THEM TO GIVE ME MONEY? TELL THEM WHAT TO DO? TELL THEM WHO

TO MARRY! NO! They are *American!* No *shiao,* no filial
duty! In America, people have *freedoms!*"

"In America, Dad, it's your duty to *her.* The old way, *goo
dai,* is only her duty to you." I took a deep breath. "We don't
do that anymore. We're Americans. Americans honor their
daughters, bear duty to them, always. Here, the stronger care
for the weak, the parent always stands up for the child." I
didn't even know that I knew that.

"What do *you* know about anything!" he cried. "You know
nothing! Nothing of duty! Only read baby book in Chinese!
Never see China! Don't know pressures." He shook his head,
retrieved his pipe, and clanged the pipe in the brown glass ashtray like a Muni cable car man ringing a bell.

"Sit." He pointed at the old hassock. I sat on the arm of the
sofa. The light from the lamp cast shadows under his eyes and
reflected on the expanse of his broad forehead, brimming with
ancient knowledge. "Not matter. Tonight, talk about school.
Not Janie. Night for memory. I ready to talk. Then you come
in, angry." He grimaced. "Always, you do it wrong. When
should be quiet, you talk. When should shout, you whisper.
Say stupid thing in restaurant, laugh in face of society lady!
Always drive Edna crazy with frowns! Not matter. I tell you,
anyway. I have great memory." He blew out his breath, pursing
lips.

He nodded. "I remember too much." He looked out the window for a long time. I glanced at Uncle Shim's watch, reminding myself to be patient, to honor my *gahng* to him, to try to
restore his *ho,* his harmony.

"You see, I not graduate. I flunk out of engineering. Never
finish college at St. John's. I did not finish with my classmates.
I last—three years."

My mouth fell open.

"Yes! True! Three years—just like you! When you fail at
West Point—I think gods curse us!"

"God. You—don't believe in gods," I said.

"Maybe now," he said, "you flunk out. End of third year,"
he said. "My grades not so good." He frowned, shaking his
head, the pain in his face something I understood so intimately.
His pain, my pain, double-double pain.

"My father say: *'Be engineer!'* Americans say: 'Improve
self, climb ladder high, tomorrow new day—always better!
Sky the limit.' Chinese say—born under stars, no choice. All
geomancy, all *yuing chi* and *yeh,* luck and karma. Born Horse,

always Horse. Once stupid, always stupid! Once second son, always worthless! Then, world go crazy—Japan invade. Reds say kill all landowners. People like my father! Foreign power push each other. Kuomintang try improve China. College students all demonstrate—no studies."

He smiled ruefully. "Easier, demonstrate, ask for justice, than do calculus. Easier, hold knees and tell school dean to go work for democracy than do studies. It was revolution. I was a leader. I had to lead."

I nodded, dumbfounded, hearing and not believing.

"That why I push so hard when you were small child, try make you *so good* in mathematics. I think: give him pain now, no pain later! Try save you from my trouble, use all my *will-power!* Still have trouble with geometry, trig, calculus! Have to study hundreds hours make trig diagram, calculus equation for you at home.

"Still have trouble with geometry, trig, calculus," he said. That was me. I couldn't believe it was him.

He shook his head again, and his eyes were moist. I couldn't watch this, and closed my own.

"I fear, inside your head, same bad brain like me, not as smart as Older Brother. Weakness for math. I try, *fu bu fu, tsi bu tsi*—father unlike father, son unlike son. I try save you. Instead," he said slowly, "I put all my trouble in box and give to you. Sorry, so sorry," he said, shaking his head bitterly.

"Oh, Dad."

Silence, neither of us able to look at the other, swallowed by a dark world full of secret, inherited curses and broken hopes.

"I thought you were so good in math . . . you had a tutor. . . ."

He nodded, lips pursed, eyes narrowing in pain. "Ha!" he cried with old pains. "You have no idea. My tutor, so oppose to modern ways, so tied to past. He scorned at me! At my American thoughts, say that K'ung Fu-tzu very happy with my failure. *Pleased* that disrespectful Second Son got price of foreign thinking. He hardened his heart. He was so *bitter, never* forgive. Say all his years with me wasted.

"You know"—he sighed deeply—"I honor my tutor. But his old books not stop Japanese tanks." His jaw hardened. "I try to be modern soldier, trained by Americans to protect my father, my mother, China. I think of my tutor, I hear his laughing. . . .

"So," he said, firmly, his lips tightly pursed, his eyes hard.

"Never look back. I not man with backward glance. No tutor. No China. Only America."

He walked into the bedroom, opened the window, and stepped onto the fire escape. I moved the curtain back and joined him, elbow to elbow, shoulder to shoulder on the small steel lattice platform, both of us looking up at the brilliantly radiant moon.

"Except tonight." He opened his hand to the moon, the impresario opening the long, dark, secret stage of memory.

"Tonight, have Liu Bei's eyes, see past long ears! You like Guan Yu and his spear. Liu Bei was the brother in the orchard with brains.

"I remember. Moon so bright like artillery flare! I remember moon shining down St. John College central courtyard, June harvest moon, 1927. Same year when snow fall in summer on rebuilt Hanlin roof, when Shanghai sun have black circle run around it, when sweat come from orange figure of Prince Min on Forbidden City roofs, midwives say so many sick baby boys, born dead.

"All fortune-tellers say, bad crops, war, death, suffering, bad year. I not superstitious. But *was* bad year. Grades not good enough to stay. I stand alone in courtyard, knowing I go in morning.

"Midnight, last day of school. Everyone else asleep. Only I awake, all St. John's. Like school belong to me, but not belong.

"It did not hurt to leave Shanghai. I had great adventure in front of me. No. It hurt to leave my teachers, my schoolmates. I was son of very important, very powerful man! My failure *his* failure. He lost face with fathers of my classmates, now, strangers to my face. Very much, so much hurt.

"Kai. Now we here, in America. Moon is round, just like China moon. But courtyard is unlimited, most peculiar, most special courtyard of all history. I come here, your mother angry with me from war, daughters grown up. No college degree, try get job.

"I so excited about come to America! With American Army, everyone has respect! You fight hard, you think good, you are honored. Here, no one want hire me. Call me 'Chinaman' and 'chink.' Me—grandson of emperor's magistrate and friend of Joseph Stilwell! No honor! But I speak English not so good. My wife die from cancer. What do with you? Need mother. Janie just a girl. I could go back Army. Help, Korean War, do what I know." He shook his head. "American father, must stay. I stay."

He stopped. I was barely breathing. He turned to me.

"You speak English like American. You American. Look big and strong, good sergeant, paratrooper. American schooling. Edna teach English. Manners. Now, you go college, finish. Study, your choice. You have children—speak English. Do good. Have good life."

Study, your choice. He faced me, and wiped the water from the wings on my chest. Blood Wings. Then, slowly, he held my shoulders. He had only held me like this when I was very small and he was angry. He shook me, like Pearl had, begging me to open my heart.

"You know, is true. I cannot hold anger for you anymore. You are my son. I am proud of you. I always proud."

I couldn't say anything. I was crying.

"Is all right, Kai," he said. "I wanted West Point too much, for me. Was *my* dream. How can you have dream when Father in your shoes, try take your heart? Your future clear, without me say where you go.

"American father *not* decide if son life good enough for him! That is *goo dai*, old ways, ancient times. You American! I American."

"Janie's American," I whispered.

He patted my shoulder, his eyes moist.

"I think of my father," he said. "How things did not work for him. How many sadness he have. Long time ago. World turn against him, blame him for everything. He not bad man."

He looked away from me as a large, single tear ran down his cheek. DIs always carry Kleenex, and I wiped away the tear.

He pretended that this had not happened. My father surveyed the sky, the old soldier knowing its portents, smelling the air, tactically measuring visibility, wind, and moisture, judging the distance between East and West. He glanced at me and looked, his eyes seeing someone behind me, behind himself.

"Perhaps I was honorable son to my father. Maybe I wrong, all many years. You know—I save my family. Everyone! I bring them to America. All children alive. All children *smart*."

I wasn't smart. "Janie most of all," I said. "She'll be the doctor, the scholar. The one you'll be proudest of. And

Megan's a great, a popular schoolteacher, the highest honor. And Jennifer's the smartest, the wisest. Right, Dad?"

He looked down at the ground and sighed, exhaling old pains that would not die.

Take command, Dad.

He nodded imperceptibly, Chinese talk, secret, subtle, but clear. Right, he had meant, silently. Janie most of all and Megan is a great teacher, Jennifer the wise one. My daughters.

He turned away from me for a while. The sound of nearby traffic on Lombard seemed to be from another world. The air was clean with hints of the sea. No cars honked. I smelled of ocean mist.

Then he said, "You are good brother, stand up for sister. You do right thing." He nodded, too sad to speak.

"You forgive me, Father?" I asked, my voice not mine.

"I will tell you now, Ding Kai, you American now. This honors me. Then we get better. Know more. Learn."

It was a Chinese answer, full of courtesy.

I smiled, my hands in my pockets in the cool night air. It was a beautiful evening. I touched the matchbook. I remembered Pearl's phone numbers. I remembered leaving her and I closed my eyes with the pain that I had never felt that day, but had been festering in me for a year. Please remember me, Pearl. Please forgive me. Ding Kai loves you.

"Hey, you guys aren't going to jump, are you?" came a concerned voice from a man on the dark street below.

My father looked down at him, then grabbed my arm, making me open my eyes.

"No," he called. "We not jumping. We climbing up American ladder!"

Abbreviations and Glossary

AAA: Army Athletic Association, a voluntary alumni group which supports Academic intercollegiate sports; often confused with an unrelated organization

AI: additional instruction, for those who require extra class time in course work; used lyrically to describe individually focused hazing upon shit magnets

Airborne: training and operations for parachute-trained infantry. Training graduates receive a silver emblem of a parachute bracketed by wings. Opposite of "leg" infantry—those without airborne qualification

All Right: abbreviated official statement on a cadet's Honor that all persons in a room are authorized, wherever they may be; also used as a social declaration to describe an excellent situation, often accompanied by a thumbs-up

animal night: slang for eating without the benefit of utensils; customarily reserved for Mulligan stew, beef ragout, and ravioli or spaghetti dinners, and induced by the same conditions that precipitate RFs

AO: area of operation, short for tactical area of operation; also used to describe an individual's personal living space within cramped barracks

AOT: summer Army Orientation Training for Second Classmen serving with actual Army units, such as at Fort Carson, Colorado

Area: space in the middle quadrangle of Central Barracks. Walking the Area takes place here.

ASP: assigned study problem, a shared-work take-home assignment; also the reptile that killed Cleopatra

BA: bare ass—bare area of the human derriere; used as a noun in conjunction with modifiers such as "mountain," "atomic," and "nuclear," when the BA is pointed at someone like a weapon, en masse, using geometric or military formations; also, bare-assed, the adjective, to describe someone who is so exposed

B-ache: bellyache, as a verb; to complain, which, at the Academy, achieved an art form

Big Dick: a risk exercise at mess hall tables, in which diners flip knives to win more, or lose all, of dessert, premised on the business principles that finance nation-states

Black Hat: cadre of the Airborne School; major aficionados of push-ups, shouting, singing while running, and the defeat of acrophobia by compelling frightened men to collide repeatedly with the earth

Blue Book: Manual of Regulations, USCC, which guides the conduct of the Corps; so called because of its blue binder; filled, in the 1960s, largely with interpolations into interpolations, unto the third and fourth generation of interpolations, upon which the IRS based its code and interpretations

boodle: food, particularly that found in cadet rooms—and usually sweets from Boodlers, small cadet cafes in the Weapons Room and the First Class Club that dispensed ice cream and cookies. Food hogs, however, considered all food "boodle."

BJ: before June—describing a lack of military respect in a Plebe's conduct with upperclassmen. In June, Plebes are "recognized" as being part of the upper classes, and can then comport themselves according to a far lower standard of human behavior.

BP: barracks policeman, a civilian building janitor

brace: correct position of military attention for a Plebe, executed by compressing the neck inward toward the spine and producing waves of wrinkles in the neck ideally equal to the age of the Plebe, to be maintained whenever outdoors or in the presence of an upperclassman

brat: for "Army brat"—child of an Army family

brown boy: a homely but warm comforter issued to each cadet. "Brown boy defilade" means to establish a defensive tactical position: to sleep under deep covers, eyes and mind closed to the sensate assault of the system.

Buckner: military training camp for Third Classmen's two-month military skills summer, on the USMA Military Reservation; emphasis on platoon tactics, patrolling, and physical fitness; named after General Simon Bolivar Buckner, CG, X Army Corps, a former Commandant of Cadets, killed at Okinawa

Bugle Notes: the "Plebe bible"—filled with poop for recitation and containing general information about the Academy

butt: a remaining fraction or portion of a whole: e.g., the four hours before midnight are a butt of a day

CIB: Combat Infantryman's Badge, a prized award for serving in the Infantry in combat, denoted by a musket mounted in the center of a blue rectangular field, with a silver oak wreath bracketing the rectangle from behind. Stars are added to the top center of the wreath for successive awards.

civvies: civilian clothes

CG: commanding general

CO: commanding officer

Code: shorthand for the Honor Code: "a cadet does not lie, cheat, or steal, or tolerate those who do"

cold: perfect and without error, as in "cold max"

Corps Squad: USMA intercollegiate team

Cow: a Second Classman, equivalent to a college junior attending night school with two full-time jobs and four children, one of whom is a well-armed juvenile delinquent. Cows are the maternal figures of the Corps, with the strongest personal leadership responsibility of the upper classes. They and Plebes are traditionally the spooniest members of the Corps.

C-rats: C-rations—canned food for field use—individually packaged meals of high caloric and questionable nutritional value, renowned for haute cuisine savoriness. Hot picks included hard and lard (ham and beans); cows and rocks (sliced beef and potatoes); lard and balls (beans and meatballs in tomato sauce). Nutritional supplements included fudge bricks, pound cake, and peaches. Accessory packs included coffee, creamer, sugar, salt and pepper, cigarettes, and toilet paper.

crimes against humanity: see EE 304

crot: slang for Plebe; derived from the original Academy

French-language primer, designed to allow cadets to read later the seminal military engineering texts, which were authored by Vauban, de Gribeauval, Montalembert, and Carnot. "Monsieur Ducrot" was the central illustrative character in that primer, making him one of the most despised mythical characters in the American-woodsmen, monolingual Corps of Cadets. New cadets on R-Day were traditionally greeted with, "Here, at last, is Mr. Ducrot," and subjected to all of the repressed frustration generated by studying the French tongue. Eventually, the name was Americanized and, like the new cadet himself, shortened, its background forgotten.

dee: deficient—not maintaining minimum proficiency in a course; opposite of "pro," proficient

detail: cadre, or duty assignment, as in First Detail Beast, which manages New Cadet Barracks for July, and Second Detail Beast, which operates it for August

DF: disposition form, a standardized Army memorandum form

DX: delete/final—equipment item dropped from inventory because either destroyed, lost, or damaged beyond repair, which frequently occurred whenever cadets were brought into contact with equipment with moving parts

DZ: drop zone: proposed target for an Airborne drop, usually several kilometers from where paratroopers actually land

EE 304: Electrical Engineering 304, a Second Class, two-semester, seven-semester-hour lab course, also known as Juice. EE 304A is first, and 304B is second semester. According to unbiased accounts, EE 304 represented a new low in human learning and was generally recognized as the responsible agent for the collapse of Western morality in the latter half of the twentieth century.

engineer: a hive—a good student in a school of good students

ES&GS: Earth, Space, and Graphic Sciences; Plebe course in Everything Known to Anyone: geology, meteorology, astronomy, cartography, terrain science, formation of the universe, and drafting, conducted in narcotized sixth-floor classrooms atop Washington Hall after cadets have double-timed up the stairs. Course analysts at the University of California at Davis reviewed this class for a week before deciding that it matched nothing ever seen in any other university, awarding no transfer credit.

fall out: the military order allowing a Plebe to release his brace—to "let his neck out," to let his chin "fall out" of a stiff, compressed bracing posture, somewhat akin to a person being released from hanging, fingernail removal, or wearing a jock-strap several sizes too small

FD: full dress—a forty-four-brass-buttoned gray tunic with a high collar, gold braid, and tails designed to (a) make the wearer appear to be a member of an earlier century and (b) choke the wearer in several places at once

find: to separate a cadet from the Corps for deficiency in studies or conduct. Separated cadets are "found."

Firstie: a First Classman, a cadet in his fourth year—academically equal to a doctoral candidate in class hours, so-cially equal to a monk in individual liberties, and penally equal to a medium-security inmate in recreational opportunities; responsible for running the Corps and normally so worn by the preceding three years that shaving, spit-shining, trou pressing, and the wearing of hats become forgotten skills

4-F: Selective Service classification for a person medically dis-qualified from the draft and military service, a status highly de-sired by vast numbers of American males in the period 1964 to 1972

frogmen: slang for underwater commandos, now called Seals, but unaccountably under control of the Department of the Navy

goat: a poor performer in academics; opposite of a hive or en-gineer

gray hog: a passionate believer in the system and in West Point, and, accordingly, deemed suspect by those still in pos-session of rational faculties

gross: significantly inadequate, extremely erroneous, blindingly dull, or startlingly below Academy standards; a favorite and conventional adjective and the companion of "puny"

grub: the act of scavenging academic tenths, or credits, for higher grades or to avoid being found for being dee

Hellcats: military band members tasked with sounding reveille with unrestrained vigor after the sounding of the cannon, and who are accordingly beloved by all cadets and remembered by them in their nighttime prayers and in their wills

hive: a successful academic performer; a bright student who quickly understands and grasps academic principles; an engineer; also used as a verb to describe effort in academics

Honor: the Code at West Point

India: an all-white, brass-buttoned, high-collared cadet uniform for formal summer events, also known as the "snow suit" for making even the most nefariously twisted cadet appear like a Sir Galahad

IOBC: Infantry Officer Basic Course at Fort Benning, Georgia, home of the Infantry and the Benning School for Boys

IRP: "immediate response, please," a vigorously shouted command offered to Plebes, encouraging them to not dally in their spoken answers to the upper classes

jodie: a cadence-based song for troops during quick-time or double-time march, named for the proverbial boy back home who is dating the soldier's girlfriend ("Your momma was there when you left / Your baby was there when you left / Jodie was there when you left / Sound off . . .")

Juice: see EE 304.

LBE: load-bearing equipment—the cartridge belt and suspenders upon which infantrymen carry pack or ruck, rations, mess kit, bedding, grenades, D-rings, first aid pack, flashlight, canteen, entrenching tool, pistol holster, ammo pouches, gas mask, foot powder, cosmetics, aftershave, magazines, and boodle

Lost Fifties: the divisions of barracks numbered in the fifties, which were the last constructed before the 1964 Academy Expansion Plan began; so called because they were on the outer periphery of barracks

LT: lieutenant

max: maximum grade on a writ. Cold max is one achieved with ease and a grubbing of extra-credit tenths. Also used as a verb

mike-mike: millimeter, derived from radio shorthand. An "81 mike-mike" was an 81mm mortar.

MP: Military Policeman—an Army cop

muck: to strain by main effort at a task

NVA: Army of North Vietnam—Communist regular forces with twenty-two years' combat experience against two better-equipped armies before the first U.S. ground forces arrived in Vietnam

oak leaf: second identical military award or decoration. A recipient of two Silver Stars would receive a gold leaf for insertion into the original ribbon to indicate a second award, described as "Silver Star with first oak leaf cluster."

OAO: one and only—*the* girlfriend

OC: officer in charge; member of the TD appointed for a twenty-four-hour period to represent the Commandant of Cadets in the maintenance of good order. OCs patrol the Academy on search-and-quill missions, looking for cadet infractions. The OC's job is never done; the OC never sleeps; his pen is never still. Some tacs, when serving as OC, performed with a commitment that reminded casual observers of the burning of Moscow.

O Club: Officers Club, adult extensions of Snuffy's, with dining and smoking rooms and at least one bar; used for receptions, dinners, and after-duty socializing. To use the club, an officer must join by paying annual dues.

OCS: Officer Candidate School—a compressed officer-commissioning program for qualified enlisted personnel

OD: olive drab, a standard, subdued, military color used with little imagination on anything that couldn't be painted white

Odin: Norse god to whom Plebes sang in loud, elongated, mass chants, in the hopes that singing his name would bring rain for cancellation of parades and inspections. Sadly, Odin was the top deity in Norse mythology, responsible for everything except the weather. Thor was the Norse god of thunder, which no doubt explains why the overwhelming majority of pleas to the heavens went unanswered.

OMI: Office of Military Instruction, which formally teaches cadets how to teach for data retention when quill and slugs cannot be used for academic reinforcement

OPE: Office of Physical Education, or oppression of physical exertion

op order: operation order, the five-paragraph military planning format for Situation (enemy and friendly forces), Mission, Execution (concept of operation, sub-unit missions, coordinating instructions), Service Support, and Command and Signal; reducible to the neumonic "SMESC"

P: professor

ping: to move with great panic in an unmilitary fashion. A ping meter is an imaginary instrument (sometimes a cotton ball on a string) by which upperclassmen can quantify the amount of ricocheting activity undertaken by a frantically animated Plebe required to perform eighteen duties in two minutes.

Plebe: a Fourth Classman, in tenure equal to a college freshman and socially equal to a condemned prisoner held in an armed, maximum-security installation surrounded by water and rocks; also known as crot, crothead, tool, dooly, dumbjohn, doowillie, beanhead, knob, smack, and smackhead

PM: Provost Marshal, chief law enforcement officer on an Army post, equal to a chief of police; manages the MPs and the Criminal Investigation Division

point man: lead man in a patrol, tasked with breaking trail, taking directions from the compass man, who follows the course dictated by the patrol leader. "Point" finds every precipice, low log, swampy bog, and rat hole on a night patrol before anyone else does, evidenced by the sounds of crashing and subdued moaning in the dead of night.

poop: information; usually, information to be spec'ed, for spouting

poop school: USMAPS, United States Military Academy Preparatory School, Fort Belvoir, Virginia, where candidates not initially admitted to West Point are specifically trained for a successful second application from the ranks. Poop schoolers frequently perform very well at the Academy, maxing tasks while their civilian counterparts muck and draw ire.

post: an order meaning "take your post," i.e., move with great purpose; also, the military reservation

present arms: salute, by hand, rifle, or saber; refers to both the action of saluting and the command to do so

pro: proficient in academics—signifying minimum competence

in a course by maintaining at least a 2.0 academic average—
and attained by grubbing, hiving, or brains

Q: quarters, as in bachelor officers quarters

quill: a Form 2-1 for recording conditions out of military order, resulting in demerits; based on the use of a nineteenth-
century pen to write the record; issued by the TD, by wheels,
ranking First Classmen who become the primary deputies of
TD policies, and by Cow squad leaders; also used as a verb;
usually used as a weapon

Rabble-Rouser: cheerleader

rack: cadet bed or cot, a sacred place where freedom and privacy can be realized in deep REM sleep; also used as a verb
("rack-out"), a hope ("hope for clothing-formation-free rack"),
and a prayer ("Please, God, let me rack-out and not dream of
being late to formation"); home of the "rack monster" which
invisibly seized cadets and threw them bodily into the rack, or
allowed them to nod off in class; also called "sack"

Ranger: graduate of Ranger School, an elite infantry skills program emphasizing patrol skills, night marches, hill negotiation,
and maximum physical endurance under duress. At one time,
all West Point graduates automatically attended Ranger and
Airborne schools.

R-Day: Reception Day, July 1, when the New Cadet class reports to West Point for the beginning of Beast Barracks and the
opportunity to test the drop resilience of their luggage and their
qualifications for the Academy choirs

Recognition: acceptance of Plebes as upperclassmen on Graduation Day; celebrated by bashing and human vandalism and a
great deal of smiling and handshaking after a year of abuse,
torture, torment, and character development. A recognized
Plebe has been accepted by an individual upperclassman before Graduation. Frequently done by an upperclassman to a
Plebe from the same hometown or high school, or players on
the same Corps Squad team. A recognized Plebe calls the recognizing upperclassman by his first name when they are not in
duty status, and can seek the upperclassman's counsel on a
friendship basis.

REMF: rear echelon motherf——. A Vietnam-era reference to
noncombat personnel assigned to the rear, with air-conditioning

and steaks, presumed by the slur to be uncaring about troops on the line

RF: rat fornication: periodic episodes of pandemonium, when community testosterone reaches critical mass and barracks mates must fight, punch, gouge, wrestle, destroy, and scream in a rowdy effort to relieve the pressure before a fatal white-out

RPG: rocket-propelled grenade used by NVA/VC

RTO: radio telephone operator: an enlisted man who carries the twenty-three-pound, backpacked PRC-25 radio for the platoon leader; a high-profile target because of the whip antenna and because the platoon leader is always next to the RTO

Rumor Control: basis for confirmation of alleged facts

San-gahng: The Three Bonds defined by K'ung Fu-tzu, prescribing the strict obedience that sons owe to fathers, subjects owe to the emperor, and wives owe to husbands. The related social concept was expressed in the comprehensive *Wu-lun,* or the Five Relationships, the first three of which are the *San-gahng.* The two non-primary relationships prescribed the respect that younger brothers owe to older brothers, and that younger friends owe to older friends.

saltpeter: chemical substance used in the manufacture of gunpowder rumored to be (1) capable of diminishing prurient impulses and (2) an ingredient in every Academy mess hall breakfast since the end of World War I, without any noticeable effect

shit magnet: Plebe who draws hazing, quill, and AI with ferromagnetic force

short round: artillery round which falls short of the target and is likely to impact in your own AO

slug: a specially packaged punishment involving both demerits and punishment tours on the Area; may include hours of confinement to room except for duties; described in shorthand as two numbers, i.e., eight and eight; sixteen, sixteen, and ten; also used in verb form

snow: to fool someone, customarily, by presenting a better appearance than conditions warrant

Snuffy's: a tavern located ten miles outside West Point, where cadets are authorized to imbibe alcoholic beverages; replaced Benny Havens's renowned tavern, which was frequented by cadets in the nineteenth century, and part of the culture where once, to be a man meant to drink to the point of insensate breathing

SOP: standard operating procedure

South Odd: South Thayer Hall Auditorium, where major lectures, evening programs, and weekend movies superior to those in the gym, but still of dubious value, are presented; also "South Aud"

spec: memorize; part of "spec and dump"—memorize, regurgitate, and instantly forget, SOP for many of the engineering courses for many cadets

spoony: militarily neat in appearance

spout: to recite spec'd poop by memory

Strac: derived from STRC, former military acronym for U.S. Strike Command, which came to be synonymous at West Point with a neat and spoony appearance

stud: poker game with five cards dealt to each player, the first one down, and the next four up, with new bets after the second, third, fourth, and fifth cards; also, a manly cadet

system: the culture of the Academy, derived from the Thayer Academic System, and modified by the disciplinary requirements of the TD and OPE

tac: company tactical officer, a member of the TD, and father confessor, inquisitional inspector, and, friend or foe, depending upon personality

tar bucket: a shako, the traditional short, black, tightly fitting, stovepipe, nineteenth-century military hat with a brass chain, chin strap, short brass-rimmed brim, an oversize brass emblem on its front, and a pom-pom or plume of feathers inserted into its flat top, designed to reduce a cadet's cranial circumference by one-half hat size per year of wear

TD: Tactical Department, responsible for the military training of cadets through the administration of command via company tacs, i.e., the system; exemplified by rigid inspections with quill for militarily disreputable quarters, equipment, or persons, leading to slugs

tenth: one-tenth of a grade point and one-thirtieth of a cold max; increment of academic grade points, which cadets gain or lose through the daily writ system

Thayer: Sylvanus Thayer, USMA Class of 1808, who reformed the Academy and created the Thayer Academic System of daily writs. Dickens described Thayer's work as "severe but well devised and manly," ample proof that Dickens never spent a night in the place.

trou: trousers. There are no pants at West Point.

USCC: United States Corps of Cadets

walking the Area: marching punishment tours in Central Area as a result of receiving excess number of demerits through quill; often a self-sustaining exercise, since cadets required to walk the Area were inspected prior to commencement of the exercise, often resulting in more demerits and more punishment tours

WFR: written final review; *see* whufer.

wheel: a Firstie with high rank. West Point's cadets are actually managed by the Corps, not officers. Key to this are six-striped Firsties, who are at the top of their class in military aptitude. Wheels drive the First and Second classes, and through them, West Point.

white-out: brain-swamping consequence of male celibacy

whufer: slang for WFR, written final review, covering all of the material within a block of instruction. Plebe math WFRs lasted two weeks but reminded history students of the siege of Leningrad.

WPR: written partial review, or whuper

Wu-lun: see *San-gahng.*

Yearling: a Third Classman; a merger of a college sophomore, a parolee in a small desert ville, and a junkyard hobo: too young to be a true upperclassman, too rattled to button his shirt, and far too experienced to be a Plebe